D0734476

MASTERPIECES OF MYSTERY AND SUSPENSE

MASTERPIECES OF MYSTERY AND SUSPENSE

Compiled by
Martin H. Greenberg

St. Martin's Press • New York

Copyright © 1988 by Doubleday Book & Music Clubs, Inc.
All Rights Reserved
Printed in the United States of America

Published by The Reader's Digest Association, Inc.,
1993, by permission of Doubleday Book & Music Clubs, Inc.

Library of Congress Cataloging-in-Publication Data

Masterpieces of mystery and suspense / compiled by Martin H. Greenberg.
    p.   cm.
   ISBN 0-312-02251-4
   1. Detective and mystery stories, English 2. Detective and
mystery stories, American. 1. Greenberg, Martin H.
PR1309.D4M37 1988
823'.0872'08--dc19   88-14753
                                   CIP

No part of this book may be used or reproduced in any manner whatsoever without
written permission except in the case of brief quotations in critical articles or
reviews. For information, address St. Martin's Press, 175 Fifth Avenue, New York,
N.Y. 10010.

ACKNOWLEDGMENTS

Grateful acknowledgment is made to the following for permission to reprint their copy-
righted material:

"The Case of the Emerald Sky" by Eric Ambler. Copyright 1940 by Eric Ambler.
Reprinted by permission of the author.

"The Splintered Monday" by Charlotte Armstrong. First published in *Ellery Queen's
Mystery Magazine.* Copyright © 1966 by Davis Publications, Inc. Reprinted by permission of Brandt & Brandt Literary Agents, Inc.

"The Cross of Lorraine" by Isaac Asimov. Copyright © 1976 by Isaac Asimov. Reprinted by permission of the author.

"Little Terror" by Robert Barnard. Copyright © 1986 by Robert Barnard. Reprinted by
permission of the author.

"Lucky Penny" by Linda Barnes. Copyright © 1985 by Linda Barnes. From *The New
Black Mask.* Reprinted by permission of Gina Maccoby Literary Agency.

"The Man Who Collected Poe" by Robert Bloch. Copyright 1951 by Robert Bloch.
Reprinted by permission of the Scott Meredith Literary Agency, Inc., 845 Third Avenue,
New York, NY 10022.

"One Thousand Dollars a Word" by Lawrence Block. Copyright © 1977 by Lawrence
Block. Reprinted by permission of the author.

"And So Died Riabouchinska" by Ray Bradbury. Copyright 1953 by Ray Bradbury;
renewed © 1981 by Ray Bradbury. Reprinted by permission of Don Congdon Associates, Inc.

"The Nuggy Bar" by Simon Brett. Copyright © 1981 by Simon Brett. First published in
Ellery Queen's Mystery Magazine as "Metaphor for Murder"; and in *Tickled to Death
and Other Stories* by Charles Scribner's Sons, 1985, and Dell Publishing, 1987. Reprinted
by permission of *the author.*

"Strictly Diplomatic" by John Dickson Carr. Copyright 1945 by John Dickson Carr. First published in *Ellery Queen's Mystery Magazine.* Reprinted by permission of Harold Ober Associates Incorporated.

"The Submarine Plans" by Agatha Christie. Reprinted by permission of Dodd, Mead & Company, Inc. from *The Under Dog and Other Stories* by Agatha Christie. Copyright 1925 by Agatha Christie. Copyright renewed 1953 by Agatha Christie Mallowan.

"The Marked Man" by Ursula Curtiss. Reprinted by permission of Dodd, Mead & Company, Inc. from *The House on Plymouth Street and Other Stories* by Ursula Curtiss. Copyright © 1972 by Ursula Curtiss.

"Milady Bigamy" by Lillian de la Torre. Copyright © 1978 by Lillian de la Torre. First published in *Ellery Queen's Mystery Magazine.* Reprinted by permission of Harold Ober Associates Incorporated.

"The Nine-to-Five Man" by Stanley Ellin. Copyright © 1964 by Stanley Ellin. Reprinted by permission of Curtis Brown, Ltd.

"There Are No Snakes in Ireland" by Frederick Forsyth. Copyright © 1982 by Frederick Forsyth. Reprinted by permission of Curtis Brown, London.

"Twenty-one Good Men and True" by Dick Francis. Copyright © 1979 by Dick Francis. Reprinted by permission of Sterling Lord Literistic, Inc.

"Have a Nice Death" by Antonia Fraser. Reprinted from *Jemima Shore's First Case and Other Stories* by Antonia Fraser, by permission of W. W. Norton & Company, Inc. and Curtis Brown Ltd., London.

"Danger Out of the Past" by Erle Stanley Gardner. Copyright 1955 by Erle Stanley Gardner. Reprinted by permission of Curtis Brown, Ltd.

"The African Tree-Beavers" by Michael Gilbert. Copyright © 1971 by Michael Gilbert. First published in *Argosy* (U. K.). Reprinted by permission of the author.

"The Parker Shotgun" by Sue Grafton. Copyright © 1986 by Sue Grafton. Reprinted by permission of The Aaron Priest Literary Agency.

"The Worst Crime Known to Man" by Reginald Hill. Copyright © 1984 by Reginald Hill. Reprinted by permission of AP Watt Ltd.

"The Theft of the Four of Spades" by Edward D. Hoch. Copyright © 1980 by Edward D. Hoch. First published in *Ellery Queen's Mystery Magazine.* Reprinted by permission of the author.

"The Victim" by P. D. James. Copyright © 1973 by P. D. James. From *Crime's Times Three,* Macmillan London Limited and St. Martin's Press. Reprinted by permission of Roberta Pryor, Inc.

"Quitters Inc." by Stephen King. From *Night Shift.* Copyright © 1978 by Stephen King. Reprinted by permission of Doubleday, a division of Bantam, Doubleday, Dell Publishing Group, Inc.

"The Homesick Buick" by John D. MacDonald. Copyright 1955 by John D. MacDonald; renewed © 1983 by John D. MacDonald Publishing, Inc. Reprinted by permission of George Diskant Associates, Inc.

"Midnight Blue" by Ross Macdonald. Copyright © 1960 by Ross Macdonald. Reprinted by permission of Harold Ober Associates, Inc.

"Death on the Air" by Dame Ngaio Marsh. Copyright 1947 by American Mercury Inc. Copyright renewed © 1975 by Ngaio Marsh. First published in the United States in *Ellery Queen's Mystery Magazine.* Reprinted by permission of Harold Ober Associates, Incorporated.

"The Honest Blackmailer" by Patricia Moyes. Copyright © 1982 by Patricia Moyes. Reprinted by permission of Curtis Brown, Ltd.

"Cat's-Paw" by Bill Pronzini. Copyright © 1983 by Bill Pronzini. First published in limited edition form by Waves Press, Richmond, VA. Reprinted by permission of the author.

"Abraham Lincoln's Clue" by Ellery Queen. Copyright © 1965 by Ellery Queen. Reprinted by permission of the agents for the author's Estate, the Scott Meredith Literary Agency, Inc., 845 Third Avenue, New York, NY 10022.

"The Fever Tree" by Ruth Rendell. Copyright © 1982 by Kingsmarkam Enterprises, Ltd. From *The Fever Tree and Other Stories of Suspense* by Ruth Rendell. Reprinted by permission of Pantheon Books, a Division of Random House, Inc., and A.D. Peters & Co.

"The Necklace of Pearls" by Dorothy L. Sayers. Copyright 1933 by Dorothy Leigh Sayers Fleming. Reprinted by permission of Harper & Row, Publishers, Inc., and David Higham Associates Limited.

"Help Wanted, Male" from *Trouble in Triplicate* by Rex Stout. Copyright 1945, renewed © 1972 by Rex Stout. Reprinted by permission of Viking Penguin, Inc.

"The Dream Is Better" by Julian Symons. Copyright © 1982 by Julian Symons. First published in *Ellery Queen's Mystery Magazine*. Reprinted by permission of the author.

"A Nice Place to Stay" by Nedra Tyre. Reprinted by permission of the Scott Meredith Literary Agency, Inc., 845 Third Avenue, New York, NY 10022.

"Never Shake a Family Tree" by Donald Westlake. Copyright © 1961 by Donald E. Westlake. Reprinted by permission of the author and by Knox Burger Associates, Ltd.

"The Dancing Detective" by Cornell Woolrich. Copyright © 1958 by Cornell Woolrich. Reprinted by the agents for the author's Estate, the Scott Meredith Literary Agency, Inc., 845 Third Avenue, New York, NY 10022.

CONTENTS

Introduction

Legendary Sleuths

Masters of the Mystery

Masters of Suspense

Masterworks of Crime and Detection

INTRODUCTION

Masterpieces of Mystery and Suspense brings together forty of the most ingenious, suspenseful stories ever written in this popular genre, covering most of the major categories, including armchair detectives, private eyes, espionage, psychological suspense, and crimes of passion and greed.

Since these works trace the development of the mystery/suspense story from near its beginnings in the late nineteenth century to the present, a brief history may be useful here.* While stories of crime are as old as civilization itself, moving from an oral tradition to written works, the *mystery* story as such did not develop until after 1820. Before that date, crime was defined as anything that the ruling classes said it was—if it was practiced by them against commoners, it wasn't crime at all. Agents of the monarchies did pursue criminals on occasion, but the deductive process that we associate with the mystery story had to await the rise of science and technology in order to be possible. In other words, the mystery story was a product of its time, much as the science fiction story arose only with the scientific age.

The great Edgar Allan Poe was clearly the first mystery writer, and was also the father of the modern psychological suspense story and the modern horror story. His *Murders in the Rue Morgue,* published in 1840, is considered the first true *detective* story. However, it took some forty-six years for the development of the first great series detective to appear, the immortal Sherlock Holmes created by Sir Arthur Conan Doyle, whose *A Study in Scarlet* may be said to be the model of the *modern* mystery story. Not only was Holmes a man of science, employing the scientific method in his calculations, but he also had his Dr. Watson, a brilliant narrative device on the part of Conan Doyle that has been much imitated but never equaled. Sherlock Holmes was such a marvelous creation that he has persisted to the present, quite a feat in this age of instant, but passing, celebrities and fads. Only three years later, William Le Queux published *Guilty Bonds,* considered by many scholars to be the first important espionage novel, advancing the field and adding a variant whose popularity continues to the present day.

The first twenty years of the new century saw the appearance of the suspense story, at first closely related to the traditional gothic tale, but furthered by such popular writers as Mary Roberts Rinehart, whose *The Circular Staircase* featured a protagonist who wished she had shown better judgment at key moments in the story. The suspense story differs profoundly from the mystery since we usually know that the central character(s) face danger before they do, and more importantly, we know *who* is after them. They are frequently victims of bad luck or fate, not really responsible for their predicament, and they have to either rise to the occasion and save themselves, or be saved by a friend or lover.

So, by roughly 1920 the three major forms of the criminous story were in place—the mystery, with its emphasis on "Who dunnit"; the suspense story, with its emphasis on danger, flight, and rescue; and the spy story, with its emphasis on international politics and high stakes.

The 1920s ushered in the so-called "Golden Age" of the mystery story. This was inaugurated by *The Mysterious Affair at Styles* by Agatha Christie, published in 1920. Along with such fine writers as Dorothy L. Sayers, Christie established a style that proved very popular and continues to be loved by millions of readers. These books were typically set in a small village, an isolated mansion, or some other semi-enclosed place like a train. The orderly world of the inhabitants is shattered by a murder: a cast of suspects is investigated by an amateur or police detective; after false leads are followed to dead ends, the murderer is unmasked and the world is once again an orderly place. Very strict rules evolved for this form—the most important being fair play—there should be a killer, the death cannot turn out to be a suicide, for example, and there could not be a supernatural explanation for the crime.

Although there were U.S. practitioners of the classic puzzle mystery, Americans were moving in a different direction. The development of "dime novels" and "pulp" magazines (magazines printed on cheap pulped paper) filled the newsstands quickly, providing entertainment for every possible fictional interest, including crime stories. The first of these magazines was *Detective Story,* which began publication during World War I. At the same time, American literature was moving toward "realism" and "naturalism"; this made the English country mystery unacceptable to the majority of American readers, especially those who lived in big cities and/or had actual experience with crime. The classic puzzle story was largely bloodless, the action nearly nonexistent or off-stage, and not at all like the real thing.

The result was the development of the "hardboiled" school of crime writing with its emphasis on fast pacing, physical action, and *private* detectives. The focus for this process was *Black Mask,* a magazine that debuted in the United States in 1920 and featured stories by Carroll John Daly, Dashiell Hammett, Frederick Nebel, Erle Stanley Gardner, and other masters of this school of crime writing.

So began the modern career of the American private eye (as opposed to the British private investigator), who has become an icon of American culture and has captured the imagination of millions of people in other cultures as well. The private eye and the mystery in general were given a tremendous boost by sound motion pictures, and beloved series detectives quickly found their way to the screen. The private detective usually operated alone and in a corrupt society, unable to trust anyone, even the police, who were often depicted as being as rotten as the criminals they pursued. The "one honorable man" in an environment of dishonor struck a chord with American and foreign readers that still resonates today. The pulp era was characterized by mostly shoddy writing—the action did not provide much of an opportunity for character development or even serious plotting, although there is much excellent material buried in those thousands of magazines. This is not to say that American mystery writers did not continue the tradition of the classic puzzle story, because they did—particularly Ellery Queen, the two New York cousins who had the brilliant idea of using their pseudonym as the name of their detective. The magazine they founded, *Ellery Queen's Mystery Magazine,* quickly established itself as a major force in the short story market in America, a role the magazine still fulfills today.

However, the police were not neglected in either England or America. In 1952 Hillary Waugh published *Last Seen Wearing,* considered by some to be the first police procedural mystery, although others would vote for Lawrence Treat's *V as in Victim* (1945). This form concentrated on the minute details of police work, including the use of scientific devices, legwork, interviewing, and other routines of the average police officer. Ed McBain (Evan Hunter) raised this to an art form with his 87th Precinct stories, perhaps the first series to feature more than two central detectives. In England, the police never suffered from the suspicion and disparagement foisted upon them by the American hardboiled school, except for a certain contempt expressed by more talented and less bumbling private or amateur detectives.

The advent of World War II affected the espionage story, moving it toward greater realism as actual events overtook fiction in many cases. These "thrillers" proved extremely popular as millions of men and women who had served in the war provided an enormous audience for the numerous novels and stories that were written during and after the fighting ended.

The 1930s and especially the 1940s saw the emergence of the "psychological" crime novel with its focus on the motivation of the criminal. This trend was given impetus by public discussion of the effects of the war on the mental health of veterans, much as recent fiction and films have focused on the "Vietnam syndrome" and its effect on the behavior of the veterans of that war. This concern reached its peak in the 1946–1955 period with the *roman noir* and its corollary, the *film noir*—books and films in which men and women found themselves trapped by fate in sometimes fatalistic (and fatal) situations not wholly of their own making. A notable author of this period was Cornell Woolrich, whose stories of desperation and despair combined with a race against time proved enormously influential, making the dark, rain-swept streets of large cities real and dangerous places. Alfred Hitchcock would mine this area with great success in a string of classic movies that themselves enriched and influenced the literature on which they were based.

In short, the crime novel began to examine what makes people human—what makes them do the things they do—the desire for success, for revenge, and for happiness. Writers also examined the darker side of the human condition, the side that is sometimes pathological, psychotic, and deranged. The deviant in society was receiving greater attention in popular and scholarly publications, and it was only a matter of time until these concerns found their way into mystery and suspense fiction. This trend was clearly linked to the concern with the mental health of returning war veterans, as mentioned above.

World War II was followed almost immediately by the onset of the Cold War, which in turn produced more espionage fiction of all types, from the jingoistic, black-and-white James Bond stories by Ian Fleming to the very gray novels of John Le Carré and everything in between. Mystery and spy fiction rather carefully follows the mood of the readers, and a good case can be made for claiming that mysteries are an excellent barometer of their times, as authors like Le Carré and Len Deighton vividly capture the mood of informed opinion in the Western democracies.

The history of the publishing of mystery books is also that of publishing in general, since such novels were a staple of fiction from an early date. The advent of the paperback book after World War II greatly widened the market for mysteries, both through inexpensive reprints of hardcover books, and through the publication of paperback originals. Writers as different as Mickey Spillane, Erle Stanley Gardner, and Agatha Christie sold tens of millions of books in paperback, while John D. MacDonald was typical of the many excellent writers who first gained fame through paperback originals. Hardcover and paperback houses soon established mystery lines, complete with identifying logos, and librarians found that mysteries enjoyed circulation levels as high or higher than for any other type of book. Book clubs fought for the right to issue editions of mysteries and The Mystery Guild was founded to cater exclusively to this huge audience. All this success was echoed in the electronic media as first radio and movies and then television embraced the form.

The audience for crime stories is extremely egalitarian—men and women in almost equal numbers (the women enjoy a slight edge here), rich and poor (the James Bond books received an enormous boost when President Kennedy mentioned his affection for them), young and old alike flock to bookstores and newsstands to find the latest book by their favorite author. The mystery, like science fiction, has a readership that knows what it likes and wants more of it, and the *series* detective has become institutionalized as the most popular format. People wanted to *know* the sleuth, and mystery writers have responded with an astounding variety of detectives—amateur, police, and private detectives; blind, gay, fat, alcoholic, and confined-to-wheelchair detectives; and a large number of ethnic detectives of every persuasion, from rabbis to American Indians, from Chinese (Robert van Gulik's Judge Dee) to Chicana (Marcia Muller's Elena Oliverez) to black (John Ball's Virgil Tibbs).

As the modern crime story developed, so did the different forms that writers worked with, and readers preferred. Some writers, like Isaac Asimov, wrote mainly *armchair* detective stories, where the investigator, through acute deductive reasoning, solves the mystery without leaving his or her chair. Others, like John Dickson Carr, specialized in the *locked-room* or related *impossible crime* story, wherein the crime occurs in a sealed place or other "impossible" situation. Still others, like Ross Macdonald, concentrated on the "why dunnit," where everything is known except the motivation of the criminal; or on the "how dunnit" (related to the impossible crime), where everything is known except how the crime was committed. A variation that gained great popularity through the "Columbo" television series was the "inverted mystery," in which the reader knows from the beginning who committed the crime, but still enjoys watching the process whereby the detective solves the case.

By the 1980s the crime story had matured to the point where some of its practitioners, including writers like Ruth Rendell and P. D. James, were among the finest writers of fiction in the English language. *Masterpieces of Mystery and Suspense* pays homage to the crime-writing field and collects forty excellent examples of the best it has to offer the discerning reader.

This book is organized into four parts. The first part presents eight of the most famous literary creations in the mystery field, from Arthur Conan Doyle's Sherlock Holmes to Ross Macdonald's Lew Archer. In the second part you'll find the criminous stories of the greatest mystery writers the genre has produced. The third section focuses on some of the most influential suspense writers of the twentieth century, with outstanding examples of their craftsmanship. Finally, the fourth part offers a variety of memorable crime and detection stories by great writers of the past and present.

I hope that you enjoy the following stories as much as I enjoyed selecting them for you.

Martin H. Greenberg
Green Bay, Wisconsin

---

* Two useful histories of mystery and crime fiction are *The Mystery Story* edited by John Ball and *Whodunit?: A Guide to Crime, Suspense, and Spy Fiction* edited by H.R.F. Keating.

LEGENDARY
SLEUTHS

Sherlock Holmes is without doubt the greatest literary creation of all time. Holmes personified the man of science, valued by the Industrial Revolution, who brought the scientific method to crime detection. Dr. Watson, Moriarty, and 221B Baker Street are almost as well known as the great sleuth himself, and are known to five generations of readers. Films, television shows, and radio dramas have all been produced to star Holmes—he is one of the very few literary creations to be brought to life by every form of mass communication, and he continues to fascinate readers in many cultures.

SIR ARTHUR CONAN DOYLE *(1859–1930), a British physician as well as a novelist and detective-story writer, based Holmes on a doctor he knew. No man ever received a greater tribute.*

The Copper Beeches
BY SIR ARTHUR CONAN DOYLE

"To the man who loves art for its own sake," remarked Sherlock Holmes, tossing aside the advertisement sheet of the *Daily Telegraph,* "it is frequently in its least important and lowliest manifestations that the keenest pleasure is to be derived. It is pleasant to me to observe, Watson, that you have so far grasped this truth that in these little records of our cases which you have been good enough to draw up, and, I am bound to say, occasionally to embellish, you have given prominence not so much to the many *causes célèbres* and sensational trials in which I have figured, but rather to those incidents which may have been trivial in themselves, but which have given room for those faculties of deduction and of logical synthesis which I have made my special province."

"And yet," said I, smiling, "I cannot quite hold myself absolved from the charge of sensationalism which has been urged against my records."

"You have erred, perhaps," he observed, taking up a glowing cinder with the tongs, and lighting with it the long cherrywood pipe which was wont to replace his clay when he was in a disputatious rather than a meditative mood—"you have erred, perhaps, in attempting to put colour and life into each of your statements, instead of confining yourself to the task of placing upon record that severe reasoning from cause to effect which is really the only notable feature about the thing."

"It seems to me that I have done you full justice in the matter," I remarked with some coldness, for I was repelled by the egotism which I had more than once observed to be a strong factor in my friend's singular character.

"No, it is not selfishness or conceit," said he, answering, as was his wont, my thoughts rather than my words. "If I claim full justice for my art, it is because it is an impersonal thing—a thing beyond myself. Crime is common. Logic is rare. Therefore it is upon the logic rather than upon the crime that you should dwell. You have degraded what should have been a course of lectures into a series of tales."

It was a cold morning of the early spring, and we sat after breakfast on either side of a cheery fire in the old room in Baker Street. A thick fog rolled down between the lines of dun-coloured houses, and the opposing windows loomed like dark, shapeless blurs, through the heavy yellow wreaths. Our gas was lit, and shone on the white cloth, and glimmer of china and metal, for the table had not been cleared yet. Sherlock Holmes had been silent all the morning, dipping continuously into the advertisement columns of a succession of papers, until at last, having apparently given up his search, he had emerged in no very sweet temper to lecture me upon my literary shortcomings.

"At the same time," he remarked, after a pause, during which he had sat puffing at his long pipe and gazing down into the fire, "you can hardly be open to a charge of sensationalism, for out of these cases which you have been so kind as to interest yourself in, a fair proportion do not treat of crime, in its legal sense, at all. The small matter in which I endeavoured to help the King of Bohemia, the singular experience of Miss Mary Sutherland, the problem connected with the man with the twisted lip, and the incident of the noble bachelor, were all matters which are outside the pale of the law. But in avoiding the sensational, I fear that you may have bordered on the trivial."

"The end may have been so," I answered, "but the methods I hold to have been novel and of interest."

"Pshaw, my dear fellow, what do the public, the great unobservant public, who could hardly tell a weaver by his tooth or a compositor by his left thumb, care about the finer shades of analysis and deduction! But, indeed, if you are trivial, I cannot blame you, for the days of the great cases are past. Man, or at least criminal man, has lost all enterprise and originality. As to my own little practice, it seems to be degenerating into an agency for recovering lost lead pencils and giving advice to young ladies from boarding-schools. I think that I have touched bottom at last, however. This note I had this morning marks my zero point, I fancy. Read it!" He tossed a crumpled letter across to me.

It was dated from Montague Place upon the proceding evening, and ran thus:

Dear Mr Holmes—I am very anxious to consult you as to whether I should or should not accept a situation which has been offered to me as governess. I shall call at half-past ten tomorrow, if I do not inconvenience you—Yours faithfully,
                                                                        Violet Hunter.

"Do you know the young lady?" I asked
"Not I."
"It is half-past ten now."
"Yes, and I have no doubt that is her ring."
"It may turn out to be of more interest than you think. You remember that the affair of the blue carbuncle, which appeared to be a mere whim at first, developed into a serious investigation. It may be so in this case also."
"Well, let us hope so! But our doubts will very soon be solved, for here, unless I am much mistaken, is the person in question."

As he spoke the door opened, and a young lady entered the room. She was plainly but neatly dressed, with a bright, quick face, freckled like a plover's egg, and with the brisk manner of a woman who has had her own way to make in the world.

"You will excuse my troubling you, I am sure," said she, as my companion rose to greet her; "but I have had a very strange experience, and as I have no parents or relations of any sort from whom I could ask advice, I thought that perhaps you would be kind enough to tell me what I should do."

"Pray take a seat, Miss Hunter. I shall be happy to do anything that I can to serve you."

I could see that Holmes was favourably impressed by the manner and speech of his new client. He looked her over in his searching fashion, and then composed himself with his lids drooping and his fingertips together to listen to her story.

"I have been a governess for five years," said she, "in the family of Colonel Spence Munro, but two months ago the Colonel received an appointment at Halifax, in Nova Scotia, and took his children over to America with him, so that I found myself without a situation. I advertised and I answered advertisements, but without success. At last the little money which I had saved began to run short, and I was at my wits' end as to what I should do.

"There is a well-known agency for governesses in the West End called Westaway's, and there I used to call about once a week in order to see whether anything had turned up which might suit me. Westaway was the name of the founder of the business, but it is really managed by Miss Stoper. She sits in her own little office, and the ladies who are seeking employment wait in an ante-room, and are then shown in one by one, when she consults her ledgers, and sees whether she has anything which would suit them.

"Well, when I called last week I was shown into the little office as usual, but I found that Miss Stoper was not alone. A prodigiously stout man with a very smiling face, and a great heavy chin which rolled down in fold upon fold over his throat, sat at her elbow with a pair of glasses on his nose, looking very earnestly at the ladies who entered. As I came in he gave quite a jump in his chair, and turned quickly to Miss Stoper:

" 'That will do,' said he; 'I could not ask for anything better. Capital! Capital!' He seemed quite enthusiastic and rubbed his hands together in the most genial fashion. He was such a comfortable-looking man that it was quite a pleasure to look at him.

" 'You are looking for a situation, miss?' he asked.

" 'Yes, sir.'

" 'As governess?'

" 'Yes, sir.'

" 'And what salary do you ask?'

" 'I had four pounds a month in my last place with Colonel Spence Munro.'

" 'Oh, tut, tut! sweating—rank sweating!' he cried, throwing his fat hands out into the air like a man who is in a boiling passion. 'How could anyone offer so pitiful a sum to a lady with such attractions and accomplishments?'

" 'My accomplishments, sir, may be less than you imagine,' said I. 'A little French, a little German, music and drawing—'

" 'Tut, tut!' he cried. 'This is all quite beside the question. The point is, have you or have you not the bearing and deportment of a lady? There it is in a nutshell. If you have not, you are not fitted for the

rearing of a child who may some day play a considerable part in the
history of the country. But if you have, why, then how could any
gentleman ask you to condescend to accept anything under the three
figures? Your salary with me, madam, would commence at a hundred
pounds a year.'

"You may imagine, Mr Holmes, that to me, destitute as I was, such
an offer seemed almost too good to be true. The gentleman, however,
seeing perhaps the look of incredulity upon my face, opened a pocket-
book and took out a note.

" 'It is also my custom,' said he, smiling in the most pleasant fashion
until his eyes were just two shining slits, amid the white creases of his
face, 'to advance to my young ladies half their salary beforehand, so
that they may meet any little expenses of their journey and their wardrobe.'

"It seemed to me that I had never met so fascinating and so thoughtful a man. As I was already in debt to my tradesmen, the advance was
a great convenience, and yet there was something unnatural about the
whole transaction which made me wish to know a little more before I
quite committed myself.

" 'May I ask where you live, sir?' said I.

" 'Hampshire. Charming rural place. The Copper Beeches, five miles
on the far side of Winchester. It is the most lovely country, my dear
young lady, and the dearest old country house.'

" 'And my duties, sir? I should be glad to know what they would
be.'

" 'One child—one dear little romper just six years old. Oh, if you
could see him killing cockroaches with a slipper! Smack! smack! smack!
Three gone before you could wink!' He leaned back in his chair and
laughed his eyes into his head again.

"I was a little startled at the nature of the child's amusement, but
the father's laughter made me think that perhaps he was joking.

" 'My sole duties, then,' I asked, 'are to take charge of a single
child?'

" 'No, no, not the sole, not the sole, my dear young lady,' he cried.
'Your duty would be, as I am sure your good sense would suggest, to
obey any little commands which my wife might give, provided always
that they were such commands as a lady might with propriety obey.
You see no difficulty, heh?'

" 'I should be happy to make myself useful.'

" 'Quite so. In dress now, for example! We are faddy people, you know—faddy, but kind-hearted. If you were asked to wear any dress which we might give you, you would not object to our little whim. Heh?'

" 'No,' said I, considerably astonished at his words.

" 'Or to sit here, or sit there, that would not be offensive to you?'

" 'Oh, no.'

" 'Or, to cut your hair quite short before you come to us?'

"I could hardly believe my ears. As you may observe, Mr Holmes, my hair is somewhat luxuriant, and of a rather peculiar tint of chestnut. It has been considered artistic. I could not dream of sacrificing it in this offhand fashion.

" 'I am afraid that that is quite impossible,' said I. He had been watching me eagerly out of his small eyes, and I could see a shadow pass over his face as I spoke.

" 'I am afraid that it is quite essential,' said he. 'It is a little fancy of my wife's, and ladies' fancies, you know, madam, ladies' fancies must be consulted. And so you won't cut your hair?'

" 'No, sir, I really could not,' I answered firmly.

" 'Ah, very well; then that quite settles the matter. It is a pity, because in other respects you would really have done very nicely. In that case, Miss Stoper, I had best inspect a few more of your young ladies.'

"The manageress had sat all this while busy with her papers without a word to either of us, but she glanced at me now with so much annoyance upon her face that I could not help suspecting that she had lost a handsome commission through my refusal.

" 'Do you desire your name to be kept upon the books?' she asked.

" 'If you please, Miss Stoper.'

" 'Well, really, it seems rather useless, since you refuse the most excellent offers in this fashion,' said she sharply. 'You can hardly expect us to exert ourselves to find another such opening for you. Good day to you, Miss Hunter.' She struck a gong upon the table, and I was shown out by the page.

"Well, Mr Holmes, when I got back to my lodgings and found little enough in the cupboard, and two or three bills upon the table, I began to ask myself whether I had not done a very foolish thing. After all, if these people had strange fads, and expected obedience on the most extraordinary matters, they were at least ready to pay for their eccentricity. Very few governesses in England are getting a hundred a year. Besides, what use was my hair to me? Many people are improved by wearing it short, and perhaps I should be among the number. Next day I was inclined to think that I had made a mistake, and by the day after I was sure of it. I had almost overcome my pride, so far as to go back to the agency and inquire whether the place was still open, when I received this letter from the gentleman himself. I have it here, and I will read it to you:

The Copper Beeches, near Winchester.

Dear Miss Hunter—Miss Stoper has very kindly given me your address, and I write from here to ask you whether you have reconsidered your decision. My wife is very anxious that you should come, for she has been much attracted by my description of you. We are willing to give thirty pounds a quarter, or £120 a year, so as to recompense you for any little inconvenience which our fads may cause you. They are not very exacting after all. My wife is fond of a particular shade of electric blue, and would like you to wear such a dress indoors in the morning. You need not, however, go to the expense of purchasing one, as we have one belonging to my dear daughter Alice (now in Philadelphia) which would, I should think, fit you very well. Then, as to sitting here or there, or amusing yourself in any manner indicated, that need cause you no inconvenience. As regards your hair, it is no doubt a pity, especially as I could not help remarking its beauty during our short interview, but I am afraid that I must remain firm upon this point, and I only hope that the increased salary may recompense you for the loss. Your duties, as far as the child is concerned, are very light. Now do try to come, and I shall meet you with the dog-cart at Winchester. Let me know your train—Yours faithfully,

Jephro Rucastle.

"That is the letter which I have just received, Mr Holmes, and my mind is made up that I will accept it. I thought, however, that before taking the final step, I should like to submit the whole matter to your consideration."

"Well, Miss Hunter, if your mind is made up, that settles the question," said Holmes, smiling.

"But you would not advise me to refuse?"

"I confess that it is not the situation which I should like to see a sister of mine apply for."

"What is the meaning of it all, Mr Holmes?"

"Ah, I have no data. I cannot tell. Perhaps you have yourself formed some opinion?"

"Well, there seems to me to be only one possible solution. Mr Rucastle seemed to be a very kind, good-natured man. Is it not possible that his wife is a lunatic, that he desires to keep the matter quiet for fear she should be taken to an asylum, and that he humours her fancies in every way in order to prevent an outbreak."

"That is a possible solution—in fact, as matters stand, it is the most probable one. But in any case it does not seem to be a nice household for a young lady."

"But the money, Mr Holmes, the money!"

"Well, yes, of course, the pay is good—too good. That is what makes me uneasy. Why should they give you £120 a year, when they could have the pick for £40? There must be some strong reason behind."

"I thought that if I told you the circumstances you would understand afterwards if I wanted your help. I should feel so much stronger if I felt that you were at the back of me."

"Oh, you may carry that feeling away with you. I assure you that your little problem promises to be the most interesting which has come my way for some months. There is something distinctly novel about some of the features. If you should find yourself in doubt or in danger—"

"Danger! What danger do you foresee?"

Holmes shook his head gravely. "It would cease to be a danger if we could define it," said he. "But at any time, day or night, a telegram would bring me down to your help."

"That is enough." She rose briskly from her chair with the anxiety all swept from her face. "I shall go down to Hampshire quite easy in my mind now. I shall write to Mr Rucastle at once, sacrifice my poor hair tonight, and start for Winchester tomorrow." With a few grateful words to Holmes she bade us both good-night, and bustled off upon her way.

"At least," said I, as we heard her quick, firm step descending the stairs, "she seems to be a young lady who is very well able to take care of herself."

"And she would need to be," said Holmes gravely; "I am much mistaken if we do not hear from her before many days are past."

It was not very long before my friend's prediction was fulfilled. A fortnight went by, during which I frequently found my thoughts turning in her direction, and wondering what strange side alley of human experience this lonely woman had strayed into. The unusual salary, the curious conditions, the light duties, all pointed to something abnormal, though whether a fad or a plot, or whether the man were a philanthropist or a villain, it was quite beyond my powers to determine. As to Holmes, I observed that he sat frequently for half an hour on end, with knitted brows and an abstracted air, but he swept the matter away with a wave of his hand when I mentioned it. "Data! data! data!" he cried impatiently. "I can't make bricks without clay." And yet he would always wind up by muttering that no sister of his should ever have accepted such a situation.

The telegram which we eventually received came late one night, just as I was thinking of turning in, and Holmes was settling down to one of those all-night researches which he frequently indulged in, when I would leave him stooping over a retort and a test-tube at night, and find him in the same position when I came down to breakfast in the morning. He opened the yellow envelope, and then, glancing at the message, threw it across to me.

"Just look up the trains in Bradshaw," said he, and turned back to his chemical studies.

The summons was a brief and urgent one.

> Please be at the Black Swan Hotel at Winchester at midday tomorrow (it said). Do come! I am at my wits' end.
>
> Hunter.

"Will you come with me?" asked Holmes, glancing up.

"I should wish to."

"Just look it up, then."

"There is a train at half-past nine," said I, glancing over my Bradshaw. "It is due at Winchester at 11:30."

"That will do very nicely. Then perhaps I had better postpone my analysis of the acetones, as we may need to be at our best in the morning."

By eleven o'clock the next day we were well upon our way to the old English capital. Holmes had been buried in the morning papers all the way down, but after we had passed the Hampshire border he threw them down, and began to admire the scenery. It was an ideal spring day, a light blue sky, flecked with little fleecy white clouds drifting across from west to east. The sun was shining very brightly, and yet there was an exhilarating nip in the air, which set an edge to a man's energy. All over the countryside, away to the rolling hills around Aldershot, the little red and grey roofs of the farm-steadings peeped out from amidst the light green of the new foliage.

"Are they not fresh and beautiful?" I cried, with all the enthusiasm of a man fresh from the fogs of Baker Street.

But Holmes shook his head gravely.

"Do you know, Watson," said he, "that it is one of the curses of a mind with a turn like mine that I must look at everything with reference to my own special subject. You look at these scattered houses, and you are impressed by their beauty. I look at them, and the only thought which comes to me is a feeling of their isolation, and of the impunity with which crime may be committed there."

"Good heavens!" I cried. "Who would associate crime with these dear old homesteads?"

"They always fill me with a certain horror. It is my belief, Watson, founded upon my experience, that the lowest and vilest alleys in London do not present a more dreadful record of sin than does the smiling and beautiful countryside."

"You horrify me!"

"But the reason is very obvious. The pressure of public opinion can do in the town what the law cannot accomplish. There is no lane so vile that the scream of a tortured child, or the thud of a drunkard's blow, does not beget sympathy and indignation among the neighbours, and then the whole machinery of justice is ever so close that a word of complaint can set it going, and there is but a step between the crime and the dock. But look at these lonely houses, each in its own fields, filled for the most part with poor ignorant folk who know little of the law. Think of the deeds of hellish cruelty, the hidden wickedness which may go on, year in, year out, in such places, and none the wiser. Had this lady who appeals to us for help gone to live in Winchester, I should never have had a fear for her. It is the five miles of country which makes the danger. Still, it is clear that she is not personally threatened."

"No. If she can come to Winchester to meet us she can get away."

"Quite so. She has her freedom."

"What *can* be the matter, then? Can you suggest no explanation?"

"I have devised seven separate explanations, each of which would cover the facts as far as we know them. But which of these is correct can only be determined by the fresh information which we shall no doubt find waiting for us. Well, there is the tower of the Cathedral, and we shall soon learn all that Miss Hunter has to tell."

The "Black Swan" is an inn of repute in the High Street, at no distance from the station, and there we found the young lady waiting for us. She had engaged a sitting-room, and our lunch awaited us upon the table.

"I am so delighted that you have come," she said earnestly, "it is so kind of you both; but indeed I do not know what I should do. Your advice will be altogether invaluable to me."

"Pray tell us what has happened to you."

"I will do so, and I must be quick, for I have promised Mr Rucastle to be back before three. I got his leave to come into town this morning, though he little knew for what purpose."

"Let us have everything in its due order." Holmes thrust his long thin legs out towards the fire, and composed himself to listen.

"In the first place, I may say that I have met, on the whole, with no actual ill-treatment from Mr and Mrs Rucastle. It is only fair to them to say that. But I cannot understand them, and I am not easy in my mind about them."

"What can you not understand?"

"Their reasons for their conduct. But you shall have it all just as it occurred. When I came down Mr Rucastle met me here, and drove me in his dog-cart to Copper Beeches. It is, as he said, beautifully situated, but it is not beautiful in itself, for it is a large square block of a house, whitewashed, but all stained and streaked with damp and bad weather. There are grounds round it, woods on three sides, and on the fourth a field which slopes down to the Southampton high-road, which curves past about a hundred yards from the front door. This ground in front belongs to the house, but the woods all round are part of Lord Southerton's preserves. A clump of copper beeches immediately in front of the hall door has given its name to the place.

"I was driven over by my employer, who was as amiable as ever, and was introduced by him that evening to his wife and the child. There was no truth, Mr Holmes, in the conjecture which seemed to us to be probable in your rooms at Baker Street. Mrs Rucastle is not mad. I found her to be a silent, pale-faced woman, much younger than her husband, not more than thirty, I should think, while he can hardly be less than forty-five. From their conversation I have gathered that they have been married about seven years, that he was a widower, and that his only child by the first wife was the daughter who has gone to Philadelphia. Mr Rucastle told me in private that the reason why she had left them was that she had an unreasoning aversion to her step-mother. As the daughter could not have been less than twenty, I can quite imagine that her position must have been uncomfortable with her father's young wife.

"Mrs Rucastle seemed to me to be colourless in mind as well as in feature. She impressed me neither favourably nor the reverse. She was a nonentity. It was easy to see that she was passionately devoted both to her husband and to her little son. Her light grey eyes wandered continually from one to the other, noting every little want and fore-stalling it if possible. He was kind to her also in his bluff, boisterous fashion, and on the whole they seemed to be a happy couple. And yet she had some secret sorrow, this woman. She would often be lost in deep thought, with the saddest look upon her face. More than once I have surprised her in tears. I have thought sometimes that it was the disposition of her child which weighed upon her mind, for I have never met so utterly spoilt and so ill-natured a little creature. He is small for his age, with a head which is quite disproportionately large. His whole life appears to be spent in an alternation between savage fits of passion and gloomy intervals of sulking. Giving pain to any creature weaker than himself seems to be his one idea of amusement, and he shows quite remarkable talent in planning the capture of mice, little birds, and insects. But I would rather not talk about the creature, Mr Holmes, and, indeed, he has little to do with my story."

"I am glad of all details," remarked my friend, "whether they seem to you to be relevant or not."

"I shall try not to miss anything of importance. The one unpleasant thing about the house, which struck me at once, was the appearance and conduct of the servants. There are only two, a man and his wife. Toller, for that's his name, is a rough, uncouth man, with grizzled hair and whiskers, and a perpetual smell of drink. Twice since I have been with them he has been quite drunk, and yet Mr Rucastle seemed to take no notice of it. His wife is a very tall and strong woman with a sour face, as silent as Mrs Rucastle, and much less amiable. They are a most unpleasant couple, but fortunately I spend most of my time in the nursery and my own room, which are next to each other in one corner of the building.

"For two days after my arrival at the Copper Beeches my life was very quiet; on the third, Mrs Rucastle came down just after breakfast and whispered something to her husband.

" 'Oh yes,' said he, turning to me, 'we are very much obliged to you, Miss Hunter, for falling in with our whims so far as to cut your hair. I assure you that it has not detracted in the tiniest iota from your appearance. We shall now see how the electric blue dress will become you. You will find it laid out upon the bed in your room, and if you would be so good as to put it on we should both be extremely obliged.'

"The dress which I found waiting for me was of a peculiar shade of blue. It was of excellent material, a sort of beige, but it bore unmistakable signs of having been worn before. It could not have been a better fit if I had been measured for it. Both Mr and Mrs Rucastle expressed a delight at the look of it which seemed quite exaggerated in its vehemence. They were waiting for me in the drawing-room, which is a very large room, stretching along the entire front of the house, with three long windows reaching down to the floor. A chair had been placed close to the central window, with its back turned towards it. In this I was asked to sit, and then Mr Rucastle, walking up and down on the other side of the room, began to tell me a series of the funniest stories that I have ever listened to. You cannot imagine how comical he was, and I laughed until I was quite weary. Mrs Rucastle, however, who has evidently no sense of humour, never so much as smiled, but sat with her hands in her lap, and a sad, anxious look upon her face. After an hour or so, Mr Rucastle suddenly remarked that it was time to commence the duties of the day, and that I might change my dress, and go to little Edward in the nursery.

"Two days later this same performance was gone through under exactly similar circumstances. Again I changed my dress, again I sat in the window, and again I laughed very heartily at the funny stories of which my employer had an immense repertoire, and which he told inimitably. Then he handed me a yellow-backed novel, and, moving my chair a little sideways, that my own shadow might not fall upon the page, he begged me to read aloud to him. I read for about ten minutes, beginning in the heart of a chapter, and then suddenly, in the middle of a sentence, he ordered me to cease and change my dress.

"You can easily imagine, Mr Holmes, how curious I became as to what the meaning of this extraordinary performance could possibly be. They were always very careful, I observed, to turn my face away from the window, so that I became consumed with the desire to see what was going on behind my back. At first it seemed to be impossible, but I soon devised a means. My hand mirror had been broken, so a happy thought seized me, and I concealed a little of the glass in my handkerchief. On the next occasion, in the midst of my laughter, I put my handkerchief up to my eyes, and was able with a little management to see all that there was behind me. I confess that I was disappointed. There was nothing.

"At least, that was my first impression. At the second glance, however, I perceived that there was a man standing in the Southampton road, a small bearded man in a grey suit, who seemed to be looking in my direction. The road is an important highway, and there are usually people there. This man, however, was leaning against the railings which bordered our field, and was looking earnestly. I lowered my handkerchief, and glanced at Mrs Rucastle to find her eyes fixed upon me with a most searching gaze. She said nothing, but I am convinced that she had divined that I had a mirror in my hand, and had seen what was behind me. She rose at once.

" 'Jephro,' said she, 'there is an impertinent fellow upon the road there who stares up at Miss Hunter.'

" 'No friend of yours, Miss Hunter?' he asked.

" 'No; I know no one in these parts.'

" 'Dear me! How very impertinent! Kindly turn round, and motion him to go away.'

" 'Surely it would be better to take no notice?'

" 'No, no, we should have him loitering here always. Kindly turn round, and wave him away like that.'

"I did as I was told, and at the same instant Mrs Rucastle drew down the blind. That was a week ago, and from that time I have not sat again in the window, nor have I worn the blue dress, nor seen the man in the road."

"Pray continue," said Holmes. "Your narrative promises to be a most interesting one."

"You will find it rather disconnected, I fear, and there may prove to be little relation between the different incidents of which I speak. On the very first day that I was at Copper Beeches, Mr Rucastle took me to a small outhouse which stands near the kitchen door. As we approached it I heard the sharp rattling of a chain, and the sound as of a large animal moving about.

" 'Look in here!' said Mr Rucastle, showing me a slit between two planks. 'Is he not a beauty?'

"I looked through, and was conscious of two glowing eyes, and of a vague figure huddled up in the darkness.

" 'Don't be frightened,' said my employer, laughing at the start which I had given. 'It's only Carlo, my mastiff. I call him mine, but really old Toller, my groom, is the only man who can do anything with him. We feed him once a day, and not too much then, so that he is always as keen as mustard. Toller lets him loose every night, and God help the trespasser whom he lays his fangs upon. For goodness' sake don't you ever on any pretext set your foot over the threshold at night, for it is as much as your life is worth.'

"The warning was no idle one, for two nights later I happened to look out of my bedroom window about two o'clock in the morning. It was a beautiful moonlight night, and the lawn in front of the house was silvered over and almost as bright as day. I was standing wrapped in the peaceful beauty of the scene, when I was aware that something was moving under the shadow of the copper beeches. As it emerged into the moonshine I saw what it was. It was a giant dog, as large as a calf, tawny-tinted, with hanging jowl, black muzzle, and huge projecting bones. It walked slowly across the lawn and vanished into the shadow upon the other side. That dreadful silent sentinel sent a chill to my heart, which I do not think that any burglar could have done.

"And now I have a very strange experience to tell you. I had, as you know, cut off my hair in London, and I had placed it in a great coil at the bottom of my trunk. One evening, after the child was in bed, I began to amuse myself by examining the furniture of my room, and by rearranging my own little things. There was an old chest of drawers in the room, the two upper ones empty and open, the lower one locked. I had filled the two first with my linen, and as I had still much to pack away, I was naturally annoyed at not having the use of the third drawer. It struck me that it might have been fastened by a mere oversight, so I took out my bunch of keys and tried to open it. The very first key fitted to perfection, and I drew the drawer open. There was only one thing in it, but I am sure that you would never guess what it was. It was my coil of hair.

"I took it up and examined it. It was of the same peculiar tint, and the same thickness. But then the impossibility of the thing obtruded itself upon me. How *could* my hair have been locked in the drawer? With trembling hands I undid my trunk, turned out the contents, and drew from the bottom my own hair. I laid the two tresses together, and I assure you they were identical. Was it not extraordinary? Puzzle as I would I could make nothing at all of what it meant. I returned the strange hair to the drawer, and I said nothing of the matter to the Rucastles, as I felt that I had put myself in the wrong by opening a drawer which they had locked.

"I am naturally observant as you may have remarked, Mr Holmes, and I soon had a pretty good plan of the whole house in my head. There was one wing, however, which appeared not to be inhabited at all. A door which faced that which led into the quarters of the Tollers opened into this suite, but it was invariably locked. One day, however, as I ascended the stair, I met Mr Rucastle coming out through this door, his keys in his hand, and a look on his face which made him a very different person to the round jovial man to whom I was accustomed. His cheeks were red, his brow was all crinkled with anger, and the veins stood out at his temples with passion. He locked the door, and hurried past me without a word or a look.

"This aroused my curiosity; so when I went out for a walk in the grounds with my charge, I strolled round to the side from which I could see the windows of this part of the house. There were four of them in a row, three of which were simply dirty, while the fourth was shuttered up. They were evidently all deserted. As I strolled up and down, glancing at them occasionally, Mr Rucastle came out to me, looking as merry and jovial as ever.

" 'Ah!' said he, 'you must not think me rude if I passed you without a word, my dear young lady. I was preoccupied with business matters.'

"I assured him that I was not offended. 'By the way,' said I, 'you seem to have quite a suite of spare rooms up there, and one of them has the shutters up.'

" 'Photography is one of my hobbies,' said he. 'I have made my darkroom up there. But, dear me! what an observant young lady we have come upon. Who would have believed it? Who would have ever believed it?' He spoke in a jesting tone, but there was no jest in his eyes as he looked at me. I read suspicion there, and annoyance, but no jest.

"Well, Mr Holmes, from the moment that I understood that there was something about that suite of rooms which I was not to know, I was all on fire to go over them. It was not mere curiosity, though I have my share of that. It was more a feeling of duty—a feeling that some good might come from my penetrating to this place. They talk of woman's instinct; perhaps it was woman's instinct which gave me that feeling. At any rate, it was there; and I was keenly on the look-out for any chance to pass the forbidden door.

"It was only yesterday that the chance came. I may tell you that, besides Mr Rucastle, both Toller and his wife find something to do in these deserted rooms, and I once saw him carrying a large black linen bag with him through the door. Recently he has been drinking hard, and yesterday evening he was very drunk; and, when I came upstairs, there was the key in the door. I have no doubt at all that he had left it there. Mr and Mrs Rucastle were both downstairs, and the child was with them, so that I had an admirable opportunity. I turned the key gently in the lock, opened the door, and slipped through.

"There was a little passage in front of me, unpapered and uncarpeted, which turned at a right angle at the farther end. Round this corner were three doors in a line, the first and third of which were open. They each led into an empty room, dusty and cheerless, with two windows in the one, and one in the other, so thick with dirt that the evening light glimmered dimly through them. The center door was closed, and across the outside of it had been fastened one of the broad bars of an iron bed, padlocked at one end to a ring in the wall, and fastened at the other with stout cord. The door itself was locked as well, and the key was not there. This barricaded door corresponded clearly with the shuttered window outside, and yet I could see by the glimmer from beneath it that the room was not in darkness. Evidently there was a skylight which let in light from above. As I stood in the passage gazing at this sinister door, and wondering what secret it might veil, I suddenly heard the sound of steps within the room, and saw a shadow pass backwards and forwards against the little slit of dim light which shone out from under the door. A mad, unreasoning terror rose up in me at the sight, Mr Holmes. My overstrung nerves failed me suddenly, and I turned and ran—ran as though some dreadful hand were behind me, clutching at the skirt of my dress. I rushed down the passage, through the door, and straight into the arms of Mr Rucastle, who was waiting outside.

" 'So,' said he, smiling, 'it was you, then. I thought it must be when I saw the door open.'

" 'Oh, I am so frightened!' I panted.

" 'My dear young lady! my dear young lady!'—you cannot think how caressing and soothing his manner was—'and what has frightened you, my dear young lady?'

"But his voice was just a little too coaxing. He overdid it. I was keenly on my guard against him.

" 'I was foolish enough to go into the empty wing,' I answered. 'But it is so lonely and eerie in this dim light that I was frightened and ran out again. Oh, it is so dreadfully still in there!'

" 'Only that?' said he, looking at me keenly.

" 'Why, what do you think?' I asked.

" 'Why do you think that I lock this door?'

" 'I am sure that I do not know.'

" 'It is to keep people out who have no business there. Do you see?' He was still smiling in the most amiable manner.

" 'I am sure if I had known—'

" 'Well, then, you know now. And if you ever put your foot over that threshold again—' here in an instant the smile hardened into a grin of rage, and he glared down at me with the face of a demon, 'I'll throw you to the mastiff.'

"I was so terrified that I do not know what I did. I suppose that I must have rushed past him into my room. I remember nothing until I found myself lying on my bed trembling all over. Then I thought of you, Mr Holmes. I could not live there longer without some advice. I was frightened of the house, of the man, of the woman, of the servants, even of the child. They were all horrible to me. If I could only bring you down all would be well. Of course I might have fled from the house, but my curiosity was almost as strong as my fears. My mind was soon made up. I would send you a wire. I put on my hat and cloak, went down to the office, which is about half a mile from the house, and then returned, feeling very much easier. A horrible doubt came into my mind as I approached the door lest the dog might be loose, but I remembered that Toller had drunk himself into a state of insensibility that evening, and I knew that he was the only one in the household who had any influence with the savage creature, or who would venture to set him free. I slipped in in safety, and lay awake half the night in my joy at the thought of seeing you. I had no difficulty in getting leave to come into Winchester this morning, but I must be back before three o'clock, for Mr and Mrs Rucastle are going on a visit, and will be away all the evening, so that I must look after the child. Now I have told you all my adventures, Mr Holmes, and I should be very glad if you could tell me what it all means, and, above all, what I should do."

Holmes and I had listened spellbound to this extraordinary story. My friend rose now, and paced up and down the room, his hands in his pockets, and an expression of the most profound gravity upon his face.

"Is Toller still drunk?" he asked.

"Yes. I heard his wife tell Mrs Rucastle that she could do nothing with him."

"That is well. And the Rucastles go out tonight?"

"Yes."

"Is there a cellar with a good strong lock?"

"Yes, the wine cellar."

"You seem to me to have acted all through this matter like a brave and sensible girl, Miss Hunter. Do you think that you could perform one more feat? I should not ask it of you if I did not think you a quite exceptional woman."

"I will try. What is it?"

"We shall be at the Copper Beeches by seven o'clock, my friend and I. The Rucastles will be gone by that time, and Toller will, we hope, be incapable. There only remains Mrs Toller, who might give the alarm. If you could send her into the cellar, on some errand, and then turn the key upon her, you would facilitate matters immensely."

"I will do it."

"Excellent! We shall then look thoroughly into the affair. Of course there is only one feasible explanation. You have been brought there to personate someone, and the real person is imprisoned in this chamber. That is obvious. As to who this prisoner is, I have no doubt that it is the daughter, Miss Alice Rucastle, if I remember right, who was said to have gone to America. You were chosen, doubtless, as resembling her in height, figure, and the colour of your hair. Hers had been cut off, very possibly in some illness through which she has passed, and so, of course, yours had to be sacrificed also. By a curious chance you came upon her tresses. The man in the road was, undoubtedly, some friend of hers—possibly her fiancé and no doubt as you wore the girl's dress, and were so like her, he was convinced from your laughter, whenever he saw you, and afterwards from your gesture, that Miss Rucastle was perfectly happy, and that she no longer desired his attentions. The dog is let loose at night to prevent him from endeavouring to communicate with her. So much is fairly clear. The most serious point in the case is the disposition of the child."

"What on earth has that to do with it?' I ejaculated.

"My dear Watson, you as a medical man are continually gaining light as to the tendencies of a child by the study of the parents. Don't you see that the converse is equally valid? I have frequently gained my first real insight into the character of parents by studying their children. This child's disposition is abnormally cruel, merely for cruelty's sake, and whether he derives this from his smiling father, as I should suspect, or from his mother, it bodes evil for the poor girl who is in their power."

"I am sure that you are right, Mr Holmes," cried our client. "A thousand things come back to me which make me certain that you have hit it. Oh, let us lose not an instant in bringing help to this poor creature."

"We must be circumspect, for we are dealing with a very cunning man. We can do nothing until seven o'clock. At that hour we shall be with you, and it will not be long before we solve the mystery."

We were as good as our word, for it was just seven when we reached the Copper Beeches, having put up our trap at the wayside public-house. The group of trees, with their dark leaves shining like burnished metal in the light of the setting sun, were sufficient to mark the house even had Miss Hunter not been standing smiling on the doorstep.

"Have you managed it?" asked Holmes.

A loud thudding noise came from somewhere downstairs. "That is Mrs Toller in the cellar," said she. "Her husband lies snoring on the kitchen rug. Here are his keys which are the duplicates of Mr Rucastle's."

"You have done well indeed!" cried Holmes, with enthusiasm. "Now lead the way, and we shall soon see the end of this black business."

We passed up the stair, unlocked the door, followed on down a passage, and found ourselves in front of the barricade which Miss Hunter had described. Holmes cut the cord and removed the transverse bar. Then he tried the various keys in the lock, but without success. No sound came from within, and at the silence Holmes' face clouded over.

"I trust that we are not too late," said he. "I think, Miss Hunter, that we had better go in without you. Now, Watson, put your shoulder to it, and we shall see whether we cannot make our way in."

It was an old rickety door and gave at once before our united strength. Together we rushed into the room. It was empty. There was no furniture save a little pallet bed, a small table, and a basketful of linen. The skylight above was open, and the prisoner gone.

"There has been some villainy here," said Holmes; "this beauty has guessed Miss Hunter's intentions, and has carried his victim off."

"But how?"

"Through the skylight. We shall soon see how he managed it." He swung himself up on to the roof. "Ah, yes," he cried, "here's the end of a long light ladder against the eaves. That is how he did it."

"But it is impossible," said Miss Hunter, "the ladder was not there when the Rucastles went away."

"He has come back and done it. I tell you that he is a clever and dangerous man. I should not be very much surprised if this were he whose step I hear now upon the stair. I think, Watson, that it would be as well for you to have your pistol ready."

The words were hardly out of his mouth before a man appeared at the door of the room, a very fat and burly man, with a heavy stick in his hand. Miss Hunter screamed and shrunk against the wall at the sight of him, but Sherlock Holmes sprang forward and confronted him.

"You villain," said he, "where's your daughter?"

The fat man cast his eyes round, and then up at the open skylight.

"It is for me to ask you that," he shrieked, "you thieves! Spies and thieves! I have caught you, have I! You are in my power. I'll serve you!" He turned and clattered down the stairs as hard as he could go.

"He's gone for the dog!" cried Miss Hunter.

"I have my revolver," said I.

"Better close the front door," cried Holmes, and we all rushed down the stairs together. We had hardly reached the hall when we heard the baying of a hound, and then a scream of agony, with a horrible worrying sound which it was dreadful to listen to. An elderly man with a red face and shaking limbs came staggering out at a side-door.

"My God!" he cried. "Someone has loosed the dog. It's not been fed for two days. Quick, quick, or it'll be too late!"

Holmes and I rushed out, and round the angle of the house, with Toller hurrying behind us. There was the huge famished brute, its black muzzle buried in Rucastle's throat, while he writhed and screamed upon the ground. Running up, I blew its brains out, and it fell over with its keen white teeth still meeting in the great creases of his neck. With much labour we separated them, and carried him, living but horribly mangled, into the house. We laid him upon the drawing-room sofa, and having despatched the sobered Toller to bear the news to his wife, I did what I could to relieve his pain. We were all assembled round him when the door opened, and a tall, gaunt woman entered the room.

"Mrs Toller!" cried Miss Hunter.

"Yes, miss. Mr Rucastle let me out when he came back before he went up to you. Ah, miss, it is a pity you didn't let me know what you were planning, for I would have told you that your pains were wasted."

"Ha!" said Holmes, looking keenly at her. "It is clear that Mrs Toller knows more about this matter than anyone else."

"Yes, sir, I do, and I am ready enough to tell what I know."

"Then pray sit down, and let us hear it, for there are several points on which I must confess that I am still in the dark."

"I will soon make it clear to you," said she; "and I'd have done so before now if I could ha' got out from the cellar. If there's police-court business over this, you'll remember that I was the one that stood your friend, and that I was Miss Alice's friend too.

"She was never happy at home, Miss Alice wasn't, from the time that her father married again. She was slighted like, and had no say in anything; but it never really became bad for her until after she met Mr Fowler at a friend's house. As well as I could learn, Miss Alice had rights of her own by will, but she was so quiet and patient, she was, that she never said a word about them, but just left everything in Mr Rucastle's hands. He knew he was safe with her; but when there was a chance of a husband coming forward, who would ask for all that the law could give him, then her father thought it time to put a stop on it. He wanted her to sign a paper so that whether she married or not, he could use her money. When she wouldn't do it, he kept on worrying her until she got brain fever, and for six weeks was at death's door. Then she got better at last, all worn to a shadow, and with her beautiful hair cut off; but that didn't make no change in her young man, and he stuck to her as true as man could be."

"Ah," said Holmes, "I think that what you have been good enough to tell us makes the matter fairly clear, and that I can deduce all that remains. Mr Rucastle, then, I presume, took to this system of imprisonment?"

"Yes, sir."

"And brought Miss Hunter down from London in order to get rid of the disagreeable persistence of Mr Fowler."

"That was it, sir."

"But Mr Fowler, being a persevering man, as a good seaman should be, blockaded the house, and, having met you, succeeded by certain arguments, metallic or otherwise, in convincing you that your interests were the same as his."

"Mr Fowler was a very kind-spoken, free-handed gentleman," said Mrs Toller serenely.

"And in this way he managed that your good man should have no want of drink, and that a ladder should be ready at the moment when your master had gone."

"You have it, sir, just as it happened."

"I am sure we owe you an apology, Mrs Toller," said Holmes, "for you have certainly cleared up everything which puzzled us. And here comes the country surgeon and Mrs Rucastle, so I think, Watson, that we had best escort Miss Hunter back to Winchester, as it seems to me that our *locus standi* now is rather a questionable one."

And thus was solved the mystery of the sinister house with the copper beeches in front of the door. Mr Rucastle survived, but was always a broken man, kept alive solely through the care of his devoted wife. They still live with their old servants, who probably know so much of Rucastle's past life that he finds it difficult to part from them. Mr Fowler and Miss Rucastle were married, by special licence, in Southampton the day after their flight, and he is now the holder of a Government appointment in the Island of Mauritius. As to Miss Violet Hunter, my friend Holmes, rather to my disappointment, manifested no further interest in her when once she had ceased to be the centre of one of his problems, and she is now the head of a private school at Walsall, where I believe that she has met with considerable success.

G.K. CHESTERTON *(1874–1936), the creator of the famous Catholic priest detective Father Brown, was the father of the clerical detective, a small but very important part of the mystery field well worked by Harry Kemelman, among others. Chesterton himself was one of the great literary figures of his time, the author of scores of books and hundreds of articles of literary and art criticism and on all sorts of social issues. His one criminous novel,* The Man Who Was Thursday *(1908), is outstanding, but it is as a short story writer that Chesterton made his contribution to crime fiction. His Father Brown tales are wonderful puzzles, among the best written of their time, even though we are told very little about the detective himself.*

"The Blue Cross" is one of Father Brown's finest and most baffling cases.

The Blue Cross
BY G. K. CHESTERTON

Between the silver ribbon of morning and the green glittering ribbon of sea, the boat touched Harwich and let loose a swarm of folk like flies, among whom the man we must follow was by no means conspicuous—nor wished to be. There was nothing notable about him, except a slight contrast between the holiday gayety of his clothes and the official gravity of his face. His clothes included a slight, pale gray jacket, a white waistcoat, and a silver straw hat with a gray-blue ribbon. His lean face was dark by contrast, and ended in a curt black beard that looked Spanish and suggested an Elizabethan ruff. He was smoking a cigarette with the seriousness of an idler. There was nothing about him to indicate the fact that the gray jacket covered a loaded revolver, that the white waistcoat covered a police card, or that the straw hat covered one of the most powerful intellects in Europe. For this was Valentin himself, the head of the Paris police and the most famous investigator of the world; and he was coming from Brussels to London to make the greatest arrest of the century.

Flambeau was in England. The police of three countries had tracked the great criminal at last from Ghent to Brussels, from Brussels to the Hook of Holland; and it was conjectured that he would take some advantage of the unfamiliarity and confusion of the Eucharistic Congress, then taking place in London. Probably he would travel as some minor clerk or secretary connected with it; but, of course, Valentin could not be certain; nobody could be certain about Flambeau.

It is many years now since this colossus of crime suddenly ceased keeping the world in a turmoil; and when he ceased, as they said after the death of Roland, there was a great quiet upon the earth. But in his best days (I mean, of course, his worst) Flambeau was a figure as statuesque and international as the Kaiser. Almost every morning the daily paper announced that he had escaped the consequences of one extraordinary crime by committing another. He was a Gascon of gigantic stature and bodily daring; and the wildest tales were told of his outburst of athletic humor; how he turned the *juge d'instruction* upside down and stood him on his head, "to clear his mind"; how he ran down the Rue de Rivoli with a policeman under each arm. It is due to him to say that his fantastic physical strength was generally employed in such bloodless though undignified scenes; his real crimes were chiefly those of ingenious and wholesale robbery. But each of his thefts was almost a new sin, and would make a story by itself. It was he who ran the great Tyrolean Dairy Company in London, with no dairies, no cows, no carts, no milk, but with some thousand subscribers. These he served by the simple operation of moving the little milk cans outside people's doors to the doors of his own customers. It was he who had kept up an unaccountable and close correspondence with a young lady whose whole letter-bag was intercepted, by the extraordinary trick of photographing his messages infinitesimally small upon the slides of a microscope. A sweeping simplicity, however, marked many of his experiments. It is said that he once repainted all the numbers in a street in the dead of night merely to divert one traveler into a trap. It is quite certain that he invented a portable pillar-box, which he put up at corners in quiet suburbs on the chance of strangers dropping postal orders into it. Lastly, he was known to be a startling acrobat; despite his huge figure, he could leap like a grasshopper and melt into the tree-tops like a monkey. Hence the great Valentin, when he set out to find Flambeau, was perfectly aware that his adventures would not end when he had found him.

But how was he to find him? On this the great Valentin's ideas were still in process of settlement.

There was one thing which Flambeau, with all his dexterity of disguise, could not cover, and that was his singular height. If Valentin's quick eye had caught a tall apple-woman, a tall grenadier, or even a tolerably tall duchess, he might have arrested them on the spot. But all along his train there was nobody that could be a disguised Flambeau, any more than a cat could be a disguised giraffe. About the people on the boat he had already satisfied himself; and the people picked up at Harwich or on the journey limited themselves with certainty to six. There was a short railway official traveling up to the terminus, three fairly short market gardeners picked up two stations afterwards, one very short widow lady going up from a small Essex town, and a very short Roman Catholic priest going up from a small Essex village. When it came to the last case, Valentin gave it up and almost laughed. The little priest was so much the essence of those Eastern flats; he had a face as round and dull as a Norfolk dumpling; he had eyes as empty as the North Sea; he had several brown paper parcels, which he was quite incapable of collecting. The Eucharistic Congress had doubtless sucked out of their local stagnation many such creatures, blind and helpless, like moles disinterred. Valentin was a skeptic in the severe style of France, and could have no love for priests. But he could have pity for them, and this one might have provoked pity in anybody. He had a large, shabby umbrella, which constantly fell on the floor. He did not seem to know which was the right end of his return ticket. He explained with a moon-calf simplicity to everybody in the carriage that he had to be careful, because he had something made of real silver "with blue stones" in one of his brown-paper parcels. His quaint blending of Essex flatness with saintly simplicity continuously amused the Frenchman till the priest arrived (somehow) at Tottenham with all his parcels, and came back for his umbrella. When he did the last, Valentin even had the good nature to warn him not to take care of the silver by telling everybody about it. But to whomever he talked, Valentin kept his eye open for some one else; he looked out steadily for any one, rich or poor, male or female, who was well up to six feet; for Flambeau was four inches above it.

He alighted at Liverpool Street, however, quite conscientiously secure that he had not missed the criminal so far. He then went to Scotland Yard to regularize his position and arrange for help in case of need; he then lit another cigarette and went for a long stroll in the streets of London. As he was walking in the streets and squares beyond Victoria, he paused suddenly and stood. It was a quaint, quiet square, very typical of London, full of an accidental stillness. The tall, flat houses round looked at once prosperous and uninhabited; the square of shrubbery in the center looked as deserted as a green Pacific islet. One of the four sides was much higher than the rest, like a dais; and the line of this side was broken by one of London's admirable accidents—a restaurant that looked as if it had strayed from Soho. It was an unreasonably attractive object, with dwarf plants in pots and long, striped blinds of lemon yellow and white. It stood specially high above the street, and in the usual patchwork way of London, a flight of steps from the street ran up to meet the front door almost as a fire-escape might run up to a first-floor window. Valentin stood and smoked in front of the yellow-white blinds and considered them long.

The most incredible thing about miracles is that they happen. A few clouds in heaven do come together into the staring shape of one human eye. A tree does stand up in the landscape of a doubtful journey in the exact and elaborate shape of a note of interrogation. I have seen both these things myself within the last few days. Nelson does die in the instant of victory; and a man named Williams does quite accidentally murder a man named Williamson; it sounds like a sort of infanticide. In short, there is in life an element of elfin coincidence which people reckoning on the prosaic may perpetually miss. As it has been well expressed in the paradox of Poe, wisdom should reckon on the unforeseen.

Aristide Valentin was unfathomably French; and the French intelligence is intelligence specially and solely. He was not "a thinking machine"; for that is a brainless phrase of modern fatalism and materialism. A machine only *is* a machine because it cannot think. But he was a thinking man, and a plain man at the same time. All his wonderful successes, that looked like conjuring, had been gained by plodding logic, by clear and commonplace French thought. The French electrify the world not by starting any paradox, they electrify it by carrying out a truism. They carry a truism so far—as in the French Revolution. But exactly because Valentin understood reason, he understood the limits of reason. Only a man who knows nothing of motors talks of motoring without petrol; only a man who knows nothing of reason talks of reasoning without strong, undisputed first principles. Here he had no strong first principles. Flambeau had been missed at Harwich; and if he was in London at all, he might be anything from a tall tramp on Wimbledon Common to a tall toastmaster at the Hôtel Métropole. In such a naked state of nescience, Valentin had a view and a method of his own.

In such cases he reckoned on the unforeseen. In such cases, when he could not follow the train of the reasonable, he coldly and carefully followed the train of the unreasonable. Instead of going to the right

places—banks, police stations, rendezvous—he systematically went to
the wrong places; knocked at every empty house, turned down every
cul de sac, went up every lane blocked with rubbish, went round every
crescent that led him uselessly out of the way. He defended this crazy
course quite logically. He said that if one had a clue this was the worst
way; but if one had no clue at all it was the best, because there was just
the chance that any oddity that caught the eye of the pursuer might be
the same that had caught the eye of the pursued. Somewhere a man
must begin, and it had better be just where another man might stop.
Something about that flight of steps up to the shop, something about
the quietude and quaintness of the restaurant, roused all the detective's
rare romantic fancy and made him resolve to strike at random. He
went up the steps, and sitting down at a table by the window, asked for
a cup of black coffee.

It was half-way through the morning, and he had not breakfasted;
the slight litter of other breakfasts stood about on the table to remind
him of his hunger; and adding a poached egg to his order, he proceeded musingly to shake some white sugar into his coffee, thinking all
the time about Flambeau. He remembered how Flambeau had escaped, once by a pair of nail scissors, and once by a house on fire; once
by having to pay for an unstamped letter, and once by getting people to
look through a telescope at a comet that might destroy the world. He
thought his detective brain as good as the criminal's, which was true.
But he fully realized the disadvantage. "The criminal is the creative
artist; the detective only the critic," he said with a sour smile, and
lifted his coffee cup to his lips slowly, and put it down very quickly. He
had put salt in it.

He looked at the vessel from which the silvery powder had come; it
was certainly a sugar-basin; as unmistakably meant for sugar as a
champagne bottle for champagne. He wondered why they should keep
salt in it. He looked to see if there were any more orthodox vessels.
Yes, there were two salt-cellars quite full. Perhaps there was some
speciality in the condiment in the salt-cellars. He tasted it; it was sugar.
Then he looked round at the restaurant with a refreshed air of interest,
to see if there were any other traces of that singular artistic taste which
puts the sugar in the salt-cellars and the salt in the sugar-basin. Except
for an odd splash of some dark fluid on one of the white-papered walls,
the whole place appeared neat, cheerful and ordinary. He rang the bell
for the waiter.

When that official hurried up, fuzzy-haired and somewhat blear-eyed at that early hour, the detective (who was not without an appreciation of the simpler forms of humor) asked him to taste the sugar and see if it was up to the high reputation of the hotel. The result was that the waiter yawned suddenly and woke up.

"Do you play this delicate joke on your customers every morning?" inquired Valentin. "Does changing the salt and sugar never pall on you as a jest?"

The waiter, when this irony grew clearer, stammeringly assured him that the establishment had certainly no such intention; it must be a most curious mistake. He picked up the sugar-basin and looked at it; he picked up the salt-cellar and looked at that, his face growing more and more bewildered. At last he abruptly excused himself, and hurrying away, returned in a few seconds with the proprietor. The proprietor also examined the sugar-basin and then the salt-cellar; the proprietor also looked bewildered.

Suddenly the waiter seemed to grow inarticulate with a rush of words.

"I zink," he stuttered eagerly, "I zink it is those two clergymen."

"What two clergymen?"

"The two clergymen," said the waiter, "that threw soup at the wall."

"Threw soup at the wall?" repeated Valentin, feeling sure this must be some singular Italian metaphor.

"Yes, yes," said the attendant excitedly, and pointing at the dark splash on the white paper; "threw it over there on the wall."

Valentin looked his query at the proprietor, who came to his rescue with fuller reports.

"Yes, sir," he said, "it's quite true, though I don't suppose it has anything to do with the sugar and salt. Two clergymen came in and drank soup here very early, as soon as the shutters were taken down. They were both very quiet, respectable people; one of them paid the bill and went out; the other, who seemed a slower coach altogether, was some minutes longer getting his things together. But he went at last. Only, the instant before he stepped into the street he deliberately picked up his cup, which he had only half emptied, and threw the soup slap on the wall. I was in the back room myself, and so was the waiter; so I could only rush out in time to find the wall splashed and the shop empty. It don't do any particular damage, but it was confounded cheek; and I tried to catch the men in the street. They were too far off though; I only noticed they went round the next corner into Carstairs Street."

The detective was on his feet, hat settled and stick in his hand. He had already decided that in the universal darkness of his mind he could only follow the first odd finger that pointed; and this finger was odd enough. Paying his bill and clashing the glass doors behind him, he was soon swinging round into the other street.

It was fortunate that even in such fevered moments his eye was cool and quick. Something in a shop-front went by him like a mere flash; yet he went back to look at it. The shop was a popular greengrocer and fruiterer's, an array of goods set out in the open air and plainly ticketed with their names and prices. In the two most prominent compartments were two heaps, of oranges and of nuts respectively. On the heap of nuts lay a scrap of cardboard, on which was written in bold, blue chalk, "Best tangerine oranges, two a penny." On the oranges was the equally clear and exact description, "Finest Brazil nuts, 4d. a lb." M. Valentin looked at these two placards and fancied he had met this highly subtle form of humor before, and that somewhat recently. He drew the attention of the red-faced fruiterer, who was looking rather sullenly up and down the street, to this inaccuracy in his advertisements. The fruiterer said nothing, but sharply put each card into its proper place. The detective, leaning elegantly on his walking-cane, continued to scrutinize the shop. At last he said, "Pray excuse my apparent irrelevance, my good sir, but I should like to ask you a question in experimental psychology and the association of ideas."

The red-faced shopman regarded him with an eye of menace; but he continued gayly, swinging his cane. "Why," he pursued, "why are two tickets wrongly placed in a greengrocer's shop like a shovel hat that has come to London for a holiday? Or, in case I do not make myself clear, what is the mystical association which connects the idea of nuts marked as oranges with the idea of two clergymen, one tall and the other short?"

The eyes of the tradesman stood out of his head like a snail's; he really seemed for an instant likely to fling himself upon the stranger. At last he stammered angrily: "I don't know what you 'ave to do with it, but if you're one of their friends, you can tell 'em from me that I'll knock their silly 'eads off, parsons or no parsons, if they upset my apples again."

"Indeed," asked the detective, with great sympathy. "Did they upset your apples?"

"One of 'em did," said the heated shopman; "rolled 'em all over the street. I'd 'ave caught the fool but for havin' to pick 'em up."

"Which way did these parsons go?" asked Valentin.

"Up that second road on the left-hand side, and then across the square," said the other promptly.

"Thanks," replied Valentin, and vanished like a fairy. On the other side of the second square he found a policeman, and said: "This is urgent, constable; have you seen two clergymen in shovel hats?"

The policeman began to chuckle heavily. "I 'ave, sir; and if you arst me, one of 'em was drunk. He stood in the middle of the road that bewildered that—"

"Which way did they go?" snapped Valentin.

"They took one of them yellow buses over there," answered the man; "them that go to Hampstead."

Valentin produced his official card and said very rapidly: "Call up two of your men to come with me in pursuit," and crossed the road with such contagious energy that the ponderous policeman was moved to almost agile obedience. In a minute and a half the French detective was joined on the opposite pavement by an inspector and a man in plain clothes.

"Well, sir," began the former, with smiling importance, "and what may—?"

Valentin pointed suddenly with his cane. "I'll tell you on the top of that omnibus," he said, and was darting and dodging across the tangle of the traffic. When all three sank panting on the top seats of the yellow vehicle, the inspector said: "We could go four times as quick in a taxi."

"Quite true," replied their leader placidly, "if we only had an idea of where we were going."

"Well, where *are* you going?" asked the other, staring.

Valentin smoked frowningly for a few seconds; then, removing his cigarette, he said: "If you *know* what a man's doing, get in front of him; but if you want to guess what he's doing, keep behind him. Stray when he strays; stop when he stops; travel as slowly as he. Then you may see what he saw and may act as he acted. All we can do is to keep our eyes skinned for a queer thing."

"What sort of queer thing do you mean?" asked the inspector.

"Any sort of queer thing," answered Valentin, and relapsed into obstinate silence.

The yellow omnibus crawled up the northern roads for what seemed

like hours on end; the great detective would not explain further, and
perhaps his assistants felt a silent and growing doubt of his errand.
Perhaps, also, they felt a silent and growing desire for lunch, for the
hours crept long past the normal luncheon hour, and the long roads of
the North London suburbs seemed to shoot out into length after length
like an infernal telescope. It was one of those journeys on which a man
perpetually feels that now at last he must have come to the end of the
universe, and then finds he has only come to the beginning of Tufnell
Park. London died away in draggled taverns and dreary scrubs, and
then was unaccountably born again in blazing high streets and blatant
hotels. It was like passing through thirteen separate vulgar cities all
just touching each other. But though the winter twilight was already
threatening the road ahead of them, the Parisian detective still sat
silent and watchful, eyeing the frontage of the streets that slid by on
either side. By the time they had left Camden Town behind, the policemen were nearly asleep; at least, they gave something like a jump as
Valentin leaped erect, struck a hand on each man's shoulder, and
shouted to the driver to stop.

They tumbled down the steps into the road without realizing why
they had been dislodged; when they looked round for enlightenment
they found Valentin triumphantly pointing his finger towards a window on the left side of the road. It was a large window, forming part of
the long facade of a gilt and palatial public-house; it was the part
reserved for respectable dining, and labeled "Restaurant." This window, like all the rest along the frontage of the hotel, was of frosted and
figured glass; but in the middle of it was a big, black smash, like a star
in the ice.

"Our cue at last," cried Valentin, waving his stick: "the place with
the broken window."

"What window? What cue?" asked his principal assistant. "Why,
what proof is there that this has anything to do with them?"

Valentin almost broke his bamboo stick with rage.

"Proof!" he cried. "Good God! the man is looking for proof! Why,
of course, the chances are twenty to one that it has *nothing* to do with
them. But what else can we do? Don't you see we must either follow
one wild possibility or else go home to bed?" He banged his way into
the restaurant, followed by his companions, and they were soon seated
at a late luncheon at a little table, and looking at the star of smashed
glass from the inside. Not that it was very informative to them even
then.

"Got your window broken, I see," said Valentin to the waiter as he paid the bill.

"Yes, sir," answered the attendant, bending busily over the change, to which Valentin silently added an enormous tip. The waiter straightened himself with mild but unmistakable animation.

"Ah, yes, sir," he said. "Very odd thing, that, sir."

"Indeed?" Tell us about it," said the detective with careless curiosity.

"Well, two gents in black came in," said the waiter; "two of those foreign parsons that are running about. They had a cheap and quiet little lunch, and one of them paid for it and went out. The other was just going out to join him when I looked at my change again and found he'd paid me more than three times too much. 'Here,' I says to the chap who was nearly out of the door, 'you've paid too much.' 'Oh,' he says, very cool, 'have we?' 'Yes,' I says, and picks up the bill to show him. Well, that was a knockout."

"What do you mean?" asked his interlocutor.

"Well, I'd have sworn on seven Bibles that I'd put 4s. on that bill. But now I saw I'd put 14s., as plain as paint."

"Well?" cried Valentin, moving slowly, but with burning eyes, "and then?"

"The parson at the door he says all serene, "Sorry to confuse your accounts, but it'll pay for the window." 'What window?' I says. 'The one I'm going to break,' he says, and smashed that blessed pane with his umbrella."

All three inquirers made an explanation; and the inspector said under his breath, "Are we after escaped lunatics?" The waiter went on with some relish for the ridiculous story:

"I was so knocked silly for a second, I couldn't do anything. The man marched out of the place and joined his friend just round the corner. Then they went so quick up Bullock Street that I couldn't catch them, though I ran round the bars to do it."

"Bullock Street," said the detective, and shot up that thoroughfare as quickly as the strange couple he pursued.

Their journey now took them through bare brick ways like tunnels; streets with few lights and even with few windows; streets that seemed built out of the blank backs of everything and everywhere. Dusk was deepening, and it was not easy even for the London policemen to guess in what exact direction they were treading. The inspector, however, was pretty certain that they would eventually strike some part of

Hampstead Heath. Abruptly one bulging gas-lit window broke the blue twilight like a bull's-eye lantern; and Valentin stopped an instant before a little garish sweetstuff shop. After an instant's hesitation he went in; he stood amid the gaudy colors of the confectionery with entire gravity and bought thirteen chocolate cigars with a certain care. He was clearly preparing an opening, but he did not need one.

An angular, elderly young woman in the shop had regarded his elegant appearance with a merely automatic inquiry; but when she saw the door behind him blocked with the blue uniform of the inspector, her eyes seemed to wake up.

"Oh," she said, "if you've come about that parcel, I've sent it off already."

"Parcel!" repeated Valentin; and it was his turn to look inquiring.

"I mean the parcel the gentleman left—the clergyman gentleman."

"For goodness' sake," said Valentin, leaning forward with his first real confession of eagerness, "for Heaven's sake tell us what happened exactly."

"Well," said the woman a little doubtfully, "the clergymen came in about half an hour ago and bought some peppermints and talked a bit, and then went off towards the Heath. But a second after, one of them runs back into the shop and says, 'Have I left a parcel?' Well, I looked everywhere and couldn't see one; so he says, 'Never mind; but if it should turn up, please post it to this address,' and he left me the address and a shilling for my trouble. And sure enough, though I thought I'd looked everywhere, I found he'd left a brown paper parcel, so I posted it to the place he said. I can't remember the address now; it was somewhere in Westminster. But as the thing seemed so important, I thought perhaps the police had come about it."

"So they have," said Valentin shortly. "Is Hampstead Heath near here?"

"Straight on for fifteen minutes," said the woman, "and you'll come right out on the open." Valentin sprang out of the shop and began to run. The other detectives followed him at a reluctant trot.

The street they threaded was so narrow and shut in by shadows that when they came out unexpectedly into the void common and vast sky they were startled to find the evening still so light and clear. A perfect dome of peacock-green sank into gold amid the blackening trees and the dark violet distances. The glowing green tint was just deep enough to pick out in points of crystal one or two stars. All that was left of the daylight lay in a golden glitter across the edge of Hampstead and that popular hollow which is called the Vale of Health. The holiday makers who roam this region had not wholly dispersed; a few couples sat shapelessly on benches; and here and there a distant girl still shrieked in one of the swings. The glory of heaven deepened and darkened around the sublime vulgarity of man; and standing on the slope and looking across the valley, Valentin beheld the thing which he sought.

Among the black and breaking groups in that distance was one especially black which did not break—a group of two figures clerically clad. Though they seemed as small as insects, Valentin could see that one of them was much smaller than the other. Though the other had a student's stoop and an inconspicuous manner, he could see that the man was well over six feet high. He shut his teeth and went forward, whirling his stick impatiently. By the time he had substantially diminished the distance and magnified the two black figures as in a vast microscope, he had perceived something else; something which startled him, and yet which he had somehow expected. Whoever was the tall priest, there could be no doubt about the identity of the short one. It was his friend of the Harwich train, the stumpy little *curé* of Essex whom he had warned about his brown paper parcels.

Now, so far as this went, everything fitted in finally and rationally enough. Valentin had learned by his inquiries that morning that a Father Brown from Essex was bringing up a silver cross with sapphires, a relic of considerable value, to show some of the foreign priests at the congress. This undoubtedly was the "silver with blue stones"; and Father Brown undoubtedly was the little greenhorn in the train. Now there was nothing wonderful about the fact that what Valentin had found out Flambeau had also found out; Flambeau found out everything. Also there was nothing wonderful in the fact that when Flambeau heard of a sapphire cross he should try to steal it; that was the most natural thing in all natural history. And most certainly there was nothing wonderful about the fact that Flambeau should have it all his own way with such a silly sheep as the man with the umbrella and the parcels. He was the sort of man whom anybody could lead on a string to the North Pole; it was not surprising that an actor like Flambeau, dressed as another priest, could lead him to Hampstead Heath. So far the crime seemed clear enough; and while the detective pitied the priest for his helplessness, he almost despised Flambeau for condescending to so gullible a victim. But when Valentin thought of all that had happened in between, of all that had led him to his triumph, he racked his brains for the smallest rhyme or reason in it. What had the stealing of a blue-and-silver cross from a priest from Essex to do with chucking soup at wall paper? What had it to do with calling nuts oranges, or with paying for windows first and breaking them afterwards? He had come to the end of his chase; yet somehow he had missed the middle of it. When he failed (which was seldom), he had usually grasped the clue, but nevertheless missed the criminal. Here he had grasped the criminal, but still he could not grasp the clue.

The two figures that they followed were crawling like black flies across the huge green contour of a hill. They were evidently sunk in conversation, and perhaps did not notice where they were going; but they were certainly going to the wilder and more silent heights of the Heath. As their pursuers gained on them, the latter had to use the undignified attitudes of the deer-stalker, to crouch behind clumps of trees and even to crawl prostrate in deep grass. By these ungainly ingenuities the hunters even came close enough to the quarry to hear the murmur of the discussion, but no word could be distinguished except the word "reason" recurring frequently in a high and almost childish voice. Once over an abrupt dip of land and a dense tangle of thickets, the detectives actually lost the two figures they were following. They did not find the trail again for an agonizing ten minutes, and then it led round the brow of a great dome of hill overlooking an amphitheater of rich and desolate sunset scenery. Under a tree in this commanding yet neglected spot was an old ramshackle wooden seat. On this seat sat the two priests still in serious speech together. The gorgeous green and gold still clung to the darkening horizon; but the dome above was turning slowly from peacock-green to peacock-blue, and the stars detached themselves more and more like solid jewels. Mutely motioning to his followers, Valentin contrived to creep up behind the big branching tree, and, standing there in deathly silence, heard the words of the strange priests for the first time.

After he had listened for a minute and a half, he was gripped by a devilish doubt. Perhaps he had dragged the two English policemen to the wastes of a nocturnal heath on an errand no saner than seeking figs on its thistles. For the two priests were talking exactly like priests, piously, with learning and leisure, about the most aerial enigmas of theology. The little Essex priest spoke the more simply, with his round face turned to the strengthening stars; the other talked with his head bowed, as if he were not even worthy to look at them. But no more innocently clerical conversation could have been heard in any white Italian cloister or black Spanish cathedral.

The first he heard was the tail of one of Father Brown's sentences, which ended: ". . . what they really meant in the Middle Ages by the heavens being incorruptible."

The taller priest nodded his bowed head and said:

"Ah, yes, these modern infidels appeal to their reason; but who can look at those millions of worlds and not feel that there may well be wonderful universes above us where reason is utterly unreasonable?"

"No," said the other priest: "reason is always reasonable, even in the last limbo, in the lost borderland of things. I know that people charge the Church with lowering reason, but it is just the other way. Alone on earth, the Church makes reason really supreme. Alone on earth, the Church affirms that God himself is bound by reason."

The other priest raised his austere face to the spangled sky and said:

"Yet who knows if in that infinite universe—?"

"Only infinite physically," said the little priest, turning sharply in his seat, "not infinite in the sence of escaping from the laws of truth."

Valentin behind his tree was tearing his finger-nails with silent fury. He seemed almost to hear the sniggers of the English detectives whom he had brought so far on a fantastic guess only to listen to the metaphysical gossip of two mild old parsons. In his impatience he lost the equally elaborate answer of the tall cleric, and when he listened again it was Father Brown who was speaking:

"Reason and justice grip the remotest and loneliest star. Look at those stars. Don't they look as if they were single diamonds and sapphires? Well, you can imagine any mad botany or geology you please. Think of forests of adamant with leaves of brilliants. Think the moon is a blue moon, a single elephantine sapphire. But don't fancy that all that frantic astronomy would make the smallest difference to the reason and justice of conduct. On plains of opal, under cliffs cut out of pearl, you would still find a notice-board, 'Thou shalt not steal.' "

Valentin was just in the act of rising from his rigid and crouching attitude and creeping away as softly as might be, felled by the one great folly of his life. But something in the very silence of the tall priest made him stop until the latter spoke. When at last he did speak, he said simply, his head bowed and his hands on his knees:

"Well, I still think that other worlds may perhaps rise higher than our reason. The mystery of heaven is unfathomable, and I for one can only bow my head."

Then, with brow yet bent and without changing by the faintest shade his attitude or voice, he added:

"Just hand over that sapphire cross of yours, will you? We're all alone here, and I could pull you to pieces like a straw doll."

The utterly unaltered voice and attitude added a strange violence to that shocking change of speech. But the guarder of the relic only seemed to turn his head by the smallest section of the compass. He seemed still to have a somewhat foolish face turned to the stars. Perhaps he had not understood. Or, perhaps, he had understood and sat rigid with terror.

"Yes," said the tall priest, in the same low voice and in the same still posture, "yes, I am Flambeau."

Then, after a pause, he said:

"Come, will you give me that cross?"

"No," said the other, and the monosyllable had an odd sound.

Flambeau suddenly flung off all his pontifical pretensions. The great robber leaned back in his seat and laughed low but long.

"No," he cried, "you won't give it me, you proud prelate. You won't give it me, you little celibate simpleton. Shall I tell you why you won't give it me? Because I've got it already in my own breast-pocket."

The small man from Essex turned what seemed to be a dazed face in the dusk, and said, with the timid eagerness of "The Private Secretary":

"Are—are you sure?"

Flambeau yelled with delight.

"Really, you're as good as a three-act farce," he cried. "Yes, you turnip, I am quite sure. I had the sense to make a duplicate of the right parcel, and now, my friend, you've got the duplicate and I've got the jewels. An old dodge, Father Brown—a very old dodge."

"Yes," said Father Brown, and passed his hand through his hair with the same strange vagueness of manner. "Yes, I've heard of it before."

The colossus of crime leaned over to the little rustic priest with a sort of sudden interest.

"*You* have heard of it?" he asked. "Where have *you* heard of it?"

"Well, I mustn't tell you his name, of course," said the little man simply. "He was a penitent, you know. He had lived prosperously for about twenty years entirely on duplicate brown paper parcels. And so, you see, when I began to suspect you, I thought of this poor chap's way of doing it at once."

"Began to suspect me?" repeated the outlaw with increased intensity. "Did you really have the gumption to suspect me just because I brought you up to this bare part of the heath?"

"No, no," said Father Brown with an air of apology. "You see, I suspected you when we first met. It's that little bulge up the sleeve where you people have the spiked bracelet."

"How in Tartarus," cried Flambeau, "did you ever hear of the spiked bracelet?"

"Oh, one's little flock, you know!" said Father Brown, arching his eyebrows rather blankly. "When I was a curate in Hartlepool, there were three of them with spiked bracelets. So, as I suspected you from the first, don't you see, I made sure that the cross should go safe, anyhow. I'm afraid I watched you, you know. So at last I saw you change the parcels. Then, don't you see, I changed them back again. And then I left the right one behind."

"Left it behind?" repeated Flambeau, and for the first time there was another note in his voice beside his triumph.

"Well, it was like this," said the little priest, speaking in the same unaffected way. "I went back to that sweetshop and asked if I'd left a parcel, and gave them a particular address if it turned up. Well, I knew I hadn't; but when I went away again I did. So, instead of running after me with that valuable parcel, they have sent it flying to a friend of mine in Westminster." Then he added rather sadly: "I learnt that, too, from a poor fellow in Hartlepool. He used to do it with handbags he stole at railway stations, but he's in a monastery now. Oh, one gets to know, you know," he added, rubbing his head again with the same sort of desperate apology. "We can't help it being priests. People come and tell us these things."

Flambeau tore a brown paper parcel out of his inner pocket and rent it in pieces. There was nothing but paper and sticks of lead inside it. He sprang to his feet with a gigantic gesture, and cried:

"I don't believe you. I don't believe a bumpkin like you could manage all that. I believe you've still got the stuff on you, and if you don't give it up—why, we're all alone, and I'll take it by force!"

"No," said Father Brown simply, and stood up also, "you won't take it by force. First, because I really haven't still got it. And, second, because we are not alone."

Flambeau stopped in his stride forward.

"Behind that tree," said Father Brown, pointing, "are two strong policemen and the greatest detective alive. How did they come here, do you ask? Why, I brought them, of course! How did I do it? Why, I'll tell you if you like! Lord bless you, we have to know twenty such things when we work among the criminal classes! Well, I wasn't sure you were a thief, and it would never do to make a scandal against one of our own clergy. So I just tested you to see if anything would make you show yourself. A man generally makes a small scene if he finds salt in his coffee; if he doesn't, he has some reason for keeping quiet. I changed the salt and sugar, and *you* kept quiet. A man generally objects if his bill is three times too big. If he pays it, he has some motive for passing unnoticed. I altered your bill, and *you* paid it."

The world seemed waiting for Flambeau to leap like a tiger. But he was held back as by a spell; he was stunned with the utmost curiosity.

"Well," went on Father Brown, with lumbering lucidity, "as you wouldn't leave any tracks for the police, of course somebody had to. At every place we went to, I took care to do something that would get us talked about for the rest of the day. I didn't do much harm—a splashed wall, spilt apples, a broken window; but I saved the cross, as the cross will always be saved. It is at Westminister by now. I rather wonder you didn't stop it with the Donkey's Whistle."

"With the what?" asked Flambeau.

"I'm glad you've never heard of it," said the priest, making a face. "It's a foul thing. I'm sure you're too good a man for a Whistler. I couldn't have countered it even with the Spots myself; I'm not strong enough in the legs."

"What on earth are you talking about?" asked the other.

"Well, I did think you'd know the Spots," said Father Brown, agreeably surprised. "Oh, you can't have gone so very wrong yet!"

"How in blazes do you know all these horrors?" cried Flambeau.

The shadow of a smile crossed the round, simple face of his clerical opponent.

"Oh, by being a celibate simpleton, I suppose," he said. "Has it never struck you that a man who does next to nothing but hear men's real sins is not likely to be wholly unaware of human evil? But, as a matter of fact, another part of my trade, too, made me sure you weren't a priest."

"What?" asked the thief, almost gaping.

"You attacked reason," said Father Brown. "It's bad theology."

And even as he turned away to collect his property, the three policemen came out from under the twilight trees. Flambeau was an artist and a sportsman. He stepped back and swept Valentin a great bow.

"Do not bow to me, *mon ami*," said Valentin with silver clearness. "Let us both bow to our master."

And they both stood an instant uncovered while the little Essex priest blinked about for his umbrella.

AGATHA CHRISTIE *(1890–1976) is without doubt the best-selling mystery writer of all time. Literally millions of her readers have read every one of her novels. Her fame rests firmly on her marvelous ability to plot, and on the development of two series detectives—Miss Marple, a senior sleuth (age seventy-four in the first book to feature her) with a cynical streak, who works out of her village of St. Mary Mead; and the fabulous Hercule Poirot, a former detective for the Belgian Sureté, whose clever use of his "little grey cells" has entranced readers since his debut in* The Mysterious Affair at Styles *in 1920.*

"The Submarine Plans" is an early case for Poirot and finds him involved in the highest ranks of the British government prior to World War I.

The Submarine Plans
BY AGATHA CHRISTIE

A note had been brought by special messenger. Poirot read it, and a gleam of excitement and interest came into his eyes as he did so. He dismissed the man with a few curt words and then turned to me.

"Pack a bag with all haste, my friend. We're going down to Sharples."

I started at the mention of the famous country place of Lord Alloway. Head of the newly formed Ministry of Defence, Lord Alloway was a prominent member of the Cabinet. As Sir Ralph Curtis, head of a great engineering firm, he had made his mark in the House of Commons, and he was now freely spoken of as *the* coming man, and the one most likely to be asked to form a ministry should the rumours as to Mr David MacAdam's health prove well founded.

A big Rolls-Royce car was waiting for us below, and as we glided off into the darkness, I plied Poirot with questions.

"What on earth can they want us for at this time of night?" I demanded. It was past eleven.

Poirot shook his head. "Something of the most urgent, without doubt."

"I remember," I said, "that some years ago there was some rather ugly scandal about Ralph Curtis, as he then was—some jugglery with shares, I believe. In the end, he was completely exonerated; but perhaps something of the kind has arisen again?"

"It would hardly be necessary for him to send for me in the middle of the night, my friend."

I was forced to agree, and the remainder of the journey was passed in silence. Once out of London, the powerful car forged rapidly ahead, and we arrived at Sharples in a little under the hour.

A pontifical butler conducted us at once to a small study where Lord Alloway was awaiting us. He sprang up to greet us—a tall, spare man who seemed actually to radiate power and vitality.

"M. Poirot, I am delighted to see you. It is the second time the Government has demanded your services. I remember only too well what you did for us during the war, when the Prime Minister was kidnapped in that astounding fashion. Your masterly deductions—and may I add, your discretion?—saved the situation."

Poirot's eyes twinkled a little.

"Do I gather then, milor', that this is another case for—discretion?"

"Most emphatically. Sir Harry and I—oh, let me introduce you— Admiral Sir Harry Weardale, our First Sea Lord—M. Poirot and—let me see, Captain—"

"Hastings," I supplied.

"I've often heard of you, M. Poirot," said Sir Harry, shaking hands. "This is a most unaccountable business, and if you can solve it, we'll be extremely grateful to you."

I liked the First Sea Lord immediately, a square, bluff sailor of the good old-fashioned type.

Poirot looked inquiringly at them both, and Alloway took up the tale.

"Of course, you understand that all this is in confidence, M. Poirot. We have had a most serious loss. The plans of the new Z type of submarine have been stolen."

"When was that?"

"Tonight—less than three hours ago. You can appreciate perhaps, M. Poirot, the magnitude of the disaster. It is essential that the loss should not be made public. I will give you the facts as briefly as possible. My guests over the weekend were the Admiral, here, his wife and son, and a Mrs Conrad, a lady well known in London society. The ladies retired to bed early—about ten o'clock; so did Mr Leonard Weardale. Sir Harry is down here partly for the purpose of discussing the construction of this new type of submarine with me. Accordingly, I asked Mr Fitzroy, my secretary, to get out the plans from the safe in the corner there, and to arrange them ready for me, as well as various other documents that bore upon the subject in hand. While he was doing this, the Admiral and I strolled up and down the terrace, smoking cigars and enjoying the warm June air. We finished our smoke and our chat, and decided to get down to business. Just as we turned at the far end of the terrace, I fancied I saw a shadow slip out of the french window here, cross the terrace, and disappear. I paid very little attention, however. I knew Fitzroy to be in this room, and it never entered my head that anything might be amiss. There, of course, I am to blame. Well, we retraced our steps along the terrace and entered this room by the window just as Fitzroy entered it from the hall.

" 'Got everything out we are likely to need, Fitzroy?' I asked.

" ' 'I think so, Lord Alloway. The papers are all on your desk,' he answered. And then he wished us both goodnight.

" 'Just wait a minute,' I said, going to the desk. 'I may want something I haven't mentioned.'

"I looked quickly through the papers that were lying there.

" 'You've forgotten the most important of the lot, Fitzroy,' I said. 'The actual plans of the submarine!'

" 'The plans are right on top, Lord Alloway.'

" 'Oh no, they're not,' I said, turning over the papers.

" 'But I put them there not a minute ago!'

" 'Well, they're not here now,' I said.

"Fitzroy advanced with a bewildered expression on his face. The thing seemed incredible. We turned over the papers on the desk; we hunted through the safe; but at last we had to make up our minds to it that the papers were gone—and gone within the short space of about three minutes while Fitzroy was absent from the room."

"Why did he leave the room?" asked Poirot quickly.

"Just what I asked him," exclaimed Sir Harry.

"It appears," said Lord Alloway, "that just when he had finished arranging the papers on my desk, he was startled by hearing a woman scream. He dashed out into the hall. On the stairs he discovered Mrs Conrad's French maid. The girl looked very white and upset, and declared that she had seen a ghost—a tall figure dressed all in white that moved without a sound. Fitzroy laughed at her fears and told her, in more or less polite language, not to be a fool. Then he returned to this room just as we entered from the window."

"It all seems very clear," said Poirot thoughtfully. "The only question is, was the maid an accomplice? Did she scream by arrangement with her confederate lurking outside, or was he merely waiting there in the hope of an opportunity presenting itself? It was a man, I suppose—not a woman you saw?"

"I can't tell you, M. Poirot. It was just a—shadow."

The Admiral gave such a peculiar snort that it could not fail to attract attention.

"M. l'Amiral has something to say, I think," said Poirot quietly, with a slight smile. "You saw this shadow, Sir Harry?"

"No, I didn't," returned the other. "And neither did Alloway. The branch of a tree flapped, or something, and then afterwards, when we discovered the theft, he leaped to the conclusion that he had seen someone pass across the terrace. His imagination played a trick on him; that's all."

"I am not usually credited with having much imagination," said Lord Alloway with a slight smile.

"Nonsense, we've all got imagination. We can all work ourselves up to believe that we've seen more than we have. I've had a lifetime of experience at sea, and I'll back my eyes against those of any landsman. I was looking right down the terrace, and I'd have seen the same if there was anything to see."

He was quite excited over the matter. Poirot rose and stepped quickly to the window.

"You permit?" he asked. "We must settle this point if possible."

He went out upon the terrace, and we followed him. He had taken an electric torch from his pocket, and was playing the light along the edge of the grass that bordered the terrace.

"Where did he cross the terrace, milor'?" he asked.

"About opposite the window, I should say."

Poirot continued to play the torch for some minutes longer, walking the entire length of the terrace and back. Then he shut it off and straightened himself up.

"Sir Harry is right—and you are wrong, milor'," he said quietly. "It rained heavily earlier this evening. Anyone who passed over that grass could not avoid leaving footmarks. But there are none—none at all."

His eyes went from one man's face to the other's. Lord Alloway looked bewildered and unconvinced; the Admiral expressed a noisy gratification.

"Knew I couldn't be wrong," he declared. "Trust my eyes anywhere."

He was such a picture of an honest old sea-dog that I could not help smiling.

"So that brings us to the people in the house," said Poirot smoothly. "Let us come inside again. Now milor', while Mr Fitzroy was speaking to the maid on the stairs, could anyone have seized the opportunity to enter the study from the hall?"

Lord Alloway shook his head.

"Quite impossible—they would have had to pass him in order to do so."

"And Mr Fitzroy himself—you are sure of him, eh?"

Lord Alloway flushed.

"Absolutely, M. Poirot. I will answer confidently for my secretary. It is quite impossible that he should be concerned in the matter in any way."

"Everything seems to be impossible," remarked Poirot rather drily. "Possibly the plans attached to themselves a little pair of wings, and flew away—*comme ça!*" He blew his lips out like a comical cherub.

"The whole thing is impossible," declared Lord Alloway impatiently. "But I beg, M. Poirot, that you will not dream of suspecting Fitzroy. Consider for one moment—had he wished to take the plans, what could have been easier for him than to take a tracing of them without going to the trouble of stealing them?"

"There milor'," said Poirot with approval, "you make a remark *bien juste*—I see that you have a mind orderly and methodical. *L'Angleterre* is happy in possessing you."

Lord Alloway looked rather embarrassed by this sudden burst of praise. Poirot returned to the matter in hand.

"The room in which you had been sittting all the evening—"

"The drawing-room? Yes?"

"That also has a window on the terrace, since I remember your saying you went out that way. Would it not be possible for someone to come out by the drawing-room window and in by this one while Mr Fitzroy was out of the room, and return the same way?"

"But we'd have seen them," objected the Admiral.

"Not if you had your backs turned, walking the other way."

"Fitzroy was only out of the room a few minutes, the time it would take us to walk to the end and back."

"No matter—it is a possibility—in fact, the only one as things stand."

"But there was no one in the drawing-room when we went out," said the Admiral.

"They may have come there afterwards."

"You mean," said Lord Alloway slowly, "that when Fitzroy heard the maid scream and went out, someone was already concealed in the drawing-room, and that they darted in and out through the windows, and only left the drawing-room when Fitzroy had returned to this room?"

"The methodical mind again," said Poirot, bowing. "You express the matter perfectly."

"One of the servants, perhaps?"

"Or a guest. It was Mrs Conrad's maid who screamed. What exactly can you tell me of Mrs Conrad?"

Lord Alloway considered for a minute.

"I told you that she is a lady well known in society. That is true in the sense that she gives large parties, and goes everywhere. But very little is known as to where she really comes from, and what her past life has been. She is a lady who frequents diplomatic and Foreign Office circles as much as possible. The Secret Service is inclined to ask— why?"

"I see," said Poirot. "And she was asked here this weekend—"

"So that—shall we say?—we might observe her at close quarters."

"Parfaitement! It is possible that she has turned the tables on you rather neatly."

Lord Alloway looked discomfited, and Poirot continued: "Tell me, milor', was any reference made in her hearing to the subjects you and the Admiral were going to discuss together?"

"Yes," admitted the other. "Sir Harry said: 'And now for our submarine! To work!' or something of that sort. The others had left the room, but she had come back for a book."

"I see," said Poirot thoughtfully. "Milor', it is very late—but this is an urgent affair. I would like to question the members of this house-party at once if it is possible."

"It can be managed, of course," said Lord Alloway. "The awkward thing is, we don't want to let it get about more than can be helped. Of course, Lady Juliet Weardale and young Leonard are all right—but Mrs Conrad, if she is not guilty, is rather a different proposition. Perhaps you could just state that an important paper is missing, without specifying what it is, or going into any of the circumstances of the disappearance?"

"Exactly what I was about to propose myself," said Poirot, beaming. "In fact, in all three cases. Monsieur the Admiral will pardon me, but even the best of wives—"

"No offence," said Sir Harry. "All women talk, bless 'em! I wish Juliet would talk a little more and play bridge a little less. But women are like that nowadays, never happy unless they're dancing or gambling. I'll get Juliet and Leonard up, shall I, Alloway?"

"Thank you. I'll call the French maid. M. Poirot will want to see her, and she can rouse her mistress. I'll attend to it now. In the meantime, I'll send Fitzroy along."

Mr Fitzroy was a pale, thin young man with pince-nez and a frigid expression. His statement was practically word for word what Lord Alloway had already told us.

"What is your own theory, Mr Fitzroy?"

Mr Fitzroy shrugged his shoulders.

"Undoubtedly someone who knew the hang of things was waiting his chance outside. He could see what went on through the window, and he slipped in when I left the room. It's a pity Lord Alloway didn't give chase then and there when he saw the fellow leave."

Poirot did not undeceive him. Instead he asked: "Do you believe the story of the French maid—that she had seen a ghost?"

"Well, hardly, M. Poirot!"

"I mean—that she really thought so?"

"Oh, as to that, I can't say. She certainly seemed rather upset. She had her hands to her head."

"Aha!" cried Poirot with the air of one who has made a discovery. "Is that so indeed—and she was without doubt a pretty girl?"

"I didn't notice particularly," said Mr. Fitzroy in a repressive voice.

"You did not see her mistress, I suppose?"

"As a matter of fact, I did. She was in the gallery at the top of the steps and was calling her—'Léonie!' Then she saw me—and of course retired."

"Upstairs," said Poirot, frowning.

"Of course, I realize that all this is very unpleasant for me—or rather would have been, if Lord Alloway had not chanced to see the man actually leaving. In any case, I should be glad if you would make a point of searching my room—and myself."

"You really wish that?"

"Certainly I do."

What Poirot would have replied I do not know, but at that moment Lord Alloway reappeared and informed us that the two ladies and Mr Leonard Weardale were in the drawing-room.

The women were in becoming négligés. Mrs Conrad was a beautiful woman of thirty-five, with golden hair and a slight tendency to *embonpoint*. Lady Juliet Weardale must have been forty, tall and dark, very thin, still beautiful, with exquisite hands and feet, and a restless, haggard manner. Her son was rather an effeminate-looking young man, as great a contrast to his bluff, hearty father as could well be imagined.

Poirot gave forth the little rigmarole we had agreed upon, and then explained that he was anxious to know if anyone had heard or seen anything that night which might assist us.

Turning to Mrs Conrad first, he asked her if she would be so kind as to inform him exactly what her movements had been.

"Let me see . . . I went upstairs. I rang for my maid. Then, as she did not put in an appearance, I came out and called her. I could hear her talking on the stairs. After she had brushed my hair, I sent her away—she was in a very curious nervous state. I read awhile and then went to bed."

"And you, Lady Juliet?"

"I went straight upstairs and to bed. I was very tired."

"What about your book, dear?" asked Mrs Conrad with a sweet smile.

"My book?" Lady Juliet flushed.

"Yes, you know, when I sent Léonie away, you were coming up the stairs. You had been down to the drawing-room for a book, you said."

"Oh yes, I did go down. I—I forgot."

Lady Juliet clasped her hands nervously together.

"Did you hear Mrs Conrad's maid scream, milady?"

"No—no, I didn't."

"How curious—because you must have been in the drawing-room at the time."

"I heard nothing," said Lady Juliet in a firmer voice.

Poirot turned to young Leonard.

"Monsieur?"

"Nothing doing. I went straight upstairs and turned in."

Poirot stroked his chin.

"Alas, I fear there is nothing to help me here. Mesdames and monsieur, I regret—I regret infinitely to have deranged you from your slumbers for so little. Accept my apologies, I pray of you."

Gesticulating and apologizing, he marshalled them out. He returned with the French maid, a pretty, impudent-looking girl. Alloway and Weardale had gone out with the ladies.

"Now, mademoiselle," said Poirot in a brisk tone, "let us have the truth. Recount to me no histories. Why did you scream on the stairs?"

"Ah, monsieur, I saw a tall figure—all in white—"

Poirot arrested her with an energetic shake of his forefinger.

"Did I not say, recount to me no histories? I will make a guess. He kissed you, did he not? M. Leonard Weardale, I mean?"

"Eh bien, monsieur, and after all, what is a kiss?"

"Under the circumstances, it is most natural," replied Poirot gallantly. "I myself, or Hastings here—but tell me just what occurred."

"He came up behind me, and caught me. I was startled, and I screamed. If I had known, I would not have screamed—but he came upon me like a cat. Then came *M. le secrétaire.* M. Leonard flew up the stairs. And what could I say? Especially to a *jeune homme comme ça— tellement comme il faut? Ma foi,* I invent a ghost."

"And all is explained," cried Poirot genially. "You then mounted to the chamber of Madame your mistress. Which is her room, by the way?"

"It is at the end, monsieur. That way."

"Directly over the study, then. *Bien,* mademoiselle, I will detain you no longer. And *la prochaine fois,* do not scream."

Handing her out, he came back to me with a smile.

"An interesting case, is it not, Hastings? I begin to have a few little ideas. *Et vous?"*

"What was Leonard Weardale doing on the stairs? I don't like that young man, Poirot. He's a thorough young rake, I should say."

"I agree with you, *mon ami."*

"Fitzroy seems an honest fellow."

"Lord Alloway is certainly insistent on that point."

"And yet there is something in his manner—"

"That is almost too good to be true? I felt it myself. On the other hand, our friend Mrs Conrad is certainly not good at all."

"And her room is over the study," I said musingly, and keeping a sharp eye on Poirot.

He shook his head with a slight smile.

"No, *mon ami,* I cannot bring myself seriously to believe that that immaculate lady swarmed down the chimney, or let herself down from the balcony."

As he spoke, the door opened, and to my great surprise, Lady Juliet Weardale flitted in.

"M. Poirot," she said somewhat breathlessly, "can I speak to you alone?"

"Milady, Captain Hastings is as my other self. You can speak before him as though he were a thing of no account, not there at all. Be seated, I pray you."

She sat down, still keeping her eyes fixed on Poirot.

"What I have to say is—rather difficult. You are in charge of this case. If the—papers were to be returned, would that end the matter? I mean, could it be done without questions being asked?"

Poirot stared hard at her.

"Let me understand you, madame. They are to be placed in my hand—is that right? And I am to return them to Lord Alloway on the condition that he asks no questions as to where I got them?"

She bowed her head. "That is what I mean. But I must be sure there will be no—publicity."

"I do not think Lord Alloway is particularly anxious for publicity," said Poirot grimly.

"You accept then?" she cried eagerly in response.

"A little moment, milady. It depends on how soon you can place those papers in my hands."

"Almost immediately."

Poirot glanced up at the clock.

"How soon, exactly?"

"Say—ten minutes," she whispered.

"I accept, milady."

She hurried from the room. I pursed my mouth up for a whistle.

"Can you sum up the situation for me, Hastings?"

"Bridge," I replied succinctly.

"Ah, you remember the careless words of Monsieur the Admiral! What a memory! I felicitate you, Hastings."

We said no more, for Lord Alloway came in, and looked inquiringly at Poirot.

"Have you any further ideas, M. Poirot? I am afraid the answers to your questions have been rather disappointing."

"Not at all, milor'. They have been quite sufficiently illuminating. It will be unnecessary for me to stay here any longer, and so, with your permission, I return at once to London."

Lord Alloway seemed dumbfounded.

"But—but what have you discovered? Do you know who took the plans?"

"Yes, milor', I do. Tell me—in the case of the papers being returned to you anonymously, you would prosecute no further inquiry?"

Lord Alloway stared at him.

"Do you mean on payment of a sum of money?"

"No, milor', returned unconditionally."

"Of course, the recovery of the plans is the great thing," said Lord Alloway slowly. He still looked puzzled and uncomprehending.

"Then I should seriously recommend you to adopt that course. Only you, the Admiral and your secretary know of the loss. Only they need know of the restitution. And you may count on me to support you in every way—lay the mystery on my shoulders. You asked me to restore the papers—I have done so. You know no more." He rose and held out his hand. "Milor', I am glad to have met you. I have faith in you—and your devotion to England. You will guide her destinies with a strong, sure hand."

"M. Poirot—I swear to you that I will do my best. It may be a fault, or it may be a virtue—but I believe in myself."

"So does every great man. Me, I am the same!" said Poirot grandiloquently.

The car came round to the door in a few minutes, and Lord Alloway bade us farewell on the steps with renewed cordiality.

"That is a great man, Hastings," said Poirot as we drove off. "He has brains, resource, power. He is the strong man that England needs to guide her through these difficult days of reconstruction."

"I'm quite ready to agree with all you say, Poirot—but what about Lady Juliet? Is she to return the papers straight to Alloway? What will she think when she finds you have gone off without a word?"

"Hastings, I will ask you a little question. Why, when she was talking with me, did she not hand me the plans then and there?"

"She hadn't got them with her."

"Perfectly. How long would it take her to fetch them from her room? Or from any hiding-place in the house? You need not answer. I will tell you. Probably about two minutes and a half! Yet she asks for ten minutes. Why? Clearly she has to obtain them from some other person, and to reason or argue with that person before they give them up. Now, what person could that be? Not Mrs Conrad, clearly, but a member of her own family, her husband or son. Which is it likely to be? Leonard Weardale said he went straight to bed. We know that to be untrue. Supposing his mother went to his room and found it empty;

supposing she came down filled with a nameless dread—he is no beauty that son of hers! She does not find him, but later she hears him deny that he ever left his room. She leaps to the conclusion that he is the thief. Hence her interview with me.

"But, *mon ami,* we know something that Lady Juliet does not. We know that her son could not have been in the study, because he was on the stairs, making love to the pretty French maid. Although she does not know it, Leonard Weardale has an alibi."

"Well, then, who did steal the papers? We seem to have eliminated everybody—Lady Juliet, her son, Mrs Conrad, the French maid—"

"Exactly. Use your little grey cells, my friend. The solution stares you in the face."

I shook my head blankly.

"But yes! If you would only persevere! See, then, Fitzroy goes out of the study; he leaves the papers on the desk. A few minutes later Lord Alloway enters the room, goes to the desk, and the papers are gone. Only two things are possible: either Fitzroy did *not* leave the papers on the desk, but put them in his pocket—and that is not reasonable, because as Alloway pointed out, he could have taken a tracing at his own convenience any time—or else the papers were still on the desk when Lord Alloway went to it—in which case they went into *his* pocket."

"Lord Alloway the thief," I said, dumbfounded. "But why? Why?"

"Did you not tell me of some scandal in the past? He was exonerated, you said. But suppose, after all, it had been true? In English public life there must be no scandal. If this were raked up and proved against him now—goodbye to his political career. We will suppose that he was being blackmailed, and the price asked was the submarine plans."

"But the man's a black traitor!" I cried.

"Oh no, he is not. He is clever and resourceful. Supposing, my friend, that he copied those plans, making—for he is a clever engineer —a slight alteration in each part which will render them quite impracticable. He hands the faked plans to the enemy's agent—Mrs Conrad, I fancy; but in order that no suspicion of their genuineness may arise, the plans must seem to be stolen. He does his best to throw no suspicion on anyone in the house, by pretending to see a man leaving the window. But there he ran up against the obstinacy of the Admiral. So his next anxiety is that no suspicion shall fall on Fitzroy."

"This is all guesswork on your part, Poirot," I objected.

"It is psychology, *mon ami.* A man who had handed over the real plans would not be overscrupulous as to who was likely to fall under suspicion. And why was he so anxious that no details of the robbery should be given to Mrs Conrad? Because he had handed over the faked plans earlier in the evening, and did not want her to know that the theft could only have taken place later."

"I wonder if you are right," I said.

"Of course I am right. I spoke to Alloway as one great man to another—and he understood perfectly. You will see."

One thing is quite certain. On the day when Lord Alloway became Prime Minister, a cheque and a signed photograph arrived; on the photograph were the words: *"To my discreet friend, Hercule Poirot—from Alloway."*

I believe that the Z type of submarine is causing great exultation in naval circles. They say it will revolutionize modern naval warfare. I have heard that a certain foreign power essayed to construct something of the same kind and the result was a dismal failure. But I still consider that Poirot was guessing. He will do it once too often one of these days.

DOROTHY L. SAYERS *(1893—1957) was one of the giants of the "Golden Age" of detective fiction. Her popularity and enduring fame rest largely on her creation of Peter Death Bredon Wimsey, a son of the Duke of Denver, and therefore a lord. Wimsey's lengthly romance with Harriet Vane and his royal manners and attitudes have charmed Ms. Sayers' loyal readership over the years. Dorothy Sayers' excellent plots showcase a flair for the original combined with good humor. She produced only thirteen mystery novels and a batch of short stories before her deep religiosity led her along other paths. Her last novel was* Busman's Honeymoon *in 1937.*

"The Necklace of Pearls" shows Ms. Sayers at her most charming, and her most whimsical, best.

The Necklace of Pearls
BY DOROTHY L. SAYERS

Sir Septimus Shale was accustomed to assert his authority once in the year and once only. He allowed his young and fashionable wife to fill his house with diagrammatic furniture made of steel; to collect advanced artists and anti-grammatical poets; to believe in cocktails and relativity and to dress as extravagantly as she pleased; but he did insist on an old-fashioned Christmas. He was a simple-hearted man, who really liked plum-pudding and cracker mottoes, and he could not get it out of his head that other people, "at bottom", enjoyed these things also. At Christmas, therefore, he firmly retired to his country house in Essex, called in the servants to hang holly and mistletoe upon the cubist electric fittings; loaded the steel sideboard with delicacies from Fortnum & Mason; hung up stockings at the heads of the polished walnut bedsteads; and even, on this occasion only, had the electric radiators removed from the modernist grates and installed wood fires and a Yule log. He then gathered his family and friends about him, filled them with as much Dickensian good fare as he could persuade them to swallow, and, after their Christmas dinner, set them down to play "Charades" and "Clumps" and "Animal, Vegetable, and Mineral" in the drawing-room, concluding these diversions by "Hide-and-Seek" in the dark all over the house. Because Sir Septimus was a very rich man, his guests fell in with this invariable programme, and if they were bored, they did not tell him so.

Another charming and traditional custom which he followed was that of presenting to his daughter Margharita a pearl on each successive birthday—this anniversary happening to coincide with Christmas Eve. The pearls now numbered twenty, and the collection was beginning to enjoy a certain celebrity, and had been photographed in the Society papers. Though not sensationally large—each one being about the size of a marrow-fat pea—the pearls were of very great value. They were of exquisite colour and perfect shape and matched to a hair's-weight. On this particular Christmas Eve, the presentation of the twenty-first pearl had been the occasion of a very special ceremony. There was a dance and there were speeches. On the Christmas night following, the more restricted family party took place, with the turkey and the Victorian games. There were eleven guests, in addition to Sir Septimus and Lady Shale and their daughter, nearly all related or connected to them in some way: John Shale, a brother, with his wife and their son and daughter Henry and Betty; Betty's fiancé, Oswald Truegood, a young man with parliamentary ambitions; George Comphrey, a cousin of Lady Shale's, aged about thirty and known as a man about town; Lavina Prescott, asked on George's account; Joyce Trivett, asked on Henry Shale's account; Richard and Beryl Dennison, distant relations of Lady Shale, who lived a gay and expensive life in town on nobody precisely knew what resources; and Lord Peter Wimsey, asked, in a touching spirit of unreasonable hope, on Margharita's account. There were also, of course, William Norgate, secretary to Sir Septimus, and Miss Tomkins, secretary to Lady Shale, who had to be there because, without their calm efficiency, the Christmas arrangements could not have been carried through.

Dinner was over—a seemingly endless succession of soup, fish, turkey, roast beef, plum-pudding, mince-pies, crystallized fruit, nuts, and five kinds of wine, presided over by Sir Septimus, all smiles, by Lady Shale, all mocking deprecation, and by Margharita, pretty and bored, with the necklace of twenty-one pearls gleaming softly on her slender throat. Gorged and dyspeptic and longing only for the horizontal position, the company had been shepherded into the drawing-room and set to play "Musical Chairs" (Miss Tomkins at the piano), "Hunt the Slipper" (slipper provided by Miss Tomkins), and "Dumb Crambo" (costumes by Miss Tomkins and Mr William Norgate). The back drawing-room (for Sir Septimus clung to these old-fashioned names) provided an admirable dressing-room, being screened by folding doors from the large drawing-room in which the audience sat on aluminium chairs, scrabbling uneasy toes on a floor of black glass under the tremendous illumination of electricity reflected from a brass ceiling.

It was William Norgate who, after taking the temperature of the meeting, suggested to Lady Shale that they should play at something less athletic. Lady Shale agreed and, as usual, suggested bridge. Sir Septimus, as usual, blew the suggestion aside.

"Bridge? Nonsense! Nonsense! Play bridge every day of your lives. This is Christmas time. Something we can all play together. How about 'Animal, Vegetable, and Mineral'?"

This intellectual pastime was a favourite with Sir Septimus; he was rather good at putting pregnant questions. After a brief discussion, it became evident that this game was an inevitable part of the programme. The party settled down to it, Sir Septimus undertaking to "go out" first and set the thing going.

Presently they had guessed among other things Miss Tomkin's mother's photograph, a gramophone record of "I want to be happy" (much scientific research into the exact composition of records, settled by William Norgate out of the *Encyclopaedia Britannica),* the smallest stickleback in the stream at the bottom of the garden, the new planet Pluto, the scarf worn by Mrs Dennison (very confusing, because it was not silk, which would be animal, or artificial silk, which would be vegetable, but made of spun glass—mineral, a very clever choice of subject), and had failed to guess the Prime Minister's wireless speech—which was voted not fair, since nobody could decide whether it was animal by nature or a kind of gas. It was decided that they should do one more word and then go on to "Hide-and-Seek." Oswald Truegood had retired into the back room and shut the door behind him while the party discussed the next subject of examination, when suddenly Sir Septimus broke in on the argument by calling to his daughter:

"Hullo, Margy! What have you done with your necklace?"

"I took it off, Dad, because I thought it might get broken in 'Dumb Crambo'. It's over here on this table. No, it isn't. Did you take it, mother?"

"No, I didn't. If I'd seen it, I should have. You are a careless child."

"I believe you've got it yourself, Dad. You're teasing."

Sir Septimus denied the accusation with some energy. Everybody got up and began to hunt about. There were not many places in that bare and polished room where a necklace could be hidden. After ten minutes' fruitless investigation, Richard Dennison, who had been seated next to the table where the pearls had been placed, began to look rather uncomfortable.

"Awkward, you know," he remarked to Wimsey.

At this moment, Oswald Truegood put his head through the folding-doors and asked whether they hadn't settled on something by now, because he was getting the fidgets.

This directed the attention of the searchers to the inner room. Margharita must have been mistaken. She had taken it in there, and it had got mixed up with the dressing-up clothes somehow. The room was ransacked. Everything was lifted up and shaken. The thing began to look serious. After half an hour of desperate energy it became apparent that the pearls were nowhere to be found.

"They must be somewhere in these two rooms, you know," said Wimsey. "The back drawing-room has no door and nobody could have gone out of the front drawing-room without being seen. Unless the windows—"

No. The windows were all guarded on the outside by heavy shutters which it needed two footmen to take down and replace. The pearls had not gone out that way. In fact, the mere suggestion that they had left the drawing-room at all was disagreeable. Because—because—

It was William Norgate, efficient as ever, who coldly and boldly, faced the issue.

"I think, Sir Septimus, it would be a relief to the minds of everybody present if we could all be searched."

Sir Septimus was horrified, but the guests, having found a leader, backed up Norgate. The door was locked, and the search was conducted—the ladies in the inner room and the men in the outer.

Nothing resulted from it except some very interesting information about the belongings habitually carried about by the average man and woman. It was natural that Lord Peter Wimsey should possess a pair of forceps, a pocket lens, and a small folding foot-rule—was he not a Sherlock Holmes in high life? But that Oswald Truegood should have two liver-pills in a screw of paper and Henry Shale a pocket edition of *The Odes of Horace* was unexpected. Why did John Shale distend the pockets of his dress-suit with a stump of red sealing-wax, an ugly little mascot, and a five-shilling piece? George Comphrey had a pair of folding scissors, and three wrapped lumps of sugar, of the sort served in restaurants and dining-cars—evidence of a not uncommon form of kleptomania; but that the tidy and exact Norgate should burden himself with a reel of white cotton, three separate lengths of string, and twelve safety-pins on a card seemed really remarkable till one remembered that he had superintended all the Christmas decorations. Richard Dennison, amid some confusion and laughter, was found to cherish a lady's garter, a powder-compact, and half a potato; the last-named, he said, was a prophylactic against rheumatism (to which he was subject), while the other objects belonged to his wife. On the ladies' side, the more striking exhibits were a little book on palmistry, three invisible hair-pins, and a baby's photograph (Miss Tomkins); a Chinese trick cigarette-case with a secret compartment (Beryl Dennison); a *very* private letter and an outfit for mending stocking-ladders (Lavinia Prescott); and a pair of eyebrow tweezers and a small packet of white powder, said to be for headaches (Betty Shale). An agitating moment followed the production from Joyce Trivett's handbag of a small string of pearls—but it was promptly remembered that these had come out of one of the crackers at dinner-time, and they were, in fact, synthetic. In short, the search was unproductive of anything beyond a general shamefacedness and the discomfort always produced by undressing and re-dressing in a hurry at the wrong time of the day.

It was then that somebody, very grudgingly and haltingly, mentioned the horrid word "Police." Sir Septimus, naturally, was appalled by the idea. It was disgusting. He would not allow it. The pearls must be somewhere. They must search the rooms again. Could not Lord Peter Wimsey, with his experience of—er—mysterious happenings, do something to assist them?

"Eh?" said his lordship. "Oh, by Jove, yes—by all means, certainly. That is to say, provided nobody supposes—eh, what? I mean to say, you don't know that I'm not a suspicious character, do you, what?"

Lady Shale interposed with authority.

"We don't think *anybody* ought to be suspected," she said, "but, if we did, we'd know it couldn't be you. You know *far* too much about crimes to want to commit one."

"All right," said Wimsey. "But after the way the place has been gone over—" He shrugged his shoulders.

"Yes, I'm afraid you won't be able to find any footprints," said Margharita. "But we may have overlooked something."

Wimsey nodded.

"I'll try. Do you all mind sitting down on your chairs in the outer room and staying there. All except one of you—I'd better have a witness to anything I do or find. Sir Septimus—you'd be the best person, I think."

He shepherded them to their places and began a slow circuit of the two rooms, exploring every surface, gazing up to the polished brazen ceiling, and crawling on hands and knees in the approved fashion across the black and shining desert of the floors. Sir Septimus followed, staring when Wimsey stared, bending with his hands upon his knees when Wimsey crawled, and puffing at intervals with astonishment and chagrin. Their progress rather resembled that of a man taking out a very inquisitive puppy for a very leisurely constitutional. Fortunately, Lady Shale's taste in furnishing made investigation easier; there were scarcely any nooks or corners where anything could be concealed.

They reached the inner drawing-room, and here the dressing-up clothes were again minutely examined, but without result. Finally, Wimsey lay down flat on his stomach to squint under a steel cabinet which was one of the very few pieces of furniture which possessed short legs. Something about it seemed to catch his attention. He rolled up his sleeve and plunged his arm into the cavity, kicked convulsively in the effort to reach farther than was humanly possible, pulled out from his pocket and extended his folding foot-rule, fished with it under the cabinet, and eventually succeeded in extracting what he sought.

It was a very minute object—in fact, a pin. Not an ordinary pin, but one resembling those used by entomologists to impale extremely small moths on the setting-board. It was about three-quarters of an inch in length, as fine as a very fine needle, with a sharp point and a particularly small head.

"Bless my soul!" said Sir Septimus. "What's that?"

"Does anybody here happen to collect moths or beetles or anything?" asked Wimsey, squatting on his haunches and examining the pin.

"I'm pretty sure they don't," replied Sir Septimus. "I'll ask them."

"Don't do that." Wimsey bent his head and stared at the floor, from which his own face stared meditatively back at him.

"I see," said Wimsey presently. "That's how it was done. All right, Sir Septimus. I know where the pearls are, but I don't know who took them. Perhaps it would be as well—for everybody's satisfaction—just to find out. In the meantime they are perfectly safe. Don't tell anyone that we've found this pin or that we've discovered anything. Send all these people to bed. Lock the drawing-room door and keep the key, and we'll get our man—or woman—by breakfast-time."

"God bless my soul," said Sir Septimus, very much puzzled.

Lord Peter Wimsey kept careful watch that night upon the drawing-room door. Nobody, however, came near it. Either the thief suspected a trap or he felt confident that any time would do to recover the pearls. Wimsey, however, did not feel that he was wasting his time. He was making a list of people who had been left alone in the back drawing-room during the playing of "Animal, Vegetable, and Mineral." The list ran as follows:

Sir Septimus Shale
Lavinia Prescott
William Norgate
Joyce Trivett and Henry Shale (together, because they had claimed to be incapable of guessing anything unaided)
Mrs Dennison
Betty Shale
George Comphrey
Richard Dennison
Miss Tomkins
Oswald Truegood

He also made out a list of the persons to whom pearls might be useful or desirable. Unfortunately, this list agreed in almost all respects with the first (always excepting Sir Septimus) and so was not very helpful. The two secretaries had both come well recommended, but that was exactly what they would have done had they come with ulterior designs; the Dennisons were notorious livers from hand to mouth; Betty Shale carried mysterious white powders in her handbag, and was known to be in with a rather rapid set in town; Henry was a harmless dilettante, but Joyce Trivett could twist him round her little finger and was what Jane Austen liked to call "expensive and dissipated"; Comphrey speculated; Oswald Truegood was rather frequently present at Epsom and Newmarket—the search for motives was only too fatally easy.

When the second housemaid and the under-footman appeared in the passage with household implements, Wimsey abandoned his vigil, but he was down early to breakfast. Sir Septimus with his wife and daughter were down before him, and a certain air of tension made itself felt. Wimsey, standing on the hearth before the fire, made conversation about the weather and politics.

The party assembled gradually, but, as though by common consent, nothing was said about pearls until after breakfast, when Oswald Truegood took the bull by the horns.

"Well now!" said he. "How's the detective getting along? Got your man, Wimsey?"

"Not yet," said Wimsey easily.

Sir Septimus, looking at Wimsey as though for his cue, cleared his throat and dashed into speech.

"All very tiresome," he said, "all very unpleasant. Hr'rm. Nothing for it but the police, I'm afraid. Just at Christmas, too. Hr'rm. Spoilt the party. Can't stand seeing all this stuff about the place." He waved his hand towards the festoons of evergreens and coloured paper that adorned the walls. "Take it all down, eh, what? No heart in it. Hr'rm. Burn the lot."

"What a pity, when we worked so hard over it," said Joyce.

"Oh, leave it, Uncle," said Henry Shale. "You're bothering too much about the pearls. They're sure to turn up."

"Shall I ring for James?" suggested William Norgate.

"No," interrupted Comphrey, "let's do it ourselves. It'll give us something to do and take our minds off our troubles."

"That's right," said Sir Septimus. "Start right away. Hate the sight of it."

He savagely hauled a great branch of holly down from the mantelpiece and flung it, crackling, into the fire.

"That's the stuff," said Richard Dennison. "Make a good old blaze!" He leapt up from the table and snatched the mistletoe from the chandelier. "Here goes! One more kiss for somebody before it's too late."

"Isn't it unlucky to take it down before the New Year?" suggested Miss Tomkins.

"Unlucky be hanged. We'll have it all down. Off the stairs and out of the drawing-room too. Somebody go and collect it."

"Isn't the drawing-room locked?" asked Oswald.

"No. Lord Peter says the pearls aren't there, wherever else they are, so it's unlocked. That's right, isn't it, Wimsey?"

"Quite right. The pearls were taken out of these rooms. I can't tell yet how, but I'm positive of it. In fact, I'll pledge my reputation that wherever they are, they're not up there."

"Oh, well," said Comphrey, "in that case, have at it! Come along, Lavinia—you and Dennison do the drawing-room and I'll do the back room. We'll have a race."

"But if the police are coming in," said Dennison, "oughtn't everything to be left just as it is?"

"Damn the police!" shouted Sir Septimus. "They don't want evergreens."

Oswald and Margharita were already pulling the holly and ivy from the staircase, amid peals of laughter. The party dispersed. Wimsey went quietly upstairs and into the drawing-room, where the work of demolition was taking place at a great rate, George having bet the other two ten shillings to a tanner that they would not finish their part of the job before he finished his.

"You mustn't help," said Lavinia, laughing to Wimsey. "It wouldn't be fair."

Wimsey said nothing, but waited till the room was clear. Then he followed them down again to the hall, where the fire was sending up a great roaring and spluttering, suggestive of Guy Fawkes' night. He whispered to Sir Septimus, who went forward and touched George Comphrey on the shoulder.

"Lord Peter wants to say something to you, my boy," he said.

Comphrey started and went with him a little reluctantly, as it seemed. He was not looking very well.

"Mr Comphrey," said Wimsey, "I fancy these are some of your property." He held out the palm of his hand, in which rested twenty-two fine, small-headed pins.

"Ingenious," said Wimsey, "but something less ingenious would have served his turn better. It was very unlucky, Sir Septimus, that you should have mentioned the pearls when you did. Of course, he hoped that the loss wouldn't be discovered till we'd chucked guessing games and taken to 'Hide-and-Seek'. Then the pearls might have been anywhere in the house, we shouldn't have locked the drawing-room door, and he could have recovered them at his leisure. He had had this possibility in his mind when he came here, obviously, and that was why he brought the pins, and Miss Shale's taking off the necklace to play 'Dumb Crambo' gave him his opportunity.

"He had spent Christmas here before, and knew perfectly well that 'Animal, Vegetable, and Mineral' would form part of the entertainment. He had only to gather up the necklace from the table when it came to his turn to retire, and he knew he could count on at least five minutes by himself while we were all arguing about the choice of a word. He had only to snip the pearls from the string with his pocket-scissors, burn the string in the grate, and fasten the pearls to the mistletoe with the fine pins. The mistletoe was hung on the chandelier, pretty high—it's a lofty room—but he could easily reach it by standing on the glass table, which wouldn't show footmarks, and it was almost certain that nobody would think of examining the mistletoe for extra berries. I shouldn't have thought of it myself if I hadn't found that pin which he had dropped. That gave me the idea that the pearls had been separated and the rest was easy. I took the pearls off the mistletoe last night—the clasp was there, too, pinned among the holly-leaves. Here they are. Comphrey must have got a nasty shock this morning. I knew he was our man when he suggested that the guests should tackle the decorations themselves and that he should do the back drawing-room —but I wish I had seen his face when he came to the mistletoe and found the pearls gone."

"And you worked it all out when you found the pin?" said Sir Septimus.

"Yes; I knew then where the pearls had gone to."

"But you never even looked at the mistletoe."

"I saw it reflected in the black glass floor, and it struck me then how much the mistletoe berries looked like pearls."

DAME NGAIO *(pronounced "Ny'o")* MARSH *(1899–1982) is the most famous writer from New Zealand. An actress and theatrical producer from 1920–1952, Dame Ngaio brought to her fiction a background in the theater. She created one of the great series detectives of the twentieth century, Inspector (later Superintendent) Roderick Alleyn, who is featured in every one of her thirty-two published novels. A good measure of the success of Dame Ngaio rests on the way she allowed Alleyn to grow emotionally, to marry his beloved Agatha Troy, and to advance in his profession. Her impact on the mystery field can be seen in her selection as a Grand Master by the Mystery Writers of America.*

"Death on the Air" finds Roderick Alleyn facing one of his most interesting and puzzling cases, set on Christmas Day.

Death on the Air
BY DAME NGAIO MARSH

On the 25th of December at 7:30 a.m. Mr. Septimus Tonks was found dead beside his wireless set.

It was Emily Parks, an under-housemaid, who discovered him. She butted open the door and entered, carrying mop, duster, and carpet-sweeper. At that precise moment she was greatly startled by a voice that spoke out of the darkness.

"Good morning, everybody," said the voice in superbly inflected syllables, "and a Merry Christmas!"

Emily yelped, but not loudly, as she immediately realized what had happened. Mr. Tonks had omitted to turn off his wireless before going to bed. She drew back the curtains, revealing a kind of pale murk which was a London Christmas dawn, switched on the light, and saw Septimus.

He was seated in front of the radio. It was a small but expensive set, specially built for him. Septimus sat in an armchair, his back to Emily, his body tilted towards the radio.

His hands, the fingers curiously bunched, were on the ledge of the cabinet under the tuning and volume knobs. His chest rested against the shelf below and his head leaned on the front panel.

He looked rather as though he was listening intently to the interior secrets of the wireless. His head was bent so that Emily could see his bald top with its trail of oiled hairs. He did not move.

"Beg pardon, sir," gasped Emily. She was again greatly startled. Mr. Tonks' enthusiasm for radio had never before induced him to tune in at seven-thirty in the morning.

"Special Christmas service," the cultured voice was saying. Mr. Tonks sat very still. Emily, in common with the other servants, was terrified of her master. She did not know whether to go or to stay. She gazed wildly at Septimus and realized that he wore a dinner-jacket. The room was now filled with the clamor of pealing bells.

Emily opened her mouth as wide as it would go and screamed and screamed and screamed. . . .

Chase, the butler, was the first to arrive. He was a pale, flabby man but authoritative. He said: "What's the meaning of this outrage?" and then saw Septimus. He went to the arm-chair, bent down, and looked into his master's face.

He did not lose his head, but said in a loud voice: "My Gawd!" And then to Emily: "Shut your face." By this vulgarism he betrayed his agitation. He seized Emily by the shoulders and thrust her towards the door, where they were met by Mr. Hislop, the secretary, in his dressing-gown. Mr. Hislop said: "Good heavens, Chase, what is the meaning—" and then his voice too was drowned in the clamor of bells and renewed screams.

Chase put his fat white hand over Emily's mouth.

"In the study if you please, sir. An accident. Go to your room, will you, and stop that noise or I'll give you something to make you." This to Emily, who bolted down the hall, where she was received by the rest of the staff who had congregated there.

Chase returned to the study with Mr. Hislop and locked the door. They both looked down at the body of Septimus Tonks. The secretary was the first to speak.

"But—but—he's dead," said little Mr. Hislop.

"I suppose there can't be any doubt," whispered Chase.

"Look at the face. Any doubt! My God!"

Mr. Hislop put out a delicate hand towards the bent head and then drew it back. Chase, less fastidious, touched one of the hard wrists, gripped, and then lifted it. The body at once tipped backwards as if it was made of wood. One of the hands knocked against the butler's face. He sprang back with an oath.

There lay Septimus, his knees and his hands in the air, his terrible face turned up to the light. Chase pointed to the right hand. Two fingers and the thumb were slightly blackened.

Ding, dong, dang, ding.

"For God's sake stop those bells," cried Mr. Hislop. Chase turned off the wall switch. Into the sudden silence came the sound of the door-handle being rattled and Guy Tonks' voice on the other side.

"Hislop! Mr. Hislop! Chase! What's the matter?"

"Just a moment, Mr. Guy." Chase looked at the secretary. "You go, sir."

So it was left to Mr. Hislop to break the news to the family. They listened to his stammering revelation in stupefied silence. It was not until Guy, the eldest of the three children, stood in the study that any practical suggestion was made.

"What has killed him?" asked Guy.

"It's extraordinary," burbled Hislop. "Extraordinary. He looks as if he'd been—"

"Galvanized," said Guy.

"We ought to send for a doctor," suggested Hislop timidly.

"Of course. Will you, Mr. Hislop? Dr. Meadows."

Hislop went to the telephone and Guy returned to his family. Dr. Meadows lived on the other side of the square and arrived in five minutes. He examined the body without moving it. He questioned Chase and Hislop. Chase was very voluble about the burns on the hand. He uttered the word "electrocution" over and over again.

"I had a cousin, sir, that was struck by lighting. As soon as I saw the hand—"

"Yes, yes," said Dr. Meadows. "So you said. I can see the burns for myself."

"Electrocution," repeated Chase. "There'll have to be an inquest."

Dr. Meadows snapped at him, summoned Emily, and then saw the rest of the family—Guy, Arthur, Phillipa, and their mother. They were clustered round a cold grate in the drawing-room. Phillipa was on her knees, trying to light the fire.

"What was it?" asked Arthur as soon as the doctor came in.

"Looks like electric shock. Guy, I'll have a word with you if you please. Phillipa, look after your mother, there's a good child. Coffee with a dash of brandy. Where are those damn maids? Come on, Guy."

Alone with Guy, he said they'd have to send for the police.

"The police!" Guy's dark face turned very pale. "Why? What's it got to do with them?"

"Nothing, as like as not, but they'll have to be notified. I can't give a certificate as things are. If it's electrocution, how did it happen?"

"But the police!" said Guy. "That's simply ghastly. Dr. Meadows, for God's sake couldn't you—?"

"No," said Dr. Meadows, "I couldn't. Sorry, Guy, but there it is."

"But can't we wait a moment? Look at him again. You haven't examined him properly."

"I don't want to move him, that's why. Pull yourself together, boy. Look here. I've got a pal in the C.I.D. —Alleyn. He's a gentleman and all that. He'll curse me like a fury, but he'll come if he's in London, and he'll make things easier for you. Go back to your mother. I'll ring Alleyn up."

That was how it came about that Chief Detective-Inspector Roderick Alleyn spent his Christmas Day in harness. As a matter of fact he was on duty, and as he pointed out to Dr. Meadows, would have had to turn out and visit his miserable Tonkses in any case. When he did arrive it was with his usual air of remote courtesy. He was accompanied by a tall, thick-set officer—Inspector Fox—and by the divisional police-surgeon. Dr. Meadows took them into the study. Alleyn, in his turn, looked at the horror that had been Septimus.

"Was he like this when he was found?"

"No. I understand he was leaning forward with his hands on the ledge of the cabinet. He must have slumped forward and been propped up by the chair arms and the cabinet."

"Who moved him?"

"Chase, the butler. He said he only meant to raise the arm. *Rigor* is well established."

Alleyn put his hand behind the rigid neck and pushed. The body fell forward into its original position.

"There you are, Curtis," said Alleyn to the divisional surgeon. He turned to Fox. "Get the camera man, will you, Fox?"

The photographer took four shots and departed. Alleyn marked the position of the hands and feet with chalk, made a careful plan of the room and turned to the doctors.

"Is it electrocution, do you think?"

"Looks like it," said Curtis. "Have to be a p.m. of course."

"Of course. Still, look at the hands. Burns. Thumb and two fingers bunched together and exactly the distance between the two knobs apart. He'd been tuning his hurdy-gurdy."

"By gum," said Inspector Fox, speaking for the first time.

"D'you mean he got a lethal shock from his radio?" asked Dr. Meadows.

"I don't know. I merely conclude he had his hands on the knobs when he died."

"It was still going when the house-maid found him. Chase turned it off and got no shock."

"Yours, partner," said Alleyn, turning to Fox. Fox stooped down to the wall switch.

"Careful," said Alleyn.

"I've got rubber soles," said Fox, and switched it on. The radio hummed, gathered volume, and found itself.

"No-oel, No-o-el," it roared. Fox cut it off and pulled out the wall plug.

"I'd like to have a look inside this set," he said.

"So you shall, old boy, so you shall," rejoined Alleyn. "Before you begin, I think we'd better move the body. Will you see to that, Meadows? Fox, get Bailey, will you? He's out in the car."

Curtis, Hislop, and Meadows carried Septimus Tonks into a spare downstairs room. It was a difficult and horrible business with that contorted body. Dr. Meadows came back alone, mopping his brow, to find Detective-Sergeant Bailey, a fingerprint expert, at work on the wireless cabinet.

"What's all this?" asked Dr. Meadows. "Do you want to find out if he'd been fooling round with the innards?"

"He," said Alleyn, "or—somebody else."

"Umph!" Dr. Meadows looked at the Inspector. "You agree with me, it seems. Do you suspect—?"

"Suspect? I'm the least suspicious man alive. I'm merely being tidy. Well, Bailey?"

"I've got a good one off the chair arm. That'll be the deceased's, won't it, sir?"

"No doubt. We'll check up later. What about the wireless?"

Fox, wearing a glove, pulled off the knob of the volume control.

"Seems to be O.K." said Bailey. "It's a sweet bit of work. Not too bad at all, sir." He turned his torch into the back of the radio, undid a couple of screws underneath the set, lifted out the works.

"What's the little hole for?" asked Alleyn.

"What's that, sir?" said Fox.

"There's a hole bored through the panel above the knob. About an eighth of an inch in diameter. The rim of the knob hides it. One might easily miss it. Move your torch, Bailey. Yes. There, do you see?"

Fox bent down and uttered a bass growl. A fine needle of light came through the front of the radio.

"That's peculiar, sir," said Bailey from the other side. "I don't get the idea at all."

Alleyn pulled out the tuning knob.

"There's another one there," he murmured. "Yes. Nice clean little holes. Newly bored. Unusual, I take it?"

"Unusual's the word, sir," said Fox.

"Run away, Meadows," said Alleyn.

"Why the devil?" asked Dr. Meadows indignantly. "What are you driving at? Why shouldn't I be here?"

"You ought to be with the sorrowing relatives. Where's your corpse-side manner?"

"I've settled them. What are you up to?"

"Who's being suspicious now?" asked Alleyn mildly. "You may stay for a moment. Tell me about the Tonkses. Who are they? What are they? What sort of a man was Septimus?"

"If you must know, he was a damned unpleasant sort of a man."

"Tell me about him."

Dr. Meadows sat down and lit a cigarette.

"He was a self-made bloke," he said, "as hard as nails and—well, coarse rather than vulgar."

"Like Dr. Johnson perhaps?"

"Not in the least. Don't interrupt. I've known him for twenty-five years. His wife was a neighbor of ours in Dorset. Isabel Foreston. I brought the children into this vale of tears and, by jove, in many ways it's been one for them. It's an extraordinary household. For the last ten years Isabel's condition has been the sort that sends these psycho-jokers dizzy with rapture. I'm only an out-of-date G.P., and I'd just say she is in an advanced stage of hysterical neurosis. Frightened into fits of her husband."

"I can't understand these holes," grumbled Fox to Bailey.

"Go on, Meadows," said Alleyn.

"I tackled Sep about her eighteen months ago. Told him the trouble was in her mind. He eyed me with a sort of grin on his face and said: 'I'm surprised to learn that my wife has enough mentality to—' But look here, Alleyn, I can't talk about my patients like this. What the devil am I thinking about."

"You know perfectly well it'll go no further unless—"

"Unless what?"

"Unless it has to. Do go on."

But Dr. Meadows hurriedly withdrew behind his professional rectitude. All he would say was that Mr. Tonks had suffered from high blood pressure and a weak heart, that Guy was in his father's city office, that Arthur had wanted to study art and had been told to read for law, and that Phillipa wanted to go on the stage and had been told to do nothing of the sort.

"Bullied his children," commented Alleyn.

"Find out for yourself. I'm off." Dr. Meadows got as far as the door and came back.

"Look here," he said, "I'll tell you one thing. There was a row here last night. I'd asked Hislop, who's a sensible little beggar, to let me know if anything happened to upset Mrs. Sep. Upset her badly, you know. To be indiscreet again, I said he'd better let me know if Sep cut up rough because Isabel and the young had had about as much of that as they could stand. He was drinking pretty heavily. Hislop rang me up at ten-twenty last night to say there'd been a hell of a row; Sep bullying Phips—Phillipa, you know; always call her Phips—in her room. He said Isabel—Mrs. Sep—had gone to bed. I'd had a big day and I didn't want to turn out. I told him to ring again in half an hour if things hadn't quieted down. I told him to keep out of Sep's way and stay in his own room, which is next to Phips' and see if she was all right when Sep cleared out. Hislop was involved. I won't tell you how. The servants were all out. I said that if I didn't hear from him in half an hour I'd ring again and if there was no answer I'd know they were all in bed and quiet. I did ring, got no answer, and went to bed myself. That's all. I'm off. Curtis knows where to find me. You'll want me for the inquest, I suppose. Goodbye."

When he had gone Alleyn embarked on a systematic prowl round the room. Fox and Bailey were still deeply engrossed with the wireless.

"I don't see how the gentleman could have got a bump-off from the instrument," grumbled Fox. "These control knobs are quite in order. Everything's as it should be. Look here, sir."

He turned on the wall switch and tuned in. There was a prolonged humming.

". . . concludes the program of Christmas carols," said the radio.

"A very nice tone," said Fox approvingly.

"Here's something, sir," announced Bailey suddenly.

"Found the sawdust, have you?" said Alleyn.

"Got it in one," said the startled Bailey.

Alleyn peered into the instrument, using the torch. He scooped up two tiny traces of sawdust from under the holes.

"'Vantage number one," said Alleyn. He bent down to the wall plug. "Hullo! A two-way adapter. Serves the radio and the radiator. Thought they were illegal. This is a rum business. Let's have another look at those knobs."

He had his look. They were the usual wireless fitments, bakelite knobs fitting snugly to the steel shafts that projected from the front panel.

"As you say," he murmured, "quite in order. Wait a bit." He produced a pocket lens and squinted at one of the shafts. "Ye-es. Do they ever wrap blotting-paper round these objects, Fox?"

"Blotting-paper!" ejaculated Fox. "They do not."

Alleyn scraped at both the shafts with his penknife, holding an envelope underneath. He rose, groaning, and crossed to the desk. "A corner torn off the bottom bit of blotch," he said presently. "No prints on the wireless, I think you said, Bailey?"

"That's right," agreed Bailey morosely.

"There'll be none, or too many, on the blotter, but try, Bailey, try," said Alleyn. He wandered about the room, his eyes on the floor; got as far as the window and stopped.

"Fox!" he said. "A clue. A very palpable clue."

"What is it?" asked Fox.

"The odd wisp of blotting-paper, no less." Alleyn's gaze traveled up the side of the window curtain. "Can I believe my eyes?"

He got a chair, stood on the seat, and with his gloved hand pulled the buttons from the ends of the curtain rod.

"Look at this." He turned to the radio, detached the control knobs, and laid them beside the ones he had removed from the curtain rod.

Ten minutes later Inspector Fox knocked on the drawing-room door and was admitted by Guy Tonks. Phillipa had got the fire going and the family was gathered round it. They looked as though they had not moved or spoken to one another for a long time.

It was Phillipa who spoke first to Fox. "Do you want one of us?"

"If you please, miss," said Fox. "Inspector Alleyn would like to see Mr. Guy Tonks for a moment, if convenient."

"I'll come," said Guy, and led the way to the study. At the door he paused. "Is he—my father—still—?"

"No, no, sir," said Fox comfortably. "It's all ship-shape in there again."

With a lift of his chin Guy opened the door and went in, followed by Fox. Alleyn was alone, seated at the desk. He rose to his feet.

"You want to speak to me?" asked Guy.

"Yes, if I may. This has all been a great shock to you, of course. Won't you sit down?"

Guy sat in the chair farthest away from the radio.

"What killed my father? Was it a stroke?"

"The doctors are not quite certain. There will have to be a *post-mortem.*"

"Good God! And an inquest?"

"I'm afraid so."

"Horrible!" said Guy violently. "What do you think was the matter? Why the devil do these quacks have to be so mysterious? What killed him?"

"They think an electric shock."

"How did it happen?"

"We don't know. It looks as if he got it from the wireless."

"Surely that's impossible. I thought they were fool-proof."

"I believe they are, if left to themselves."

For a second undoubtedly Guy was startled. Then a look of relief came into his eyes. He seemed to relax all over.

"Of course," he said, "he was always monkeying about with it. What had he done?"

"Nothing."

"But you said—if it killed him he must have done something to it."

"If anyone interfered with the set it was put right afterwards."

Guy's lips parted but he did not speak. He had gone very white.

"So you see," said Alleyn, "your father could not have done anything."

"Then it was not the radio that killed him."

"That we hope will be determined by the *post-mortem.*"

"I don't know anything about wireless," said Guy suddenly. "I don't understand. This doesn't seem to make sense. Nobody ever touched the thing except my father. He was most particular about it. Nobody went near the wireless."

"I see. He was an enthusiast?"

"Yes, it was his only enthusiasm except—except his business."

"One of my men is a bit of an expert," Alleyn said. "He says this is a remarkably good set. You are not an expert you say. Is there anyone in the house who is?"

"My young brother was interested at one time. He's given it up. My father wouldn't allow another radio in the house."

"Perhaps he may be able to suggest something."

"But if the thing's all right now—"

"We've got to explore every possibility."

"You speak as if—as—if—"

"I speak as I am bound to speak before there has been an inquest," said Alleyn. "Had anyone a grudge against your father, Mr. Tonks?"

Up went Guy's chin again. He looked Alleyn squarely in the eyes.

"Almost everyone who knew him," said Guy.

"Is that an exaggeration?"

"No. You think he was murdered, don't you?"

Alleyn suddenly pointed to the desk beside him.

"Have you ever seen those before?" he asked abruptly. Guy stared at two black knobs that lay side by side on an ashtray.

"Those?" he said. "No. What are they?"

"I believe they are the agents of your father's death."

The study door opened and Arthur Tonks came in.

"Guy," he said, "what's happening? We can't stay cooped up together all day. I can't stand it. For God's sake what happened to him?"

"They think those things killed him," said Guy.

"Those?" For a split second Arthur's glance slewed to the curtainrods. Then, with a characteristic flicker of his eyelids, he looked away again.

"What do you mean?" he asked Alleyn.

"Will you try one of those knobs on the shaft of the volume control?"

"But," said Arthur, "they're metal."

"It's disconnected," said Alleyn.

Arthur picked one of the knobs from the tray, turned to the radio, and fitted the knob over one of the exposed shafts.

"It's too loose," he said quickly, "it would fall off."

"Not if it was packed—with blotting-paper, for instance."

"Where did you find these things?" demanded Arthur.

"I think you recognized them, didn't you? I saw you glance at the curtain-rod."

"Of course I recognized them. I did a portrait of Phillipa against those curtains when—he—was away last year. I've painted the damn things."

"Look here," interrupted Guy, "exactly what are you driving at, Mr. Alleyn? If you mean to suggest that my brother—"

"I!" cried Arthur. "What's it got to do with me? Why should you suppose—."

"I found traces of blotting-paper on the shafts and inside the metal knobs," said Alleyn. "It suggested a substitution of the metal knobs for the bakelite ones. It is remarkable, don't you think, that they should so closely resemble one another? If you examine them, of course, you find they are not identical. Still, the difference is scarcely perceptible."

Arthur did not answer this. He was still looking at the wireless.

"I've always wanted to have a look at this set," he said surprisingly.

"You are free to do so now," said Alleyn politely. "We have finished with it for the time being."

"Look here," said Arthur suddenly, "suppose metal knobs were substituted for bakelite ones, it couldn't kill him. He wouldn't get a shock at all. Both the controls are grounded."

"Have you noticed those very small holes drilled through the panel?" asked Alleyn. "Should they be there, do you think?"

Arthur peered at the little steel shafts. "By God, he's right, Guy," he said. "That's how it was done."

"Inspector Fox," said Alleyn, "tells me those holes could be used for conducting wires and that a lead could be taken from the—transformer, is it?—to one of the knobs."

"And the other connected to earth," said Fox. "It's a job for an expert. He could get three hundred volts or so that way."

"That's not good enough," said Arthur quickly; "there wouldn't be enough current to do any damage—only a few hundredths of an amp."

"I'm not an expert," said Alleyn, "but I'm sure you're right. Why were the holes drilled then? Do you imagine someone wanted to play a practical joke on your father?"

"A practical joke? On *him?*" Arthur gave an unpleasant screech of laughter. "Do you hear that, Guy?"

"Shut up," said Guy. "After all, he is dead."

"It seems almost too good to be true, doesn't it?"

"Don't be a bloody fool, Arthur. Pull yourself together. Can't you see what this means? They think he's been murdered."

"Murdered! They're wrong. None of us had the nerve for that, Mr.

Inspector. Look at me. My hands are so shaky they told me I'd never be able to paint. That dates from when I was a kid and he shut me up in the cellars for a night. Look at me. Look at Guy. He's not so vulnerable, but he caved in like the rest of us. We were conditioned to surrender. Do you know—"

"Wait a moment," said Alleyn quietly. "Your brother is quite right, you know. You'd better think before you speak. This may be a case of homicide."

"Thank you, sir," said Guy quickly. "That's extraordinarily decent of you. Arthur's a bit above himself. It's a shock."

"The relief, you mean," said Arthur. "Don't be such an ass. I didn't kill him and they'll find it out soon enough. Nobody killed him. There must be some explanation."

"I suggest that you listen to me," said Alleyn. "I'm going to put several questions to both of you. You need not answer them, but it will be more sensible to do so. I understand no one but your father touched this radio. Did any of you ever come into this room while it was in use?"

"Not unless he wanted to vary the program with a little bullying," said Arthur.

Alleyn turned to Guy, who was glaring at his brother.

"I want to know exactly what happened in this house last night. As far as the doctors can tell us, your father died not less than three and not more than eight hours before he was found. We must try to fix the time as accurately as possible."

"I saw him at about a quarter to nine," began Guy slowly. "I was going out to a supper-party at the Savoy and had come downstairs. He was crossing the hall from the drawing-room to his room."

"Did you see him after a quarter to nine, Mr. Arthur?"

"No. I heard him, though. He was working in here with Hislop. Hislop had asked to go away for Christmas. Quite enough. My father discovered some urgent correspondence. Really, Guy, you know, he was pathological. I'm sure Dr. Meadows thinks so."

"When did you hear him?" asked Alleyn.

"Some time after Guy had gone. I was working on a drawing in my room upstairs. It's above his. I heard him bawling at little Hislop. It must have been before ten o'clock, because I went out to a studio party at ten. I heard him bawling as I crossed the hall."

"And when," said Alleyn, "did you both return?"

"I came home at about twenty past twelve," said Guy immediately.

"I can fix the time because we had gone on to Chez Carlo, and they had a midnight stunt there. We left immediately afterwards. I came home in a taxi. The radio was on full blast."

"You heard no voices?"

"None. Just the wireless."

"And you, Mr. Arthur?"

"Lord knows when I got in. After one. The house was in darkness. Not a sound."

"You had your own key?"

"Yes," said Guy. "Each of us has one. They're always left on a hook in the lobby. When I came in I noticed Arthur's was gone."

"What about the others? How did you know it was his?"

"Mother hasn't got one and Phips lost hers weeks ago. Anyway, I knew they were staying in and that it must be Arthur who was out."

"Thank you," said Arthur ironically.

"You didn't look in the study when you came in," Alleyn asked him.

"Good Lord, no," said Arthur as if the suggestion was fantastic. "I say," he said suddenly, "I suppose he was sitting here—dead. That's a queer thought." He laughed nervously. "Just sitting here, behind the door in the dark."

"How do you know it was in the dark?"

"What d'you mean? Of course it was. There was no light under the door."

"I see. Now do you two mind joining your mother again? Perhaps your sister will be kind enough to come in here for a moment. Fox, ask her, will you?"

Fox returned to the drawing-room with Guy and Arthur and remained there, blandly unconscious of any embarrassment his presence might cause the Tonkses. Bailey was already there, ostensibly examining the electric points.

Phillipa went to the study at once. Her first remark was characteristic. "Can I be of any help?" asked Phillipa.

"It's extremely nice of you to put it like that," said Alleyn. "I don't want to worry you for long. I'm sure this discovery has been a shock to you."

"Probably," said Phillipa. Alleyn glanced quickly at her. "I mean," she explained, "that I suppose I must be shocked but I can't feel anything much. I just want to get it all over as soon as possible. And then think. Please tell me what has happened."

Alleyn told her they believed her father had been electrocuted and that the circumstances were unusual and puzzling. He said nothing to suggest that the police suspected murder.

"I don't think I'll be much help," said Phillipa, "but go ahead."

"I want to try to discover who was the last person to see your father or speak to him."

"I should think very likely I was," said Phillipa composedly. "I had a row with him before I went to bed."

"What about?"

"I don't see that it matters."

Alleyn considered this. When he spoke again it was with deliberation.

"Look here," he said, "I think there is very little doubt that your father was killed by an electric shock from his wireless set. As far as I know the circumstances are unique. Radios are normally incapable of giving a lethal shock to anyone. We have examined the cabinet and are inclined to think that its internal arrangements were disturbed last night. Very radically disturbed. Your father may have experimented with it. If anything happened to interrupt or upset him, it is possible that in the excitement of the moment he made some dangerous readjustment."

"You don't believe that, do you?" asked Phillipa calmly.

"Since you ask me," said Alleyn, "no."

"I see," said Phillipa; "you think he was murdered, but you're not sure." She had gone very white, but she spoke crisply. "Naturally you want to find out about my row."

"About everything that happened last evening," amended Alleyn.

"What happened was this," said Phillipa; "I came into the hall some time after ten. I'd heard Arthur go out and had looked at the clock at five past. I ran into my father's secretary, Richard Hislop. He turned aside, but not before I saw . . . not quickly enough. I blurted out: 'You're crying.' We looked at each other. I asked him why he stood it. None of the other secretaries could. He said he had to. He's a widower with two children. There have been doctor's bills and things. I needn't tell you about his . . . about his damnable servitude to my father nor about the refinements of curelty he'd had to put up with. I think my father was mad, really mad, I mean. Richard gabbled it all out to me higgledy-piggledy in a sort of horrified whisper. He's been here two years, but I'd never realized until that moment that we . . . that . . ." A faint flush came into her cheeks. "He's such a funny little man. Not at all the sort I've always thought . . . not good-looking or exciting or anything."

She stopped, looking bewildered.

"Yes?" said Alleyn.

"Well, you see—I suddenly realized I was in love with him. He realized it too. He said: 'Of course, it's quite hopeless, you know. Us, I mean. Laughable, almost.' Then I put my arms round his neck and kissed him. It was very odd, but it seemed quite natural. The point is my father came out of his room into the hall and saw us."

"That was bad luck," said Alleyn.

"Yes, it was. My father really seemed delighted. He almost licked his lips. Richard's efficiency had irritated my father for a long time. It was difficult to find excuses for being beastly to him. Now, of course . . . He ordered Richard to the study and me to my room. He followed me upstairs. Richard tried to come too, but I asked him not to. My father . . . I needn't tell you what he said. He put the worst possible construction on what he'd seen. He was absolutely foul, screaming at me like a madman. He was insane. Perhaps it was D. Ts. He drank terribly, you know. I dare say it's silly of me to tell you all this."

"No," said Alleyn.

"I can't feel anything at all. Not even relief. The boys are frankly relieved. I can't feel afraid either." She stared meditatively at Alleyn. "Innocent people needn't feel afraid, need they?"

"It's an axiom of police investigation," said Alleyn and wondered if indeed she was innocent.

"It just *can't* be murder," said Phillipa. "We were all too much afraid to kill him. I believe he'd win even if you murdered him. He'd hit back somehow." She put her hands to her eyes. "I'm all muddled."

"I think you are more upset than you realized. I'll be as quick as I can. Your father made this scene in your room. You say he screamed. Did anyone hear him?"

"Yes. Mummy did. She came in."

"What happened?"

"I said: 'Go away, darling, it's all right.' I didn't want her to be involved. He nearly killed her with the things he did. Sometimes he'd . . . we never knew what happened between them. It was all secret, like a door shutting quietly as you walk along a passage."

"Did she go away?"

"Not at once. He told her he'd found out that Richard and I were lovers. He said . . . it doesn't matter. I don't want to tell you. She was terrified. He was stabbing at her in some way I couldn't understand. Then, quite suddenly, he told her to go to her own room. She went at once and he followed her. He locked me in. That's the last I saw of him, but I heard him go downstairs later."

"Were you locked in all night?"

"No. Richard Hislop's room is next to mine. He came up and spoke through the wall to me. He wanted to unlock the door, but I said better not in case—he—came back. Then, much later, Guy came home. As he passed my door I tapped on it. The key was in the lock and he turned it."

"Did you tell him what had happened?"

"Just that there'd been a row. He only stayed a moment."

"Can you hear the radio from your room?"

She seemed surprised.

"The wireless? Why, yes. Faintly."

"Did you hear it after your father returned to the study?"

"I don't remember."

"Think. While you lay awake all that long time until your brother came home?"

"I'll try. When he came out and found Richard and me, it was not going. They had been working, you see. No, I can't remember hearing it at all unless—wait a moment. Yes. After he had gone back to the study from mother's room I remember there was a loud crash of static. Very loud. Then I think it was quiet for some time. I fancy I heard it again later. Oh, I've remembered something else. After the static my bedside radiator went out. I suppose there was something wrong with the electric supply. That would account for both, wouldn't it? The heater went on again about ten minutes later."

"And did the radio begin again then, do you think?"

"I don't know. I'm very vague about that. It started again sometime before I went to sleep."

"Thank you very much indeed. I won't bother you any longer now."

"All right," said Phillipa calmly, and went away.

Alleyn sent for Chase and questioned him about the rest of the staff and about the discovery of the body. Emily was summoned and dealt with. When she departed, awestruck but complacent, Alleyn turned to the butler.

"Chase," he said, "had your master any peculiar habits?"

"Yes, sir."

"In regard to the wireless?"

"I beg pardon, sir. I thought you meant generally speaking."

"Well, then, generally speaking."

"If I may so, sir, he was a mass of them."

"How long have you been with him?"

"Two months, sir, and due to leave at the end of this week."

"Oh. Why are you leaving?"

Chase produced the classic remark of his kind.

"There are some things," he said, "that flesh and blood will not stand, sir. One of them's being spoke to like Mr. Tonks spoke to his staff."

"Ah. His peculiar habits, in fact?"

"It's my opinion, sir, he was mad. Stark, staring."

"With regard to the radio. Did he tinker with it?"

"I can't say I've ever noticed, sir. I believe he knew quite a lot about wireless."

"When he turned the thing, had he any particular method? Any characteristic attitude or gesture?"

"I don't think so, sir. I never noticed, and yet I've often come into the room when he was at it. I can seem to see him now, sir."

"Yes, yes," said Alleyn swiftly. "That's what we want. A clear mental picture. How was it now? Like this?"

In a moment he was across the room and seated in Septimus's chair. He swung round to the cabinet and raised his right hand to the tuning control.

"Like this?"

"No, sir," said Chase promptly, "that's not him at all. Both hands it should be."

"Ah." Up went Alleyn's left hand to the volume control. "More like this?"

"Yes, sir," said Chase slowly. "But there's something else and I can't recollect what it was. Something he was always doing. It's in the back of my head. You know, sir. Just on the edge of my memory, as you might say."

"I know."

"It's a kind—something—to do with irritation," said Chase slowly. "Irritation? His?"

"No. It's no good, sir. I can't get it."

"Perhaps later. Now look here, Chase, what happened to all of you last night? All the servants, I mean."

"We were all out, sir. It being Christmas Eve. The mistress sent for

me yesterday morning. She said we could take the evening off as soon
as I had taken in Mr. Tonks's grog-tray at nine o'clock. So we went,"
ended Chase simply.

"When?"

"The rest of the staff got away about nine. I left at ten past, sir, and
returned about eleven-twenty. The others were back then, and all in
bed. I went straight to bed myself, sir."

"You came in by a back door, I suppose?"

"Yes, sir. We've been talking it over. None of us noticed anything
unusual."

"Can you hear the wireless in your part of the house?"

"No, sir."

"Well," said Alleyn, looking up from his notes, "that'll do, thank
you."

Before Chase reached the door Fox came in.

"Beg pardon, sir," said Fox, "I just want to take a look at the *Radio
Times* on the desk."

He bent over the paper, wetted a gigantic thumb, and turned a page.

"That's it, sir," shouted Chase suddenly. "That's what I tried to
think of. That's what he was always doing."

"But what?"

"Licking his fingers, sir. It was a habit," said Chase. "That's what he
always did when he sat down to the radio. I heard Mr. Hislop tell the
doctor it nearly drove him demented, the way the master couldn't
touch a thing without first licking his fingers."

"Quite so," said Alleyn. "In about ten minutes, ask Mr. Hislop if he
will be good enough to come in for a moment. That will be all, thank
you, Chase."

"Well, sir," remarked Fox when Chase had gone, "if that's the case
and what I think's right, it'd certainly make matters worse."

"Good heavens, Fox, what an elaborate remark. What does it
mean?"

"If metal knobs were substituted for bakelite ones and fine wires
brought through those holes to make contact, then he'd get a bigger
bump if he tuned in with *damp* fingers."

"Yes. And he always used both hands. Fox!"

"Sir."

"Approach the Tonkses again. You haven't left them alone, of
course?"

"Bailey's in there making out he's interested in the light switches.

He's found the main switchboard under the stairs. There's signs of a blown fuse having been fixed recently. In a cupboard underneath there are odd lengths of flex and so on. Same brand as this on the wireless and the heater."

"Ah, yes. Could the cord from the adapter to the radiator be brought into play?"

"By gum," said Fox, "you're right! That's how it was done, Chief. The heavier flex was cut away from the radiator and shoved through. There was a fire, so he wouldn't want the radiator and wouldn't notice."

"It might have been done that way, certainly, but there's little to prove it. Return to the bereaved Tonkses, my Fox, and ask prettily if any of them remember Septimus's peculiarities when tuning his wireless."

Fox met little Mr. Hislop at the door and left him alone with Alleyn. Phillipa had been right, reflected the Inspector, when she said Richard Hislop was not a noticeable man. He was nondescript. Grey eyes, drab hair; rather pale, rather short, rather insignificant; and yet last night there had flashed up between those two the realization of love. Romantic but rum, thought Alleyn.

"Do sit down," he said. "I want you, if you will, to tell me what happened between you and Mr. Tonks last evening."

"What happened?"

"Yes. You all dined at eight, I understand. Then you and Mr. Tonks came in here?"

"Yes."

"What did you do?"

"He dictated several letters."

"Anything unusual take place?"

"Oh, no."

"Why did you quarrel?"

"Quarrel!" The quiet voice jumped a tone. "We did not quarrel, Mr. Alleyn."

"Perhaps that was the wrong word. What upset you?"

"Phillipa has told you?"

"Yes. She was wise to do so. What was the matter, Mr. Hislop?"

"Apart from the . . . what she told you . . . Mr. Tonks was a difficult man to please. I often irritated him. I did so last night."

"In what way?"

"In almost every way. He shouted at me. I was startled and nervous, clumsy with papers, and making mistakes. I wasn't well. I blundered and then . . . I . . . I broke down. I have always irritated him. My very mannerisms—"

"Had he no irritating mannerisms, himself?"

"He! My God!"

"What were they?"

"I can't think of anything in particular. It doesn't matter does it?"

"Anything to do with the wireless, for instance?"

There was a short silence.

"No," said Hislop.

"Was the radio on in here last night, after dinner?"

"For a little while. Not after—after the incident in the hall. At least, I don't think so. I don't remember."

"What did you do after Miss Phillipa and her father had gone upstairs?"

"I followed and listened outside the door for a moment." He had gone very white and had backed away from the desk.

"And then?"

"I heard someone coming. I remembered Dr. Meadows had told me to ring him up if there was one of the scenes. I returned here and rang him up. He told me to go to my room and listen. If things got any worse I was to telephone again. Otherwise I was to stay in my room. It is next to hers."

"And you did this?" He nodded. "Could you hear what Mr. Tonks said to her?"

"A—a good deal of it."

"What did you hear?"

"He insulted her. Mrs. Tonks was there. I was just thinking of ringing Dr. Meadows up again when she and Mr. Tonks came out and went along the passage. I stayed in my room."

"You did not try to speak to Miss Phillipa?"

"We spoke through the wall. She asked me not to ring Dr. Meadows, but to stay in my room. In a little while, perhaps it was as much as twenty minutes—I really don't know—I heard him come back and go downstairs. I again spoke to Phillipa. She implored me not to do anything and said that she herself would speak to Dr. Meadows in the morning. So I waited a little longer and then went to bed."

"And to sleep?"

"My God, no!"

"Did you hear the wireless again?"

"Yes. At least I heard static."

"Are you an expert on wireless?"

"No. I know the ordinary things. Nothing much."

"How did you come to take this job, Mr. Hislop?"

"I answered an advertisement."

"You are sure you don't remember any particular mannerism of Mr. Tonks's in connection with the radio?"

"No."

"And you can tell me no more about your interview in the study that led to the scene in the hall?"

"No."

"Will you please ask Mrs. Tonks if she will be kind enough to speak to me for a moment?"

"Certainly," said Hislop, and went away.

Septimus's wife came in looking like death. Alleyn got her to sit down and asked her about her movements on the preceding evening. She said she was feeling unwell and dined in her room. She went to bed immediately afterwards. She heard Septimus yelling at Phillipa and went to Phillipa's room. Septimus accused Mr. Hislop and her daughter of "terrible things." She got as far as this and then broke down quietly. Alleyn was very gentle with her. After a little while he learned that Septimus had gone to her room with her and had continued to speak of "terrible things."

"What sort of things?" asked Alleyn.

"He was not responsible," said Isabel. "He did not know what he was saying. I think he had been drinking."

She thought he had remained with her for perhaps a quarter of an hour. Possibly longer. He left her abruptly and she heard him go along the passage, past Phillipa's door, and presumably downstairs. She had stayed awake for a long time. The wireless could not be heard from her room. Alleyn showed her the curtain knobs, but she seemed quite unable to take in their significance. He let her go, summoned Fox, and went over the whole case.

"What's your idea on the show?" he asked when he had finished.

"Well, sir," said Fox, in his stolid way, "on the face of it the young gentlemen have got alibis. We'll have to check them up, of course, and I don't see we can go much further until we have done so."

"For the moment," said Alleyn, "let us suppose Masters Guy and Arthur to be safely established behind cast-iron alibis. What then?"

"Then we've got the young lady, the old lady, the secretary, and the servants."

"Let us parade them. But first let us go over the wireless game. You'll have to watch me here. I gather that the only way in which the radio could be fixed to give Mr. Tonks his quietus is like this: Control knobs removed. Holes bored in front panel with fine drill. Metal knobs substituted and packed with blotting paper to insulate them from metal shafts and make them stay put. Heavier flex from adapter to radiator cut and the ends of the wires pushed through the drilled holes to make contact with the new knobs. Thus we have a positive and negative pole. Mr. Tonks bridges the gap, gets a mighty wallop as the current passes through him to the earth. The switchboard fuse is blown almost immediately. All this is rigged by murderer while Sep was upstairs bullying wife and daughter. Sep revisited study some time after ten-twenty. Whole thing was made ready between ten, when Arthur went out, and the time Sep returned—say, about ten-forty-five. The murderer reappeared, connected radiator with flex, removed wires, changed back knobs, and left the thing tuned in. Now I take it that the burst of static described by Phillipa and Hislop would be caused by the short-circuit that killed our Septimus?"

"That's right."

"It also affected all the heaters in the house. *Vide* Miss Tonks's radiator."

"Yes. He put all that right again. It would be a simple enough matter for anyone who knew how. He'd just have to fix the fuse on the main switchboard. How long do you say it would take to—what's the horrible word?—to recondition the whole show?"

"M'm," said Fox deeply. "At a guess, sir, fifteen minutes. He'd have to be nippy."

"Yes," agreed Alleyn. "He or she."

"I don't see a female making a success of it," grunted Fox. "Look here, Chief, you know what I'm thinking. Why did Mr. Hislop lie about deceased's habit of licking his thumbs? You say Hislop told you he remembered nothing and Chase says he overheard him saying the trick nearly drove him dippy."

"Exactly," said Alleyn. He was silent for so long that Fox felt moved to utter a discreet cough.

"Eh?" said Alleyn. "Yes, Fox, yes. It'll have to be done." He consulted the telephone directory and dialed a number.

"May I speak to Dr. Meadows? Oh, it's you, is it? Do you remember

Mr. Hislop telling you that Septimus Tonks's trick of wetting his fingers nearly drove Hislop demented. Are you there? You don't? Sure? All right. All right. Hislop rang you up at ten-twenty, you said? And you telephoned him? At eleven. Sure of the times? I see. I'd be glad if you'd come round. Can you? Well, do if you can."

He hung up the receiver.

"Get Chase again, will you, Fox?"

Chase, recalled, was most insistent that Mr. Hislop had spoken about it to Dr. Meadows.

"It was when Mr. Hislop had flu, sir. I went up with the doctor. Mr. Hislop had a high temperature and was talking very excited. He kept on and on, saying the master had guessed his ways had driven him crazy and that the master kept on purposely to aggravate. He said if it went on much longer he'd . . . he didn't know what he was talking about, sir, really."

"What did he say he'd do?"

"Well, sir, he said he'd—he'd do something desperate to the master. But it was only his rambling, sir. I daresay he wouldn't remember anything about it."

"No," said Alleyn, "I daresay he wouldn't." When Chase had gone he said to Fox: "Go and find out about those boys and their alibis. See if they can put you on to a quick means of checking up. Get Master Guy to corroborate Miss Phillipa's statement that she was locked in her room."

Fox had been gone for some time and Alleyn was still busy with his notes when the study door burst open and in came Dr. Meadows.

"Look here, my giddy sleuth-hound," he shouted, "what's all this about Hislop? Who says he disliked Sep's abominable habits?"

"Chase does. And don't bawl at me like that. I'm worried."

"So am I, blast you. What are you driving at? You can't imagine that . . . that poor little broken-down hack is capable of electrocuting anybody, let alone Sep?"

"I have no imagination," said Alleyn wearily.

"I wish to God I hadn't called you in. If the wireless killed Sep, it was because he'd monkeyed with it."

"And put it right after it had killed him?"

Dr. Meadows stared at Alleyn in silence.

"Now," said Alleyn, "you've got to give me a straight answer, Meadows. Did Hislop, while he was semi-delirious, say that this habit of Tonks's made him feel like murdering him?"

"I'd forgotten Chase was there," said Dr. Meadows.

"Yes, you'd forgotten that."

"But even if he did talk wildly, Alleyn, what of it? Damn it, you can't arrest a man on the strength of a remark made in delirium."

"I don't propose to do so. Another motive has come to light."

"You mean—Phips—last night?"

"Did he tell you about that?"

"She whispered something to me this morning. I'm very fond of Phips. My God, are you sure of your grounds?"

"Yes," said Alleyn. "I'm sorry. I think you'd better go, Meadows."

"Are you going to arrest him?"

"I have to do my job."

There was a long silence.

"Yes," said Dr. Meadows at last. "You have to do your job. Good-bye, Alleyn."

Fox returned to say that Guy and Arthur had never left their parties. He had got hold of two of their friends. Guy and Mrs. Tonks confirmed the story of the locked door.

"It's a process of elimination," said Fox. "It must be the secretary. He fixed the radio while deceased was upstairs. He must have dodged back to whisper through the door to Miss Tonks. I suppose he waited somewhere down here until he heard deceased blow himself to blazes and then put everything straight again, leaving the radio turned on."

Alleyn was silent.

"What do we do now, sir?" asked Fox.

"I want to see the hook inside the front-door where they hang their keys."

Fox, looking dazed, followed his superior to the little entrance hall.

"Yes, there they are," said Alleyn. He pointed to a hook with two latch-keys hanging from it. "You could scarcely miss them. Come on, Fox."

Back in the study they found Hislop with Bailey in attendance.

Hislop looked from one Yard man to another.

"I want to know if it's murder."

"We think so," said Alleyn.

"I want you to realize that Phillipa—Miss Tonks—was locked in her room all last night."

"Until her brother came home and unlocked the door," said Alleyn.

"That was too late. He was dead by then."

"How do you know when he died?"

"It must have been when there was that crash of static."

"Mr. Hislop," said Alleyn, "why would you not tell me how much that trick of licking his fingers exasperated you?"

"But—how do you know! I never told anyone."

"You told Dr. Meadows when you were ill."

"I don't remember." He stopped short. His lips trembled. Then, suddenly he began to speak.

"Very well. It's true. For two years he's tortured me. You see, he knew something about me. Two years ago when my wife was dying, I took money from the cash-box in that desk. I paid it back and thought he hadn't noticed. He knew all the time. From then on he had me where he wanted me. He used to sit there like a spider. I'd hand him a paper. He'd wet his thumbs with a clicking noise and a sort of complacent grimace. Click, click. Then he'd thumb the papers. He knew it drove me crazy. He'd look at me and then . . . click, click. And then he'd say something about the cash. He'd never quite accused me, just hinted. And I was impotent. You think I'm insane. I'm not. I could have murdered him. Often and often I've thought how I'd do it. Now you think I've done it. I haven't. There's the joke of it. I hadn't the pluck. And last night when Phillipa showed me she cared, it was like Heaven—unbelievable. For the first time since I've been here I *didn't* feel like killing him. And last night someone else *did!*"

He stood there trembling and vehement. Fox and Bailey, who had watched him with bewildered concern, turned to Alleyn. He was about to speak when Chase came in. "A note for you, sir," he said to Alleyn. "It came by hand."

Alleyn opened it and glanced at the first few words. He looked up. "You may go, Mr. Hislop. Now I've got what I expected—what I fished for."

When Hislop had gone they read the letter.

Dear Alleyn,

Don't arrest Hislop. I did it. Let him go at once if you've arrested him and don't tell Phips you ever suspected him. I was in love with Isabel before she met Sep. I've tried to get her to divorce him, but she wouldn't because of the kids. Damned nonsense, but there's no time to discuss it now. I've got to be quick. He suspected us. He reduced her to a nervous wreck. I was afraid she'd go under altogether. I thought it all out. Some weeks ago I took Phips's key from the hook inside the

front door. I had the tools and the flex and wire all ready. I
knew where the main switchboard was and the cupboard. I
meant to wait until they all went away at the New Year, but
last night when Hislop rang me I made up my mind to act at
once. He said the boys and servants were out and Phips locked
in her room. I told him to stay in his room and to ring me up
in half an hour if things hadn't quieted down. He didn't ring
up. I did. No answer, so I knew Sep wasn't in his study.

I came round, let myself in, and listened. All quiet upstairs,
but the lamp still on in the study, so I knew he would come
down again. He'd said he wanted to get the midnight broad-
cast from somewhere.

I locked myself in and got to work. When Sep was away last
year, Arthur did one of his modern monstrosities of paintings
in the study. He talked about the knobs making good pattern.
I noticed then that they were very like the ones on the radio
and later on I tried one and saw that it would fit if I packed it
up a bit. Well, I did the job just as you worked it out, and it
only took twelve minutes. Then I went into the drawing-room
and waited.

He came down from Isabel's room and evidently went
straight to the radio. I hadn't thought it would make such a
row, and half expected someone would come down. No one
came. I went back, switched off the wireless, mended the fuse
in the main switchboard, using my torch. Then I put everything right in the study.

There was no particular hurry. No one would come in while
he was there and I got the radio going as soon as possible to
suggest he was at it. I knew I'd be called in when they found
him. My idea was to tell them he had died of a stroke. I'd been
warning Isabel it might happen at any time. As soon as I saw
the burned hand I knew that cat wouldn't jump. I'd have tried
to get away with it if Chase hadn't gone round bleating about
electrocution and burned fingers. Hislop saw the hand. I
daren't do anything but report the case to the police, but I
thought you'd never twig the knobs. One up to you.

I might have bluffed through if you hadn't suspected Hislop. Can't let you hang the blighter. I'm enclosing a note to
Isabel, who won't forgive me, and an official one for you to

use. You'll find me in my bedroom upstairs. I'm using cyanide. It's quick.

I'm sorry, Alleyn. I think you knew, didn't you? I've bungled the whole game, but if you will be a supersleuth . . . Good-bye.

Henry Meadows

Millions of readers are familiar with the great detectives of fiction, but those who read REX STOUT*'s (1886–1975) stories of his wonderful creation Nero Wolfe are also totally familiar with the living quarters of their favorite sleuth (as the readers of Sherlock Holmes know all about 221B Baker Street). Stout produced a group of workers and friends for Wolfe without peer in the mystery field—the invaluable Archie Goodwin, his great chef Fritz Brenner, Inspector Cramer, Archie's girl Lily Rowan, and private eye Saul Panzer—all fully developed characters who graced the door of Nero's home somewhere on West Thirty-fifth Street in Manhattan. The almost forty novels and story collections featuring these characters constitute one of the foundations of the modern detective genre. Their creator was an active, politically aware man who served his fellow writers well as President of the Mystery Writers of America, President of the Author's Guild, and later as President of the Authors League of America.*

Wolfe himself, with his giant appetite and love of plants, is as interesting as ever in the complex plot twists of "Help Wanted, Male."

Help Wanted, Male
BY REX STOUT

He paid us a visit the day he stopped the bullet.

Ben Jensen was a publisher, a politician, and, in my opinion, a dope. I had had a sneaking idea that he would have gone ahead and bought the inside Army dope that Captain Root had offered to sell him if he had been able to figure out a way of using it without any risk of losing a hunk of hide. But he had played it safe and had cooperated with Nero Wolfe like a good little boy. That had been a couple of months before.

Now, early on a Tuesday morning, he phoned to say he wanted to see Wolfe. When I told him that Wolfe would be occupied with the orchids, as usual, until eleven o'clock, he fussed a little and made a date for eleven sharp. He arrived five minutes ahead of time, and I escorted him into the office and invited him to deposit his big, bony frame in the red leather chair.

After he sat down he asked me, "Don't I remember you? Aren't you Major Goodwin?"

"Yep."

"You're not in uniform."

"I was just noticing," I said, "that you need a haircut. At your age, with your gray hair, it looks better trimmed. More distinguished. Shall we continue with the personal remarks?"

There was the clang of Wolfe's personal elevator out in the hall, and a moment later Wolfe entered, exchanged greetings with the caller and got himself, all of his two hundred and sixty-some pounds lowered into his personal chair behind his desk.

Ben Jensen said, "Something I wanted to show you—got it in the mail this morning," and took an envelope from his pocket and stood up to hand it across. Wolfe glanced at the envelope, removed a piece of paper from it and glanced at that, and passed them along to me. The envelope was addressed to Ben Jensen, neatly hand-printed in ink. The piece of paper had been clipped from something, all four edges, with scissors or a sharp knife, and it had printed on it, not by hand, in large, black type:

YOU ARE ABOUT TO DIE—
AND I WILL WATCH YOU DIE!

Wolfe murmured, "Well, sir?"

"I can tell you," I put in, "free for nothing, where this came from."

Jensen snapped at me, "You mean who sent it?"

"Oh, no. For that I would charge. It was clipped from an ad for a movie called *Meeting at Dawn*. The movie of the century. I saw the ad last week in *The American Magazine*. I suppose it's in all the magazines. If you could find—"

Wolfe made a noise at me and murmured again at the fidgeting Jensen, "Well, sir?"

"What am I going to do?" Jensen demanded.

"I'm sure I don't know. Have you any notion who sent it?"

"No. None at all." Jensen sounded grieved. "Damn it, I don't like it. It's not just the usual junk from an anonymous crank. Look at it! It's direct and to the point. I think someone's going to try to kill me, and I don't know who or why or when or how. I suppose tracing it is out of the question, but I want some protection. I want to buy it from you."

I put up a hand to cover a yawn. I knew there would be nothing doing—no case, no fee, no excitement. In the years I had been living in

Nero Wolfe's house on West 35th Street, acting as goad, prod, lever, irritant, and chief assistant in the detective business, I had heard him tell at least fifty scared people, of all conditions and ages, that if someone had determined to kill them and was going to be stubborn about it, he would probably succeed.

On occasion, when the bank balance was doing a dive, he had furnished Cather or Durkin or Panzer or Keems as a bodyguard at a 100 percent markup, but now they were all very busy fighting Japs, and anyhow we had just deposited a five-figure check from a certain client.

Jensen got sore, naturally, but Wolfe only murmured at him that he might succeed in interesting the police, or that we would be glad to give him a list of reliable detective agencies which would provide companions for his movements as long as he remained alive—at sixty bucks for twenty-four hours. Jensen said that wasn't it, he wanted to hire Wolfe's brains. Wolfe merely made a face and shook his head. Then Jensen wanted to know what about Goodwin? Wolfe said that Major Goodwin was an officer in the United States Army.

"He's not in uniform," Jensen growled.

Wolfe was patient. "Officers in Military Intelligence on special assignments," he explained, "have freedoms. Major Goodwin's special assignment is to assist me in various projects entrusted to me by the Army. For which I am not paid. I have little time now for my private business. I think, Mr. Jensen, you should move and act with reasonable precaution for awhile. For example, in licking the flaps of envelopes—such things as that. Examine the strip of mucilage. Nothing is easier than to remove mucilage from an envelope flap and replace it with a mixture containing a deadly poison. Any door you open, anywhere, stand to one side and fling the door wide with a push or a pull before crossing the sill. Things like that."

"Good God," Jensen muttered.

Wolfe nodded. "That's how it is. But keep in mind that this fellow has severely restricted himself, if he's not a liar. He says he will watch you die. That greatly limits him in method and technique. He or she has to be there when it happens. So I advise prudence and a decent vigilance. Use your brains, but give up the idea of renting mine. No panic is called for. . . . Archie, how many people have threatened to take my life in the past ten years?"

I pursued my lips. "Oh, maybe twenty-two."

"Pfui." He scowled at me. "At least a hundred. And I am not dead yet, Mr. Jensen."

Jensen pocketed his clipping and envelope and departed, no better off than when he came except for the valuable advice about licking envelopes and opening doors. I felt kind of sorry for him and took the trouble to wish him good luck as I escorted him to the front door and let him out to the street, and even used some breath to tell him that if he decided to try an agency, Cornwall & Mayer had the best men.

Then I went back to the office and stood in front of Wolfe's desk, facing him, and pulled my shoulders back and expanded my chest. I took that attitude because I had some news to break to him and thought it might help to look as much like an army officer as possible.

"I have an appointment," I said, "at nine o'clock Thursday morning, in Washington, with General Carpenter."

Wolfe's brows went up a millimeter. "Indeed?"

"Yes, sir. At my request. I wish to take an ocean trip. I want to get a look at a Jap. I would like to catch one, if it can be done without much risk, and pinch him and make some remarks to him. I have thought up a crushing remark to make to a Jap and would like to use it."

"Nonsense." Wolfe was placid. "Your three requests to be sent overseas have been denied."

"Yeah, I know." I kept my chest out. "But that was just colonels and old Fife. Carpenter will see my point. I admit you're a great detective, the best orchid-grower in New York, a champion eater and beer-drinker, and a genius. But I've been working for you a hundred years —anyhow, a lot of years—and this is a hell of a way to spend a war. I'm going to see General Carpenter and lay it out. Of course he'll phone you. I appeal to your love of country, your vanity, your finer instincts what there is of them, and your dislike of Japs. If you tell Carpenter it would be impossible for you to get along without me, I'll put pieces of gristle in your crabmeat and sugar in your beer."

Wolfe opened his eyes and glared at me. The mere suggestion of sugar in his beer made him speechless.

That was Tuesday. The next morning, Wednesday, the papers head-lined the murder of Ben Jensen on the front page. Eating breakfast in the kitchen with Fritz, as usual, I was only halfway through the report in the *Times* when the doorbell rang, and when I answered it I found on the stoop our old friend, Inspector Cramer, of the homicide squad.

Nero Wolfe said, "Not interested, not involved, and not curious."

He was a sight, as he always was when propped up in bed with his breakfast tray. The custom was for Fritz, his chef, to deliver the tray to his room on the second floor at eight o'clock. It was now 8:15, and already down the gullet were the peaches and cream, most of the bacon, and two thirds of the eggs, not to mention coffee and the green tomato jam. The black silk coverlet was folded back, and you had to look to tell where the yellow percale sheet ended and the yellow pajamas began. Few people except Fritz and me ever got to see him like that, but he had stretched a point for Inspector Cramer, who knew that from nine to eleven he would be up in the plant-rooms with the orchids, and unavailable.

"In the past dozen years," Cramer said in his ordinary growl, without any particular feeling, "you have told me, I suppose, in round figures, ten million lies."

The commas were chews on his unlighted cigar. He looked the way he always did when he had been working all night—peevish and put upon but under control, all except his hair, which had forgotten where the part went.

Wolfe, who was hard to rile at breakfast, swallowed toast and jam and then coffee, ignoring the insult.

Cramer said, "He came to see you yesterday morning, twelve hours before he was killed. You don't deny that."

"And I have told you what for," Wolfe said politely. "He had received that threat and said he wanted to hire my brains. I declined to work for him and he went away. That was all."

"Why did you decline to work for him? What had he done to you?"

"Nothing." Wolfe poured coffee. "I don't do that kind of work. A man whose life is threatened anonymously is either in no danger at all, or his danger is so acute and so ubiquitous that his position is hopeless. My only previous association with Mr. Jensen was in connection with an attempt by an army captain named Root to sell him inside army information for political purposes. Together we got the necessary evidence, and Captain Root was court-martialed. Mr. Jensen was impressed, so he said, by my handling of that case. I suppose that was why he came to me when he decided that he wanted help."

"Did he think the threat came from someone connected with Captain Root?"

"No. Root wasn't mentioned. He said he had no idea who intended to kill him."

Cramer humphed. "That's what he told Tim Cornwall, too. Cornwall thinks you passed because you knew or suspected it was too hot to handle. Naturally, Cornwall is bitter. He has lost his best man."

"Indeed," Wolfe said mildly. "If that was his best man . . ."

"So Cornwall says," Cramer insisted, "and he's dead. Name of Doyle; been in the game twenty years, with a good record. The picture as we've got it doesn't necessarily condemn him. Jensen went to Cornwall & Mayer yesterday about noon, and Cornwall assigned Doyle as a guard.

"We've traced all their movements—nothing special. In the evening Doyle went along to a meeting at a midtown club. They left the club at eleven-twenty, and apparently went straight home, on the subway or bus, to the apartment house where Jensen lived on Seventy-third Street near Madison. It was eleven-forty-five when they were found dead on the sidewalk at the entrance to the apartment house. Both shot in the heart with a thirty-eight, Doyle from behind and Jensen from the front. We have the bullets. No powder marks. No nothing."

Wolfe murmured sarcastically, "Mr. Cornwall's best man."

"Nuts," Cramer objected to the sarcasm. "He was shot in the back. There's a narrow passage ten paces away where the guy could have hid. Or the shots could have come from a passing car, or from across the street. We haven't found anybody who heard the shots. The doorman was in the basement stoking the water heater, the excuse for that being that they're short of men like everybody else. The elevator man was on his way to the tenth floor with a passenger, a tenant. The bodies were discovered by two women on their way home from a movie. It must have happened not more than a minute before they came by, but they had just got off a Madison Avenue bus at the corner."

Wolfe got out of bed, which was an operation deserving an audience. He glanced at the clock on the bed table. It was 8:35.

"I know, I know," Cramer growled. "You've got to get dressed and get upstairs to your horticulture. . . . The tenant going up in the elevator was a prominent doctor who barely knew Jensen by sight. The two women who found the bodies are Seventh Avenue models who never heard of Jensen. The elevator man has worked there over twenty years without displaying a grudge, and Jensen was a generous tipper and popular with the bunch. The doorman is a fat nitwit who was hired two weeks ago only because of the manpower situation and doesn't know the tenants by name.

"Beyond those, all we have is the population of New York City and the guests who arrive and depart daily and nightly. That's why I came to you, and for the lord's sake give me what you've got. You can see that I need it."

"Mr. Cramer." The mountain of yellow pajamas moved. "I repeat. I am not interested, not involved, and not curious." Wolfe headed for the bathroom.

Exit Cramer—mad.

Back in the office there was the morning mail. I was getting toward the bottom of the stack without encountering anything startling or promising when I slit another envelope, and there it was.

I stared at it. I picked up the envelope and stared at that. I don't often talk to myself, but I said, loud enough for me to hear, "My goodness." Then I left the rest of the mail for later and went and mounted the three flights to the plant-rooms on the roof. Proceeding through the first three departments, past everything from rows of generating flasks to Cattleya hybrids covered with blooms, I found Wolfe in the potting-room, with Theodore Horstmann, the orchid nurse, examining a crate of sphagnum that had just arrived.

"Well?" he demanded, with no sign of friendliness. The general idea was that when he was up there I interrupted him at my peril.

"I suppose," I said carelessly, "that I shouldn't have bothered you, but I ran across something in the mail that I thought you'd find amusing," and I put them on the bench before him, side by side: the envelope with his name and address printed on it by hand, in ink, and the piece of paper that had been clipped from something with scissors or a sharp knife, reading in large, black type, printed, but not by hand:

YOU ARE ABOUT TO DIE— AND I WILL WATCH YOU DIE!

"It sure is a coincidence," I remarked, grinning at him.

Wolfe said without any perceptible quiver, "I'll look over the mail at eleven o'clock as usual."

It was the grand manner, all right. Seeing he was impervious, I retrieved the exhibits without a word, returned to the office, and busied myself with the chores.

It was eleven on the dot when he came down, and began the routine. Not until Fritz had brought the beer and he had irrigated his interior did he lean back in his chair, let his eyes go half shut, and observe, "You will, of course, postpone your trip to Washington."

I let my frank, open countenance betray surprise. "I can't. I have an appointment with a Lieutenant General. Anyhow, why?" I indicated the envelope and clipping on his desk. "That tomfoolery? No panic is called for. I doubt the urgency of your peril. A man planning a murder doesn't spend his energy clipping pieces out of adver—"

"You are going to Washington?"

"Yes, sir. I have a date. Of course, I could phone Carpenter and tell him your nerves are a little shaky on account of an anony—"

"When do you leave?"

"I have a seat on the six o'clock train."

"Very well. Then we have the day. Your notebook."

Wolfe leaned forward to pour beer and drink, and then leaned back again. "I offer a comment on your jocosity. When Mr. Jensen called here yesterday and showed us that thing, we had no inkling of the character of the person who had sent it. It might have been merely the attempt of a coward to upset his digestion.

"However, we no longer enjoy that ignorance. This person not only promptly killed Mr. Jensen, with wit equal to his determination, but also killed Mr. Doyle, a stranger, whose presence could not have been foreseen. We now know that this person is cold-blooded, ruthless, quick to decide and to act, and an egomaniac."

"Yes, sir. I agree. If you go to bed and stay there until I get back from Washington, letting no one but Fritz enter the room, I may not be able to control my tongue when with you, but actually I will understand and I won't tell anybody. You need a rest, anyway. And don't lick any envelopes."

"Bah." Wolfe wiggled a finger at me. "That thing was not sent to you. Presumably you are not on the agenda."

"Yes, sir."

"And this person is dangerous and requires attention."

"I agree."

Wolfe shut his eyes. "Very well. Take notes as needed. . . . It may be assumed, if this person means business with me as he did with Mr. Jensen, that this is connected with the case of Captain Root. I had no other association with Mr. Jensen. . . . Learn the whereabouts of Captain Root."

"The court-martial gave him three years in the cooler."

"I know it. Is he there? Also, what about that young woman, his fiancée, who raised such a ruction about it? Her name is Jane Geer." Wolfe's eyes half opened for an instant. "You have a habit of knowing how to locate personable young women without delay. Have you seen that one recently?"

"Oh," I said offhand, "I sort of struck up an acquaintance with her. I guess I can get in touch with her. But I doubt—"

"Do so. I want to see her. . . . Excuse me for interrupting, but you have a train to catch. . . . Also, inform Inspector Cramer of this development and suggest that he investigate Captain Root's background, his relatives and intimates, anyone besides Miss Geer who might thirst for vengeance at his disgrace. I'll do that. If Captain Root is in prison, arrange with General Fife to bring him here. I want to have a talk with him. . . . Where is the clipping received yesterday by Mr. Jensen? Ask Mr. Cornwall and Mr. Cramer. There is the possibility that this is not another one like it, but the same one."

I shook my head. "No, sir. This one is clipped closer to the printing at the upper right."

"I noticed that, but ask, anyway. Inspect the chain bolts on the doors and test the night gong in your room. Fritz will sleep in your room tonight. I shall speak to Fritz and Theodore. All of this can easily be attended to by telephone except Miss Geer, and that is your problem. When will you return from Washington?"

"I should be able to catch a noon train back—my appointment's at nine. Getting here around five." I added earnestly, "If I can clear it with Carpenter to cross the ocean, I will, of course, arrange not to leave until this ad-clipper has been attended to."

"Don't hurry back on my account. Or alter your plans. You receive a salary from the Government." Wolfe's tone was dry, sharp, and icy. He went on with it: "Please get General Fife on the phone. We'll begin by learning about Captain Root."

The program went smoothly, all except the Jane Geer number. If it hadn't been for her I'd have been able to make the six o'clock train with hours to spare. Fife reported back on Root in thirty minutes, to the effect Root was in the clink on government property down in Maryland, and would be transported to New York without delay for an interview with Wolfe.

Cornwall said he had turned the clipping and envelope Jensen had received over to Inspector Cramer, and Cramer verified it and said he had it. When I had explained the situation, Cramer emitted a hoarse chuckle, and said offensively, "So Wolfe is not interested, involved, or curious." I knew Wolfe would have a visit from him. Not pleasant.

On Jane Geer the luck was low. When, before noon, I phoned the advertising agency she worked for, I was told that she was somewhere on Long Island admiring some client's product for which she was to produce copy. When I finally did get her after four o'clock, she went willful on me, presumably because she regarded my phoning five times in one day as evidence that my primal impulses had been aroused and I was beginning to pant. She would not come to Nero Wolfe's place unless I bought her a cocktail first. So I met her a little after five at the Stork Club.

She had put in a full day's work, but, looking at her, you might have thought she had come straight from an afternoon nap.

She darted her brown eyes at me. "Let me," she said, "see your right forefinger."

I poked it at her. She rubbed its tip gently with the tip of her own. "I wondered if it had a callus. After dialing my number five times in less than five hours."

She sipped her Tom Collins, bending her head to get her lips to the straw. A strand of her hair slipped forward over an eye and a cheek, and I reached across and used the same finger to put it back in place.

"I took that liberty," I told her, "because I wish to have an unobstructed view of your lovely phiz. I want to see if you turn pale."

"Overwhelmed by you so near?"

"No, I know that reaction—I correct for it. Anyhow, I doubt if I'm magnetic right now, because I'm sore at you for making me miss a train."

"I didn't phone you this time. You phoned me."

"Okay." I drank. "You said on the phone that you still don't like Nero Wolfe and you wouldn't go to see him unless you knew what for, and maybe not even then. So this is what for: He wants to ask you whether you intend to kill him yourself or hire the same gang that you got to kill Jensen and Doyle."

"Mercy." She looked my face over. "You'd better put your humor on a diet. It's taking on weight."

I shook my head. "Ordinarily, I would enjoy playing catch with you, as you are aware, but I can't miss all the trains. Because Wolfe's life has been threatened in the same manner as Jensen's was, the supposition is that Jensen was murdered for revenge, for what he did to Captain Root. Because of the cutting remarks you made when Root was trapped, and your general attitude, there is a tendency to want to know what you have been doing lately."

"Nero Wolfe seriously thinks I—did that? Or had it done?"

"I didn't say so. He wants to discuss it."

Her eyes flashed. Her tone took on an edge: "It is also extremely corny. And the police. Have you kindly arranged that when Wolfe finishes with me I proceed to headquarters?"

"Listen, Tiger-eyes." She let me cut her off, which was a pleasant surprise. "Have you noticed me sneaking up on you from behind? If so, draw it for me. I have explained a situation. Your name has not been mentioned to the police, though they have consulted us. But since the police are onto the Root angle they are apt to get a steer in your direction without us, and it wouldn't hurt if Wolfe had already satisfied himself that you wouldn't kill a fly."

"By what process?" She was scornful. "I suppose he asks me if I ever committed murder, and I smile and say no, and he apologizes and gives me an orchid."

"Not quite. He's a genius. He asks you questions like do you bait your own hook when you go fishing, and you reveal yourself without knowing it."

"It sounds fascinating." Her eyes suddenly changed. "I wonder," she said.

"What is it?—and we'll both wonder."

"Sure." Her eyes had changed more. "This wouldn't by any chance be a climax you've been working up to? You, with a thousand girls and women, so that you have to issue ration books so many minutes to a coupon, and yet finding so much time for me? Leading up to this idiotic frame—"

"Turn that one off," I broke in, "or I'll begin to get suspicious, myself. You know darned well why I have found time for you, having a mirror as you do. I have been experimenting to test my emotional reaction to form, color, touch, and various perfumes, and I have been deeply grateful for your cooperation. I thank you—but that is all."

"Ha, ha." She stood up, her eyes not softening nor her tone melting. "I am going to see Nero Wolfe. I welcome an opportunity to reveal myself to Nero Wolfe. Do I go or are you taking me?"

I took her. I paid the check and we went out and got a taxi.

But she didn't get to see Wolfe.

Since chain-bolt orders were in effect, my key wouldn't let us in and I had to ring the doorbell for Fritz. I had just pushed the button, when who should appear, mounting the steps to join us on the stoop, but the army officer that they use for a model when they want to do a picture conveying the impression that masculine comeliness will win the war. I admit he was handsome; I admitted it to myself right then, when I first saw him. He looked preoccupied and concentrated, but, even so, he found time for a glance at Jane.

At that moment the door swung open and I spoke to Fritz:

"Okay, thanks. Is Mr. Wolfe in the office?"

"No, he's up in his room."

"All right; I'll take it." Fritz departed, and I maneuvered into position to dominate the scene, on the doorsill facing out. I spoke to the masculine model: "Yes, Major? This is Nero Wolfe's place."

"I know it is." He had a baritone voice that suited him to a T. "I want to see him. My name is Emil Jensen. I am the son of Ben Jensen, who was killed last night."

"Oh." There wasn't much resemblance, but that's nature's lookout. I have enough to do. "Mr. Wolfe has an appointment. It would be handy if I could tell him what you want."

"I want to—consult him. If you don't mind. I'd rather tell him." He smiled to take the sting off. Probably Psychological Warfare Branch.

"I'll see. Come on in."

I made room for Jane, and he followed her. After attending to the bolt I escorted them to the office, invited them to sit, and went to the phone on my desk and buzzed Wolfe's room.

"Yes?" Wolfe's voice came.

"Archie. Miss Geer is here. Also, Major Emil Jensen just arrived. He is the son of Ben Jensen and prefers to tell you what he wants to consult you about."

"Give them both my regrets. I am engaged and can see no one."

"Engaged for how long?"

"Indefinitely. I can make no appointments for this week."

"But you may remember—"

"Archie! Tell them that please." The line died.

So I told them that. They were not pleased. The Lord knows what kind of performance Jane would have put on if she hadn't been restrained by the presence of a stranger; as it was, she didn't have to fumble around for pointed remarks. Jensen wasn't indignant, but he sure was stubborn. During an extended conversation that got nowhere, I noticed a gradual increase in their inclination to cast sympathetic glances at each other.

I thought it might help matters along, meaning that they might clear out sooner if I changed the subject, so I said emphatically, "Miss Geer, this is Major Jensen."

He got to his feet, bowed to her like a man who knows how to bow, and told her, "How do you do? It looks as if it's hopeless, at least for this evening, for both of us. I'll have to hunt a taxi, and it would be a pleasure if you'll let me drop you."

So they left together. Going down the stoop, which I admit was moderately steep, he indicated not obtrusively that he had an arm there, and she rested her fingers in the bend of it to steady herself. That alone showed astonishing progress in almost no time at all, for she was by no means a born clinger.

Oh, well, I was a major too. I shrugged indifferently as I shut the door. Then I sought Wolfe's room, knocked, and was invited in.

Standing in the doorway to his bathroom, facing me, his old-fashioned razor in his hand, all lathered up, he demanded brusquely, "What time is it?"

"Six-thirty."

"When is the next train?"

"Seven o'clock. But what the hell, apparently there is going to be work to do. I can put it off to next week."

"No. It's on your mind. Get that train."

I tried one more stab. "My motive is selfish. If, while I am sitting talking to Carpenter in the morning, word comes that you have been killed, or even temporarily disabled, he'll blame me and I won't stand a chance. So for purely selfish reasons—"

"Confound it!" he barked. "You'll miss that train! I have no intention of getting killed. Get out of here!"

I faded. . . .

After the war I intended to run for Congress and put through laws about generals. I have a theory that generals should be rubbed liberally with neat's-foot oil before being taken out and shot. Though I doubt if I would have bothered with the oil in the case of General Carpenter that morning if I had had a free hand.

I was a major. So I sat and said yessir yessir yessir, while he told me that he had given me the appointment only because he thought I wanted to discuss something of importance, and that I would stay where I was put, and shut my trap about it. When it was all over, he observed that since I was in Washington I might as well confer with the staff on various cases, finished and unfinished, and I would report immediately to Colonel Dickey.

I doubt if I made a good impression, considering my state of mind. They kept me around, conferring, all day Thursday and most of Friday. I phoned Wolfe that I was detained. By explaining the situation on 35th Street I could have got permission to beat it back to New York, but I wasn't going to give that collection of brass headgear an excuse to giggle around that Nero Wolfe didn't have brains enough to keep on breathing, in his own house, without me there to look after him. Wolfe would have had my scalp.

But I was tempted to hop a plane when, late Thursday evening, I saw the ad in the *Star*. I had been too busy all day to take more than a glance at the New York papers I'd been following for news of the Jensen case. I was alone in my hotel room when it caught my eye, bordered and spaced to make a spot:

WANTED, A MAN

weighing about 260–270, around 5 ft. 11; 45–55 years old, medium in coloring, waist not over 48, capable of easy and normal movement. Temporary. Hazardous. $100 a day. Send photo with letter. Box 292 Star.

I read it through four times, stared at it disapprovingly for an additional two minutes, and then reached for the phone and put in a New York call. I got Fritz Brenner on the phone, and he assured me Wolfe was all right.

Getting ready for bed, I tried to figure out in what manner, if I were making preparations to kill Nero Wolfe, I could make use of an assistant, hired on a temporary basis at a hundred bucks a day, who was a physical counterpart of Wolfe. The two schemes I devised weren't very satisfactory, and the one I hit on after I got my head on the pillow was even worse, so I flipped the switch on the nervous system and let the muscles quit. . . .

In the morning I finished conferring and made tracks for New York.

Arriving at Wolfe's house on 35th Street a little before eleven, I gave the button three short pushes as usual, and in a moment there were footsteps, and the curtain was pulled aside and Fritz was peering at me through the glass panel. Satisfied, he let me in.

I saw Wolfe was in the office, since the door to it was open and the light shining through, so I breezed down the hall and on in.

"I am a fug—" I began, and stopped. Wolfe's chair behind his desk, his own chair and no one else's under any circumstances, was occupied by the appropriate mass of matter in comparatively human shape—in other words, by a big, fat man—but it wasn't Nero Wolfe. I had never seen him before.

Fritz, who had stayed to bolt the door, came at me from behind, talking. The occupant of the chair neither moved nor spoke, but merely leered at me. Fritz was telling me that Mr. Wolfe was up in his room.

The specimen in the chair said in a husky croak, "I suppose you're Goodwin. Archie. Have a good trip?"

I stared at him. In a way I wished I was back at the Pentagon, and in another way I wished I had come sooner.

He said, "Fritz, bring me another highball."

Fritz said, "Yes, sir."

He said, "Have a good trip, Archie?"

That was enough of that. I marched out to the hall and up a flight, went to Wolfe's door and tapped on it, and called, "Archie!" Wolfe's voice told me to come in.

He was seated in his number two chair, under the light, reading a book. He was fully dressed, and there was nothing in his appearance to indicate that he had lost his mind.

I did not intend to give him the satisfaction of sitting there smirking and enjoying fireworks. "Well," I said casually, "I got back. If you're sleepy we can wait till morning for conversation."

"I'm not sleepy." He closed the book, with a finger inserted at his page. "Are you going overseas?"

"You know damn well I'm not." I sat down. "We can discuss that at some future date when I'm out of the Army. It's a relief to find you all alive and well around here. It's very interesting down in Washington. Everybody on their toes."

"No doubt. Did you stop in the office downstairs?"

"I did. So you put that ad in the *Star* yourself. How do you pay him —cash every day? Did you figure out the deductions for income tax and social security? I sat down at my desk and began to report to him. I thought it was you. Until he ordered Fritz to bring him a highball, and I know you hate highballs. Deduction. It reminds me of the time your daughter from Yugoslavia showed up—"

"Archie. Shut up."

Wolfe put the book down and shifted in his chair, with the routine grunts. When the new equilibrium was established he said, "You will find details about him on a slip of paper in the drawer of your desk. He is a retired architect named H. H. Hackett, out of funds, and an unsurpassed nincompoop with the manners of a wart hog. I chose him, from those answering the advertisement, because his appearance and build were the most suitable and he is sufficiently an ass to be willing to risk his life for a hundred dollars a day."

"If he keeps on calling me 'Archie' the risk will become—"

"If you please." Wolfe wiggled a finger at me. "Do you think the idea of him sitting there in my chair is agreeable to me? He may be dead tomorrow or the next day. I told him that. This afternoon he went to Mr. Ditson's place in a taxicab to look at orchids, and came back ostentatiously carrying two plants. Tomorrow afternoon you will drive him somewhere and bring him back, and again in the evening. Dressed for the street, wearing my hat and lightweight coat, carrying my stick, he would deceive anyone except you."

"Yes, sir. But why couldn't you just stay in the house? You do, anyway. And be careful who gets in. Until . . ."

"Until what?"

"Until the bird that killed Jensen is caught."

"Bah!" He glared at me. "By whom? By Mr. Cramer? What do you suppose he is doing now? Pfui! Major Jensen, Mr. Jensen's son, arriving home on leave from Europe five days ago, learned that during his absence his father had sued his mother for divorce. The father and son quarreled, which was not unique. But Mr. Cramer has a hundred men trying to collect evidence that will convict Major Jensen of killing his father! Utterly intolerable asininity. For what motive could Major Jensen have for killing me?"

"Well, now." My eyebrows were up. "I wouldn't just toss it in the wastebasket. What if the major figured that sending you the same kind of message he sent his father would make everybody react the way you are doing?"

Wolfe shook his head. "He didn't. Unless he's a born fool. He would have known that merely sending me that thing would be inadequate, that he would have to follow it up by making good on the threat; and he hasn't killed me, and I doubt if he intends to. General Fife has looked up his record for me. Mr. Cramer is wasting his time, his men's energy, and the money of the people of New York. I am handicapped. The men I have used and can trust have gone to war. You bounce around thinking only of yourself, deserting me. I am confined to this room, left to my own devices, with a vindictive, bloodthirsty maniac waiting an opportunity to kill me."

He sure was piling it on. But I knew better than to contribute a note of skepticism when he was in one of his romantic moods, having been fired for that once; and, besides, I wouldn't have signed an affidavit that he was exaggerating the situation. So I only asked him, "What about Captain Root? Did they bring him?"

"Yes. He was here today and I talked with him. He has been in that prison for over a month and asserts that this cannot possibly be connected with him or his. He says Miss Geer has not communicated with him for six weeks or more. His mother is teaching school at Danforth, Ohio; that has been verified by Mr. Cramer; she is there. His father, who formerly ran a filling station at Danforth, abandoned wife and son ten years ago, and is said to be working in a war plant in Oklahoma. Wife and son prefer not to discuss him. No brother or sister. According to Captain Root, there is no one on earth who would conceivably undertake a ride on the subway, let alone multiple murder, to avenge him."

"He might just possibly be right."

"Nonsense. There was no other slightest connection between Mr. Jensen and me. I've asked General Fife to keep Root in New York and to request the prison authorities to look over his effects there if he has any."

"When you get an idea in your head—"

"I never do. As you mean it. I react to stimuli. In this instance I am reacting in the only way open to me. The person who shot Mr. Jensen and Mr. Doyle is bold to the point of rashness. He can probably be tempted to proceed with his program." . . .

I went up to my room.

The gong was a dingus under my bed. The custom was that when I retired at night I turned a switch, and if anyone put his foot down in the hall within ten feet of Wolfe's door the gong gonged. It had been installed on account of a certain occurrence some years previously, when Wolfe had got a knife stuck in him. The thing had never gone off except when we tested it, and in my opinion never would but I never failed to switch it on, because if Wolfe had stepped into the hall some night and the gong hadn't sounded it would have caused discussion.

This night, with a stranger in the house, I was glad it was there.

In the morning breakfast was all over the place. Afterward I spent an hour up in the plant-rooms with Wolfe.

We got to details. Jane Geer was making a nuisance of herself. I understood now, of course, why Wolfe had refused to see her Wednesday evening. After sending me to get her he had conceived the strategy of hiring a double, and he didn't want her to get a look at the real Nero Wolfe, because if she did she would be less likely to be deceived by the counterfeit and go to work on him.

She had phoned several times, insisting on seeing him, and had come to the house Friday morning and argued for five minutes with Fritz through the three-inch crack which the chain bolt permitted the door to open to. Now Wolfe had an idea for one of his elaborate charades. I was to phone her to come to see Wolfe at six o'clock that afternoon. When she came I was to take her in to Hackett. Wolfe would coach Hackett for the interview.

I looked skeptical.

Wolfe said, "It will give her a chance to kill Mr. Hackett."

I snorted. "With me right there to tell her when to cease firing."

"I admit it is unlikely, but it will give me an opportunity to see her and hear her. I shall be at the hole."

So that was really the idea. He would be in the passage, a sort of alcove, at the kitchen end of the downstairs hall, looking through into the office by means of the square hole in the wall. The hole was camouflaged on the office side by a picture that was transparent one way. He loved to have an excuse to use it.

Major Jensen had phoned once and been told that Wolfe was engaged; apparently he wasn't as persistent as Jane.

When I got down to the office Hackett was there in Wolfe's chair, eating cookies and getting crumbs on the desk.

From the phone on my desk I got Jane Geer at her office. "Archie," I told her.

She snapped, "Archie who?"

"Oh, come, come. We haven't sicked the police onto you, have we? Nero Wolfe wants to see you."

"He does? Ha, ha. He doesn't act like it."

"He has reformed. I showed him a lock of your hair. I showed him a picture of Elsa Maxwell and told him it was you. This time he won't let me come after you."

"Neither will I."

"Okay. Be here at six o'clock and you will be received. Six o'clock today P.M. Will you?"

She admitted that she would.

I made a couple of other calls and did some miscellaneous chores. But I found that my jaw was getting clamped tighter and tighter on account of an irritating noise. Finally I spoke to the occupant of Wolfe's chair: "What kind of cookies are those?"

"Gingersnaps." Evidently the husky croak was his normal voice.

"I didn't know we had any."

"We didn't. I asked Fritz. He doesn't seem to know about ginger-snaps, so I walked over to Ninth Avenue and got some."

"When? This morning?"

"Just a little while ago."

I turned to my phone, buzzed the plant-rooms, got Wolfe, and told him, "Mr. Hackett is sitting in your chair eating gingersnaps. Just a little while ago he walked to Ninth Avenue and bought them. If he pops in and out of the house whenever he sees fit, what are we getting for our hundred bucks?"

Wolfe spoke to the point. I hung up and turned to Hackett and spoke to the point. He was not to leave the house except as instructed by Wolfe or me. He seemed unimpressed.

"All right," he said; "if that's the bargain I'll keep it. But there's two sides to a bargain. I was to be paid daily in advance, and I haven't been paid for today. A hundred dollars net."

I took five twenties from the expense wallet and forked it over.

"I must say," he commented, folding the bills neatly and stuffing them in his waistband pocket, "this is a large return for a small effort. I am aware that I may earn it—ah, suddenly and unexpectedly." He leaned toward me. "Though I may tell you confidentially, Archie, that I expect nothing to happen. I am sanguine by nature."

"Yeah," I told him, "me too."

I opened the drawer of my desk, the middle one on the right, where I kept armament, got out the shoulder holster and put it on, and selected the gun that was my property—the other two belonged to Wolfe. There were only three cartridges in it, so I pulled the drawer open farther to get to the ammunition compartment, and filled the cylinder.

As I shoved the gun into the holster. I happened to glance at Hackett, and saw that he had a new face. The line of his lips was tight, and his eyes looked startled, wary.

"It hadn't occurred to me before," he said, and his voice had changed too. "This Mr. Wolfe is quite an article, and you're his man. I am doing this with the understanding that someone may mistake me for Mr. Wolfe and try to kill me, but I have only his word for it that this is actually the situation. If it's more complicated than that, and the intention is for you to shoot me yourself, I want to say emphatically that that would not be fair."

I grinned at him sympathetically, trying to make up for my blunder, realizing that I should not have dressed for the occasion in his presence. The sight of the gun, a real gun and real cartridges, had scared him stiff.

"Listen," I told him earnestly; "you said a minute ago that you expect nothing to happen. You may be right. I'm inclined to agree with you. But in case somebody does undertake to perform, I am wearing this little number"—I patted under my arm where the gun was—"for two purposes: first, to keep you from getting hurt; and, second, if you do get hurt, to hurt him worse."

It seemed to satisfy him, for his eyes got less concentrated, but he didn't resume with the gingersnaps. At least, I had accomplished that much.

To tell the truth, by the time the afternoon was over and I had him back in the house again, a little after five-thirty, I had to maintain a firm hold on such details as gingersnaps and his calling me "Archie" to keep from admiring him. During that extended expedition we made stops at the Metropolitan Museum of Art, the Botanical Gardens, and three or four stores. He occupied the rear seat, of course, because Wolfe always did, and the mirror showed me that he sat back comfortably, taking in the sights, a lot more imperturbable than Wolfe, himself, ever was in a car.

When we made one of our stops and Hackett got out to cross the sidewalk, he was okay. He didn't hurry or dodge or jerk or weave, but just walked. In Wolfe's hat and coat and stick, he might even have fooled me. I had to hand it to him, in spite of the fact that the whole show struck me as the biggest bust Wolfe had ever concocted.

Back in the house, I left Hackett in the office and went to the kitchen, where Wolfe was sitting at the big table drinking beer.

I reported: "They tried to get him from the top of the Palisades with a howitzer, but missed him. He was a little bruised on his left elbow from the revolving door at Rusterman's but otherwise unhurt."

Wolfe grunted. "How did he behave?"

"Okay."

Wolfe grunted again. "After dark we may more reasonably expect results. I repeat what I told you at noon; you will take an active part in the interview with Miss Geer, but you will restrain yourself. If you permit yourself to get fanciful, there is no telling what the effect may be on Mr. Hackett. As you know, his instructions are precise, but his discipline is questionable. See that she speaks up, so I can hear her. Seat her at the corner of my desk farthest from you, so I will have a good view of her face."

"Yes, sir."

But, as it turned out, I wasn't able to obey orders. It was then nearly six o'clock. When the doorbell rang, a few minutes later, and I went to answer it, glancing in at the office on my way down the hall to make sure that Hackett didn't have his feet up on the desk, I opened the door, to find that Miss Geer hadn't ventured alone on the streets of the great city, after all. Major Emil Jensen was there with her.

"Well," I said brightly, "two on one hook?"

Jensen said hello. Jane volunteered, "Major Jensen decided to come on the spur of the moment. We were having cocktails." She looked me up and down; it was true that I was blocking the way. "May we come in?"

Certainly I could have told Jensen we had only one extra chair so he had better go for a walk, but if there was going to be anything accomplished by having either of those two get the idea that Hackett was Nero Wolfe, I would have picked him for the experiment rather than her. On the other hand, with Hackett primed only for her, it would have been crowding our luck to confront him with both of them, and, anyway, I couldn't take such a chance on my own hook. I needed advice from headquarters. So I decided to herd them into the front room, ask them to wait, and go consult Wolfe.

"Sure," I said hospitably; "enter." I had got them seated, and was headed for the hall before noticing an unfortunate fact: The door from the front room to the office was standing open. That was careless of me, but I hadn't expected complications. If they moved across, as they naturally would, Hackett, sitting in the office, would be in plain sight. But what the hell, that was what he was there for. So I kept going, down the hall to the turn into the alcove at the far end, found Wolfe there ready to take position at the peephole, and muttered to him:

"She brought an outsider along. Major Jensen. I put them in the front room. The door into the office is open. Well?"

He scowled at me. He whispered, "Confound it. Return to the front room by way of the office, closing that door as you go. Tell Major Jensen to wait, that I wish to speak with Miss Geer privately. Take her to the office by way of the hall, and when you—"

Somebody fired a gun.

At least, that's what it sounded like, and the sound didn't come from outdoors. The walls and the air vibrated. Judging by the noise, I might have fired it myself, but I hadn't. I moved. In three jumps I was at the door to the office. Hackett was sitting there, looking startled and speechless. I dashed through to the front room. Jensen and Jane were there, on their feet, she off to the right and he to the left, both also startled and speechless, staring at each other. Their hands were empty, except for Jane's bag. I might have been inclined to let it go for Hackett biting a gingersnap if it hadn't been for the smell. I knew that smell.

I snapped at Jensen, "Well?"

"Well yourself." He had transferred the stare to me. "What the hell was it?"

"Did you fire a gun?"

"No. Did you?"

I pivoted to Jane. "Did you?"

"You—you idiot," she stammered, trying not to tremble. "Why would I fire a gun?"

"Let me see the one in your hand," Jensen demanded.

I looked at my hand and was surprised to see a gun in it. I must have snatched it from the holster automatically en route. "Not it," I said. I poked the muzzle to within an inch of Jensen's nose. "Was it?"

He sniffed. "No."

I said, "But a gun was fired inside here. Do you smell it?"

"Certainly I smell it."

"Okay. Let's join Mr. Wolfe and discuss it. Through there." I indicated the door to the office with a flourish of the gun.

Jane started jabbering about a put-up job, but I followed Jensen into the other room.

"This is Mr. Nero Wolfe," I said. "Sit down." I was using my best judgment, and figured I was playing it right, because Wolfe was nowhere in sight. I had to decide what to do with them while I found the gun and maybe the bullet.

Jane was still trying to jabber, but she stopped when Jensen blurted, "Wolfe has blood on his head!"

I glanced at Hackett. He was standing up behind the desk, leaning forward with his hand on the desk, staring wildly at the three of us. Blood dribbled down the side of his neck.

I took in breath and yelled, "Fritz!"

He appeared instantly, probably having been standing by in the hall, and when he came I handed him my gun. "If anybody reaches for a handkerchief, shoot."

"Those instructions," Jensen said sharply, "are dangerous if he—"

"He's all right."

"I would like you to search me." Jensen stuck his hands toward the ceiling.

"That," I said, "is more like it," and crossed to him and explored him from neck to ankles, invited him to relax in a chair, and turned to Jane. She darted me a look of lofty disgust.

I remarked, "If you refuse to stand inspection and then you happen to make a gesture and Fritz shoots you in the tummy, don't blame me."

She darted more looks, but took it. I felt her over not quite as comprehensively as I had Jensen, took her bag and glanced in it, and returned it to her, and then stepped around Wolfe's desk to examine Hackett. After Jensen had announced the blood, he had put his hand up to feel and was staring at the red on his fingers with his big jaw hanging open.

"My head?" he croaked. "Is it my head?"

The exhibition he was making of himself was no help to Nero Wolfe's reputation for intrepidity.

After a brief look I told him distinctly, "No, sir. Nothing but a nick in the upper outside corner of your ear."

"I am not—hurt?"

I could have murdered him. Instead, I told Fritz, standing there with my gun, that unnecessary movements were still forbidden, and took Hackett to the bathroom in the far corner and shut the door behind us. While I showed him the ear in the mirror and dabbed on some iodine and taped on a bandage, I told him to stay in there until his nerves calmed down and then rejoin us, act detached and superior, and let me do the talking.

As I reappeared in the office, Jane shot at me, "Did you search *him?*"

I ignored her and circled around Wolfe's desk for a look at the back of the chair. The head-rest was upholstered with brown leather; and about eight inches from the top and a foot from the side edge, a spot that would naturally have been on a line behind Hackett's left ear as he sat, there was a hole in the leather. I looked behind and there was another hole on the rear side. I look at the wall back of the chair and found still another hole, torn into the plaster.

From the bottom drawer of my desk I got a screwdriver and hammer, and started chiseling, ran against a stud, and went to work with the point of my knife. When I finally turned around I held a small object between my thumb and finger. As I did so, Hackett emerged from the bathroom.

"Bullet," I said informatively. "Thirty-eight. Passed through Mr. Wolfe's ear and the back of his chair, and ruined the wall."

Jane sputtered. Jensen sat and gazed at me with narrowed eyes. Hackett shuddered.

"It could be," Jensen said coldly, "that Wolfe fired that bullet himself."

"Yeah?" I returned his gaze. "Mr. Wolfe would be glad to let you inspect his face for powder marks."

"He washed them off in the bathroom," Jane snapped.

"They don't wash off." . . . I continued to Jensen, "I'll lend you a magnifying glass. You can examine the chair, too."

By gum, he took me up. He nodded and rose, and I got the glass from Wolfe's desk, the big one. First he went over the chair, the portion in the neighborhood of the bullet hole, and then crossed to Hackett and gave his face and ear a look. Hackett stood still with his lips compressed and his eyes straight ahead. Jensen gave me back the glass and returned to his seat.

I asked him, "Did Mr. Wolfe shoot himself in the ear?"

"No," he admitted. "Not unless he had the gun wrapped."

"Sure." My tone cut slices off of him. "He tied a pillow around it, held it at arm's length, pointing it at his ear, and pulled the trigger. How would you like to try demonstrating it? Keeping the bullet within an inch of your frontal lobe?"

He never stopped gazing at me. "I am," he declared, "being completely objective. With some difficulty."

"If I understand what happened—" Hackett began, but I cut him off.

"Excuse me, sir. The bullet helps, but the gun would help still more. Let's be objective, too. We might possibly find the object in the front room." I moved, touching his elbow to take him along. "Fritz, see that they stay put."

"I," said Jensen, getting up, "would like to be present—"

"The hell you would." I wheeled on him. My voice may have gone up a notch. "Sit down, brother. I am trying not to fly off the handle. Whose house is this, anyway, with bullets zipping around?"

He had another remark to contribute, and so did Jane, but I disregarded them and wangled Hackett ahead of me into the front room and shut the soundproof door.

"It seems incredible to me," Hackett said, choosing his words carefully, "that one of them could have shot at me from in here, through the open door, without me seeing anything."

"You said that before, in the bathroom. You also said you didn't remember whether your eyes were open or shut, or where you were looking, when you heard the shot."

I moved my face to within fourteen inches of his. "See here. If you are suspecting that I shot at you, or that Wolfe did, you have got fleas or other insects playing tag in your brain and should have it attended to. One thing alone: The way the bullet went, straight past your ear and into the chair-back, it had to come from in front, the general direction of that door and this room. It couldn't have come from the door in the hall or anywhere else, because we haven't got a gun that shoots a curve. Now, you will sit down and keep still."

He grumbled, but obeyed. I surveyed the field. On the assumption that the gun had been fired in that room, I adopted the theory that either it was still there or it had been transported or propelled without. As for transportation, I had got there not more than five seconds after the shot and found them there staring at each other. As for propulsion, the windows were closed and the Venetian blinds down. I preferred the first alternative.

I began to search, but I had the curious feeling that I probably wouldn't find the gun, no matter how thoroughly I looked; I have never understood why.

If it was a hunch, it was a bad day for hunches, because when I came to the big vase on the table between the windows and peeked into it and saw something white, and stuck my hand in, I felt the gun. Getting it by the trigger guard, I lifted it out. Judging by smell, it had been fired recently, but of course it had had time to cool off. It was an old Granville thirty-eight, next door to rusty. The white object I had seen was an ordinary cotton handkerchief, man's size, with a tear in it through which the butt of the gun protruded. With proper care about touching, I opened the cylinder and found there were five loaded cartridges and one shell.

Hackett was there beside me, trying to say things. I got brusque with him:

"Yes, it's a gun, recently fired, and not mine or Wolfe's. Is it yours? No? Good. Okay, keep your shirt on. We're going back in there, and there will be sufficient employment for my brain without interference from you. Do not try to help me. If this ends as it ought to, you'll get an extra hundred. Agreed?"

I'll be damned if he didn't say, "Two hundred. I was shot at. I came within an inch of getting killed."

I told him he'd have to talk the second hundred out of Wolfe, and opened the door to the office and followed him through. He detoured around Jane Geer and went and sat in the chair he had just escaped being a corpse in. I swiveled my own chair to face it out.

Jensen demanded sharply, "What have you got there?"

"This," I said cheerfully, "is a veteran revolver, a Granville thirty-eight, which has been fired not too long ago." I lowered it onto my desk. "Fritz, give me back my gun."

He brought it. I kept it in my hand.

"Thank you. I found this other affair in the vase on the table in there, dressed in a handkerchief. Five unused cartridges and one used. It's a stranger here. Never saw it before. It appears to put the finishing touch on a critical situation."

Jane exploded. She called me an unspeakable rat. She said she wanted a lawyer and intended to go to one immediately. She called Hackett three or four things. She said it was the dirtiest frame-up in history. "Now," she told Hackett, "I know damned well you framed Captain Root! I let that skunk Goodwin talk me out of it! But you won't get away with it this time!"

Hackett was trying to talk back to her, making his voice louder and louder, and when she stopped for breath he could be heard:

". . . will not tolerate it! You come here and try to kill me! You nearly do kill me! Then you abuse me about a Captain Root, and I have never heard of Captain Root!" He was putting real feeling into it; apparently he had either forgotten that he was supposed to be Nero Wolfe, or had got the notion, in all the excitement, that he really was Nero Wolfe. He was proceeding, "Young lady, listen to me! I will not—"

She turned and made for the door. I was immediately on my feet and after her, but halfway across the room I put on the brake, because the doorway had suddenly filled up with a self-propelled massive substance and she couldn't get through. She stopped, goggle-eyed, and then fell back a couple of paces.

The massive substance advanced, halted, and used its mouth: "How do you do? I am Nero Wolfe."

He did it well, at top form, and it was quite an effect. Nobody made a chirp. He moved forward, and Jane retreated again.

Wolfe stopped at the corner of his desk and wiggled a finger at Hackett. "Take another chair, sir, if you please?"

Hackett sidled out, without a word, and went to the red leather chair. Wolfe leaned over to peer at the hole in the back of his own chair, and then at the hole in the plaster, grunted, and got himself seated.

"This," Jensen said, "makes it a farce."

Jane snapped, "I'm going," and headed for the door, but I had been expecting that, and with only two steps had her by the arm with a good grip and was prepared to give her the twist if she went thorny on me. Jensen sprang to his feet with both of his hands fists. Evidently in the brief space of forty-eight hours it had developed to the point where the sight of another man laying hands on his Jane started his adrenalin spurting in torrents.

"Stop it!" Wolfe's voice was a whip. It turned us into a group of statuary. "Miss Geer, you may leave shortly, if you still want to, after I have said something. Mr. Jensen, sit down. Archie, go to your desk, but be ready to use the gun. One of them is a murderer."

"That's a lie!" Jensen was visibly breathing. "And who the hell are you?"

"I introduced myself, sir. That gentleman is my temporary employee. When my life was threatened I hired him to impersonate me."

Jane spat at him, "You fat coward!"

He shook his head. "No, Miss Geer. It is no great distinction not to be a coward, but I can claim it. Not cowardice. Conceit convinced me that only I could catch the person daring and witty enough to kill me. I wished to be alive to do so."

He turned abruptly to me: "Archie, get Inspector Cramer on the phone."

Jane and Jensen both started talking at once, with vehemence.

Wolfe cut them off: "If you please! In a moment I shall offer you an alternative: the police or me. Meanwhile, Mr. Cramer can help." He glanced at Hackett. "If you want to get away from this uproar, there is your room upstairs . . ."

"I think I'll stay here," Hackett declared. "I'm a little interested in this myself, since I nearly got killed."

"Cramer on," I told Wolfe.

He lifted his phone from the cradle. "How do you do, sir? . . . No.

. . . No, I have a request to make. If you'll send a man here right away, I'll give him a revolver and a bullet. First, examine the revolver for fingerprints and send me copies. Second, trace the revolver if possible. Third, fire a bullet from it and compare it both with the bullet I am sending you and with the bullets that killed Mr. Jensen and Mr. Doyle. Let me know the results. That's all. . . . No. . . . Confound it, no! If you come yourself you will be handed the package at the door and not admitted. I'm busy."

As he hung up I said, "Does Cramer get the handkerchief, too?"

"Let me see it."

I handed the gun to him, with its butt still protruding through the tear in the handkerchief. Wolfe frowned as he saw that the handkerchief had no laundry mark or any other mark and was a species that could be bought in almost any dry-goods store.

"We'll keep the handkerchief," Wolfe said.

Jensen demanded, "What the devil was it doing there?"

Wolfe's eyes went shut. He was, of course, tasting Jensen's expression, tone of voice, and mental longitude and latitude, to try to decide whether innocent curiosity was indicated or a camouflage for guilt. He always shut his eyes when he tasted. In a moment they opened again halfway.

"If a man has recently shot a gun," he said, "and has had no opportunity to wash, an examination of his hand will furnish incontestable proof. You probably know that. One of you, the one who fired that shot, certainly does. The handkerchief protected the hand. Under a microscope it would be found to contain many minute particles of explosives and other residue. The fact that it is a man's handkerchief doesn't help. Major Jensen would naturally possess a man's handkerchief. Miss Geer could buy or borrow one."

"You asked me to stay while you said something." Jane snapped. She and Jensen were back in their chairs. "You haven't said anything yet. Where were *you* when the shot was fired?"

"Pfui." Wolfe sighed. "Fritz, pack the gun and bullet in a carton, carefully with tissue paper, and give it to the man when he comes. First, bring me beer. Do any of you want beer?"

Evidently no one did.

"Very well, Miss Geer. To assume, or pretend to assume, some elaborate hocus-pocus by the inmates of this house is inane. At the moment the shot was fired, I was standing near the kitchen talking with

Mr. Goodwin. Since then I have been at a spot from which part of this room can be seen and voices heard."

His eyes went to Jensen and back to Jane. "One of you two people is apt to make a mistake, and I want to prevent it if possible. I have not yet asked you where you were and what you were doing at the instant the shot was fired. Before I do so I want to say this, that even with the information at hand it is demonstrable that the shot came from the direction of that door to the front room, which was standing open. Mr. Hackett could not have fired it; you, Mr. Jensen, satisfied yourself of that. Mr. Brenner was in the kitchen. Mr. Goodwin and I were together. I warn you—one of you—that this is sufficiently provable to satisfy a jury in a murder trial.

"Now, what if you both assert that at the instant you heard the shot you were together, close together perhaps, looking at each other? For the one who fired the gun that would be a blessing, indeed. For the other it might be disastrous in the end, for when the truth is disclosed, as it will be, the question of complicity will arise. . . . How long have you two known each other?"

Jane's teeth were holding her lower lip. She removed them. "I met him day before yesterday. Here."

"Indeed. Is that correct, Mr. Jensen?"

"Yes."

Wolfe's brows were up. "Hardly long enough to form an attachment to warrant any of the more costly forms of sacrifice. Unless the spark was exceptionally hot, not long enough to weld you into collusion for murder. I hope you understand, Miss Geer, that all that is wanted here is the truth. Where were you and what were you doing when you heard the shot?"

"I was standing by the piano. I had put my bag on the piano and was opening it."

"Which way were you facing?"

"Toward the window."

"Were you looking at Mr. Jensen?"

"Not at the moment, no."

"Thank you." Wolfe's eyes moved. "Mr. Jensen?"

"I was in the doorway to the hall, looking down the hall and wondering where Goodwin had gone to. For no particular reason. I was not at that moment looking at Miss Geer."

Wolfe poured beer, which Fritz had brought. "Now we are ready to decide something." He took them both in. "Miss Geer, you said you wanted to go to a lawyer, heaven protect you. But it would not be sensible to permit either of you to walk out of here, to move and act at your own will and discretion. Since that bullet was intended for me, I reject the notion utterly. On the other hand, we can't proceed intelligently until I get a report from Mr. Cramer. There is time to be passed."

Wolfe heaved a sigh. "Archie, take them to the front room and stay there till I send for you. Fritz will answer the bell."

Two hours of stony silence grow tiresome.

I appreciated the break in the monotony when, a little before nine, I heard the doorbell, and Fritz came in. He said, "Archie, Mr. Wolfe wants you in the office. Inspector Cramer is there with Sergeant Stebbins. I am to stay here."

If the situation in the front room had been unjovial, the one in the office was absolutely grim. One glance at Wolfe was enough to see that he was in a state of uncontrollable fury, because his forefinger was making the same circle, over and over, on the surface of his desk. Hackett was not in the room, but Sergeant Purley Stebbins was standing by the wall, looking official. Inspector Cramer was in the red leather chair, with his face about the color of the chair.

Wolfe tapped a piece of paper on his desk. "Look at this, Archie."

I went and looked. It was a search warrant.

Wowie! I was surprised that Cramer was still alive, or Wolfe, either.

Cramer growled, holding himself in, "I'll try to forget what you just said, Wolfe. It was totally uncalled for. Damn it, you have given me a run-around too many times. There I was with that gun. A bullet fired from it matched the bullet you sent me and also the two that killed Jensen and Doyle. That's the gun, and you sent it to me. All right; then you've got a client, and when you've got a client you keep him right in your pocket. I would have been a fool to come here and start begging you. I've begged you before."

He started to get up. "We're going to search this house."

"If you do you'll never catch the murderer of Mr. Jensen and Mr. Doyle."

Cramer dropped back in the chair. "I won't?"

"No, sir."

"You'll prevent me?"

"Bah!" Wolfe was disgusted. "Next you'll be warning me formally that obstruction of justice is a crime. I didn't say that the murderer wouldn't be caught, I said you wouldn't catch him. Because I already have."

Cramer said, "The hell you have."

"Yes, sir. Your report on the gun and bullets settles it. But I confess the matter is a little complicated, and I do give you a formal warning: You are not equipped to handle it. I am." Wolfe shoved the warrant across the desk. "Tear that thing up."

Cramer shook his head. "You see, Wolfe, I know you. Lord, don't I know you! But I'm willing to have a talk before I execute it."

"No, sir." Wolfe was murmuring again: "I will not submit to duress. I would even prefer to deal with District Attorney Skinner. Tear it up, or proceed to execute it."

That was a dirty threat. Cramer's opinion of Skinner was that he was one of the defects of our democratic system of government. Cramer looked at the warrant, at Wolfe, at me, and back at the warrant. Then he picked it up and tore.

"Can the gun be traced?" Wolfe said.

"No. The number's gone. It dates from about nineteen-ten. And there are no prints on it that are worth anything. Nothing but smudges."

Wolfe nodded. "Naturally. A much simpler technique than wiping it clean or going around in gloves. . . . The murderer is in this house."

"I suspected he was. Is he your client?"

"The main complication," Wolfe said, in his purring tone, "is this: There are a man and a woman in that front room. Granting that one of them is the murderer, which one?"

Cramer frowned at him. "You didn't say anything about granting. You said that you have caught the murderer."

"So I have. He or she is in there, under guard. I suppose I'll have to tell you what happened, if I expect you to start your army of men digging, and it looks as though that's the only way to go about it. I have no army. To begin with, when I received that threat, I hired a man who resembles me—"

Purley Stebbins nearly bit the end of his tongue off, trying to get it all in his notebook.

Wolfe finished. Cramer sat scowling. Wolfe purred, "Well, sir, there's the problem. I doubt if it can be solved with what we have, or what is available on the premises. You'll have to get your men started."

"I wish," Cramer growled, "I knew how much dressing you put on that."

"Not any. I have only one concern in this. I have no client. I withheld nothing and added nothing."

"Maybe." Cramer straightened up like a man of action. "Okay, we'll proceed on that basis and find out. First of all I want to ask them some questions."

"I suppose you do." Wolfe detested sitting and listening to someone else ask questions. "You are handicapped, of course, by your official status. Which one do you want first?"

Cramer stood up. "I've got to see that room before I talk to either of them. I want to see where things are. Especially that vase."

Jane was seated on the piano bench. Jensen was on the sofa, but arose as we entered. Fritz was standing by a window.

Wolfe said, "This is Inspector Cramer, Miss Geer."

She didn't make a sound or move a muscle.

Wolfe said, "I believe you've met the inspector, Mr. Jensen."

"Yes, I have." Jensen's voice had gone unused so long it squeaked, and he cleared his throat. "So the agreement not to call in the police was a farce, too." He was bitter.

"There was no such agreement. I said that Mr. Cramer couldn't be kept out of it indefinitely. The bullet that was fired at me—at Mr. Hackett—came from the gun that was found in that vase," Wolfe pointed at it—"and so did those that killed your father and Mr. Doyle. So the field has become—ah, restricted."

"I insist," Jane put in, in a voice with no resemblance to any I had ever heard her use before, "on my right to consult a lawyer."

"Just a minute, now," Cramer told her in the tone he thought was soothing. "We're going to talk this over, but wait till I look around a little."

He proceeded to inspect things, and so did Sergeant Stebbins. They considered distances, and the positions of various objects. Then there was this detail: From what segment of that room could a gun send a bullet through the hole in Wolfe's chair and the one in the wall? They were working on that together when Wolfe turned to Fritz and asked him, "What happened to the other cushion?"

Fritz was taken aback. "Other cushion?"

"There were six velvet cushions on that sofa. Now there are only five. Did you remove it?"

"No, sir." Fritz gazed at the sofa and counted. "That's right. They've been rearranged to take up the space. I don't understand it. They were all here yesterday."

"Are you sure of that?"

"Yes, sir. Positive."

"Look for it. Archie, help him."

It seemed like an odd moment to send out a general alarm for a sofa cushion, but since I had nothing else to do at the moment I obliged.

I finally told Wolfe, "It's gone. It isn't in here."

He muttered at me, "I see it isn't."

I stared at him. There was an expression on his face that I knew well. It wasn't exactly excitement, though it always stirred excitement in me. His neck was rigid, as if to prevent any movement of the head, so as not to disturb the brain, his eyes were half shut and not seeing anything, and his lips were moving, pushing out, then relaxing, then pushing out again.

Suddenly he turned and spoke: "Mr. Cramer! Please leave Mr. Stebbins in here with Miss Geer and Mr. Jensen. You can stay here, too, or come with me, as you prefer. Fritz and Archie, come." He headed for the office.

Cramer, knowing Wolfe's tones of voice almost as well as I did, came with us.

Wolfe waited until he was in his chair before he spoke: "I want to know if that cushion is on the premises. Search the house from the cellar up—except the south room; Mr. Hackett is in there lying down. Start in here."

Cramer barked, "What the hell is all this about?"

"I'll give you an explanation," Wolfe told him, "when I have one. I'm going to sit here and work, now, and must not be disturbed."

He leaned back and closed his eyes, and his lips started moving. Cramer slid farther back in his chair, crossed his legs, and got out a cigar and sank his teeth in it.

Half an hour had passed while I searched the office, when I heard Wolfe let out a grunt. I nearly toppled off the stepladder turning to look at him. He was in motion. He picked up his wastebasket, which was kept at the far corner of his desk, inspected it, shook his head, put it down again, and began opening the drawers of his desk. The first two, the one at the top and the one in the middle, apparently didn't get him anything, but when he yanked out the double-depth one at the bottom, as far as it would go, he looked in, bent over closer to see better, then closed the drawer and announced, "I've found it."

In those three little words there was at least two tons of self-satisfaction and smirk.

We all goggled at him.

He looked at me: "Archie. Get down off that thing, and don't fall. Look in your desk and see if one of my guns has been fired."

I stepped down and went and opened the armament drawer. The first one I picked up was innocent. I tried the second with a sniff and a look, and reported, "Yes, sir. There were six cartridges, and now there are five. Same as the cushions. The shell is here."

"Tchah! The confounded ass! . . . Tell Miss Geer and Mr. Jensen that they may come in here if they care to hear what happened, or they may go home or anywhere else. We don't need them. Take Mr. Stebbins with you upstairs and bring Mr. Hackett down here. Use caution, and search him with great care. He is an extremely dangerous man."

Naturally, Jane and Jensen voted for joining the throng in the office, and their pose during the balloting was significant. They stood facing each other, with Jensen's right hand on Jane's left shoulder, and Jane's right hand, or perhaps just the fingers, on Jensen's left forearm. I left it to them to find the way to the office alone, told Purley Stebbins what our job was, and took him upstairs with me.

It was approximately ten minutes later that we delivered our cargo in the office. Even though Mr. Hackett staged one of the most convincing demonstrations of unwillingness to cooperate that I have ever encountered.

We got him to the office in one piece, nothing really wrong with any of us that surgical gauze wouldn't fix. We propped him in a chair.

I said, "He was reluctant."

I'll say one thing for Wolfe—I've never seen him gloat over a guy about to get it. He was contemplating Hackett more as an extraordinary object that deserved study.

I said, "Purley thinks he knows him."

Purley, as was proper, spoke to his superior: "I swear, Inspector, I'm sure I've seen him somewhere, but I can't remember."

Wolfe nodded. "A uniform makes a difference. I suggest that he was in uniform."

"Uniform?" Purley scowled. "Army?"

Wolfe shook his head. "Mr. Cramer told me Wednesday morning that the doorman on duty at the apartment house at the time Mr. Jensen and Mr. Doyle were killed was a fat nitwit who had been hired two weeks ago and didn't know the tenants by name, and also that he claimed to have been in the basement stoking the water heater at the moment the murders were committed. A phone call would tell us whether he is still working there."

"He isn't," Cramer growled. "He left Wednesday afternoon because he didn't like a place where people were murdered. I never saw him. Some of my men did."

"Yeah," Purley said, gazing at Hackett's face. "By God, it's him."

"He is," Wolfe declared, "a remarkable combination of fool and genius. He came to New York determined to kill Mr. Jensen and me. By the way, Mr. Hackett, you look a little dazed. Can you hear what I'm saying?"

Hackett made no sound.

"I guess you can," Wolfe went on. "This will interest you. I requested Military Intelligence to have an examination made of the effects of Captain Root at the prison in Maryland. A few minutes ago I phoned for a report, and got it. Captain Root was lying when he stated that he was not in communication with his father and had not been for years. There are several letters from his father among his belongings, dated in the past two months, and they make it evident that his father, whose name is Thomas Root, regards him as a scion to be proud of. To the point of mania."

Wolfe wiggled a finger at Hackett. "I offer the conjecture that you are in a position to know whether that is correct or not. Is it?"

"One more day," Hackett said in his husky croak. His hands were twitching. "One more day," he repeated.

Wolfe nodded. "I know. One more day and you would have killed me, with the suspicion centered on Miss Geer or Mr. Jensen, or both, on account of your flummery here this afternoon. And you would have disappeared."

Jensen popped up. "You haven't explained the flummery."

"I shall, Mr. Jensen." Wolfe got more comfortable in his chair. "But first that performance Tuesday evening."

He was keeping his eyes on Hackett. "That was a masterpiece. You decided to kill Mr. Jensen first, which was lucky for me, and, since all apartment house service staffs are short-handed, got a job there as doorman with no difficulty. All you had to do was await an opportunity, with no passers-by or other onlookers. It came the day after you mailed the threat, an ideal situation in every respect except the presence of the man he had hired to guard him.

"Arriving at the entrance to the apartment house, naturally they would have no suspicion of the doorman in uniform. Mr. Jensen probably nodded and spoke to you. With no one else in sight, and the elevator man ascending with a passenger, it was too good an opportunity to lose. Muffling the revolver with some piece of cloth, you shot Mr. Doyle in the back, and when Mr. Jensen whirled at the sound you shot him in the front, and skedaddled for the stairs to the basement and started stoking the water heater. I imagine the first thing you fed it was the cloth with which you had muffled the gun."

Wolfe moved his eyes. "Does that rattle anywhere, Mr. Cramer?"

"It sounds tight from here," Cramer said.

"That's good. Because it is for those murders that Mr. Hackett—or Mr. Root, I suppose I should say—must be convicted. He can't be electrocuted for hacking a little gash in his own ear." Wolfe's eyes moved again, to me. "Archie, did you find any tools in his pockets?"

"Only a boy scout's dream," I told him. "One of those knives with scissors, awl, nail file . . ."

"Let the police have it to look for traces of blood. Just the sort of thing Mr. Cramer does best."

"The comedy can wait," Cramer growled. "I'll take it as is for Tuesday night and go on from there."

Wolfe heaved a sigh. "You're rushing past the most interesting point of all: Mr. Hackett's answering my advertisement for a man. Was he sufficiently acute to realize that its specifications were roughly a description of me, suspect that I was the advertiser, and proceed to take advantage of it to approach me? Or was it merely that he was short of funds and attracted by the money offered?

"Actually, I am sure that he saw it as precisely the kind of opportunity I meant it to be—an opportunity to kill Nero Wolfe. Nor was my insertion of the advertisement a mere shot in the dark. I was very sure we were dealing with a dangerous killer and a bold ingenious personality.

"Accordingly, Archie, when, after you had left to meet Miss Geer, I looked out the window and saw this fellow pass by, and saw him again three times in the next three hours in the vicinity of the house, it occurred to me that a lion is much safer in a cage even if you have to be in the cage with him. I thought the advertisement should provide proper enticement for a character who had shown complete disregard for danger in his previous attempt at murder. . . .

"In any event, having answered the advertisement and received a message from me, he was, of course, delighted, and doubly delighted when he was hired.

"Now, from the moment he got in here, Mr. Root was concocting schemes, rejecting, considering, revising; and no doubt relishing the situation enormously. The device of the handkerchief to protect a hand firing a gun was no doubt a part of one of those schemes.

"This morning he learned that Miss Geer was to call on me at six o'clock, and he was to impersonate me. After lunch, in here alone, he got a cushion from the sofa in there, wrapped his revolver in it, and fired a bullet through the back of this chair into the wall.

"He stuffed the cushion into the rear compartment of the bottom right-hand drawer of this desk, then put the gun in his pocket."

"If the hole had been seen, the bullet would have been found," Cramer muttered.

"I have already pronounced him," Wolfe said testily, "an unsurpassable fool. Even so, he knew that Archie would be out with him the rest of the afternoon, and I would be in my room. I had made a remark which informed him that I would not sit in that chair again until he was permanently out of it. At six o'clock Miss Geer arrived, unexpectedly accompanied by Mr. Jensen. They were shown into the front room, and that door was open. Mr. Root's brain moved swiftly, and so did the rest of him. He got one of my guns from Archie's desk, returned to this chair, opened the drawer where he had put the cushion, fired a shot into the cushion, dropped the gun in, and shut the drawer."

Wolfe sighed again. "Archie came dashing in, cast a glance at Mr. Root seated here, and went on to the front room. Mr. Root grasped the opportunity to do two things: return my gun to the drawer of Archie's desk, and use a blade of his knife, I would guess the awl, to tear a gash in the corner of his ear. That, of course, improved the situation for him. What improved it vastly more was the chance that came soon after, when Archie took him to the bathroom and left him there. He might have found another chance, but that was perfect. He entered the front room from the bathroom, put his own gun, handkerchief attached, in the vase, and returned to the bathroom, and later rejoined the others here.

"It was by no means utterly preposterous if I had not noticed the absence of that cushion. Since this desk sits flush with the floor, no sign of the bullet fired into the bottom drawer would be visible unless the drawer was opened, and why should it be? It was unlikely that Archie would have occasion to find that one of my guns in his desk had been fired, and what if he did? Mr. Root knows how to handle a gun without leaving fingerprints, which is simple."

Cramer slowly nodded. "I'm not objecting. I'll buy it. But you must admit you've described quite a few things you can't prove."

"I don't have to. Neither do you. As I said before, Mr. Root will be put on trial for the murder of Mr. Jensen and Mr. Doyle, not for his antics here in my house."

Cramer stood up. "Let's go, Mr. Root."

Back in the office, Wolfe, in his own chair with only one bullet hole that could easily be repaired, and with three bottles of beer on a tray in front of him, was leaning back, the picture of a man at peace.

He murmured at me, "Archie, remind me in the morning to telephone Mr. Viscardi about that tarragon."

"Yes, sir." I sat down. "And if I may, sir, I would like to offer a man-eating tiger weighing around two hundred and sixty pounds capable of easy and normal movement. We could station him behind the big cabinet, and when you enter he could leap on you from the rear."

It didn't faze him. He was enjoying the feel of his chair and I doubt if he heard me.

ROSS MACDONALD *is a pseudonym used by Kenneth Millar (1915–1983), a onetime professor of English (Ph.D., 1951). He also wrote as John Macdonald and John Ross Macdonald, but because of confusion with authors John D. MacDonald and Philip MacDonald, he resorted to "Ross." Ross Macdonald worked in the tradition of Dashiell Hammett and Raymond Chandler, with a detective, Lew Archer, who is perhaps the greatest creation of the hardboiled school of crime writing. An introspective man like his creator, Archer solved crimes in thirteen novels and two collections of short stories, and he also learned a great deal about himself (Macdonald's readers usually found out something about* themselves *as well). It is quite probable that Mr. Millar has received more critical attention than almost any of his contemporaries, and it is richly deserved.*

"Midnight Blue" is an Archer story that is truly unforgettable.

Midnight Blue
BY ROSS MACDONALD

It had rained in the canyon during the night. The world had the colored freshness of a butterfly just emerged from the chrysalis stage and trembling in the sun. Actual butterflies danced in flight across free spaces of air or played a game of tag without any rules among the tree branches. At this height there were giant pines among the eucalyptus trees.

I parked my car where I usually parked it, in the shadow of the stone building just inside the gates of the old estate. Just inside the posts, that is—the gates had long since fallen from their rusted hinges. The owner of the country house had died in Europe, and the place had stood empty since the war. It was one reason I came here on the occasional Sunday when I wanted to get away from the Hollywood rat race. Nobody lived within two miles.

Until now, anyway. The window of the gatehouse overlooking the drive had been broken the last time that I'd noticed it. Now it was patched up with a piece of cardboard. Through a hole punched in the middle of the cardboard, bright emptiness watched me—human eye's bright emptiness.

"Hello," I said.

A grudging voice answered: "Hello."

The gatehouse door creaked open, and a white-haired man came out. A smile sat strangely on his ravaged face. He walked mechanically, shuffling in the leaves, as if his body was not at home in the world. He wore faded denims through which his clumsy muscles bulged like animals in a sack. His feet were bare.

I saw when he came up to me that he was a huge old man, a head taller than I was and a foot wider. His smile was not a greeting or any kind of a smile that I could respond to. It was the stretched, blind grimace of a man who lived in a world of his own, a world that didn't include me.

"Get out of here. I don't want trouble. I don't want nobody messing around."

"No trouble," I said. "I came up to do a little target shooting. I probably have as much right here as you have."

His eyes widened. They were as blue and empty as holes in his head through which I could see the sky.

"Nobody has the rights here that I have. I lifted up mine eyes unto the hills and the voice spoke and I found sanctuary. Nobody's going to force me out of my sanctuary."

I could feel the short hairs bristling on back of my neck. Though my instincts didn't say so, he was probably a harmless nut. I tried to keep my instincts out of my voice.

"I won't bother you. You don't bother me. That should be fair enough."

"You bother me just *being* here. I can't stand people. I can't stand cars. And this is twice in two days you come up harrying me and harassing me."

"I haven't been here for a month."

"You're an Ananias liar." His voice whined like a rising wind. He clenched his knobbed fists and shuddered on the verge of violence.

"Calm down, old man," I said. "There's room in the world for both of us."

He looked around at the high green world as if my words had snapped him out of a dream.

"You're right," he said in a different voice. "I have been blessed, and I must remember to be joyful. Joyful. Creation belongs to all of us poor creatures." His smiling teeth were as long and yellow as an old horse's. His roving glance fell on my car. "And it wasn't you who come up here last night. It was a different automobile. I remember."

He turned away, muttering something about washing his socks, and dragged his horny feet back into the gatehouse. I got my targets, pistol, and ammunition out of the trunk, and locked the car up tight. The old man watched me through his peephole, but he didn't come out again.

Below the road, in the wild canyon, there was an open meadow backed by a sheer bank which was topped by the crumbling wall of the estate. It was my shooting gallery. I slid down the wet grass of the bank and tacked a target to an oak tree, using the butt of my heavy-framed twenty-two as a hammer.

While I was loading it, something caught my eye—something that glinted red, like a ruby among the leaves. I stooped to pick it up and found it was attached. It was a red-enameled fingernail at the tip of a white hand. The hand was cold and stiff.

I let out a sound that must have been loud in the stillness. A jay bird erupted from a manzanita, sailed up to a high limb of the oak, and yelled down curses at me. A dozen chickadees flew out of the oak and settled in another at the far end of the meadow.

Panting like a dog, I scraped away the dirt and wet leaves that had been loosely piled over the body. It was the body of a girl wearing a midnight-blue sweater and skirt. She was a blonde, about seventeen. The blood that congested her face made her look old and dark. The white rope with which she had been garrotted was sunk almost out of sight in the flesh of her neck. The rope was tied at the nape in what is called a granny's knot, the kind of knot that any child can tie.

I left her where she lay and climbed back up to the road on trembling knees. The grass showed traces of the track her body had made where someone had dragged it down the bank. I looked for tire marks on the shoulder and in the rutted, impacted gravel of the road. If there had been any, the rain had washed them out.

I trudged up the road to the gatehouse and knocked on the door. It creaked inward under my hand. Inside there was nothing alive but the spiders that had webbed the low black beams. A dustless rectangle in front of the stone fireplace showed where a bedroll had lain. Several blackened tin cans had evidently been used as cooking utensils. Gray embers lay on the cavernous hearth. Suspended above it from a spike in the mantel was a pair of white cotton work socks. The socks were wet. Their owner had left in a hurry.

It wasn't my job to hunt him. I drove down the canyon to the highway and along it for a few miles to the outskirts of the nearest town. There a drab green box of a building with a flag in front of it housed the Highway Patrol. Across the highway was a lumberyard, deserted on Sunday.

"Too bad about Ginnie," the dispatcher said when she had radioed the local sheriff. She was a thirtyish brunette with fine black eyes and dirty fingernails. She had on a plain white blouse, which was full of her.

"Did you know Ginnie?"

"My younger sister knows her. They go—they went to high school together. It's an awful thing when it happens to a young person like that. I knew she was missing—I got the report when I came on at eight —but I kept hoping that she was just off on a lost weekend, like. Now there's nothing to hope for, is there?" Her eyes were liquid with feeling. "Poor Ginnie. And poor Mr. Green."

"Her father?"

"That's right. He was in here with her high school counselor not more than an hour ago. I hope he doesn't come back right away. I don't want to be the one that has to tell him.

"How long has the girl been missing?"

"Just since last night. We got the report here about 3 A.M., I think. Apparently she wandered away from a party at Cavern Beach. Down the pike a ways." She pointed south toward the mouth of the canyon.

"What kind of a party was it?"

"Some of the kids from the Union High School—they took some wienies down and had a fire. The party was part of graduation week. I happen to know about it because my young sister Alice went. I didn't want her to go, even if it was supervised. That can be a dangerous beach at night. All sorts of bums and scroungers hang out in the caves. Why, one night when I was a kid I saw a naked man down there in the moonlight. He didn't have a woman with him either."

She caught the drift of her words, did a slow blush, and checked her loquacity. I leaned on the plywood counter between us.

"What sort of girl was Ginnie Green?"

"I wouldn't know. I never really knew her."

"Your sister does."

"I don't let my sister run around with girls like Ginnie Green. Does that answer your question?"

"Not in any detail."

"It seems to me you ask a lot of questions."

"I'm naturally interested, since I found her. Also, I happen to be a private detective."

"Looking for a job?"

"I can always use a job."

"So can I, and I've got one and I don't intend to lose it." She softened the words with a smile. "Excuse me; I have work to do."

She turned to her shortwave and sent out a message to the patrol cars that Virginia Green had been found. Virginia Green's father heard it as he came in the door. He was a puffy gray-faced man with red-rimmed eyes. Striped pajama bottoms showed below the cuffs of his trousers. His shoes were muddy, and he walked as if he had been walking all night.

He supported himself on the edge of the counter, opening and shutting his mouth like a beached fish. Words came out, half strangled by shock.

"I heard you say she was dead, Anita."

The woman raised her eyes to his, "Yes. I'm awfully sorry, Mr. Green."

He put his face down on the counter and stayed there like a penitent, perfectly still. I could hear a clock somewhere, snipping off seconds, and in the back of the room the L.A. police signals like muttering voices coming in from another planet. Another planet very much like this one, where violence measured out the hours.

"It's my fault," Green said to the bare wood under his face. "I didn't bring her up properly. I haven't been a good father."

The woman watched him with dark and glistening eyes ready to spill. She stretched out an unconscious hand to touch him, pulled her hand back in embarrassment when a second man came into the station. He was a young man with crew-cut brown hair, tanned and fit-looking in a Hawaiian shirt. Fit-looking except for the glare of sleeplessness in his eyes and the anxious lines around them.

"What is it, Miss Brocco? What's the word?"

"The word is bad." She sounded angry. "Somebody murdered Ginnie Green. This man here is a detective and he just found her body up in Trumbull Canyon."

The young man ran his fingers through his short hair and failed to get a grip on it, or on himself. "My God! That's terrible!"

"Yes," the woman said. "You were supposed to be looking after her, weren't you?"

They glared at each other across the counter. The tips of her breasts pointed at him through her blouse like accusing fingers. The young man lost the glaring match. He turned to me with a wilted look.

"My name is Connor, Franklin Connor, and I'm afraid I'm very much to blame in this. I'm counselor at the high school, and I was supposed to be looking after the party, as Miss Brocco said."

"Why didn't you?"

"I didn't realize. I mean, I thought they were all perfectly happy and safe. The boys and girls had pretty well paired off around the fire. Frankly, I felt rather out of place. They aren't children, you know. They were all seniors, they had cars. So I said good night and walked home along the beach. As a matter of fact, I was hoping for a phone call from my wife."

"What time did you leave the party?"

"It must have been nearly eleven. The ones who hadn't paired off had already gone home."

"Who did Ginnie pair off with?"

"I don't know. I'm afraid I wasn't paying too much attention to the kids. It's graduation week, and I've had a lot of problems—"

The father, Green, had been listening with a changing face. In a sudden yammering rage his implosive grief and guilt exploded outward.

"It's your business to know! By God, I'll have your job for this. I'll make it *my* business to run you out of town."

Connor hung his head and looked at the stained tile floor. There was a thin spot in his short brown hair, and his scalp gleamed through it like bare white bone. It was turning into a bad day for everybody, and I felt the dull old nagging pull of other people's trouble, like a toothache you can't leave alone.

The sheriff arrived, flanked by several deputies and an HP sergeant. He wore a western hat and a rawhide tie and a blue gabardine business suit which together produced a kind of gun-smog effect. His name was Pearsall.

I rode back up the canyon in the right front seat of Pearsall's black Buick, filling him in on the way. The deputies' Ford and an HP car followed us, and Green's new Oldsmobile convertible brought up the rear.

The sheriff said: "The old guy sounds like a looney to me."

"He's a loner, anyway."

"You never can tell about them hoboes. That's why I give my boys instructions to roust 'em. Well, it looks like an open-and-shut case."

"Maybe. Let's keep our minds open anyway, Sheriff."

"Sure. Sure. But the old guy went on the run. That shows consciousness of guilt. Don't worry, we'll hunt him down. I got men that know these hills like you know your wife's geography."

"I'm not married."

"Your girl friend, then." He gave me a sideways leer that was no gift. "And if we can't find him on foot, we'll use the air squadron."

"You have an air squadron?"

"Volunteer, mostly local ranchers. We'll get him." His tires squealed on a curve. "Was the girl raped?"

"I didn't try to find out. I'm not a doctor. I left her as she was."

The sheriff grunted. "You did the right thing at that."

Nothing had changed in the high meadow. The girl lay waiting to have her picture taken. It was taken many times, from several angles. All the birds flew away. Her father leaned on a tree and watched them go. Later he was sitting on the ground.

I volunteered to drive him home. It wasn't pure altruism. I'm incapable of it. I said when I had turned his Oldsmobile:

"Why did you say it was your fault, Mr Green?"

He wasn't listening. Below the road four uniformed men were wrestling a heavy covered aluminum stretcher up the steep bank. Green watched them as he had watched the departing birds, until they were out of sight around a curve.

"She was so young," he said to the back seat.

I waited, and tried again. "Why did you blame yourself for her death?"

He roused himself from his daze. "Did I say that?"

"In the Highway Patrol office you said something of the sort."

He touched my arm. "I didn't mean I killed her."

"I didn't think you meant that. I'm interested in finding out who did."

"Are you a cop—a policeman?"

"I have been."

"You're not with the locals."

"No. I happen to be a private detective from Los Angeles. The name is Archer."

He sat and pondered this information. Below and ahead the summer sea brimmed up in the mouth of the canyon.

"You don't think the old tramp did her in?" Green said.

"It's hard to figure out how he could have. He's a strong-looking old buzzard, but he couldn't have carried her all the way up from the beach. And she wouldn't have come along with him of her own accord."

It was a question, in a way.

"I don't know," her father said. "Ginnie was a little wild. She'd do a thing *because* it was wrong, *because* it was dangerous. She hated to turn down a dare, especially from a man."

"There were men in her life?"

"She was attractive to men. You saw her, even as she is." He gulped. "Don't get me wrong. Ginnie was never a *bad* girl. She was a little headstrong, and I made mistakes. That's why I blame myself."

"What sort of mistakes, Mr. Green?"

"All the usual ones, and some I made up on my own." His voice was bitter. "Ginnie didn't have a mother, you see. Her mother left me years ago, and it was as much my fault as hers. I tried to bring her up myself. I didn't give her proper supervision. I run a restaurant in town, and I don't get home nights till after midnight. Ginnie was pretty much on her own since she was in grade school. We got along fine when I was there, but I usually wasn't there.

"The worst mistake I made was letting her work in the restaurant over the weekends. That started about a year ago. She wanted the money for clothes, and I thought the discipline would be good for her. I thought I could keep an eye on her, you know. But it didn't work out. She grew up too fast, and the night work played hell with her studies. I finally got the word from the school authorities. I fired her a couple of months ago, but I guess it was too late. We haven't been getting along too well since then. Mr. Connor said she resented my indecision, that I gave her too much responsibility and then took it away again."

"You've talked her over with Connor?"

"More than once, including last night. He was her academic counselor, and he was concerned about her grades. We both were. Ginnie finally pulled through, after all, thanks to him. She was going to graduate. Not that it matters now, of course.

Green was silent for a time. The sea expanded below us like a second blue dawn. I could hear the roar of the highway. Green touched my elbow again, as if he needed human contact.

"I oughtn't to've blown my top at Connor. He's a decent boy, he means well. He gave my daughter hours of free tuition this last month. And he's got troubles of his own, like he said."

"What troubles?"

"I happen to know his wife left him, same as mine. I shouldn't have borne down so hard on him. I have a lousy temper, always have had." He hesitated, then blurted out as if he had found a confessor: "I said a terrible thing to Ginnie at supper last night. She always has supper with me at the restaurant. I said if she wasn't home when I got home last night that I'd wring her neck."

"And she wasn't home," I said. And somebody wrung her neck, I didn't say.

The light at the highway was red. I glanced at Green. Tear tracks glistened like small tracks on his face.

"Tell me what happened last night."

"There isn't anything much to tell," he said. "I got to the house about twelve-thirty, and, like you said, she wasn't home. So I called Al Brocco's house. He's my night cook, and I knew his youngest daughter Alice was at the moonlight party on the beach. Alice was home all right."

"Did you talk to Alice?"

"She was in bed asleep. Al woke her up, but I didn't talk to her. She told him she didn't know where Ginnie was. I went to bed, but I couldn't sleep. Finally I got up and called Mr. Connor. That was about one-thirty. I thought I should get in touch with the authorities, but he said no, Ginnie had enough black marks against her already. He came over to the house and waited for a while and then we went down to Cavern Beach. There was no trace of her. I said it was time to call in the authorities, and he agreed. We went to his beach house, because it was nearer, and called the sheriff's office from there. We went back to the beach with a couple of flashlights and went through the caves. He stayed with me all night. I give him that."

"Where are these caves?"

"We'll pass them in a minute. I'll show you if you want. But there's nothing in any of the three of them."

Nothing but shadows and empty beer cans, discarded contraceptives, the odor of rotting kelp. I got sand in my shoes and sweat under my collar. The sun dazzled my eyes when I half-walked, half-crawled, from the last of the caves.

Green was waiting beside a heap of ashes.

"This is where they had the wienie roast," he said.

I kicked the ashes. A half-burned sausage rolled along the sand. Sand fleas hopped in the sun like fat on a griddle. Green and I faced each other over the dead fire. He looked out to sea. A seal's face floated like a small black nose cone beyond the breakers. Farther out a water skier slid between unfolding wings of spray.

Away up the beach two people were walking toward us. They were small and lonely and distinct as Chirico figures in the long white distance.

Green squinted against the sun. Red-rimmed or not, his eyes were good. "I believe that's Mr. Connor. I wonder who the woman is with him."

They were walking as close as lovers, just above the white margin of the surf. They pulled apart when they noticed us, but they were still holding hands as they approached.

"It's Mrs. Connor," Green said in a low voice.

"I thought you said she left him."

"That's what he told me last night. She took off on him a couple of weeks ago, couldn't stand a high school teacher's hours. She must have changed her mind."

She looked as though she had a mind to change. She was a hard-faced blonde who walked like a man. A certain amount of style took the curse off her stiff angularity. She had on a madras shirt, mannishly cut, and a pair of black Capri pants that hugged her long, slim legs. She had good legs.

Connor looked at us in complex embarrassment. "I thought it was you from a distance, Mr. Green. I don't believe you know my wife."

"I've seen her in my place of business." He explained to the woman: "I run the Highway Restaurant in town."

"How do you do," she said aloofly, then added in an entirely different voice: "You're Virginia's father, aren't you? I'm so sorry."

The words sounded queer. Perhaps it was the surroundings; the ashes on the beach, the entrances to the caves, the sea, and the empty sky which dwarfed us all. Green answered her solemnly.

"Thank you, ma'am. Mr. Connor was a strong right arm to me last night. I can tell you." He was apologizing. And Connor responded:

"Why don't you come to our place for a drink? It's just down the beach. You look as if you could use one, Mr. Green. You, too," he said to me. "I don't believe I know your name."

"Archer. Lew Archer."

He gave me a hard hand. His wife interposed. "I'm sure Mr. Green and his friend won't want to be bothered with us on a day like this. Besides, it isn't even noon yet, Frank."

She was the one who didn't want to be bothered. We stood around for a minute, exchanging grim, nonsensical comments on the beauty of the day. Then she led Connor back in the direction they had come from. Private Property, her attitude seemed to say: Trespassers will be fresh-frozen.

I drove Green to the Highway Patrol station. He said that he was feeling better, and could make it home from there by himself. He thanked me profusely for being a friend in need to him, as he put it. He followed me to the door of the station, thanking me.

The dispatcher was cleaning her fingernails with an ivory-handled file. She glanced up eagerly.

"Did they catch him yet?"

"I was going to ask you the same question, Miss Brocco."

"No such luck. But they'll get him," she said with female vindictiveness. "The sheriff called out his air squadron, and he sent to Ventura for bloodhounds."

"Big deal."

She bridled. "What do you mean by that?"

"I don't think the old man of the mountain killed her. If he had, he wouldn't have waited till this morning to go on the lam. He'd have taken off right away."

"Then why did he go on the lam at all?" The word sounded strange in her prim mouth.

"I think he saw me discover the body, and realized he'd be blamed."

She considered this, bending the long nail file between her fingers. "If the old tramp didn't do it, who did?"

"You may be able to help me answer that question."

"Me help you? How?"

"You know Frank Connor, for one thing."

"I know him. I've seen him about my sister's grades a few times."

"You don't seem to like him much."

"I don't like him, I don't dislike him. He's just blah to me."

"Why? What's the matter with him?"

Her tight mouth quivered, and let out words: "*I* don't know what's the matter with him. He can't keep his hands off of young girls."

"How do you know that?"

"I heard it."

"From your sister Alice?"

"Yes. The rumor was going around the school, she said."

"Did the rumor involve Ginnie Green?"

She nodded. Her eyes were black as fingerprint ink.

"Is that why Connor's wife left him?"

"I wouldn't know about that. I never even laid eyes on Mrs. Connor."

"You haven't been missing much."

There was a yell outside, a kind of choked ululation. It sounded as much like an animal as a man. It was Green. When I reached the door, he was climbing out of his convertible with a heavy blue revolver in his hand.

"I saw the killer," he cried out exultantly.

"Where?"

He waved the revolver toward the lumberyard across the road. "He poked his head up behind that pile of white pine. When he saw me, he ran like a deer. I'm going to get him."

"No. Give me the gun."

"Why? I got a license to carry it. And use it."

He started across the four-lane highway, dodging through the moving patterns of the Sunday traffic as if he were playing parcheesi on the kitchen table at home. The sounds of brakes and curses split the air. He had scrambled over the locked gate of the yard before I got to it. I went over after him.

Green disappeared behind a pile of lumber. I turned the corner and saw him running halfway down a long aisle walled with stacked wood and floored with beaten earth. The old man of the mountain was running ahead of him. His white hair blew in the wind of his own movement. A burlap sack bounced on his shoulders like a load of sorrow and shame.

"Stop or I'll shoot!" Green cried.

The old man ran on as if the devil himself were after him. He came to a cyclone fence, discarded his sack, and tried to climb it. He almost got over. Three strands of barbed wire along the top of the fence caught and held him struggling.

I heard a tearing sound, and then the sound of a shot. The huge old body espaliered on the fence twitched and went limp, fell heavily to the earth. Green stood over him breathing through his teeth.

I pushed him out of the way. The old man was alive, though there was blood in his mouth. He spat it onto his chin when I lifted his head.

"You shouldn't ought to of done it. I come to turn myself in. Then I got ascairt."

"Why were you scared?"

"I watched you uncover the little girl in the leaves. I knew I'd be blamed. I'm one of the chosen. They always blame the chosen. I been in trouble before."

"Trouble with girls?" At my shoulder Green was grinning terribly.

"Trouble with cops."

"For killing people?" Green said.

"For preaching on the street without a license. The voice told me to preach to the tribes of the wicked. And the voice told me this morning to come in and give my testimony."

"What voice?"

"The great voice." His voice was little and weak. He coughed red.

"He's as crazy as a bedbug," Green said.

"Shut up." I turned back to the dying man. "What testimony do you have to give?"

"About the car I seen. It woke me up in the middle of the night, stopped in the road below my sanctuary."

"What kind of car?"

"I don't know cars. I think it was one of them foreign cars. It made a noise to wake the dead."

"Did you see who was driving it."

"No. I didn't go near. I was ascairt."

"What time was this car in the road?"

"I don't keep track of time. The moon was down behind the trees."

Those were his final words. He looked up at the sky with his sky-colored eyes, straight into the sun. His eyes changed color.

Green said: "Don't tell them. If you do, I'll make a liar out of you. I'm a respected citizen in this town. I got a business to lose. And they'll believe me ahead of you, mister."

"Shut up."

He couldn't. "The old fellow was lying anyway. You know that. You heard him say yourself that he heard voices. That proves he's a psycho. He's a psycho killer. I shot him down like you would a mad dog, and I did right."

He waved the revolver.

"You did wrong, Green, and you know it. Give me that gun before it kills somebody else."

He thrust it into my hand suddenly. I unloaded it, breaking my fingernails in the process, and handed it back to him empty. He nudged up against me.

"Listen, maybe I did do wrong. I had provocation. It doesn't have to get out. I got a business to lose."

He fumbled in his hip pocket and brought out a thick sharkskin wallet. "Here. I can pay you good money. You say that you're a private eye; you know how to keep your lip buttoned."

I walked away and left him blabbering beside the body of the man he had killed. They were both victims, in a sense, but only one of them had blood on his hands.

Miss Brocco was in the HP parking lot. Her bosom was jumping with excitement.

"I heard a shot."

"Green shot the old man. Dead. You better send in for the meat wagon and call off your bloody dogs."

The words hit her like slaps. She raised her hand to her face, defensively. "Are you mad at me? Why are you mad at me?"

"I'm mad at everybody."

"You still don't think he did it."

"I know damned well he didn't. I want to talk to your sister."

"Alice? What for?"

"Information. She was on the beach with Ginnie Green last night. She may be able to tell me something."

"You leave Alice alone."

"I'll treat her gently. Where do you live?"

"I don't want my little sister dragged into this filthy mess."

"All I want to know is who Ginnie paired off with."

"I'll ask Alice. I'll tell you."

"Come on, Miss Brocco, we're wasting time. I don't need your permission to talk to your sister, after all. I can get the address out of the phone book if I have to."

She flared up and then flared down.

"You win. We live on Orlando Street, 224. That's on the other side of town. You will be nice to Alice, won't you? She's bothered enough as it is about Ginnie's death."

"She really was a friend of Ginnie's, then?"

"Yes. I tried to break it up. But you know how kids are—two motherless girls, they stick together. I tried to be like a mother to Alice."

"What happened to your own mother?"

"Father—I mean, she died." A greenish pallor invaded her face and turned it to old bronze. "Please. I don't want to talk about it. I was only a kid when she died."

She went back to her muttering radios. She was quite a woman, I thought as I drove away. Nubile but unmarried, probably full of untapped Mediterranean passions. If she worked an eight-hour shift and started at eight, she'd be getting off about four.

It wasn't a large town, and it wasn't far across it. The highway doubled as its main street. I passed the Union High School. On the green playing field beside it a lot of kids in mortarboards and gowns were rehearsing their graduation exercises. A kind of pall seemed to hang over the field. Perhaps it was in my mind.

Farther along the street I passed Green's Highway Restaurant. A dozen cars stood in its parking space. A couple of white-uniformed waitresses were scooting around behind the plate-glass windows.

Orlando Street was a lower-middle-class residential street bisected by the highway. Jacaranda trees bloomed like low small purple clouds among its stucco and frame cottages. Fallen purple petals carpeted the narrow lawn in front of the Brocco house.

A thin, dark man, wiry under his T-shirt, was washing a small red Fiat in the driveway beside the front porch. He must have been over fifty, but his long hair was as black as an Indian's. His Sicilian nose was humped in the middle by an old break.

"Mr. Brocco?"

"That's me."

"Is your daughter Alice home?"

"She's home."

"I'd like to speak to her."

He turned off his hose, pointing its dripping nozzle at me like a gun. "You're a little old for her, ain't you?"

"I'm a detective investigating the death of Ginnie Green."

"Alice don't know nothing about that."

"I've just been talking to your older daughter at the Highway Patrol office. She thinks Alice may know something."

He shifted on his feet. "Well, if Anita says it's all right."

"It's okay, Dad," a girl said from the front door. "Anita just called me on the telephone. Come in, Mister—Archer isn't it?"

"Archer."

She opened the screen door for me. It opened directly into a small square living room containing worn green frieze furniture and a television set which the girl switched off. She was a handsome, serious-looking girl, a younger version of her sister with ten years and ten pounds subtracted and a pony tail added. She sat down gravely on the edge of the chair, waving her hand at the chesterfield. Her movements were languid. There were blue depressions under her eyes. Her face was sallow.

"What kind of questions do you want to ask me? My sister didn't say."

"Who was Ginnie with last night?"

"Nobody. I mean, she was with me. She didn't make out with any of the boys." She glanced from me to the blind television set, as if she felt caught between. "It said on the television that she was with a man, that there was medical evidence to prove it. But I didn't see her with no man. Any man."

"Did Ginnie go with men?"

She shook her head. Her pony tail switched and hung limp. She was close to tears.

"You told Anita she did."

"I did not!"

"Your sister wouldn't lie. You passed on a rumor to her—a high school rumor that Ginnie had had something to do with one man in particular."

The girl was watching my face in fascination. Her eyes were like a bird's, bright and shallow and fearful.

"Was the rumor true?"

She shrugged her thin shoulders. "How would I know?"

"You were good friends with Ginnie."

"Yes. I was." Her voice broke on the past tense. "She was a real nice kid, even if she was kind of boy crazy."

"She was boy crazy, but she didn't make out with any of the boys last night."

"Not while I was there."

"Did she make out with Mr. Connor?"

"No. He wasn't there. He said he was going home. He lives up the beach."

"What did Ginnie do?"

"I don't know. I didn't notice."

"You said she was with you. Was she with you all evening?"

"Yes." Her face was agonized. "I mean no."

"Did Ginnie go away, too?"

She nodded.

"In the same direction Mr. Connor took? The direction of his house?"

Her head moved almost imperceptibly downward.

"What time was that, Alice?"

"About eleven o'clock, I guess."

"And Ginnie never came back from Mr. Connor's house?"

"I don't know. I don't know for certain that she went there."

"But Ginnie and Mr. Connor were good friends?"

"I guess so."

"How good? Like a boy friend and a girl friend?"

She sat mute, her birdlike stare unblinking.

"Tell me, Alice."

"Afraid of Mr. Connor?"

"No. Not him."

"Has someone threatened you—told you not to talk?"

Her head moved in another barely perceptible nod.

"Who threatened you, Alice? You'd better tell me for your own protection. Whoever did threaten you is probably a murderer."

She burst into frantic tears. Brocco came to the door.

"What goes on in here?"

"Your daughter is upset. I'm sorry."

"Yeah, and I know who upset her. You better get out of here or you'll be sorrier."

He opened the screen door and held it open, his head poised like a dark and broken ax. I went out past him. He spat after me. The Broccos were a very emotional family.

I started back toward Connor's beach house on the south side of town but ran into a diversion on the way. Green's car was parked in the lot beside his restaurant. I went in.

The place smelled of grease. It was almost full of late Sunday lunchers seated in booths and at the U-shaped breakfast bar in the middle. Green himself was sitting on a stool behind the cash register counting money. He was counting it as if his life and his hope of heaven depended on the colored paper in his hands.

He looked up, smiling loosely and vaguely. "Yes, sir?" Then he recognized me. His face went through a quick series of transformations and settled for a kind of boozy shame. "I know I shouldn't be here working on a day like this. But it keeps my mind off my troubles. Besides, they steal you blind if you don't watch 'em. And I'll be needing the money."

"What for, Mr. Green?"

"The trial." He spoke the word as if it gave him a bitter satisfaction.

"Whose trial?"

"Mine. I told the sheriff what the old guy said. And what I did. I know what I did. I shot him down like a dog, and I had no right to. I was crazy with my sorrow, you might say."

He was less crazy now. The shame in his eyes was clearing. But the sorrow was still there in their depths, like stone at the bottom of a well.

"I'm glad you told the truth, Mr. Green."

"So am I. It doesn't help him, and it doesn't bring Ginnie back. But at least I can live with myself."

"Speaking of Ginnie," I said. "Was she seeing quite a lot of Frank Connor?"

"Yeah. I guess you could say so. He came over to help her with her studies quite a few times. At the house, and at the library. He didn't charge me any tuition, either."

"That was nice of him. Was Ginnie fond of Connor?"

"Sure she was. She thought very highly of Mr. Connor."

"Was she in love with him?"

"In love? Hell, I never thought of anything like that. Why?"

"Did she have dates with Connor?"

"Not to my knowledge," he said. "If she did, she must done it behind my back." His eyes narrowed to two red swollen slits. "You think Frank Connor had something to do with her death?"

"It's a possibility. Don't go into a sweat now. You know where that gets you."

"Don't worry. But what about this Connor? Did you get something on him? I thought he was acting queer last night."

"Queer in what way?"

"Well, he was pretty tight when he came to the house. I gave him a stiff snort, and that straightened him out for a while. But later on, down on the beach, he got almost hysterical. He was running around like a rooster with his head chopped off."

"Is he a heavy drinker?"

"I wouldn't know. I never saw him drink before last night at my house." Green narrowed his eyes. "But he tossed down a triple bourbon like it was water. And remember this morning, he offered us a drink on the beach. A drink in the morning, that isn't the usual thing, especially for a high school teacher."

"I noticed that."

"What else have you been noticing?"

"We won't go into it now," I said. "I don't want to ruin a man unless and until I'm sure he's got it coming."

He sat on his stool with his head down. Thought moved murkily under his knitted brows. His glance fell on the money in his hands. He was counting tens.

"Listen, Mr. Archer. You're working on this case on your own, aren't you? For free?"

"So far."

"So go to work for me. Nail Connor for me, and I'll pay you whatever you ask."

"Not so fast," I said. "We don't know that Connor is guilty. There are other possibilities."

"Such as?"

"If I tell you, can I trust you not to go on a shooting spree?"

"Don't worry," he repeated. "I've had that."

"Where's your revolver?"

"I turned it in to Sheriff Pearsall. He asked for it."

We were interrupted by a family group getting up from one of the booths. They gave Green their money and their sympathy. When they were out of hearing, I said:

"You mentioned that your daughter worked here in the restaurant for a while. Was Al Brocco working here at the same time?"

"Yeah. He's been my night cook for six-seven years. Al is a darned good cook. He trained as a chef on the Italian line." His slow mind, punchy with grief, did a double-take. "You wouldn't be saying that he messed around with Ginnie?"

"I'm asking you."

"Shucks, Al is old enough to be her father. He's all wrapped up in his own girls, Anita in particular. He worships the ground she walks on. She's the mainspring of that family."

"How did he get on with Ginnie?"

"Very well. They kidded back and forth. She was the only one who could ever make him smile. Al is a sad man, you know. He had a tragedy in his life."

"His wife's death?"

"It was worse than that," Green said. "Al Brocco killed his wife with his own hand. He caught her with another man and put a knife in her."

"And he's walking around loose?"

"The other man was a Mex," Green said in an explanatory way. "A wetback. He couldn't even talk the English language. The town hardly blamed Al, the jury gave him manslaughter. But when he got out of the pen, the people at the Pink Flamingo wouldn't give him his old job back—he used to be chef there. So I took him on. I felt sorry for his girls, I guess, and Al's been a good worker. A man doesn't do a thing like that twice, you know."

He did another slow mental double-take. His mouth hung open. I could see the gold in its corners.

"Let's hope not."

"Listen here," he said. "You go to work for me, eh? You nail the guy, whoever he is. I'll pay you. I'll pay you now. How much do you want?"

I took a hundred dollars of his money and left him trying to comfort himself with the rest of it. The smell of grease stayed in my nostrils.

Connor's house clung to the edge of a low bluff about halfway between the HP station and the mouth of the canyon where the thing had begun: a semi-cantilevered redwood cottage with a closed double garage fronting the highway. From the grapestake-fenced patio in the angle between the garage and the front door a flight of wooden steps climbed to the flat roof which was railed as a sun deck. A second set of steps descended the fifteen or twenty feet to the beach.

I tripped on a pair of garden shears crossing the patio to the garage window. I peered into the interior twilight. Two things inside interested me: a dismasted flattie sitting on a trailer, and a car. The sailboat interested me because its cordage resembled the white rope that had strangled Ginnie. The car interested me because it was an imported model, a low-slung Triumph two-seater.

I was planning to have a closer look at it when a woman's voice screeked overhead like a gull's:

"What do you think you're doing?"

Mrs. Connor was leaning over the railing on the roof. Her hair was in curlers. She looked like a blonde Gorgon. I smiled up at her, the way that Greek whose name I don't remember must have smiled.

"Your husband invited me for a drink, remember? I don't know whether he gave me a rain check or not."

"He did not! Go away! My husband is sleeping!"

"Ssh. You'll wake him up. You'll wake up the people in Forest Lawn."

She put her hand to her mouth. From the expression on her face she seemed to be biting her hand. She disappeared for a moment, and then came down the steps with a multi-colored silk scarf over her curlers. The rest of her was sheathed in a white satin bathing suit. Against it her flesh looked like brown wood.

"You get out of here," she said. "Or I shall call the police."

"Fine. Call them. I've got nothing to hide."

"Are you implying that we have?"

"We'll see. Why did you leave your husband?"

"That's none of your business."

"I'm making it my business, Mrs. Connor. I'm a detective investigating the murder of Ginnie Green. Did you leave Frank on account of Ginnie Green?"

"No. No! I wasn't even aware—" Her hand went to her mouth again. She chewed on it some more.

"You weren't aware that Frank was having an affair with Ginnie Green?"

"He wasn't."

"So you say. Others say different."

"What others? Anita Brocco? You can't believe anything *that* woman says. Why, her own father is a murderer, everybody in town knows that."

"Your own husband may be another, Mrs. Connor. You might as well come clean with me."

"But I have nothing to tell you."

"You can tell me why you left him."

"That is a private matter, between Frank and me. It has nothing to do with anybody but us." She was calming down, setting her moral forces in a stubborn, defensive posture.

"There's usually only the one reason."

"I had my reasons. I said they were none of your business. I chose for reasons of my own to spend a month with my parents in Long Beach."

"When did you come back?"

"This morning."

"Frank called me. He said he needed me." She touched her thin breast absently, pathetically, as if perhaps she hadn't been much needed in the past.

"Needed you for what?"

"As his wife," she said. "He said there might be tr—" Her hand went to her mouth again. She said around it: "Trouble."

"Did he name the kind of trouble?"

"No."

"What time did he call you?"

"Very early, around seven o'clock."

"That was more than an hour before I found Ginnie's body."

"He knew she was missing. He spent the whole night looking for her."

"Why would he do that, Mrs. Connor?"

"She was his student. He was fond of her. Besides, he was more or less responsible for her."

"Responsible for her death?"

"How dare you say a thing like that!"

"If he dared to do it, I can dare to say it."

"He didn't!" she cried. "Frank is a good man. He may have his faults, but he wouldn't kill anyone. I know him."

"What are his faults?"

"We won't discuss them."

"Then may I have a look in your garage?"

"What for? What are you looking for?"

"I'll know when I find it." I turned toward the garage door.

"You mustn't go in there," she said intensely. "Not without Frank's permission."

"Wake him up and we'll get his permission."

"I will not. He got no sleep last night."

"Then I'll just have a look without his permission."

"I'll kill you if you go in there."

She picked up the garden shears and brandished them at me—a sick-looking lioness defending her overgrown cub. The cub himself opened the front door of the cottage. He slouched in the doorway groggily, naked except for white shorts.

"What goes on, Stella?"

"This man has been making the most horrible accusations."

His blurred glance wavered between us and focused on her. "What did he say?"

"I won't repeat it."

"I will, Mr. Connor. I think you were Ginnie Green's lover, if that's the word. I think she followed you to this house last night, around midnight. I think she left it with a rope around her neck."

Connor's head jerked. He started to make a move in my direction. Something inhibited it, like an invisible leash. His body slanted toward me, static, all the muscles taut. It resembled an anatomy specimen with the skin off. Even his face seemed bone and teeth.

I hoped he'd swing on me and let me hit him. He didn't. Stella Connor dropped the garden shears. They made a noise like the dull clank of doom.

"Aren't you going to deny it, Frank?"

"I didn't kill her. I swear I didn't. I admit that we—that we were together last night, Ginnie and I."

"Ginnie and I?" the woman repeated incredulously.

His head hung down. "I'm sorry, Stella. I didn't want to hurt you more than I have already. But it has to come out. I took up with the girl after you left. I was lonely and feeling sorry for myself. Ginnie kept hanging around. One night I drank too much and let it happen. It happened more than once. I was so flattered that a pretty young girl—"

"You fool!" she said in a deep, harsh voice.

"Yes, I'm a moral fool. That's no surprise to you, is it?"

"I thought you respected your pupils, at least. You mean to say you brought her into our own house, into our own bed?"

"You'd left. It wasn't ours any more. Besides, she came of her own accord. She wanted to come. She loved me."

She said with grinding contempt: "You poor, groveling ninny. And to think you had the gall to ask me to come back here, to make you look respectable."

I cut in between them. "Was she here last night, Connor?"

"She was here. I didn't invite her. I wanted her to come, but I dreaded it, too. I knew that I was taking an awful chance. I drank quite a bit to numb my conscience—"

"What conscience?" Stella Connor said.

"I have a conscience," he said without looking at her. "You don't know the hell I've been going through. After she came, after it happened last night, I drank myself unconscious."

"Do you mean after you killed her?" I said.

"I didn't kill her. When I passed out, she was perfectly all right. She was sitting up drinking a cup of instant coffee. The next thing I knew, hours later, her father was on the telephone and she was gone."

"Are you trying to pull the old blackout alibi? You'll have to do better than that."

"I can't. It's the truth."

"Let me into your garage."

He seemed almost glad to be given an order, a chance for some activity. The garage wasn't locked. He raised the overhead door and let the daylight into the interior. It smelled of paint. There were empty cans of marine paint on a bench beside the sailboat. Its hull gleamed virgin white.

"I painted my flattie last week," he said inconsequentially.

"You do a lot of sailing?"

"I used to. Not much lately."

"No," his wife said from the doorway. "Frank changed his hobby to women. Wine and women."

"Lay off, eh?" His voice was pleading.

She looked at him from a great and stony silence.

I walked around the boat, examining the cordage. The starboard jib line had been sheared off short. Comparing it with the port line, I found that the missing piece was approximately a yard long. That was the length of the piece of white rope that I was interested in.

"Hey!" Connor grabbed the end of the cut line. He fingered it as if it was a wound in his own flesh. "Who's been messing with my lines? Did you cut it, Stella?"

"I never go near your blessed boat," she said.

"I can tell you where the rest of that line is, Connor. A line of similar length and color and thickness was wrapped around Ginnie Green's neck when I found her."

"Surely you don't believe I put it there?"

I tried to, but I couldn't. Small-boat sailers don't cut their jib lines, even when they're contemplating murder. And while Connor was clearly no genius, he was smart enough to have known that the line could easily be traced to him. Perhaps someone else had been equally smart.

I turned to Mrs. Connor. She was standing in the doorway with her legs apart. Her body was almost black against the daylight. Her eyes were hooded by the scarf on her head.

"What time did you get home, Mrs. Connor?"

"About ten o'clock this morning. I took a bus as soon as my husband called. But I'm in no position to give him an alibi."

"An alibi wasn't what I had in mind. I suggest another possibility, that you came home twice. You came home unexpectedly last night, saw the girl in the house with your husband, waited in the dark till the girl came out, waited with a piece of rope in your hands—a piece of rope you'd cut from your husband's boat in the hope of getting him punished for what he'd done to you. But the picture doesn't fit the frame, Mrs. Connor. A sailor like your husband wouldn't cut a piece of line from his own boat. And even in the heat of murder he wouldn't tie a granny's knot. His fingers would automatically tie a reef knot. That isn't true of a woman's fingers."

She held herself upright with one long, rigid arm against the doorframe.

"I wouldn't do anything like that. I wouldn't do that to Frank."

"Maybe you wouldn't in daylight, Mrs. Connor. Things have different shapes at midnight."

"And hell hath no fury like a woman scorned? Is that what you're thinking? You're wrong. I wasn't here last night. I was in bed in my father's house in Long Beach. I didn't even know about that girl and Frank."

"Then why did you leave him?"

"He was in love with another woman. He wanted to divorce me and marry her. But he was afraid—afraid that it would affect his position in town. He told me on the phone this morning that it was all over with the other woman. So I agreed to come back to him." Her arm dropped to her side.

"He said that it was all over with Ginnie?"

Possibilities were racing through my mind. There was the possibility that Connor had been playing reverse English, deliberately and clumsily framing himself in order to be cleared. But that was out of far left field.

"Not Ginnie," his wife said. "The other woman was Anita Brocco. He met her last spring in the course of work and fell in love—what *he* calls love. My husband is a foolish, fickle man."

"Please, Stella. I said it was all over between me and Anita, and it is."

She turned on him in quiet savagery. "What does it matter now? If it isn't one girl it's another. Any kind of female flesh will do to poultice your sick little ego."

Her cruelty struck inward and hurt her. She stretched out her hand toward him. Suddenly her eyes were blind with tears.

"Any flesh but mine, Frank," she said brokenly.

Connor paid no attention to his wife.

He said to me in a hushed voice:

"My God, I never thought. I noticed her car last night when I was walking home along the beach."

"Whose car?"

"Anita's red Fiat. It was parked at the viewpoint a few hundred yards from here." He gestured vaguely toward town. "Later, when Ginnie was with me, I thought I heard someone in the garage. But I was too drunk to make a search." His eyes burned into mine. "You say a woman tied that knot?"

"All we can do is ask her."

We started toward my car together. His wife called after him:

"Don't go, Frank. Let him handle it."

He hesitated, a weak man caught between opposing forces.

"I need you," she said. "We need each other."

I pushed him in her direction.

It was nearly four when I got to the HP station. The patrol cars had gathered like homing pigeons for the change in shift. Their uniformed drivers were talking and laughing inside.

Anita Brocco wasn't among them. A male dispatcher, a fat-faced man with pimples, had taken her place behind the counter.

"Where's Miss Brocco?" I asked.

"In the ladies' room. Her father is coming to pick her up any minute."

She came out wearing lipstick and a light beige coat. Her face turned beige when she saw my face. She came toward me in slow motion, leaned with both hands flat on the counter. Her lipstick looked like fresh blood on a corpse.

"You're a handsome woman, Anita. Too bad about you."

"Too bad." It was half a statement and half a question. She looked down at her hands.

"Your fingernails are clean now. They were dirty this morning. You were digging in the dirt last night, weren't you?"

"No."

"You were, though. You saw then together and you couldn't stand it. You waited in ambush with a rope, and put it around her neck. Around your own neck, too."

She touched her neck. The talk and laughter had subsided around us. I could hear the tick of the clock again, and the muttering signals coming in from inner space.

"What did you use to cut the rope with, Anita? The garden shears?"

Her red mouth groped for words and found them. "I was crazy about him. She took him away. It was all over before it started. I didn't know what to do with myself. I wanted him to suffer."

"He suffering. He's going to suffer more."

"He deserved to. He was the only man—" She shrugged in a twisted way and looked down at her breast. "I didn't want to kill her, but when I saw them together—I saw them through the window. I saw her take off her clothes and put them on. Then I thought of the night my father—when he—when there was all the blood in Mother's bed. I had to wash it out of the sheets."

The men around me were murmuring. One of them, a sergeant, raised his voice.

"Did you kill Ginnie Green?"

"Yes."

"Are you ready to make a statement?" I said.

"Yes. I'll talk to Sheriff Pearsall. I don't want to talk here, in front of my friends." She looked around doubtfully.

"I'll take you downtown."

"Wait a minute." She glanced once more at her empty hands. "I left my purse in the—in the back room. I'll go and get it."

She crossed the office like a zombie, opened a plain door, closed it behind her. She didn't come out. After a while we broke the lock and went in after her.

Her body was cramped on the narrow floor. The ivory-handled nail file lay by her right hand. There were bloody holes in her white blouse and in the white breast under it. One of them had gone as deep as her heart.

Later Al Brocco drove up in her red Fiat and came into the station.

"I'm a little late," he said to the room in general. "Anita wanted me to give her car a good cleaning. Where is she, anyway?"

The sergeant cleared his throat to answer Brocco.

All us poor creatures, as the old man of the mountain had said that morning.

ELLERY QUEEN *was the name used by two cousins, Frederic Dannay (Daniel Nathan, 1905–1982) and Manfred B. Lee (Manford Lepofsky, 1905–1971), for their mystery fiction. However, in one of the most inspired ideas in publishing, they also used the Queen name for their most famous series detective. Ellery the creation and Ellery the creator both prospered, and the rest is history. Although their novels and stories were great successes, both commercially and critically, it should not be forgotten that they founded the field's most successful magazine, the one that carries their created name, as well as the Mystery Writers of America. Everyone who loves crime fiction is deeply in their debt.*

"Abraham Lincoln's Clue" is an ingeniously clever story that mixes American history with a wonderful puzzle.

Abraham Lincoln's Clue
BY ELLERY QUEEN

The case began on the outskirts of an upstate-New York city with the dreadful name of Eulalia, behind the flaking shutters of a fat and curlicued house with architectural dandruff, recalling for all the world some blowsy ex-Bloomer Girl from the Gay Nineties of its origin.

The owner, a formerly wealthy man named DiCampo, possessed a grandeur not shared by his property, although it was no less fallen into ruin. His falcon's face, more Florentine then Victorian, was—like the house—ravaged by time and the inclemencies of fortune; but haughtily so, and indeed DiCampo wore his scurfy purple velvet house jacket like the prince he was entitled to call himself, but did not. He was proud, and stubborn, and useless; and he had a lovely daughter named Bianca, who taught at a Eulalia grade school and, through marvels of economy, supported them both.

How Lorenzo San Marco Borghese-Ruffo DiCampo came to this decayed estate is no concern of ours. The presence there this day of a man named Harbidger and a man named Tungston, however, is to the point: they had come, Harbidger from Chicago, Tungston from Philadelphia, to buy something each wanted very much, and DiCampo had summoned them in order to sell it. The two visitors were collectors, Harbidger's passion being Lincoln, Tungston's Poe.

The Lincoln collector, an elderly man who looked like a migrant fruit picker, had plucked his fruits well: Harbidger was worth about $40,000,000, every dollar of which was at the beck of his mania for Lincolniana. Tungston, who was almost as rich, had the aging body of a poet and the eyes of a starving panther, armament that had served him well in the wars of Poeana.

"I must say, Mr. DiCampo," remarked Harbidger, "that your letter surprised me." He paused to savor the wine his host had poured from an ancient and honorable bottle (DiCampo had filled it with California claret before their arrival). "May I ask what has finally induced you to offer the book and document for sale?"

"To quote Lincoln in another context, Mr. Harbidger," said Di-Campo with a shrug of his wasted shoulders, " 'the dogmas of the quiet past are inadequate to the stormy present.' In short, a hungry man sells his blood."

"Only if it's of the right type," said old Tungston, unmoved. "You've made that book and document less accessible to collectors and historians, DiCampo, than the gold in Fort Knox. Have you got them here? I'd like to examine them."

"No other hand will ever touch them except by right of ownership." Lorenzo DiCampo replied bitterly. He had taken a miser's glee in his lucky finds, vowing never to part with them; now forced by his need to sell them, he was like a suspicion-caked old prospector who, stumbling at last on pay dirt, draws cryptic maps to keep the world from stealing the secret of its location. "As I informed you gentlemen, I represent the book as bearing the signatures of Poe and Lincoln, and the document as being in Lincoln's hand; I am offering them with the customary proviso that they are returnable if they should prove to be not as represented; and if this does not satisfy you," and the old prince actually rose, "let us terminate our business here and now."

"Sit down, sit down, Mr. DiCampo," Harbidger said.

"No one is questioning your integrity," snapped old Tungston. "It's just that I'm not used to buying sight unseen. If there's a money-back guarantee, we'll do it your way."

Lorenzo DiCampo reseated himself stiffly. "Very well, gentlemen. Then I take it you are both prepared to buy?"

"Oh, yes!" said Harbidger. "What is your price?"

"Oh, no," said DiCampo. "What is your bid?"

The Lincoln collector cleared his throat, which was full of slaver. "If the book and document are as represented, Mr. DiCampo, you might hope to get from a dealer or realize at auction—oh—$50,000. I offer you $55,000."

"$56,000," said Tungston.

"$57,000," said Harbidger.

"$58,000," said Tungston.

"$59,000," said Harbidger.

Tungston showed his fangs. "$60,000," he said.

Harbidger fell silent, and DiCampo waited. He did not expect miracles. To these men, five times $60,000 was of less moment than the undistinguished wine they were smacking their lips over; but they were veterans of many a hard auction-room campaign, and a collector's victory tastes very nearly as sweet for the price as for the prize.

So the impoverished prince was not surprised when the Lincoln collector suddenly said, "Would you be good enough to allow Mr. Tungston and me to talk privately for a moment?"

DiCampo rose and strolled out of the room, to gaze somberly through a cracked window at the jungle growth that had once been his Italian formal gardens.

It was the Poe collector who summoned him back. "Harbidger has convinced me that for the two of us to try to outbid each other would simply run the price up out of all reason. We're going to make you a sporting proposition."

"I've proposed to Mr. Tungston, and he has agreed," nodded Harbidger, "that our bid for the book and document be $65,000. Each of us is prepared to pay that sum, and not a penny more."

"So that is how the screws are turned," said DiCampo, smiling. "But I do not understand. If each of you makes the identical bid, which of you gets the book and document?"

"Ah," grinned the Poe man, "that's where the sporting proposition comes in."

"You see, Mr. DiCampo," said the Lincoln man, "we are going to leave that decision to you."

Even the old prince, who had seen more than his share of the astonishing, was astonished. He looked at the two rich men really for the first time. "I must confess," he murmured, "that your compact is an amusement. Permit me?" He sank into thought while the two collectors sat expectantly. When the old man looked up he was smiling like a fox. "The very thing, gentlemen! From the typewritten copies of the document I sent you, you both know that Lincoln himself left a clue to a theoretical hiding place for the book which he never explained. Some time ago I arrived at a possible solution to the President's little mystery. I propose to hide the book and document in accordance with it."

"You mean whichever of us figures out your interpretation of the Lincoln clue and finds the book and document where you will hide them, Mr. DiCampo, gets both for the agreed price?"

"That is it exactly."

The Lincoln collector looked dubious. "I don't know . . ."

"Oh, come, Harbidger," said Tungston, eyes glittering. "A deal is a deal. We accept, DiCampo! Now what?"

"You gentlemen will of course have to give me a little time. Shall we say three days?"

Ellery let himself into the Queen apartment, tossed his suitcase aside, and set about opening windows. He had been out of town for a week on a case, and Inspector Queen was in Atlantic City attending a police convention.

Breathable air having been restored, Ellery sat down to the week's accumulation of mail. One envelope made him pause. It had come by air-mail special delivery, it was postmarked four days earlier, and in the lower left corner, in red, flamed the word URGENT. The printed return address on the flap said; *L.S.M.B.-R. DiCampo, Post Office Box 69, Southern District, Eulalia, N.Y.* The initials of the name had been crossed out and "Bianca" written above them.

The enclosure, in a large agitated female hand on inexpensive notepaper, said:

> Dear Mr. Queen,
> The most important detective book in the world has disappeared. Will you please find it for me?
> Phone me on arrival at the Eulalia RR station or airport and I will pick you up.
>
> > Bianca DiCampo

A yellow envelope then caught his eye. It was a telegram, dated the previous day:

WHY HAVE I NOT HEARD FROM YOU STOP AM IN DESPERATE
NEED YOUR SERVICES

BIANCA DICAMPO

He had no sooner finished reading the telegram than the telephone on his desk trilled. It was a long-distance call.

"Mr. Queen?" throbbed a contralto voice. "Thank heaven I've finally got through to you! I've been calling all day—"

"I've been away," said Ellery, "and you would be Miss Bianca Di-Campo of Eulalia. In two words, Miss DiCampo: Why me?"

"In two words, Mr. Queen: Abraham Lincoln."

Ellery was startled. "You plead a persuasive case," he chuckled. "It's true, I'm an incurable Lincoln addict. How did you find out? Well, never mind. Your letter refers to a book, Miss DiCampo. Which book?"

The husky voice told him, and certain other provocative things as well. "So will you come, Mr. Queen?"

"Tonight if I could! Suppose I drive up first thing in the morning. I ought to make Eulalia by noon. Harbidger and Tungston are still around, I take it?"

"Oh, yes. They're staying at a motel downtown."

"Would you ask them to be there?"

The moment he hung up Ellery leaped to his bookshelves. He snatched out his volume of *Murder for Pleasure,* the historical work on detective stories by his good friend Howard Haycraft, and found what he was looking for on page 26:

And . . . young William Dean Howells thought it significant praise to assert of a nominee for President of the United States:

> The bent of his mind is mathematical and metaphysical, and he is therefore pleased with the absolute and logical method of Poe's tales and sketches, in which the problem of mystery is given, and wrought out into everyday facts by processes of cunning analysis. It is said that he suffers no year to pass without a perusal of this author.

Abraham Lincoln subsequently confirmed this statement, which appeared in his little-known "campaign biography" by Howells in 1860 . . . The instance is chiefly notable, of course, for its revelation of a little-suspected affinity between two great Americans . . .

Very early the next morning Ellery gathered some papers from his files, stuffed them into his briefcase, scribbled a note for his father, and ran for his car, Eulalia-bound.

He was enchanted by the DiCampo house, which looked like something out of Poe by Charles Addams; and, for other reasons, by Bianca, who turned out to be a genetic product supreme of northern Italy, with titian hair and Mediterranean blue eyes and a figure that needed only some solid steaks to qualify her for Miss Universe competition. Also, she was in deep mourning; so her conquest of the Queen heart was immediate and complete.

"He died of a cerebral hemorrhage, Mr. Queen," Bianca said, dabbing at her absurd little nose. "In the middle of the second night after his session with Mr. Harbidger and Mr. Tungston."

So Lorenzo San Marco Borghese-Ruffo DiCampo was unexpectedly dead, bequeathing the lovely Bianca near-destitution and a mystery.

"The only things of value father really left me are that book and the Lincoln document. The $65,000 they now represent would pay off father's debts and give me a fresh start. But I can't find them, Mr. Queen, and neither can Mr. Harbidger and Mr. Tungston—who'll be here soon, by the way. Father hid the two things, as he told them he would; but where? We've ransacked the place."

"Tell me more about the book, Miss DiCampo."

"As I said over the phone, it's called *The Gift: 1845*. The Christmas annual that contained the earliest appearance of Edgar Allan Poe's *The Purloined Letter.*"

"Published in Philadelphia by Carey & Hart? Bound in red?" At Bianca's nod Ellery said, "You understand that an ordinary copy of *The Gift: 1845* isn't worth more than about $50. What makes your father's copy unique is that double autograph you mentioned."

"That's what he said, Mr. Queen. I wish I had the book here to show you—that beautifully handwritten *Edgar Allan Poe* on the flyleaf, and under Poe's signature the signature *Abraham Lincoln.*"

"Poe's own copy, once owned, signed, and read by Lincoln," Ellery said slowly. "Yes, that would be a collector's item for the ages. By the way, Miss DiCampo, what's the story behind the other piece—the Lincoln document?"

Bianca told him what her father had told her.

One morning in the spring of 1865, Abraham Lincoln opened the rosewood door of his bedroom in the southwest corner of the second floor of the White House and stepped out into the red-carpeted hall at the unusually late hour—for him—of 7:00 A.M.; he was more accustomed to beginning his work day at six.

But (as Lorenzo DiCampo had reconstructed events) Mr. Lincoln that morning had lingered in his bedchamber. He had awakened at his usual hour but, instead of leaving immediately on dressing for his office, he had pulled one of the cane chairs over to the round table, with its gas-fed reading lamp, and sat down to reread Poe's *The Purloined Letter* in his copy of the 1845 annual; it was a dreary morning, and the natural light was poor. The President was alone; the folding doors to Mrs. Lincoln's bedroom remained closed.

Impressed as always with Poe's tale, Mr. Lincoln on this occasion was struck by a whimsical thought; and, apparently finding no paper handy, he took an envelope from his pocket, discarded its enclosure, slit the two short edges so that the envelope opened out into a single sheet, and began to write on the blank side.

"Describe it to me, please."

"It's a long envelope, one that must have contained a bulky letter. It is addressed to the White House, but there is no return address, and father was never able to identify the sender from the handwriting. We do know that the letter came through the regular mails, because there are two Lincoln stamps on it, lightly but unmistakably canceled."

"May I see your father's transcript of what Lincoln wrote out that morning on the inside of the envelope?"

Bianca handed him a typewritten copy and, in spite of himself, Ellery felt goose flesh rise as he read:

Apr. 14, 1865

Mr. Poe's The Purloined Letter is a work of singular originality. Its simplicity is a master-stroke of cunning, which never fails to arouse my wonder.

Reading the tale over this morning has given me a "notion." Suppose I wished to hide a book, this very book, perhaps? Where best to do so? Well, as Mr. Poe in his tale hid a letter *among letters,* might not a book be hidden *among books?* Why, if this very copy of the tale were to be deposited in a library and on purpose not recorded—would not the Library of Congress make a prime depository!—well might it repose there, undiscovered, for a generation.

On the other hand, let us regard Mr. Poe's "notion" turn-about: Suppose the book were to be placed, not amongst other

books, but *where no book would reasonably be expected?* (I
may follow the example of Mr. Poe, and, myself, compose a
tale of "ratiocination"!)

The "notion" beguiles me, it is nearly seven o'clock. Later
to-day, if the vultures and my appointments leave me a few
moments of leisure, I may write further of my imagined hiding-place.

In self-reminder: The hiding-place of the book is in 30d,
which

Ellery looked up. "The document ends there?"

"Father said that Mr. Lincoln must have glanced again at his watch,
and shamefacedly jumped up to go to his office, leaving the sentence
unfinished. Evidently he never found the time to get back to it."

Ellery brooded. Evidently indeed. From the moment when Abraham
Lincoln stepped out of his bedroom that Good Friday morning, finger-
ing his thick gold watch on its vest chain, to bid the still-unrelieved
night guard his customary courteous "Good morning" and make for
his office at the other end of the hall, his day was spoken for. The usual
patient push through the clutching crowd of favor-seekers, many of
whom had bedded down all night on the hall carpet; sanctuary in his
sprawling office, where he read official correspondence by 8:00 A.M.
having breakfast with his family—Mrs. Lincoln chattering away about
plans for the evening, 12-year-old Tad of the cleft palate lisping a
complaint that "nobody asked me to go," and young Robert Lincoln,
just returned from duty, bubbling with stories about his hero Ulysses
Grant and the last days of the war; then back to the presidential office
to look over the morning newspapers (which Lincoln had once remarked he "never" read, but these were happy days, with good news
everywhere), sign two documents, and signal the soldier at the door to
admit the morning's first caller, Speaker of the House Schuyler Colfax
(who was angling for a Cabinet post and had to be tactfully handled);
and so on throughout the day—the historic Cabinet meeting at 11:00
A.M., attended by General Grant himself, that stretched well into the
afternoon; a hurried lunch at almost half-past two with Mrs. Lincoln
(had this 45-pounds-underweight man eaten his usual midday meal of
a biscuit, a glass of milk, and an apple?); more visitors to see in his
office (including the unscheduled Mrs. Nancy Bushrod, escaped slave
and wife of an escaped slave and mother of three small children, weeping that Tom, a soldier in the Army of the Potomac, was no longer

getting his pay: "You are entitled to your husband's pay. Come this time tomorrow," and the tall President escorted her to the door, bowing her out "like I was a natural-born lady"); the late afternoon drive in the barouche to the Navy Yard and back with Mrs. Lincoln; more work, more visitors, into the evening . . . until finally, at five minutes past 8:00 P.M., Abraham Lincoln stepped into the White House formal coach after his wife, waved, and sank back to be driven off to see a play he did not much want to see, *Our American Cousin,* at Ford's Theatre . . .

Ellery mused over that black day in silence. And, like a relative hanging on the specialist's yet undelivered diagnosis, Bianca DiCampo sat watching him with anxiety.

Harbidger and Tungston arrived in a taxi to greet Ellery with the fervor of castaways grasping at a smudge of smoke on the horizon.

"As I understand it, gentlemen," Ellery said when he had calmed them down, "neither of you has been able to solve Mr. DiCampo's interpretation of the Lincoln clue. If I succeed in finding the book and paper where DiCampo hid them, which of you gets them?"

"We intend to split the $65,000 payments to Miss DiCampo," said Harbidger, "and take joint ownership of the two pieces."

"An arrangement," growled old Tungston, "I'm against on principle, in practice, and by plain horse sense."

"So am I," sighed the Lincoln collector, "but what else can we do?"

"Well," and the Poe man regarded Bianca DiCampo with the icy intimacy of the cat that long ago marked the bird as its prey, "Miss DiCampo, who now owns the two pieces, is quite free to renegotiate a sale on her own terms."

"Miss DiCampo," said Miss DiCampo, giving Tungston stare for stare, "considers herself bound by her father's wishes. His terms stand."

"In all likelihood, then," said the other millionaire, "one of us will retain the book, the other the document, and we'll exchange them every year, or some such thing." Harbidger sounded unhappy.

"Only practical arrangement under the circumstances," grunted Tungston, and *he* sounded unhappy. "But all this is academic, Queen, unless and until the book and document are found."

Ellery nodded. "The problem, then, is to fathom DiCampo's interpretation of that *30d* in the document. 30d . . . I notice, Miss Di-Campo—or, may I? Bianca?—that your father's typewritten copy of the Lincoln holograph text runs the *3* and *0* and *d* together—no spacing in between. Is that the way it occurs in the longhand?"

"Yes."

"Hmm. Still . . . 30d . . . Could *d* stand for *days* . . . or the British *pence* . . . *or died,* as used in obituaries? Do any of these make sense to you, Bianca?"

"No."

"Did your father have any special interest in, say, pharmacology? chemistry? physics? algebra? electricity? Small *d* is an abbreviation used in all those." But Bianca shook her splendid head. "Banking? Small *d* for *dollars, dividends?*"

"Hardly," the girl said with a sad smile.

"How about theatricals? Was your father ever involved in a play production? Small *d* stands for *door* in playscript stage directions."

"Mr. Queen, I've gone through every darned abbreviation my dictionary lists, and I haven't found one that has a point of contact with any interest of my father's."

Ellery scowled. "At that—I assume the typewritten copy is accurate —the manuscript shows no period after the *d,* making an abbreviation unlikely. 30d . . . let's concentrate on the number. Does the number 30 have any significance for you?"

"Yes, indeed," said Bianca, making all three men sit up. But then they sank back. "In a few years it will represent my age, and that has enormous significance. But only for me, I'm afraid."

"You'll be drawing wolf whistles at twice thirty," quoth Ellery warmly. "However! Could the number have cross-referred to anything in your father's life or habits?"

"None that I can think of Mr. Queen. And," Bianca said, having grown roses in her cheeks, "thank you."

"I think," said old Tungston testily, "we had better stick to the subject."

"Just the same, Bianca, let me run over some 'thirty' associations as they come to mind. Stop me if one of them hits a nerve. The Thirty Tyrants—was your father interested in classical Athens? Thirty Years' War—in Seventeenth Century European history? Thirty all—did he play or follow tennis? Or . . . did he ever live at an address that included the number 30?"

Ellery went on and on, but to each suggestion Bianca DiCampo could only shake her head.

"The lack of spacing, come to think of it, doesn't necessarily mean that Mr. DiCampo chose to view the clue that way," said Ellery thoughtfully. "He might have interpreted it arbitrarily as 3-space-*O-d.*"

"Three od?" echoed old Tungston. "What the devil could that mean?"

"Od? Od is the hypothetical force or power claimed by Baron von Reichenbach—in 1850, wasn't it?—to pervade the whole of nature. Manifests itself in magnets, crystals, and such, which according to the excited Baron explained animal magnetism and mesmerism. Was your father by any chance interested in hypnosis, Bianca? Or the occult?"

"Not in the slightest."

"Mr. Queen," exclaimed Harbidger, "are you serious about all this —this semantic sludge?"

"Why, I don't know," said Ellery. "I never know till I stumble over something. Od . . . the word was used with prefixes, too—*biod,* the force of animal life; *elod,* the force of electricity; and so forth. *Three* od . . . or *triod,* the triune force—it's all right, Mr. Harbidger, it's not ignorance on your part, I just coined the word. But it does rather suggest the Trinity, doesn't it? Bianca, did your father tie up to the Church in a personal, scholarly, or any other way? No? That's too bad, really, because Od—capitalized—has been a minced form of the word God since the Sixteenth Century. Or . . . you wouldn't happen to have three Bibles on the premises, would you? Because—"

Ellery stopped with the smashing abruptness of an ordinary force meeting an absolutely immovable object. The girl and the two collectors gaped. Bianca had idly picked up the typewritten copy of the Lincoln document. She was not reading it, she was simply holding it on her knees; but Ellery, sitting opposite her, had shot forward in a crouch, rather like a pointer, and he was regarding the paper in her lap with a glare of pure discovery.

"That's it!" he cried.

"What's it, Mr. Queen?" the girl asked, bewildered.

"Please—the transcript!" He plucked the paper from her. "Of course. Hear this: 'On the other hand, let us regard Mr. Poe's "notion" turn-about.' *Turn-about.* Look at the 30d 'turn-about'—as I just saw it!"

He turned the Lincoln message upside down for their inspection. In that position the 30d became:

"Poe!" exploded Tungston.

"Yes, crude but recognizable," Ellery said swiftly. "So now we read the Lincoln clue as: 'The hiding-place of the book is in *poe!'"*

There was a silence.

"In Poe," said Harbidger blankly.

"In Poe?" muttered Tungston. "There are only a couple of trade editions of Poe in DiCampo's library, Harbidger, and we went through those. We looked in every book here."

"He might have meant among the Poe books in the *public* library. Miss DiCampo—"

"Wait." Bianca sped away. But when she came back she was drooping. "It isn't. We have two public libraries in Eulalia, and I know the head librarian in both. I just called them. Father didn't visit either library."

Ellery gnawed a fingernail. "Is there a bust of Poe in the house, Bianca? Or any other Poe-associated object, aside from books?"

"I'm afraid not."

"Queer," he mumbled. "Yet I'm positive your father interpreted 'the hiding-place of the book' as being 'in Poe.' So he'd have hidden it 'in Poe' . . ."

Ellery's mumbling dribbled away into a tormented sort of silence: his eyebrows worked up and down, Groucho Marx fashion; he pinched the tip of his nose until it was scarlet; he yanked at his unoffending ears; he munched on his lip . . . until, all at once, his face cleared; and he sprang to his feet. "Bianca, may I use your phone?"

The girl could only nod, and Ellery dashed. They heard him telephoning in the entrance hall, although they could not make out the words. He was back in two minutes.

"One thing more," he said briskly, "and we're out of the woods. I suppose your father had a key ring or a key case, Bianca? May I have it, please?"

She fetched a key case. To the two millionaires it seemed the sorriest of objects, a scuffed and dirty tan leatherette case. But Ellery received it from the girl as if it were an artifact of historic importance from a newly discovered IV Dynasty tomb. He unsnapped it with concentrated love; he fingered its contents like a scientist. Finally he decided on a certain key.

"Wait here!" Thus Mr. Queen; and exit, running.

"I can't decide," old Tungston said after a while, "whether that fellow is a genius or an escaped lunatic."

Neither Harbidger nor Bianca replied. Apparently they could not decide, either.

They waited through twenty elongated minutes; at the twenty-first they heard his car, champing. All three were in the front doorway as Ellery strode up the walk.

He was carrying a book with a red cover, and smiling. It was a compassionate smile, but none of them noticed.

"You—" said Bianca. "—found—" said Tungston. "—the book!" shouted Harbidger. "Is the Lincoln holograph in it?"

"It is," said Ellery. "Shall we all go into the house, where we may mourn in decent privacy?"

"Because," Ellery said to Bianca and the two quivering collectors as they sat across a refectory table from him, "I have foul news. Mr. Tungston, I believe you have never actually seen Mr. DiCampo's book. Will you now look at the Poe signature on the flyleaf?"

The panther claws leaped. There, toward the top of the flyleaf, in faded inkscript, was the signature *Edgar Allan Poe*.

The claws curled, and old Tungston looked up sharply. "DiCampo never mentioned that it's a full autograph—he kept referring to it as 'the Poe signature.' Edgar *Allan* Poe . . . Why, I don't know of a single instance after his West Point days when Poe wrote out his middle name in an autograph! And the earliest he could have signed this 1845 edition is obviously when it was published, which was around the fall of 1844. In 1844 he'd surely have abbreviated the 'Allan,' signing 'Edgar *A.* Poe,' the way he signed everything! This is a forgery."

"My God," murmured Bianca, clearly intending no impiety; she was as pale as Poe's Lenore. "Is that true, Mr. Queen?"

"I'm afraid it is," Ellery said sadly. "I was suspicious the moment you told me the Poe signature on the flyleaf contained the 'Allan.' And if the Poe signature is a forgery, the book itself can hardly be considered Poe's own copy."

Harbidger was moaning. "And the Lincoln signature underneath the Poe, Mr. Queen! DiCampo never told me it reads *Abraham* Lincoln—the full Christian name. Except on official documents, Lincoln practically always signed his name '*A.* Lincoln.' Don't tell me this Lincoln autograph is a forgery, too?"

Ellery forbore to look at poor Bianca. "I was struck by the 'Abraham' as well, Mr. Harbidger, when Miss DiCampo mentioned it to me, and I came equipped to test it. I have here"—and Ellery tapped the pile of documents he had taken from his briefcase—"facsimiles of Lincoln signatures from the most frequently reproduced of the historic documents he signed. Now I'm going to make a precise tracing of the Lincoln signature on the flyleaf of the book."—he proceeded to do so —"and I shall superimpose the tracing on the various signatures of the authentic Lincoln documents. So."

He worked rapidly. On his third superimposition Ellery looked up. "Yes. See here. The tracing of the purported Lincoln signature from the flyleaf fits in minutest detail over the authentic Lincoln signature on this facsimile of the Emancipation Proclamation. It's a fact of life that's tripped many a forger that *nobody ever writes his name exactly the same way twice.* There are always variations. If two signatures are identical, then, one must be a tracing of the other. So the 'Abraham Lincoln' signed on this flyleaf can be dismissed without further consideration as a forgery also. It's a tracing of the Emancipation Proclamation signature.

"Not only was this book not Poe's own copy; it was never signed— and therefore probably never owned—by Lincoln. However your father came into possession of the book, Bianca, he was swindled."

It was the measure of Bianca DiCampo's quality that she said quietly, "Poor, poor father," nothing more.

Harbidger was poring over the worn old envelope on whose inside appeared the dearly beloved handscript of the Martyr President. "At least," he muttered, "we have *this.*"

"Do we?" asked Ellery gently. "Turn it over, Mr Harbidger."

Harbidger looked up, scowling. "No! You're not going to deprive me of this, too!"

"Turn it over," Ellery repeated in the same gentle way. The Lincoln collector obeyed reluctantly. "What do you see?"

"An authentic envelope of the period! With two authentic Lincoln stamps!"

"Exactly. And the United States has never issued postage stamps depicting living Americans; you have to be dead to qualify. The earliest U.S. stamp showing a portrait of Lincoln went on sale April 15, 1866 —a year to the day after his death. Then a living Lincoln could scarcely have used this envelope, with these stamps on it, as writing paper. The document is spurious, too. I am so very sorry, Bianca."

Incredibly, Lorenzo DiCampo's daughter managed a smile with her *"Non importa, signor."* He could have wept for her. As for the two collectors, Harbidger was in shock; but old Tungston managed to croak, "Where the devil did DiCampo hide the book, Queen? And how did you know?"

"Oh, that," said Ellery, wishing the two old men would go away so that he might comfort this admirable creature. "I was convinced that DiCampo interpreted what we now know was the forger's, not Lincoln's, clue as *30d* read upside down; or, crudely, *Poe.* But 'the hiding-place of the book is in Poe' led nowhere.

"So I reconsidered, P, o, e. If those three letters of the alphabet didn't mean Poe, what could they mean? Then I remembered something about the letter you wrote me, Bianca. You'd used one of your father's envelopes, on the flap of which appeared his address: *Post Office Box 69, Southern District, Eulalia, N.Y.* If there was a Southern District in Eulalia, it seemed reasonable to conclude that there were post offices for other points of the compass, too. As, for instance, an Eastern District. Post Office Eastern, P.O. East. P.O.E."

"Poe!" cried Bianca.

"To answer your question, Mr. Tungston: I phoned the main post office, confirmed the existence of a Post Office East, got directions as to how to get there, looked for a postal box key in Mr. DiCampo's key case, found the right one, located the box DiCampo had rented especially for the occasion, unlocked it—and there was the book." He added, hopefully, "And that is that."

"And that *is* that," Bianca said when she returned from seeing the two collectors off. "I'm not going to cry over an empty milk bottle, Mr. Queen. I'll straighten out father's affairs somehow. Right now all I can think of is how glad I am he didn't live to see the signatures and documents declared forgeries publicly, as they would surely have been when they were expertized."

"I think you'll find there's still some milk in the bottle, Bianca."

"I beg your pardon?" said Bianca.

Ellery tapped the pseudo—Lincolnian envelope. "You know, you didn't do a very good job describing this envelope to me. All you said was that there were two canceled Lincoln stamps on it."

"Well, there are."

"I can see you misspent your childhood. No, little girls don't collect things, do they? Why, if you'll examine these 'two canceled Lincoln stamps,' you'll see that they're a great deal more than that. In the first place, they're not separate stamps. They're a vertical pair—that is, one stamp is joined to the other at the horizontal edges. Now look at this upper stamp of the pair."

The Mediterranean eyes widened. "It's upside down, isn't it?"

"Yes, it's upside down," said Ellery, "and what's more, while the pair have perforations all around, there are no perforations between them, where they're joined.

"What you have here, young lady—and what our unknown forger didn't realize when he fished around for an authentic White House cover of the period on which to perpetrate the Lincoln forgery—is what stamp collectors might call a double printing error: a pair of 1866 black 15-cent Lincolns imperforate horizontally, with one of the pair printed upside down. No such error of the Lincoln issue has ever been reported. You're the owner, Bianca, of what may well be the rarest item in U.S. philately, and the most valuable."

The world will little note, nor long remember.

But don't try to prove it by Bianca DiCampo.

MASTERS OF
THE MYSTERY

Britain's RUTH RENDELL *(1930–) has a background in journalism, but her style is anything but journalistic. Indeed, she is one of the finest stylists working in the mystery field, whose ability to write about characters with insight and feeling has won her a devoted following of readers and considerable critical success. She writes both series novels and wonderful individual works like* The Killing Doll *(1984). Her series sleuth, Chief Inspector Reginald Wexford of the Kingsmarkham police force in Sussex, is one of the best realized detectives in fiction. Although he has problems, he also has a meaningful family life and is a reasonably happy man, a refreshing change from the numerous moody, introspective types common today.*

"The Fever Tree" won an Edgar Award as the finest short story of 1974, and should be regarded as one of the ten best mystery short stories of the 1970s.

The Fever Tree
BY RUTH RENDELL

Where malaria is, there grows the fever tree.

It has the feathery fern-like leaves, fresh green and tender, that are common to so many trees in tropical regions. Its shape is graceful with an air of youth, of immaturity, as if every fever tree is still waiting to grow up. But the most distinctive thing about it is the color of its bark, which is the yellow of an unripe lemon. The fever trees stand out from among the rest because of their slender yellow trunks.

Ford knew what the tree was called and he could recognize it but he didn't know what its botanical name was. Nor had he ever heard why it was called the fever tree, whether the tribesmen used its leaves or bark or fruits as a specific against malaria or if it simply took its name from its warning presence wherever the malaria-carrying mosquito was. The sight of it in Ntsukunyane seemed to promote a fever in his blood.

An African in khaki shorts and shirt lifted up the bar for them so that their car could pass through the opening in the wire fence. Inside it looked no different from outside, the same bush, still, silent, unstirred by wind, stretching away on either side. Ford, driving the two miles along the tarmac road to the reception hut, thought of how it would be if he turned his head and saw Marguerite in the passenger seat beside him. It was an illusion he dared not have and was allowed to keep for perhaps a minute. Tricia shattered it. She began to belabor him with schoolgirl questions, uttered in a bright and desperate voice.

Another African, in a fancier, more decorated uniform, took their booking voucher and checked it against a ledger. You had to pay weeks in advance for the privilege of staying here. Ford had booked the day after he had said goodbye to Marguerite and returned, forever, to Tricia.

"My wife wants to know the area of Ntsukunyane," he said.

"Four million acres."

Ford gave the appropriate whistle. "Do we have a chance of seeing leopard?"

The man shrugged, smiled. "Who knows? You may be lucky. You're here a whole week, so you should see lion, elephant, hippo, cheetah maybe. But the leopard is nocturnal and you must be back in camp by six p.m." He looked at his watch. "I advise you to get on now, sir, if you're to make Thaba before they close the gates."

Ford got back into the car. It was nearly four. The sun of Africa, a living presence, a personal god, burned through a net of haze. There was no wind. Tricia, in a pale yellow sun dress with frills, had hung her arm outside the open window and the fair downy skin was glowing red. He told her what the man had said and he told her about the notice pinned inside the hut: It is strictly forbidden to bring firearms into the game reserve, to feed the animals, to exceed the speed limit, to litter.

"And most of all you mustn't get out of the car," said Ford.

"What, not ever?" said Tricia, making her pale blue eyes round and naive and marble-like.

"That's what it says."

She pulled a face. "Silly old rules!"

"They have to have them," he said.

In here as in the outside world. It is strictly forbidden to fall in love, to leave your wife, to try and begin anew. He glanced at Tricia to see if the same thoughts were passing through her mind. Her face wore its arch expression, winsome.

"A prize," she said, "for the first one to see an animal."

"All right." He had agreed to this reconciliation, to bring her on this holiday, this second honeymoon, and now he must try. He must work at it. It wasn't just going to happen as love had sprung between him and Marguerite, unsought and untried for. "Who's going to award it?" he said.

"You are if it's me and I am if it's you. And if it's me I'd like a presy from the camp shop. A very nice pricey presy."

Ford was the winner. He saw a single zebra come out from among the thorn trees on the right-hand side, then a small herd.

"Do I get a present from the shop?" he asked.

He could sense rather than see her shake her head with calculated coyness. "A kiss," she said and pressed warm dry lips against his cheek.

It made him shiver a little. He slowed down for the zebra to cross the road. The thorn bushes had spines on them two inches long. By the roadside grew a species of wild zinnia with tiny flowers, coral red, and these made red drifts among the coarse pale grass. In the bush were red anthills with tall peaks like towers on a castle in a fairy story. It was thirty miles to Thaba.

He drove on just within the speed limit, ignoring Tricia as far as he could whenever she asked him to slow down. They weren't going to see one of the big predators, anyway, not this afternoon, he was certain of that, only impala and zebra and maybe a giraffe. On business trips in the past he'd taken time off to go to Serengeti and Kruger and he knew.

He got the binoculars out for Tricia and adjusted them and hooked them round her neck, for he hadn't forgotten the binoculars and cameras she had dropped and smashed in the past through failing to do that, and her tears afterward. The car wasn't air-conditioned and the heat lay heavy and still between them. Ahead of them, as they drove westward, the sun was sinking in a dull yellow glare. The sweat flowed out of Ford's armpits and between his shoulder blades, soaking his already wet shirt and laying a cold sticky film on his skin.

A stone pyramid with arrows on it, set in the middle of a junction of roads, pointed the way to Thaba, to the main camp at Waka-suthu and to Hippo Bridge over the Suthu River. On top of it a baboon sat with her gray fluffy infant on her knees. Tricia yearned to it, stretching out her arms. She had never had a child. The baboon began picking fleas out of its baby's scalp. Tricia gave a little nervous scream, half disgusted, half joyful. Ford drove down the road to Thaba and in through the entrance to the camp ten minutes before they closed the gates for the night.

The dark comes down fast in Africa. Dusk is of short duration and no sooner have you noticed it than it is gone and night has fallen. In the few moments of dusk pale things glimmer brightly and birds murmur. In the camp at Thaba were a restaurant and a shop, round huts with thatched roofs, and wooden chalets with porches. Ford and Tricia had been assigned a chalet on the northern perimeter, and from their porch, across an expanse of turf and beyond the high wire fence, you could see the Suthu River flowing smoothly and silently between banks of tall reeds.

Dusk had just come as they walked up the wooden steps, Ford carrying their cases. It was then that he saw the fever trees, two of them, their ferny leaves bleached to gray by the twilight but their trunks a sharper, stronger yellow than in the day.

"Just as well we took our anti-malaria pills," said Ford as he pushed open the door. When the light was switched on he could see two mosquitos on the opposite wall. "*Anopheles* is the malaria carrier, but unfortunately they don't announce whether they're *anopheles* or not."

Twin beds, a table, lamps, an air conditioner, a fridge, a door, standing open, to lavatory and shower. Tricia dropped her makeup case, without which she went nowhere, onto the bed by the window. The light wasn't very bright. None of the lights in the camp were because the electricity came from a generator. They were a small colony of humans in a world that belonged to the animals, a reversal of the usual order of things. From the window you could see other chalets, other dim lights, other parked cars. Tricia talked to the two mosquitos.

"Is your name Anna Phyllis? No, darling, you're quite safe. She says she's Mary Jane and her husband's John Henry."

Ford managed to smile. He had accepted and grown used to Tricia's facetiousness until he had encountered Marguerite's wit. He shoved his case, without unpacking it, into the cupboard and went to have a shower.

Tricia stood on the porch, listening to the cicadas, thousands of them. It had gone pitch-dark while she was hanging up her dresses and the sky was punctured all over with bright stars.

She had got Ford back from that woman and now she had to keep him. She had lost some weight and bought a lot of new clothes and had highlights put in her hair. Men had always made her feel frightened, starting with her father when she was a child. It was then, when a child, that she had purposely begun *playing* the child with its cajolements and its winning little ways. She had noticed that her father was kinder and more forbearing toward little girls than toward her mother.

Ford had married a little girl, clinging and winsome, and had liked it well enough till he met a grown woman.

Tricia knew all that, but now she knew no better how to keep him than by the old methods, as weary and stale to her as she guessed they might be to him. Standing there on the porch, she half wished she were alone and didn't have to have a husband, didn't, for the sake of convention and pride, for support and society, have to hold on tight to him. She listened wistfully for a lion to roar out there in the bush beyond the fence, but there was no sound except the cicadas.

Ford came out in a toweling robe.

"What did you do with the mosquito stuff? The spray?"

Frightened at once, she said, "I don't know."

"What d'you mean, you don't know? You must know. I gave you the aerosol at the hotel and said to put it in that makeup case of yours."

She opened the case although she knew the mosquito stuff wasn't there. Of course it wasn't there. She could see it on the bathroom shelf in the hotel, left behind because it was too bulky. She bit her lip, looked sideways at Ford.

"We can get some more at the shop."

"Tricia, the shop closes at seven and it's now ten past."

"We can get some in the morning."

"Mosquitos happen to be most active at night." He rummaged with his hands among the bottles and jars in the case. "Look at all this useless rubbish. 'Skin cleanser,' 'pearlized foundation,' 'moisturizer'— like some young model girl. I suppose it didn't occur to you to bring the anti-mosquito spray and leave the 'pearlized foundation' behind."

Her lip trembled. She could feel herself, almost involuntarily, rounding her eyes, forming her mouth into the shape of lisping. "We did 'member to take our pills."

"That won't stop the damn things biting." He went back into the shower and slammed the door.

Marguerite wouldn't have forgotten to bring that aerosol. Tricia knew he was thinking of Marguerite again, that his head was full of her, that she had entered his thoughts powerfully and insistently on the long drive to Thaba. She began to cry. The tears went on running out of her eyes and wouldn't stop, so she changed her dress while she cried and the tears came through the powder she put on her face.

They had dinner in the restaurant. Tricia, in pink flowered crepe, was the only dressed-up woman there, and while once she would have fancied that the other diners looked at her in admiration, now she thought it must be with derision. She ate her small piece of overcooked hake and her large piece of overcooked, bread-crumbed veal, and watched the red weals from mosquito bites coming up on Ford's arms.

There were no lights on in the camp but those which shone from the windows of the main building and from the chalets. Gradually the lights went out and it became very dark. In spite of his mosquito bites, Ford fell asleep at once but the noise of the air conditioning kept Tricia awake. At eleven she switched it off and opened the window. Then she did sleep but she awoke again at four, lay awake for half an hour, got up, put on her clothes, and went out.

It was still dark but the darkness was lifting as if the thickest veil of it had been withdrawn. A heavy dew lay on the grass. As she passed under the merula tree, laden with small green apricot-shaped fruits, a flock of bats flew out from its branches and circled her head. If Ford had been with her she would have screamed and clung to him but because she was alone she kept silent. The camp and the bush beyond the fence were full of sound. The sounds brought to Tricia's mind the paintings of Hieronymus Bosch, imps and demons and dreadful homunculi which, if they had uttered, might have made noises like these, gruntings and soft whistles and chirps and little thin squeals.

She walked about, waiting for the dawn, expecting it to come with drama. But it was only a gray pallor in the sky, a paleness between parting black clouds, and the feeling of let-down frightened her as if it were a symbol or an omen of something more significant in her life than the coming of morning.

Ford woke up, unable at first to open his eyes for the swelling from mosquito bites. There were mosquitos like threads of thistledown on the walls, all over the walls. He got up and staggered, half blind, out of the bedroom and let the water from the shower run on his eyes. Tricia came and stared at his face, giggling nervously and biting her lip.

The camp gates opened at five thirty and the cars began their exodus. Tricia had never passed a driving test and Ford couldn't see, so they went to the restaurant for breakfast instead. When the shop opened, Ford bought two kinds of mosquito repellent, and impatiently, because he could no longer bear her apologies and her pleading eyes, a necklace of ivory beads for Tricia and a skirt with giraffes printed on it. At nine o'clock, when the swelling round Ford's eyes had subsided a little, they set off in the car, taking the road for Hippo Bridge.

The day was humid and thickly hot. Ford had counted the number of mosquito bites he had had and the total was twenty-four. It was hard to believe that two little tablets of quinine would be proof against twenty-four bites, some of which must certainly have been inflicted by *anopheles*. Hadn't he seen the two fever trees when they arrived last night? Now he drove the car slowly and doggedly, hardly speaking, his swollen eyes concealed behind sunglasses.

By the Suthu River and then by a water hole he stopped and they watched. But they saw nothing come to the water's edge unless you counted the log which at last disappeared, thus proving itself to have been a crocodile. It was too late in the morning to see much apart from the marabout storks which stood one-legged, still and hunched, in a clearing or on the gaunt branch of a tree. Through binoculars Ford stared at the bush which stretched in unbroken, apparently untenanted, sameness to the blue ridge of mountains on the far horizon.

There could be no real fever from the mosquito bites. If malaria were to come it wouldn't be yet. But Ford, sitting in the car beside Tricia, nevertheless felt something like a delirium of fever. It came perhaps from the gross irritation of the whole surface of his body, from the tender burning of his skin and from his inability to move without setting up fresh torment. It affected his mind too, so that each time he looked at Tricia a kind of panic rose in him. Why had he done it? Why had he gone back to her? Was he mad? His eyes and his head throbbed as if his temperature were raised.

Tricia's pink jeans were too tight for her and the frills on her white voile blouse ridiculous. With the aid of the binoculars she had found a family of small gray monkeys in the branches of a peepul tree and she was cooing at them out of the window. Presently she opened the car door, held it just open, and turned to look at him the way a child looks at her father when he has forbidden something she nevertheless longs and means to do.

They hadn't had sight of a big cat or an elephant, they hadn't even seen a jackal. Ford lifted his shoulders.

"Okay. But if a ranger comes along and catches you we'll be in deep trouble."

She got out of the car, leaving the door open. The grass which began at the roadside and covered the bush as far as the eye could see was long and coarse. It came up above Tricia's knees. A lioness or a cheetah lying in it would have been entirely concealed. Ford picked up the binoculars and looked the other way to avoid watching Tricia who had once again forgotten to put the camera strap round her neck. She was making overtures to the monkeys who shrank away from her, embracing each other and burying heads in shoulders, like menaced refugees in a sentimental painting.

Ford moved the glasses slowly. About a hundred yards from where a small herd of buck grazed uneasily, he saw the two cat faces close together, the bodies nestled together, the spotted backs. Cheetah. It came into his mind how he had heard that they were the fastest animals on earth.

He ought to call to Tricia and get her back at once into the car. He didn't call. Through the glasses he watched the big cats that reclined there so gracefully, satiated, at rest, yet with open eyes. Marguerite would have liked them; she loved cats, she had a Burmese, as lithe and slim and poised as one of these wild creatures.

Tricia got back into the car, exclaiming about how sweet the monkeys were. He started the car and drove off without saying anything to her about the cheetahs.

Later, at about five in the afternoon, she wanted to get out of the car again and he didn't stop her. She walked up and down the road, talking to mongooses. In something over an hour it would be dark. Ford imagined starting up the car and driving back to the camp without her. Leopards were nocturnal hunters, waiting till dark.

The swelling around his eyes had almost subsided now but his neck and arms and hands ached from the stiffness of the bites. The mongooses fled into the grass as Tricia approached, whispering to them, hands outstretched. A car with four men in it was coming along from the Hippo Bridge direction. It slowed down and the driver put his head out. His face was brick-red, thick-featured, his hair corrugated blond, and his voice had the squashed vowel accent of the white man born in Africa.

"The lady shouldn't be out on the road like that."

"I know," Ford said. "I've told her."

"Excuse me, d'you know you're doing a very dangerous thing, leaving your car?"

The voice had a hectoring boom. Tricia blushed. She bridled, smiled, bit her lip, though she was in fact very afraid of this man who was looking at her as if he despised her, as if she disgusted him. When he got back to camp, would he betray her?

"Promise you won't tell on me?" she faltered, her head on one side.

The man gave an exclamation of anger and withdrew his head. The car moved forward. Tricia gave a skip and a jump into the passenger seat beside Ford. They had under an hour to get back to Thaba and Ford followed the car with the four men in it.

At dinner they sat at adjoining tables. Tricia wondered how many people they had told, for she fancied that some of the diners looked at her with curiosity or antagonism. The man with fair curly hair they called Eric boasted loudly of what he and his companions had seen that day, a whole pride of lions, two rhinoceros, hyena, and the rare sable antelope.

"You can't expect to see much down that Hippo Bridge road, you know," he said to Ford. "All the game's up at Sotingwe. You take the Sotingwe road first thing tomorrow and I'll guarantee you lions."

He didn't address Tricia, he didn't even look at her. Ten years before men in restaurants had turned their heads to look at her and though she had feared them, she had basked, trembling, in their gaze. Walking across the grass, back to their chalet, she held on to Ford's arm.

"For God's sake, mind my mosquito bites," said Ford.

He lay awake a long while in the single bed a foot away from Tricia's, thinking about the leopard out there beyond the fence that hunted by night. The leopard would move along the branch of a tree and drop upon its prey. Lionesses hunted in the early morning and brought the kill to their mate and the cubs. Ford had seen all that sort of thing on television. How cheetahs hunted he didn't know except that they were very swift. An angry elephant would lean on a car and crush it or smash a windshield with a blow from its foot.

It was too dark for him to see Tricia but he knew she was awake, lying still, sometimes holding her breath. He heard her breath released in an exhalation, a sigh, that was audible above the rattle of the air conditioner.

Years ago he had tried to teach her to drive. They said a husband should never try to teach his wife, he would have no patience with her and make no allowances. Tricia's progress had never been maintained, she had always been liable to do silly reckless things and then he had shouted at her. She took a driving test and failed and she said this was because the examiner had bullied her. Tricia seemed to think no one should ever raise his voice to her, and at one glance from her all men should fall slaves at her feet.

He would have liked her to be able to take a turn at driving. There was no doubt you missed a lot when you had to concentrate on the road. But it was no use suggesting it. Theirs was one of the first cars in the line to leave the gates at five thirty, to slip out beyond the fence into the gray dawn, the still bush. At the stone pyramid, on which a family of baboons sat clustered, Ford took the road for Sotingwe.

A couple of miles up they came upon the lions. Eric and his friends were already there, leaning out of the car windows with cameras. The lions, two full-grown lionesses, two lioness cubs and a lion cub with his mane beginning to sprout, were lying on the roadway. Ford stopped and parked the car on the opposite side to Eric.

"Didn't I say you'd be lucky up here?" Eric called to Tricia. "Not got any ideas about getting out and investigating, I hope."

Tricia didn't answer him or look at him. She looked at the lions. The sun was coming up, radiating the sky with a pinkish-orange glow, and a little breeze fluttered all the pale green, fern-like leaves. The larger of the adult lionesses, bored rather than alarmed by Eric's elaborate photographic equipment, got up slowly and strolled into the bush, in among the long dry grass and the red zinnias. The cubs followed her, the other lioness followed her. Through his binoculars Ford watched them stalk with proud lifted heads, walking, even the little ones, in a graceful, measured, controlled way. There were no impala anywhere, no giraffe, no wildebeest. The world here belonged to the lions.

All the game was gathered at Sotingwe, near the water hole. An elephant with ears like punkahs was powdering himself with red earth blown out through his trunk. Tricia got out of the car to photograph the elephant and Ford didn't try to stop her. He scratched his mosquito bites which had passed the burning and entered the itchy stage.

Once more Tricia had neglected to pass the camera strap around her neck. She made her way down to the water's edge and stood at a safe distance—was it a safe distance? Was any distance safe in here?—looking at a crocodile. Ford thought, without really explaining to himself or even fully understanding what he meant, that it was the wrong time of day, it was too early. They went back to Thaba for breakfast.

At breakfast and again at lunch Eric was full of what he had seen. He had taken the dirt road that ran down from Sotingwe to Suthu Bridge and there, up in a tree near the water, had been a leopard. Malcolm had spotted it first, stretched out asleep on a branch, a long way off but quite easy to see through field glasses.

"Massive great fella with your authentic square-type spots," said Eric, smoking a cigar.

Tricia, of course, wanted to go to Suthu Bridge, so Ford took the dirt road after they had had their siesta. Malcolm described exactly where he had seen the leopard which might, for all he knew, still be sleeping on its branch.

"About half a mile up from the bridge. You look over on your left and there's a sort of clearing with one of those trees with yellow trunks in it. This chap was on a branch on the right side of the clearing."

The dirt road was a track of crimson earth between green verges. Ford found the clearing with the single fever tree but the leopard had gone. He drove slowly down to the bridge that spanned the sluggish green river. When he switched off the engine it was silent and utterly still, the air hot and close, nothing moving but the mosquitos that danced in their haphazard yet regular measure above the surface of the water.

Tricia was getting out of the car as a matter of course now. This time she didn't even trouble to give him the coy glance that asked permission. She was wearing a red and white striped sundress with straps that were too narrow and a skirt that was too tight. She ran down to the water's edge, took off a sandal, and dipped in a daring foot. She laughed and twirled her foot, dabbling the dry round stones with water drops. Ford thought how he had loved this sort of thing when he had first met her, and now he was going to have to bear it for the rest of his life. He broke into a sweat as if his temperature had suddenly risen.

She was prancing about on the stones and in the water, holding up her skirt. There were no animals to be seen. All afternoon they had seen nothing but impala, and the sun was moving down now, beginning to color the hazy pastel sky. Tricia, on the opposite bank, broke another Ntsukunyane rule and picked daisies, tucking one behind each ear. With a flower between her teeth like a Spanish dancer, she swayed her hips and smiled.

Ford turned the ignition key and started the car. It would be dark in just over an hour and long before that they would have closed the gates at Thaba. He moved the car forward, reversed, making what Tricia, no doubt, would call a three-point turn. Facing toward Thaba now, he put the shift into drive, his foot on the accelerator, and took a deep breath as the sweat trickled between his shoulder blades. The heat made mirages on the road and out of them a car was coming. Ford stopped and switched off the engine. It wasn't Eric's car but one belonging to a couple of young Americans on holiday. The boy raised his hand in a salute at Ford.

Ford called out to Tricia, "Come on or we'll be late."

She got into the car, dropping her flowers onto the roadway. Ford

had been going to leave her there, that was how much he wanted to be
rid of her. Her body began to shake and she clasped her hands tightly
together so that he shouldn't see. He had been going to drive away and
leave her there to the darkness and the lions, the leopard that hunted
by night. He had been driving away, only the Americans' car had come
along.

She was silent, thinking about it. The American turned back soon
after they did and followed them up the dirt road. Impala stood
around the solitary fever tree, listening perhaps to inaudible sounds or
scenting invisible danger. The sky was smoky yellow with sunset.
Tricia thought about what Ford must have intended to do—drive back
to camp just before they closed the gates, watch the darkness come
down, knowing she was out there, say not a word of her absence to
anyone—and who would miss her? Eric? Malcolm? Ford wouldn't
have gone to the restaurant and in the morning when they opened the
gates he would have driven away. No need even to check out at Ntsukunyane where you paid weeks in advance.

The perfect murder. Who would search for her, not knowing there
was need for search? And if her bones were found? One set of bones,
human, impala, waterbuck, looks very much like another when the
jackals have been at it and the vultures. And when he reached home he
would have said he had left her for Marguerite . . .

He was nicer to her that evening, gentler. Because he was afraid she
had guessed or might guess the truth of what had happened at Sotingwe?

"We said we'd have champagne one night. How about now? No time
like the present."

"If you like," Tricia said.

She felt sick all the time, she had no appetite. Ford toasted them in
champagne.

"To us!"

He ordered the whole gamut of the menu, soup, fish, wiener
schnitzel, creme brulee. She picked at her food, thinking how he had
meant to kill her. She would never be safe now, for having failed once
he would try again. Not the same method perhaps but some other.
How was she to know he hadn't already tried? Perhaps, for instance,
he had substituted aspirin for those quinine tablets, or when they were
back at the hotel in Mombasa he might try to drown her. She would
never be safe unless she left him.

Which was what he wanted, which would be the next best thing to her death. Lying awake in the night, she thought of what leaving him would mean—going back to live with her mother while he went to Marguerite. He wasn't asleep either. She could hear the sound of his irregular wakeful breathing. She heard the bed creak as he moved in it restlessly, the air conditioner grinding, the whine of a mosquito.

Now, if she hadn't already been killed, she might be wandering out there in the bush, in terror in the dark, afraid to take a step but afraid to remain still, fearful of every sound yet not knowing which sound most to fear. There was no moon. She had taken note of that before she came to bed and had seen in her diary that tomorrow the moon would be new. The sky had been overcast at nightfall and now it was pitch-dark. The leopard could see, perhaps by the light of the stars or with an inner instinctive eye more sure than simple vision, and would drop silently from its branch to sink its teeth into the lifted throat.

The mosquito that had whined stung Ford in several places on his face and neck and on his left foot. He had forgotten to use the repellent the night before. Early in the morning, at dawn, he got up and dressed and went for a walk round the camp. There was no one about but one of the African staff, hosing down a guest's car. Squeaks and shufflings came from the bush beyond the fence.

Had he really meant to rid himself of Tricia by throwing her, as one might say, to the lions? For a mad moment, he supposed, because fever had got into his blood, poison into his veins. She knew, he could tell that. In a way it might be all to the good, her knowing; it would show her how hopeless the marriage was that she was trying to preserve.

The swellings on his foot, though covered by his sock, were making the instep bulge through the sandal. His foot felt stiff and burning and he became aware that he was limping slightly. Supporting himself against the trunk of a fever tree, his skin against its cool, dampish, yellow bark, he took off his sandal and felt his swollen foot tenderly with his fingertips. Mosquitos never touched Tricia; they seemed to shirk contact with her pale dry flesh.

She was up when he hobbled in; she was sitting on her bed, painting her fingernails. How could he live with a woman who painted her fingernails in a game reserve?

They didn't go out till nine. On the road to Waka-suthu, Eric's car met them, coming back.

"There's nothing down there for miles, you're wasting your time."

"Okay," said Ford. "Thanks."

"Sotingwe's the place. Did you see the leopard yesterday?"

Ford shook his head.

"Oh, well, we can't all be lucky."

Elephants were playing in the river at Hippo Bridge, spraying each other with water and nudging heavy shoulders. Ford thought that was going to be the high spot of the morning until they came upon the kill. They didn't actually see it. The kill had taken place some hours before, but the lioness and her cubs were still picking at the carcase, at a blood-blackened rib cage.

They sat in the car and watched. After a while the lions left the carcase and walked away in file through the grass, but the little jackals were already gathered, a pack of them, posted behind trees. Ford came back that way again at four and by then the vultures had moved in, picking the bones.

It was a hot day of merciless sunshine, the sky blue and perfectly clear. Ford's foot was swollen to twice its normal size. He noticed that Tricia hadn't once left the car that day, nor had she spoken girlishly to him or giggled or given him a roguish kiss. She thought he had been trying to kill her, a preposterous notion really. The truth was he had only been giving her a fright, teaching her how stupid it was to flout the rules and leave the car.

Why should he kill her, anyway? He could leave her, he *would* leave her, and once they were back in Mombasa he would tell her so. The thought of it made him turn to her and smile. He had stopped by the clearing where the fever tree stood, yellow of bark, delicate and fern-like of leaf, in the sunshine like a young sapling in springtime.

"Why don't you get out any more?"

She faltered, "There's nothing to see."

"No?"

He had spotted the porcupine with his naked eye but he handed her the binoculars. She looked and she laughed with pleasure. That was the way she used to laugh when she was young, not from amusement but delight. He shut his eyes.

"Oh, the sweetie porky-pine!"

She reached on to the back seat for the camera. And then she hesitated. He could see the fear, the caution, in her eyes. Silently he took the key out of the ignition and held it out to her on the palm of his hand. She flushed. He stared at her, enjoying her discomfiture, indignant that she should suspect him of such baseness.

She hesitated but she took the key. She picked up the camera and opened the car door, holding the key on its fob in her left hand and the camera in her right. He noticed she hadn't passed the strap of the camera, his treasured Pentax, round her neck. For the thousandth time he could have told her but he lacked the heart to speak. His swollen foot throbbed and he thought of the long days at Ntsukunyane that remained to them. Marguerite seemed infinitely far away, farther even than at the other side of the world where she was.

He knew Tricia was going to drop the camera some fifteen seconds before she did so. It was because she had the key in her other hand. If the strap had been round her neck it wouldn't have mattered. He knew how it was when you held something in each hand and lost your grip or your footing. You had no sense then, in that instant, of which of the objects was valuable and mattered and which was not. Tricia held on to the key and dropped the camera. The better to photograph the porcupine, she had mounted on to the twisted roots of a tree, roots that looked as hard as a flight of stone steps.

She gave a little cry. At the sounds of the crash and the cry the porcupine erected its quills. Ford jumped out of the car, wincing when he put his foot to the ground, hobbling through the grass to Tricia who stood as if petrified with fear of him. The camera, the pieces of camera, had fallen among the gnarled, stone-like tree roots. He dropped onto his knees, shouting at her, cursing her.

Tricia began to run. She ran back to the car and pushed the key into the ignition. The car was pointing in the direction of Thaba and the clock on the dashboard shelf said five thirty-five. Ford came limping back, waving his arms at her, his hands full of broken pieces of camera. She looked away and put her foot down hard on the accelerator.

The sky was clear orange with sunset, black bars of the coming night lying on the horizon. She found she could drive when she had to, even though she couldn't pass a test. A mile along the road she met the American couple. The boy put his head out.

"Anything worth going down there for?"

"Not a thing," said Tricia. "You'd be wasting your time."

The boy turned his car round and followed her back. It was two minutes to six when they entered Thaba, the last cars to do so, and the gates were closed behind them.

Like his countryman Eric Ambler, DICK FRANCIS *(1920–) is
an Officer of the Order of the British Empire, but there the
similarities end. Mr. Francis has built his career around one
subject—horse racing—a field he knows firsthand, since he was
a successful professional jockey from 1948 to 1957 (and National Hunt Champion in 1953 and 1954) and after his retirement served as racing correspondent for the* Sunday Express
from 1957 to 1973. His first novel, Dead Cert, *appeared in
1962 and he has since published over twenty-five others to great
acclaim and commercial success, including* Reflex *(1980),*
Banker *(1982),* Proof *(1984),* Bolt *(1986), and* Hot Money
(1988).

*Dick Francis' fiction frequently involves such themes as the
meaning of tragedy and the importance of decisions and judg-
ments in a man's life. "Twenty-one Good Men and True"
shows his skill at plotting, and also has a racetrack setting.*

Twenty-one Good
Men and True
BY DICK FRANCIS

Arnold Roper whistled breathily while he boiled his kettle and
spooned instant own-brand economy-pack coffee into the old blue souvenir from Brixham. Unmelodic and without rhythm, the whistling
was nonetheless an expression of content, both with things in general
and with the immediate prospect ahead. Arnold Roper, as usual, was
going to the races; and as usual, if he had a bet he would win. Neat,
methodical, professional, he would operate his unbeatable system and
grow richer, the one following the other as surely as chickens and eggs.

Arnold Roper at forty-five was one of nature's bachelors, a lean-
bodied, handy man accustomed to looking after himself, a man who
found the chatter of companionship a nuisance. Like a sailor, though
he had never been to sea, he kept his surroundings polished and ship-
shape, ordering his life in plastic dustbin liners and reheated take-away
food.

The one mild problem on Arnold Roper's horizon was his wealth.
The getting of the money was his most intense enjoyment. The spending of it was something he postponed to a remote and dreamlike fu-

ture, when he would exchange his sterile flat for a warm, unending idyll under tropical palms. It was the interim storage of the money which was currently causing him, if not positive worry, at least occasional frowns of doubt. He might, he thought, as he stirred dried milk grains into the brownish brew, have to find space for yet another wardrobe in his already crowded bedroom.

If anyone had told Arnold Roper he was a miser, he would have denied it indignantly. True, he lived frugally, but by habit rather than obsession; and he never took out his wealth just to look at it, and count, and gloat. He would not have admitted as miserliness the warm feeling that stole over him every night as he lay down to sleep, smiling from the knowledge that all around him, filling two oak-veneered bargain-sale bedroom suites, was a ton or two of negotiable paper.

It was not that Arnold Roper distrusted banks. He knew, too, that money won by betting could not be lost by tax. He would not have kept his growing gains physically around him were it not that his unbeatable system was also a splendid fraud.

The best frauds are only ever discovered by accident, and Arnold could not envisage any such accident happening to *him*.

Jamie Finland woke to his customary darkness and thought three disconnected thoughts with the first second of consciousness. The sun is shining. It is Wednesday. They are racing today here at Ascot.

He stretched out a hand and put his fingers delicately down on the top of his bedside tape recorder. There was a cassette lying there. Jamie smiled, slid the cassette into the recorder and switched on.

His mother's voice spoke to him. "Jamie, don't forget the man is coming to mend the television at ten-thirty and please put the washing into the machine, there's a dear, as I am so pushed this morning, and would you mind having yesterday's soup again for lunch. I've left it in a saucepan, ready. Don't lose all that ten quid this afternoon or I'll cut the plug off your stereo. Home soon after eight, love."

Jamie Finland's thirty-eight-year-old mother supported them both on her earnings as an agency nurse, and she had made a fair job, her son considered, of bringing up a child who could not see. He rose gracefully from bed and put on his clothes: blue shirt, blue jeans. "Blue is Jamie's favourite colour," his mother would say, and her friends would say, "Oh, yes?" politely and she could see them thinking, how could he possibly know? But Jamie could identify blue as surely as his mother's voice, and red, and yellow, and every colour in the spectrum, and long as it was daylight. "I can't see in the dark," he had said when he was six, and only his mother, from watching his sureness by day and his stumbling by night, had understood what he meant. Walking radar, she called him. Like many young blind people, he could sense the wavelength of light, and distinguish the infinitesimal changes of frequency reflected from coloured things close to him. Strangers thought him uncanny. Jamie believed everyone could see that way if they wanted to, and could not himself clearly understand what they meant by sight.

He made and ate some toast and thankfully opened the door to the television fixer. "In my room," he said, leading the way. "We've got sound but no picture." The television fixer looked at the blind eyes and shrugged. If the boy wanted a picture he was entitled to it, same as everyone else who paid their rental. "Have to take it back to the work-shop," he said, judiciously pressing buttons.

"The races are on," Jamie said. "Can you fix it by then?"

"Races? Oh, yeah. Well . . . tell you what: I'll lend you another set. Got one in the van . . ." He staggered off with the invalid and returned with the replacement. "Not short of radios, are you?" he said, looking around. "What do you want six for?"

"I leave them tuned to different things," Jamie said. "That one"—he pointed accurately—"listens to aircraft, that one to the police, those three are on ordinary radio stations, and this one, local broadcasts."

"What you need is a transmitter. Put you in touch with all the world."

"I'm working on it," Jamie said. "Starting today."

He closed the door after the man and wondered whether betting on a certainty was a crime.

Greg Simpson had no such qualms. He paid his way into the Ascot paddock, bought a race card, and ambled off to add a beer and sand-wich to a comfortable paunch. Two years now, he thought, munching, since he had first set foot on the turf; two years since he had exchanged his principles for prosperity and been released from paralyzing depres-sion. They seemed a distant memory now, those fifteen months in the wilderness, the awful humiliating collapse of his seemingly secure pen-sionable world. No comfort in knowing that mergers and cutbacks had thrown countless near-top managers like himself onto the redundancy heap. At fifty-two, with long success-strewn experience and genuine administrative skill, he had expected that he at least would find another suitable post easily; but door after door closed, and a regretful chorus of "Sorry, Greg," "Sorry, old chap," "Sorry, Mr. Simpson, we need someone younger," had finally thrust him into agonized despair. And it was just when, in spite of all their anxious economies, his wife had had to deny their two children even the money to go swimming that he had seen the curious advertisement:

Jobs offered to mature respectable persons who must have been unwillingly unemployed for at least twelve months.

Part of his mind told him he was being invited to commit a crime, but he had gone nonetheless to the subsequently arranged interview, in a London pub, and he had been relieved, after all, to meet the very ordinary man holding out salvation. A man like himself, middle-aged, middle-educated, wearing a suit and tie and indoor skin.

"Do you go to the races?" Arnold Roper asked. "Do you gamble? Do you follow the horses?"

"No," Greg Simpson said prudishly, seeing the job prospect disappear but feeling all the same superior. "I'm afraid not."

"Do you bet on dogs? Go to Bingo? Do the pools? Play bridge? Feel attracted by roulette?"

Greg Simpson silently shook his head and prepared to leave.

"Good," said Arnold Roper cheerfully. "Gamblers are no good to me. Not for this job."

Greg Simpson relaxed into a glow of self-congratulation on his own virtue. "What job?" he said.

Arnold Roper wiped out Simpson's smirk. "Going to the races," he said bluntly. "Betting when I say bet, and never at any other time. You would have to go to race meetings most days, like any other job. You would be betting on certainties, and after every win I would expect you to send me twenty-five pounds. Anything you made above that would be yours. It is foolproof, and safe. If you go about it in a businesslike way, and don't get tempted into the mug's game of backing your own fancy, you'll do very well. Think it over. If you're interested, meet me here again tomorrow."

Betting on certainties . . . every one a winner. Arnold Roper had been as good as his word, and Greg Simpson's lifestyle had returned to normal. His qualms had evaporated once he learned that even if the fraud was discovered, he himself would not be involved. He did not know how his employer acquired his infallible information, and if he speculated, he didn't ask. He knew his employer only as John Smith, and had never met him since those first two days, but he heeded his warning that if he failed to attend the specified race meetings or failed to send his twenty-five-pound payment, the bounty would stop dead.

Simpson finished his sandwich and went down to mingle with the bookmakers as the horses cantered to the post for the start of the first race.

From high in the stands, Arnold Roper looked down through powerful binoculars, spotting his men one by one. The perfect work force, he thought, smiling to himself; no absenteeism, no union troubles, no complaints. There were twenty-one of them at present on his register, all contentedly receiving his information, all dutifully returning their moderate levies, and none of them knowing of the existence of the others. In an average week they would all bet for him twice; in an average week, after expenses, he added a thousand in readies to his bedroom.

In the five years since he had begun in a small way to put his scheme into operation, he had never picked a defaulter. The thinking-it-over time gave the timid and the honest an easy way out; and if Arnold himself had doubts, he simply failed to return on day two. The rest, added one by one to the fold, lived comfortably with quiet minds and prayed that their benefactor would never be rumbled.

Arnold himself couldn't see why he ever should be. He put down the binoculars and began in his methodical fashion to get on with his day's work. There was always a good deal to see to in the way of filling in forms, testing equipment and checking that the nearby telephone was working. Arnold never left anything to chance.

Down at the starting gate, sixteen two-year-olds bucked and skittered as they were led by the handlers into the stalls. Two-year-old colts, thought the starter resignedly, looking at his watch, could behave like a pack of prima donnas in a heat wave in Milan. If they didn't hurry with that chestnut at present squealing and backing away determinedly, he would let the other runners off without him. He was all too aware of the television cameras pointing his way, mercilessly awaiting his smallest error. Starters who got the races off minutes late were unpopular. Starters who got the races off early were asking for official reprimands and universal curses, because of the fiddles that had been worked in the past on premature departures.

The starter ruled the chestnut out of the race and pulled his lever at time plus three minutes twenty seconds, entering the figures meticulously in his records. The gates crashed open, the fifteen remaining colts roared out of the stalls, and along the stands the serried ranks of race glasses followed their progress over the five-furlong sprint.

Alone in his special box, the judge watched intently. A big pack of two-year-olds over five furlongs were often a problem, presenting occasionally even to his practised eyes a multiple dead heat. He had learned all the horses by name and all the colours by heart, a chore he shared every day with the race-reading commentators, and from long acquaintance he could recognize most of the jockeys by their riding style alone, but still the ignominy of making a mistake flitted uneasily through his dreams. He squeezed his eyeballs, and concentrated.

Up in his aerie, the television commentator looked through his high-magnification binoculars, which were mounted rock-steady like a telescope, and spoke unhurriedly into his microphone. "Among the early leaders are Breakaway and Middle Park, followed closely by Pickup, Jetset, Darling Boy and Gumshoe. . . . Coming to the furlong marker, the leaders are bunched, with Jetset, Darling Boy, Breakaway all showing. . . . One furlong out, there is nothing to choose between Darling Boy, Jetset, Gumshoe, Pickup. . . . In the last hundred yards. . . . Jetset, Darling Boy . . ."

The colts stretched their necks, the jockeys swung their whips, the crowd rose on tiptoes and yelled in a roar which drowned the commentary, and in his box the judge's eyes ached with effort. Darling Boy, Jetset, Gumshoe and Pickup swept past the winning post abreast, and an impersonal voice over the widespread loudspeakers announced calmly, "Photograph. Photograph."

Half a mile away in his own room, Jamie Finland listened to the race on television and tried to imagine the pictures on the screen. Racing was misty to him. He knew the shape of the horses from handling toys and riding a rocker, but their size and speed were mysterious; he had no conception at all of a broad sweep of railed racecourse, or of the size or appearance of trees.

As he grew older, Jamie was increasingly aware that he had drawn lucky in the material stakes, and he had become in his teens protective rather than rebellious, which touched his hard-pressed mother sometimes to tears. It was for her sake that he had welcomed the television fixer, knowing that, for her, sound without pictures was almost as bad as pictures without sound for himself. Despite a lot of trying, he could pick up little from the screen through his ultrasensitive fingertips. Electronically produced colours gave him none of the vibrations of natural light.

He sat hunched with tension at his table, the telephone beside his right hand and one of his radios at his left. There was no telling, he thought, whether the bizarre thing would happen again, but if it did, he would be ready.

"One furlong out, nothing to choose . . ." said the television commentator, his voice rising to excitement-inducing crescendo. "In the last hundred yards, Jetset, Darling Boy, Pickup and Gumshoe . . . At the post, all in a line . . . Perhaps Pickup got there in the last stride, but we'll have to wait for the photograph. Meanwhile, let's see the closing stages of the race again. . . ."

The television went back on its tracks, and Jamie waited intently with his fingers over the quick, easy numbers of the push-button telephone.

On the racecourse, the crowds buzzed like agitated bees round the bookmakers, who were transacting deals as fast as they could. Photo finishes were always popular with serious gamblers, who bet with fervour on the outcome. Some punters really believed in the evidence of their own quick eyes: others found it a chance to hedge their main bet or even recoup a positive loss. A photo was the second chance, the life belt to the drowning, the temporary reprieve from torn-up tickets and anticlimax.

"Six to four on Pickup," shouted young Billy Hitchins hoarsely, from his prime bookmaking pitch in the front row facing the stands. "Six to four on Pickup." A rush of customers descending from the crowded steps enveloped him. "A tenner, Pickup—right, sir. Five on Gumshoe—right, sir. Twenty, Pickup—you're on, sir. Fifty? Yeah, if you like. Fifty at evens, Jetset—why not?" Billy Hitchins, in whose opinion Darling Boy had taken the race by a nostril, was happy to rake in the money.

Greg Simpson accepted Billy Hitchins's ticket for an even fifty on Jetset and hurried to repeat his bet with as many bookmakers as he could reach. There was never much time between the arrival of the knowledge and the announcement of the winner. Never much, but always enough. Two minutes at least. Sometimes as much as five. A determined punter could strike five or six bets in that time, given a thick skin and a ruthless use of elbows. Greg reckoned he could burrow to the front of the closest of throngs after all those years of rush-hour commuting on the Underground, and he managed, that day at Ascot, to lay out all the cash he had brought with him; all four hundred pounds of it, all at evens, all on Jetset.

Neither Billy Hitchins, nor any of his colleagues, felt the slightest twinge of suspicion. Sure, there was a lot of support for Jetset, but so there was for the three other horses, and in a multiple finish like this one a good deal of money always changed hands. Billy Hitchins welcomed it, because it gave him, too, a chance of making a second profit on the race.

Greg noticed one or two others scurrying with wads to Jetset, and wondered, not for the first time, if they, too, were working for Mr. Smith. He was sure he'd seen them often at other meetings, but he felt no inclination at all to accost one of them and ask. Safety lay in anonymity; for him, for them, and for John Smith.

In his box, the judge pored earnestly over the black-and-white print, sorting out which nose belonged to Darling Boy and which to Pickup. He could discern the winner easily enough, and had murmured its number aloud as he wrote it on the pad beside him. The microphone linked to the public announcement system waited mutely at his elbow for him to make his decision on second and third places, a task seeming increasingly difficult. Number two or number eight. But which was which?

It was quiet in his box, the scurrying and shouting among the bookmakers' stands below hardly reaching him through the window glass.

At his shoulder a racecourse official waited patiently, his job only to make the actual announcement, once the decision was made. With a bright light and a magnifying glass, the judge studied the noses. If he got them wrong, a thousand knowledgeable photoreaders would let him know it. He wondered if he should see about a new prescription for his glasses. Photographs never seemed so sharp in outline these days.

Greg Simpson thought regretfully that the judge was overdoing the delay. If he had known he would have so much time, he would have brought with him more than four hundred. Still, four hundred clear profit (less betting tax) was a fine afternoon's work; and he would send Mr. Smith his meagre twenty-five with a grateful heart. Greg Simpson smiled contentedly, and briefly, as if touching a lucky talisman, he

fingered the tiny transistorized hearing aid he wore unobtrusively under hair and trilby behind his left ear.

Jamie Finland listened intently, head bent, his curling dark hair
falling onto the radio with which he eavesdropped on aircraft. The
faint hiss of the carrier wave reached him unchanged, but he waited
with quickening pulse and a fluttering feeling of excitement. If it didn't
happen, he thought briefly, it would be very boring indeed.

Although he was nerve-strainingly prepared, he almost missed it.
The radio spoke one single word, distantly, faintly, without emphasis:
"Eleven." The carrier wave hissed on, as if never disturbed, and it took
Jamie's brain two whole seconds to light up with a laugh of joy.

He pressed the buttons and connected himself to the local bookmaking firm.

"Hullo? This is Jamie Finland. I have a ten-pound credit arranged
with you for this afternoon. Well . . . please, will you put it all on the
result of the photo finish of this race they've just run at Ascot? On
number eleven, please."

"Eleven?" echoed a matter-of-fact voice at the other end. "Jetset?"

"That's right," Jamie said. "Eleven. Jetset."

"Right. Jamie Finland, even tenner on Jetset. Right?"

"Right," Jamie said. "I was watching it on the box."

"Don't we all, chum," said the voice in farewell, clicking off.

Jamie sat back in his chair with a tingling feeling of mischief. If
eleven really had won, he was surely plain robbing the bookie. But who
could know? How could anyone ever know? He wouldn't even tell his
mother, because she would disapprove and might make him give the
winnings back. He imagined her voice if she came home and found he
had turned her ten pounds into twenty. He also imagined it if she
found he had lost it all on the first race, betting on the result of a photo
finish that he couldn't even see.

He hadn't told her that it was because of the numbers on the radio
he had wanted to bet at all. He'd said that he knew people often bet
from home while they were watching racing on television. He'd said it
would give him a marvellous new interest, if he could do that while she
was out at work. He had persuaded her without much trouble to lend
him a stake and arrange things with the bookmakers, and he wouldn't
have done it at all if the certainty factor had been missing.

When he'd first been given the radio which received aircraft frequencies, he had spent hours and days listening to the calls of the jetliners

thundering overhead on their way in and out of Heathrow; but the fascination had worn off, and gradually he tuned in less and less. By accident one day, having twiddled the tuning knob aimlessly without finding an interesting channel, he forgot to switch the set off. In the afternoon, while he was listening to the Ascot televised races, the radio suddenly emitted one word. "Twenty-three."

Jamie switched the set off but took little real notice until the television commentator, announcing the result of the photo finish, spoke almost as if in echo. "Twenty-three . . . Swanlake, number twenty-three, is the winner."

How *odd,* Jamie thought. He left the tuning knob undisturbed, and switched the aircraft radio on again the following Saturday, along with Kempton Park races on television. There were two photo finishes, but no voice of God on the ether. Ditto nil results from Doncaster, Chepstow and Epsom persuaded him, shrugging, to put it down to coincidence, but with the rearrival of a meeting at Ascot, he decided to give it one more try.

"Five," said the radio quietly; and later, "Ten." And duly, numbers five and ten were given the verdict by the judge.

The judge, deciding he could put off the moment no longer, handed his written-down result to the waiting official, who leaned forward and drew the microphone to his mouth.

"First, number eleven," he said. "A dead heat for second place between number two and number eight. First, Jetset. Dead heat for second, Darling Boy and Pickup. The distance between first and second a short head. The fourth horse was number twelve."

The judge leaned back in his chair and wiped the sweat from his forehead. Another photo finish safely past . . . but there was no doubt they were testing to his nerves.

Arnold Roper picked up his binoculars, the better to see the winning punters collect from the bookmakers. His twenty-one trusty men had certainly had time today for a thorough killing. Greg Simpson, in particular, was sucking honey all along the line; but then Greg Simpson, with his outstanding managerial skills, was always, in Arnold's view, the one most likely to do best. Greg's success was as pleasing to Arnold as his own.

Billy Hitchins handed Greg his winnings without a second glance, and paid out, too, to five others whose transistor hearing aids were safely hidden by hair. He reckoned he had lost, altogether, on the photo betting, but his book for the race itself had been robustly healthy. Billy Hitchins, not displeased, switched his mind attentively to the next event.

Jamie Finland laughed aloud and banged his table with an ecstatic fist. Someone, somewhere, was talking through an open microphone, and if Jamie had had the luck to pick up the transmission, why shouldn't he? Why shouldn't he? He thought of the information as an accident, not a fraud, and he waited with uncomplicated pleasure for another bunch of horses to finish nose to nose. Betting on certainties, he decided, quietening his conscience, was not a crime if you come by the information innocently.

After the fourth race he telephoned to bet on number fifteen, increasing his winnings to thirty-five pounds.

Greg Simpson went home at the end of the afternoon with a personal storage problem almost as pressing as Arnold's. There was a limit, he discovered, to the amount of ready cash one could stow away in an ordinary suit, and he finally had to wrap the stuff in the *Sporting Life* and carry it home under his arm, like fish and chips. Two in one day, he thought warmly. A real clean-up. A day to remember. And there was always tomorrow, back here at Ascot, and Saturday at Sandown, and next week, according to the list which had arrived anonymously on the usual postcard, Newbury and Windsor. With a bit of luck, he could soon afford a new car, and Joan could book the skiing holiday with the children.

Billy Hitchins packed away his stand and equipment, and with the help of his clerk carried them the half mile along the road to his betting shop in Ascot High Street. Billy at eighteen had horrified his teachers by ducking university and apprenticing his bright mathematical brain to his local bookie. Billy at twenty-four had taken over the business, and now, three years later, was poised for expansion. He had had a good day on the whole, and after totting up the total, and locking the safe, he took his betting-shop manager along to the pub.

"Funny thing," said the manager over the second beer. "That new account, the one you fixed up yesterday, with that nurse."

"Oh, yes . . . the nurse. Gave me ten quid in advance. They don't often do that." He drank his Scotch and water.

"Yeah . . . Well, this Finland, while he was watching the telly, he phoned in two bets, both on the results of the photos, and he got it right both times."

"Can't have that," said Billy, with mock severity.

"He didn't place other bets, see? Unusual, that."

"What did you say his name was?"

"Jamie Finland."

The barmaid leaned towards them over the bar, her friendly face smiling and the pink sweater leaving little to the imagination. "Jamie Finland?" she said. "Ever such a nice boy, isn't he? Shame about him being blind."

"What?" said Billy.

The barmaid nodded. "Him and his mother, they live just down the road in those new flats, next door to my sister. He stays home most of the time, studying and listening to his radios. And you'd never believe it, but he can tell colours, he can really. My sister says it's really weird, but he told her she was wearing a green coat, and she was."

"I don't believe it," Billy said.

"It's true as God's my judge," said the barmaid, offended.

"No . . ." Billy said. "I don't believe that even if he can tell a green coat from a red, he could distinguish colours on a television screen with three or four horses crossing the line abreast. You can't do it often even if you can see." He sat and thought. "It could be a coincidence," he said. "On the other hand, I lost a lot today on those photos." He thought longer. "We all took a caning over those photos. I heard several of the other bookies complaining about the run on Jetset . . ." He frowned. "I don't see how it could be rigged . . ."

Billy put his glass down with a crash which startled the whole bar.

"Did you say Jamie Finland listens to radios? What radios?"

"How should I know?" said the barmaid, bridling.

"He lives near the course," Billy said, thinking feverishly. "So just suppose he somehow overheard the photo result before it was given on the loudspeakers. But that doesn't explain the delay . . . how there was time for him—and probably quite a lot of others who heard the same thing—to get their money on."

"I don't know what you're on about," said the barmaid.

"I think I'll pop along and see Jamie Finland," said Billy Hitchins. "And ask who or what he heard . . . if he heard anything at all."

"Bit far-fetched," said the manager judiciously. "The only person who could delay things long enough would be the judge."

"Oh, my God," said Billy, awe-struck. "What about the judge?"

Arnold Roper did not know about the long fuse being lit in the pub. To Arnold, Billy Hitchins was a name on a bookmaker's stand. He could not suppose that brainy Billy Hitchins would drink in a pub where the barmaid had a sister who lived next door to a blind boy who had picked up his discreet transmissions on a carelessly left on radio which, unlike most, was capable of receiving 110 to 140 megahertz on VHF.

Arnold Roper travelled serenely homewards with his walkie-talkie-type transmitter hidden as usual inside his inner jacket pocket, its short aerial retracted now, safely out of sight. The line-of-sight low-powered frequency he used was in his opinion completely safe, as only a passing aircraft was likely to receive it, and no pilot on earth would connect a simple number spoken on the air with the winner of the photo finish down at Ascot, or Epsom, or Newmarket, or York.

Back on the racecourse, Arnold had carefully packed away and securely locked up the extremely delicate and expensive apparatus which belonged to the firm that employed him. Arnold Roper was not the judge. Arnold Roper's job lay in operating the photo-finish camera. It was he who watched the print develop; he who could take his time delivering it to the judge; he who always knew the winner first.

No less a critic than Carolyn Heilbron ("Amanda Cross") con-
siders PHYLLIS DOROTHY JAMES *(1921–) to be "one of the*
leading detective novelists of this day or any day." Ms. James
has two extremely popular series detectives—Adam Dalgliesh of
Scotland Yard and Cordelia Gray, a particularly convincing
private eye—and she uses her background with the National
Health Service and Criminal Policy Department of the Home
Office in Great Britain to wonderful effect in her books. An
Unsuitable Job for a Woman *(1972) is considered her master-*
piece to date, but this writer prefers her magnificent Death of
an Expert Witness *(1977).*

"The Victim" is a brilliant, moving story that demonstrates
why Ms. James is admired by critics and readers alike.

The Victim
BY P. D. JAMES

You know Princess Ilsa Mancelli, of course. I mean by that that you
must have seen her on the cinema screen; on television; pictured in
newspapers arriving at airports with her latest husband; relaxing on
their yacht; be-jewelled at first nights, gala nights, at any night and in
any place where it is obligatory for the rich and successful to show
themselves. Even if, like me, you have nothing but bored contempt for
what I believe is called the international jet set, you can hardly live in
the modern world and not know Ilsa Mancelli. And you can't fail to
have picked up some scraps about her past. The brief and not particularly successful screen career, when even her heart-stopping beauty
couldn't quite compensate for the paucity of talent; the succession of
marriages, first to the producer who made her first film and who broke
a twenty-year-old marriage to get her; then to a Texan millionaire;
lastly to a prince. About two months ago I saw a nauseatingly sentimental picture of her with her two-day-old son in a Rome nursing
home. So it looks as if this marriage, sanctified as it is by wealth, a title
and maternity may be intended as her final adventure.

The husband before the film producer is, I notice, no longer mentioned. Perhaps her publicity agent fears that a violent death in the
family, particularly an unsolved violent death, might tarnish her bright
image. Blood and beauty. In the early stages of her career they hadn't

been able to resist that cheap, vicarious thrill. But not now. Nowadays her early history, before she married the film producer, has become a little obscure, although there is a suggestion of poor but decent parentage and early struggles suitably rewarded. I am the most obscure part of that obscurity. Whatever you know, or think you know, of Ilsa Mancelli, you won't have heard about me. The publicity machine has decreed that I be nameless, faceless, unremembered, that I no longer exist. Ironically, the machine is right; in any real sense, I don't.

I married her when she was Elsie Bowman, aged seventeen. I was assistant librarian at our local branch library and fifteen years older, a thirty-two-year-old virgin, a scholar *manqué,* thin faced, a little stooping, my meagre hair already thinning. She worked on the cosmetic counter of our High Street store. She was beautiful then, but with a delicate, tentative, unsophisticated loveliness which gave little promise of the polished mature beauty which is hers today. Our story was very ordinary. She returned a book to the library one evening when I was on counter duty. We chatted. She asked my advice about novels for her mother. I spent as long as I dared finding suitable romances for her on the shelves. I tried to interest her in the books I liked. I asked her about herself, her life, her ambitions. She was the only woman I had been able to talk to. I was enchanted by her, totally and completely besotted.

I used to take my lunch early and make surreptitious visits to the store, watching her from the shadow of a neighbouring pillar. There is one picture which even now seems to stop my heart. She had dabbed her wrist with scent and was holding out a bare arm over the counter so that a prospective customer could smell the perfume. She was totally absorbed, her young face gravely preoccupied. I watched her, silently, and felt the tears smarting my eyes.

It was a miracle when she agreed to marry me. Her mother (she had no father) was reconciled if not enthusiastic about the match. She didn't, as she made it abundantly plain, consider me much of a catch. But I had a good job with prospects; I was educated; I was steady and reliable; I spoke with a grammar school accent which, while she affected to deride it, raised my status in her eyes. Besides, any marriage for Elsie was better than none. I was dimly aware when I bothered to think about Elsie in relation to anyone but myself that she and her mother didn't get on.

Mrs Bowman made, as she described it, a splash. There was a full choir and a peal of bells. The church hall was hired and a sit-down meal, ostentatiously unsuitable and badly cooked, was served to eighty guests. Between the pangs of nervousness and indigestion I was conscious of smirking waiters in short white jackets, a couple of giggling bridesmaids from the store, their freckled arms bulging from pink taffeta sleeves, hearty male relatives, red faced and with buttonholes of carnation and waving fern, who made indelicate jokes and clapped me painfully between the shoulders. There were speeches and warm champagne. And, in the middle of it all, Elsie my Elsie, like a white rose.

I suppose that it was stupid of me to imagine that I could hold her. The mere sight of our morning faces, smiling at each other's reflection in the bedroom mirror, should have warned me that it couldn't last. But, poor deluded fool, I never dreamed that I might lose her except by death. Her death I dared not contemplate, and I was afraid for the first time of my own. Happiness had made a coward of me. We moved into a new bungalow, chosen by Elsie, sat in new chairs chosen by Elsie, slept in a befrilled bed chosen by Elsie. I was so happy that it was like passing into a new phase of existence, breathing a different air, seeing the most ordinary things as if they were newly created. One isn't necessarily humble when greatly in love. Is it so unreasonable to recognize the value of a love like mine, to believe that the beloved is equally sustained and transformed by it?

She said that she wasn't ready to start a baby and, without her job, she was easily bored. She took a brief training in shorthand and typing at our local Technical College and found herself a position as shorthand typist at the firm of Collingford and Major. That, at least, was how the job started. Shorthand typist, then secretary to Mr Rodney Collingford, then personal secretary, then confidential personal secretary; in my bemused state of uxorious bliss I only half registered her progress from occasionally taking his dictation when his then secretary was absent to flaunting his gifts of jewellery and sharing his bed.

He was everything I wasn't. Rich (his father had made a fortune from plastics shortly after the war and had left the factory to his only son), coarsely handsome in a swarthy fashion, big muscled, confident, attractive to women. He prided himself on taking what he wanted. Elsie must have been one of his easiest pickings.

Why, I still wonder, did he want to marry her? I thought at the time that he couldn't resist depriving a pathetic, under-privileged, unattractive husband of a prize which neither looks nor talent had qualified him to deserve. I've noticed that about the rich and successful. They can't bear to see the undeserving prosper. I thought that half the satis-

faction for him was in taking her away from me. That was partly why I
knew that I had to kill him. But now I'm not so sure. I may have done
him an injustice. It may have been both simpler and more complicated
than that. She was, you see—she still is—so very beautiful.

I understand her better now. She was capable of kindness, good
humour, generosity even, provided she was getting what she wanted.
At the time we married, and perhaps eighteen months afterwards, she
wanted me. Neither her egoism nor her curiosity had been able to
resist such a flattering, overwhelming love. But for her, marriage
wasn't permanency. It was the first and necessary step towards the
kind of life she wanted and meant to have. She was kind to me, in bed
and out, while I was what she wanted. But when she wanted someone
else, then my need of her, my jealousy, my bitterness, she saw as a
cruel and wilful denial of her basic right, the right to have what she
wanted. After all, I'd had her for nearly three years. It was two years
more than I had any right to expect. She thought so. Her darling
Rodney thought so. When my acquaintances at the library learnt of
the divorce I could see in their eyes that they thought so too. And she
couldn't see what I was so bitter about. Rodney was perfectly happy to
be the guilty party; they weren't, she pointed out caustically, expecting
me to behave like a gentleman. I wouldn't have to pay for the divorce.
Rodney would see to that. I wasn't being asked to provide her with
alimony. Rodney had more than enough. At one point she came close
to bribing me with Rodney's money to let her go without fuss. And yet
—was it really as simple as that? She had loved me, or at least needed
me, for a time. Had she perhaps seen in me the father that she had lost
at five years old?

During the divorce, through which I was, as it were, gently pro-
cessed by highly paid legal experts as if I were an embarrassing but
expendable nuisance to be got rid of with decent speed, I was only able
to keep sane by the knowledge that I was going to kill Collingford. I
knew that I couldn't go on living in a world where he breathed the
same air. My mind fed voraciously on the thought of his death,
savoured it, began systematically and with dreadful pleasure to plan it.

A successful murder depends on knowing your victim, his character,
his daily routine, his weaknesses, those unalterable and betraying habits which make up the core of personality. I knew quite a lot about
Rodney Collingford. I knew facts which Elsie had let fall in her first
weeks with the firm, typing pool gossip. I knew the fuller and rather
more intimate facts which she had disclosed in those early days of her

enchantment with him, when neither prudence nor kindness had been able to conceal her obsessive preoccupation with her new boss. I should have been warned then. I knew, none better, the need to talk about the absent lover.

What did I know about him? I knew the facts that were common knowledge, of course. That he was wealthy; aged thirty; a notable amateur golfer; that he lived in an ostentatious mock-Georgian house on the banks of the Thames looked after by over-paid but non-resident staff; that he owned a cabin cruiser; that he was just over six feet tall; that he was a good business man but reputedly close-fisted; that he was methodical in his habits. I knew a miscellaneous and unrelated set of facts about him, some of which would be useful, some important, some of which I couldn't use. I knew—and this was rather surprising—that he was good with his hands and liked making things in metal and wood. He had built an expensively-equipped and large workroom in the grounds of his house and spent every Thursday evening working there alone. He was a man addicted to routine. This creativity, however mundane and trivial, I found intriguing, but I didn't let myself dwell on it. I was interested in him only so far as his personality and habits were relevant to his death. I never thought of him as a human being. He had no existence for me apart from my hate. He was Rodney Collingford, my victim.

First I decided on the weapon. A gun would have been the most certain, I supposed, but I didn't know how to get one and was only too well aware that I wouldn't know how to load or use it if I did. Besides, I was reading a number of books about murder at the time and I realized that guns, however cunningly obtained, were easy to trace. And there was another thing. A gun was too impersonal, too remote. I wanted to make physical contact at the moment of death. I wanted to get close enough to see that final look of incredulity and horror as he recognized, simultaneously, me and his death. I wanted to drive a knife into his throat.

I bought it two days after the divorce. I was in no hurry to kill Collingford. I knew that I must take my time, must be patient, if I were to act in safety. One day, perhaps when we were old, I might tell Elsie. But I didn't intend to be found out. This was to be the perfect murder. And that meant taking my time. He would be allowed to live for a full year. But I knew that the earlier I bought the knife the more difficult it would be, twelve months later, to trace the purchase. I didn't buy it locally. I went one Saturday morning by train and bus to a north-east suburb and found a busy ironmongers and general store just off the High Street. There was a variety of knives on display. The blade of the one I selected was about six inches long and was made of strong steel screwed into a plain wooden handle. I think it was probably meant for cutting lino. In the shop its razor-sharp edge was protected by a strong cardboard sheath. It felt good and right in my hand. I stood in a small queue at the pay desk and the cashier didn't even glance up as he took my notes and pushed the change towards me.

But the most satisfying part of my planning was the second stage. I wanted Collingford to suffer. I wanted him to know that he was going to die. It wasn't enough that he should realise it in a last second before I drove in the knife or in that final second before he ceased to know anything for ever. Two seconds of agony, however horrible, weren't an adequate return for what he had done to me. I wanted him to know that he was a condemned man, to know it with increasing certainty, to wonder every morning whether this might be his last day. What if this knowledge did make him cautious, put him on his guard? In this country, he couldn't go armed. He couldn't carry on his business with a hired protector always at his side. He couldn't bribe the police to watch him every second of the day. Besides, he wouldn't want to be thought a coward. I guessed that he would carry on, ostentatiously normal, as if the threats were unreal or derisory, something to laugh about with his drinking cronies. He was the sort to laugh at danger. But he would never be sure. And, by the end, his nerve and confidence would be broken. Elsie wouldn't know him for the man she had married.

I would have liked to have telephoned him but that, I knew, was impracticable. Calls could be traced; he might refuse to talk to me; I wasn't confident that I could disguise my voice. So the sentence of death would have to be sent by post. Obviously, I couldn't write the notes or the envelopes myself. My studies in murder had shown me how difficult it was to disguise handwriting and the method of cutting out and sticking together letters from a newspaper seemed messy, very time consuming and difficult to manage wearing gloves. I knew, too, that it would be fatal to use my own small portable typewriter or one of the machines at the library. The forensic experts could identify a machine.

And then I hit on my plan. I began to spend my Saturdays and occasional half days journeying round London and visiting shops where they sold secondhand typewriters. I expect you know the kind

of shop; a variety of machines of different ages, some practically obsolete, others hardly used, arranged on tables where the prospective pur-
chaser may try them out. There were new machines too, and the proprietor was usually employed in demonstrating their merits or
discussing hire purchase terms. The customers wandered desultorily
around, inspecting the machines, stopping occasionally to type out an
exploratory passage. There were little pads of rough paper stacked
ready for use. I didn't, of course, use the scrap paper provided. I came
supplied with my own writing materials, a well-known brand sold in
every stationer's and on every railway bookstall. I bought a small supply of paper and envelopes once every two months and never from the
same shop. Always, when handling them, I wore a thin pair of gloves,
slipping them on as soon as my typing was complete. If someone were
near, I would tap out the usual drivel about the sharp brown fox or all
good men coming to the aid of the party. But if I were quite alone I
would type something very different.

"This is the first comunication, Collingford. You'll be getting them
regularly from now on. They're just to let you know that I'm going to
kill you."

"You can't escape me, Collingford. Don't bother to inform the police. They can't help you."

"I'm getting nearer, Collingford. Have you made your will?"

"Not long now, Collingford. What does it feel like to be under sentence of death?"

The warnings weren't particularly elegant. As a librarian I could
think of a number of apt quotations, which would have added a touch
of individuality or style, perhaps even of sardonic humour, to the bald
sentence of death. But I dared not risk originality. The notes had to be
ordinary, the kind of threat which anyone of his enemies, a worker, a
competitor, a cuckolded husband, might have sent.

Sometimes I had a lucky day. The shop would be large, well supplied, nearly empty. I would be able to move from typewriter to typewriter and leave with perhaps a dozen or so notes and addressed envelopes ready to send. I always carried a folded newspaper in which I
could conceal my writing pad and envelopes and into which I could
quickly slip my little stock of typed messages.

It was quite a job to keep myself supplied with notes and I discovered interesting parts of London and fascinating shops. I particularly
enjoyed this part of my plan. I wanted Collingford to get two notes a
week, one posted on Sunday and one on Thursday. I wanted him to

come to dread Friday and Monday mornings when the familiar typed envelope would drop on his mat. I wanted him to believe the threat was real. And why should he not believe it? How could the force of my hate and resolution not transmit itself through paper and typescript to his gradually comprehending brain?

I wanted to keep an eye on my victim. It shouldn't have been difficult; we lived in the same town. But our lives were worlds apart. He was a hard and sociable drinker. I never went inside a public house, and would have been particularly ill at ease in the kind of public house he frequented. But, from time to time, I would see him in the town. Usually he would be parking his Jaguar, and I would watch his quick, almost furtive, look to left and right before he returned to lock the door. Was it my imagination that he looked older, that some of the confidence had drained out of him?

Once, when walking by the river on a Sunday in early spring, I saw him manoeuvring his boat through Teddington Lock. Ilsa—she had, I knew, changed her name after her marriage—was with him. She was wearing a white trouser suit, her flowing hair was bound by a red scarf. There was a party. I could see two more men and a couple of girls and hear high female squeals of laughter. I turned quickly and slouched away as if I were the guilty one. But not before I had seen Collingford's face. This time I couldn't be mistaken. It wasn't, surely, the tedious job of getting his boat unscratched through the lock that made his face look so grey and strained.

The third phase of my planning meant moving house. I wasn't sorry to go. The bungalow, feminine, chintzy, smelling of fresh paint and the new shoddy furniture which she had chosen, was Elsie's home not mine. Her scent still lingered in cupboards and on pillows. In these inappropriate surroundings I had known greater happiness than I was ever to know again. But now I paced restlessly from room to empty room, fretting to be gone.

It took me four months to find the house I wanted. It had to be on or very near to the river within two or three miles upstream of Collingford's house. It had to be small and reasonably cheap. Money wasn't too much of a difficulty. It was a time of rising house prices and the modern bungalow sold at three hundred pounds more than I had paid for it. I could get another mortgage without difficulty if I didn't ask for too much, but I thought it likely that, for what I wanted, I should have to pay cash.

The house agents perfectly understood that a man on his own found a three-bedroom bungalow too large for him and, even if they found me rather vague about my new requirements and irritatingly imprecise about the reasons for rejecting their offerings, they still sent me orders to view. And then, suddenly on an afternoon in April, I found exactly what I was looking for. It actually stood on the river, separated from it only by a narrow tow path. It was a one-bedroom shack-like wooden bungalow with a tiled roof, set in a small neglected plot of sodden grass and overgrown flower beds. There had once been a wooden landing stage but now the two remaining planks, festooned with weeds and tags of rotted rope, were half submerged beneath the slime of the river. The paint on the small veranda had long ago flaked away. The wallpaper of twined roses in the sitting room was blotched and faded. The previous owner had left two old cane chairs and a ramshackle table. The kitchen was pokey and ill-equipped. Everywhere there hung a damp miasma of depression and decay. In summer, when the neighbouring shacks and bungalows were occupied by holidaymakers and weekenders it would, no doubt, be cheerful enough. But in October, when I planned to kill Collingford, it would be as deserted and isolated as a disused morgue. I bought it and paid cash. I was even able to knock two hundred pounds off the asking price.

My life that summer was almost happy. I did my job at the library adequately. I lived alone in the shack, looking after myself as I had before my marriage. I spent my evenings watching television. The images flickered in front of my eyes almost unregarded, a monochrome background to my bloody and obsessive thoughts.

I practised with the knife until it was as familiar in my hand as an eating utensil. Collingford was taller than I by six inches. The thrust then would have to be upward. It made a difference to the way I held the knife and I experimented to find the most comfortable and effective grip. I hung a bolster on a hook in the bedroom door and lunged at a marked spot for hours at a time. Of course, I didn't actually insert the knife; nothing must dull the sharpness of its blade. Once a week, a special treat, I sharpened it to an even keener edge.

Two days after moving into the bungalow I bought a dark blue untrimmed track suit and a pair of light running shoes. Throughout the summer I spent an occasional evening running on the tow path. The people who owned the neighbouring chalets, when they were there which was infrequently, got used to the sound of my television through the closed curtains and the sight of my figure jogging past their windows. I kept apart from them and from everyone and summer passed into autumn. The shutters were put up on all the chalets except mine. The tow path became mushy with falling leaves. Dusk fell early, and the summer sights and sounds died on the river. And it was October.

He was due to die on Thursday October 17th, the anniversary of the final decree of divorce. It had to be a Thursday, the evening which he spent by custom alone in his workshop, but it was a particularly happy augury that the anniversary should fall on a Thursday. I knew that he would be there. Every Thursday for nearly a year I had padded along the two and a half miles of the footpath in the evening dusk and had stood briefly watching the squares of light from his windows and the dark bulk of the house behind.

It was a warm evening. There had been a light drizzle for most of the day but, by dusk, the skies had cleared. There was a thin white sliver of moon and it cast a trembling ribbon of light across the river. I left the library at my usual time, said my usual good-nights. I knew that I had been my normal self during the day, solitary, occasionally a little sarcastic, conscientious, betraying no hint of the inner tumult.

I wasn't hungry when I got home but I made myself eat an omelette and drink two cups of coffee. I put on my swimming trunks and hung around my neck a plastic toilet bag containing the knife. Over the trunks I put on my track suit, slipping a pair of thin rubber gloves into the pocket. Then, at about quarter past seven, I left the shack and began my customary gentle trot along the tow path.

When I got to the chosen spot opposite to Collingford's house I could see at once that all was well. The house was in darkness but there were the customary lighted windows of his workshop. I saw that the cabin cruiser was moored against the boathouse. I stood very still and listened. There was no sound. Even the light breeze had died and the yellowing leaves on the riverside elms hung motionless. The tow path was completely deserted. I slipped into the shadow of the hedge where the trees grew thickest and found the place I had already selected. I put on the rubber gloves, slipped out of the track suit, and left it folded around my running shoes in the shadow of the hedge. Then, still watching carefully to left and right, I made my way to the river.

I knew just where I must enter and leave the water. I had selected a place where the bank curved gently, where the water was shallow and the bottom was firm and comparatively free of mud. The water struck very cold, but I expected that. Every night during that autumn I had bathed in cold water to accustom my body to the shock. I swam across the river with my methodical but quiet breast stroke, hardly disturbing the dark surface of the water. I tried to keep out of the path of moon-light but, from time to time, I swam into its silver gleam and saw my red gloved hands parting in front of me as if they were already stained with blood.

I used Collingford's landing stage to clamber out the other side. Again I stood still and listened. There was no sound except for the constant moaning of the river and the solitary cry of a night bird. I made my way silently over the grass. Outside the door of his work-room, I paused again. I could hear the noise of some kind of machin-ery. I wondered whether the door would be locked, but it opened easily when I turned the handle. I moved into a blaze of light.

I knew exactly what I had to do. I was perfectly calm. It was over in about four seconds. I don't think he really had a chance. He was absorbed in what he had been doing, bending over a lathe, and the sight of an almost naked man, walking purposely towards him, left him literally impotent with surprise. But, after that first paralysing second, he knew me. Oh yes, he knew me! Then I drew my right hand from behind my back and struck. The knife went in as sweetly as if the flesh had been butter. He staggered and fell. I had expected that and I let myself go loose and fell on top of him. His eyes were glazed, his mouth opened and there was a gush of dark red blood. I twisted the knife viciously in the wound, relishing the sound of tearing sinews. Then I waited. I counted five deliberately, then raised myself from his prone figure and crouched behind him before withdrawing the knife. When I withdrew it there was a fountain of sweet smelling blood which curved from his throat like an arch. There is one thing I shall never forget. The blood must have been red, what other colour could it have been? But, at the time and for ever afterwards, I saw it as a golden stream.

I checked my body for blood stains before I left the workshop and rinsed my arms under the cold tap at his sink. My bare feet made no marks on the wooden block flooring. I closed the door quietly after me and, once again, stood listening. Still no sound. The house was dark and empty.

The return journey was more exhausting than I had thought possi-ble. The river seemed to have widened and I thought that I should never reach my home shore. I was glad I had chosen a shallow part of the stream and that the bank was firm. I doubt whether I could have drawn myself up through a welter of mud and slime. I was shivering violently as I zipped-up my track suit and it took me precious seconds to get on my running shoes. After I had run about a mile down the tow path I weighted the toilet bag containing the knife with stones from the path and hurled it into the middle of the river. I guessed that they would drag part of the Thames for the weapon but they could hardly search the whole stream. And, even if they did, the toilet bag was one sold at the local chain store which anyone might have bought, and I was confident that the knife could never be traced to me. Half an hour later I was back in my shack. I had left the television on and the news was just ending. I made myself a cup of hot cocoa and sat to watch it. I felt drained of thought and energy as if I had just made love. I was conscious of nothing but my tiredness, my body's coldness gradually returning to life in the warmth of the electric fire, and a great peace.

He must have had quite a lot of enemies. It was nearly a fortnight before the police got round to interviewing me. Two officers came, a Detective Inspector and a Sergeant, both in plain clothes. The Sergeant did most of the talking; the other just sat, looking round at the sitting room, glancing out at the river, looking at the two of us from time to time from cold grey eyes as if the whole investigation were a necessary bore. The Sergeant said the usual reassuring platitudes about just a few questions. I was nervous, but that didn't worry me. They would expect me to be nervous. I told myself that, whatever I did, I mustn't try to be clever. I mustn't talk too much. I had decided to tell them that I spent the whole evening watching television, confident that no one would be able to refute this. I knew that no friends would have called on me. I doubted whether my colleagues at the library even knew where I lived. And I had no telephone so I need not fear that a caller's ring had gone unanswered during that crucial hour and a half.

On the whole it was easier than I had expected. Only once did I feel myself at risk. That was when the Inspector suddenly intervened. He said in a harsh voice:

"He married your wife didn't he? Took her away from you, some people might say. Nice piece of goods, too, by the look of her. Didn't you feel any grievance? Or was it all nice and friendly? You take her, old chap. No ill feelings. That kind of thing?"

It was hard to accept the contempt in his voice but if he hoped to provoke me he didn't succeed. I had been expecting this question. I was prepared. I looked down at my hands and waited a few seconds before I spoke. I knew exactly what I would say.

"I could have killed Collingford myself when she first told me about him. But I had to come to terms with it. She went for the money you see. And if that's the kind of wife you have, well she's going to leave you sooner or later. Better sooner than when you have a family. You tell yourself 'good riddance'. I don't mean I felt that at first, of course. But I did feel it in the end. Sooner than I expected, really."

That was all I said about Elsie then or ever. They came back three times. They asked if they could look round my shack. They looked round it. They took away two of my suits and the track suit for examination. Two weeks later they returned them without comment. I never knew what they suspected, or even if they did suspect. Each time they came I said less, not more. I never varied my story. I never allowed them to provoke me into discussing my marriage or speculating about the crime. I just sat there, telling them the same thing over and over again. I never felt in any real danger. I knew that they had dragged some lengths of the river but that they hadn't found the weapon. In the end they gave up. I always had the feeling that I was pretty low on their list of suspects and that, by the end, their visits were merely a matter of form.

It was three months before Elsie came to me. I was glad that it wasn't earlier. It might have looked suspicious if she had arrived at the shack when the police were with me. After Collingford's death I hadn't seen her. There were pictures of her in the national and local newspapers, fragile in sombre furs and black hat at the inquest, bravely controlled at the crematorium, sitting in her drawing room in afternoon dress and pearls with her husband's dog at her feet, the personification of loneliness and grief.

"I can't think who could have done it. He must have been a madman. Rodney hadn't an enemy in the world."

That statement caused some ribald comment at the library. One of the assistants said:

"He's left her a fortune I hear. Lucky for her she had an alibi. She was at a London theatre all the evening, watching *Macbeth.* Otherwise, from what I've heard of our Rodney Collingford, people might have started to get ideas about his fetching little widow."

Then he gave me a sudden embarrassed glance, remembering who the widow was.

And so one Friday evening, she came. She drove herself and was alone. The dark green Saab drove up at my ramshackle gate. She came into the sitting room and looked around in a kind of puzzled contempt. After a moment, still not speaking, she sat in one of the fireside chairs and crossed her legs, moving one caressingly against the other. I hadn't seen her sitting like that before. She looked up at me. I was standing stiffly in front of her chair, my lips dry. When I spoke I couldn't recognize my own voice.

"So you've come back?" I said.

She stared at me, incredulous, and then she laughed:

"To you? Back for keeps? Don't be silly, darling! I've just come to pay a visit. Besides, I wouldn't dare to come back, would I? I might be frightened that you'd stick a knife into my throat."

I couldn't speak. I stared at her, feeling the blood drain from my face. Then I heard her high, rather childish voice. It sounded almost kind.

"Don't worry, I shan't tell. You were right about him, darling, you really were. He wasn't at all nice really. And mean! I didn't care so much about your meanness. After all, you don't earn so very much do you? But he had half a million! Think of it, darling. I've been left half a million! And he was so mean that he expected me to go on working as his secretary even after we were married. I typed all his letters! I really did! All that he sent from home, anyway. And I had to open his post every morning unless the envelopes had a secret little sign on them he'd told his friends about to show that they were private."

I said through bloodless lips:

"So all my notes—"

"He never saw them, darling. Well, I didn't want to worry him, did I? And I knew they were from you. I knew when the first one arrived. You never could spell communication, could you? I noticed that when you used to write to the house agents and the solicitor before we were married. It made me laugh considering that you're an educated librarian and I was only a shop assistant."

"So you knew all the time. You knew that it was going to happen."

"Well, I thought that it might. But he really was horrible, darling. You can't imagine. And now I've got half a million! Isn't it lucky that I have an alibi? I thought you might come on that Thursday. And Rodney never did enjoy a serious play."

After that brief visit I never saw or spoke to her again. I stayed in the shack, but life became pointless after Collingford's death. Planning his murder had been an interest, after all. Without Elsie and without my victim there seemed little point in living. And, about a year after his death, I began to dream. I still dream, always on a Monday and Friday. I live through it all again: the noiseless run along the tow path over the mush of damp leaves; the quiet swim across the river; the silent opening of his door; the upward thrust of the knife; the vicious turn in the wound; the animal sound of tearing tissues; the curving stream of golden blood. Only the homeward swim is different. In my dream the river is no longer a cleansing stream, luminous under the sickle moon, but a cloying, impenetrable, slow moving bog of viscous blood through which I struggle in impotent panic towards a steadily receding shore.

I know about the significance of the dream. I've read all about the psychology of guilt. Since I lost Elsie I've done all my living through books. But it doesn't help. And I no longer know who I am. I know who I used to be, our local Assistant Librarian, gentle, scholarly, timid, Elsie's husband. But then I killed Collingford. The man I was couldn't have done that. He wasn't that kind of person. So who am I? It isn't really surprising, I suppose, that the Library Committee suggested so tactfully that I ought to look for a less exacting job. A less exacting job than the post of Assistant Librarian? But you can't blame them. No one can be efficient and keep his mind on the job when he doesn't know who he is.

Sometimes, when I'm in a public house—and I seem to spend most of my time there nowadays since I've been out of work—I'll look over someone's shoulder at a newspaper photograph of Elsie and say:

"That's the beautiful Ilsa Mancelli. I was her first husband."

I've got used to the way people sidle away from me, the ubiquitous pub bore, their eyes averted, their voices suddenly hearty. But sometimes, perhaps because they've been lucky with the horses and feel a spasm of pity for a poor deluded sod, they push a few coins over the counter to the barman before making their way to the door, and buy me a drink.

ROBERT BARNARD *(1936–) is a distinguished academic with books such as* Imagery and Theme in the Novels of Dickens *and* A Short History of English Literature *to his credit, along with an excellent study of the work of Agatha Christie,* A Talent to Deceive. *Although an Englishman, he taught for many years at the Universities of Bergen and Tromso in Norway.*

Robert Barnard's fiction is in the tradition of the English village mystery of the "Golden Age," with out-of-the-way settings and a closed group of suspicious characters, spiced with his satiric wit. Of his more than fifteen novels, several feature Scotland's Yard's Perry Trethowan, although the series sleuth is absent from most of Mr. Barnard's writings.

You wouldn't want to meet this "Little Terror" in an English village, or anywhere else.

Little Terror
BY ROBERT BARNARD

It was Albert Wimpole's first holiday on his own for—oh, he didn't know how long: since he was in his late teens it must have been. Because after Mum died, Dad always liked to tag along with him, and though Dad was quite lively, and certainly no trouble at all, still, it was not quite the same, because Albert was a considerate person, conscientious, and naturally he adapted a lot to Dad's ways. Now Dad had decided, regretfully, that he couldn't quite manage it this year, his arthritis being what it was. So Albert was going to enjoy Portugal on his own. A small thrill of anticipation coursed through his slightly old-maidish veins. Who knew what adventures he might meet with? What encounters he might have? On the first day, though, he decided not to go down to the Carcavelos beach, because the breeze was rather high. At the hotel pool it was nice and sheltered.

"Hello."

The voice came from behind his ear. Albert's heart sank, but he was a courteous man, and he turned round on his sunbed in order to respond. He saw, without joy, a pink, ginger-haired boy, with evilly curious eyes.

"Hello," said Albert, and began to turn back.

"How old are you?"

"How old? Let me see now . . . I'm forty-two."

The carroty boy thought.

"That's not three score years and ten, is it?"

"No, it's not, I'm glad to say. In fact, it's not much more than half way there."

"*I've* not even used up the ten," said the child.

"I can see that. You've got an awful lot left."

"Yes. Still, I wouldn't say you were *old,* yet," said the boy.

"Thank you very much," said Albert, and turned over thankfully as the boy left, but not before he had caught sight of the boy's parents, waving in his direction in a friendly fashion. They were heavy, unattractive people of about his own age, or older. Perhaps the Menace was a late blessing, the result of some virulent fertility drug, and spoilt accordingly.

When Albert had been by the pool a couple of hours, he got ready to leave. No sense in overdoing the sunshine on the first day of your holiday. You pay for that if you do, Dad always said, and he was right. As he was just preparing to make his move, the ginger-haired head appeared once more close to his.

"What's your name?"

"My name's Wimpole. What's yours?"

"Terry."

"Ah—short for 'Terror', I suppose."

"No, it isn't, silly. It's short for Terence. Everybody knows that. And I think Wimpole is a jolly funny name. Do you know what happens to you when you die?"

The abrupt change in the topic caught Albert on the hop, and he paused a moment before replying.

"That's something people have been discussing for quite a long time."

"No, it's not, stupid. You lie there still, and you don't breathe, and you don't even twitch, and you don't have dreams, because you're dead."

"I see. Yes, I did know that."

"Then they put you in a box, and either they put you in the ground and throw earth all over you, or they cre-mate you. That means they burn you up, like Guy Fawkes Night."

"I must be getting along," said Albert, and indeed he did begin to feel a burning sensation on his shoulders.

"You know, you don't *necessarily* die at three score years and ten."

"That's a comfort."

"My Gran was seventy-four, and that's more, isn't it? My friend Wayne Catherick said she was past it."

"Well, it's nice to think I might stagger on a bit longer than seventy," said Albert, who had gathered together his things and now began to make his way out.

"Terry's taken quite a fancy to you," said Little Terror's parents as he walked past them. Albert smiled politely.

The next morning Albert ventured on the beach. He walked half a mile towards the fortress, then laid out his towel and settled down. At first the breeze worried him a little, because he knew people often sunburned badly in a breeze, but by half past ten it had died down, and things had become quite idyllic.

"There's Wimpole!" came the well-known voice. Against his wiser instincts Albert looked up. Terry was standing over him, and pointing, as if he were some unusual sea creature.

"We won't intrude," said Terry's parents, settling themselves down two or three yards away, and beginning to remove clothes from their remarkably ill-proportioned bodies. Terry, however, intruded.

While his parents just lay there tanning those fleshy bodies of theirs (Albert prided himself on keeping in good trim), Terry confined himself to questions like "What's that?" and to giving information about his friend Wayne Catherick. When his parents went down to dabble their toes in the freezing Atlantic, Terry's conversation reverted to the topics of yesterday.

"When you're cre-mated," he said, "they shoot your body into a great big oven. Then when you're all burnt up, they put the ashes into a bottle, and you can put flowers in front of it if you want to."

"I think I'll be buried."

"Or they can scatter the ashes somewhere. Like over Scotland, or into the sea. Do you know what Wayne says, Wimpole?"

"No. What does Wayne say?"

"He says my Gran's ashes ought to have been scattered over Tesco's supermarket, because she ate so much."

"That's a very nasty thing for Wayne to say."

"No, it's not. It's true, Wimpole. She was eating us out of house and home. Wayne says she took the food from out of our mouths. She just sat up there in her bedroom, eating. Sometimes I had to go up and get her tray, and she hadn't finished, and it was disgusting. She used to spray me with bits. I could have had chocolate cream sponge every day if she hadn't taken the food from out of my mouth."

"I don't think chocolate cream sponge every day would have been very good for you."

"Yes, it would. *And* I had to keep quiet, *every* morning and *every* night because she was *asleep.* It wasn't fair."

"You *have* made a hit," said Terry's mother, coming back. "It's nice for you, seeing as you're on your own, isn't it?"

The next day Albert waited in his room until he saw them trailing down to the beach. Then he made his way to the pool, and gratefully sank down on a lilo. Though his sunbathing had been in shorter doses than he had intended, the red was beginning to turn to a respectable brown. Half an hour later Terry was sitting beside him, telling him about Wayne.

"It was awfully breezy on the beach," Terry's dad called out, in a friendly way. "You were wise to come here."

"Wayne's dad has a sports shop," said Terry. "I got my costume there. Wayne's got an Auntie Margaret and two grannies. His grannies aren't dead!" he ended, emphatically, as if he had scored a definite point there.

"That's nice," said Albert. "Grannies are always nice to little boys, aren't they?"

"Ha!" said Little Terror, latching back on to his grievance with the tenacity of a politician. "Mine wasn't, Wimpole. I had to be as quiet as quiet, all the time. And her up there stuffing food into her mouth and dribbling, and spitting out crumbs. I don't call that nice. It was disgusting. I was glad when she died and they put her in the oven."

"I'm sure that your mummy and daddy would be very upset if they heard you say that."

"That's why I don't say it when they're there," said Terry, simply. "I expect they quite wanted her to live."

The next day Albert went to the beach at Estoril, then caught the bus to Sintra in the afternoon. When he got back to the hotel the dinner hour was almost over, and Terry and his parents were tucking into enormous slices of caramel cake.

"We missed you today," said Terry's mum, reproachfully, as he passed their table.

When Terry's parents got up to go, they came over and introduced themselves properly. They were the Mumfords, they said. And they had something to ask Albert.

"One doesn't like *putting* on people, but Terry's so fond of you, and it is a *bit* difficult shopping with him tagging along, and we wondered if you *could* keep an eye on him one afternoon so we could go into Lisbon. After all, it's not much fun for a child, watching his parents trying on shoes, is it?"

Albert thought the request an outrageous one. All his instincts cried out against agreeing. Why should he ruin a day of his holidays looking after someone else's repellent (and tedious) child? All his natural instincts told him to say no. All his middle-class instincts told him he had to say yes. He said yes.

"Let me see—I have places I'm planning to go to, and some friends I have to see . . ." he improvised, untruthfully.

"Oh—friends in Portugal," said Mrs Mumford, in a tone of voice which seemed to be expressing either scepticism or disapproval.

"Shall we say Monday?"

Monday was five days away, and the Mumfords would obviously have preferred some earlier day, but *their* middle-class instincts forced them not to quibble, but to accept and to thank him gratefully.

The next day was a day of rest for Albert: the Mumfords went on one of the tours—to Nazaré and Fatima. When he went past their table at dinner time, Mrs Mumford enthused to him about the shrine of Fatima.

"It was a real religious experience," she said. "I expect Terry will want to tell you about it."

Albert repressed a shudder, out of consideration for any Portuguese waiter who might be listening. He merely smiled and went on to his table.

The next day he took the train to Queluz, and the day after he spent exploring the little back streets of Lisbon, then in the afternoon walking up the broad avenue to the park. But all the time Monday was approaching inexorably, and short of going down with beri-beri, Albert could see no way of avoiding his stewardship of the repulsive and necrophilic Terry.

On Monday morning (it turned out, without explanation, to be a whole day's shopping Terry's parents were planning), after the Mumfords had trailed off towards the train for Lisbon, Albert took Terry into Carcavelos and filled him unimaginably full of ice-cream. He hoped it would make him ill or sleepy, but it did neither. When Albert suggested a very light lunch, Terry demanded roast pork at one of the town's little restaurants. Portions were substantial, and he ate with gusto. All this eating at least kept him quiet. Far from responding to suggestions that he have an afternoon's nap, Terry demanded to be taken to the hotel swimming pool. Terry's parents had impressed upon Albert most forcefully that Terry was not allowed to use the diving board, but while Albert was still fussing around removing his own clothes, he saw that Terry was already up there, and preparing to throw himself into the water.

"This is a suicide dive!" yelled the child. "I want to be cremated!"

"You've got to be drowned first," muttered Albert. Ten seconds later he was in the pool, fishing out the sobbing, gasping boy. Respect for the susceptibilities of parents prevented Albert giving him a good belting, but he was able to pummel him pretty satisfyingly on the pretext of getting water out of his lungs. He commanded him to lie still for at least ten minutes.

"Would I be in heaven now, if I had drowned, Wimpole?" Terry asked, after five.

Albert did not think it wise to go into alternative destinations for his soul. His parents might be namby-pamby as theologians.

"I believe there is some period of waiting."

"Like on the platform, before the train comes in?" asked Terry. "I bet once I started I'd have gone fast. Like a space-shot. Whoosh! You wouldn't have been able to see me, I'd have gone so fast."

"I expect you're right," said Albert, reading his P. D. James.

"I bet Grandma didn't go fast like that. I can't see it. She was enormous. Wayne's mum called her unwiel . . ."

"Unwieldy."

"That's right. It means enormous. Colossal. Like a great, fat pig."

"You know your mother wouldn't like hearing you say that."

"She isn't," said Terry, dismissively. "Anyway, you can't expect to go to heaven like a space-shot if you eat enough for three elephants. *And* if you're bad-tempered and make everyone's life a misery."

Terry lay quiet for a bit, watching other children in the pool, children with whom he habitually refused to play. Then, out of the corner of his eye, Albert was aware that he was being watched, slyly, out of the corner of Terry's eye.

"My grandma died of an overdose," Terry said.

"An overdose of you?" asked Albert, though he knew it was useless to venture humour on this horrible child.

"No, stupid. An overdose of medicine. She had it in a glass by the side of her bed, so she could take it while Mummy was out at work. Mummy does half days at the librerry. And Gran's medicine was left in the glass by her bed. So she didn't have to get up and go to any trouble to get it. Fat old pig!"

"Terry—if I hear any more words like that about your gran I'm going to take you and lock you in your room. In fact, I don't wish to hear any more about your gran at all."

"All right," said Terry, equably. "Only it's funny the medicine was in the cupboard, and she'd have to get up and get it to give herself an overdose, isn't it? 'Cos it was left by her bed like that every day."

"I expect she felt bad, and thought she needed more," suggested Albert.

"Maybe," said Terry.

Then he took himself off once more to the pool, and began showing off in front of the smaller children. Before very long he was on the diving board again, and Albert was in the pool rescuing him. It was during the third time this happened that the Mumfords arrived back at the hotel.

"I do hope he hasn't been any trouble," said Mrs Mumford. "Now say thank you to Mr Wimpole, Terry."

For the remainder of the holiday the sun shone with a terrible brightness. Albert grew inventive about where he spent his days. He took the bus and ferry out to Sesimbra, he found little beaches on the Estoril coast where fishermen still mended their nets and tourists were never seen. He took the train up to Coimbra, and only rejected Oporto because he calculated that he would only have two hours to spend there before he would have to travel back. He had none of the spicy or sad romantic adventures he had hoped for—what lonely, middle-aged person does on holiday, unless he pays for them?—but he arrived back at the hotel for dinner tired and not dissatisfied with his days.

"My, you *have* got a lot of friends in Portugal," said the Mumfords, who were now spending all their days by the pool. "We've made good friends with Manuel, the waiter there," explained Dad Mumford. "He's introduced us to this lovely restaurant run by his uncle. They're wonderful to Terry there, and they really do us proud at lunchtime."

So the Mumfords had found they could do without him.

Eventually it was time to go home. On the bus to the airport Albert hung back, and selected a seat well away from Terry. At the airport there was a slight delay, while the plane was refuelled and cleaned, and restocked with plastic food. In any case, Albert knew that there he would not be able to escape the Mumfords entirely.

"Do you think you could just keep an eye on Terry for one *minute* while we go to the duty free shop?" his mum asked. There was something in the tone of voice as she asked it, as if she knew he had considered their earlier request an encroachment, and she regretted having to ask again so obviously selfish a person.

"Of course," said Albert.

"I'll tell you how she died," said Terry, as their heavy footsteps faded away across the marble halls.

"I don't wish to know."

"Yes, you do. She was lying up there, and Wayne and I were playing in my bedroom—*quietly*. How can you play quietly? And we were pretty fed up. And she called out, and called, and called. And when we went in, she said she'd got stuck on one side, and couldn't get over, and her leg had gone to sleep. She hadn't had her afternoon medicine yet. And while Wayne pretended to push her, I got the bottle from the cupboard, and I emptied some of it into her glass, and then I put it back in the cupboard. Then I went and pushed with Wayne, and finally we got her over. She said she was ever so grateful. She said, 'Now I can go off.' We laughed and laughed when we got back to my room. She went off all right!"

"I'm not believing any of this, Terry."

"Believe it or not, I don't care," said Terry. "It's true. That's how the old pig died."

"It's an awful swindle in there," said the Mumfords, coming back from the duty free shop. "Hardly any cheaper than in England. I shouldn't bother to go."

"I'll just take a look," said Albert, escaping.

Albert did not enjoy his flight home at all, though he bought no less than three of the little bottles of white wine they sell with the meal. He was examining the story and re-examining it with the brain of one who was accustomed to weighing up stories likely and unlikely (for Albert worked in a tax office). On the face of it, it was incredible—that a small boy (or was it two small boys?) should kill someone in this simple, almost foolproof way. Yet there had been in the last few years murder cases—now and again, yet often enough—involving children horribly young. And in England too, not in America, where people like Albert imagined such things might be common occurrences.

Albert shook his head over the stewed fish that turned out to be braised chicken. How was he to tell? And if he said nothing, how terrible might be the consequences that might ensue! If adult murderers are inclined to kill a second time, how much more likely must a child be—one who has got away with it, and rejoices in his cleverness. Even the boy's own parents would not be safe, in the unlikely event of their ever crossing his will. What sort of figure would Albert make if he went to the police *then* with his story. Reluctantly, for he foresaw little but embarrassment and ridicule, Albert decided he would have to go to them and tell his tale. In his own mind he could not tell whether Little Horror's story was true or not. It would have to be left to trained minds to come to a conclusion.

At Gatwick Albert was first out of the plane, through Passport Control and Customs in no time, and out to his car, which was miraculously unscathed by the attentions of vandals or thieves. As he drove off towards Hull and home, Albert suddenly realised, with a little moue of distaste, that his holiday had had its little spice of adventure after all.

"Well!" said Terry's dad, when the police had finally left. "We know who we have to thank for *that!*"

"There wasn't much point in keeping it secret, was there? He was the only one Terry talked to at all. And he seemed such a nice man!"

"I'm going to write him a stiff letter," fumed Terry's dad. "I know he works in the tax office in Hull. Interfering, troublemaking little twerp!"

"It could have been serious, you know. I hope you make him realise that. It could have been very embarrassing. If we hadn't been able to give him the names and addresses of *both* Terry's grannies . . . Oh, Good Lord! What *are* they going to say?"

"The police are going to be very tactful. The inspector told me so at the door. I think they'll probably just make enquiries of neighbours. Or pretend to be council workers, and get them talking. Just so's they make sure they are who we say they are."

"*My* mother will find out," said Mrs Mumford, with conviction and foreboding. "She's got a nose! . . . And how am I going to explain it to her? I'll never forgive that Wimpole!"

Later that night, as they were undressing for bed, Terry's mum, who had been thinking, said to Terry's dad, "Walter: you don't think we ought to have told them about Wayne Catherick's gran, do you?"

"What about her?"

"Old Mrs Corfitt, who lived next door. Should we have told them that she died of an overdose?"

"No. 'Course not. What's it to do with Terry? They said the old lady got confused and gave herself an extra lot."

"I suppose it would just have caused more trouble," agreed Mrs Mumford. "And as you say, it was nothing to do with Terry, was it?"

She turned out the light.

"Well," she said, as she prepared for sleep, "I hope next time we go on holiday Terry finds someone nicer than *that* to make friends with!"

JULIAN SYMONS *(1912–) has an interesting literary background, having been a leading young English poet in the 1930s,
then moving into the crime fiction field with his first novel,* The
Immaterial Murder Case, *in 1945. While concentrating his efforts on mystery writing, he still found time to write volumes of
literary and social criticism, as well as verse. Julian Symons has
been a regular book critic for London's* Sunday Times *since
1958. His excellent mystery novels and short stories continue to
appear with regularity, with some thirty books to date. Mr.
Symons is especially known for his critical study of crime fiction,* Bloody Murder *(1972;* Mortal Consequences, *in the
United States), one of the best one-volume histories available.
In addition, he was a co-founder of the Crime Writers Association and has served as President of the prestigious Detection
Club in Great Britain.*

*As in many of Mr. Symon's mysteries, the most interesting
thing about "The Dream Is Better" is the powerful psychological suspense.*

The Dream Is Better
BY JULIAN SYMONS

1. ANDREW BLOOD'S MANUSCRIPT

I think of the misery of the past and the peace of the present. I think of
the women who almost blasted my life, Jean and Olga, and then of
Helen, who has brought me happiness.

In retrospect, the past seems to have been nothing but a series of
defeats and humiliations. I know the need to put them down on paper.
Helen is here today and sits on the other side of the room. I tell her of
my intention and she approves with the serenity that is her nature.
Jean and Olga were furious, frantic, and deceitful. I had thought that
to be the nature of all women except my mother, but Helen has shown
me otherwise. She brings to my mind Edgar Allan Poe's lines:

> *"Helen, thy beauty is to me
> Like those Nicean barks of yore,*

That gently, o'er a perfumed sea,
The weary, wayworn wanderer bore
To his own native shore."

With Helen I am at peace. It is not my fault that such peace has been reached through travail and through blood. The last may be thought appropriate, since my name is Andrew John Blood.

My father was an inspector in the revenue service, what is sometimes called an income-tax collector, although of course he did not collect taxes in person but was responsible only for assessing the sums owing and sending out the necessary notices. The occupation is respectable but not popular, and boys at school would jeer at me because of it. The combination of my surname and my father's occupation led them to call me bloodsucker.

"Watch out, don't let him get near you, he'll suck your blood!" they would cry. "My dad says it's what his dad does for a living!" They would go on to make sucking noises, so that often I ran home in tears. My mother comforted me and said that they were only teasing.

It would have been useless to speak to my father. He had only two interests in life, his work and his stamp collection. He was especially concerned with Nineteenth Century stamps of Chile, Peru, and Ecuador, and engaged in long correspondence about them. Once, when I was making a drawing, I knocked over the India ink I was using and ruined several pages of stamps. He showed no outward anger but afterwards had as little to do with me as possible. I have affections—yes, indeed I have affections, and of the purest kind—but I could feel no emotion when he stepped absentmindedly off the pavement one day (his mind perhaps on some Peruvian stamp issue), was knocked over by a lorry and instantly killed. After the funeral my mother said that I must be the man of the house and look after her now. I was thirteen years old.

What can I say about Mother? Her photograph, in an old-fashioned silver frame, is on the table at which I write. Her head is a little to one side, and she has the wistful and apologetic expression that I remember so well. Looking at the photograph, I see that she was a pretty woman. I was always said to look like her and be a pretty child, but this never occurred to me at the time, I suppose because for years I was so close to her.

I was an only child and she fussed over me, making sure that I always had clean linen, cooking and washing up, keeping my bedroom tidy and making the bed. Even when I got my first job as an apprentice draughtsman in a big engineering firm (I had always been good at making neat accurate drawings), I never had to dry a plate or a dish, and never hung up a jacket or put away a pair of shoes. My mother had said that I must look after her, but what she meant was that with my father gone she would have more time to look after me. We were constant companions and needed nobody else.

We lived in a small town in the southeast of England. Our house was about forty years old, with a bow window in front, a living room, dining room, and three bedrooms. It was a replica of the others in the road, for they had all been built at the same time. Here I lived for the first thirty years of my life.

Looking back on that time, which seems very long ago, I cannot say I was unhappy. I enjoyed my work in the drawing office of my firm. I bought a small car and used it to take Mother for a spin in the country and dinner at a little country inn, or to go with her to the town repertory theatre. She was fond of a good play.

Occasionally, late at night in my room, I wrote poems about girls, visionary girls who were an ideal for me as they were for Poe. In no way did they resemble the coarse creatures I met at the office, with their constant giggling and their vulgar jokes. Such girls were no worse than the men, but I expected that they would be better.

I was twenty-seven years of age when I met Jean.

My mother liked to go to the Conservative Party bazaar. This was held during the summer, in the grounds of Ampleton House, home of Lord and Lady Ampleton. The stalls were erected on the big central lawn, but there were tree-lined avenues on either side, down which one could walk, with little paths off them that led to cunningly created arbors and small waterfalls.

It was an enchanting place. Of course, Mother expected me to accompany her but, once arrived, she soon found people she knew and on this occasion immediately met Mrs. Wilson, the Party secretary. I knew that she was occupied for at least half an hour, so that I was free to wander. I walked down one of the avenues, and then stood still at the vision I saw at the other end of it.

The avenue sloped upwards and the girl I saw was at the top of the slope, so that she was outlined against the blue sky. Her figure was slim and elegant, her bright golden hair was shoulder length, and her distant profile—for she was turned away from me—looked exquisitely delicate. I made no approach to her, for at that moment all I wanted was to keep this perfection in my memory. But she began to move towards me and to my surprise smiled and waved a hand. When we were a yard or two apart, she spoke to me by name and told me that she was Jean Merton.

She laughed, a low musical sound. "You won't know me but I've heard a lot about you. I'm Mrs. Wilson's niece."

When seen so close she lacked the perfection of beauty I had imagined from a distance, but there was a charm and eagerness about her that overwhelmed me. Her eyes danced with pleasure and she said outright how delighted she was to meet me.

"Aunt Wilson would bring me along, though I knew it would be an awful drag. But now it's different. Come and help me buy jam and honey—I said I'd take some back. And I've got to get a bit of something or other for my younger sister, Nancy. She likes bright and gaudy bits of jewelry." She took my hand as though that was the most natural thing in the world, and it seemed natural to me also.

We bought half a dozen things at the fair, including a one-eyed elephant Jean said she must have because he looked so pathetic, and by the time we found Mrs. Wilson and my mother I knew I was in love. If you think that is ridiculous you fail to understand the spell that may be cast by beauty. I had learned various facts about Jean—that she had some sort of secretarial job, was four years younger than me, and so on —but they were unimportant. She was the most beautiful person I had ever seen, and I wanted to be with her always.

I said something of this to my mother when we returned home. She listened with a smile that changed to a frown. When I had done, she said, "Andrew, you are twenty-seven years old. How many girls have you taken out?"

"None. There was nobody I liked."

"Your father died before telling you things you should have known. And then, perhaps I have been selfish. I had hoped we would always be together until—" Her voice faltered. I told her that of course I would never leave her, but she continued.

"You are an unworldly boy, a dreamer. That has always been so, and I would not wish you different. From what I hear, I am not sure that Jean Merton is the right girl for you. Perhaps there is no right girl. You may find that girls are not like your dreams, that always the dream is better."

I hardly listened. I had already arranged to take Jean to a concert the following evening.

In the following days I took Jean to the concert, to a traveling art
exhibition that had come to our Town Hall, and to the cinema—a film
with Woody Allen she wanted to see. After the film we went to dinner
at the Venezia, which was said to be the best restaurant in town. I
cannot remember what we ate and drank. There remains in my mind
only the vision of her on the other side of the table, her laugh, her
flickering fingers as she made a point about the film, her hair shining
gold, whether in daylight at the art exhibition or in the subdued light
of the Venezia.

Her family home was a little way outside town. She did not live
there but in a small block of flats near the town center. When I took
her back that night she invited me in, saying that she had a bottle of
cognac. I said that I had drunk both a glass of sherry and some wine.

"Don't be so stuffy, Andrew. Come up anyway."

The apartment was small, a bed-sitting room, kitchenette and bath.
She poured the brandy, then came and sat beside me.

"Andrew."

"Yes?"

"You like me, don't you? If you like me, kiss me." I put an arm
round her and our lips met, hers pressed against mine.

"I shall begin to think you don't like me," she murmured, and the
words seemed to break the bond that had kept me almost silent. I said
that liking was not the word, that for me she was a thing of beauty,
and that beautiful things should be worshipped. She ran a hand
through my hair and said that I was a funny boy, she'd never met
anybody like me.

I drove home that night in a daze. On the following night I asked
Jean to marry me.

We had spent part of the evening in the lounge bar of the County
Hotel. Jean liked sitting in pubs and bars, saying that they had a
wonderful atmosphere. She was fond of a drink called a whiskey sour,
which looked pleasant but seemed to me to have a curious taste. I
thought that she both drank and smoked too much.

That night she seemed nervous, lighting cigarettes and putting them
out half-smoked. I asked what was the matter and she said that her
work was boring—sometimes she felt she couldn't face it for another
day.

At that I spoke. The words came out of their own volition. "Why
not give it up?"

"What do you mean?"

"Give it up. Marry me."

I put down the pen now and visualize the scene clearly—a scene utterly remote from this little room. The bar was dim, with purple-shaded wall lights. Canned music played softly. Jean's features were slightly blurred, in a way that enhanced her beauty. Her gaze looked beyond me, as though she saw our future together. She said nothing, and I was content to let the moment rest.

Then a man's voice spoke from behind my left ear "Who's this?" it said.

"Jerry," Jean said. "Jerry Wilson, this is Andrew Blood. Andrew has just asked me to marry him." The man gave a kind of snort. "And I've said yes," she told him.

"Don't be bloody stupid." The man took his hands out of his pockets. They were large and covered with hair, like a monkey's. He used obscene words to her, words I shall not write down, and was gone.

I should have known the truth then, although I could not have imagined all of it. Jean said that the man was somebody she used to know and that he was really rather awful. She also said again that she would marry me.

"You are making a mistake," my mother said when I told her. "I don't say that only because I shall miss you. She is not Miss Right. I could tell you things I have heard—"

I refused to listen to them.

We went together to buy the engagement ring, a simple circle of diamonds. I met her father and mother. He was a farmer and evidently well-to-do. They were polite to me, but seemed to greet the news with some reserve, which was a matter of indifference to me.

I have never cared for other people or felt the need of friends, having always been content with life at home, but I told my colleagues in the drawing office. There were congratulations, mixed with the kind of jokes I dislike, although I endured them. The department manager called me in, congratulated me, said that they were pleased with my work and that my salary would be raised. He said also that he and the rest of them hoped to meet my future wife. I made some reply, I don't know what. I had no wish that Jean should meet any of them. My private life had nothing to do with my work.

The engagement was announced in the local paper. I saw Jean most evenings and she often came to lunch on Sunday. Mother was an excellent cook, took special pains with these lunches, and was polite to Jean, but I could see it was all on the surface.

Jean said more than once that Mother didn't like her.

"She doesn't want to lose her pretty baby boy. And she thinks I smoke too much—I can see her counting the number of cigarettes each time I light one." Of course I said that wasn't true, although I knew there was something in it. "And she expects to be paid compliments every time she cooks a meal. I can cook, you know. I'll make dinner for us tomorrow night."

And she did. Each of the courses was from a recipe originated by a great chef and had some complicated sauce or dressing. I really preferred Mother's simpler cooking, but of course I said everything was wonderful. Afterwards we sat on the sofa. I kissed her, and within a few moments she made a suggestion to me which, again, I shall not write down, accompanying it with physical actions. I said as gently as possible that I did not care for or approve that kind of thing, certainly not until we were married.

She lay back and stared at me. I could see that she was angry, but anger made her more beautiful than ever. She said I had better go home, and I left her.

I heard nothing from her after that. I telephoned her office and was told that she was on a week's holiday. I rang the flat but there was no reply.

When the week had passed, she called and said that she would like to see me. The place was the lounge of the County Hotel, where I had proposed to her. When I arrived she was already there, a whisky sour in front of her. She pushed a little box across to me.

"One ring, returned," she said. "Engagement finished."

I stared at her unbelievingly.

"It was a mistake. I should never have said yes. You want to know why I did? You'll hardly believe it in these days of the pill—or perhaps you've never heard of the pill, I'd forgotten what you're like—but Jerry had got me pregnant. He didn't want the kid and I did, or I thought so. So when you turned up I said yes. I was going to try to make you believe the kid was yours, but there wasn't much chance of that, was there? I don't think I could have gone through with it anyway, but it doesn't matter now. I had an abortion. Jerry and I are getting married."

I took the ring and looked at it wonderingly. I could feel tears forming in my eyes, tears not of self-pity but of regret at losing so much beauty. Jean finished her drink.

"It would never have done, and you must know that. I like the way you look, but you don't really need anyone but your mother."

That was the end of it. I told Mother that the engagement was broken. She said that she was pleased for my sake and with her wonderful discretion never uttered another word about it. I sold the ring back for half what I paid for it. There were jokes at the office, but I ignored them and after a while they stopped. I have said already that I had no close friends.

Mother and I settled down to our old life together. She said sometimes that Miss Right would come along one day, although she hoped it would be after she had gone. Sometimes she added that this might not be long. I told her not to talk like that and paid no attention to what she said.

Then one day, nearly two years after the parting from Jean, I came home and found Mother dead. It seemed that she had a heart condition of which she had never told me. She had gone upstairs to lie down in the afternoon, as she often did, and had passed out of life without pain.

I was stunned. In the days and weeks that followed I realized how much I had depended upon her for everything. I knew I must change my life. I sold the house, got rid of the furniture and most of Mother's possessions, although I could not bring myself to dispose of some things, like her jewelry. That was a terrible time and I cannot write more about it.

The doctor was concerned for me and said that I should go away to recover from the shock. I did so, and found Helen. Again, I shall not write about this. When I returned I bought an apartment and lived there contentedly. Through Helen I have learned to cook, to wash and iron clothes, and through her the flat is kept in a way that would have made Mother proud. I never spoke of her to the people I worked with, feeling it was better so.

So passed weeks, and months. I have made what happened sound sudden but it was gradual. I recovered from the shocks of Jean's betrayal and Mother's death, like somebody slowly emerging from severe illness who becomes a little stronger each day. With Helen's help I recovered my serenity so that the past was wiped out as though it had never been.

And then Olga entered my life—Olga from central Europe, Olga Kreisky.

Olga's parents had been refugees who came to this country just before the war, and although she was born in England she spoke with a distinct foreign accent. She had some architectural training and came to the office as a draughtsman. She was a large woman, large in a way that people call motherly, although my mother had been fine-boned and delicate, as I am.

Olga was, I suppose, about my own age, although because of her size she seemed to me older. I do not know why she should have taken an interest in me, but she did so from the beginning. She would sit at the same table with me in the canteen and would say that I did not eat enough, I should have ordered the batter pudding or the macaroni and cheese. I would reply that I was not hungry and in any case did not care for starchy foods.

"But you are so thin, And-rew"—almost from the start she called me Andrew, dwelling lovingly on the name. "You should put flesh on your bones. It is because you cook for yourself, that is not good. A man on his own never eats properly."

She told me she lived with her sister, who would be getting married soon. "Then I am on my own too, but never fear, I shall go on making my soups and puddings, and my schnitzels. You must come round, And-rew, and I cook for you my special wiener schnitzel. You will not feel hungry afterwards, I can tell you." She laughed heartily and her plump cheeks wobbled.

Mother taught me always to be polite and I hope I have not forgotten my manners. I said I had a poor digestion and must be very careful. She said she knew of many special health foods and she could prepare those too. I stopped using the canteen, but it did not free me from her. She would come over to my drawing board to see what I was working on and, leaning over so that I felt the pressure of her bosom, praise my skill and neatness.

She made sure that she left the office when I did, and at first I made the foolish mistake of giving her a lift in my car, with the result that I was invited indoors to meet her sister. She introduced me as "My dear friend And-rew" and her sister Nadia said she had heard much about me. How could she have done when there was nothing to hear? I stopped driving to work in the car.

Olga wanted to see my flat, saying she was sure it needed a woman's touch. I avoided giving her the address. I knew it would be disastrous for her to meet Helen. I had to endure a great deal of what I believe is called "ribbing" about Olga at the office. I said nothing, I showed my supreme indifference, both to the dolts surrounding me and to Olga, but Olga's skin was hippopotamus-thick. She began to bring pies and sandwiches to the office, insisting that we share them for lunch. I did not know how to refuse without rudeness. I nearly told her of Helen at home, who would prepare anything I wished, but refrained.

The strain on my nerves grew. I thought of changing my job, but feared that Olga might follow me elsewhere. Her round fat face, her huge udders, the whole bulk of her began to obsess me. I had nightmares in which the weight of her flesh bore me down, so that I wriggled unavailingly beneath her. Yet I could not have imagined the nightmare that happened.

I had returned from work at the usual time, looking forward to my evening at home with Helen. A steak and salad, cheese and coffee, then an hour or two in front of the television. When the bell rang, Helen answered it. That was a mistake, for outside stood Olga, her arms full of brown paper parcels. It was dark in the hall, so that at first she did not see she was speaking to Helen.

"And-rew, I have been a naughty girl. You will not tell me your address, it is not in the phonebook, but I get it from the accounts department. But you forgive me, And-rew, when you see what I have here for us to eat. There is smoked salmon and then a special Hungarian sausage with noodles—"

At that moment she realized she was talking to Helen. And she began to laugh.

Her laughter roused me to fury. If she had not laughed I might have told her just to go away. But she laughed, this fat European cow laughed at my Helen. I pulled her inside the door and then towards the kitchen. She dropped the groceries. Then we were in the kitchen. I took the knife with which I had been trimming the steak and plunged it into the fat creature who had insulted Helen.

I cannot say what else I did with the knife. I was sane before the action, I am perfectly sane now, but I admit that for those moments I was mad. Mad, but greatly provoked. I do not excuse my action, yet surely all must agree that I was greatly provoked. When it was over, and the screaming had stopped, I looked at the thing on the floor and saw blood, blood everywhere. I felt that this was something ordained, that I had fulfilled my name. There had been eggs among the groceries and they had broken, so that in one place the yellow eggs yolks were mixed with the red blood. When the police came I was trying to clear up the mess on the kitchen floor.

Such are the events that brought me to this room. I have set them down at Dr. Glasser's suggestion, and should like to add that I am happy to have retired from the world and grateful for the opportunity to live here and to receive visits from Helen.

2. THE IRONIES OF DR. GLASSER

Dr. Glasser's office was large and square. The walls were white and covered with framed certificates testifying to the doctor's psychiatric eminence. In person the doctor was tall, with an aquiline nose and a fine head of grey hair. There was something ironical in his gaze and in his manner, as though he found the world even more absurd than he had expected.

His visitor—small, tubby, with innocent eyes behind gold-rimmed spectacles—was named Johnson. He was a vice-president of the Mental Patients' Reform League. He put down the sheets of paper, which were written in a neat and elegant hand.

"Most interesting. And remarkably coherent, it seems to me."

"Yes, Andrew is perfectly coherent. It is a classic case, textbook material." Dr. Glasser steepled his fingers and looked up at the ceiling, as though he were lecturing. "The child is ignored by the father, attachment to the mother becomes total. Every woman met is seen not as a real person but in terms of the mother. Because of the incest taboo the sex act cannot be contemplated with any woman, they must all be remade in the mother's image. The experience with Jean was unfortunate, but it would have been much the same with any woman who desired sexual relations. For the reasons I have given, the sex act fills Andrew with horror."

Mr. Johnson moved uneasily. "I understand. But my point is—"

Dr. Glasser in flow was not easily checked. "He rejects it with violence. The injuries inflicted on poor Olga Kreisky were savage, far more than is indicated in the manuscript. There were mutilations."

"Very distressing. But all this was several years ago."

"Six years."

"As you know, the League's concern is that far too many patients are kept in homes, when they would be perfcctly capable of leading normal lives. I understand Andrew still makes technical drawings."

"He does indeed. Very good ones."

"So that he is obviously capable of work. From his record, his behavior here has been exemplary. If he were let out on condition that he lives with this Helen, who I suppose might be called a mother-substitute, and to whom he is evidently devoted, would he be a danger to the community? But first, would you agree that Helen is a mother-substitute?"

The doctor turned his ironical gaze on Mr. Johnson. "I would."

"And would he be a danger to other people?"

"Perhaps not."

Mr. Johnson took off his glasses, polished them, and said earnestly, "Only perhaps? You agreed that his behavior has been exemplary."

"I did."

"Then why should he not be released?"

"Suppose somebody else insulted Helen?"

Mr. Johnson was taken aback. "Why should that happen? Helen has been remarkably faithful to him—she is clearly devoted. I understand from the document that she pays visits. Perhaps they might marry."

Dr. Glasser sighed. "Come along, Mr. Johnson. We will speak to this exemplary patient."

They left the room, took a lift, walked down a corridor, then down another at right angles to it. On either side were doors with names on them. The doors had keyholes but lacked handles. In a room between the corridors four male nurses sat playing cards. Little Mr. Johnson was uneasily conscious that they were all big men. The doctor spoke to one of them, who accompanied them. He opened one of the doors with a key from a bunch at his waist and said, "Andrew, here's Dr. Glasser to see you."

They entered a small sitting room, simply furnished. Several drawings were pinned up on the walls, some machinery, one of Dr. Glasser, and two of a woman Mr. Johnson supposed to be Helen. A man who sat reading in an armchair put down his book. He was small and had neat, almost doll-like features. "Good afternoon, Doctor."

"Andrew, this is Mr. Johnson from the Mental Patients' Reform League. He enjoyed your manuscript."

"Did you really? I'm so pleased." A smile touched the neat features. "It's all true, you know, every word. I was provoked, but I did very wrong. Just for the moment I went mad, although I am perfectly sane now, have been for years. Look at what I'm reading." He held up the book. *"Persuasion,* Jane Austen. I like to read about the past, it's so much more civilized than the present."

Mr. Johnson asked in his earnest way, "Supposing you were released, would you like that?" Andrew Blood considered, then nodded.

"You would take a job, use your technical skills?" Another nod. "And live with Helen? Perhaps get married?"

A look of uncertainty, even alarm, touched the neat features. Andrew Blood looked questioningly at the doctor, who said softly, "If Helen is here, Andrew, we'd be delighted to meet her."

The uncertain look was replaced by a charming smile. Andrew jumped up and went to an inner room. The nurse began to say something, but was checked by Dr. Glasser. It was perhaps no more than two or three minutes, although it seemed longer to Mr. Johnson, before the figure appeared in the doorway.

It was small and wore a wig of grey hair, permanently waved. The face below it was that of Andrew Blood, but it had been powdered to a dead whiteness and lipstick crudely applied so that it looked like a clown's face. The figure wore an oatmeal-colored twin set with a rope of imitation pearls round the neck and high-heeled shoes. It came mincingly across the room, held out a ringed hand, and said in a falsetto voice, "How do you do?"

The figure was ludicrous in itself, but it was the words and the falsetto voice that broke Mr. Johnson's composure. He was unable to refrain from laughter. The sounds were loud in the little room, and although he put a hand over his mouth laughter continued to bubble up.

That was one moment. In the next he was on the floor, hands were tearing at his face and throat, a high voice was screaming abuse. His face had been badly scratched and his spectacles knocked off, although not broken, before the doctor and nurse managed to pull the figure off him.

Back in the office Dr. Glasser poured a tot of whiskey and apologized. "Forgive me for practising that little deceit. I should have told you that Andrew was Helen, but I thought visual evidence would be more convincing. Of course, I could not know that you would laugh. That was an insult to Helen, and Andrew was outraged by it, as he was when Olga Kreisky laughed."

"And Helen is—"

"Hardly Poe's Helen, as you will have gathered from her appearance. Helen was the name of Andrew's mother. She was the center of his life, and when she died he recreated her. Those were some of her old clothes. Andrew said in the manuscript that he could not bring himself to dispose of them. He is a small neat man, and they fit him reasonably well.

"I told you it was a classic case and so it is, not of transvestism but of personality transfer. It occurs only among those who cannot face the physical aspects of life. Mrs. Blood understood that when she told him there might be no right girl for him, that he would always be one of those for whom the dream is better."

JOHN D. MACDONALD *(1916–1986) was one of the great masters of American fiction for over thirty-five years. His series character, Travis McGee, began his career as a recoverer of stolen property and developed into a full-fledged private detective over the course of more than twenty novels, each one of which included a color in its title. Travis, like his creator, had a strong moral streak in him, especially in regard to environmental issues. Prior to the appearance of Travis McGee, Mr. MacDonald wrote hundreds of stories for the pulp magazines and also published some forty novels. These books—for example,* The Damned *(1952),* Cry Hard, Cry Fast *(1955), and* The Executioners *(1958)—are among the finest suspense novels of their time.*

Mr. MacDonald brought to his writing an ability to plot, a just-right hard-edged dialogue, and above all, believable characters. "The Homesick Buick" shows him at the top of his form.

The Homesick Buick
BY JOHN D. MACDONALD

To get to Leeman, Texas, you go southwest from Beaumont on Route 90 for approximately thirty miles and then turn right on a two-lane concrete farm road. Five minutes from the time you turn, you will reach Leeman. The main part of town is six lanes wide and five blocks long. If the hand of a careless giant should remove the six gas stations, the two theatres, Willows' Hardware Store, the Leeman National Bank, the two big air-conditioned five-and-dimes, the Sears store, four cafés, Rightsinger's dress shop, and The Leeman House, a twenty-room hotel, there would be very little left except the supermarket and four assorted drugstores.

On October 3rd, 1949, a Mr. Stanley Woods arrived by bus and carried his suitcase over to The Leeman House. In Leeman there is no social distinction of bus, train, or plane, since Leeman has neither airport facilities nor railroad station.

On all those who were questioned later, Mr. Stanley Woods seemed to have made very little impression. They all spoke of kind of a medium-size fella in his thirties, or it might be his forties. No, he wasn't fat, but he wasn't thin either. Blue eyes? Could be brown. Wore a grey suit, I think. Can't remember whether his glasses had rims or not. If they did have rims, they were probably gold.

But all were agreed that Mr. Stanley Woods radiated quiet confidence and the smell of money. According to the cards that were collected here and there, Mr. Woods represented the Groston Precision Tool Company of Atlanta, Georgia. He had deposited in the Leeman National a certified cheque for twelve hundred dollars and the bank had made the routine check of looking up the credit standing of Groston. It was Dun & Bradstreet double-A, but, of course, the company explained later that they had never heard of Mr. Stanley Woods. Nor could the fake calling cards be traced. They were of a type of paper and type face which could be duplicated sixty or a hundred times in every big city in the country.

Mr. Woods' story, which all agreed on, was that he was ". . . nosing around to find a good location for a small plant. Decentralisation, you know. No, we don't want it right in town."

He rented Tod Bishner's car during the day. Tod works at the Shell station on the corner of Beaumont and Lone Star Streets and doesn't have any use for his Plymouth sedan during the day. Mr. Woods drove around all the roads leading out of town and, of course, real estate prices were jacked to a considerable degree during his stay.

Mr. Stanley Woods left Leeman rather suddenly on the morning of October 17th under unusual circumstances.

The first person to note a certain oddness was Miss Trilla Price on the switchboard at the phone company. Her local calls were all right but she couldn't place Charley Anderson's call to Houston, nor, when she tried, could she raise Beaumont. Charley was upset because he wanted to wangle an invitation to go visit his sister over the coming weekend.

That was at five minutes of nine. It was probably at the same time that a car with two men in it parked on Beaumont Street, diagonally across from the bank, and one of the two men lifted the hood and began to fiddle with the electrical system.

Nobody agrees from what direction the Buick came into town. There was a man and a girl in it and they parked near the drugstore. No one seems to know where the third car parked, or even what kind of car it was.

The girl and the man got out of the Buick slowly, just as Stanley Woods came down the street from the hotel.

In Leeman the bank is open on weekdays from nine until two. And so, at nine o'clock, C. F. Hethridge, who is, or was, the chief teller, raised the green shades on the inside of the bank doors and unlocked the doors. He greeted Mr. Woods, who went on over to the high counter at the east wall and began to ponder over his cheque book.

At this point, out on the street, a very peculiar thing happened. One of the two men in the first car strolled casually over and stood beside the Buick. The other man started the motor of the first car, drove down the street, and made a wide U-turn to swing in and park behind the Buick.

The girl and the man had gone over to Bob Kimball's window. Bob is second teller, and the only thing he can remember about the girl is that she was blonde and a little hard-looking around the mouth, and that she wore a great big alligator shoulder-bag. The man with her made no impression on Bob at all, except that Bob thinks the man was on the heavy side.

Old Rod Harrigan, the bank guard, was standing beside the front door, yawning, and picking his teeth with a broken match.

At this point C. F. Hethridge heard the buzzer on the big time-vault and went over and swung the door wide and went in to get the money for the cages. He was out almost immediately, carrying Bob's tray over to him. The girl was saying something about cashing a cheque and Bob had asked her for identification. She had opened the big shoulder-bag as her escort strolled over to the guard. At the same moment the girl pulled out a small vicious-looking revolver and aimed it between Bob's eyes, her escort sapped old Rod Harrigan with such gusto that it was four that same afternoon before he came out of it enough to talk. And then, of course, he knew nothing.

C. F. Hethridge bolted for the vault and Bob, wondering whether he should step on the alarm, looked over the girl's shoulder just in time to see Stanley Woods aim carefully and bring Hethridge down with a slug through the head, catching him on the fly, so to speak.

Bob says that things were pretty confusing and that the sight of Hethridge dying so suddenly sort of took the heart out of him. Anyway, there was a third car and it contained three men, two of them equipped with empty black-leather suitcases. They went into the vault, acting as though they had been all through the bank fifty times. They stepped over Hethridge on the way in, and on the way out again.

About the only cash they overlooked was the cash right in front of Bob, in his teller's drawer.

As they all broke for the door, Bob dropped and pressed the alarm button. He said later that he held his hands over his eyes, though what good that would do him, he couldn't say.

Henry Willows is the real hero. He was fuddying around in his hardware store when he heard the alarm. With a reaction-time remarkable in a man close to seventy, he took a little twenty-two rifle, slapped a clip into it, trotted to his store door, and quickly analysed the situation. He saw Mr. Woods, whom he recognised, plus three strangers and a blonde woman coming out of the bank pretty fast. Three cars were lined up, each one with a driver. Two of the men coming out of the bank carried heavy suitcases. Henry levelled on the driver of the lead car, the Buick, and shot him in the left temple, killing him outright. The man slumped over the wheel, his body resting against the horn ring, which, of course, added its blare to the clanging of the bank alarm.

At that point a slug, later identified as having come from a Smith and Wesson Police Positive, smashed a neat hole in Henry's plate-glass store window, radiating cracks in all directions. Henry ducked, and by the time he got ready to take a second shot, the two other cars were gone. The Buick was still there. He saw Bob run out of the bank, and later on he told his wife that he had his finger on the trigger and his sights lined up before it came to him that it was Bob Kimball.

It was agreed that the two cars headed out toward Route 90 and, within two minutes, Hod Abrams and Lefty Quinn had roared out of town in the same direction in the only police car. They were followed by belligerent amateurs to whom Henry Willows had doled out fire-arms. But on the edge of town all cars ran into an odd obstacle. The road was liberally sprinkled with metal objects shaped exactly like the jacks that little girls pick up when they bounce a ball, except they were four times normal size and all the points were sharpened. No matter how a tyre hit one, it was certain to be punctured.

The police car swerved to a screaming stop, nearly tipping over. The Stein twins, boys of nineteen, managed to avoid the jacks in their souped-up heap until they were hitting eighty. When they finally hit one, the heap rolled over an estimated ten times, killing the twins outright.

So that made four dead. Hethridge, the Stein twins, and one unidentified bank robber.

Nobody wanted to touch the robber, and he stayed right where he was until the battery almost ran down and the horn squawked into silence. Hod Abrams commandeered a car, and he and Lefty rode back into town and took charge. They couldn't get word out by phone and within a very short time they found that some sharpshooter with a high-powered rifle had gone to work on the towers of local station WLEE and had put the station out of business.

Thus, by the time the Texas Rangers were alerted and ready to set up road blocks, indecision and confusion had permitted an entire hour to pass.

The Houston office of the FBI assigned a detail of men to the case and, from the Washington headquarters, two bank-robbery experts were dispatched by plane to Beaumont. Reporters came from Houston and Beaumont and the two national press services, and Leeman found itself on the front pages all over the country because the planning behind the job seemed to fascinate the average joe.

Mr. Woods left town on that particular Thursday morning. The FBI from Houston was there by noon, and the Washington contingent arrived late Friday. Everyone was very confident. There was a corpse and a car to work on. These would certainly provide the necessary clues to indicate which outfit had pulled the job, even though the method of the robbery did not point to any particular group whose habits were known.

Investigation headquarters were set up in the local police station and Hod and Lefty, very important in the beginning, had to stand around outside trying to look as though they knew what was going on.

Hethridge, who had been a cold, reserved, unpopular man, had, within twenty-four hours, fifty stories invented about his human kindness and generosity. The Stein twins, heretofore considered to be trash who would be better off in prison, suddenly became proper sons of old Texas.

Special Agent Randolph A. Sternweister who, fifteen years before, had found a law office to be a dull place, was in charge of the case, being the senior of the two experts who had flown down from Washington. He was forty-one years old, a chain smoker, a chubby man with incongruous hollow cheeks and hair of a shade of grey which his wife, Clare, tells him is distinguished.

The corpse was the first clue. Age between thirty and thirty-two. Brown hair, thinning on top. Good teeth, with only four small cavities, two of them filled. Height, five foot eight and a quarter; weight, a hundred and forty-eight. No distinguishing scars or tattoos. X-ray plates showed that the right arm had been fractured years before. His clothes were neither new nor old. The suit had been purchased in

Chicago. The shirt, underwear, socks, and shoes were all national brands, in the medium-price range. In his pockets they found an almost full pack of cigarettes, a battered Zippo lighter, three fives and a one in a cheap, trick billclip, eighty-five cents in change, a book of matches advertising a nationally known laxative, a white bone button, two wooden kitchen matches with blue and white heads, and a pencilled map, on cheap notebook paper, of the main drag of Leeman—with no indication as to escape route. His fingerprint classification was teletyped to the Central Bureau files and the answer came back that there was no record of him. It was at this point that fellow workers noted that Mr. Sternweister became a shade irritable.

The next search of the corpse was more minute. No specific occupational callouses were found on his hands. The absence of laundry marks indicated that his linen, if it had been sent out, had been cleaned by a neighbourhood laundress. Since Willows had used a .22 hollowpoint, the hydraulic pressure on the brain fluids had caused the eyes of Mr. X to bulge in a disconcerting fashion. A local undertaker, experienced in the damage caused by the average Texas automobile accident, replaced the bulging eyeballs and smoothed out the expression for a series of pictures which were sent to many points. The Chicago office reported that the clothing store which had sold the suit was large and that the daily traffic was such that no clerk could identify the customer from the picture; nor was the youngish man known to the Chicago police.

Fingernail scrapings were put in a labelled glassine envelope, as well as the dust vacuumed from pants cuffs and other portions of the clothing likely to collect dust. The excellent lab in Houston reported back that the dust and scrapings were negative to the extent that the man could not be tied down to any particular locality.

In the meantime the Buick had been the object of equal scrutiny. The outside was a mass of prints from the citizens of Leeman who had peered morbidly in at the man leaning against the horn ring. The plates were Mississippi licence plates and, in checking with the Bureau of Motor Vehicle Registration, it was found that the plates had been issued for a 1949 Mercury convertible which had been almost totally destroyed in a head-on collision in June, 1949. The motor number and serial number of the Buick were checked against central records and it was discovered that the Buick was one which disappeared from Chapel Hill, North Carolina, on the 5th July, 1949. The insurance company, having already replaced the vehicle, was anxious to take possession of the stolen car.

Pictures of Mr. X, relayed to Chapel Hill, North Carolina, and to myriad points in Mississippi, drew a large blank. In the meantime a careful dusting of the car had brought out six prints, all different. Two of them turned out to be on record. The first was on record through the cross-classification of Army prints. The man in question was found working in a gas station in Lake Charles, Louisiana. He had a very difficult two hours until a bright police officer had him demonstrate his procedure for brushing out the front of a car. Ex-Sergeant Golden braced his left hand against the dashboard in almost the precise place where the print had been found. He was given a picture of Mr. X to study. By that time he was so thoroughly annoyed at the forces of law and order that it was impossible to ascertain whether or not he had ever seen the man in question. But due to the apparent freshness of the print it was established—a reasonable assumption—that the gangsters had driven into Texas from the East.

The second print on record was an old print, visible when dust was carefully blown off the braces under the dismantled front seat. It belonged to a garage mechanic in Chapel Hill who once had a small misunderstanding with the forces of law and order and who was able to prove, through the garage work orders, that he had repaired the front-seat mechanism when it had jammed in April, 1949.

The samples of road dirt and dust taken from the fender well and the frame members proved nothing. The dust was proved, spectroscopically, to be from deep in the heart of Texas, and the valid assumption, after checking old weather reports, was that the car had come through some brisk thunderstorms en route.

Butts in the ashtray of the car showed that either two women, or one woman with two brands of lipstick, had ridden recently as a passenger. Both brands of lipstick were of shades which would go with a fair-complexioned blonde, and both brands were available in Woolworth's, Kress, Kresge, Walgreens—in fact, in every chain outfit of any importance.

One large crumb of stale whole-wheat bread was found on the floor mat, and even Sternweister could make little of that, despite the fact that the lab was able to report that the bread had been eaten in conjunction with liverwurst.

Attention was given to the oversized jacks which had so neatly punctured the tyres. An ex-OSS officer reported that similar items had been scattered on enemy roads in Burma during the late war and, after examining the samples, he stated confidently that the OSS merchandise had been better made. A competent machinist looked them over and stated with assurance that they had been made by cutting eighth-inch rod into short lengths, grinding them on a wheel, putting them in a jig, and spot-welding them. He said that the maker did not do much of a job on either the grinding or the welding, and that the jig itself was a little out of line. An analysis of the steel showed that it was a Jones & Laughlin product that could be bought in quantity at any wholesaler and in a great many hardware stores.

The auditors, after a careful examination of the situation at the bank, reported that the sum of exactly $94,725 had disappeared. They recommended that the balance remaining in Stanley Woods' account of $982.80 be considered as forfeited, thus reducing the loss to $93,742.20. The good citizens of Leeman preferred to think that Stanley had withdrawn his account.

Every person who had a glimpse of the gang was cross-examined. Sternweister was appalled at the difficulty involved in even establishing how many there had been. Woods, the blonde, and the stocky citizen were definite. And then there were two with suitcases—generally agreed upon. Total, so far—five. The big question was whether each car had a driver waiting. Some said no—that the last car in line had been empty. Willows insisted angrily that there had been a driver behind each wheel. Sternweister at last settled for a total of eight, seven of whom escaped.

No one had taken down a single licence number. But it was positively established that the other two cars had been either two- or four-door sedans in dark blue, black, green, or maroon, and that they had been either Buicks, Nashes, Oldsmobiles, Chryslers, Pontiacs, or Packards—or maybe Hudsons. And one lone woman held out for convertible Cadillacs. For each person that insisted that they had Mississippi registration, there was one equally insistent on Louisiana, Texas, Alabama, New Mexico, and Oklahoma. And one old lady said that she guessed she knew a California plate when she saw one.

On Saturday morning, nine days after the sudden blow to the FDIC, Randolph Sternweister paced back and forth in his suite at the hotel, which he shared with the number two man from the Washington end, one Buckley Weed. Weed was reading through the transcripts of the testimony of the witnesses, in vain hope of finding something to which insufficient importance had been given. Weed, though lean, a bit stooped, and only thirty-one, had, through osmosis, acquired most of the personal mannerisms of his superior. Sternweister had noticed this and for the past year had been on the verge of mentioning it. As Weed had acquired Sternweister's habit of lighting one cigarette off the last half-inch of the preceding one, any room in which the two of them remained for more than an hour took on the look and smell of any hotel room after a Legion convention.

"Nothing," Sternweister said. "Not one censored, unmentionable, unprintable, unspeakable thing! My God, if I ever want to kill anybody, I'll do it in the Pennsy Station at five-fifteen.

"The Bureau has cracked cases when the only thing it had to go on was a human hair or a milligram of dust. My God, we've got a whole automobile that weighs nearly two tons, and a whole corpse! They'll think we're down here learning to rope calves. You know what?"

"What, Ran?"

"I think this was done by a bunch of amateurs. There ought to be a law restricting the practice of crime to professionals. A bunch of wise amateurs. And you can bet your loudest argyles, my boy, that they established identity, hideout, the works, before they knocked off that vault. Right now, blast their souls, they're being seven average citizens in some average community, making no splash with that ninety-four grand. People didn't used to move around so much. Since the war they've been migrating all over the place. Strangers don't stick out like sore thumbs any more. See anything in those transcripts?"

"Nothing."

"Then stop rattling paper. I can't think. Since a week ago Thursday fifty-one stolen cars have been recovered in the south and southwest. And we don't know which two, if any, belonged to this mob. We don't even know which route they took away from here. Believe it or not— nobody saw 'em!"

As the two specialists stared bleakly at each other, a young man of fourteen named Pink Dee was sidling inconspicuously through the shadows in the rear of Louie's Garage. (Tow car service—open 24 hours.) Pink was considered to have been the least beautiful baby, the most unprepossessing child, in Leeman, and he gave frank promise of growing up to be a rather coarse joke on the entire human race. Born with a milk-blue skin, dead white hair, little reddish weak eyes, pipe-cleaner bones, narrow forehead, no chin, beaver teeth, a voice like an unoiled hinge, nature had made the usual compensation. His reaction-time was exceptional. Plenty of more rugged and more normal children had found out that Pink Dee could hit you by the time you had the word out of your mouth. The blow came from an outsize, knobbly fist at the end of a long thin arm, and he swung it with all the abandon of a bag of rocks on the end of a rope. The second important item about Pink Dee came to light when the Leeman School System started giving IQ's. Pink's was higher than they were willing to admit the first time, as it did not seem proper that the only genius in Leeman should be old Homer Dee's only son. Pink caught on, and the second time he was rated he got it down into the cretin class. The third rating was ninety-nine and everybody seemed happy with that.

At fourteen Pink was six foot tall and weighed a hundred and twenty pounds. He peered at the world through heavy lenses and maintained, in the back room of his home on Fountain Street, myriad items of apparatus, some made, some purchased. There he investigated certain electrical and magnetic phenomena, having tired of building radios, and carried on a fairly virulent correspondence on the quantum theory with a Cal Tech professor who was under the impression that he was arguing with someone of more mature years.

Dressed in his khakis, the uniform of Texas, Pink moved through the shadows, inserted the key he had filched into the Buick door, and then into the ignition lock. He turned it on in order to activate the electrical gimmicks, and then turned on the car radio. As soon as it warmed up he pushed the selective buttons, carefully noting the dial. When he had the readings he tuned in to WLEE to check the accuracy of the dial. When WLEE roared into a farm report, Louie appeared and dragged Pink out by the thin scruff of his neck.

"What the hell?" Louie said.

Being unable to think of any adequate explanation, Pink wriggled away and loped out.

Pink's next stop was WLEE, where he was well known. He found the manual he wanted and spent the next twenty minutes with it.

Having been subjected to a certain amount of sarcasm from both Sternweister and Weed, Hod Abrams and Lefty Quinn were in no mood for the approach Pink Dee used.

"I demand to see the FBI," Pink said firmly, the effect spoiled a bit by the fact that his voice change was so recent that the final syllable was a reversion to his childhood squeaky-hinge voice.

"He demands," Hod said to Lefty.

"Go away, Pink," Lefty growled, "before I stomp on your glasses."

"I am a citizen who wishes to speak to a member of a Federal agency," Pinky said with dignity.

"A citizen, maybe. A taxpayer, no. You give me trouble, kid, and I'm going to warm your pants right here in this lobby."

Maybe the potential indignity did it. Pink darted for the stairs leading up from the lobby. Hod went roaring up the stairs after him and Lefty grabbed the elevator. They both snared him outside Sternweister's suite and found that they had a job on their hands. Pink bucked and contorted like a picnic on which a hornet's nest had just fallen.

The door to the suite opened and both Sternweister and Weed glared out, their mouths open.

"Just . . . just a fresh . . . kid," Hod Abrams panted.

"I know where the crooks are!" Pink screamed.

"He's nuts," Lefty yelled.

"Wait a minute," Randolph Sternweister ordered sharply. They stopped dragging Pink but still clung to him. "I admit he doesn't look as though he knew his way home, but you can't tell. You two wait outside. Come in here, young man."

Pink marched erectly into the suite, selected the most comfortable chair, and sank into it, looking smug.

"Where are they?"

"Well, I don't know exactly . . ."

"Outside!" Weed said with a thumb motion.

". . . but I know how to find out."

"Oh, you know how to find out, eh? Keep talking, I haven't laughed in nine days," Sternweister said.

"Oh, I had to do a little checking first," Pink said in a lofty manner. "I stole the key to the Buick and got into it to test something."

"Kid, experts have been over that car, half-inch by half-inch."

"Please don't interrupt me, sir. And don't take that attitude. Because, if it turns out I have something, and I know I have, you're going to look as silly as anything."

Sternweister flushed and then turned pale. He held hard to the edge of a table. "Go ahead," he said thickly.

"I am making an assumption that the people who robbed our bank started out from some hideout and then went back to the same one. I am further assuming that they were in their hideout some time, while they were planning the robbery."

Weed and Sternweister exchanged glances. "Go on."

"So my plan has certain possible flaws based on these assumptions, but at least it uncovers one possible pattern of investigation. I know that the car was stolen from Chapel Hill. That was in the paper. And I know the dead man was in Chicago. So I checked Chicago and Chapel Hill a little while ago."

"Checked them?"

"At the radio station, of course. Modern car radios are easy to set to new stations by altering the push buttons. The current settings of the push buttons do not conform either to the Chicago or the Chapel Hill areas. There are six stations that the radio in the Buick is set for and . . ."

Sternweister sat down on the couch as though somebody had clubbed him behind the knees. "Agh!" he said.

"So all you have to do," Pink said calmly, "is to check areas against the push-button settings until you find an area *where all six frequencies are represented by radio stations in the immediate geographical vicinity.* It will take a bit of statistical work, of course, and a map of the country, and a supply of push pins should simplify things, I would imagine. Then, after the area is located, I would take the Buick there and, due to variations in individual sets and receiving conditions, you might be able to narrow it down to within a mile or two. Then by showing the photograph of the dead gangster around at bars and such places . . ."

And that was why, on the following Wednesday, a repainted Buick with new plates and containing two agents of the Bureau roamed through the small towns near Tampa on the West Florida Coast, and how they found that the car radio in the repainted Buick brought in Tampa, Clearwater, St. Pete, Orlando, Winter Haven, and Dunedin on the push buttons with remarkable clarity the closer they came to a little resort town called Tarpon Springs. On Thursday morning at four, the portable floodlights bathed three beach cottages in a white glare, and the metallic voice of the P.A. system said, "You are surrounded. Come out with your hands high. You are surrounded."

The shots, a few moments later, cracked with a thin bitterness against the heavier sighing of the Gulf of Mexico. Mr. Stanley Woods, or, as the blonde later stated, Mr. Grebbs Fainstock, was shot, with poetic justice, through the head, and that was the end of resistance.

On Pink Dee Day in Leeman, the president of the Leeman National Bank turned over the envelope containing the reward. It came to a bit less than six per cent of the recovered funds, and it is ample to guarantee, at some later date, a Cal Tech degree.

In December the Sternweisters bought a new car. When Claire demanded to know why Randolph insisted on delivery *sans* car radio, his only answer was a hollow laugh.

She feels that he has probably been working too hard.

*Perry Mason, Della Street, Paul Drake, Lieutenant Tragg, and
Hamilton Burger are known to tens of millions of readers and
viewers as the chief characters of* ERLE STANLEY GARDNER*'s
(1889–1987) famous series of eighty-two novels, all of which
end in an exciting courtroom scene. Mr. Gardner knew of what
he wrote for he was a practicing lawyer for nearly twenty years
before becoming a full-time writer. Despite the great success of
the Perry Mason stories, many readers prefer the twenty-nine
"A.A. Fair" novels that pair tiny Donald Lam and obese Bertha
Cool and feature broad humor and wild plotting.*

*Mr. Gardner achieved great fame and wealth during his life-
time and his books still sell in the millions all over the world.
The reasons for his success are easy to discover—his fans loved
the predictable courtroom scenes, the dizzying plots, and the
rapid, page-turning pace of his novels. "Danger Out of the
Past" vividly illustrates all of these qualities, but without Perry
Mason or a courtroom.*

Danger Out of the Past
BY ERLE STANLEY GARDNER

The roadside restaurant oozed an atmosphere of peaceful prosperity. It
was a green-painted building set in a white graveled circle in the triangle where the two main highways joined.

Five miles beyond, a pall of hazy smog marked the location of the
city; but out here at the restaurant the air was pure and crystal clear.

George Ollie slid down from the stool behind the cash register and
walked over to look out of the window. His face held an expression
which indicated physical well-being and mental contentment.

In the seven short years since he had started working as a cook over
the big range in the rear he had done pretty well for himself—exceptionally well for a two-time loser—although no one here knew that, of
course. Nor did *anyone* know of that last job where a confederate had
lost his head and pulled the trigger . . .

But all that was in the past. George Ollie, president of a luncheon
club, member of the Chamber of Commerce, had no connection with
that George Ollie who had been prisoner number 56289.

In a way, however, George owed something of his present prosperity
to his criminal record. When he had started work in the restaurant,

that bank job which had been "ranked" preyed on his mind. For three years he had been intent on keeping out of circulation. He had stayed in his room nights and had perforce saved all the money that he had made.

So, when the owner's heart had given out and it became necessary for him to sell almost on a moment's notice, George was able to make a down payment in cash. From then on, hard work, careful management, and the chance relocation of a main highway had spelled prosperity for the ex-con.

George turned away from the window, looked over the tables at the symmetrical figure of Stella, the head waitress, as she bent over the table taking the orders of the family that had just entered.

Just as the thrill of pride swept through George whenever he looked at the well-kept restaurant, the graveled parking place, and the constantly accelerating stream of traffic which furnished him with a constantly increasing number of customers—so did George thrill with a sense of possessive pride whenever he looked at Stella's smoothly curved figure.

There was no question but what Stella knew how to wear clothes. Somewhere, George thought, there must in Stella's past have been a period of prosperity, a period when she had worn the latest Parisian models with distinction. Now she wore the light-blue uniform, with the white starched cuffs above the elbow and the white collar, with that same air of distinction. She not only classed up the uniforms but she classed up the place.

When Stella walked, the lines of her figure rippled smoothly beneath the clothes. Customers looking at her invariably looked again. Yet Stella was always demure, never forward. She smiled at the right time and in the right manner. If the customer tried to get intimate, Stella always managed to create an atmosphere of urgency so that she gave the impression of an amiable, potentially willing young woman too busy for intimacies.

George could tell from the manner in which she put food down at a table and smilingly hurried back to the kitchen, as though on a matter of the greatest importance, just what was being said by the people at the table—whether it was an appreciative acknowledgement of skillful service, good-natured banter, or the attempt on the part of predatory males to make a date.

But George had never inquired into Stella's past. Because of his own history he had a horror of anything that even hinted of an attempt to inquire into one's past. The present was all that counted.

Stella herself avoided going to the city. She went on a shopping trip once or twice a month, attended an occasional movie, but for the rest stayed quietly at home in the little motel a couple of hundred yards down the roadway.

George was aroused from his reverie by a tapping sound. The man at the counter was tapping a coin on the mahogany. He had entered from the east door and George, contemplating the restaurant, hadn't noticed him.

During this period of slack time in the afternoon Stella was the only waitress on duty. Unexpectedly half a dozen tables had filled up and Stella was busy.

George departed from his customary post at the cash register to approach the man. He handed over a menu, filled a glass with water, arranged a napkin, spoon, knife, and fork, and stood waiting.

The man, his hat pulled well down on his forehead, tossed the menu to one side with a gesture almost of contempt.

"Curried shrimp."

"Sorry," George explained affably, "that's not on the menu today."

"Curried shrimp," the man repeated.

George raised his voice. Probably the other was hard of hearing. "We don't have them today, sir. We have . . ."

"You heard me," the man said. "Curried shrimp. Go get 'em."

There was something about the dominant voice, the set of the man's shoulders, the arrogance of manner, that tugged at George's memory. Now that he thought back on it, even the contemptuous gesture with which the man had tossed the menu to one side without reading it meant something.

George leaned a little closer.

"Larry!" he exclaimed in horror.

Larry Giffen looked up and grinned. "Georgie!" The way he said the name was contemptuously sarcastic.

"When . . . when did you . . . how did you get out?"

"It's okay, Georgie," Larry said. "*I* went out through the front door. Now go get me the curried shrimp."

"Look, Larry," George said, making a pretense of fighting the feeling of futility this man always inspired, "the cook is cranky. I'm having plenty of trouble with the help and . . ."

"You heard me," Larry interrupted. "Curried shrimp!"

George met Larry's eyes, hesitated, turned away toward the kitchen.

Stella paused beside the range as he was working over the special curry sauce.

"What's the idea?" she asked.

"A special."

Her eyes studied his face. "How special?"

"Very special."

She walked out.

Larry Giffen ate the curried shrimp. He looked around the place with an air of proprietorship.

"Think maybe I'll go in business with you, Georgie."

George Ollie knew from the dryness in his mouth, the feeling of his knees, that that was what he had been expecting.

Larry jerked his head toward Stella. "She goes with the joint."

Ollie, suddenly angry and belligerent, took a step forward. "She doesn't go with anything."

Giffen laughed, turned on his heel, started toward the door, swung back, said, "I'll see you after closing tonight," and walked out.

It wasn't until the period of dead slack that Stella moved close to George.

"Want to tell me?" she asked.

He tried to look surprised. "What?"

"Nothing."

"I'm sorry, Stella. I can't."

"Why not?"

"He's dangerous."

"To whom?"

"To you—to both of us."

She made a gesture with her shoulder. "You never gain anything by running."

He pleaded with her. "Don't get tangled in it, Stella. You remember last night the police were out here for coffee and doughnuts after running around like mad—those two big jobs, the one on the safe in the bank, the other on the theater safe?"

She nodded.

"I should have known then," he told her. "That's Larry's technique. He never leaves them anything to work on. Rubber gloves so there are no fingerprints. Burglar alarms disconnected. Everything like clockwork. No clues. No wonder the police were nuts. Larry Giffen never leaves them a clue."

She studied him. "What's he got on *you?*"

George turned away, then faced her, tried to speak, and couldn't.

"Okay," she said, "I withdraw the question."

Two customers came in, Stella escorted them to a table and went on with the regular routine. She seemed calmly competent, completely unworried. George Ollie, on the other hand, couldn't get his thoughts together. His world had collapsed. Rubber-glove Giffen must have found out about that bank job with the green accomplice, otherwise he wouldn't have dropped in.

News travels fast in the underworld. Despite carefully cultivated changes in his personal appearance, some smart ex-con while eating at the restaurant must have "made" George Ollie. He had said nothing to George, but had reserved the news as an exclusive for the ears of Larry Giffen. The prison underworld knew Big Larry might have use for George—as a farmer might have use for a horse.

And now Larry had "dropped in."

Other customers arrived. The restaurant filled up. The rush-hour waitresses came on. For two and a half hours there was so much business that George had no chance to think. Then business began to slacken. By eleven o'clock it was down to a trickle. At midnight George closed up.

"Coming over?" Stella asked.

"Not tonight," George said. "I want to do a little figuring on a purchase list."

She said nothing and went out.

George locked the doors, put on the heavy double bolts, and yet, even as he turned out the lights and put the bars in place, he knew that bolts wouldn't protect him from what was coming.

Larry Giffen kicked on the door at twelve-thirty.

George, in the shadows, pretended not to hear. He wondered what Larry would do if he found that George had ignored his threat, had gone away and left the place protected by locks and the law.

Larry Giffen knew better. He kicked violently on the door, then turned and banged it with his heel—banged it so hard that the glass rattled and threatened to break.

George hurried out of the shadows and opened the door.

"What's the idea of keeping me waiting, Georgie?" Larry asked with a solicitude that was overdone to the point of sarcasm. "Don't you want to be chummy with your old friend?"

George said, "Larry, I'm on the square. I'm on the legit. I'm staying that way."

Larry threw back his head and laughed. "You know what happens to rats, Georgie."

"I'm no rat, Larry. I'm going straight, that's all. I've paid my debts to the law and to you."

Larry showed big yellowed teeth as he grinned. "Ain't that nice, Georgie. *All* your debts paid! Now how about that National Bank job where Skinny got in a panic because the cashier didn't get 'em up fast enough?"

"I wasn't in on that, Larry."

Larry's grin was triumphant. "Says you! You were handling the getaway car. The cops got one fingerprint from the rearview mirror. The FBI couldn't classify that one print, but if anyone ever started 'em checking it with *your* file, Georgie, your fanny would be jerked off that cushioned stool by the cash register and transferred to the electric chair—the hot seat, George . . . You never did like the hot seat, Georgie."

George Ollie licked dry lips. His forehead moistened with sweat. He wanted to say something but there was nothing he could say.

Larry went on talking. "I pulled a couple of jobs here. I'm going to pull just one more. Then I'm moving in with you, Georgie. I'm your new partner. You need a little protection. I'm giving it to you."

Larry swaggered over to the cash register, rang up No Sale, pulled the drawer open, raised the hood over the roll of paper to look at the day's receipts.

"Now, Georgie," he said, regarding the empty cash drawer, "you shouldn't have put away all that dough. Where is it?"

George Ollie gathered all the reserves of his self-respect. "Go to hell," he said. "I've been on the square and I'm going to stay on the square."

Larry strode across toward him. His open left hand slammed against the side of George's face with staggering impact.

"You're hot," Larry said, and his right hand swung up to the other side of George's face. "You're hot, Georgie," and his left hand came up from his hip.

George made a pretense at defending himself but Larry Giffen, quick as a cat, strong as a bear, came after him. "You're hot." . . . Wham . . . "You're hot." . . . Wham . . . "You're hot, Georgie."

At length Larry stepped back. "I'm taking a half interest. You'll run it for me when I'm not here, Georgie. You'll keep accurate books. You'll do all the work. Half of the profits are mine. I'll come in once in a while to look things over. Be damn certain that you don't try any cheating, Georgie.

"You wouldn't like the hot squat, Georgie. You're fat, Georgie. You're well fed. You've teamed up with that swivel-hipped babe, Georgie. I could see it in your eye. She's class, and she goes with the place, Georgie. Remember, I'm cutting myself in for a half interest. I'm leaving it to you to see there isn't any trouble."

George Ollie's head was in a whirl. His cheeks were stinging from the heavy-handed slaps of the big man. His soul felt crushed under a weight. Larry Giffen knew no law but the law of power, and Larry Giffen, his little malevolent eyes glittering with sadistic gloating, was on the move, coming toward him again, hoping for an opportunity to beat up on him.

George hadn't known when Stella had let herself in. Her key had opened the door smoothly.

"What's he got on you, George?" she asked.

Larry Giffen swung to the sound of her voice. "Well, well, little Miss Swivel-hips," he said. "Come here, Swivel-hips. I'm half owner in the place now. Meet your new boss."

She stood still, looking from him to George Ollie.

Larry turned to George.

"All right, Georgie, where's the safe? Give me the combination to the safe, Georgie. As your new partner I'll need to have it. I'll handle the day's take. Later on you can keep books, but right now, I need money. I have a heavy date tonight."

George Ollie hesitated a moment, then moved back toward the kitchen.

"I said give *me* the combination to the safe," Larry Giffen said, his voice cracking like a whip.

Stella was looking at him. George had to make it a showdown. "The dough's back here," he said. He moved toward the rack where the big butcher knives were hanging.

Larry Giffen read his mind. Larry had always been able to read him like a book.

Larry's hand moved swiftly. A snub-nosed gun nestled in Larry's big hand.

There was murder in the man's eye but his voice remained silky and taunting.

"Now, Georgie, you must be a good boy. Don't act rough. Remember, Georgie, I've done my last time. No one takes Big Larry alive. Give me the combination to the safe, Georgie. And I don't want any fooling!"

George Ollie reached a decision. It was better to die fighting than to be strapped into an electric chair. He ignored the gun, kept moving back toward the knife rack.

Big Larry Giffen was puzzled for a moment. George had always collapsed like a flat tire when Larry had given an order. This was a new George Ollie. Larry couldn't afford to shoot. He didn't want noise and he didn't want to kill.

"Hold it, Georgie! You don't need to get rough." Larry put away his gun. "You're hot on that bank job, Georgie. Remember I can send you to the hot squat. That's all the argument I'm going to use, Georgie. You don't need to go for a shiv. Just tell me to walk out, Georgie, and I'll leave. Big Larry doesn't stay where he isn't welcome.

"But you'd better welcome me, Georgie boy. You'd better give me the combination to the safe. You'd better take me in as your new partner. Which is it going to be, Georgie?"

It was Stella who answered the question. Her voice was calm and clear. "Don't hurt him. You'll get the money."

Big Larry looked at her. His eyes changed expression. "Now that's the sort of a broad *I* like. Tell your new boss where the safe is. Start talking, babe, and remember you go with the place."

"There isn't any safe," George said hurriedly. "I banked the money."

Big Larry grinned. "You're a liar. You haven't left the place. I've been casing the joint. Go on, babe, tell me where the hell that safe is. Then Georgie here will give his new partner the combination."

"Concealed back of the sliding partition in the pie counter," Stella said.

"Well, well, well," Larry Giffen observed, "isn't *that* interesting?"

"Please don't hurt him," Stella pleaded. "The shelves lift out . . ."

"Stella!" George Ollie said sharply. "Shut up!"

"The damage has been done now, Georgie boy," Giffen said.

He slid back the glass doors of the pie compartment, lifted out the shelves, put them on the top of the counter, then slid back the partition disclosing the safe door.

"Clever, Georgie boy, clever! You called on your experience, didn't you? And now the combination, Georgie."

Ollie said, "You can't get away with it, Larry. I won't . . ."

"Now, Georgie boy, don't talk that way. I'm your partner. I'm in here fifty-fifty with you. You do the work and run the place and I'll take my half from time to time—But you've been holding out on me for a while, Georgie boy, so everything that's in the safe is part of my half. Come on with the combination—Of course, I could make a spindle job on it, but since I'm a half owner in the joint I hate to damage any of the property. Then you'd have to buy a new safe. The cost of that would have to come out of your half. You couldn't expect *me* to pay for a new safe."

Rubber-glove Giffen laughed at his little joke.

"I said to hell with you," George Ollie said.

Larry Giffen's fist clenched. "I guess you need a damn good working over, Georgie boy. You shouldn't be disrespectful . . ."

Stella's voice cut in. "Leave him alone. I said you'd get the money. George doesn't want any electric chair."

Larry turned back to her. "I like 'em sensible, sweetheart. Later on, I'll tell you about it. Right now it's all business. Business before pleasure. Let's go."

"Ninety-seven four times to the right," Stella said.

"Well, well, well," Giffen observed. "She knows the combination. We both know what that means, Georgie boy, don't we?"

George, his face red and swollen from the impact of the slaps, stood helpless.

"It means she really is part of the place," Giffen said. "I've got a half interest in you too, girlie. I'm looking forward to collecting on that too. Now what's the rest of the combination?"

Giffen bent over the safe; then, suddenly thinking better of it, he straightened, slipped the snub-nosed revolver into his left hand, and said, "Just so you don't get ideas, Georgie boy—but you wouldn't, you know. You don't like the idea of the hot squat."

Stella, white-faced and tense, called out the numbers. Larry Giffen spun the dials on the safe, swung the door open, opened the cash box.

"Well, well, well," he said, sweeping the bills and money into his pocket. "It *was* a good day, wasn't it?"

Stella said, "There's a hundred-dollar bill in the ledger."

Big Larry pulled out the ledger. "So there is, so there is," he said, surveying the hundred-dollar bill with the slightly torn corner. "Girlie, you're a big help. I'm glad you go with the place. I think we're going to get along swell."

Larry straightened, backed away from the safe, stood looking at George Ollie.

"Don't look like that Georgie boy. It isn't so bad. I'll leave you enough profit to keep you in business and keep you interested in the work. I'll just take off most of the cream. I'll drop in to see you from time to time, and, of course, Georgie boy, you won't tell anybody that you've seen me. Even if you did it wouldn't do any good because I came out the front door, Georgie boy. I'm smart. I'm not like you. I don't have something hanging over me where someone can jerk the rug out from under me at any time.

"Well, Georgie boy, I've got to be toddling along. I've got a little job at the supermarket up the street. They put altogether too much confidence in that safe they have. But I'll be back in a couple of hours, Georgie boy. I've collected on part of my investment and now I want to collect on the rest of it. You wait up for me, girlie. You can go get some shut-eye, Georgie."

Big Larry looked at Stella, walked to the door, stood for a moment searching the shadows, then melted away into the darkness.

"You," Ollie said to Stella, his voice showing his heartsickness at her betrayal.

"What?" she asked.

"Telling him about the safe—about that hundred dollars, giving him the combination . . ."

She said, "I couldn't stand to have him hurt you."

"You and the things you can't stand," Ollie said. "You don't know Rubber-glove Giffen. You don't know what you're in for now. You don't . . ."

"Shut up," she interrupted. "If you're going to insist on letting other people do your thinking for you, I'm taking on the job."

He looked at her in surprise.

She walked over to the closet, came out with a wrecking bar. Before he had the faintest idea of what she had in mind she walked over to the cash register, swung the bar over her head, and brought it down with crashing impact on the front of the register. Then she inserted the point of the bar, pried back the chrome steel, jerked the drawer open. She went to the back door, unlocked it, stood on the outside, inserted the end of the wrecking bar, pried at the door until she had crunched the wood of the door jamb.

George Ollie was watching her in motionless stupefaction. "What the devil are you doing?" he asked. "Don't you realize . . . ?"

"Shut up," she said. "What's this you once told me about a spindle job? Oh, yes, you knock off the knob and punch out the spindle—"

She walked over to the safe and swung the wrecking bar down on the knob of the combination, knocking it out of its socket, letting it roll crazily along the floor. Then she went to the kitchen, picked out a towel, polished the wrecking bar clean of fingerprints.

"Let's go," she said to George Ollie.

"Where?" he asked.

"To Yuma," she said. "We eloped an hour and a half ago—or hadn't you heard? We're getting married. There's no delay or red tape in Arizona. As soon as we cross the state line we're free to get spliced. You need someone to do your thinking for you. I'm taking the job.

"And," she went on, as George Ollie stood there, "in this state a husband can't testify against his wife, and a wife can't testify against her husband. In view of what I know now it might be just as well."

George stood looking at her, seeing something he had never seen before—a fierce, possessive something that frightened him at the same time it reassured him. She was like a panther protecting her young.

"But I don't get it," George said. "What's the idea of wrecking the place, Stella?"

"Wait until you see the papers," she told him.

"I still don't get it," he told her.

"You will," she said.

George stood for another moment. Then he walked toward her. Strangely enough he wasn't thinking of the trap but of the smooth contours under her pale blue uniform. He thought of Yuma, of marriage and of security, of a home.

It wasn't until two days later that the local newspaper were available in Yuma. There were headlines on an inside page:

RESTAURANT BURGLARIZED WHILE PROPRIETOR ON HONEYMOON
BIG LARRY GIFFEN KILLED IN GUN BATTLE WITH OFFICERS

The newspaper account went on to state that **Mrs.** George Ollie had telephoned the society editor from Yuma stating that George Ollie and she had left the night before and had been married in the Gretna Green across the state line. The society editor had asked her to hold the phone and had the call switched to the police.

Police asked to have George Ollie put on the line. They had a surprise for him. It seemed that when the merchant patrolman had made his regular nightly check of Ollie's restaurant at 1 A.M., he found it had been broken into. Police had found a perfect set of fingerprints on the cash register and on the safe. Fast work had served to identify the fingerprints as those of Big Larry Giffen, known in the underworld as Rubber-glove Giffen because of his skill in wearing rubber gloves and never leaving fingerprints. This was one job that Big Larry had messed up. Evidently he had forgotten his gloves.

Police had mug shots of Big Larry and in no time at all they had out a general alarm.

Only that afternoon George Ollie's head waitress and part-time cashier had gone to the head of the police burglary detail. "In case we should ever be robbed," she had said, "I'd like to have it so you could get a conviction when you get the man who did the job. I left a hundred-dollar bill in the safe. I've torn off a corner. Here's the torn corner. You keep it. That will enable you to get a conviction if you get the thief."

Police thought it was a fine idea. It was such a clever idea they were sorry they couldn't have used it to pin a conviction on Larry Giffen.

But Larry had elected to shoot it out with the arresting officers. Knowing his record, officers had been prepared for this. After the sawed-off shotguns had blasted the life out of Big Larry the police had found the bloodstained hundred-dollar bill in his pocket when his body was stripped at the morgue.

Police also found the loot from three other local jobs on him, cash amounting to some seven thousand dollars.

Police were still puzzled as to how it happened that Giffen, known to the underworld as the most artistic box man in the business, had done such an amateurish job at the restaurant. Giffen's reputation was that he had never left a fingerprint or a clue.

Upon being advised that his place had been broken into, George Ollie, popular restaurant owner, had responded in a way which was perfectly typical of honeymooners the world over.

"The hell with business," he had told the police. "I'm on my honeymoon."

ERIC AMBLER *(1909–) is best known as one of the fathers of the modern spy story.* His novels A Coffin for Dimitrious *and* Dirty Story *helped to establish espionage fiction as an important genre of contemporary literature. However, Mr. Ambler is also a fine practitioner of the "straight" detective story. His tales, like this one, concerning the exploits of Dr. Jan Czissar, a Czech refugee who unofficially aids certain investigations of Scotland Yard, are excellent examples of his range and talent. Mr. Ambler's place in literary history is secure and can be demonstrated by his receipt of four British Crime Writer Awards, an Edgar Award from the Mystery Writers of America, and the Grand Master Award for lifetime achievement from the latter organization. He is also an Officer of the Order of the British Empire, one of only a few popular writers to be so honored.*

"The Case of the Emerald Sky" contains several of the elements that have made Eric Ambler a popular writer for over fifty years—authenticity, great suspense, and a skill for narrative that keeps the reader turning the pages.

The Case of the Emerald Sky

BY ERIC AMBLER

Assistant Commissioner Mercer of Scotland Yard stared, without speaking, at the card which Sergeant Flecker had placed before him. There was no address, simply:

DR. JAN CZISSAR
Late Prague Police

It was an inoffensive-looking card. An onlooker, who knew only that Dr. Czissar was a refugee Czech with a brilliant record of service in the criminal investigation department of the Prague police, would have been surprised at the expression of dislike that spread slowly over the assistant commissioner's healthy face.

Yet, had the same onlooker known the circumstances of Mercer's first encounter with Dr. Czissar, he would not have been surprised. Just one week had elapsed since Dr. Czissar had appeared out of the blue with a letter of introduction from the mighty Sir Herbert at the home office, and Mercer was still smarting as a result of the meeting.

Sergeant Flecker had seen and interpreted the expression. Now he spoke.

"Out, sir?"

Mercer looked up sharply. "No, sergeant. In, but too busy," he snapped.

Half an hour later Mercer's telephone rang.

"Sir Herbert to speak to you from the Home Office, sir," said the operator.

Sir Herbert said, "Hello, Mercer, is that you?" And then, without waiting for a reply: "What's this I hear about your refusing to see Dr. Czissar?"

Mercer jumped but managed to pull himself together. "I did not refuse to see him, Sir Herbert," he said with iron calm. "I sent down a message that I was too busy to see him."

Sir Herbert snorted. "Now look here, Mercer; I happen to know that it was Dr. Czissar who spotted those Seabourne murderers for you. Not blaming you, personally, of course, and I don't propose to mention the matter to the commissioner. You can't be right every time. We all know that as an organization there's nothing to touch Scotland Yard. My point is, Mercer, that you fellows ought not to be above learning a thing or two from a foreign expert. Clever fellows, these Czechs, you know. No question of poaching on your preserves. Dr. Czissar wants no publicity. He's grateful to this country and eager to help. Least we can do is to let him. We don't want any professional jealousy standing in the way."

If it were possible to speak coherently through clenched teeth, Mercer would have done so. "There's no question either of poaching on preserves or of professional jealousy, Sir Herbert. I was, as Dr. Czissar was informed, busy when he called. If he will write for an appointment, I shall be pleased to see him."

"Good man," said Sir Herbert cheerfully. "But we don't want any of this red tape business about writing in. He's in my office now. I'll send him over. He's particularly anxious to have a word with you about this Brock Park case. He won't keep you more than a few minutes. Goodby."

Mercer replaced the telephone carefully. He knew that if he had replaced it as he felt like replacing it, the entire instrument would have been smashed. For a moment or two he sat quite still. Then, suddenly, he snatched the telephone up again.

"Inspector Cleat, please." He waited. "Is that you, Cleat? Is the commissioner in? . . . I see. Well, you might ask him as soon as he comes in if he could spare me a minute or two. It's urgent. Right."

He hung up again, feeling a little better. If Sir Herbert could have words with the commissioner, so could he. The old man wouldn't stand for his subordinates being humiliated and insulted by pettifogging politicians. Professional jealousy!

Meanwhile, however, this precious Dr. Czissar wanted to talk about the Brock Park case. Right! Let him! He wouldn't be able to pull that to pieces. It was absolutely watertight. He picked up the file on the case which lay on his desk.

Yes, absolutely watertight.

Three years previously, Thomas Medley, a widower of 60 with two adult children, had married Helena Merlin, a woman of 42. The four had since lived together in a large house in the London suburb of Brock Park. Medley, who had amassed a comfortable fortune, had retired from business shortly before his second marriage, and had devoted most of his time since to his hobby, gardening. Helena Merlin was an artist, a landscape painter, and in Brock Park it was whispered that her pictures sold for large sums. She dressed fashionably and smartly, and was disliked by her neighbors. Harold Medley, the son aged 25, was a medical student at a London hospital. His sister, Janet, was three years younger, and as dowdy as her stepmother was smart.

In the early October of that year, and as a result of an extra heavy meal, Thomas Medley had retired to bed with a bilious attack. Such attacks had not been unusual. He had had an enlarged liver, and had been normally dyspeptic. His doctor had prescribed in the usual way. On his third day in bed the patient had been considerably better. On the fourth day, however, at about four in the afternoon, he had been seized with violent abdominal pains, persistent vomiting, and severe cramps in the muscles of his legs.

These symptoms had persisted for three days, on the last of which there had been convulsions. He had died that night. The doctor had certified the death as being due to gastroenteritis. The dead man's estate had amounted to, roughly £110,000. Half of it went to his wife. The remainder was divided equally between his two children.

A week after the funeral, the police had received an anonymous letter suggesting that Medley had been poisoned. Subsequently, they had received two further letters. Information had then reached them that several residents in Brock Park had received similar letters, and that the matter was the subject of gossip.

Medley's doctor was approached later. He had reasserted that the death had been due to gastroenteritis, but admitted that the possibility of the condition having been brought by the willful administration of poison had not occurred to him. The body had been exhumed by license of the home secretary, and an autopsy performed. No traces of poison had been found in the stomach; but in the liver, kidneys and spleen a total of 1.751 grains of arsenic had been found.

Inquiries had established that on the day on which the poisoning symptoms had appeared, the deceased had had a small luncheon consisting of breast of chicken, spinach (canned), and one potato. The cook had partaken of spinach from the same tin without suffering any ill effects. After his luncheon, Medley had taken a dose of the medicine prescribed for him by the doctor. It had been mixed with water for him by his son, Harold.

Evidence had been obtained from a servant that, a fortnight before the death, Harold had asked his father for £100 to settle a racing debt. He had been refused. Inquiries had revealed that Harold had lied. He had been secretly married for some time, and the money had been needed not to pay racing debts but for his wife, who was about to have a child.

The case against Harold had been conclusive. He had needed money desperately. He had quarrelled with his father. He had known that he was the heir to a quarter of his father's estate. As a medical student in a hospital, he had been in a position to obtain arsenic. The poisoning that appeared had shown that the arsenic must have been administered at about the time the medicine had been taken. It had been the first occasion on which Harold had prepared his father's medicine.

The coroner's jury had boggled at indicting him in their verdict, but he had later been arrested and was now on remand. Further evidence from the hospital as to his access to supplies of arsenical drugs had been forthcoming. He would certainly be committed for trial.

Mercer sat back in his chair. A watertight case. Sentences began to form in his mind. "This Dr. Czissar, Sir Charles, is merely a time-wasting crank. He's a refugee and his sufferings have probably unhinged him a little. If you could put the matter to Sir Herbert, in that light . . ."

And then, for the second time that afternoon, Dr. Czissar was announced.

Mercer was angry, yet, as Dr. Czissar came into the room, he became conscious of a curious feeling of friendliness toward him. It was not entirely the friendliness that one feels toward an enemy one is about to destroy. In his mind's eye he had been picturing Dr. Czissar as an ogre. Now, Mercer saw that, with his mild eyes behind their thick spectacles, his round, pale face, his drab raincoat and his unfurled umbrella, Dr. Czissar was, after all, merely pathetic. When, just inside the door, Dr. Czissar stopped, clapped his umbrella to his side as if it were a rifle, and said loudly: "Dr. Jan Czissar. Late Prague Police, At your service." Mercer very nearly smiled.

Instead he said: "Sit down, doctor. I am sorry I was too busy to see you earlier."

"It is so good of you . . ." began Dr. Czissar earnestly.

"Not at all, doctor. You want, I hear, to compliment us on our handling of the Brock Park case."

Dr. Czissar blinked. "Oh, no, Assistant Commissioner Mercer," he said anxiously. "I would like to compliment, but it is too early, I think. I do not wish to seem impolite, but . . ."

Mercer smiled complacently. "Oh, we shall convict our man, all right, doctor. I don't think you need to worry."

Dr. Czissar's anxiety became painful to behold. "Oh, but I do worry. You see—" He hesitated differently. "—he is not guilty."

Mercer hoped that the smile with which he greeted the statement did not reveal his secret exultation. He said blandly, "Are you aware, doctor, of all the evidence against him?"

"I attended the inquest," said Dr. Czissar mournfully. "But there will be more evidence from the hospital, no doubt. This young Mr. Harold could no doubt have stolen enough arsenic to poison a regiment without the loss being discovered."

The fact that the words had been taken out of his mouth disconcerted Mercer only slightly. He nodded. "Exactly."

A faint, thin smile stretched the doctor's full lips. He settled his glasses on his nose. Then he cleared his throat, swallowed hard and leaned forward. "Attention, please," he said sharply.

For some reason that he could not fathom, Mercer felt his self-confidence ooze suddenly away. He had seen that same series of actions, ending with the peremptory demand for attention, performed once before, and it had been the prelude to humiliation, to . . . He pulled himself up sharply. The Brock Park case was water-tight. He was being absurd.

"I'm listening," he said.

"Good." Dr. Czissar wagged one solemn finger. "According to the medical evidence given at the inquest, arsenic was found in the liver, kidneys and spleen. No?"

Mercer nodded firmly. "One point seven five one grains. That shows that much more than a fatal dose had been administered. Much more."

Dr. Czissar's eyes gleamed. "Ah, yes. Much more. It is odd, is it not, that so much was found in the kidneys?"

"Nothing odd at all about it."

"Let us leave the point for the moment. Is it not true, Assistant Commissioner Mercer, that all postmortem tests for arsenic are for arsenic itself and not for any particular arsenic salt?"

Mercer frowned. "Yes, but it's unimportant. All arsenic salts are deadly poisons. Besides, when arsenic is absorbed by the human body, it turns to the sulphide. I don't see what you are driving at, doctor."

"My point is this, Assistant Commissioner, that usually it is impossible to tell from a delayed autopsy which form of arsenic was used to poison the body. You agree? It might be arsenious oxide; or one of the arsenates or arsenites, copper arsenite, for instance; or it might be a chloride, or it might be an organic compound of arsenic."

"Precisely."

"But," continued Dr. Czissar, "what sort of arsenic should we expect to find in a hospital, eh?"

Mercer pursed his lips. "I see no harm in telling you, doctor, that Harold Medley could easily have secured supplies of either salvarsan or neosalvarsan. They are both important drugs."

"Yes, indeed," said Dr. Czissar. "Very useful in one-tenth of a gram doses, but very dangerous in larger quantities." He stared at the ceiling. "Have you seen any of Helena Merlin's paintings, Assistant Commissioner?"

The sudden change of subject took Mercer unawares. He hesitated. Then: "Oh, you mean Mrs. Medley. No, I haven't seen any of her paintings."

"Such a chic, attractive woman," said Dr. Czissar. "After I had seen her at the inquest I could not help wishing to see some of her work. I found some in a gallery near Bond St." He sighed. "I had expected something clever, but I was disappointed. She paints what she thinks instead of what is."

"Really? I'm afraid, doctor, that I must . . ."

"I felt," persisted Dr. Czissar, bringing his cowlike eyes once more to Mercer's, "that the thoughts of a woman who thinks of a field as blue and of a sky as emerald green must be a little strange."

"Modern stuff, eh?" said Mercer shortly. "I don't much care for it, either. And now, doctor, if you've finished, I'll ask you to excuse me. I . . ."

"Oh, but I have not finished yet," said Dr. Czissar kindly. "I think, Assistant Commissioner, that a woman who paints a landscape with a green sky is not only strange, but also interesting, don't you? I asked the gentlemen at the gallery about her. She produces only a few pictures—about six a year. He offered to sell me one of them for 15 guineas. She earns £100 a year from her work. It is wonderful how expensively she dresses on that sum."

"She had a rich husband."

"Oh, yes. A curious household, don't you think? The daughter Janet is especially curious. I was so sorry that she was so much upset by the evidence at the inquest."

"A young woman probably would be upset at the idea of her brother being a murderer," said Mercer drily.

"But to accuse herself so violently of the murder. That was odd."

"Hysteria. You get a lot of it in murder cases." Mercer stood up and held out his hand. "Well, doctor, I'm sorry you haven't been able to upset our case this time. If you'll leave your address with the sergeant as you go. I'll see that you get a pass for the trial," he added with relish.

But Dr. Czissar did not move. "You are going to try this young man for murder, then?" he said slowly. "You have not understood what I have been hinting at?"

Mercer grinned. "We've got something better than hints, doctor—a first-class circumstantial case against young Medley. Motive, time and method of administration, source of the poison. Concrete evidence, doctor! Juries like it. If you can produce one scrap of evidence to show that we've got the wrong man, I'll be glad to hear it."

Dr. Czissar's back straightened, and his cowlike eyes flashed. He said, sharply, "I, too, am busy. I am engaged on a work on medical jurisprudence. I desire only to see justice done. I do not believe that on the evidence you have you can convict this young man under English law; but the fact of his being brought to trial could damage his career as a doctor. Furthermore, there is the real murderer to be considered. Therefore, in a spirit of friendliness, I have come to you instead of going to Harold Medley's legal advisers. I will now give you your evidence."

Mercer sat down again. He was very angry. "I am listening," he said grimly; "but if you . . ."

"Attention, please," said Dr. Czissar. He raised a finger. "Arsenic was found in the dead man's kidneys. It is determined that Harold Medley could have poisoned his father with either salvarsan or neosalvarsan. There is a contradiction there. Most inorganic salts of arsenic, white arsenic, for instance, are practically insoluble in water, and if a quantity of such a salt had been administered, we might expect to find traces of it in the kidneys. Salvarsan and neosalvarsan, however, are compounds of arsenic and are very soluble in water. If either of them had been administered through the mouth, we should *not* expect to find arsenic in the kidneys."

He paused; but Mercer was silent.

"In what form, therefore, was the arsenic administered?" he went on. "The tests do not tell us, for they detect only the presence of the element, arsenic. Let us then look among the inorganic salts. There is white arsenic, that is arsenious oxide. It is used for dipping sheep. We should not expect to find it in Brock Park. But Mr. Medley was a gardener. What about sodium arsenite, the weed-killer? But we heard at the inquest that the weed-killer in the garden was of the kind harmful only to weeds. We come to copper arsenite. Mr. Medley was, in my opinion, poisoned by a large dose of copper arsenite."

"And on what evidence," demanded Mercer, "do you base that opinion?"

"There is, or there has been, copper arsenite in the Medleys' house." Dr. Czissar looked at the ceiling. "On the day of the inquest, Mrs. Medley wore a fur coat. I have since found another fur coat like it. The price of the coat was 400 guineas. Inquiries in Brock Park have told me that this lady's husband, besides being a rich man, was also a very mean and unpleasant man. At the inquest, his son told us that he had kept his marriage a secret because he was afraid that his father would stop his allowance or prevent his continuing studies in medicine. Helena Medley had expensive tastes. She had married this man so that she could indulge them. He had failed her. That coat she wore, Assistant Commissioner, was unpaid for. You will find, I think, that she had other debts, and that a threat had been made by one of the creditors to approach her husband. She was tired of this man so much older than she was—this man who did not even justify his existence by spending his fortune on her. She poisoned her husband. There is no doubt of it."

"The commissioner to speak to you, sir," said the operator.

"All right. Hello . . . Hello, Sir Charles. Yes, I did want to speak to you urgently. It was—" He hesitated. "—it was about the Brock Park case. I think that we will have to release young Medley. I've got hold of some new medical evidence that . . . Yes, yes, I realize that, Sir Charles, and I'm very sorry that . . . All right, Sir Charles, I'll come immediately."

He replaced the telephone and went.

"Nonsense!" said Mercer. "Of course we know that she was in debt. We are not fools. But lots of women are in debt. It doesn't make them murderers. Ridiculous!"

"All murderers are ridiculous," agreed Dr. Czissar solemnly; "especially the clever ones."

"But how on earth . . . ?" began Mercer.

Dr. Czissar smiled gently. "It was the spinach that the dead man had for luncheon before the symptoms of poisoning began that interested me," he said. "Why give spinach when it is out of season? Canned vegetables are not usually given to an invalid with gastric trouble. And then, when I saw Mrs. Medley's paintings, I understood. The emerald sky, Assistant Commissioner. It was a fine, rich emerald green, that sky—*the sort of emerald green that the artist gets when there is aceto-arsenite of copper in the paint!* The firm which supplies Mrs. Medley with her working materials will be able to tell you when she bought it. I suggest, too, that you take the picture—it is in the Summons Gallery—and remove a little of the sky for analysis. You will find that the spinach was prepared at her suggestion and taken to her husband's bedroom by her. Spinach is *green* and *slightly bitter* in taste. *So is copper arsenite.*" He sighed. "If there had not been anonymous letters . . ."

"Ah!" interrupted Mercer. "The anonymous letters! Perhaps you know . . ."

"Oh, yes," said Dr. Czissar simply. "The daughter Janet wrote them. Poor child! She disliked her smart stepmother and wrote them out of spite. Imagine her feelings when she found that she had—how do you say?—put a noose about her brother's throat. It would be natural for her to try to take the blame herself." He looked at his watch. "But it is late and I must get to the museum reading-room before it closes." He stood up, clapped his umbrella to his side, clicked his heels and said loudly: "Dr. Jan Czissar. Late Prague Police. At your service!"

JOHN DICKSON CARR *(1906–1977) was often thought of as an Englishman because many of his stories were set in the British Isles, where he lived from 1932 to 1948, but he was born in Uniontown, Pennsylvania, and graduated from Haverford College. A Grand Master of the Mystery Writers of America and long–time book reviewer for* Ellery Queen's Mystery Magazine, *his most famous creation—who appeared in twenty-three novels and dozens of short stories—is undoubtedly Dr. Gideon Fell, a G. K. Chesterton look-alike whose speciality was the "impossible" crime and the locked-room mystery. Carr's analysis of the locked-room mystery, which appears in his novel* The Three Coffins *(1935), is must reading for all lovers of this form of the genre.*

"Strictly Diplomatic" is both a spy story and a mystery–with a difference.

Strictly Diplomatic
BY JOHN DICKSON CARR

Now that he was nearly at the end of his rest-cure, Dermot had never felt so well in his life.

He leaned back in the wicker chair, flexing his muscles. He breathed deeply. Below him the flattish lands between France and Belgium sloped to the river: a slow Flemish river dark green with the reflection of its banks. Half a mile away he could see the houses of the town, with the great glass roof of the spa smoky in autumn sunshine. Behind him —at the end of the arbor—was the back of the hotel, now denuded of its awnings.

They had taken down the awnings; they were closing up many of the bedrooms. Only a few guests now pottered about the terrace. A crisp tang had come into the air: work, and the thunder of London again, now loomed up as a pleasant prospect. Once, hardly a month ago, it had been a nightmare of buses charging straight at you, like houses loose; a place where nerves snapped, and you started to run.

Even with that noise in his ears, he had not wanted to go away.

"But I can't take a holiday now!" he had told the doctor.

"Holiday?" snorted the doctor. "Do you call it a holiday? Your trouble is plain overwork, a complaint we don't often get nowadays. Why don't you relax? Not hard up, are you?"

"No, it isn't that."

"You're too conscientious," the doctor had said, rather enviously.

"No. It's not a virtue," said Dermot, as honestly as he could. "I can't help it. Every second I'm away from work, I'm worrying about it until I get back. I'm built like that. I can't relax. I can't even get drunk."

The doctor grunted.

"Ever try falling in love?"

"Not since I was nineteen. And, anyway, it's not something you can take down like a box of pills and dose yourself with. Or at least I can't."

"Well," said the doctor, surveying him. "I know a rising barrister who's going to come a cropper unless you get out of this. Now I warn you. You get off to the Continent this week. There's a spa I know—Ile St. Cathérine. The waters won't do you any harm; and the golf will do you good."

Here the doctor, who was an old friend of Andrew Dermot's, grinned raffishly.

"What you want," he added, "is adventure. In the grand manner. I hear there's a fenced-off area near Ile St. Cathérine, bayonets and all. The casino is probably full of beautiful slant-eyed spies with jade earrings. Forget you're turning into such a moss-back. Pick up one of the beautiful slant-eyed spies, and go on the razzle-dazzle with her. It'll do you all the good in the world."

Alone on the lawn behind his hotel, Dermot laughed aloud. Old Foggy had been right, in a way. But he had gone one less or one better than that. He had fallen in love.

Anyone less like a slant-eyed spy than Betty Weatherill would be difficult to imagine. In face even the tension which tautened nerves in the rest of Europe did not exist in Ile St. Cathérine. It was a fat, friendly, rather stodgy sort of place. Looking round the spa—where fountains fell, and people got very excited on the weighing-machines— Dermot wondered at old Foggy's notion of bayonets. He felt soothed, and free. Bicycle-bells tingled in the streets under once-gilded houses. At night, when you ordered thin wine by the glass, a band played beneath lights in the trees. A mild flutter in roulette at the casino caused excitement; and one Belgian burgher was caught bringing his supper in a paper packet.

Dermot first saw Betty Weatherill on the morning after his arrival.

It was at breakfast. There were not many guests at the hotel: a fat Dutchman eating cheese for breakfast, half a dozen English people, a foreign envoy, a subdued French couple. And, of course, the sturdy girl who sat alone at the sun-steeped table by the windows.

Dermot's nerves were still raw from the journey. When he first saw her he felt a twinge of what he thought was envy at her sheer health. It flashed out at him. He had an impression of a friendly mouth, a sun-tanned complexion; of eagerness, and even naïveté. It disturbed him like the clattering coffee-cups. He kept looking round at her, and looking round again, though he did not understand why.

He played execrable golf that day.

He saw her again next morning. They ran into each other buying stamps at the cash-desk. They both smiled slightly, and Dermot felt embarrassed. He had been trying to remember whether the color of her hair was fair or chestnut; it was, he saw, a light brown. That afternoon his golf was even worse. It was absurd that he, thirty-five years old, should seem as stale and crumpled as an old poster against a wall. He was a nerve-ridden fool. He fell to thinking of her again.

On the following day they went so far as to say good morning. On the third day he took his nerve in both hands, and plumped down at the breakfast-table next to hers.

"I *can't* do it," he heard her say, half-laughing.

The words gave him a start. Not a ladies' man, this move of his had struck him as distinctly daring. Yet he felt the communication between them, an uncomfortable awareness of each other's presence. He looked up, to find her eyes fixed on him.

"Do what?" he asked quickly.

"Manage Continental breakfasts," she answered, as though they were old friends discussing a problem of mutual importance. "I know I shouldn't, but every day I order bacon and eggs."

After that their acquaintance was off at a gallop.

Her name was Betty Weatherill. She was twenty-eight, and came from Brighton. She had been a schoolmistress (incongruous idea); but she had come into a small inheritance and, as she confessed, was blue-ing part of it. He had never met a girl who seemed so absolutely right: in what she said, in what she did, in her response to any given remark.

That afternoon they went to the fair and ate hot dogs and rode round and round on the wooden horses to the panting music of an electric piano. That night they dressed for the casino; and Andrew Dermot, shuffling roulette-counters, felt no end of an experienced gay-dog. And the knowledge came to him, with a kind of shock, "Good lord, I'm alive."

Betty was popular at the hotel. The proprietor, Monsieur Gant, knew her quite well and was fond of her. Even the fat Dr. Vanderver, of the Sylvanian Embassy, gave her a hoarse chuckle of appreciation whenever she went by. Not that she had no difficulties. There was, it appeared, some trouble about her passport. She had several times to go to the prefecture of police—from which she emerged flushed, and as near angry as it was possible for her to be.

As for Dermot, he was in love and he knew it. That was why he exulted when he sat by the teatable on the lawn behind the hotel, at half-past five on that lazy, veiled autumn afternoon, waiting for Betty to join him. The lawn was dotted with little tables, but he was alone. The remains of tea and sandwiches were piled on a tray. Dermot was replete; no outside alarms troubled Ile St. Cathérine; no black emblems threw shadows.

This was just before he received the greatest shock of his life.

"Hello!" said Betty. "Sorry I'm late." She came hurrying out of the arbor, with the breathless smile she always wore when she was excited. She glanced quickly round the lawn, deserted except for a waitress slapping at crumbs. Dermot got up.

"You're not late," he told her. "But you swore to me you were going to have tea in town, so I went ahead." He looked at her suspiciously. "Did you?"

"Did I what?"

"Have tea."

"Yes, of course."

For no reason that he could analyze, a chill of uneasiness came to Dermot. His nightmares were cured. But it was as though an edge of the nightmare returned. Why? Only because the atmosphere suddenly seemed wrong, because the expression of her eyes was wrong. He drew out a chair for her.

"Sure you wouldn't like another cup? Or a sandwich?"

"Well—"

Now he thought he must be a fool reading huge meanings into trifles. But the impression persisted. He gave an order to the waitress, who removed the tea-tray and disappeared into the arbor. Betty had taken a cigarette out of her handbag; but, when he tried to light it for her, the cigarette slipped out of her fingers, rolled on the table.

"Oh, damn," she whispered. Now he was looking into her eyes from a short distance away; they seemed the eyes of a slightly older, wiser woman. They were hazel eyes, the whites very clear against a sun-tanned face. The heavy lids blinked.

"I want to know what's wrong," Dermot said.

"There's nothing wrong," said Betty, shaking her head. "Only—I wanted to talk to you. I'm afraid I've got to leave here."

"When?"

"Tonight."

Dermot sat up. It seemed to him that there was a stranger sitting across from him, and that all his plans were toppling.

"If you must, you must," he said. "But I've got to go myself at the beginning of the week. I thought we were going to leave together."

"I can't. Very shortly"—she spoke with some intensity—"I hope I can explain to you what a beast I am. All I can tell you now is that it's not altogether safe for me to be here."

"Safe? In this place?"

Betty was not listening. She was wearing white, as he always remembered afterwards, with a white handbag. Again she had opened this handbag, and was going through it in something of a hurry.

"Derry." She spoke sharply. "You haven't seen my compact, have you? The white ivory one with the red band?" She looked round. "It didn't fall out when I opened my handbag before?"

"No, I don't think so, I didn't see it."

"I must have left it back in my room. Please excuse me. I'll be back in half a tick."

And she got to her feet, snapped shut the catch of the handbag.

Dermot also got up. It would not be fair to say that he exploded. He was a mild-mannered man who arrived at all emotions with difficulty. But in the past few minutes he felt that a door had opened on a world he could not understand.

"Look here, Betty," he said. "I don't know what's got into you; but I insist on knowing. If there's anything wrong, just tell me and we'll put it right. If—"

"I'll be back in a moment," she assured him.

And, disregarding the hand he put out, she hurried back through the arbor.

Dermot sat down heavily, and stared after her. A veiled sun had turned the sky to grey, making dingy the cloths of the little tables on the lawn. The cloths fluttered under a faint breeze.

He contemplated the arbor, which was a very special sort of arbor.

Monsieur Gant, the proprietor of the Hotel Suchard, had imported it from Italy and was very proud of it. Stretching back a full twenty yards to the rear terrace of the hotel, it made a sort of tunnel composed of tough interlaced vines which in summer were heavy with purplish-pink blossom. A line of tables ran beside it, with lights from above. Inside the arbor, at night, Chinese lanterns hung from the roof. It was one of the romantic features of the hotel. But at the moment—cramped, unlighted, hooded with thick foliage—it was a tunnel which suggested unpleasant images.

"A good place for a murder," Betty had once laughed.

Andrew Dermot could hear his watch ticking. He wished she would come back.

He lit a cigarette and smoked it to a stump; but she had not returned. He got to his feet, stamping on the chilling grass. For the first time he glanced across the tea-table at Betty's empty chair. It was a wicker chair. And, lying on the seat in plain view, was a white ivory compact with a red band.

So that was it! She had been too much upset to notice the compact, of course. She was probably still searching her room for it.

He picked up the compact and went after her.

Inside the arbor it was almost dark, but chinks and glimmers of light flickered through interlaced vines and showed him an arched tunnel some ten feet high, with a floor of packed sand. There was a stagnant smell of dying blossom; the Judas tree, did they call it? Obscurely, he was relieved to find the gnat-stung arbor empty. He hurried along its length to the arch of light at the end, and emerged on a red-tiled terrace where there were more tables under the windows.

"Good eefening, Mr. Dermot," said an affable voice.

Dermot checked his rush.

He almost stumbled over Dr. Henrik Vanderver of the Sylvanian Embassy, who was sitting near the arbor, smoking a cigar with relish, and looking at him through thick-lensed spectacles.

"Ha, ha, ha!" said Dr. Vanderver, laughing uproariously and for no apparent reason; as was his custom.

"Good evening, Dr. Vanderver," said Dermot. His uneasiness had gone; he felt again a nerve-ridden fool. "Sorry to barge into you like that. Is Miss Weatherill down yet?"

Dr. Vanderver was proud of his English.

"Down?" he repeated, drawing down his eyebrows as though to illustrate.

"From her room, I mean."

"De young lady," said Vanderver, "iss with you. I have seen her go through dere"—he pointed to the arbor—"fifteen, twenty minutes ago."

"Yes, I know. But she came back here to get a compact."

Vanderver was now anxious about his English.

"Please?" he prompted, cupping his hand behind his ear.

"I said she came back here to get a compact. You know. This kind of thing." Dermot held it up. "She walked back through the arbor—"

"My friend," said Vanderver with sudden passion, "I do not know if I have understood you. Nobody has come back through this arbor while I am sitting here."

"But that's impossible."

"Please?"

Dermot thought he saw the explanation. "You mean you haven't been sitting here all the time?"

"My friend," said Vanderver, taking out a watch and shaking it, "I am sitting here one hour more—more!—where I sit always and smoke my cigar before I dress. Yes?"

"Well, Doctor?"

"I have seen the young lady go through, yes. But I have not seen her come back. I haf not seen nobody. In all dat time the only liffing soul I see on this terrace is the maid which gather up your tea-tray and bring it back here."

The terrace, always dark in the shadow of the arbor, was growing more dusky.

"Dr. Vanderver, listen to me." Dermot spoke coldly and sharply; he found Vanderver's thick-lensed spectacles turning on him with hypnotic effect. "That is not what I mean. I remember the maid going back through the arbor with the tray. But Miss Weatherill was with me then. I mean later. L-a-t-e-r, several minutes later. You saw Miss Weatherill come out through here about ten minutes ago, didn't you?"

"No."

"But you must have! I saw her go into the arbor on my side, and I never took my eyes off the entrance. She isn't in the arbor now; see for yourself. She must have come out here."

"So!" said Vanderver, tapping the table with magnificent dignity. "Now I tell *you* something. I do not know what you think has happened to the young lady. Perhaps de goblins ketch her, yes? Perhaps she dissolved to electrons and bust, yes?" Dark blood suffused his face.

"Now I will haf no more of this. I settle it. I tell you." He thrust out his thick neck. "Nobody," he said flatly, "hass come back through this arbor at all."

By nine o'clock that night, terror had come to the Hotel Suchard.

Until then Monsieur Gant, the manager, had refrained from summoning the police. At first Monsieur Gant appeared to think that everybody was joking. He only began to gesticulate, and to run from room to room, when it became clear that Betty Weatherill was not to be found either in the hotel or in the grounds. If the testimony were to be believed—and neither Dermot nor Vanderver would retract one word—then Betty Weatherill had simply walked into the arbor, and there had vanished like a puff of smoke.

It was certain that she had not left the arbor by (say) getting out through the vines. The vines grew up from the ground in a matted tangle like a wire cage, so trained round their posts from floor to arch that it would be impossible to penetrate them without cutting. And nowhere were they disturbed in any way. There was not—as one romantic under-porter suggested—an underground passage out of the tunnel. It was equally certain that Betty could not have been hiding in the arbor when Dermot walked through it. There was no place there to hide in.

This became only too clear when the Chinese lanterns were lighted in the greenish tunnel, and Monsieur Gant stood on a stepladder to shake frantically at the vine-walls—with half the domestic staff twittering behind him. This was a family matter, in which everybody took part.

Alys Marchand, in fact, was the backstairs-heroine of the occasion. Alys was the plump waitress who had been sent to fetch fresh tea and sandwiches not fifteen minutes before Betty's disappearance, but who had not brought them back because of a disagreement with the cook as to what hours constituted feev-o'clock-tay.

Apart from Dermot, Alys had been the last person to see Betty Weatherill in the flesh. Alys had passed unscathed through the arbor. To Monsieur Gant she described, with a wealth of gesture, how she had taken the order for tea and sandwiches from Monsieur Dermot. She showed how she had picked up the big tray, whisking a cloth over its debris like a conjuror. A pink-cheeked brunette, very neat in her black frock and apron, she illustrated how she had walked back through the arbor towards the hotel.

Had she seen Dr. Vanderver on this occasion?

She had.

Where was he?

At the little table on the terrace. He was smoking a cigar, and sharpening a big horn-handled knife on a small whetstone block he carried in his pocket.

"That," interposed Vanderver, in excellent French, "is a damned lie."

It was very warm in the arbor, under the line of Chinese lanterns. Vanderver stood against the wall. He seemed less bovine when he spoke French. But a small bead of perspiration had appeared on his forehead, up by the large vein near the temple; and the expression of his eyes behind the thick spectacles turned Andrew Dermot cold.

"It is true as I tell you," shrieked Alys, turning round her dark eyes. "I told my sister Clothilde, and Gina and Odette too, when I went to the kitchen. He thrusts it into his pocket—quick, so!—when he sees me."

"There are many uses for knives," said Monsieur Gant, hastily and nervously. "At the same time, perhaps it would be as well to telephone the police. You are an advocate, Monsieur Dermot. You agree?"

Dermot did agree.

He had been keeping tight hold of his nerves. In fact, he found the cold reason of his profession returning to him; and it was he who directed matters. Instead of bringing back the nightmare, this practical situation steadied him. He saw the issue clearly now. It became even more clear when there arrived, amid a squad of plainclothes men, none other than Monsieur Lespinasse, the *juge d'instruction*.

After examining the arbor, M. Lespinasse faced them all in the manager's office. He was a long, lean, melancholy man with hollow cheeks, and the Legion of Honor in his buttonhole. He had hard uncomfortable eyes, which stared down at them.

"You understand," said Lespinasse, "we appear to have here a miracle. Now I am a realist. I do not believe in miracles."

"That is good," said Dermot grimly, in his careful French. "You have perhaps formed a theory?"

"A certainty," said Lespinasse.

The hard uncomfortable eyes turned on Dermot.

"From our examination," said Lespinasse, "it is certain that Mlle. Weatherill did not leave the arbor by any secret means. You, monsieur, tell one story." He looked at Vanderver. "You, monsieur, tell another."

He looked back at Dermot. "It is therefore evident that one of you must be telling a lie."

Vanderver protested at this.

"I remind you," Vanderver growled, with a significant look, "that it will be unwise for you to make mistakes. As an acting representative of His Majesty the King of Sylvania, I enjoy immunities. I enjoy privileges—"

"Diplomatic privileges," said Monseur Lespinasse. "That is no concern of mine. My concern is that you do not break the civil law."

"I have broken no law!" said Vanderver, purple in the face. "I have told no lie!"

The *juge d'instruction* held up his hand.

"And I tell you in return," he said sharply, "that either your story or Monsieur Dermot's must be untrue. Either the young lady never went into the arbor, in which case Monsieur Dermot is telling a falsehood. Or else she did go in, and for some reason you choose to deny that you saw her come out. In which case—" Again he held up his hand. "It is only fair to warn you, Dr. Vanderver, that Miss Weatherill told me you might try to kill her."

They could hear a clock ticking in the overcrowded room.

"Kill?" said Vanderver.

"That is what I said."

"But I did not know her!"

"Evidently she knew you," answered M. Lespinasse. His sallow face was alive with bitterness; he fingered the rosette in his buttonhole. Then he took a step forward. "Miss Weatherill several times came to me at the prefecture of police. She told me of your—murderous activities in the past. I did not choose to believe her. It was too much of a responsibility. Responsibility! Now this happens, and I must take the responsibility for it at least. One more question, if you please. What have you to say to the maid's story of the horn-handled knife?"

Vanderver's voice was hoarse. "I never owned such a knife. I never saw one. I call you a son of—"

"It will not be necessary to finish," said the *juge d'instruction*. "On the contrary, *we* shall finish." He snapped his fingers, and one of the plainclothes men brought into the room an object wrapped in a newspaper.

"Our search of the arbor," continued M. Lespinasse, "was perhaps more thorough than that of Monsieur Gant. This was found buried in the sand floor only a few feet away from where monsieur was sitting."

There were more than damp stains of sand on the bright, wafer-thin blade in the newspaper; there were others. Monsieur Lespinasse pointed to them.

"Human blood," he said.

At eleven o'clock Andrew Dermot was able to get out of the room.

They told him afterwards that he had made an admirable witness; that his replies had been calm, curt, and to the point; and that he had even given sound advice on details of legal procedure, contrasting those of England with those of the present country.

He did not remember this. He knew only that he must get out into the air and stop himself from thinking of Betty.

He stood on the front terrace of the hotel, as far removed as possible from the arbor in whose floor the knife had been buried. Half a mile away the lights of the principal street in the town, the Promenade des Francais, twinkled with deathly pallor. A cool wind swept the terrace.

They took Vanderver down the front steps and bundled him into a car. There was a chain round Vanderver's wrists; his legs shook so that they had to push him up into the car. The car roared away, with a puff of smoke from the exhaust—carbon monoxide, which meant death— and only the *juge d'instruction* remained behind searching Vanderver's room for some clue as to why a sudden, meaningless murder had been done at dusk beside a commonplace hotel.

Andrew Dermot put his hands to his temples, pressing hard.

Well, that was that.

He sat down on the terrace. The little round tables had red tops, and the color did not please him, but he remained. He ordered brandy, which he could not taste. The brandy was brought to him by the same under-porter who had suggested an underground passage in the arbor, and who, agog, seemed to want to entertain him with speculations about motives for murder. Dermot chased him away.

But if Betty had to go—"go" was hardly the word for that—where was the sense in it? Why? Why? Vanderver was presumably not a homicidal maniac. Besides, all Dermot's legal instincts were bewildered by so clumsy a crime. If Vanderver were guilty, why had he from the first persisted in that unnecessary lie of saying Betty had never come out of the arbor? Why hadn't he simply faded away, never professing to have seen anything at all? Why thrust himself at that entrance as though determined to ensure suspicion for himself?

What Dermot had not permitted himself to wonder was where Betty herself might be.

But suppose Vanderver had been telling the truth?

Nonsense! Vanderver could not be telling the truth. People do not vanish like soap-bubbles out of guarded tunnels.

Presently they would be turning out the lights here on this windy, deserted terrace. The Hotel Suchard was ready, in any case, to close its doors for the winter; it would close its doors very early tonight. Behind him, in lighted windows, glowed the lounge, the smoking-room, the dining-room where he had first seen Betty. The head porter, his footsteps rapping on hardwood, darkened first the dining-room and then the lounge. Dermot would have to go upstairs to his room and try to sleep.

Getting to his feet, he walked through the thick-carpeted hall. But he could not help it. He must have one more look at the arbor.

It was veritable tunnel now: a black shape inside which, for twenty yards, Chinese lanterns glowed against the roof. The sand was torn where the knife had been dug out. Near that patch, two shovels had been propped against the wall in readiness for deeper excavations next morning. It was when he noted those preparations, and realized what they meant, that Dermot's mind turned black; he had reached his lowest depth.

He was so obsessed by it that he did not, at first, hear footfalls on the tiled terrace. He turned round. Two persons had come out to join him —but they came by different windows, and they stopped short and stared at each other as much as they stared at him.

One of these persons was M. Lespinasse, the *juge d'instruction.*

The other was Betty Weatherill.

"And now, mademoiselle," roared Lespinasse, "perhaps you will be good enough to explain the meaning of this ridiculous and indefensible trick?"

M. Lespinasse, his cheek-bones even more formidable, was carrying a briefcase and a valise. He let both fall.

"I had to do it," said Betty, addressing Dermot. "I *had* to do it, my dear."

She was not smiling at him. Dermot felt that presently, in the sheer relief of nerves, they would both be shouting with laughter. At the moment he only knew that she was there, and that he could touch her.

"One moment," said Lespinasse, coldly interrupting what was going on. "You do well, Monsieur Dermot, to demand an explanation—"

"But I don't. So long as she's—"

"—of this affair." The *juge d'instruction* raised his voice. "I can now tell you, in fact I came downstairs to tell you, *how* Miss Weatherill played this trick. What I do not know is why she did it."

Betty whirled round. "You know how?"

"I know, mademoiselle," snapped the other, "that you planned this foolishness and carried it out with the assistance of Alys Marchand, who deserves a formidable stroke of the boot behind for her part in the affair. When I found Alys ten minutes ago capering round her room waving a packet of thousand-franc notes, her behavior seemed to call for some explanation." He looked grim. "Alys was very shortly persuaded to give one."

Then he turned to Dermot.

"Let me indicate what happened, and you shall confirm it! Miss Weatherill asked you to meet her here, even specifying the table you were to occupy, and said she would arrive after tea?"

"Yes," said Dermot.

"At half-past five she came through the arbor—first making certain that Dr. Vanderver was on the terrace in the place he always occupied, every day, to smoke a cigar at that hour?"

"I—yes."

"Miss Weatherill was easily persuaded to have a fresh cup of tea?"

"Well, I asked her to."

"The waitress, Alys, was then pottering round for no apparent reason among otherwise deserted tables?"

"She was."

"You gave the order to Alys," said Monsieur Lespinasse grimly. "She picked up your tray—a big tray—whisking over it a large cloth to cover the dishes? Just as we later saw her do?"

"I admit it."

"Alys then walked away from you through the arbor. As she did so," leered Lespinasse, so intent that he made a face, "Miss Weatherill distracted your attention by getting a light for her cigarette. And kept your attention fixed on herself by dropping the cigarette, and pretending an agitation she did not feel."

Dermot gave a quick look at Betty. Whatever else this might be, it was not a hoax or a joke. Betty's face was white.

"Miss Weatherill held your attention," said Lespinasse, "so that Alys could slip back out of the arbor unnoticed. *Alys did not really go through the arbor at all!* Carrying the tray, she merely darted round the side of the arbor and returned unseen to the hotel by another way.

"Miss Weatherill was then ready to play the rest of the comedy.

'Discovering' the loss of her compact, *she* enters the arbor. Halfway up, in the darkness, is lying a stage-property these two have already left there. This is another tray: like the first, and covered with a cloth. But this cloth does not cover dishes. It covers—"

Monsieur Lespinasse broke off.

He looked flustered and dishevelled, but in his wicked eye there was a gleam of admiration.

"Monsieur Dermot, I tell you a psychological truth. The one person in this world whose features nobody can remember are those of a waitress. You see her at close range; yet you do not see her. Should you doubt this, the next time in your abominable London you go into a Lyons or an A.B.C., try calling for your bill in a hurry and see if you can identify the particular young lady who served you with a cup of tea. I know it. So did Miss Weatherill.

"She was already wearing a thin black frock under her white one. The tray in the arbor contained the other properties by which a blonde is changed into a brunette, white stockings and shoes change to black, a tanned complexion is heightened to a vivid ruddiness. It was the clumsiest possible disguise because it needed to be no more. Dr. Vanderver never glanced twice at the black-clad figure in cap and apron who walked out of the arbor carrying a tray. He saw no black wig; he saw no false complexion; he saw nothing. In his mind there registered, 'waitress-has-passed': no more. Thus Miss Weatherill, inexpertly got up as Alys, passed safely through the dense shadow which the arbor casts on the terrace—carrying before her the tray whose cloth nearly hid the discarded white dress, stockings, and shoes."

The *juge d'instruction* drew a deep, whistling breath.

"Very well!" he said. "But what I wish to know is: *why?*"

"You don't see it even yet?" asked Betty.

"My deepest apologies," said Lespinasse, "if I am dense. But I do not see it. You cannot have liked cutting yourself so that you might get real blood to put on the knife you buried. But why? How does all this nonsense help us, when Dr. Vanderver has committed no crime?"

"Because he's Embassy," answered Bettty simply.

"Mademoiselle?"

"He has diplomatic immunity," said Betty. "The government can't search him; can't even touch him. And so, you see, I had to get him arrested by the *civil* authorities so that his papers could be searched."

She turned to Dermot.

"Derry, I'm sorry," she went on. "That is, I'm sorry I'm not quite the candid-camera schoolmistress burbling to high heaven that I pretended to be. But I want to be just that. I want to enjoy myself. For the first time in all my life, I've enjoyed myself in the last month. What I mean is: I want to be with you, that's all. So, now that I'm chucking the beastly job—"

Monsieur Lespinasse swore softly. After remaining rigid for a moment, he picked up the brief-case and the valise he had dropped.

Both were in green leather stamped in gold with the royal arms of Sylvania.

"—and of course," Betty was saying almost wildly, "the fellow's name wasn't 'Dr. Vanderver,' and he's no more a neutral than I am. Only he'd got that job on forged credentials, and he was safe. So I had to keep telling the *juge d'instruction* I suspected him of being a murderer. His real name is Karl Heinrich von Arnheim; and when Sir George—you know to whom I refer, Monsieur Lespinasse—asked me to go after him—"

Monsieur Lespinasse could not break the lock of the brief-case. So he opened a wicked-looking knife of his own to slit the leather; and so he found the secret.

"The English," he said, "are not bad." He waved the knife, which glittered against the light from the windows. "Dr. Vanderver will not, I think, leave the police station after all." He swept Betty Weatherill a profound bow. "The complete plans," he added, "of the underground fortifications whose fall would break the whole line of defense along this front."

A long career filled with fine novels and stories earned
MICHAEL GILBERT*(1912–) the coveted Grand Master Award of*
the Mystery Writers of America in 1987. A solicitor and partner
in a major London legal firm, Mr. Gilbert frequently includes
events surrounding the law, solicitors, and courts in his fiction,
which now totals more than two dozen novels, numerous radio
and television scripts, and hundreds of short stories. Michael
Gilbert is especially adept at the espionage story, and his collec-
tion Game Without Rules *(1967) contains some of the best*
writing ever done in that genre. Among his series characters is
the estimable Patrick Petrella, Detective Chief Inspector of the
Metropolitan Police, who appears in some masterful police
procedurals.

"The African Tree-Beavers" is not a procedural, but it is one
of the most fascinating and challenging mysteries you will ever
read.

The African Tree-Beavers
BY MICHAEL GILBERT

Like many practical and unimaginative men, Mr Calder believed in
certain private superstitions. He would never take a train which left at
one minute to the hour, distrusted the number twenty-nine, and refused to open any parcel or letter on which the stamp had been fixed
upside down. This, incidentally, saved his life when he refused to open
an innocent-looking parcel bearing the imprint of a bookseller from
whom he had made many purchases in the past, but which proved, on
this occasion, to contain three ounces of tri-toluene and a contact fuse.
Mr Behrens sneered at the superstition, but agreed that his friend was
lucky.

Mr Calder also believed in coincidences. To be more precise, he
believed in a specific law of coincidence. If you heard a new name, or a
hitherto unknown fact, twice within twelve hours, you would hear it
again before a further twelve hours was up. Not all the schoolmasterly
logic of Mr Behrens could shake him in this belief. If challenged to
produce an example he will cite the case of the Reverend Francis
Osbaldestone.

The first time Mr Calder heard this name was at eleven o'clock at
night, at the Old Comrades' Reunion of the infantry regiment with

which he had fought for a memorable eight months in the Western Desert in 1942. He attended these reunions once every three years. His real interest was not in reminiscences of the war, but in observation of what had taken place since. It delighted him to see that a Motor Transport Corporal, whom he remembered slouching round in a pair of oily denims, should have become a prosperous garage proprietor, and that the Orderly Room Clerk, who had sold places on the leave roster, had developed his talents, first as a bookmakers' runner, and now as a bookmaker; and that the God-like Company Sergeant-Major should have risen no higher than commissionaire in a block of flats at Putney, and would be forced, if he met him in ordinary life, to call his former clerk, 'Sir'.

Several very old friends were there. Freddie Faulkner, who had stayed on in the army and had risen to command the battalion, surged through the crowd and pressed a large whisky into his hand. Mr Calder accepted it gratefully. One of the penalties of growing old, he had found, was a weak bladder for beer.

Colonel Faulkner shouted above the roar of conversation, "When are you going to keep your promise?"

"What promise?" said Mr Calder. "How many whiskies *is* this? Three or four?"

"I thought I'd get you a fairly large one. It's difficult to get near the bar. Have you forgotten? You promised to come and look me up."

"I hadn't forgotten. It's difficult to get away."

"Nonsense. You're a bachelor. You can up-sticks whenever you like."

"It's difficult to leave Rasselas behind."

"That dog of yours? For God's sake! Where do you think I live? In Hampstead Garden Suburb? Bring him with you! He'll have the time of his life. He can chase anything that moves, except my pheasants."

"He's a very well-behaved dog," said Mr Calder, "and does exactly what I tell him. If you really want me—"

"Certainly I do. Moreover, I can introduce Rasselas to another animal lover. Our rector. Francis Osbaldestone. A remarkable chap. Now get your diary out, and fix a date. . . ."

It was ten o'clock on the following morning when the name cropped up next. Mr Calder was stretched in one chair in front of the fire, his eyes shut, nursing the lingering remains of a not disagreeable hangover. Mr Behrens was in the other chair, reading the Sunday newspapers. Rasselas occupied most of the space between them.

Mr Behrens said, "Have you read this? It's very interesting. There's a clergyman who performs miracles."

"The biggest miracle any clergyman can perform nowadays," said Mr Calder sleepily, "is to get people to come to church."

"Oh, they come to *his* church all right. Full house, every Sunday. Standing-room only."

"How does he do it?"

"Personal attraction. He's equally successful with animals. However savage or shy they are, he can make them come to him, and behave themselves."

"He ought to try it on a bull."

"He has. Listen to this: *On one occasion, a bull got loose and threatened some children who were picnicking in a field. The rector, who happened to be passing, quelled the bull with a few well-chosen words. The children were soon taking rides on the bull's back.*"

"Animal magnetism."

"I suppose, if you'd met St Francis of Assisi, you'd have sniffed and said, 'Animal magnetism.' "

"He was a saint."

"How do you know this man isn't?"

"He may be. But it would need more than a few tricks with animals to convince me."

"Then what about miracles? *On another occasion, the rector was woken on a night of storm by an alarm of fire. The verger ran down to the rectory to tell the rector that a barn had been struck by lightning. The telephone line to the nearest town with a fire brigade was down. The rector said, 'Not a moment to lose. The bells must be rung.' As he spoke, the bells started to ring themselves.*"

Mr Calder snorted.

"It's gospel truth," Mr Behrens said. "Mr Penny, the verger, vouches for it. He says that by the time he got back to his cottage, where the only key of the bell-chamber is kept, and got across with it to the church, the bells had *stopped* ringing. He went up into the belfry. There was no one there. The ropes were on their hooks. Everything was in perfect order. At that moment, the brigade arrived. They had heard the bells, and were in time to save the barn."

Mr Calder said, "It sounds like a tall story to me. What do you think, Rasselas?" The dog showed his long white teeth in a smile. "He agrees. What is the name of this paragon?"

"He is the Reverend Francis Osbaldestone."

"Rector of Hedgeborn, in the heart of rural Norfolk."

"Do you know him?"

"I heard his name for the first time at about eleven o'clock last night."

"In that case," said Mr Behrens, "according to the fantastic rules propounded and believed in by you, you will hear it again before ten o'clock this evening."

It was at this precise moment that the telephone rang.

Since Mr Calder's telephone number was not only ex-directory, but was changed every six months, his incoming calls were likely to be matters of business. He was not surprised, therefore, to recognise the voice of Mr Fortescue, who was the Manager of the Westminster Branch of the London and Home Counties Bank, and other things besides.

Mr Fortescue said, "I'd like to see you and Behrens, as soon as possible. Shall we say tomorrow afternoon?"

"Certainly," said Mr Calder. "Can you give me any idea what it's about?"

"You'll find it all in your *Observer*. An article about a clergyman who performs miracles. Francis Osbaldestone."

"Ah!" said Mr Calder

"You sound pleased about something," said Mr Fortescue.

Mr Calder said, "You've just proved a theory."

"I understand," said Mr Fortescue, "that you know Colonel Faulkner quite well, in the army."

"He was my company commander," said Mr Calder.

"Would you say he was an imaginative man?"

"I should think he's got about as much imagination as a No. 11 bus."

"Or a man who would be easily deluded?"

"I'd hate to try."

Mr Fortescue pursed his lips primly, and said, "That was my impression, too. Do you know Hedgeborn?"

"Not the village. But I know that part of Norfolk. It's fairly primitive. The army had a battle school near there during the war. They were a bit slow about handing it back, too."

"I seem to remember," said Mr Behrens, "that there was a row about it. Questions in Parliament. Did they give it back in the end?"

"Most of it. They kept Snelsham Manor, with its park. After all the trouble at Porton Experimental Station, they moved the gas section down to Cornwall, and transferred the Bacterial Warfare Establishment to Snelsham, which is less than two miles from Hedgeborn."

"I can understand," said Mr Calder, "that Security would keep a careful eye on an establishment like Snelsham. But why should they be alarmed by a saintly parson two miles down the valley?"

"You are not aware of what happened last week?"

"Ought we to be?"

"It has been kept out of the press. It's bound to leak out sooner or later. Your saintly parson led what I can only describe as a village task force. It was composed of the members of the Parochial Church Council, and a couple of dozen of the villagers and farmers. They broke into Snelsham Manor."

"But, good God," said Calder, "the security arrangements must have been pretty ropy."

"The security was adequate: a double wire fence, patrolling guards and dogs. The village blacksmith cut the fence in two places. A farm tractor dragged it clear. They had no trouble with the guards, who were armed with truncheons. The farmers had shot-guns."

"And the dogs?"

"They made such a fuss of the rector that he was, I understand, in some danger of being licked to death."

"What did they do when they got in?" said Behrens.

"They broke into the experimental wing and liberated twenty rabbits, a dozen guinea-pigs and nearly fifty rats."

Mr Behrens started to laugh, and managed to turn it into a cough when he observed Mr Fortescue's eyes on him.

"I hope you don't think it was funny, Behrens. A number of the rats had been infected with Asiatic plague. They *hope* that they recaptured or destroyed the whole of that batch."

"Has no action been taken against the rector?"

"Naturally. The police were informed. An inspector and a sergeant drove over from Thetford to see the rector. They were refused access."

"Refused?"

"They were told," said Mr Fortescue gently, "that if they attempted to lay hands on the rector they would be resisted—by force."

"But surely—" said Mr Behrens. And stopped.

"Yes," said Mr Fortescue. "Do think before you say anything. Try to visualize the unparalleled propaganda value to our friends in the various CND and Peace Groups if an armed force had to be despatched to seize a village clergyman."

Mr Behrens said, "I'm visualizing it. Do you think one of the more enterprising bodies—the International Brotherhood Group occurs to me as a possibility—might have planted someone in Hedgeborn? Someone who is using the rector's exceptional influence—"

"It's a possibility. You must remember that the Bacterial Warfare Wing has only been there for two years. If anyone *has* been planted, it has been done comparatively recently."

"How long has the rector been there?" said Mr Calder.

"Eighteen months."

"I see."

"The situation is full of possibilities, I agree. I suggest you tackle it from both ends. I should suppose, Behrens, that there are few people who know more about the IBG and its ramifications than you do. Can you find out whether they have been active in this area recently?"

"I'll do my best."

"We can none of us do more than our best," agreed Mr Fortescue. "And you, Calder, must go down to Hedgeborn immediately. I imagine that Colonel Faulkner would invite you?"

"I have a standing invitation," said Mr Calder. "For the shooting."

Hedgeborn has changed in the last four hundred years, but not very much. The church was built in the reign of Charles the Martyr, and the Manor in the reign of Anne the Good. There is a village smithy, where a farmer can still get his horses shod. He can also buy diesel oil for his tractor. The cottages have thatched roofs, and television aerials.

Mr Calder leaned out of his bedroom window at the Manor and surveyed the village, asleep under a full moon. He could see the church, at the far end of the village street, perched on a slight rise, its bell-tower outlined against the sky. There was a huddle of cottages round it. The one with a light in it would belong to Mr Penny, the verger, who had come running down the street to tell the rector that Farmer Alsop's farm was on fire. If he leaned out of the window, Mr Calder could just see the roof of the rectory, at the far end of the street, masked by trees.

Could there be any truth in the story of the bells? It had seemed fantastic in London. It seemed less so now.

A soft knock at the door heralded the arrival of Stokes, once the Colonel's batman, now his factotum.

"Would you care for a nightcap before you turn in, sir?"

"Certainly not," said Mr Calder. "Not after that lovely dinner. Did you cook it yourself?"

Stokes looked gratified. "It wasn't what you might call hote kweezeen."

"It was excellent. Tell me, don't you find things a bit quiet down here?"

"I'm used to it, sir. I was born here."

"I didn't realize that," said Mr Calder.

"I saw you looking at the smithy this afternoon. Enoch Clavering's my first cousin. Come to that, we're mostly first or second cousins. Alsops, and Stokes, and Vowles, and Claverings."

"It would have been Enoch who cut down the fence at Snelsham Manor?"

"That's right, sir." Stokes' voice was respectful, but there was a hint of wariness in it. "How did you know about that, if you don't mind me asking? It hasn't been in the papers."

"The colonel told me."

"Oh, of course. All the same, I do wonder how *he* knew about Enoch cutting down the fence. He wasn't with us."

"With *you?*" said Mr Calder. "Do I gather, Stokes, that you took part in this—this enterprise?"

"Well, naturally, sir. Seeing I'm a member of the Parochial Church Council. Would there be anything more?"

"Nothing more," said Mr Calder. "Goodnight."

He lay awake for a long time, listening to the owls talking to each other in the elms. . . .

"It's true," said Colonel Faulkner next morning. "We are a bit inbred. All Norfolk men are odd. It makes us just a bit odder, that's all."

"Tell me about your rector."

"He was some sort of missionary, I believe. In darkest Africa. Got malaria very badly, and was invalided out."

"From darkest Africa to darkest Norfolk. What do you make of him?"

The colonel was lighting his after-breakfast pipe, and took time to think about that. He said, "I just don't know, Calder. Might be a saint. Might be a scoundrel. He's got a touch with animals. No denying that."

"What about the miracles?"

"No doubt they've been exaggerated in the telling. But—well—that business of the bells . . . I can give chapter and verse for that. There only *is* one key to the bell-chamber. I remember what a fuss there was when it was mislaid last year. And no-one could have got it from Penny's cottage, opened the tower up, rung the bells, *and* put the key back without someone seeing him. Stark impossibility."

"How many bells rang?"

"The tenor and the treble. That's the way we always ring them for an alarm. One of the farmers across the valley heard them, got out of bed, spotted the fire, and phoned for the brigade."

"Two bells," said Mr Calder thoughtfully. "So one man *could* have rung them."

"If he could have got in."

"Quite so." Mr Calder was looking at a list. "There are three people I should like to meet. A man called Smedley . . ."

"The rector's warden. I'm people's warden. He's my opposite number. Don't like him much."

"Miss Martin, your organist. I believe she has a cottage near the church. And Mr Smallpiece, your village postmaster."

"Why those three?"

"Because," said Calder, "apart from the rector himself, they are the only people who have come to live in this village during the past two years—so Stokes tells me."

"He ought to know," said the Colonel. "He's related to half the village."

Mr Smedley lived in a small, dark cottage. It was tucked away behind the Viscount Townshend public house, which had a signboard outside it with a picture of the Second Viscount looking remarkably like the turnip which had become associated with his name.

Mr Smedley was old and thin, and inclined to be cautious. He thawed very slightly when he discovered that his visitor was the son of Canon Calder of Salisbury.

"A world authority on monumental brasses," he said. "You must be proud of him."

"I'd no idea."

"Yes, indeed. I have a copy somewhere of a paper he wrote on the brasses at Verden, in Hanover. A most scholarly work. We have some fine brasses in the church here, too. Not as old or as notable as Stoke d'Abernon, but very fine."

"It's an interesting village altogether. You've been getting into the papers."

"I'd no idea that our brasses were *that* famous."

"Not your brasses. Your rector. He's been written up as a miracle-worker."

"I'm not surprised."

"Oh, why?"

Mr Smedley blinked maliciously, and said, "I'm not surprised at the ability of the press to cheapen anything it touches."

"But *are* they miracles?"

"You'll have to define your terms. If you accept the Shavian definition of a miracle as an event which creates faith, then certainly, yes. They are miracles."

It occurred to Mr Calder that Mr Smedley was enjoying this conversation more than he was. He said, "You know quite well what I mean. Is there a rational explanation for them?"

"Again, it depends what you mean by rational."

"I mean," said Mr Calder bluntly, "are they miracles or conjuring tricks?"

Mr Smedley considered the matter, his head on one side. Then he said, "Isn't that a question which you should put to the rector? After all, if they are conjuring tricks, he must be the conjurer."

"I was planning to do just that," said Mr Calder, and prepared to take his leave.

When he was at the door, his host checked him by laying a claw-like hand on his arm. He said, "Might I offer a word of advice? This is not an ordinary village. I suppose the word which would come most readily to mind is—primitive. I don't mean anything sinister. But, being so isolated, it has grown up rather more slowly than the outside world. And another thing . . ." Mr Smedley paused, and Mr Calder was reminded of an old black crow, cautiously approaching a tempting morsel, wondering whether he dared to seize it. "I ought to warn you that the people here are very fond of their rector. If what they regarded as divine manifestations were described by you as conjuring tricks, well —you see what I mean."

"I see what you mean," said Mr Calder. He went out into the village street, took a couple of deep breaths, and made his way to the post office.

The post office was dark, dusty and empty. He could hear the postmaster, in the back room, wrestling with a manual telephone exchange. He realised, as he listened, that Mr Smallpiece was no Norfolkman. His voice suggested that he had been brought up within sound of Bow Bells. When he emerged, Mr Calder confirmed the diagnosis. If Mr Smedley was a country crow, Mr Smallpiece was a cockney sparrow.

Mr Smallpiece said, "Nice to see a new face around. You'll be staying with the colonel. I 'ope his aunt gets over it."

"Gets over what?"

"Called away ten minutes ago. The old lady 'ad a fit. Not the first one neither. If you ask me, she 'as one whenever she feels lonely."

"Old people are like that," agreed Mr Calder. "Your job must keep you very busy."

" 'Oh, I am the cook and the captain bold, and the mate of the Nancy brig', " agreed Mr Smallpiece. "I work the exchange—eighteen lines— deliver the mail, sell stamps, send telegrams, and run errands. 'Owever, there's no overtime in this job, and what you don't get paid for you don't get thanked for." He looked at the clock above the counter, which showed five minutes to twelve, pushed the hand on five minutes, turned a card in the door from 'Open' to 'Closed', and said, "Since the colonel won't be back much before two, what price a pint at the Viscount?"

"You take the words out of my mouth," said Mr Calder. "What happens if anyone wants to ring up someone whilst you're out?"

"Well, they can't, can they?" said Mr Smallpiece.

When the colonel returned—his aunt, Mr Calder was glad to learn, was much better—he reported the negative results of his inquiries to date.

"If you want to see Miss Martin, you can probably kill two birds with one stone. She goes along to the rectory most Wednesdays, to practise the harmonium. You'll find the rectory at the far end of the street. The original one was alongside the church, but it was burned down about a hundred years ago. I'm afraid it isn't an architectural gem. Built in the worst style of Victorian ecclesiastical red brick."

Mr Calder, as he lifted the heavy wrought-iron knocker, was inclined to agree. The house was not beautiful. But it had a certain old-fashioned dignity and solidity.

The rector answered the door himself. Mr Calder had hardly known what to expect. A warrior-ecclesiastic in the Norman mould? A fanatical priest, prepared to face stake and faggots for his faith? A subtle Jesuit living by the Rule of Ignatius Loyola in solitude and prayer? What he had not been prepared for was a slight, nondescript man with an apologetic smile who said, "Come in, come in. Don't stand on ceremony. We never lock our doors here. I know you, don't I? Wait! You're Mr Calder, and you're staying at the Manor. *What* a lovely dog! A genuine Persian deerhound of the royal breed. What's his name?"

"He's called Rasselas."

"Rasselas," said the rector. He wasn't looking at the dog, but was staring over his shoulder, as though he could see something of interest behind him in the garden. "Rasselas." The dog gave a rumbling growl. The rector said, "Rasselas," again, very softly. The rumble changed to a snarl. The rector stood perfectly still, and said nothing. The snarl changed back into a rumble.

"Well, that's much better," said the rector. "Did you see? He was fighting me. I wonder why."

"He's usually very well behaved with strangers."

"I'm sure he is. Intelligent, too. Why should he have *assumed* that I was an enemy? You heard him assuming it, didn't you?"

"I heard him changing his mind, too."

"I was able to reassure him. The interesting point is, why should he have started with hostile thoughts? I trust he didn't derive them from you? But I'm being fanciful. Why should you have thoughts about us at all? Come along in and meet our organist, Miss Martin. Such a helpful person, and a spirited performer on almost any instrument."

The opening of an inner door had released a powerful blast of Purcell's overture to *Dido and Aeneas,* played on the harmonium with all stops out.

"Miss Martin. *Miss Martin!*"

"I'm so sorry, Rector. I didn't hear you."

"This is Mr Calder. He's a wartime friend of Colonel Faulkner. Curious that such an evil thing as war should have produced the fine friendships it did."

"Good sometimes comes out of evil, don't you think?"

"No," said the rector. "I'm afraid I don't believe that at all. Good sometimes comes in spite of evil. A very different proposition."

"A beautiful rose," said Miss Martin, "can grow on a dunghill."

"Am I the rose, and Colonel Faulkner the dunghill, or vice-versa?"

Miss Martin tittered. The rector said, "Let that be a warning to you not to take an analogy too far."

"I have to dash along now, but please stay. Miss Martin will do the honours. Have a cup of tea. You will? Splendid."

Over the teacups, as Mr. Calder was wondering how to bring the conversation round to the point he required, Miss Martin did it for him. She said, "This is a terrible village for gossip, Mr Calder. Although you've hardly been down here two days, people are already beginning to wonder what you're up to. Particularly as you've been getting round, talking to people."

"I am naturally gregarious," said Mr Calder.

"Now, now. You won't pull the wool over *my* eyes. I know better. You've been sent."

Mr Calder said, trying to keep the surprise out of his voice, "Sent by whom?"

"I'll mention no names. We all know that there are sects and factions in the Church who would find our rector's teachings abhorrent to their own narrow dogma. And who would be envious of his growing reputation."

"Oh, I see," said Mr Calder.

"I'm not asking you to tell me if my guess is correct. What I do want to impress on you is that there is nothing exaggerated in these stories. I'll give you one instance which I can vouch for myself. It was a tea-party we were giving for the Brownies. I'd made a terrible miscalculation. The most appalling disaster faced us. *There wasn't enough to eat.* Can you imagine it?"

"Easily," said Mr Calder, with a shudder.

"I called the rector aside, and told him. He just smiled, and said, 'Look in that cupboard, Miss Martin.' I simply stared at him. It was a cupboard I use myself for music and anthems. I have the only key. I walked over and unlocked it. And what do you think I found? A large plate of freshly cut bread and butter, and two plates of biscuits."

"Enough to feed the five thousand."

"It's odd you should say that. It was the precise analogy that occurred to me."

"Did you tell people about this?"

"I don't gossip. But one of my helpers was there. She must have spread the story. Ah, here is the rector. Don't say a word about it to him. He denies it all, of course."

"I'm glad to see that Miss Martin has been looking after you," said the rector. "A thought has occurred to me. Do you sing?"

"Only under duress."

"Recite, perhaps? We are getting up a village concert. Miss Martin is a tower of strength in such matters. . . ."

"It would appear from his reports," said Mr Fortescue, "that your colleague is entering fully into the life of the village. Last Saturday, according to the *East Anglian Gazette,* he took part in a village concert in aid of the RSPCA. He obliged with a moving rendering of *The Wreck of the Hesperus."*

"Good gracious!" said Mr Behrens. "How very versatile!"

"He would not, however, appear to have advanced very far in the matter I sent him down to investigate. He thinks that the rector is a perfectly sincere enthusiast. He has his eye on three people, any one of whom *might* have been planted in the village to work on him. Have you been able to discover anything?"

"I'm not sure," said Mr Behrens. "I've made the round of our usual contacts. I felt that the International Brotherhood Group was the most likely. It's a line they've tried with some success in the past. Stirring up local prejudice, and working it up into a national campaign. You remember the schoolchildren who trespassed on that missile base in Scotland and were roughly handled?"

"Were alleged to have been roughly handled."

"Yes. It was a put-up job. But they made a lot of capital out of it. I have a line on their chief organizer. My contact thinks they *are* up to something. Which means they've got an agent planted in Hedgeborn."

"Or that the rector is their agent."

"Yes. The difficulty will be to prove it. Their security is rather good."

Mr Fortescue considered the matter, running his thumb down the angle of his prominent chin. He said, "Might you be able to contrive, through your contact, to transmit a particular item of information to their agent in Hedgeborn?"

"I might. But I hardly see—"

"In medicine," said Mr Fortescue, "I am told that, when it proves impossible to clear up a condition by direct treatment, it is sometimes possible to precipitate an artificial crisis which *can* be dealt with."

"Always bearing in mind that, if we do precipitate a crisis, poor old Calder will be in the middle of it."

"Exactly," said Mr Fortescue.

It was on the Friday of the second week of his stay that Mr Calder noticed the change. There was no open hostility. No one attacked him. No one was even rude to him. It was simply that he had ceased to be acceptable to the village. People who had been prepared to chat with him in the bar of the Viscount Townshend now had business of their own to discuss when he appeared. Mr Smedley did not answer his knock, although he could see him through the front window, reading a book. Mr Smallpiece avoided him in the street.

It was like the moment, in a theatre, when the iron safety-curtain descends, cutting off the actors and all on the stage from the audience. Suddenly, he was on one side. The village was on the other.

By the Saturday, the atmosphere had become so oppressive that Mr Calder decided to do something about it. Stokes had driven the Colonel into Thetford on business. He was alone in the house. He decided, on the spur of the moment, to have a word with the rector.

Although it was a fine afternoon, the village street was completely empty. As he walked, he noted the occasional stirring of a curtain, and knew that he was not unobserved, but the silence of the early autumn afternoon lay heavily over everything. On this occasion he had left a strangely subdued Rasselas behind.

His knock at the rectory door was unanswered. Remembering the rector saying, "We never lock our doors here," he turned the handle and went in. The house was silent. He took a few steps along the hall, and stopped. The door on his left was ajar. He looked in. The rector was there. He was kneeling at a carved prie-dieu, as motionless as if he had himself been part of the carving. If he had heard Mr Calder's approach, he took absolutely no notice of it. Feeling extremely foolish, Mr Calder withdrew by the way he had come.

Walking back down the street, he was visited by a recollection of his days with the Military Mission in wartime Albania. The mission had visited a remote village, and had been received with the same silent disregard. They had usually been well received, and it had puzzled them. When he returned to the village some months later, Mr Calder had learned the truth. The village had caught an informer, and were waiting for the mission to go before they dealt with him. He had heard what they had done to the informer, and, although he was not naturally queasy, it had turned his stomach. . . .

That evening, Stokes waited on them in unusual silence. When he had gone, the colonel said, "Whatever it is, it's tomorrow."

"How do you know?"

"I'm told that the rector has been fasting since Thursday. Also that morning service tomorrow has been cancelled, and Evensong brought forward to four o'clock. That's when it'll break."

"It will be a relief," said Mr Calder.

"Stokes thinks you ought to leave tonight. He thinks I shall be all right. You might not be."

"That was thoughtful of Stokes. But I'd as soon stay. That is, unless you want to get rid of me."

"Glad to have you," said the colonel. "Besides, if they see you've gone, they may put it off. Then we shall have to start all over again."

"Did you contact the number I asked you to?"

"Yes. From a public call-box in Thetford."

"And what was the answer?"

"It was so odd," said the colonel, "that I was afraid I might get it wrong, and I wrote it down."

He handed Mr Calder a piece of paper. Mr Calder read it carefully, folded it up, and put it in his pocket.

"Is it good news or bad?"

"I'm not sure," said Mr Calder. "But I can promise you one thing. You'll hear a sermon tomorrow which you won't forget."

When the rector stepped into the pulpit, his face was pale and composed, but it was no longer gentle. Mr Calder wondered how he could ever have considered him nondescript. There was a blazing conviction about the man, a fire and a warmth which lit up the whole church. This was no longer the gentle St Francis. This was Peter the Hermit, "Whose eyes were a flame and whose tongue was a sword."

He stood for a moment, upright and motionless. Then he turned his head slowly, looking from face to face in the crowded congregation, as if searching for support and guidance from his flock. When he started to speak, it was in a quiet, almost conversational voice.

"The anti-Christ has raised his head once more. The Devil is at his work again. We deceived ourselves into thinking that we had dealt him a shrewd blow. We were mistaken. Our former warning has not been heeded. I fear that it will have to be repeated, and this time more strongly."

The colonel looked anxiously at Mr Calder, who mouthed the word, "Wait."

"Far from abandoning the foul work at Snelsham Manor, I have learned that it is not only continuing, but intensifying. More of God's creatures are being imprisoned and tortured by methods which would have shamed the Gestapo. In the name of science, mice, small rabbits, guinea-pigs and hamsters are being put to obscene and painful deaths. Yesterday, a cargo of African tree-beavers, harmless and friendly little animals, arrived at this . . . at this scientific slaughter-house. They are to be inoculated with a virus which will first paralyse their limbs, then cause them to go mad with pain, and, finally, die. The object of the experiment is to hold off the moment of death as long as possible. . . ."

Mr Calder, who was listening with strained attention, had found it difficult to hear the closing sentence, and realized that the rector was now speaking against a ground-swell of noise.

The noise burst out suddenly into a roar. The rector's voice rode over the tumult like a trumpet.

"Are we going to allow this?"

A second roar crashed out with startling violence.

"We will pull down this foul place, stone by stone. We will purge what remains with fire. All who will help, follow me!"

"What do we do?" said the Colonel.

"Sit still," said Mr Calder.

In a moment they were alone in their pew, with a hundred angry faces round them. The rector, still standing in the pulpit, quelled the storm with an upraised hand. He said, "We will have no bloodshed. We cannot fight evil with evil. Those who are not with us are against us. Enoch, take one of them. Two of you the other. Into the vestry with them!"

Mr Calder said, "Go with it. Don't fight."

As they were swirled down the aisle, the colonel saw one anxious face in the crowd. He shouted, "Are you in this, too, Stokes?" The next moment they were in the vestry. The door had clanged shut, and they heard the key turn in the lock. The thick walls and nine inches of stout oak cut down the sound, but they could hear the organ playing. It sounded like Miss Martin's idea of the *Battle Hymn of the Republic*.

"Well," said the colonel. "What do we do now?"

"We give them five minutes to get to the rectory. There'll be some sort of conference there, I imagine."

"And then?"

Mr Calder had seated himself on a pile of hassocks, and sat there, swinging his short legs. He said, "As we have five minutes to kill, maybe I'd better put you in the picture. Why don't you sit down?"

The colonel grunted, and subsided.

Mr Calder said, "Hasn't it struck you that the miracles we've been hearing about were of two quite different types?"

"I don't follow you."

"One sort was simple animal magnetism. No doubt about that. I saw the rector operating on Rasselas. Nearly hypnotized the poor dog. The other sort—well, there's been a lot of talk about them, but I've only heard any real evidence of two. The bells that rang themselves and the food that materialized in a locked cupboard. Isolate them from the general hysteria, and what do they amount to? You told me yourself that the key of the vestry had been mislaid."

"You think someone stole it? Had it copied?"

"Of course."

"Who?"

"Oh," said Mr Calder impatiently, "the person who organized the other miracles, of course. I think it's time we got out of here, don't you?"

"How?"

"Get someone to unlock the door. I notice they left the key in it. There must be some sane folk about."

The colonel said, "Seeing that the nearest farm likely to be helpful to us is a good quarter of a mile away, I'd be interested to know how you intend to shout for help."

"Follow me up that ladder," said Mr Calder. "I'll show you."

In the crowded room at the rectory the rector said, "Is that clear? They'll be expecting us on the southern side, where we attacked before, so we'll come through the woods, on the north. Stokes, can you get the colonel's Land Rover up that side?"

"Easily enough, Rector."

"Have the grappling irons laid out at the back. Tom's tractor follows you. Enoch, how long to cut the wire?"

"Ten seconds."

This produced a rumbling laugh.

"Good. We don't want any unnecessary delay. We drive the tractors straight through the gap and ride in on the back of them. The fire-raising material will be in the trailers behind the rear tractor. The Scouts can see to that under you, Mr Smedley."

"Certainly, Rector. Scouts are experts at lighting fires."

"Excellent. Now, the diversion at the front gate. That will be under

you, Miss Martin. You'll have the Guides and Brownies. You demand
to be let in. When they refuse, you all start screaming. If you can get
hold of the sentry, I suggest you scratch him."

"I'll let Matilda Briggs do *that*," said Miss Martin.

Enoch Clavering touched the rector on the arm and said, "Listen."
Then he went over to the window and opened it.

"What is it, Enoch?"

"I thought I heard the bells some minutes ago, but I didn't like to
interrupt. They've stopped now. It's like it was the last time. The bells
rang themselves. What does it signify?"

"It means," said the rector cheerfully, "that I've been a duffer. I
ought to have seen that the trap-door to the belfry was padlocked. Our
prisoners must have climbed up and started clapping the tenor and the
treble. Since they've stopped, I imagine someone heard them and let
them out."

Miss Martin said, "What are we going to do?"

"What we're not going to do is lose our heads. Stokes, you've immo-
bilized the colonel's car?"

Stokes nodded.

"And you've put the telephone line out of communication, Mr
Smallpiece?"

"Same as last time."

"Then I don't see how they can summon help in under half an hour.
We should have ample time to do all we have to."

"I advise you against it," said Mr Calder.

He was standing in the doorway, one hand in his pocket. He looked
placid, but determined. Behind him they could see the great dog, Rasselas, his head almost level with Mr Calder's shoulder, his amber eyes
glowing.

For a moment there was complete silence. Then a low growl of
anger broke out from the crowded room. The rector said, "Ah, Calder.
Tell me who let you out?"

"Jack Collins. And he's gone in his own car to Thetford. The police
will be here in half an hour."

"Then they will be too late."

"That's just what I was afraid of," said Mr Calder. "It's why I came
down as fast as I could, to stop you."

There was another growl, louder and more menacing. Enoch Clavering stepped forward. He said, "Bundle him down into the cellar,
Rector, and let's get on with it."

"I shouldn't try it," said Mr Calder. His voice was still peaceful. "First, because if you put a hand on me this dog will have that hand off. Secondly, because the colonel is outside in the garden. He's got a shotgun, and he'll use it, if he has to."

The rector said gently, "You mustn't think you can frighten us. The colonel won't shoot. He's not a murderer. And Rasselas won't attack me. Will you, Rasselas?"

"You've got this all wrong," said Mr Calder. "My object is to prevent *you* attacking *us*. Just long enough for me to tell you two things. First, the gurads at Snelsham have been doubled. They are armed. And they have orders to shoot. What you're leading your flock to isn't a jamboree, like last time. It's a massacre."

"I think he's lying," said Mr Smedley.

"There's one way of finding out," said Mr Calder. "But it's not the real point. The question which really matters—what our American friends would refer to as the sixty-four thousand dollar question—is, have any of you ever seen a tree-beaver?"

The question fell into a sudden pool of silence.

"Come, come," said Mr Calder. "There must be some naturalists here. Rector, I see the *Universal Encyclopaedia of Wild Life* on your shelf. Would you care to turn its pages and give us a few facts about the habits of this curious creature?"

The reactor said, with a half-smile of comprehension on his face, "What are you getting at, Mr Calder?"

"I can save you some unnecessary research. The animal does not exist. Indeed, it could not exist. Beavers live in rivers, not in trees. The animal was invented by an old friend of mine, a Mr Behrens. And, having invented this remarkable animal, he thought it would be a pity to keep it all to himself. He had news of its arrival at Snelsham passed to a friend of his, who passed it on to a subversive organization known as the International Brotherhood Group. Who, in turn, passed it to you, Rector, through their local agent."

The rector was smiling now. He said, "So I have been led up the garden path. *Sancta simplicitas!* Who is this agent?"

"That's easy. Who told you about the tree-beavers?"

There was a flurry of movement. A shout, a crash, and the sound of a shot. . . .

"It is far from clear," said Mr Calder, "whether Miss Martin intended to shoot the rector or me. In fact Rasselas knocked her over, and she shot herself. As soon as they realized they had been fooled, the village closed its ranks. They concocted a story that Miss Martin, who was nervous of burglars, was known to possess a revolver, a relic of the last war. She must have been carrying it in her handbag, and the supposition was that, in pulling it out to show to someone, it had gone off and killed her. It was the thinnest story you ever heard, and the Coroner was suspicious as a cat. But he couldn't shake them. And, after all, it was difficult to cast doubt on the evidence of the entire Parochial Church Council, supported by their rector. The verdict was accidental death."

"Excellent," said Mr Fortescue. "It would have been hard to prove anything. In spite of your beavers. How did the rector take it?"

"Very well indeed. I had to stay for the inquest, and made a point of attending Evensong on the following Sunday. The church was so full that it was difficult to find a seat. The rector preached an excellent sermon, on the text, 'Render unto Caesar the things that are Caesar's'."

"A dangerous opponent," said Mr Fortescue. "On the whole, I cannot feel sorry that the authorities should have decided to close Snelsham Manor."

MASTERS OF
SUSPENSE

As a British citizen who traveled the world as a journalist,
FREDERICK FORSYTH *(1938–) witnessed the Cold War, conflict
in the Third World, and political intrigue in the capitals of
Europe. He worked for both Reuters and the BBC, rising to
Assistant Diplomatic Correspondent before becoming a full-
time writer. His novels have become best-selling "thrillers" and
have in fact spawned an entire subgenre.* The Day of the Jackal
and The Dogs of War *were both successful films.*

*Few can match Mr. Forsyth's ability to hold readers spell-
bound, and few writers can equal him at the top of his form, as
in the Edgar Award–winning "There Are No Snakes in Ireland," one of a small number of short stories produced by this
outstanding talent.*

There Are No Snakes in Ireland

BY FREDERICK FORSYTH

McQueen looked across his desk at the new applicant for a job with
some scepticism. He had never employed such a one before. But he
was not an unkind man, and if the job-seeker needed the money and
was prepared to work, McQueen was not averse to giving him a
chance.

"You know it's damn hard work?" he said in his broad Belfast accent.

"Yes, sir," said the applicant.

"It's a quick in-and-out job, ye know. No questions, no pack drill.
You'll be working on the lump. Do you know what that means?"

"No, Mr. McQueen."

"Well, it means you'll be paid well but you'll be paid in cash. No red
tape. Geddit?"

What he meant was there would be no income tax paid, no National
Health contributions deducted at source. He might also have added
that there would be no National Insurance cover and that the Health
and Safety standards would be completely ignored. Quick profits for all
were the order of the day, with a fat slice off the top for himself as the
contractor. The job-seeker nodded his head to indicate he had "god-
dit" though in fact he had not. McQueen looked at him speculatively.

"You say you're a medical student, in your last year at the Royal Victoria?" Another nod. "On the summer vacation?"

Another nod. The applicant was evidently one of those students who needed money over and above his grant to put himself through medical school. McQueen, sitting in his dingy Bangor office running a hole-and-corner business as a demolition contractor with assets consisting of a battered truck and a ton of second-hand sledgehammers, considered himself a self-made man and heartily approved of the Ulster Protestant work ethic. He was not one to put down another such thinker, whatever he looked like.

"All right," he said, "you'd better take lodgings here in Bangor. You'll never get from Belfast and back in time each day. We work from seven in the morning until sundown. It's work by the hour, hard but well paid. Mention one word to the authorities and you'll lose the job like shit off a shovel. OK?"

"Yes, sir. Please, when do I start and where?"

"The truck picks the gang up at the main station yard every morning at six-thirty. Be there Monday morning. The gang foreman is Big Billie Cameron. I'll tell him you'll be there."

"Yes, Mr. McQueen." The applicant turned to go.

"One last thing," said McQueen, pencil poised. "What's your name?"

"Harkishan Ram Lal," said the student. McQueen looked at his pencil, the list of names in front of him and the student.

"We'll call you Ram," he said, and that was the name he wrote down on the list.

The student walked out into the bright July sunshine of Bangor, on the north coast of County Down, Northern Ireland.

By that Saturday evening he had found himself cheap lodgings in a dingy boarding house halfway up Railway View Street, the heart of Bangor's bed-and-breakfast land. At least it was convenient to the main station from which the works truck would depart every morning just after sun-up. From the grimy window of his room he could look straight at the side of the shored embankment that carried the trains from Belfast into the station.

It had taken him several tries to get a room. Most of those houses with a B-and-B notice in the window seemed to be fully booked when he presented himself on the doorstep. But then it was true that a lot of casual labour drifted into the town in the height of summer. True also that Mrs. McGurk was a Catholic and she still had rooms left.

He spent Sunday morning bringing his belongings over from Belfast, most of them medical textbooks. In the afternoon he lay on his bed and thought of the bright hard light on the brown hills of his native Punjab. In one more year he would be a qualified physician, and after another year of intern work he would return home to cope with the sicknesses of his own people. Such was his dream. He calculated he could make enough money this summer to tide himself through to his finals and after that he would have a salary of his own.

On the Monday morning he rose at a quarter to six at the bidding of his alarm clock, washed in cold water and was in the station yard just after six. There was time to spare. He found an early-opening café and took two cups of black tea. It was his only sustenance. The battered truck, driven by one of the demolition gang, was there at a quarter past six and a dozen men assembled near it. Harkishan Ram Lal did not know whether to approach them and introduce himself, or wait at a distance. He waited.

At twenty-five past the hour the foreman arrived in his own car, parked it down a side road and strode up to the truck. He had McQueen's list in his hand. He glanced at the dozen men, recognized them all and nodded. The Indian approached. The foreman glared at him.

"Is youse the darkie McQueen has put on the job?" he demanded.

Ram Lal stopped in his tracks. "Harkishan Ram Lal," he said. "Yes."

There was no need to ask how Big Billie Cameron had earned his name. He stood 6 feet and 3 inches in his stockings but was wearing enormous nail-studded steel-toed boots. Arms like tree trunks hung from huge shoulders and his head was surmounted by a shock of ginger hair. Two small, pale-lashed eyes stared down balefully at the slight and wiry Indian. It was plain he was not best pleased. He spat on the ground.

"Well, get in the fecking truck," he said.

On the journey out to the work site Cameron sat up in the cab which had no partition dividing it from the back of the lorry, where the dozen labourers sat on two wooden benches down the sides. Ram Lal was near the tailboard next to a small, nut-hard man with bright blue eyes, whose name turned out to be Tommy Burns. He seemed friendly.

"Where are youse from?" he asked with genuine curiosity.

"India," said Ram Lal. "The Punjab."

"Well, which?" said Tommy Burns.

Ram Lal smiled. "The Punjab is a part of India," he said.

Burns thought about this for a while. "You Protestant or Catholic?" he asked at length.

"Neither," said Ram Lal patiently. "I am a Hindu."

"You mean you're not a Christian?" asked Burns in amazement.

"No. Mine is the Hindu religion."

"Hey," said Burns to the others, "your man's not a Christian at all." He was not outraged, just curious, like a small child who has come across a new and intriguing toy.

Cameron turned from the cab up front. "Aye," he snarled, "a heathen."

The smile dropped off Ram Lal's face. He stared at the opposite canvas wall of the truck. By now they were well south of Bangor, clattering down the motorway towards Newtownards. After a while Burns began to introduce him to the others. There was a Craig, a Munroe, a Patterson, a Boyd and two Browns. Ram Lal had been long enough in Belfast to recognize the names as being originally Scottish, the sign of the hard Presbyterians who make up the backbone of the Protestant majority of the Six Counties. The men seemed amiable and nodded back at him.

"Have you not got a lunch box, laddie?" asked the elderly man called Patterson.

"No," said Ram Lal, "it was too early to ask my landlady to make one up."

"You'll need lunch," said Burns, "aye, and breakfast. We'll be making tay ourselves on a fire."

"I will make sure to buy a box and bring some food tomorrow," said Ram Lal.

Burns looked at the Indian's rubber-soled soft boots. "Have you not done this kind of work before?" he asked.

Ram Lal shook his head.

"You'll need a pair of heavy boots. To save your feet, you see."

Ram Lal promised he would also buy a pair of heavy ammunition boots from a store if he could find one open late at night. They were through Newtownards and still heading south on the A21 towards the small town of Comber. Craig looked across at him.

"What's your real job?" he asked.

"I'm a medical student at the Royal Victoria in Belfast," said Ram Lal. "I hope to qualify next year."

Tommy Burns was delighted. "That's near to being a real doctor," he said. "Hey, Big Billie, if one of us gets a knock young Ram could take care of it."

Big Billie grunted. "He's not putting a finger on me," he said.

That killed further conversation until they arrived at the work site. The driver had pulled northwest out of Comber and two miles up the Dundonald road he bumped down a track to the right until they came to a stop where the trees ended and saw the building to be demolished.

It was a huge old whiskey distillery, a sheer-sided, long derelict. It had been one of two in these parts that had once turned out good Irish whiskey but had gone out of business years before. It stood beside the River Comber, which had once powered its great waterwheel as it flowed down from Dundonald to Comber and on to empty itself in Strangford Lough. The malt had arrived by horse-drawn cart down the track and the barrels of whiskey had left the same way. The sweet water that had powered the machines had also been used in the vats. But the distillery had stood alone, abandoned and empty for years.

Of course the local children had broken in and found it an ideal place to play. Until one had slipped and broken a leg. Then the county council had surveyed it, declared it a hazard and the owner found himself with a compulsory demolition order.

He, scion of an old family of squires who had known better days, wanted the job done as cheaply as possible. That was where McQueen came in. It could be done faster but more expensively with heavy machinery; Big Billie and his team would do it with sledges and crowbars. McQueen had even lined up a deal to sell the best timbers and the hundreds of tons of mature bricks to a jobbing builder. After all, the wealthy nowadays wanted their new houses to have "style" and that meant looking old. So there was a premium on antique sun-bleached old bricks and genuine ancient timber beams to adorn the new-look-old "manor" houses of the top executives. McQueen would do all right.

"Right lads," said Big Billie as the truck rumbled away back to Bangor. "There it is. We'll start with the roof tiles. You know what to do."

The group of men stood beside their pile of equipment. There were great sledgehammers with 7-pound heads; crowbars 6 feet long and over an inch thick; nailbars a yard long with curved split tips for extracting nails; short-handled, heavy-headed lump hammers and a variety of timber saws. The only concessions to human safety were a number of webbing belts with dogclips and hundreds of feet of rope.

Ram Lal looked up at the building and swallowed. It was four storeys high and he hated heights. But scaffolding is expensive.

One of the men unbidden went to the building, prised off a plank door, tore it up like a playing card and started a fire. Soon a billycan of water from the river was boiling away and tea was made. They all had their enamel mugs except Ram Lal. He made a mental note to buy that also. It was going to be thirsty, dusty work. Tommy Burns finished his own mug and offered it, refilled, to Ram Lal.

"Do they have tea in India?" he asked.

Ram Lal took the proffered mug. The tea was ready-mixed, sweet and off-white. He hated it.

They worked through the first morning perched high on the roof. The tiles were not to be salvaged, so they tore them off manually and hurled them to the ground away from the river. There was an instruction not to block the river with falling rubble. So it all had to land on the other side of the building, in the long grass, weeds, broom and gorse which covered the area round the distillery. The men were roped together so that if one lost his grip and began to slither down the roof, the next man would take the strain. As the tiles disappeared, great yawning holes appeared between the rafters. Down below them was the floor of the top storey, the malt store.

At ten they came down the rickety internal stairs for breakfast on the grass, with another billycan of tea. Ram Lal ate no breakfast. At two they broke for lunch. The gang tucked into their piles of thick sandwiches. Ram Lal looked at his hands. They were nicked in several places and bleeding. His muscles ached and he was very hungry. He made another mental note about buying some heavy work gloves.

Tommy Burns held up a sandwich from his own box. "Are you not hungry, Ram?" he asked. "Sure, I have enough here."

"What do you think you're doing?" asked Big Billie from where he sat across the circle round the fire.

Burns looked defensive. "Just offering the lad a sandwich," he said.

"Let the darkie bring his own fecking sandwiches," said Cameron. "You look after yourself."

The men looked down at their lunch boxes and ate in silence. It was obvious no one argued the toss with Big Billie.

"Thank you, I am not hungry," said Ram Lal to Burns. He walked away and sat by the river where he bathed his burning hands.

By sundown when the truck came to collect them half the tiles on the great roof were gone. One more day and they would start on the rafters, work for saw and nailbar.

Throughout the week the work went on, and the once proud building was stripped of its rafters, planks and beams until it stood hollow and open, its gaping windows like open eyes staring at the prospect of its imminent death. Ram Lal was unaccustomed to the arduousness of this kind of labour. His muscles ached endlessly, his hands were blistered, but he toiled on for the money he needed so badly.

He had acquired a tin lunch box, enamel mug, hard boots and a pair of heavy gloves, which no one else wore. Their hands were hard enough from years of manual work. Throughout the week Big Billie Cameron needled him without let-up, giving him the hardest work and positioning him on the highest points once he had learned Ram Lal hated heights. The Punjabi bit on his anger because he needed the money. The crunch came on the Saturday.

The timbers were gone and they were working on the masonry. The simplest way to bring the edifice down away from the river would have been to plant explosive charges in the corners of the side wall facing the open clearing. But dynamite was out of the question. It would have required special licences in Northern Ireland of all places, and that would have alerted the tax man. McQueen and all his gang would have been required to pay substantial sums in income tax, and McQueen in National Insurance contributions. So they were chipping the walls down in square-yard chunks, standing hazardously on sagging floors as the supporting walls splintered and cracked under the hammers.

During lunch Cameron walked round the building a couple of times and came back to the circle round the fire. He began to describe how they were going to bring down a sizable chunk of one outer wall at third-floor level. He turned to Ram Lal.

"I want you up on the top there," he said. "When it starts to go, kick it outwards."

Ram Lal looked up at the section of wall in question. A great crack ran along the bottom of it.

"That brickwork is going to fall at any moment," he said evenly. "Anyone sitting on top there is going to come down with it."

Cameron stared at him, his face suffusing, his eyes pink with rage where they should have been white. "Don't you tell me my job; you do as you're told, you stupid fecking nigger." He turned and stalked away.

Ram Lal rose to his feet. When his voice came, it was in a hard-edged shout. *"Mister Cameron . . ."*

Cameron turned in amazement. The men sat open-mouthed. Ram Lal walked slowly up to the big ganger.

"Let us get one thing plain," said Ram Lal, and his voice carried clearly to everyone else in the clearing. "I am from the Punjab in northern India. I am also a Kshatria, member of the warrior caste. I may not have enough money to pay for my medical studies, but my ancestors were soldiers and princes, rulers and scholars, two thousand years ago when yours were crawling on all fours dressed in skins. Please do not insult me any further."

Big Billie Cameron stared down at the Indian student. The whites of his eyes had turned a bright red. The other labourers sat in stunned amazement.

"Is that so?" said Cameron quietly. "Is that so, now? Well, things are a bit different now, you black bastard. So what are you going to do about that?"

On the last word he swung his arm, open-palmed, and his hand crashed into the side of Ram Lal's face. The youth was thrown bodily to the ground several feet away. His head sang. He heard Tommy Burns call out, "Stay down, laddie. Big Billie will kill you if you get up."

Ram Lal looked up into the sunlight. The giant stood over him, fists bunched. He realized he had not a chance in combat against the big Ulsterman. Feelings of shame and humiliation flooded over him. His ancestors had ridden, sword and lance in hand, across plains a hundred times bigger than these six counties, conquering all before them.

Ram Lal closed his eyes and lay still. After several seconds he heard the big man move away. A low conversation started among the others. He squeezed his eyes tighter shut to hold back the tears of shame. In the blackness he saw the baking plains of the Punjab and men riding over them; proud, fierce men, hook-nosed, bearded, turbaned, black-eyed, the warriors from the land of Five Rivers.

Once, long ago in the world's morning, Iskander of Macedon had ridden over these plains with his hot and hungry eyes; Alexander, the young god, whom they called The Great, who at twenty-five had wept because there were no more worlds to conquer. These riders were the descendants of his captains, and the ancestors of Harkishan Ram Lal.

He was lying in the dust as they rode by, and they looked down at him in passing. As they rode each of them mouthed one single word to him. Vengeance.

Ram Lal picked himself up in silence. It was done, and what still had to be done had to be done. That was the way of his people. He spent the rest of the day working in complete silence. He spoke to no one and no one spoke to him.

That evening in his room he began his preparations as night was about to fall. He cleared away the brush and comb from the battered dressing table and removed also the soiled doily and the mirror from its stand. He took his book of the Hindu religion and from it cut a page-sized portrait of the great goddess Shakti, she of power and justice. This he pinned to the wall above the dressing table to convert it into a shrine.

He had bought a bunch of flowers from a seller in front of the main station, and these had been woven into a garland. To one side of the portrait of the goddess he placed a shallow bowl half-filled with sand, and in the sand stuck a candle which he lit. From his suitcase he took a cloth roll and extracted half a dozen joss sticks. Taking a cheap, narrow-necked vase from the bookshelf, he placed them in it and lit the ends. The sweet, heady odour of the incense began to fill the room. Outside, big thunderheads rolled up from the sea.

When his shrine was ready he stood before it, head bowed, the garland in his fingers, and began to pray for guidance. The first rumble of thunder rolled over Bangor. He used not the modern Punjabi but the ancient Sanskrit, language of prayer. *"Devi Shakti . . . Maa . . . .Goddess Shakti . . . great mother . . ."*

The thunder crashed again and the first raindrops fell. He plucked the first flower and placed it in front of the portrait of Shakti.

"I have been grievously wronged. I ask vengeance upon the wrong-doer . . ." He plucked the second flower and put it beside the first.

He prayed for an hour while the rain came down. It drummed on the tiles above his head, streamed past the window behind him. He finished praying as the storm subsided. He needed to know what form the retribution should take. He needed the goddess to send him a sign.

When he had finished, the joss sticks had burned themselves out and the room was thick with their scent. The candle guttered low. The flowers all lay on the lacquered surface of the dressing table in front of the portrait. Shakti stared back at him unmoved.

He turned and walked to the window to look out. The rain had stopped but everything beyond the panes dripped water. As he watched, a dribble of rain sprang from the guttering above the window and a trickle ran down the dusty glass, cutting a path through the grime. Because of the dirt it did not run straight but meandered sideways, drawing his eye farther and farther to the corner of the window as he followed its path. When it stopped he was staring at the corner of his room, where his dressing gown hung on a nail.

He noticed that during the storm the dressing-gown cord had slipped and fallen to the floor. It lay coiled upon itself, one knotted end hidden from view, the other lying visible on the carpet. Of the dozen tassels only two were exposed, like a forked tongue. The coiled dressing-gown cord resembled nothing so much as a snake in the corner. Ram Lal understood. The next day he took a train to Belfast to see the Sikh.

Ranjit Singh was also a medical student, but he was more fortunate. His parents were rich and sent him a handsome allowance. He received Ram Lal in his well-furnished room at the hostel.

"I have received word from home," said Ram Lal. "My father is dying."

"I am sorry," said Ranjit Singh, "you have my sympathies."

"He asks to see me. I am his first born. I should return."

"Of course," said Singh. "The first-born son should always be by his father when he dies."

"It is a matter of the air fare," said Ram Lal. "I am working and making good money. But I do not have enough. If you will lend me the balance I will continue working when I return and repay you."

Sikhs are no strangers to moneylending if the interest is right and repayment secure. Ranjit Singh promised to withdraw the money from the bank on Monday morning.

That Sunday evening Ram Lal visited Mr. McQueen at his home at Groomsport. The contractor was in front of his television set with a can of beer at his elbow. It was his favourite way to spend a Sunday evening. But he turned the sound down as Ram Lal was shown in by his wife.

"It is about my father," said Ram Lal. "He is dying."

"Oh, I'm sorry to hear that, laddie," said McQueen.

"I should go to him. The first-born son should be with his father at this time. It is the custom of our people."

McQueen had a son in Canada whom he had not seen for seven years.

"Aye," he said, "that seems right and proper."

"I have borrowed the money for the air fare," said Ram Lal. "If I went tomorrow I could be back by the end of the week. The point is, Mr. McQueen, I need the job more than ever now; to repay the loan and for my studies next term. If I am back by the weekend, will you keep the job open for me?"

"All right," said the contractor. "I can't pay you for the time you're away. Nor keep the job open for a further week. But if you're back by the weekend, you can go back to work. Same terms, mind."

"Thank you," said Ram, "you are very kind."

He retained his room in Railway View Street but spent the night at his hostel in Belfast. On the Monday morning he accompanied Ranjit Singh to the bank where the Sikh withdrew the necessary money and gave it to the Hindu. Ram took a taxi to Aldergrove airport and the shuttle to London where he bought an economy-class ticket on the next flight to India. Twenty-four hours later he touched down in the blistering heat of Bombay.

On the Wednesday he found what he sought in the teeming bazaar at Grant Road Bridge. Mr. Chatterjee's Tropical Fish and Reptile Emporium was almost deserted when the young student, with his textbook on reptiles under his arm, wandered in. He found the old proprietor sitting near the back of his shop in half-darkness, surrounded by his tanks of fish and glass-fronted cases in which his snakes and lizards dozed through the hot day.

Mr. Chatterjee was no stranger to the academic world. He supplied several medical centres with samples for study and dissection, and occasionally filled a lucrative order from abroad. He nodded his white-bearded head knowledgeably as the student explained what he sought.

"Ah yes," said the old Gujerati merchant, "I know the snake. You are in luck. I have one, but a few days arrived from Rajputana."

He led Ram Lal into his private sanctum and the two men stared silently through the glass of the snake's new home.

Echis carinatus, said the textbook, but of course the book had been written by an Englishman, who had used the Latin nonmenclature. In English, the saw-scaled viper, smallest and deadliest of all his lethal breed.

Wide distribution, said the textbook, being found from West Africa eastwards and northwards to Iran, and on to India and Pakistan. Very adaptable, able to acclimatize to almost any environment, from the moist bush of western Africa to the cold hills of Iran in winter to the baking hills of India.

Something stirred beneath the leaves in the box.

In size, said the textbook, between 9 and 13 inches long and very slim. Olive brown in colour with a few paler spots, sometimes hardly distinguishable, and a faint undulating darker line down the side of the body. Nocturnal in dry, hot weather, seeking cover during the heat of the day.

The leaves in the box rustled again and a tiny head appeared.

Exceptionally dangerous to handle, said the textbook, causing more deaths than even the more famous cobra, largely because of its size which makes it so easy to touch unwittingly with hand or foot. The author of the book had added a footnote to the effect that the small but lethal snake mentioned by Kipling in his marvellous story "Rikki-Tikki-Tavy" was almost certainly not the krait, which is about 2 feet long, but more probably the saw-scaled viper. The author was obviously pleased to have caught out the great Kipling in a matter of accuracy.

In the box, a little black forked tongue flickered towards the two Indians beyond the glass.

Very alert and irritable, the long-gone English naturalist had concluded his chapter on *Echis carinatus.* Strikes quickly without warning. The fangs are so small they make a virtually unnoticeable puncture, like two tiny thorns. There is no pain, but death is almost inevitable, usually taking between two and four hours, depending on the body-weight of the victim and the level of his physical exertions at the time and afterwards. Cause of death is invariably a brain haemorrhage.

"How much do you want for him?" whispered Ram Lal.

The old Gujerati spread his hands helplessly. "Such a prime specimen," he said regretfully, "and so hard to come by. Five hundred rupees."

Ram Lal clinched the deal at 350 rupees and took the snake away in a jar.

For his journey back to London Ram Lal purchased a box of cigars, which he emptied of their contents and in whose lid he punctured twenty small holes for air. The tiny viper, he knew, would need no food for a week and no water for two or three days. It could breathe on an infinitesimal supply of air, so he wrapped the cigar box, resealed and with the viper inside it among his leaves, in several towels whose thick sponginess would contain enough air even inside a suitcase.

He had arrived with a handgrip, but he bought a cheap fibre suitcase and packed it with clothes from market stalls, the cigar box going in the centre. It was only minutes before he left his hotel for Bombay airport that he closed and locked the case. For the flight back to London he checked the suitcase into the hold of the Boeing airliner. His hand baggage was searched, but it contained nothing of interest.

The Air India jet landed at London Heathrow on Friday morning and Ram Lal joined the long queue of Indians trying to get into Britain. He was able to prove he was a medical student and not an immigrant, and was allowed through quite quickly. He even reached the luggage carousel as the first suitcases were tumbling onto it, and saw his own in the first two dozen. He took it to the toilet, where he extracted the cigar box and put it in his handgrip.

In the Nothing-to-Declare channel he was stopped all the same, but it was his suitcase that was ransacked. The customs officer glanced in his shoulder bag and let him pass. Ram Lal crossed Heathrow by courtesy bus to Number One Building and caught the midday shuttle to Belfast. He was in Bangor by teatime and able at last to examine his import.

He took a sheet of glass from the bedside table and slipped it carefully between the lid of the cigar box and its deadly contents before opening wide. Through the glass he saw the viper going round and round inside. It paused and stared with angry black eyes back at him. He pulled the lid shut, withdrawing the pane of glass quickly as the box top came down.

"Sleep, little friend," he said, "if your breed ever sleep. In the morning you will do Shakti's bidding for her."

Before dark he bought a small screw-top jar of coffee and poured the contents into a china pot in his room. In the morning, using his heavy gloves, he transferred the viper from the box to the jar. The enraged snake bit his glove once, but he did not mind. It would have recovered its venom by midday. For a moment he studied the snake, coiled and cramped inside the glass coffee jar, before giving the top a last, hard twist and placing it in his lunch box. Then he went to catch the works truck.

Big Billie Cameron had a habit of taking off his jacket the moment he arrived at the work site, and hanging it on a convenient nail or twig. During the lunch break, as Ram Lal had observed, the giant foreman never failed to go to his jacket after eating, and from the right-hand pocket extract his pipe and tobacco pouch. The routine did not vary. After a satisfying pipe, he would knock out the dottle, rise and say,

"Right, lads, back to work," as he dropped his pipe back into the pocket of his jacket. By the time he turned round everyone had to be on their feet.

Ram Lal's plan was simple but foolproof. During the morning he would slip the snake into the right-hand pocket of the hanging jacket. After his sandwiches the bullying Cameron would rise from the fire, go to his jacket and plunge his hand into the pocket. The snake would do what great Shakti had ordered that he be brought halfway across the world to do. It would be he, the viper, not Ram Lal, who would be the Ulsterman's executioner.

Cameron would withdraw his hand with an oath from the pocket, the viper hanging from his finger, its fangs deep in the flesh. Ram Lal would leap up, tear the snake away, throw it to the ground and stamp upon its head. It would by then be harmless, its venom expended. Finally, with a gesture of disgust he, Ram Lal, would hurl the dead viper far into the River Comber, which would carry all evidence away to the sea. There might be suspicion, but that was all there would ever be.

Shortly after eleven o'clock, on the excuse of fetching a fresh sledge-hammer, Harkishan Ram Lal opened his lunch box, took out the coffee jar, unscrewed the lid and shook the contents into the right-hand pocket of the hanging jacket. Within sixty seconds he was back at his work, his act unnoticed.

During lunch he found it hard to eat. The men sat as usual in a circle round the fire; the dry old timber baulks crackled and spat, the billycan bubbled above them. The men joshed and joked as ever, while Big Billie munched his way through the pile of doorstep sandwiches his wife had prepared for him. Ram Lal had made a point of choosing a place in the circle near to the jacket. He forced himself to eat. In his chest his heart was pounding and the tension in him rose steadily.

Finally Big Billie crumpled the paper of his eaten sandwiches, threw it in the fire and belched. He rose with a grunt and walked towards his jacket. Ram Lal turned his head to watch. The other men took no notice. Billie Cameron reached his jacket and plunged his hand into the right-hand pocket. Ram Lal held his breath. Cameron's hand rummaged for several seconds and then withdrew his pipe and pouch. He began to fill the bowl with fresh tobacco. As he did so he caught Ram Lal staring at him.

"What are youse looking at?" he demanded belligerently.

"Nothing," said Ram Lal, and turned to face the fire. But he could not stay still. He rose and stretched, contriving to half turn as he did so. From the corner of his eye he saw Cameron replace the pouch in the pocket and again withdraw his hand with a box of matches in it. The foreman lit his pipe and pulled contentedly. He strolled back to the fire.

Ram Lal resumed his seat and stared at the flames in disbelief. Why, he asked himself, why had great Shakti done this to him? The snake had been her tool, her instrument brought at her command. But she had held it back, refused to use her own implement of retribution. He turned and sneaked another glance at the jacket. Deep down in the lining at the very hem, on the extreme left-hand side, something stirred and was still. Ram Lal closed his eyes in shock. A hole, a tiny hole in the lining, had undone all his planning. He worked the rest of the afternoon in a daze of indecision and worry.

On the truck ride back to Bangor, Big Billie Cameron sat up front as usual, but in view of the heat folded his jacket and put it on his knees. In front of the station Ram Lal saw him throw the still-folded jacket onto the back seat of his car and drive away. Ram Lal caught up with Tommy Burns as the little man waited for his bus.

"Tell me," he asked, "does Mr. Cameron have a family?"

"Sure," said the little labourer innocently, "a wife and two children."

"Does he live far from here?" said Ram Lal. "I mean, he drives a car."

"Not far," said Burns, "up on the Kilcooley estate. Ganaway Gardens, I think. Going visiting are you?"

"No, no," said Ram Lal, "see you Monday."

Back in his room Ram Lal stared at the impassive image of the goddess of justice.

"I did not mean to bring death to his wife and children," he told her. "They have done nothing to me."

The goddess from far away stared back and gave no reply.

Harkishan Ram Lal spent the rest of the weekend in an agony of anxiety. That evening he walked to the Kilcooley housing estate on the ring road and found Ganaway Gardens. It lay just off Owenroe Gardens and opposite Woburn Walk. At the corner of Woburn Walk there was a telephone kiosk, and here he waited for an hour, pretending to make a call, while he watched the short street across the road. He thought he spotted Big Billie Cameron at one of the windows and noted the house.

He saw a teenage girl come out of it and walk away to join some friends. For a moment he was tempted to accost her and tell her what demon slept inside her father's jacket, but he dared not.

Shortly before dusk a woman came out of the house carrying a shopping basket. He followed her down to the Clandeboye shopping centre, which was open late for those who took their wage packets on a Saturday. The woman he thought to be Mrs. Cameron entered Stewarts supermarket and the Indian student trailed round the shelves behind her, trying to pluck up the courage to approach her and reveal the danger in her house. Again his nerve failed him. He might, after all, have the wrong woman, even be mistaken about the house. In that case they would take him away as a madman.

He slept ill that night, his mind racked by visions of the saw-scaled viper coming out of its hiding place in the jacket lining to slither, silent and deadly, through the sleeping council house.

On the Sunday he again haunted the Kilcooley estate, and firmly identified the house of the Cameron family. He saw Big Billie clearly in the back garden. By mid-afternoon he was attracting attention locally and knew he must either walk boldly up to the front door and admit what he had done, or depart and leave all in the hands of the goddess. The thought of facing the terrible Cameron with the news of what deadly danger had been brought so close to his children was too much. He walked back to Railway View Street.

On Monday morning the Cameron family rose at a quarter to six, a bright and sunny August morning. By six the four of them were at breakfast in the tiny kitchen at the back of the house, the son, daughter and wife in their dressing gowns, Big Billie dressed for work. His jacket was where it had spent the weekend, in a closet in the hallway.

Just after six his daughter Jenny rose, stuffing a piece of marmaladed toast into her mouth.

"I'm away to wash," she said.

"Before ye go, girl, get my jacket from the press," said her father, working his way through a plate of cereal. The girl reappeared a few seconds later with the jacket, held by the collar. She proffered it to her father. He hardly looked up.

"Hang it behind the door," he said. The girl did as she was bid, but the jacket had no hanging tab and the hook was no rusty nail but a smooth chrome affair. The jacket hung for a moment, then fell to the kitchen floor. Her father looked up as she left the room.

"Jenny," he shouted, "pick the damn thing up."

No one in the Cameron household argued with the head of the family. Jenny came back, picked up the jacket and hung it more firmly. As she did, something thin and dark slipped from its folds and slithered into the corner with a dry rustle across the linoleum. She stared at it in horror.

"Dad, what's that in your jacket?"

Big Billie Cameron paused, a spoonful of cereal halfway to his mouth. Mrs. Cameron turned from the cooker. Fourteen-year-old Bobby ceased buttering a piece of toast and stared. The small creature lay curled in the corner by the row of cabinets, tight-bunched, defensive, glaring back at the world, tiny tongue flickering fast.

"Lord save us, it's a snake," said Mrs. Cameron.

"Don't be a bloody fool, woman. Don't you know there are no snakes in Ireland? Everyone knows that," said her husband. He put down the spoon. "What is it, Bobby?"

Though a tyrant inside and outside his house, Big Billie had a grudging respect for the knowledge of his young son, who was good at school and was being taught many strange things. The boy stared at the snake through his owlish glasses.

"It must be a slowworm, Dad," he said. "They had some at school last term for the biology class. Brought them in for dissection. From across the water."

"It doesn't look like a worm to me," said his father.

"It isn't really a worm," said Bobby. "It's a lizard with no legs."

"Then why do they call it a worm?" asked his truculent father.

"I don't know," said Bobby.

"Then what the hell are you going to school for?"

"Will it bite?" asked Mrs. Cameron fearfully.

"Not at all," said Bobby. "It's harmless."

"Kill it," said Cameron senior, "and throw it in the dustbin."

His son rose from the table and removed one of his slippers, which he held like a flyswat in one hand. He was advancing, bare-ankled towards the corner, when his father changed his mind. Big Billie looked up from his plate with a gleeful smile.

"Hold on a minute, just hold on there, Bobby," he said, "I have an idea. Woman, get me a jar."

"What kind of a jar?" asked Mrs. Cameron.

"How should I know what kind of a jar? A jar with a lid on it."

Mrs. Cameron sighed, skirted the snake and opened a cupboard. She examined her store of jars.

"There's a jamjar, with dried peas in it," she said.

"Put the peas somewhere else and give me the jar," commanded Cameron. She passed him the jar.

"What are you going to do, Dad?" asked Bobby.

"There's a darkie we have at work. A heathen man. He comes from a land with a lot of snakes in it. I have in mind to have some fun with him. A wee joke, like. Pass me that oven glove, Jenny."

"You'll not need a glove," said Bobby. "He can't bite you."

"I'm not touching the dirty thing," said Cameron.

"He's not dirty," said Bobby. "They're very clean creatures."

"You're a fool, boy, for all your school learning. Does the Good Book not say: 'On thy belly shalt thou go, and dust shalt thou eat . . .'? Aye, and more than dust, no doubt. I'll not touch him with me hand."

Jenny passed her father the oven glove. Open jamjar in his left hand, right hand protected by the glove, Big Billie Cameron stood over the viper. Slowly his right hand descended. When it dropped, it was fast; but the small snake was faster. Its tiny fangs went harmlessly into the padding of the glove at the centre of the palm. Cameron did not notice, for the act was masked from his view by his own hands. In a trice the snake was inside the jamjar and the lid was on. Through the glass they watched it wriggle furiously.

"I hate them, harmless or not," said Mrs. Cameron. "I'll thank you to get it out of the house."

"I'll be doing that right now," said her husband, "for I'm late as it is."

He slipped the jamjar into his shoulder bag, already containing his lunch box, stuffed his pipe and pouch into the right-hand pocket of his jacket and took both out to the car. He arrived at the station yard five minutes late and was surprised to find the Indian student staring at him fixedly.

"I suppose he wouldn't have the second sight," thought Big Billie as they trundled south to Newtownards and Comber.

By mid-morning all the gang had been let into Big Billie's secret joke on pain of a thumping if they let on to "the darkie." There was no chance of that; assured that the slowworm was perfectly harmless, they too thought it a good leg-pull. Only Ram Lal worked on in ignorance, consumed by his private thoughts and worries.

At the lunch break he should have suspected something. The tension was palpable. The men sat in a circle around the fire as usual, but the conversation was stilted and had he not been so preoccupied he would have noticed the half-concealed grins and the looks darted in his direction. He did not notice. He placed his own lunch box between his knees and opened it. Coiled between the sandwiches and the apple, head back to strike, was the viper.

The Indian's scream echoed across the clearing, just ahead of the roar of laughter from the labourers. Simultaneously with the scream, the lunch box flew high in the air as he threw it away from himself with all his strength. All the contents of the box flew in a score of directions, landing in the long grass, the broom and gorse all around them.

Ram Lal was on his feet, shouting. The gangers rolled helplessly in their mirth, Big Billie most of all. He had not had such a laugh in months.

"It's a snake," screamed Ram Lal, "a poisonous snake. Get out of here, all of you. It's deadly."

The laughter redoubled; the men could not contain themselves. The reaction of the joke's victim surpassed all their expectations.

"Please, believe me. It's a snake, a deadly snake."

Big Billie's face was suffused. He wiped tears from his eyes, seated across the clearing from Ram Lal, who was standing looking wildly round.

"You ignorant darkie," he gasped, "don't you know? There are no snakes in Ireland. Understand? There aren't any."

His sides ached with laughing and he leaned back in the grass, his hands behind him to support him. He failed to notice the two pricks, like tiny thorns, that went into the vein on the inside of the right wrist.

The joke was over and the hungry men tucked into their lunches. Harkishan Ram Lal reluctantly took his seat, constantly glancing round him, a mug of steaming tea held ready, eating only with his left hand, staying clear of the long grass. After lunch they returned to work. The old distillery was almost down, the mountains of rubble and savable timbers lying dusty under the August sun.

At half past three Big Billie Cameron stood up from his work, rested on his pick and passed a hand across his forehead. He licked at a slight swelling on the inside of his wrist, then started work again. Five minutes later he straightened up again.

"I'm not feeling so good," he told Patterson, who was next to him. "I'm going to take a spell in the shade."

He sat under a tree for a while and then held his head in his hands.

At a quarter past four, still clutching his splitting head, he gave one convulsion and toppled sideways. It was several minutes before Tommy Burns noticed him. He walked across and called to Patterson.

"Big Billie's sick," he called. "He won't answer me."

The gang broke and came over to the tree in whose shade the foreman lay. His sightless eyes were staring at the grass a few inches from his face. Patterson bent over him. He had been long enough in the labouring business to have seen a few dead ones.

"Ram," he said, "you have medical training. What do you think?"

Ram Lal did not need to make an examination, but he did. When he straightened up he said nothing, but Patterson understood.

"Stay here all of you," he said, taking command. "I'm going to phone an ambulance and call McQueen." He set off down the track to the main road.

The ambulance got there first, half an hour later. It reversed down the track and two men heaved Cameron onto a stretcher. They took him away to Newtownards General Hospital, which has the nearest casualty unit, and there the foreman was logged in as DOA—dead on arrival. An extremely worried McQueen arrived thirty minutes after that.

Because of the unknown circumstance of the death an autopsy had to be performed and it was, by the North Down area pathologist, in the Newtownards municipal mortuary to which the body had been transferred. That was on the Tuesday. By that evening the pathologist's report was on its way to the office of the coroner for North Down, in Belfast.

The report said nothing extraordinary. The deceased had been a man of forty-one years, big-built and immensely strong. There were upon the body various minor cuts and abrasions, mainly on the hands and wrists, quite consistent with the job of navvy, and none of these were in any way associated with the cause of death. The latter, beyond a doubt, had been a massive brain haemorrhage, itself probably caused by extreme exertion in conditions of great heat.

Possessed of this report, the coroner would normally not hold an inquest, being able to issue a certificate of death by natural causes to the registrar at Bangor. But there was something Harkishan Ram Lal did not know.

Big Billie Cameron had been a leading member of the Bangor council of the outlawed Ulster Volunteer Force, the hard-line Protestant paramilitary organization. The computer at Lurgan, into which all deaths in the province of Ulster, however innocent, are programmed, threw this out and someone in Lurgan picked up the phone to call the Royal Ulster Constabulary at Castlereagh.

Someone there called the coroner's office in Belfast, and a formal inquest was ordered. In Ulster death must not only be accidental; it must be seen to be accidental. For certain people, at least. The inquest was in the Town Hall at Bangor on the Wednesday. It meant a lot of trouble for McQueen, for the Inland Revenue attended. So did two quiet men of extreme Loyalist persuasion from the UVF council. They sat at the back. Most of the dead man's workmates sat near the front, a few feet from Mrs. Cameron.

Only Patterson was called to give evidence. He related the events of the Monday, prompted by the coroner, and as there was no dispute none of the other labourers was called, not even Ram Lal. The coroner read the pathologist's report aloud and it was clear enough. When he had finished, he summed up before giving his verdict.

"The pathologist's report is quite unequivocal. We have heard from Mr. Patterson of the events of that lunch break, of the perhaps rather foolish prank played by the deceased upon the Indian student. It would seem that Mr. Cameron was so amused that he laughed himself almost to the verge of apoplexy. The subsequent heavy labour with pick and shovel in the blazing sun did the rest, provoking the rupture of a large blood vessel in the brain or, as the pathologist puts it in more medical language, a cerebral haemorrhage. This court extends its sympathy to the widow and her children, and finds that Mr. William Cameron died of accidental causes."

Outside on the lawns that spread before Bangor Town Hall McQueen talked to his navvies.

"I'll stand fair by you, lads," he said. "The job's still on, but I can't afford not to deduct tax and all the rest, not with the Revenue breathing down my neck. The funeral's tomorrow, you can take the day off. Those who want to go on can report on Friday."

Harkishan Ram Lal did not attend the funeral. While it was in progress at the Bangor cemetery he took a taxi back to Comber and asked the driver to wait on the road while he walked down the track. The driver was a Bangor man and had heard about the death of Cameron.

"Going to pay your respects on the spot, are you?" he asked.

"In a way," said Ram Lal.

"That the manner of your people?" asked the driver.

"You could say so," said Ram Lal.

"Aye, well, I'll not say it's any better or worse than our way, by the graveside," said the driver, and prepared to read his paper while he waited.

Harkishan Ram Lal walked down the track to the clearing and stood where the camp fire had been. He looked around at the long grass, the broom and the gorse in its sandy soil.

"Visha serp," he called out to the hidden viper. "O venomous snake, can you hear me? You have done what I brought you so far from the hills of Rajputana to achieve. But you were supposed to die. I should have killed you myself, had it all gone as I planned, and thrown your foul carcass in the river.

"Are you listening, deadly one? Then hear this. You may live a little longer but then you will die, as all things die. And you will die alone, without a female with which to mate, because there are no snakes in Ireland."

The saw-scaled viper did not hear him, or if it did, gave no hint of understanding. Deep in its hole in the warm sand beneath him, it was busy, totally absorbed in doing what nature commanded it must do.

At the base of a snake's tail are two overlapping plate-scales which obscure the cloaca. The viper's tail was erect, the body throbbed in ancient rhythm. The plates were parted, and from the cloaca, one by one, each an inch long in its transparent sac, each as deadly at birth as its parent, she was bringing her dozen babies into the world.

CHARLOTTE ARMSTRONG *(1905–1969) was a respected Broadway playwright before she turned to suspense fiction in the early
1940s. She achieved considerable success, particularly after her
novel* The Unsuspected *(1947) was made into a memorable
Hollywood movie. Ms. Armstrong continued her association
with nonprint media over the years, writing several of the most
interesting scripts for* Alfred Hitchcock Presents. *As a novelist
she specialized in putting sympathic characters into dangerous
positions, and then getting them out in rousing and tension-
packed finales. But her short fiction is even better, and can be
found in collections such as* The Albatross *(1957) and* I See
You *(1966).*

"The Splintered Monday" is suspense fiction at its very best.

The Splintered Monday
BY CHARLOTTE ARMSTRONG

Mrs. Sarah Brady awakened in the guest room of her nephew Jeff's
house, and for a moment or two was simply glad for the clean page of a
new day. Then she found her bookmark between the past and the
future. Oh, yes. Her sister, Alice, had died on Monday, been buried on
Wednesday. (Poor Alice.) This was Saturday. Mrs. Brady's daughter,
Del, was coming, late today, to drive her mother back home tomorrow.

Now that she knew where she was, Mrs. Brady cast a brief prayer
into time and space, then put her lean old feet to the floor.

The house was very still. For days now it had seemed muffled, everyone moving slowly in a quiet gloom, sweetened by mutually considerate behavior. Mrs. Brady had a feeling that her own departure would
signal a lift of some kind in the atmosphere. And she did not particularly like the idea.

She trotted into the guest bathroom to wash herself, examining expertly the state of her health. Mrs. Brady had an uncertain heart, but
she had lived with it a long time, and she knew how to manage. Still,
she tried to get along with as few drugs as she successfully could, so
she opened the medicine cabinet, peered at her bottle of pills, but did
not touch it.

No, on the whole, she thought, it would be better to get through the morning without a pill—at least, to see how it would go. She dressed herself briskly and set forth into the hall.

It was going to be a lovely summer day, weather-wise.

The door of the enormous front bedroom stood wide and her sister's bed, neatly made, shouted that poor Alice was gone. Mrs. Brady sampled the little recurring shock. It was not exactly lessening, but it was changing character. Yes, it was going over from feeling to thinking. She could perceive with her mind the hole in the fabric, the loss of a presence, the absence of a force.

But Mrs. Brady found herself frowning slightly as she proceeded downstairs and back through the house to the breakfast room. This was her last day here. And her last chance? Had she *cause* to feel offended? Or to feel whatever this uneasiness of hers could be called?

Henny, the cook-housekeeper and general factotum, came at once with her orange juice. She was a big, rawboned, middle-aged woman with a golden cross dangling at her throat. Henny still had that sad and wary look in her big eyes. She had been much subdued, too much subdued, since Alice's death.

She had taken to being very solicitous, treating Mrs. Brady as if *she* were an invalid. Yet Mrs. Brady and Henny had been good friends for many years. They had set up between them a kind of boisterous relationship, with a running gag that Mrs. Brady was a great nuisance to have around, and Henny, whenever Mrs. Brady visited, wished only to see the last of her.

Perhaps that gag was no longer in good taste—not today, not yet. But the continued coddling rather annoyed Mrs. Brady, who had never asked for it in the beginning and didn't particularly like it now.

When Henny brought her eggs, Mrs. Brady said, "It's surely hard to get used to Alice not being up there, in that room—she was there for so long. When did she last get out and go anywhere?"

"I don't remember, Miz Sarah." Henny obviously wanted to escape.

"Tell me, you last saw her right after she'd had her lunch on Monday?"

"Yes, Ma'am," said Henny, looking miserable.

"And so did I," said Mrs. Brady. "Karen didn't think we should tell her we were going downtown. I didn't even speak to her."

"No. No. You don't want to feel bad about that. Look, you spent the whole morning with her." Henny seemed to be cooing and she was not a cooing woman. "You couldn't know. Miz Del will be here for dinner, I guess. Right?"

"That's right. Henny?"

"Your eggs are getting cold, Miz Sarah."

"Henny," repeated Mrs. Brady sternly, "is there something I haven't been told?"

Henny was startled. Her eyes rolled, and her hand clutched at the cross. "I don't know what you mean. I just don't want to talk about it. I don't think you should talk about it, either."

"Why on earth shouldn't I talk about it?"

"I mean . . . Well, you've got to go on," mumbled Henny, "and what's the good of talking about it? Poor thing. I mean, she's probably better off."

Then Henny put her head down and seemed to butt through the swinging door into the kitchen.

Mrs. Brady began to eat her eggs, reflecting on the contradiction of the golden cross and the horror of death—if that was what Henny was trying to be rid of, by calling death "better off."

Well, Mrs. Brady herself was not so crazy about the idea of dying, but she accepted the fact that one inevitably would. It was presumptuous, in her opinion, to say that poor Alice might be better off. Maybe so. But maybe not.

Maybe Henny felt guilty because, during that seemingly normal afternoon, Henny herself had gone up to the third floor to "lie down," as usual, and had not made even a token resistance to the coming of the angel of death, by being alert to his imminence. Nobody had expected Alice to die—not on Monday.

Shock? Maybe I *am* still shocked, she thought. But it didn't click, as the truth should.

Bobby Conley came shuffling in.

"Good morning," said his great-aunt. "No school today?"

"Nope," said Bobby, getting into his chair in a young way that was far more difficult a physical feat than simply sitting down. "But I better hit the books some." Bobby was twenty, and away at college during the winters. He was taking some summer courses, locally.

"Del is coming to fetch me," said Mrs. Brady.

Bobby grunted that he knew. Henny came in with his juice and a mound of toast. Mrs. Brady poured his coffee.

"How do you feel about your parents flying off to Germany and France?" she asked him.

"That's okay," said Bobby. "I'll be living on campus, anyhow."

"And Suzanne back in boarding school. You'll be able to keep an eye on her."

Bobby gave her one blank look, as if to say, How antique to think that anybody should keep an eye on anybody. "Oh, sure," he said tolerantly.

His sister, Suzanne, bounced in, looking like something out of science fiction, with her hair wound on huge rollers all over her small head. "I don't want anything to eat, Henny. I'm reducing."

Mrs. Brady cocked an eye at the bare waistline, exposed between two pieces of cloth, that seemed to her to be tiny enough to snap in a strong breeze. But she said nothing. She was not in firm touch with these young people. They had seemed fond of her, in earlier days, but even Susie, at fifteen, had grown away. They went their own ways. And, of course, they should. Mrs. Brady thought they'd had a better break than their father.

Sarah Brady had always felt a kind of responsibility for her nephew, Jeffrey, because she could see, better than anyone else, how he had been burdened all his life. Poor Alice had believed that to be born a beautiful female was all the Lord had ever required of her, and that to have been widowed in her early thirties was surely a preposterous error of some kind. It couldn't happen to her! Poor Alice, with no personal resources, but plenty of money, had taken to the one hobby that appealed to her: she had gone in for ill health.

Sarah understood as much as there was to understand. Alice had been the golden-haired pet, the pampered darling, whereas she, Sarah, three years younger, had been the "clever" one. And the lucky one, thought Sarah now. It may be better to be born lucky than good-looking. She smiled to herself and sighed.

Alice's one child, Jeffrey, had been at his mother's mercy all his life.

But poor Alice, dead or alive, didn't seem to bother Jeffrey's children.

"You were at the beach, Susie, all day Monday," said Mrs. Brady musingly. "But Bobby, you came home for lunch and you were in your room, studying, right across the hall from your grandmother."

They both looked at her like owls.

"I didn't bother her," said Bobby, chewing.

It was Henny who had found Alice, and had called the doctor, after Henny's customary "lie down."

"And she didn't bother you, eh?" Mrs. Brady said.

Suzanne looked at her with round eyes. "If you just didn't tell her you were going anywhere."

And Mrs. Brady thought, *Touché?* Or was the girl thinking of her father?

But Susie was thinking of herself. "I never told her when I was going to the beach. She'd just have a big fit about sharks." One brown shoulder shrugged. "Or chaperones."

Bobby said, "She didn't even know I was going to summer school to pull up my grades. She'd have had a big fit about that too."

"No, it wasn't easy to tell her anything," admitted Mrs. Brady with a thoughtful air. "It never was. *I* don't operate that way. *I'll* have a big fit if I think the world is kept a secret from me."

They were eyeing her. With skepticism? Amusement? Pity? Or with a touch of wonder? Ah, thought Mrs. Brady, they are not as indifferent to death as they pretend.

"So she didn't cry out? Didn't ring her bell? You didn't hear a thing?"

"Nope," said Bobby. "Not a croak out of her." Then he turned his face to her, quickly. "I didn't mean to put it . . . I'm sorry." And for one brief moment Mrs. Brady saw an awed and shaken boy, who had never before been across the hall from where someone had died.

But now Karen came in and said, "Good morning, all." She had come in quietly. Her hand touched the young girl's shoulder. Suzanne sat perfectly still under it. Then Karen touched her stepson's hair lightly. Bobby did not flinch.

Mrs. Brady was thinking, They won't give themselves away.

Henny came to serve the mistress of the house with her normal air of devotion. This was Karen's house now. She was a pretty woman, in her thirties, small, compact, well-groomed, gracious in manner. She had been a nurse, hired to take care of poor Alice during one especially trying bout, almost six years ago. Karen and her patient had taken to each other. And when the patient's widowed son had married the nurse, whatever else it may have been, it had seemed a useful and practical arrangement.

Karen's control and gentle good manners, perhaps enhanced by her nurse's training, had been a saving and a soothing influence, all around. She was the one person, Mrs. Brady reflected, who had always given poor Alice her needed dollop of sympathy, who had never, so far as Mrs. Brady knew, been driven to protest, to say, in one way or another, Oh, for pity's sake, cheer up!

When the young people left, Mrs. Brady took another cup of coffee which she didn't want and wasn't supposed to have. She said to Karen, "You know, I've been feeling something—I don't know exactly what. But I hate to go away tomorrow without getting *at* whatever it is. Why do I feel as if I were getting special treatment—the kind that Alice always got?"

"Why, Aunt Sarah," said Karen, smiling, "Of course, you are getting special treatment. We are all so fond of you. Don't you think we realize you have lost your only sister? Oh, it is too bad that this had to happen during your visit. Poor Alice always so looked forward to seeing you."

She did? thought Mrs. Brady. She found that her feet were shuffling, her toes curling. Normally, she appreciated Karen's soothing ways, but not today, somehow.

"I hope you aren't feeling unhappy because you and I went off on a lark on Monday," said Karen gently. "Don't feel that way. Please? There was just no reason to think we shouldn't have gone. There were people in the house. We mustn't be tempted to feel guilty, must we?"

Mrs. Brady examined this. No, she thought, but then, to my best knowledge, I have not been tempted to feel guilty.

"You'll be home, back in your own place," Karen was saying, "with all the things you find to do and I know you'll just go on, because you always have." Karen had butter in her mouth. "Now, tell me, is there something Del likes to eat, especially, that I could order for dinner?"

"Nothing special," said Mrs. Brady, rather shortly. "She eats what she's given." She felt, suddenly, that she would be very glad to see her own child. "So do I," she added, "usually."

"Dear Aunt Sarah," said Karen fondly, "as if you've ever been a bit of trouble. But you know, Jeffrey is the one who has been hit the hardest. Don't you think we must try—just to go on? And let time heal? He's going to accept that European assignment. I encouraged him to. Don't you think that's wise? To get away from this house will be so good for him—new scenes and new experiences to help him forget."

"Oh, yes. *I* think it's wise for him to accept that offer," said Sarah Brady. "I thought so before, and told him so, as you know."

"He thinks so much of your judgment," said Karen, "and so do I. It is only the shock—I think we must just plunge into our plans. Let's see. You'll be busy packing today, I suppose?"

"Yes." Mrs. Brady thought to herself, and *that* will take *all* of twenty minutes. She couldn't figure out why she felt so cross.

Karen excused herself, to make her marketing lists, and Mrs. Brady went upstairs, moving through the big pleasantly furnished house with a strong sense of its eclipse. This house was going to be closed. Jeffrey and Karen would be off, abroad, the children away at schools. What will Henny do? she wondered. But Henny was a household jewel who could write her own ticket, having become as valuable as a rare antique.

Mrs. Brady went back to thinking of Monday. She couldn't help it.

Just after lunch, on Monday, Karen had invited her to ride along downtown, while Alice rested. Mrs. Brady, who loved to prowl the streets when she was feeling spry enough, had accepted gladly.

She had gone to get her things, discovered with pleasure a legitimate errand of her own, and then had passed her sister's bedroom door. Karen, in the doorway with a tray in her hands, had made a "shushing" mouth. Alice was not to be told that they were going out. Mrs. Brady had supposed at the time—and still supposed—that to teli Alice would have meant at least five minutes of listening to Alice bemoan the fact that she couldn't go too, or the fact that she was being abandoned.

So Sarah had merely glanced in, seen her sister's head—still golden, courtesy of dye—and the prow of her sister's nice straight nose (which had always made her own nose seem even more knobby than it needed to seem), taken the sense of her sister's lair, perfumed, and cluttered with the thousand things that Alice had for her bodily comfort, and heard her sister say, "I wish to rest now," in her piteous, imperious manner. I must be allowed to do exactly as I wish at all times, said Alice's manner, because I am so ill.

Mrs. Brady remembered Karen's saying that Henny needn't bother, Karen would take the tray down; remembered Henny's dive for the stairs-going-up; remembered seeing Bobby, flat on his stomach on the bed, a book on the floor, and his head hanging over it; remembered how the car had pussyfooted out of the driveway, and Karen's sad mischievous smile, when they were finally running free, on their way through the small city to its center.

Mrs. Brady had happily considered what she could, in all conscience, shop for. (She lived very frugally in a tiny apartment, not far from her daughter Del's house.) Karen had discussed a new bedspread for Suzanne and socks for Bobby, and her dentist appointment.

"You won't mind waiting for me, Aunt Sarah?"

"I think I'd rather poke around by myself and take the bus back," Mrs. Brady had said.

"But it's three blocks to walk, from the bus to the house."

"I don't mind. Besides, I have a little errand to do."

"Can't I do it for you?"

"No. No. It's all right, you see, when the three blocks end in a soft chair."

"Well . . . if you insist."

So Mrs. Brady had enjoyed herself in the department store, inspecting bedspreads, and had advised about socks, and then, deposited on the sidewalk near Karen's dentist's building, she had gone her own way. Not far. Not for long. She had that little errand, which gave her a bit of a purpose, and she had accomplished it, and then window-shopped her way to the bus stop, and a bus had come before she was *too* tired . . .

When she had come back into this house, Dr. Clarke was already there, and Henny was weeping. Bobby was in the living room, numb and dumb and dry eyed. Jeffrey had been notified. And Alice was dead.

Almost as soon as Mrs. Brady had reached her own bathroom, and taken one of her pills against the shock and strain, she'd heard Karen running up the stairs. But Karen did not need her, and then she had heard Jeffrey's voice below. So she had hurried down to stand by, been delegated to watch for Suzanne and break the news gently—as Monday had splintered out of the shape of an ordinary Monday.

Remembering, Mrs. Brady shook her head. But there was no shaking the nagging notion out of it. She couldn't help imagining that there *was* something she hadn't been told.

So she marched into her bathroom and took a pill to fortify herself. She intended to fare forth. She intended to see her nephew alone. She really had not—not since, not yet.

It was almost eleven when Mrs. Brady finally made it, by bus, to Jeffrey's office, identified herself to his receptionist, and could not help but feel gratified when Jeffrey came blasting out of his inner recess.

"Aunt Sarah, what the dickens are you doing here?" He was a tall man, a bit thick in the middle these days; his hair was graying; his long face had acquired a permanent look of slight anxiety. He was a quiet man, who ran well in light harness, grateful for peace whenever he got it.

"I won't have another chance to see you alone, Jeff."

"Will you come in?" The anxiety on his face deepened. "Or better still, let's go down to the drug store and have a coffee break."

"All right." She wouldn't risk another coffee. No matter. So he took her down in the elevator and they sat in a leatherette booth. The place was familiar. Mrs. Brady had lived in this town, herself, ten years ago. The druggist knew her. The young girl who tended the snack counter was friendly. Mrs. Brady felt personally comfortable. She ordered a piece of Danish pastry.

But now to business. Studying her nephew's face, she said, "Jeff, it's true. Poor Alice didn't *like* it. We both knew that she wouldn't. I'm sorry that your last talk with her, on Monday morning, had to be even as unpleasant as it was. But I can only say to you that *I* still think you were right to decide to go to Europe, and right to tell her that you *had* decided to go."

"Why, sure, Aunt Sarah," he said, not looking up. "I know that. And don't *you* worry about it for a minute."

"Alice would have been perfectly safe, with all the arrangements you made, and no more miserable than usual. As far as we could *know.*"

"I agree. Please, Aunt Sarah, don't think for a moment that anyone is blaming *you*—for your advice or for anything else in the world."

"Oh, Jeff." His Aunt felt impatient with him. "Of course, you're not blaming me. I don't understand why there has to be any thought of blame. *I* happen to know that the Lord is running this world and hasn't yet appointed me to do it. Or you, either." She was sputtering, as of old.

He was smiling at her. "I'm all right, Aunt Sarah," he said affectionately. "It takes a little time, that's all."

"I'm leaving tomorrow."

"I'm glad—" he began, and quickly stopped.

Oh, yes, he was glad she was going. It only confirmed what Mrs. Brady had been feeling. Well? Perhaps, she must concede that she *could* be a bit of a nuisance, too. After all, Jeff was a grown man. He didn't need his Auntie to stiffen him. Or shouldn't. Time would pass, time would heal. Heal what? The truth was, a burden had been lifted from Jeff and his household. All that eternal pussyfooting would be over. Fresh winds would blow.

But they were not blowing—not yet. Was the household guilty of being just a little *too* glad? And *too* soon?

No. She still sensed that she, Sarah Brady, was being treated too gently, in some way. She couldn't pinpoint one single piece of clear evidence—but she knew in her bones that she was being "handled."

So? Had Sarah Brady come to such a pass? She didn't relish it. Why, Alice was the one who always had to be handled. All her life. In fact, that was how Alice managed the rest of the world. If it did not behave just as she wished, she simply insisted that it *seem* to—at least within her range. And had always won, because it was easier to do it that way —Alice having such a very small and narrow range.

But not I, thought Sarah. No, not I!

"I *thought* you were glad I was leaving," she said flatly.

"Not for my sake," said Jeff, too quickly. "But I want you to be busy and forget. Live your own life, Aunt Sarah." He was smiling, but she didn't like either the look or the sound of him. "You have always told me that I ought to live mine."

Forget? thought Sarah, bristling within. Even poor Alice deserved better than to be forgotten as fast as possible. Furthermore, it *isn't* possible. Alice was what she was, and she will remain a part of our lives as long as we live.

"Oh, I say a good many things," she admitted. "For better or for worse, I have always been one to trot out what's on my mind. Well, then, right now, I keep having this nagging feeling that there is something that I *ought* to say. Or do. Or know."

"All you have to do is be yourself," said Jeff, somewhat fatuously. He patted her hand. "It'll be nice to see Del. She doesn't mind three hundred miles in one day, and the same again tomorrow."

"That sort of thing doesn't bother Del," said Mrs. Brady lightly, seeing clearly that her nephew was getting rid of her.

She refused Jeff's offer to send her home in a cab, insisting that she enjoyed the bus ride. On one of her good days, the truth was, she certainly did. But she wasn't feeling as well now as she might.

When Jeff kissed her brow goodbye and said, pseudo-gaily, "Don't you worry about a thing," Mrs. Brady was contrarily convinced that there was something she *ought* to worry about.

She stood on the sidewalk and listened to one word turn into another in her mind. "Handled"? No, she was being "spared." Well! She, Sarah Brady, was not going to stand for being "spared!" Not yet and not ever—not if she could help it.

Mrs. Brady walked back into the drug store to look in the phone book, but there were several Dr. Clarkes. She had no clue. Then the druggist hailed her. "Anything else I can do for you, today, Mrs. Brady?"

"Please, Mr. Fredericks, do you happen to know which Dr. Clarke took care of my sister?"

"Surely. Dr. Josephus Clarke. You want his phone number?"

"I want his address," she said thoughtfully.

"He's in the same building where your Dr. Crane used to be."

"Oh, is he? Thank you." Now Mrs. Brady had her bearings.

Then the druggist said, "I was sure sorry to hear about your sister. A long illness, I guess." Was he, too, delicately implying cause for rejoicing?

Mrs. Brady came into the doctor's waiting room, feeling like a dirty spy. The girl who took her name seemed totally confused to hear that she wasn't a patient. Mrs. Brady had to wait out the doctor's appointments for almost two hours.

So she sat and turned the leaves of old magazines, and watched the people come and go, and pondered how to ask a question, when it was the question that she wanted to find out. Or whether there was one.

At last she was given her five minutes. "I am Mrs. Conley's sister, Sarah Brady."

"We met," the doctor said, "in sad and unfortunate circumstances. What can I do for you. Mrs. Brady?" He was benign.

"I don't know. You could tell me, please, *why* my sister died on Monday."

"Why? I . . . don't quite understand."

"I mean, should we have suspected?"

"Oh, no. Certainly not," said the doctor. "I see. I see. You have been feeling that you should have been at her side? That's a very common feeling, Mrs. Brady, but it really isn't rational. I'm sure you know what I mean." He was tolerant, gentle.

"You took care of her, as they say, for a long time?" She was groping.

The doctor said, with a sad smile, "I did all I could, Mrs. Brady."

"Of course you did," she burst out. "I'm not here to hint that you didn't. But what did my sister die of? Maybe that's how I should have put it."

"How shall I tell you?" He seemed to be countering. He was watching her, quite warily. "In a lay term? Heart failure? . . . I don't quite understand what troubles, you, Mrs. Brady. But if you like, I can assure you that there is no need for you to be troubled—no need at all. We must accept these things."

"Dr. Clarke, I am *not* like my sister."

He made no direct response to this. "It is very easy to imagine things, in grief," he went on. "But when you have a bit of a heart problem, as you do, it is wise to learn serenity."

"I have a very good doctor," she snapped, "who has taught me to deal with my heart."

"I'm sure you have."

"Perhaps you know him? Dr. Crane?"

"By reputation. A very good man," he purred. "You are looking well."

Mrs. Brady shook her feathers. She was making a fine mess out of this interview. But the doctor was not. He was "handling" her expertly. In fact, he was getting rid of her. Expertly. Like Jeff.

Mrs. Brady found the old familiar bus stop. She supposed she must have put his back up, as the expression goes. I, said Sarah Brady to herself, am a terrible detective.

Well, it wasn't her *way,* to go snooping around corners and behind people's backs. It just never *had* been her way and she didn't really know how to do it. She, too, was what she was—a vinegary old soul— and her whole past wasn't going to let her be anything else. In the meantime, she hadn't found out a single blessed thing.

Wait. She had. Dr. Clarke had been told that *she,* Sarah, had a heart problem. Now, why was he told that?

Ah, now she was *sure* that she was being "spared" and "handled" and it was beginning to make her good and mad.

She almost trotted the three blocks to the house, brisk with anger, and had steam left over to pack her things with great dispatch. Then Del roared into the driveway. And when Del came, in her long-legged still puppylike way, there was a lift in the atmosphere. Something about Del. She was a young mother now, with a house of her own to run. But Del refused to be anything but cheerful. *She* didn't have to be tactful. It was impossible to be offended by her—Del was as open as the day.

"Sorry I couldn't make it to Aunt Alice's funeral," she said, "but Georgie was down with chicken pox. Sally isn't due to get them till Tuesday. So here I am. Hi, kids!"

Bobby and Suzanne regarded Del with a kind of suspicious delight. Dinner was almost easy.

Afterward, Del began to yawn. She said she went to bed with the sun these days. Why fight it? Her kids were up and roistering every dawn.

But Mrs. Brady didn't want Del to leave her side until she had said what she was going to say. She would still tear some veils. There was that anger still in her, still energizing her.

She said, rather abruptly, to the assembly in the living room, "I won't have another chance. So I want to ask you, right here and now, what's going on in this house? I've been poking around all day, trying to find out what's been hanging over my head. But I'm no detective. So now I am *asking*. Why are you keeping secrets from me? What have I ever done to make you insult me by keeping the truth away from me?"

"Why, Mama!" said Del, with nothing but surprise.

Jeff looked at Mrs. Brady with a reddening face. The others seemed to hold their breath. "I am sorry," Jeff said stiffly, "If you feel we've been insulting you, Aunt Sarah. That's the last thing any of us would want to do."

"Oh, Aunt Sarah," said Karen with gentle woe, "how can it be an insult to try not to keep talking about unhappy things?"

"I don't want to talk about unhappy things *because* they are unhappy," said Sarah. "I know how Alice trained you all—to keep unhappy things outside her door. But I don't like things kept outside *my* door—*any* things. And, as far as I know, I don't deserve to be treated this way."

Jeff was looking stricken and his wife put her hand on his knee. "Oh, Aunt Sarah, dear," she said softly, "you mustn't, you really mustn't. I'm so sorry that you feel as you do. I wish you didn't. Del?" She looked to Del for help.

But Del said, "I don't know what Mom's talking about."

"Neither do I," said Suzanne abruptly, from the heap she was on a floor cushion.

Mrs. Brady kept sternly to her course. "I want to know why you are all handling me with kid gloves. In fact, I think I want to know exactly what happened here on Monday."

"Children," said Karen, "she's had a shock. She's—"

But Bobby sat up in his chair and used his spine. "I know what she means," the boy said.

Mrs. Brady nodded to her unexpected ally. Karen's hands were moving in a protective flutter, but now Jeffrey said, "The fact is, we can't be quite sure what did happen. If we chose not to tell you of a certain possibility, that was because it is very distressing to think about, and it certainly need not be true."

"There," said Karen. "Now, surely, that is no insult. When is it an insult to be kind? Del, dear, would you like something to eat or drink, before bed?"

Del said cheerfully, "You won't brush her off that easily."

And Jeffrey said painfully, "No, I guess not."

Karen said, "Oh, Jeff, this is *too* bad. Oh, please, all of you. Let it go. It's all over. There is nothing anybody can do or even really *know.*"

But Bobby said, "I guess you'd better tell us, Dad."

And Suzanne said, with a burst of anger, "Don't you think we can take it?"

And Mrs. Brady was nodding and sparkling her approval. These kids will do, she thought.

So Jeffrey lifted his head and spoke in a blurting way. "All right. There is a possibility that my mother took her own life."

"Doesn't the doctor know that?" asked Del, breaking the silent moment of shock with an air of intelligent interest.

Karen said, "No, No. That is, he suspects that she may have had too much of her medicine. By accident. Or just in ignorance. He doesn't know, you see, that she happened to be feeling rather upset and hurt that day."

Bobby was on his feet. "Oh, come on, Dad! You know darned well Grandmother never would have cared *that* much. So you told her you were taking off to Europe—so what? Listen, *she* knew she'd have a ball, bossing a crew of nurses and telling everybody how you ran out on her. Well, it's the truth!" He looked around, belligerently.

Suzanne said, "She was spoiled rotten—we all know that. But nothing was going to get *her* down."

Karen said, "Oh, my dears. Oh, I don't think this is very kind. You are making your father feel very bad. None of us want him feeling any worse. Please?"

Del said, "I don't see what you're all so upset about."

And Karen said, "There now. That is *very* sensible. Isn't it?"

"It certainly is," snapped Mrs. Brady. "You haven't said a word so far that was worth keeping secret. You think she might have, in one of her moods, taken too much medicine on purpose? But the doctor thinks not? I can't see anything in *that* worth lying to me about."

"But we can't *know,*" said Karen, "and why should *you* be worried?"

Mrs. Brady answered in ringing tones. "Why not? I'm alive."

Her nephew looked at her and said, "I beg your pardon, Aunt Sarah. We should have told you. I think you knew that your heart medicine is the same as hers? And you knew that her pills were very much weaker than yours—almost placebos, in fact? Karen spoke to you of that, didn't she? The day you unpacked."

"Yes."

"Well, my mother evidently crossed over to your room on Monday, took your bottle of pills, got back into bed, and then swallowed enough to be too many for her. She took them herself—no doubt of that. So it just seemed—after the doctor had gone—"

Jeff began to flounder. "When we found—we didn't want to—we felt—" He put his hands over his eyes. "For Bobby's sake, who didn't notice that she crossed the hall, and for your sake, Aunt Sarah, who *did* encourage me to tell my mother I was going away—well, we saw no reason, since we can't be *sure* of the truth, why you should be tortured by this doubt."

"By which *you* are being tortured?" said Mrs. Brady. Then she closed her mouth and set herself to manage her treacherous heart.

"It is perfectly possible—in fact, it is probable," Jeff said, straining to believe, "that she forgot. Or never realized that your pills were so much stronger. It may have been just that her own supply was low—"

Del said alertly, "Mama?"

Sarah Brady had shrunken in the chair. She was hunched there like a little old monkey, and the agitation of her heart was now visible to all.

Her daughter came to her and said again," Mama?"

"Get my handbag—pills," Mrs. Brady mumbled through numb lips.

Karen said, "Oh, Aunt Sarah!" She clapped her hands and called, "Henny! Bring a glass of water—quickly." She stood by Mrs. Brady and her nurse's fingers felt for the pulse. Sarah kept breathing as slowly and as deeply as she could.

Bobby said, "Listen, everybody! If I'd seen her, which I didn't, I wouldn't have known to *do* anything. It's a lot of malarkey! Keeping stuff from *me.*"

Suzanne said, "Listen, if Grandmother had *wanted* to kill herself she'd have done it. What's the difference how? But I'll never believe she *did* do it."

Henny was there and Del ran up with the handbag. Del grabbed the glass of water, pushing Karen away Mrs. Brady swallowed a pill, then some water, and sighed.

In a few moments she said, "How do you know she took *my* pills?"

"Oh, Miz Sarah," wailed Henny, "Why did you have to find out about that? It was me who saw your bottle under her bed—after the doctor went."

"And who," said Mrs. Brady, lifting her voice a little, but not looking up, "put it back in my room?"

"Me," said Henny. "Miz Karen, she recognized it. And she said—and Mr. Conley, he felt so terrible—so they both said, Well, the *least* said the better. *I* didn't want you to feel bad, either." Henny was ready to weep. "Listen, you got to pray Miz Alice didn't sin, not that way."

Mrs. Brady shook her head. "Jeff, did you see this bottle, *my* bottle, on Monday?"

"Yes, I saw it." Her nephew bent forward, alarmed for her. "Now don't worry, Aunt Sarah—forget it. We shouldn't have told you."

Mrs. Brady could feel her blood beginning to flow less turbulently.

"I can't," she said. "I can't forget it. My bottle was downtown when Alice died—I *know* it was!"

"Why, no," said Jeff. "I'm sorry; Aunt Sarah, it couldn't have been —it was under Alice's bed."

"I *was* surprised," said Mrs. Brady in a stronger voice, "to see so many of my pills gone at noon. But I carry Dr. Crane's prescription with me all the time, so after Karen left me and went to the dentist, I dropped into Mr. Fredericks' drug store."

In the silence that followed, she looked only at Karen.

"Oh, but then *she* must have—" said Karen. "Poor Alice must have—"

Mrs. Brady sighed again. No. Definitely not. Alice, dead, had put no bottle under her deathbed.

She said, without anger, "I guess you wouldn't have talked them quite so desperately into 'sparing' me if you hadn't finally noticed Mr. Fredericks' name and *Monday's date* on this label? Oh, Karen, I told you I had an errand to do on Monday!"

No one spoke.

"When did Henny find it where you put it?" Mrs. Brady pressed on. "After I'd brought it back from Fredericks' drug store, of course. But by that time Alice was already dead of what you'd given her. At noon, was it, before we went downtown, when *you* took away her tray?"

"No," said Jeff. "No. *No!*"

"If there is another secret around," said Aunt Sarah sadly, "please trot it out."

In a moment Karen said sullenly. "She's buried. Now we can go to Europe. We can all live, for a change." The skin of her face was suddenly mottled, and her eyes had clouded over. "She was going to raise such a fuss. Jeff wouldn't have stood up to it—he'd have given in, the way he always did. She wasn't any good, even to herself. You all know that. *I* had to take it, all day, every day. You can call it mercy."

But no one was calling it mercy. The two children had drawn close to their father. Henny went to stand behind them. Jeffrey Conley stared at his second wife with wide and terrified eyes.

"You can do what you want," whined Karen viciously, "but you had all better stop and think. What good will it do to let the truth out now?"

The room was still, without an answer.

Mrs. Brady took another sip of water, although her heart felt steadier now as she sensed the old familiar comfort that always sustained her.

"The quality of truth," she said, "is that it's really there. Poor Alice taught me that."

It was Del who said, "I'll call the police—it has to be done. I'll do it."

Poor Karen.

His biographer, Francis M. Nevins, Jr., has called CORNELL
WOOLRICH *(1903–1968) the "Poe of the twentieth century"
and "the poet of the shadows," and he is certainly right. Mr.
Woolrich was the greatest suspense writer of his generation, almost single-handedly establishing the* noir *style of hard-edged
fiction that characterized the post–World War II period. A re-
cluse who lived with his mother in New York City hotel rooms
until her death, he produced such major works as* The Bride
Wore Black *(1940),* Night Has a Thousand Eyes *(1945), and*
Phantom Lady *(1945). The hallmarks of his style—the race
against the clock, the amnesiac, the betraying woman—became
obsessions for this tortured genius.*

*Mr. Woolrich also used rich, vivid settings for his stories,
places such as seedy hotels, cheap bars, and carnival sideshows,
and he chose a downtrodden dance hall to tell of "The Dancing
Detective," one of the best stories by a man told from a woman's point of view. For those of you too young to know the lingo,
"jives" are customers and "goona-gooing" is flirting.*

The Dancing Detective
BY CORNELL WOOLRICH

Patsy Marino was clocking us as usual when I barged in through the
foyer. He had to look twice at his watch to make sure it was right
when he saw who it was. Or pretended he had to, anyway. It was the
first time in months I'd breezed in early enough to climb into my
evening dress and powder up before we were due on the dance floor.

Marino said, "What is the matter, don't you feel well?"

I snapped, "D'ya have to pass a medical examination to get in here
and earn a living?" and gave him a dirty look across the frayed alley-
cat I wore on my shoulder.

"The reason I asked is you're on time. Are you sure you are feeling
well?" he pleaded sarcastically.

"Keep it up and you won't be," I promised, but soft-pedaled it so he
couldn't quite get it. He was my bread and butter after all.

The barn looked like a morgue. It always did before eight—or so I'd
heard. They didn't have any of the "pash" lights on yet, those smoky
red things around the walls that gave it atmosphere. There wasn't a cat
in the box, just five empty gilt chairs and the coffin. They had all the

full-length windows overlooking the main drag open to get some venti-
lation in, too. It didn't seem like the same place at all; you could
actually breathe fresh air in it!

My high heels going back to the dressing room clicked hollowly in
the emptiness, and my reflection followed me upside down across the
waxed floor, like a ghost. It gave me a spooky feeling, like tonight was
going to be a bad night. And whenever I get a spooky feeling, it turns
out to be a bad night all right.

I shoved the dressing-room door in and started, "Hey, Julie, why
didn't you wait for me, ya getting too high-hat?" Then I quit again.

She wasn't here either. If she wasn't at either end, where the hell was
she?

Only Mom Henderson was there, reading one of tomorrow morning's tabs. "Is it that late?" she wanted to know when she saw me.

"Aw, lay off," I said. "It's bad enough I gotta go to work on an
empty stomach." I slung my cat-pelt on a hook. Then I sat down and
took off my pumps and dumped some foot powder in them, and put
them back on again.

"I knocked on Julie's door on my way over," I said, "and didn't get
any answer. We always have a cup of java together before we come to
work. I don't know how I'm going to last the full fifteen rounds. . . ."

An unworthy suspicion crossed my mind momentarily: Did Julie
purposely dodge me to get out of sharing a cup of coffee with me like I
always took with her other nights? They allowed her to make it in her
rooming house because it had a fire escape; they wouldn't allow me to
make it in mine. I put it aside as unfair. Julie wasn't that kind; you
could have had the shirt off her back—only she didn't wear a shirt, just
a brassiere.

"Matter?" Mom sneered. "Didn't you have a nickel on you to buy
your own?"

Sure I did. Habit's a funny thing, though. Got used to taking it with
a sidekick and—I didn't bother going into it with the old slob.

"I got a feeling something's going to happen tonight," I said, hunching my shoulders.

"Sure," said Mom. "Maybe you'll get fired."

I thumbed my nose at her and turned the other way around on my
chair. She went back to the paper. "There haven't been any good
murders lately," she lamented. "Damn it, I like a good, juicy murder
wanst in a while."

"You're building yourself up to one right in here." I scowled into the mirror at her.

She didn't take offense; she wasn't supposed to, anyway. "Was you here when that thing happened to that Southern girl, Sally, I think was her name?"

"No!" I snapped. "Think I'm as old as you? Think I been dancing here all my life?"

"She never showed up to work one night, and they found her . . . That was only, let's see now"—she figured it out on her fingers— "three years ago."

"Cut it out!" I snarled. "I feel low enough as it is."

Mom was warming up now. "Well, for that matter, how about the Fredericks kid? That was only a little while before you come here, wasn't it?"

"I know," I cut her short. "I remember hearing all about it. Do me a favor and let it lie."

She parked one finger up alongside her mouth. "You know," she breathed confidentially, "I've always had a funny feeling one and the same guy done away with both of them."

"If he did, I know who I wish was third on his list!" I was glowering at her, when thank God the rest of the chain gang showed up and cut the death watch short. The blonde came in, and then the Raymond tramp, and the Italian frail, and all the rest of them—all but Julie.

I said, "She was never as late as this before!" and they didn't even know who or what I was talking about. Or care. Great bunch.

A slush pump started to tune up outside, so I knew the cats had come in, too.

Mom Henderson got up, sighed. "Me for the white tiles and rippling waters," and waddled out to her beat.

I opened the door on a crack and peeped out, watching for Julie. The pash lights were on now and there were customers already buying tickets over the bird cage. All the other taxi dancers were lining up— but not Julie.

Somebody behind me yelled, "Close that door! Think we're giving a free show in here?"

"You couldn't interest anyone in that secondhand hide of yours even with a set of dishes thrown in!" I squelched absentmindedly, without even turning to find out who it was. But I closed it anyway.

Marino came along and banged on it and hollered, "Outside, you in there! What do I pay you for anyway?" and somebody yelled back, "I often wonder!"

The cats exploded into a razzmatazz just then with enough oompah to be heard six blocks away, so it would pull them in off the pave. Once they were in, it was up to us. We all came out single file, to a fate worse than death, me last. They were putting the ropes up, and the mirrored tops started to go around in the ceiling and scatter flashes of light all over everything, like silver rain.

Marino said, "Where you goin', Ginger?" and when he used your front name like that, it meant he wasn't kidding.

I said, "I'm going to phone Julie a minute, find out what happened to her."

"You get out there and goona-goo!" he said roughly. "She knows what time the session begins! How long's she been working here, anyway?"

"But she'll lose her job, you'll fire her," I wailed.

He hinged his watch. "She is fired already," he said flatly.

I knew how she needed that job, and when I want to do a thing, I do it. A jive artist was heading my way, one of those barnacles you can't shake off once they fasten on you. I knew he was a jive because he'd bought enough tickets to last him all week; a really wise guy only buys them from stretch to stretch. The place might burn down for all he knows.

I grabbed his ticket and tore it quick, and Marino turned and walked away. So then I pleaded, "Gimme a break, will you? Lemme make a phone call first. It won't take a second."

The jive said, "I came in here to danst."

"It's only to a girl friend," I assured him. "And I'll smile pretty at you the whole time." *(Clink! Volunteer* 8-IIII.) "And I'll make it up to you later, I promise I will." I grabbed him quick by the sleeve. "Don't go way, stand here!"

Julie's landlady answered. I said, "Did Julie Bennett come back yet?"

"I don't know," she said. "I ain't seen her since yesterday."

"Find out for me, will ya?" I begged. "She's late and she'll lose her job over here."

Marino spotted me, came back and thundered, "I thought I told you—"

I waved the half ticket in his puss. "I'm working," I said. "I'm on this gentleman's time," and I goona-gooed the jive with teeth and eyes, one hand on his arm.

He softened like ice cream in a furnace. He said, "It's all right, Mac," and felt big and chivalrous or something. About seven cents' worth of his dime was gone by now.

Marino went away again, and the landlady came down from the second floor and said, "She don't answer her door, so I guess she's out."

I hung up and I said, "Something's happened to my girl friend. She ain't there and she ain't here. She wouldn'ta quit cold without telling me."

The goona-goo was beginning to wear off the jive by this time. He fidgeted, said, "Are you gonna danst or are you gonna stand there looking blue?"

I stuck my elbows out. "Wrap yourself around this!" I barked impatiently. Just as he reached, the cats quit and the stretch was on.

He gave me a dirty look. "Ten cents shot to hell!" and he walked off to find somebody else.

I never worry about a thing after it's happened, not when I'm on the winning end anyway. I'd put my call through, even if I hadn't found out anything. I got back under the ropes, and kept my fingers crossed to ward off garlic eaters.

By the time the next stretch began, I knew Julie wasn't coming anymore that night. Marino wouldn't have let her stay even if she had, and I couldn't have helped her get around him anymore, by then, myself. I kept worrying, wondering what had happened to her, and that creepy feeling about tonight being a bad night came over me stronger than ever, and I couldn't shake it off no matter how I goona-gooed.

The cold orangeade they kept buying me during the stretches didn't brace me up any either. I wasn't allowed to turn it down, because Marino got a cut out of the concession profits.

The night was like most of the others, except I missed Julie. I'd been more friendly with her than the rest of the girls, because she was on the square. I had the usual run of freaks.

"With the feet, with the feet," I said wearily, "lay off the belt-buckle crowding."

"What am I supposed to do, build a retaining wall between us?"

"You're supposed to stay outside the three-mile limit," I flared, "and not try to go mountain climbing in the middle of the floor. Do I look like an Alp?" And I glanced around to see if I could catch Marino's eye.

The guy quit pawing. Most of them are yellow like that. But on the other hand, if a girl complains too often, the manager begins to figure her for a troublemaker. "Wolf!" you know, so it don't pay.

It was about twelve when they showed up, and I'd been on the floor three and a half hours straight, with only one more to go. There are worse ways of earning a living. You name them. I knew it was about twelve because Duke, the front man, had just wound up "The Lady Is a Tramp," and I knew the sequence of his numbers and could tell the time of night by them, like a sailor can by bells. Wacky, eh? Half past —"Limehouse Blues."

I gandered at them when I saw them come into the foyer, because customers seldom come in that late. Not enough time left to make it worth the general admission fee. There were two of them: One was a fat, bloated little guy, the kind we call a belly wopper, the other was a pip. He wasn't tall, dark, and handsome because he was medium height, light-haired, and clean-cut-looking without being pretty about it, but if I'd had any dreams left, he coulda moved right into them. Well, I didn't, so I headed for the dressing room to count up my ticket stubs while the stretch was on; see how I was making out. Two cents out of every dime when you turn them in.

They were standing there sizing the barn up, and they'd called Marino over to them. Then the three of them turned around and looked at me just as I made the door, and Marino thumbed me. I headed over to find out what was up. Duke's next was a rumba, and I said to myself, "If I draw the kewpie, I'm going to have kittens all over the floor."

Marino said, "Get your things, Ginger." I thought one of them was going to take me out; they're allowed to do that, you know, only they've got to make it up with the management for taking you out of circulation. It's not as bad as it sounds; you can still stay on the up and up, sit with them in some laundry and listen to their troubles. It's all up to you yourself.

I got the backyard sable and got back just in time to hear Marino say something about, "Will I have to go bail for her?"

Fat said, "Naw, naw, we just want her to build up the background a little for us."

Then I tumbled, got jittery, squawked, "What is this, a pinch? What've I done? Where you taking me?"

Marino soothed, "They just want you to go with them, Ginger. You be a good girl and do like they ast." Then he said something to them I couldn't figure. "Try to keep the place here out of it, will you, fellas? I been in the red for six months as it is."

I cowered along between them like a lamb being led to the slaughter, looking from one to the other. "Where you taking me?" I wailed, going down the stairs.

Maiden's Prayer answered, in the cab. "To Julie Bennett's, Ginger." They'd gotten my name from Marino, I guess.

"What's she done?" I half sobbed.

"May as well tell her now, Nick," Fat suggested. "Otherwise she'll take it big when we get there."

Nick said, quietly as he could, "Your friend Julie met up with some tough luck, babe." He took his finger and he passed it slowly across his neck.

I took it big right there in the cab, Fat to the contrary. "Ah, no!" I whispered, holding my head. "She was on the floor with me only last night! Just this time last night we were in the dressing room together having a smoke, having some laughs! No! She was my only friend!" And I started to bawl like a two-year-old, straight down my makeup onto the cab floor.

Finally this Nick, after acting embarrassed as hell, took a young tent out of his pocket, said, "Have yourself a time on this, babe."

I was still working on it when I went up the rooming-house stairs sandwiched between them. I recoiled just outside the door. "Is she—is she still in there?"

"Naw, you won't have to look at her," Nick reassured me.

I didn't, because she wasn't in there anymore, but it was worse than if she had been. Oh, God, that sheet, with one tremendous streak down it as if a chicken had been—! I swiveled, played puss-in-the-corner with the first thing I came up against, which happened to be this Nick guy's chest. He sort of stood still like he liked the idea. Then he growled, "Turn that damn thing over out of sight, will you?"

The questioning, when I was calm enough to take it, wasn't a grill, don't get that idea. It was just, as they'd said, to fill out her background. "When was the last time you saw her alive? Did she go around much, y'know what we mean? She have any particular steady?"

"I left her outside the house door downstairs at one-thirty this morning, last night, or whatever you call it," I told them. "We walked home together from Joyland right after the session wound up. She didn't go around at all. She never dated the boys afterward and neither did I."

The outside half of Nick's left eyebrow hitched up at this, like when a terrier cocks its ear at something. "Notice anyone follow the two of you?"

"In our racket they always do; it usually takes about five blocks to wear them out, though, and this is ten blocks from Joyland."

"You walk after you been on your pins all night?" Fat asked, aghast.

"We should take a cab, on our earnings! About last night, I can't swear no one followed us, because I didn't look around. That's a come-on, if you do that."

Nick said, "I must remember that," absentmindedly.

I got up my courage, faltered, "Did it—did it happen right in here?"

"Here's how it went: She went out again after she left you the first time—"

"I knew her better than that!" I yipped. "Don't start that. Balloon Lungs, or I'll let you have this across the snout!" I swung my catpiece at him.

He grabbed up a little box, shook it in my face. "For this," he said. "Aspirin! Don't try to tell us different, when we've already checked with the all-night drugstore over on Sixth!" He took a couple of heaves, cooled off, sat down again. "She went out, but instead of lock-ing the house door behind her, she was too lazy or careless; shoved a wad of paper under it to hold it on a crack till she got back. In that five minutes or less, somebody who was watching from across the street slipped in and lay in wait for her in the upper hallway out here. He was too smart to go for her on the open street, where she might have had a chance to yell."

"How'd he know she was coming back?"

"The unfastened door woulda told him that; also the drug clerk tells us she showed up there fully dressed, but with her bare feet stuck in a pair of carpet slippers to cool 'em. The killer musta spotted that, too."

"Why didn't she yell out here in the house, with people sleeping all around her in the different rooms?" I wondered out loud.

"He grabbed her too quick for that, grabbed her by the throat just as she was opening her room door, dragged her in, closed the door, fin-ished strangling her on the other side of it. He remembered later to come out and pick up the aspirins that had dropped and rolled all over out there. All but one, which he overlooked and we found. She wouldn't 've stopped to take one outside her door. That's how we know about that part of it."

I kept seeing that sheet, which was hidden now, before me all over again. I couldn't help it, I didn't want to know, but still I had to know. "But if he strangled her, where did all that blood"—I gestured sickly —"come from?"

Fat didn't answer, I noticed. He shut up all at once, as if he didn't want to tell me the rest of it, and looked kind of sick himself. His eyes gave him away. I almost could have been a detective myself, the way I pieced the rest of it together just by following his eyes around the room. He didn't know I was reading them, or he wouldn't have let them stray like that.

First they rested on the little portable phonograph she had there on a table. By using bamboo needles she could play it late at night, soft, and no one would hear it. The lid was up and there was a record on the turntable, but the needle was worn down halfway, all shredded, as though it had been played over and over.

Then his eyes went to a flat piece of paper, on which were spread out eight or ten shiny new dimes; I figured they'd been put aside like that, on paper, for evidence. Some of them had little brown flecks on them, bright as they were. Then lastly his eyes went down to the rug; it was all pleated up in places, especially along the edges, as though something heavy, inert, had been dragged back and forth over it.

My hands flew up to my head and I nearly went wacky with horror. I gasped it out because I hoped he'd say no, but he didn't, so it was yes. "You mean he danced with her *after* she was gone? Gave her dead body a dime each time, stabbed her over and over while he did?"

There was no knife, or whatever it had been, left around, so either they'd already sent it down for prints or *he'd* taken it out with him again.

The thought of what must have gone on here in this room, of the death dance that must have taken place . . . All I knew was that I wanted to get out of here into the open, couldn't stand it anymore. Yet before I lurched out, with Nick holding me by the elbow, I couldn't resist glancing at the label of the record on the portable: "Poor Butterfly."

Stumbling out the door I managed to say, "She didn't put that on there. She hated that piece, called it a drip. I remembered once I was up here with her and started to play it, and she snatched it off, said she couldn't stand it, wanted to bust it then and there, but I kept her from doing it. She was off love and men, and it's a sort of a mushy piece, that was why. She didn't buy it, they were all thrown in with the machine when she picked it up secondhand."

"Then we know his favorite song, if that means anything. If she couldn't stand it, it would be at the bottom of the stack of records, not near the top. He went to the trouble of skimming through them to find something he liked."

"With her there in his arms already!" That thought was about the finishing touch, on top of all the other horror. We were on the stairs going down, and the ground floor seemed to come rushing up to meet me. I could feel Nick's arm hook around me just in time, like an anchor, and then I did a clothespin act over it. And that was the first time I didn't mind being pawed.

When I could see straight again, he was holding me propped up on a stool in front of a lunch counter a couple doors down, holding a cup of coffee to my lips.

"How's Ginger?" he said gently.

"Fine," I dribbled mournfully all over my lap. "How's Nick?"

And on that note the night of Julie Bennett's murder came to an end.

Joyland dance hall was lonely next night. I came in late, and chewing cloves, and for once Marino didn't crack his whip over me. Maybe even he had a heart. "Ginger," was all he said as I went hurrying by, "don't talk about it while you're on the hoof, get me? If anyone asks you, you don't know nothing about it. It's gonna kill business."

Duke, the front man, stopped me on my way to the dressing room. "I hear they took you over there last night," he started.

"Nobody took nobody nowhere, schmaltz," I snapped. He wore feathers on his neck, that's why I called him that; it's the word for long-haired musicians in our lingo.

I missed her worse in the dressing room than I was going to later on out in the barn; there'd be a crowd out there around me, and noise and music, at least. In here it was like her ghost was powdering its nose alongside me at the mirror the whole time. The peg for hanging up her things still had her name penciled under it.

Mom Henderson was having herself a glorious time; you couldn't hear yourself think, she was jabbering away so. She had two tabloids with her tonight, instead of just one, and she knew every word in all of them by heart. She kept leaning over the gals' shoulders, puffing down their necks: "And there was a dime balanced on each of her eyelids when they found her, and another one across her lips, and he stuck one in each of her palms and folded her fingers over it, mind ye! D'ye ever hear of anything like it? Boy, he sure must've been down on you taxis—"

I yanked the door open, planted my foot where it would do the most good, and shot her out into the barn. She hadn't moved that fast from one place to another in twenty years. The other girls just looked at me, and then at one another, as much as to say, "Touchy, isn't she?"

"Get outside and break it down; what do I pay you for anyway?" Marino yelled at the door. A gobstick tootled plaintively, out we trooped like prisoners in a lockstep, and another damn night had started in.

I came back in again during the tenth stretch ("Dinah" and "Have You Any Castles, Baby?") to take off my kicks a minute and have a smoke. Julie's ghost came around me again. I could still hear her voice in my ears, from the night before last! "Hold that match, Gin. I'm trying to duck a cement mixer out there. Dances like a slap-happy pug. Three little steps to the right, as if he were priming for a standing broad jump. I felt like screaming, For Pete's sake, if you're gonna jump, jump!"

And me, "What're you holding your hand for, been dancing upside down?"

"It's the way he holds it. Bends it back on itself and folds it under. Like this, look. My wrist's nearly broken. And look what his ring did to me!" she had shown me a strawberry-sized bruise.

Sitting there alone, now, in the half-light, I said to myself, "I bet *he* was the one! I bet *that's* who it was! Oh, if I'd only gotten a look at him, if I'd only had her point him out to me! If he enjoyed hurting her that much while she was still alive, he'd have enjoyed dancing with her after she was dead." My cigarette tasted rotten. I threw it down and got out of there in a hurry, back into the crowd.

A ticket was shoved at me and I ripped it without looking up. Gliding backward, all the way around on the other side of the barn, a voice finally said a little over my ear, "How's Ginger?"

I looked up and saw who it was said, "What're you dong here?"

"Detailed here," Nick said.

I shivered to the music. "Do you expect him to show up *again,* after what he's done already?"

"He's a dance-hall killer," Nick said. "He killed Sally Arnold and the Fredericks girl, both from this same mill, and he killed a girl in

Chicago in between. The prints on Julie Bennett's phonograph records match those in two of the other cases, and in the third case—where there were no prints—the girl was holding a dime clutched in her hand. He'll show up again sooner or later. There's one of us cops detailed to every one of these mills in the metropolitan area tonight, and we're going to keep it up until he does."

"How do you know what he looks like?" I asked.

He didn't answer for a whole bar. "We don't," he admitted finally. "That's the hell of it. Talk about being invisible in a crowd! We only know he isn't through yet, he'll keep doing it until we get him!"

I said, "He was here that night, he was right up here on this floor with her that night, before it happened; I'm sure of it!" And I sort of moved in closer. Me, who was always griping about being held too tight. I told him about the impression the guy's ring had left on her hand, and the peculiar way he'd held it, and the way he'd danced.

"You've got something there," he said, and left me flat on the floor and went over to phone it in.

Nick picked me up again next dance.

He said, shuffling off, "That was him all right who danced with her. They found a freshly made impression still on her hand, a little offside from the first, which was almost entirely obliterated by then. Meaning the second had been made after death, and therefore stayed uneffaced, just like a pinhole won't close up in the skin after death. They made an impression of it with moulage, my lieutenant just tells me. Then they filled that up with wax, photographed it through a magnifying lens, and now we know what kind of a ring he's wearing. A seal ring shaped like a shield, with two little jewel splinters, one in the upper right-hand corner, the other in the lower left."

"Any initials on it?" I gaped, awestricken.

"Nope, but something just as good. He can't get it off, unless he has a jeweler or locksmith file it off, and he'll be afraid to do that now. The fact that it would press so deeply into her hand proves that he can't get it off, the flesh of his finger has grown around it; otherwise it would have had a little give to it, the pressure would have shifted the head of it around a little."

He stepped all over my foot, summed up, "So we know how he dances, know what his favorite song is, 'Poor Butterfly,' know what kind of a ring he's wearing. And we know he'll be back sooner or later."

That was all well and good, but I had my own health to look out for;

the way my foot was throbbing! I hinted gently as I could. "You can't do very much watching out for him, can you, if you keep dancing around like this?"

"Maybe you think I can't. And if I just stand there with my back to the wall it's a dead giveaway. He'd smell me a mile away and duck out again. Keep it quiet what I'm doing here, don't pass it around. Your boss knows, of course, but it's to his interest to cooperate. A screwball like that can put an awful dent in his receipts."

"You're talking to the original sphinx," I assured him. "I don't pal with the rest of these twists anyway. Julie was the only one I was ever chummy with."

When the session closed and I came downstairs to the street, Nick was hanging around down there with the other lizards. He came over to me and took my arm and steered me off like he owned me.

"What's this?" I said.

He said, "This is just part of the act, make it look like the McCoy."

"Are you sure?" I said to myself, and I winked to myself without him seeing me.

All the other nights from then on were just a carbon copy of that one, and they started piling up by sevens. Seven, fourteen, twenty-one. Pretty soon it was a month since Julie Bennett had died. And not a clue as to who the killer was, where he was, what he looked like. Not a soul had noticed him that night at Joyland, too heavy a crowd. Just having his prints on file was no good by itself.

She was gone from the papers long ago, and she was gone from the dressing-room chatter, too, after a while, as forgotten as though she'd never lived. Only me, I remembered her, because she'd been my pal. And Nick Ballestier, he did because that was his job. I suppose Mom Henderson did, too, because she had a morbid mind and loved to linger on gory murders. But outside of us three, nobody cared.

They did it the wrong way around, Nick's superiors at homicide, I mean. I didn't try to tell him that, because he would have laughed at me. He would have said, "Sure! A dance-mill pony knows more about running the police department than the commissioner does himself! Why don't you go down there and show 'em how to do it?"

But what I mean is, the dance mills didn't need all that watching in the beginning, the first few weeks after it happened, like they gave them. Maniac or not, anyone would have known he wouldn't show up *that* soon after. They needn't have bothered detailing anyone at all to watch the first few weeks. He was lying low then. It was only after a month or so that they should have begun watching real closely for him. Instead they did it just the reverse. For a whole month Nick was there nightly. Then after that he just looked in occasionally, every second night or so, without staying through the whole session.

Then finally I tumbled that he'd been taken off the case entirely and was just coming for—er, the atmosphere. I put it up to him unexpectedly one night. "Are you still supposed to come around here like this?"

He got all red, admitted, "Naw, we were all taken off this duty long ago. I—er, guess I can't quit because I'm in the habit now or something."

"Oh, yeah?" I said to myself knowingly. I wouldn't have minded that so much, only his dancing didn't get any better, and the wear and tear on me was something awful. It was like trying to steer a steamroller around the place.

"Nick," I finally pleaded one night, when he pinned me down with one of his size twelves and then tried to push me out from under with the rest of him, "be a detective all over the place, only please don't ask me to dance anymore, I can't take it."

He looked innocently surprised. "Am I that bad?"

I tried to cover up with a smile at him. He'd been damn nice to me even if he couldn't dance.

When he didn't show up at all the next night, I thought maybe I'd gone a little too far, offended him maybe. But the big hulk hadn't looked like the kind that was sensitive about his dancing, or anything else for that matter. I brought myself up short with a swift, imaginary kick in the pants at this point. What the heck's the matter with *you?* I said to myself. You going soft? Didn't I tell you never to do that! And I reached for the nearest ticket, and tore it, and I goona-gooed with a, "Grab yourself an armful, mister, it's your dime."

I got through that night somehow but I had that same spooky feeling the next night like I'd had *that* night—like tonight was going to be a bad night. Whenever I got that spooky feeling, it turns out to be a bad night all right. I tried to tell myself it was because Nick wasn't around. I'd got used to him, that was all, and now he'd quit coming, and the hell with it. But the feeling wouldn't go away. Like something was going to happen before the night was over. Something bad.

Mom Henderson was sitting in there reading tomorrow morning's tab. "There hasn't been any good juicy murders lately," she mourned over the top of it. "Damn it, I like a good murder y'can get your teeth into wanst in a while!"

"Ah, dry up, you ghoul!" I snapped. I took off my shoes and dumped powder into them, put them on again. Marino came and knocked on the door. "Outside, freaks! What do I pay you for anyway?"

Someone jeered, "I often wonder!" and Duke, the front man, started to gliss over the coffin, and we all came out single file, me last, to a fate worse than death.

I didn't look up at the first buyer, just stared blindly at a triangle of shirtfront level with my eyes. It kept on like that for a while; always that same triangle of shirtfront. Mostly white, but sometimes blue, and once it was lavender, and I wondered if I ought to lead. The pattern of the tie across it kept changing too, but that was all.

> *Butchers and barbers and rats from the harbors*
> *Are the sweethearts my good luck has brought me.*

"Why so downcast, Beautiful?"

"If you were standing where I am, looking where you are, you'd be downcast too."

That took care of him. And then the stretch.

Duke went into a waltz, and something jarred for a minute. My timetable. This should have been a gut bucket (low-down swing music) and it wasn't. He'd switched numbers on me, that's what it was. Maybe a request. For waltzes they killed the pash lights and turned on a blue circuit instead, made the place cool and dim with those flecks of silver from the mirror-top raining down.

I'd had this white shirt triangle with the diamond pattern before; I remembered the knitted tie, with one tier unraveled on the end. I didn't want to see the face, too much trouble to look up. I hummed the piece mentally, to give my blank mind something to do. Then words seemed to drop into it, fit themselves to it, of their own accord, without my trying, so they must have belonged to it. "Poor butterfly by the blossoms waiting."

My hand ached, he was holding it so darned funny. I squirmed it, tried to ease it, and he held on all the tighter. He had it bent down and back on itself. . . .

"The moments pass into hours . . ."

Gee, if there's one thing I hate it's a guy with a ring that holds your mitt in a straitjacket! And he didn't know the first thing about waltzing. Three funny little hops to the right, over and over and over. It was getting my nerves on edge. "If you're gonna jump, jump!" Julie's voice came back to me from long ago. She'd run into the same kind of a . . .

"I just must die, poor butterfly!"

Suddenly I was starting to get a little scared and a whole lot excited. I kept saying to myself, Don't look up at him, you'll give yourself away. I kept my eyes on the knitted tie that had one tier unraveled. The lights went white and the stretch came on. We separated, he turned his back on me and I turned mine on him. We walked away from each other without a word. They don't thank you, they're paying for it.

I counted five and then I looked back over my shoulder, to try to see what he was like. He looked back at me at the same time, and we met each other's looks. I managed to slap on a smile, as though I'd only looked back because he'd made a hit with me, and that I hoped he'd come around again.

There was nothing wrong with his face, not just to look at anyway. It was no worse than any of the others around. He was about forty, maybe forty-five, hair still dark. Eyes speculative, nothing else, as they met mine. But he didn't answer my fake smile, maybe he could see through it. We both turned away again and went about our business.

I looked down at my hand, to see what made it hurt so. Careful not to raise it, careful not to bend my head, in case he was still watching. Just dropped my eyes to it. There was a red bruise the size of a small strawberry on it, from where his ring had pressed into it the whole time. I knew enough not to go near the box. I caught Duke's eye from where I was and hitched my head at him, and we got together sort of casually over along the wall.

"What'd you play "Poor Butterfly' for that last time?" I asked.

"Request number," he said.

I said, "Don't point, and don't look around, but whose request was it?"

He didn't have to. "The guy that was with you the last two times. Why?" I didn't answer, so then he said, "I get it." He didn't at all. "All right, chiseler," he said, and handed me two dollars and a half, splitting a fiver the guy had slipped him to play it. Duke thought I was after a kickback.

I took it. It was no good to tell him. What could he do? Nick Ballestier was the one to tell. I broke one of the singles at the orange-ade concession—for nickels. Then I started to work my way over toward the phone, slow and aimless. I was within a yard of it when the cats started up again!

And suddenly *he* was right next to me, he must have been behind me the whole time.

"Were you going any place?" he asked.

I thought I saw his eyes flick to the phone, but I wasn't positive. One thing sure, there wasn't speculation in them any more, there was— decision.

"No place," I said meekly. "I'm at your disposal," I thought, If I can only hold him here long enough, maybe Nick'll show up.

Then just as we got to the ropes, he said, "Let's skip this. Let's go out to a laundry and sit a while."

I said, smooth on the surface, panic-stricken underneath, "But I've already torn your ticket, don't you want to finish this one out at least?" And tried to goona-goo him for all I was worth, but it wouldn't take. He turned around and flagged Marino, to get his okay.

His back was to me, and across his shoulder I kept shaking my head, more and more violently, to Marino—no, no, I don't want to go with him. Marino just ignored me. It meant more money in his pocket this way.

When I saw that the deal was going through, I turned like a streak, made the phone, got my buffalo in it. It was no good trying to tell Marino, he wouldn't believe me, he'd think I was just making it up to get out of going out with the guy. Or if I raised the alarm on my own, he'd simply duck down the stairs before anyone could stop him and vanish again. Nick was the only one to tell, Nick was the only one who'd know how to nail him here.

I said, "Police headquarters, quick! Quick!" and turned and looked over across the barn. But Marino was already alone out there. I couldn't see where the guy had gone, they were milling around so, looking over their prospects for the next one.

A voice came on and I said, "Is Nick Ballestier there? Hurry up, get him for me."

Meanwhile Duke had started to break it down again; real corny. It must have carried over the open wire. I happened to raise my eyes, and there was a shadow on the wall in front of me, coming across my shoulders from behind me. I didn't move, held steady, listening.

I said, "All right, Peggy, I just wanted to know when you're gonna pay me back that five bucks you owe me," and I killed it.

Would he get it when they told him? They'd say, "A girl's voice asked for you, Nick, from somewhere where there was music going on, and we couldn't make any sense out of what she said, and she hung up without waiting." A pretty slim thread to hold all your chances on.

I stood there afraid to turn. His voice said stonily, "Get your things, let's go. Suppose you don't bother any more tonight about your five dollars." There was a hidden meaning, a warning, in it.

There was no window in the dressing room, no other way out but the way I'd come in, and he was right there outside the door. I poked around all I could, mourning, Why don't Nick come? and, boy, I was scared. A crowd all around me and no one to help me. He wouldn't stay; the only way to hang onto him for Nick was to go with him and pray for luck. I kept casing him through the crack of the door every minute or so. I didn't think he saw me, but he must have. Suddenly his heel scuffed at it brutally, and made me jump about an inch off the floor.

"Quit playing peek-a-boo, I'm waiting out here!" he called in sourly.

I grabbed up Mom Henderson's tab and scrawled across it in lipstick; "Nick: He's taking me with him, and I don't know where to. Look for my ticket stubs. Ginger."

Then I scooped up all the half tickets I'd accumulated all night long and shoved them loose into the pocket of my coat. Then I came sidling out to him. I thought I heard the phone on the wall starting to ring, but the music was so loud I couldn't be sure. We went downstairs and out on the street.

A block away I said, "There's a joint. We all go there a lot from our place," and pointed to Chan's. He said, "Shut up!" I dropped one of the dance checks on the sidewalk. Then I began making a regular trail of them.

The neon lights started to get fewer and fewer, and pretty soon we were in a network of dark lonely side streets. My pocket was nearly empty now of tickets. My luck was he didn't take a cab. He didn't want anyone to remember the two of us together, I guess.

I pleaded, "Don't make me walk anymore, I'm awfully tired."

He said, "We're nearly there, it's right ahead." The sign on the next corner up fooled me; there was a chop-suey joint, there, only a second-class laundry, but I thought that was where we were going.

But in between us and it there was a long dismal block, with tumble-down houses and vacant lots on it. And I'd run out of dance checks. All my take gone, just to keep alive. He must have worked out the whole setup carefully ahead of time, known I'd fall for that sign in the distance that we *weren't* going to.

Sure, I could have screamed out at any given step of the way, collected a crowd around us. But you don't understand. Much as I wanted to get away from him, there was one thing I wanted even more: to hold him for Nick. I didn't just want him to slip away into the night, and then do it all over again at some future date. And that's what would happen if I raised a row. They wouldn't believe me in a pinch, they'd think it was some kind of shakedown on my part. He'd talk himself out of it or scram before a cop came.

You have to live at night like I did to know the real callousness of passersby on the street, how seldom they'll horn in, lift a finger to help you. Even a harness cop wouldn't be much good, would only weigh my story against his, end up by sending us both about our business.

Maybe the thought came to me because I spotted a cop ahead just then, loitering toward us. I could hardly make him out in the gloom, but the slow steady walk told me. I didn't really think I was going to do it until we came abreast of him.

The three of us met in front of a boarded-up condemned house. Then, as though I saw my last chance slipping away—because Nick couldn't bridge the gap between me and the last of the dance checks anymore, it was too wide—I stopped dead.

I began in a low tense voice, "Officer, this man here—"

Julie's murderer had involuntarily gone on a step without me. That put him to the rear of the cop. The whole thing was so sudden, it must have been one of those knives that shot out of their own hilts. The cop's eyes rolled, I could see them white in the darkness, and he coughed right in my face, warm, and he started to come down on top of me, slow and lazy. I sidestepped and he fell with a soft thud and rocked a couple of times with his own fall and then lay still.

But the knife was already out of him long ago, and its point was touching my side. And where the cop had been a second ago, *he* was now. We were alone together again.

He said in a cold, unexcited voice, "Go ahead, scream, and I'll give it to you right across him."

I didn't, I just pulled in all my breath.

He said, "Go ahead, down there," and steered me with his knife down a pair of steps into the dark areaway of the boarded-up house it had happened in front of. "Stand there, and if you make a sound—you know what I told you." Then he did something to the cop with his feet, and the cop came rolling down into the areaway after me.

I shrank back and my back was against the boarded-up basement door. It moved a little behind me. I thought, This must be where he's taking me. If it is, then it's open. I couldn't get out past him, but maybe I could get *in* away from him.

I turned and clawed at the door, and the whole framed barrier swung out a little, enough to squeeze in through. He must have been hiding out in here, coming and going through here, all these weeks. No wonder they hadn't found him.

The real basement door behind it had been taken down out of the way. He'd seen what I was up to, and he was already wriggling through the gap after me. I was stumbling down a pitch-black hallway by then.

I found stairs going up by falling down on top of them full length. I sobbed, squirmed up the first few on hands and knees, straightened up as I went.

He stopped to light a match. I didn't have any, but his helped me too, showed me the outline of things. I was on the first-floor hall now, flitting down it. I didn't want to go up too high—he'd only seal me in some dead end up there—but I couldn't stand still down here.

A broken-down chair grazed the side of my leg as I went by, and I turned, swung it up bodily, went back a step and pitched it down over the stairwell on top of him. I don't know if it hurt him at all but his match went out.

He said a funny thing then. "You always had a temper, Muriel."

I didn't stand there listening. I'd seen an opening in the wall farther ahead, before the match went out. Just a blackness. I dived through it and all the way across with swimming motions, until I hit a jutting mantel slab over some kind of fireplace. I crouched down and tucked myself in under it. It was one of those huge old-fashioned ones. I groped over my head and felt an opening there, lined with rough brickwork and furry with cobwebs, but it wasn't wide enough to climb up through. I squeezed into a corner of the fireplace and prayed he wouldn't spot me.

He'd lit another match, and it came into the room after me, but I could only see his legs from the fireplace opening, it cut him off at the waist. I wondered if he could see me; he didn't come near where I was.

The light got a little stronger, and he'd lit a candle stump. But still his legs didn't come over to me, didn't bend down, or show his face peering in at me. His legs just kept moving to and fro around the room. It was awfully hard, after all that running, to keep my breath down.

Finally he said out loud, "Chilly in here," and I could hear him rattling newspapers, getting them together. It didn't sink in for a minute what was going to happen next. I thought. Has he forgotten me? Is he that crazy? Am I going to get away with it? But there'd been a malicious snicker in his remark; he was crazy like a fox.

Suddenly his legs came over straight to me; without bending down to look, he was stuffing the papers in beside me. I couldn't see out anymore past them. I heard the scrape of a match against the floorboards. Then there was the momentary silence of combustion. I was sick, I wanted to die quick, but I didn't want to die that way. There was the hum of rising flame, and a brightness just before me, the papers all turned gold. I thought, Oh, Nick! Nick! Here I go!

I came plunging out, scattering sparks and burning newspapers.

He said, smiling, pleased with himself, casual, "Hello, Muriel. I thought you didn't have any more use for me? What are you doing in my house?" He still had the knife—with the cop's blood on it.

I said, "I'm not Muriel, I'm Ginger Allen from the Joyland. Oh, mister, please let me get out of here, please let me go!" I was so scared and so sick I went slowly to my knees. "Please!" I cried up at him.

He said, still in that casual way, "Oh, so you're not Muriel? You didn't marry me the night before I embarked for France, thinking I'd be killed, that you'd never see me again, that you'd get my soldier's pension?" And then getting a little more vicious, "But I fooled you, I was shell-shocked but I didn't die. I came back even if it was on a stretcher. And what did I find? You hadn't even waited to find out! You'd married another guy and you were both living on my pay. You tried to make it up to me, though, didn't you, Muriel? Sure; you visited me in the hospital, bringing me jelly. The man in the next cot died from eating it. Muriel, I've looked for you high and low ever since, and now I've found you."

He moved backward, knife still in hand, and stood aside, and there was an old battered relic of a phonograph standing there on an empty packing case. It had a great big horn to it, to give it volume. He must have picked it up off some ash heap, repaired it himself. He released the catch and cranked it up a couple of times and laid the needle into the groove.

"We're going to dance, Muriel, like we did that night when I was in my khaki uniform and you were so pretty to look at. But it's going to have a different ending this time."

He came back toward me. I was still huddled there, shivering. "No!" I moaned. "Not me! You killed her, you killed her over and over again. Only last month, don't you remember?"

He said with pitiful simplicity, like the tortured thing he was, "Each time I think I have, she rises up again." He dragged me to my feet and caught me to him, and the arm with the knife went around me, and the knife pressed into my side.

The horrid thing over there was blaring into the emptiness, loud enough to be heard out on the street: "Poor Butterfly." It was horrible, it was ghastly.

And in the candle-lit pallor, with great shadows of us looming on the wall, like two crazed things we started to go round and round. I couldn't hold my head up on my neck; it hung way back over my shoulders like an overripe apple. My hair got loose and went streaming out as he pulled me and turned me and dragged me around. . . .

"I just must die, poor butterfly!"

Still holding me to him, he reached in his pocket and brought out a palmful of shiny dimes, and flung them in my face.

Then a shot went off outside in front of the house. It sounded like right in the areaway where the knifed cop was. Then five more in quick succession. The blare of the music must have brought the stabbed cop to. He must've got help.

He turned his head toward the boarded-up windows to listen. I tore myself out of his embrace, stumbled backward, and the knife point seemed to leave a long circular scratch around my side, but he didn't jam it in in time, let it trail off me.

I got out into the hall before he could grab me again, and the rest of it was just kind of a flight nightmare. I don't remember going down the stairs to the basement; I think I must have fallen down them without hurting myself—just like a drunk does.

Down there a headlight came at me from the tunnellike passage. It must have been just a pocket torch, but it got bigger and bigger, then went hurtling on by. Behind it a long succession of serge-clothed figures brushed by me.

I kept trying to stop each one, saying, "Where's Nick? Are you Nick?"

Then a shot sounded upstairs. I heard a terrible death cry. "Muriel!" and that was all.

When I next heard anything it was Nick's voice. His arm was around me and he was kissing the cobwebs and tears off my face.

"How's Ginger?" he asked.

"Fine," I said, "and how's Nick?"

Everyone knows that RAY BRADBURY *(1920–) is one of the finest contemporary writers of science fiction, fantasy, and supernatural horror. What is not as well known is that he produced a number of mystery and suspense stories early in his career, tales that appeared in magazines such as* Dime Mystery Magazine, Detective Tales, *and* Flynn's Detective Fiction, *carrying titles such as "Dead Men Rise Up Never" and "Corpse Carnival." Several decades later he produced an excellent hardboiled crime novel,* Death Is a Lonely Business *(1985).*

"And So Died Riabouchinska," from The Saint Detective Magazine, *was the basis for a fine* Alfred Hitchcock Presents *episode starring Claude Rains and a young Charles Bronson.*

And So Died Riabouchinska
BY RAY BRADBURY

The cellar was cold cement and the dead man was cold stone and the air was filled with an invisible fall of rain, while the people gathered to look at the body as if it had been washed in on an empty shore at morning. The gravity of the earth was drawn to a focus here in this single basement room—a gravity so immense that it pulled their faces down, bent their mouths at the corners and drained their cheeks. Their hands hung weighted and their feet were planted so they could not move without seeming to walk underwater.

A voice was calling, but nobody listened.

The voice called again, and only after a long time did the people turn and look, momentarily, into the air. They were at the seashore in November and this was a gull crying over their heads in the gray color of dawn. It was a sad crying, like the birds going south for the steel winter to come. It was an ocean sounding the shore so far away that it was only a whisper of sand and wind in a seashell.

The people in the basement room shifted their gaze to a table and a golden box resting there, no more than twenty-four inches long, inscribed with the name RIABOUCHINSKA. Under the lid of this small coffin the voice at last settled with finality, and the people stared at the box, and the dead man lay on the floor, not hearing the soft cry.

"Let me out, let me out, oh, please, please, someone let me out."

And finally Mr. Fabian, the ventriloquist, bent and whispered to the golden box, "No, Ria, this is serious business. Later. Be quiet, now, that's a good girl." He shut his eyes and tried to laugh.

From under the polished lid her calm voice said, "Please don't laugh. You should be much kinder now after what's happened."

Detective Lieutenant Krovitch touched Fabian's arm. "If you don't mind, we'll save your dummy act for later. Right now there's all *this* to clean up." He glanced at the woman, who had now taken a folding chair. "Mrs. Fabian." He nodded to the young man sitting next to her. "Mr. Douglas, you're Mr. Fabian's press agent and manager?"

The young man said he was. Krovitch looked at the face of the man on the floor. "Fabian, Mrs. Fabian, Mr. Douglas—all of you say you don't know this man who was murdered here last night, never heard the name Ockham before. Yet Ockham earlier told the stage manager he knew Fabian and had to see him about something vitally important."

The voice in the box began again quietly.

Krovitch shouted. "*Damn* it, Fabian!"

Under the lid, the voice laughed. It was like a muffled bell ringing.

"Pay no attention to her, Lieutenant," said Fabian.

"Her? Or *you,* damn it! What is this? Get together, you two!"

"We'll never be together," said the quiet voice, "never again after tonight."

Krovitch put out his hand. "Give me the key, Fabian."

In the silence there was the rattle of the key in the small lock, the squeal of the miniature hinges as the lid was opened and laid back against the tabletop.

"Thank you," said Riabouchinska.

Krovitch stood motionless, just looking down and seeing Riabouchinska in her box and not quite believing what he saw.

The face was white and it was cut from marble or from the whitest wood he had ever seen. It might have been cut from snow. And the neck that held the head which was as dainty as a porcelain cup with the sun shining through the thinness of it, the neck was also white. And the hands could have been ivory and they were thin small things with tiny fingernails and whorls on the pads of the fingers, little delicate spirals and lines.

She was all white stone, with light pouring through the stone and light coming out of the dark eyes with blue tones beneath like fresh mulberries. He was reminded of milk glass and of cream poured into a crystal tumbler. The brows were arched and black and thin and the cheeks were hollowed and there was a faint pink vein in each temple and a faint blue vein barely visible above the slender bridge of the nose, between the shining dark eyes.

Her lips were half parted and it looked as if they might be slightly damp, and the nostrils were arched and modeled perfectly, as were the ears. The hair was black and it was parted in the middle and drawn back of the ears and it was real—he could see every single strand of hair. Her gown was as black as her hair and draped in such a fashion as to show her shoulders, which were carved wood as white as a stone that has lain a long time in the sun. She was very beautiful. Krovitch felt his throat move, and then he stopped and did not say anything.

Fabian took Riabouchinska from her box. "My lovely lady," he said. "Carved from the rarest imported woods. She's appeared in Paris, Rome, Istanbul. Everyone in the world loves her and thinks she's really human, some sort of incredibly delicate midget creature. They won't accept that she was once part of many forests growing far away from cities and idiotic people."

Fabian's wife, Alyce, watched her husband, not taking her eyes from his mouth. Her eyes did not blink once in all the time he was telling of the doll he held in his arms. He in turn seemed aware of no one but the doll; the cellar and its people were lost in a mist that settled everywhere.

But finally the small figure stirred and quivered. "Please, don't talk about me! You know Alyce doesn't like it."

"Alyce never has liked it."

"Shh, don't!" cried Riabouchinska. "Not here, not now." And then, swiftly, she turned to Krovitch and her tiny lips moved: "How did it all happen? Mr. Ockham, I mean, Mr. Ockham."

Fabian said, "You'd better go to sleep now, Ria."

"But I don't want to," she replied. "I've as much right to listen and talk, I'm as much a part of this murder as Alyce or—or Mr. Douglas even!"

The press agent threw down his cigarette. "Don't drag me into this, you—" And he looked at the doll as if it had suddenly become six feet tall and were breathing there before him.

"It's just that I want the truth to be told." Riabouchinska turned her head to see all of the room. "And if I'm locked in my coffin there'll be no truth, for John's a consummate liar and I must watch after him, isn't that right, John?"

"Yes," he said, his eyes shut, "I suppose it is."

"John loves me best of all the women in the world, and I love him and try to understand his wrong way of thinking."

Krovitch hit the table with his fist. "God damn, oh, God *damn* it, Fabian! If you think you can—"

"I'm helpless," said Fabian.

"But she's—"

"I know, I know what you want to say," said Fabian quietly, looking at the detective. "She's in my throat, is that it? No, no. She's not in my throat. She's somewhere else. I don't know. Here, or here." He touched his chest, his head.

"She's quick to hide. Sometimes there's nothing I can do. Sometimes she is only herself, nothing of me at all. Sometimes she tells me what to do and I must do it. She stands guard; she reprimands me; is honest where I am dishonest, good when I am wicked as all the sins that ever were. She lives a life apart. She's raised a wall in my head and lives there, ignoring me if I try to make her say improper things, cooperating if I suggest the right words and pantomime." Fabian sighed. "So if you intend going on, I'm afraid Ria must be present. Locking her up will do no good, no good at all."

Lieutenant Krovitch sat silently for the better part of a minute, then made his decision. "All right. Let her stay. It just may be, by God, that before the night's over I'll be tired enough to ask even a ventriloquist's dummy questions."

Krovitch unwrapped a fresh cigar, lit it, and puffed smoke. "So you don't recognize the dead man, Mr. Douglas?"

"He looks vaguely familiar. Could be an actor."

Krovitch swore. "Let's all stop lying, what do you say? Look at Ockham's shoes, his clothing. It's obvious he needed money and came here tonight to beg, borrow, or steal some. Let me ask you this, Douglas. Are you in love with Mrs. Fabian?"

"Now, wait just a moment!" cried Alyce Fabian.

Krovitch motioned her down. "You sit there, side by side, the two of you. I'm not exactly blind. When a press agent sits where the husband should be sitting, consoling the wife, well! The way you look at the marionette's coffin, Mrs. Fabian, holding your breath when she appears. You make fists when she talks. Hell, you're obvious."

"If you think for one moment I'm jealous of a stick of wood!"

"Aren't you?"

"No, no, I'm not!"

Fabian moved. "You needn't tell him anything, Alyce."

"Let her!"

They all jerked their heads and stared at the small figurine, whose mouth was now slowly shutting. Even Fabian looked at the marionette as if it had struck him a blow.

After a long while Alyce Fabian began to speak.

"I married John seven years ago because he said he loved me and because I loved him and I loved Riabouchinska. At first, anyway. But then I began to see that he really lived all of his life and paid most of his attentions to her and I was a shadow waiting in the wings every night.

"He spent fifty thousand dollars a year on her wardrobe—a hundred thousand dollars for a dollhouse with gold and silver and platinum furniture. He tucked her in a small satin bed each night and talked to her. I thought it was all an elaborate joke at first and I was wonderfully amused. But when it finally came to me that I was indeed merely an assistant in his act, I began to feel a vague sort of hatred and distrust— not for the marionette, because after all it wasn't her doing—but I felt a terrible growing dislike and hatred for John, because it *was* his fault. He, after all, was the control, and all of his cleverness and natural sadism came out through his relationship with the wooden doll.

"And when I finally became very jealous, how silly of me! It was the greatest tribute I could have paid him and the way he had gone about perfecting the art of throwing his voice. It was all so idiotic, it was all so strange. And yet I knew that something had hold of John, just as people who drink have a hungry animal somewhere in them, starving to death.

"So I moved back and forth from anger to pity, from jealousy to understanding. There were long periods when I didn't hate him at all, and I never hated the thing that Ria was in him, for she was the best half, the good part, the honest and the lovely part of him. She was everything that he never let himself try to be."

Alyce Fabian stopped talking and the basement room was silent.

"Tell about Mr. Douglas," said a voice, whispering.

Mrs. Fabian did not look up at the marionette. With an effort she finished it out. "When the years passed and there was so little love and understanding from John, I guess it was natural I turned to—Mr. Douglas."

Krovitch nodded. "Everything begins to fall into place. Mr. Ockham was a very poor man, down on his luck, and he came to this theater tonight because he knew something about you and Mr. Douglas. Perhaps he threatened to speak to Mr. Fabian if you didn't buy him off. That would give you the best of reasons to get rid of him."

"That's even sillier than all the rest," said Alyce Fabian tiredly. "I didn't kill him."

"Mr. Douglas might have and not told you."

"Why kill a man?" said Douglas. "John knew all about us."

"I did indeed," said John Fabian, and laughed.

He stopped laughing and his hand twitched, hidden in the snowflake interior of the tiny doll, and her mouth opened and shut, opened and shut. He was trying to make her carry the laughter on after he had stopped, but there was no sound save the little empty whisper of her lips moving and gasping, while Fabian stared down at the little face and perspiration came out, shining, upon his cheeks.

The next afternoon Lieutenant Krovitch moved through the theater darkness backstage, found the iron stairs, and climbed with great thought, taking as much time as he deemed necessary on each step, up to the second-level dressing rooms. He rapped on one of the thin-paneled doors.

"Come in," said Fabian's voice from what seemed a great distance.

Krovitch entered and closed the door and stood looking at the man who was slumped before his dressing mirror. "I have something I'd like to show you," Krovitch said. His face showing no emotion whatever, he opened a manila folder and pulled out a glossy photograph, which he placed on the dressing table.

John Fabian raised his eyebrows, glanced quickly up at Krovitch, and then settled slowly back in his chair. He put his fingers to the bridge of his nose and massaged his face carefully, as if he had a headache. Krovitch turned the picture over and began to read from the typewritten data on the back. "Name, Miss Ilyana Riamonova. One hundred pounds. Blue eyes. Black hair. Oval face. Born 1914, New York City. Disappeared 1934. Believed a victim of amnesia. Of Russo-Slav parentage. Et cetera. Et cetera."

Fabian's lip twitched.

Krovitch laid the photograph down, shaking his head thoughtfully. "It was pretty silly of me to go through police files for a picture of a marionette. You should have heard the laughter at headquarters. *God.* Still, here she is—Riabouchinska. *Not* papier-mâché, *not* wood, *not* a puppet, but a woman who once lived and moved around and—disappeared." He looked steadily at Fabian. "Suppose you take it from there?"

Fabian half smiled. "There's nothing to it at all. I saw this woman's picture a long time ago, liked her looks, and copied my marionette after her."

"Nothing to it at all." Krovitch took a deep breath and exhaled, wiping his face with a huge handkerchief. "Fabian, this very morning I shuffled through a stack of *Billboard* magazines that high. In the year 1934 I found an interesting article concerning an act which played on a second-rate circuit, known as Fabian and Sweet William. Sweet William was a little boy dummy. There was a girl assistant—Ilyana Riamonova. No picture of her in the article, but I at least had a name, the name of a real person, to go on. It was simple to check police files then and dig up this picture. The resemblance, needless to say, between the live woman on one hand and the puppet on the other is nothing short of incredible. Suppose you go back and tell your story over again, Fabian."

"She was my assistant, that's all. I simply used her as a model."

"You're making me sweat," said the detective. "Do you think I'm a fool? Do you think I don't know love when I see it? I've watched you handle the marionette; I've seen you talk to it; I've seen how you make it react to you. You're in love with the puppet naturally, because you loved the original woman very, very much. I've lived too long not to sense that. Hell, Fabian, stop fencing around."

Fabian lifted his pale slender hands, turned them over, examined them, and let them fall.

"All right. In 1934 I was billed as Fabian and Sweet William. Sweet William was a small bulb-nosed boy dummy I carved a long time ago. I was in Los Angeles when this girl appeared at the stage door one night. She'd followed my work for years. She was desperate for a job and she hoped to be my assistant. . . ."

He remembered her in the half-light of the alley behind the theater and how startled he was at her freshness and eagerness to work with and for him and the way the cool rain touched softly down through the narrow alleyway and caught in small spangles through her hair, melting in dark warmness, and the rain beaded upon her white porcelain hand holding her coat together at her neck.

He saw her lips' motion in the dark and her voice, separated off on another sound track, it seemed, speaking to him in the autumn wind, and he remembered that without his saying yes or no or perhaps, she was suddenly on the stage with him, in the great pouring bright light, and in two months he, who had always prided himself on his cynicism and disbelief, had stepped off the rim of the world after her, plunging down a bottomless place of no limit and no light anywhere.

Arguments followed, and more than arguments—things said and done that lacked all sense and sanity and fairness. She had edged away from him at last, causing his rages and remarkable hysterias. Once he burned her entire wardrobe in a fit of jealousy. She had taken this quietly. But then one night he handed her a week's notice, accused her of monstrous disloyalty, shouted at her, seized her, slapped her again and again across the face, bullied her about and thrust her out the door, slamming it!

She disappeared that night.

When he found the next day that she was really gone and there was nowhere to find her, it was like standing in the center of a titanic explosion. All the world was smashed flat and all the echoes of the explosion came back to reverberate at midnight, at four in the morning, at dawn, and he was up early, stunned, with the sound of coffee simmering and the sound of matches being struck and cigarettes lit and himself trying to shave and looking at mirrors that were sickening in their distortion.

He clipped out all the advertisements that he took in the papers and pasted them in neat rows in a scrapbook—all the ads describing her and telling about her and asking for her back. He even put a private detective on the case. People talked. The police dropped by to question him. There was more talk.

But she was gone like a piece of white, incredibly fragile tissue paper, blown over the sky and down. A record of her was sent to the largest cities, and that was the end of it for the police. But not for Fabian. She might be dead or just running away, but wherever she was he knew that somehow and in some way he would have her back.

One night he came home, bringing his own darkness with him, and collapsed upon a chair, and before he knew it he found himself speaking to Sweet William in the totally black room.

"William, it's all over and done. I can't keep it up!"

And William cried, "Coward! Coward!" from the air above his head, out of the emptiness. "You can get her back if you want!"

Sweet William squeaked and clappered at him in the night. "Yes, you can! *Think!*" he insisted. "Think of a way. You can do it. Put me aside, lock me up. Start all over."

"Start all over?"

"Yes," whispered Sweet William, and darkness moved within darkness. "Yes. Buy wood. Buy fine new wood. Buy hard-grained wood. Buy beautiful fresh new wood. And carve. Carve slowly and carve carefully. Whittle away. Cut delicately. Make the little nostrils so. And cut her thin black eyebrows round and high, so, and make her cheeks in small hollows. Carve, carve . . ."

"No! It's foolish. I could never do it!"

"Yes, you could. Yes you could, could, could, could . . ."

The voice faded, a ripple of water in an underground stream. The stream rose up and swallowed him. His head fell forward. Sweet William sighed. And then the two of them lay like stones buried under a waterfall.

The next morning, John Fabian bought the hardest, finest-grained piece of wood that he could find and brought it home and laid it on the table, but could not touch it. He sat for hours staring at it. It was impossible to think that out of this cold chunk of material he expected his hands and his memory to re-create something warm and pliable and familiar. There was no way even faintly to approximate that quality of rain and summer and the first powderings of snow upon a clear pane of glass in the middle of a December night. No way, no way at all to catch the snowflake without having it melt swiftly in your clumsy fingers.

And yet Sweet William spoke out, sighing and whispering, after midnight, "You can do it. Oh, yes, yes, you can do it!"

And so he began. It took him an entire month to carve her hands into things as natural and beautiful as shells lying in the sun. Another month, and the skeleton, like a fossil imprint he was searching out, stamped and hidden in the wood, was revealed, all febrile and so infinitely delicate as to suggest the veins in the white flesh of an apple.

And all the while Sweet William lay mantled in dust in his box that was fast becoming a very real coffin. Sweet William croaking and wheezing some feeble sarcasm, some sour criticism, some hint, some help, but dying all the time, fading, soon to be untouched, soon to be like a sheath molted in summer and left behind to blow in the wind.

As the weeks passed and Fabian molded and scraped and polished the new wood, Sweet William lay longer and longer in stricken silence, and one day as Fabian held the puppet in his hand Sweet William seemed to look at him a moment with puzzled eyes and then there was a death rattle in his throat.

And Sweet William was gone.

Now as he worked, a fluttering, a faint motion of speech began far back in his throat, echoing and reechoing, speaking silently like a breeze among dry leaves. And then for the first time he held the doll in a certain way in his hands, and memory moved down his arms and into his fingers and from his fingers into the hollowed wood and the tiny hands flickered and the body became suddenly soft and pliable and her eyes opened and looked up at him.

And the small mouth opened the merest fraction of an inch and she was ready to speak and he knew all of the things that she must say to him; he knew the first and the second and the third things he would have her say. There was a whisper, a whisper, a whisper.

The tiny head turned this way gently, that way gently. The mouth half opened again and began to speak. And as it spoke he bent his head and he could feel the warm breath—of *course* it was there!—coming from her mouth; and when he listened very carefully, holding her to his head, his eyes shut, wasn't *it* there too, softly, *gently*—the beating of her heart?

Krovitch sat in a chair for a full minute after Fabian stopped talking. Finally he said, "I *see*. And your wife?"

"Alyce? She was my second assistant, of course. She worked very hard and, God help her, she loved me. It's hard now to know why I ever married her. It was unfair of me."

"What about the dead man—Ockham?"

"I never saw him before you showed me his body in the theater basement yesterday."

"Fabian," said the detective.

"It's the truth!"

"Fabian."

"The truth, the truth, damn it, I swear it's the truth!"

"The truth." There was a whisper like the sea coming in on the gray shore at early morning. The water was ebbing in a fine lace on the sand. The sky was cold and empty. There were no people on the shore. The sun was gone. And the whisper said again, "The truth."

Fabian sat up straight and took hold of his knees with his thin hands. His face was rigid. Krovitch found himself making the same motion he had made the day before—looking at the gray ceiling as if it were a November sky and a lonely bird going over and away, gray within the cold grayness.

"The truth." Fading. "The truth."

Krovitch lifted himself and moved as carefully as he could to the far side of the dressing room where the golden box lay open and inside the box the thing that whispered and talked and could laugh sometimes and could sometimes sing. He carried the golden box over and set it down in front of Fabian and waited for him to put his living hand within the gloved delicate hollowness, waited for the fine small mouth to quiver and the eyes to focus. He did not have to wait long.

"The first letter came a month ago."

"No."

"The first letter came a month ago."

"No, *no!*"

"The letter said, 'Riabouchinska, born 1914, died 1934. Born again in 1935.' Mr. Ockham was a juggler. He'd been on the same bill with John and Sweet William years before. He remembered that once there had been a woman, before there was a puppet."

"No, that's not true!"

"Yes," said the voice.

Snow was falling in silences and even deeper silences through the dressing room. Fabian's mouth trembled. He stared at the blank walls as if seeking some new door by which to escape. He half rose from his chair. "Please—"

"Ockham threatened to tell about us to everyone in the world."

Krovitch saw the doll quiver, saw the fluttering of the lips, saw Fabian's eyes widen and fix and his throat convulse and tighten as if to stop the whispering.

"I—I was in the room when Mr. Ockham came. I lay in my box and I listened and heard, and I *knew.*" The voice blurred, then recovered and went on. "Mr. Ockham threatened to tear me up, burn me into ashes if John didn't pay him a thousand dollars. Then suddenly there was a falling sound. A cry. Mr. Ockham's head must have struck the floor. I heard John cry out and I heard him swearing, I heard him sobbing. I heard a gasping and a choking sound."

"You heard nothing! You're deaf, you're blind! You're wood!" cried Fabian.

"But I *hear!*" she said, and stopped as if someone had put a hand to her mouth.

Fabian had leaped to his feet now and stood with the doll in his hand. The mouth clapped twice, three times, then finally made words. "The choking sound stopped. I heard John drag Mr. Ockham down the stairs under the theater to the old dressing rooms that haven't been used in years. Down, down, down, I heard them going away and away —down . . ."

Krovitch stepped back as if he were watching a motion picture that had suddenly grown monstrously tall. The figures terrified and frightened him, they were immense, they towered! They threatened to inundate him with size. Someone had turned up the sound so that it screamed.

He saw Fabian's teeth, a grimace, a whisper, a clenching. He saw the man's eyes squeeze shut.

Now the soft voice was so high and faint it trembled toward nothingness.

"I'm not made to live this way. This way. There's nothing for us now. Everyone will know, everyone will. Even when you killed him and I lay asleep last night, I dreamed. I knew, I realized. We both knew, we both realized that these would be our last days, our last hours. Because while I've lived with your weakness and I've lived with your lies, I can't live with something that kills and hurts in killing. There's no way to go on from here. How *can* I live alongside such knowledge? . . ."

Fabian held her into the sunlight which shone dimly through the small dressing room window. She looked at him and there was nothing in her eyes. His hand shook and, in shaking, made the marionette tremble, too. Her mouth closed and opened, closed and opened, closed and opened, again and again and again. Silence.

Fabian moved his fingers unbelievingly to his own mouth. A film slid across his eyes. He looked like a man lost in the street, trying to remember the number of a certain house, trying to find a certain window with a certain light. He swayed about, staring at the walls, at Krovitch, at the doll, at his free hand, turning the fingers over, touching his throat, opening his mouth. He listened.

Miles away in a cave, a single wave came in from the sea and whispered down in foam. A gull moved soundlessly, not beating its wings— a shadow.

"She's gone. She's gone. I can't find her. She's run off. I can't find her. I can't find her. I try, I try, but she's run away off far. Will you help me? Will you help me find her? Will you help me find her? Will you please help me find her?"

Riabouchinska slipped bonelessly from his limp hand, folded over and glided noiselessly down to lie upon the cold floor, her eyes closed, her mouth shut.

Fabian did not look at her as Krovitch led him out the door.

The talented STEPHEN KING *(1947–) is a publishing genre in himself. Virtually every one of his many books reaches number one on the bestseller lists, and his works are collected avidly by millions of readers. No recent writer has had as many of his novels and stories filmed as has Mr. King, whose career took off with the publication of* Carrie *and continued with such superior works of horror and suspense as* The Shining, Firestarter, Cujo, Salem's Lot, Misery, *and his latest, the science fiction thriller* The Tommyknockers. *A born storyteller, he richly deserves his success, which he has shared with his fellow writers by expanding the market for modern horror.*

"Quitters, Inc." is one of Mr. King's very rare forays outside the supernatural. A superior mystery, "The Doctor's Case," appeared in The New Adventures of Sherlock Holmes *in 1987. The present story is one of the most suspenseful you will ever read, and contains an unforgettably chilling ending.*

Quitters, Inc.
BY STEPHEN KING

Morrison was waiting for someone who was hung up in the air traffic jam over Kennedy International when he saw a familiar face at the end of the bar and walked down.

"Jimmy? Jimmy McCann?"

It was. A little heavier than when Morrison had seen him at the Atlanta Exhibition the year before, but otherwise he looked awesomely fit. In college he had been a thin, pallid chain smoker buried behind huge horn-rimmed glasses. He had apparently switched to contact lenses.

"Dick Morrison?"

"Yeah. You look great." He extended his hand and they shook.

"So do you," McCann said, but Morrison knew it was a lie. He had been overworking, overeating, and smoking too much. "What are you drinking?"

"Bourbon and bitters," Morrison said. He hooked his feet around a bar stool and lighted a cigarette. "Meeting someone, Jimmy?"

"No. Going to Miami for a conference. A heavy client. Bills six million. I'm supposed to hold his hand because we lost out on a big special next spring."

"Are you still with Crager and Barton?"

"Executive veep now."

"Fantastic! Congratulations! When did all this happen?" He tried to tell himself that the little worm of jealousy in his stomach was just acid indigestion. He pulled out a roll of antacid pills and crunched one in his mouth.

"Last August. Something happened that changed my life." He looked speculatively at Morrison and sipped his drink. "You might be interested."

My God, Morrison thought with an inner wince. Jimmy McCann's got religion.

"Sure," he said, and gulped at his drink when it came.

"I wasn't in very good shape," McCann said. "Personal problems with Sharon, my dad died—heart attack—and I'd developed this hacking cough. Bobby Crager dropped by my office one day and gave me a fatherly little pep talk. Do you remember what those are like?"

"Yeah." He had worked at Crager and Barton for eighteen months before joining the Morton Agency. "Get your butt in gear or get your butt out."

McCann laughed. "You know it. Well, to put the capper on it, the doc told me I had an incipient ulcer. He told me to quit smoking." McCann grimaced. "Might as well tell me to quit breathing."

Morrison nodded in perfect understanding. Nonsmokers could afford to be smug. He looked at his own cigarette with distaste and stubbed it out, knowing he would be lighting another in five minutes.

"Did you quit?" he asked.

"Yes, I did. At first I didn't think I'd be able to—I was cheating like hell. Then I met a guy who told me about an outfit over on Forty-sixth Street. Specialists. I said what do I have to lose and went over. I haven't smoked since."

Morrison's eyes widened. "What did they do? Fill you full of some drug?"

"No." He had taken out his wallet and was rummaging through it. "Here it is. I knew I had one kicking around." He laid a plain white business card on the bar between them.

QUITTERS, INC.
Stop Going Up in Smoke!
237 East 46th Street
Treatments by Appointment

"Keep it, if you want," McCann said. "They'll cure you. Guaranteed."

"How?"

"I can't tell you," McCann said.

"Huh? Why not?"

"It's part of the contract they make you sign. Anyway, they tell you how it works when they interview you."

"You signed a *contract?*"

McCann nodded.

"And on the basis of that—"

"Yep." He smiled at Morrison, who thought: Well, it's happened. Jim McCann has joined the smug bastards.

"Why the great secrecy if this outfit is so fantastic? How come I've never seen any spots on TV, billboards, magazine ads—"

"They get all the clients they can handle by word of mouth."

"You're an advertising man, Jimmy. You can't believe that."

"I do," McCann said. "They have a ninety-eight percent cure rate."

"Wait a second," Morrison said. He motioned for another drink and lit a cigarette. "Do these guys strap you down and make you smoke until you throw up?"

"No."

"Give you something so that you get sick every time you light—"

"No, it's nothing like that. Go and see for yourself." He gestured at Morrison's cigarette. "You don't really like that, do you?"

"Nooo, but—"

"Stopping really changed things for me," McCann said. "I don't suppose it's the same for everyone, but with me it was just like dominoes falling over. I felt better and my relationship with Sharon improved. I had more energy, and my job performance picked up."

"Look, you've got my curiosity aroused. Can't you just—"

"I'm sorry, Dick. I really can't talk about it." His voice was firm.

"Did you put on any weight?"

For a moment he thought Jimmy McCann looked almost grim. "Yes. A little too much, in fact. But I took it off again. I'm about right now. I was skinny before."

"Flight 206 now boarding at Gate 9," the loudspeaker announced.

"That's me," McCann said, getting up. He tossed a five on the bar. "Have another, if you like. And think about what I said, Dick. Really." And then he was gone, making his way through the crowd to the escalators. Morrison picked up the card, looked at it thoughtfully, then tucked it away in his wallet and forgot it.

The card fell out of his wallet and onto another bar a month later. He had left the office early and had come here to drink the afternoon away. Things had not been going so well at the Morton Agency. In fact, things were bloody horrible.

He gave Henry a ten to pay for his drink, then picked up the small card and reread it—237 East Forty-sixth Street was only two blocks over; it was a cool, sunny October day outside, and maybe, just for chuckles—

When Henry brought his change, he finished his drink and then went for a walk.

Quitters, Inc., was in a new building where the monthly rent on the office space was probably close to Morrison's yearly salary. From the directory in the lobby, it looked to him like their offices took up one whole floor, and that spelled money. Lots of it.

He took the elevator up and stepped off into a lushly carpeted foyer and from there into a gracefully appointed reception room with a wide window that looked out on the scurrying bugs below. Three men and one woman sat in the chairs along the walls, reading magazines. Business types, all of them. Morrison went to the desk.

"A friend gave me this," he said, passing the card to the receptionist. "I guess you'd say he's an alumnus."

She smiled and rolled a form into her typewriter. "What is your name, sir?"

"Richard Morrison."

Clack-clackety-clack. But very muted clacks; the typewriter was an IBM.

"Your address?"

"Twenty-nine Maple Lane, Clinton, New York."

"Married?"

"Yes."

"Children?"

"One." He thought of Alvin and frowned slightly. "One" was the wrong word. "A half" might be better. His son was mentally retarded and lived at a special school in New Jersey.

"Who recommended us to you, Mr. Morrison?"

"An old school friend. James McCann."

"Very good. Will you have a seat? It's been a very busy day."

"All right."

He sat between the woman, who was wearing a severe blue suit, and a young executive type wearing a herringbone jacket and modish sideburns. He took out his pack of cigarettes, looked around, and saw there were no ashtrays.

He put the pack away again. That was all right. He would see this little game through and then light up while he was leaving. He might even tap some ashes on their maroon shag rug if they made him wait long enough. He picked up a copy of *Time* and began to leaf through it.

He was called a quarter of an hour later, after the woman in the blue suit. His nicotine center was speaking quite loudly now. A man who had come in after him took out a cigarette case, snapped it open, saw there were no ashtrays, and put it away—looking a little guilty, Morrison thought. It made him feel better.

At last the receptionist gave him a sunny smile and said, "Go right in, Mr. Morrison."

Morrison walked through the door beyond her desk and found himself in a indirectly lit hallway. A heavyset man with white hair that looked phony shook his hand, smiled affably, and said, "Follow me, Mr. Morrison."

He led Morrison past a number of closed, unmarked doors and then opened one of them about halfway down the hall with a key. Beyond the door was an austere little room walled with drilled white cork panels. The only furnishings were a desk with a chair on either side. There was what appeared to be a small oblong window in the wall behind the desk, but it was covered with a short green curtain. There was a picture on the wall to Morrison's left—a tall man with iron-gray hair. He was holding a sheet of paper in one hand. He looked vaguely familiar.

"I'm Vic Donatti," the heavyset man said. "If you decide to go ahead with our program, I'll be in charge of your case."

"Pleased to know you," Morrison said. He wanted a cigarette very badly.

"Have a seat."

Donatti put the receptionist's form on the desk, and then drew another form from the desk drawer. He looked directly into Morrison's eyes. "Do you want to quit smoking?"

Morrison cleared his throat, crossed his legs, and tried to think of a way to equivocate. He couldn't. "Yes," he said.

"Will you sign this?" He gave Morrison the form. He scanned it quickly. The undersigned agrees not to divulge the methods or techniques or et cetera, et cetera.

"Sure," he said, and Donatti put a pen in his hand. He scratched his name, and Donatti signed below it. A moment later the paper disappeared back into the desk drawer. Well, he thought ironically, I've taken the pledge. He had taken it before. Once it had lasted for two whole days.

"Good," Donatti said. "We don't bother with propaganda here, Mr. Morrison. Questions of health or expense or social grace. We have no interest in why you want to stop smoking. We are pragmatists."

"Good," Morrison said blankly.

"We employ no drugs. We employ no Dale Carnegie people to sermonize you. We recommend no special diet. And we accept no payment until you have stopped smoking for one year."

"My God," Morrison said.

"Mr. McCann didn't tell you that?"

"No."

"How is Mr. McCann, by the way? Is he well?"

"He's fine."

"Wonderful. Excellent. Now . . . just a few questions, Mr. Morrison. These are somewhat personal, but I assure you that your answers will be held in strictest confidence."

"Yes?" Morrison asked noncommittally.

"What is your wife's name?"

"Lucinda Morrison. Her maiden name was Ramsey."

"Do you love her?"

Morrison looked up sharply, but Donatti was looking at him blandly. "Yes, of course," he said.

"Have you ever had marital problems? A separation, perhaps?"

"What has that go to do with kicking the habit?" Morrison asked. He sounded a little angrier than he had intended, but he wanted—hell, he *needed*—a cigarette.

"A great deal," Donatti said. "Just bear with me."

"No. Nothing like that." Although things *had* been a little tense just lately.

"You just have the one child?"

"Yes. Alvin. He's in a private school."

"And which school is it?"

"That," Morrison said grimly, "I'm not going to tell you."

"All right," Donatti said agreeably. He smiled disarmingly at Morrison. "All your questions will be answered tomorrow at your first treatment."

"How nice," Morrison said, and stood.

"One final question," Donatti said. "You haven't had a cigarette for over an hour. How do you feel?"

"Fine," Morrison lied. "Just fine."

"Good for you!" Donatti exclaimed. He stepped around the desk and opened the door. "Enjoy them tonight. After tomorrow, you'll never smoke again."

"Is that right?"

"Mr. Morrison," Donatti said solemnly, "we guarantee it."

He was sitting in the outer office of Quitters, Inc., the next day promptly at three. He had spent most of the day swinging between skipping the appointment the receptionist had made for him on the way out and going in a spirit of mulish cooperation—*Throw your best pitch at me, buster.*

In the end, something Jimmy McCann had said convinced him to keep the appointment—*It changed my whole life.* God knew his own life could do with some changing. And then there was his own curiosity. Before going up in the elevator, he smoked a cigarette down to the filter. Too damn bad if it's the last one, he thought. It tasted horrible.

The wait in the outer office was shorter this time. When the receptionist told him to go in, Donatti was waiting. He offered his hand and smiled, and to Morrison the smile looked almost predatory. He began to feel a little tense, and that made him want a cigarette.

"Come with me," Donatti said, and led the way down to the small room. He sat behind the desk again, and Morrison took the other chair.

"I'm very glad you came," Donatti said. "A great many prospective clients never show up again after the initial interview. They discover they don't want to quit as badly as they thought. It's going to be a pleasure to work with you on this."

"When does the treatment start?" Hypnosis, he was thinking. It must be hypnosis.

"Oh, it already has. It started when we shook hands in the hall. Do you have cigarettes with you, Mr. Morrison?"

"Yes."

"May I have them, please?"

Shrugging, Morrison handed Donatti his pack. There were only two or three left in it, anyway.

Donatti put the pack on the desk. Then, smiling into Morrison's eyes, he curled his right hand into a fist and began to hammer it down on the pack of cigarettes, which twisted and flattened. A broken cigarette end flew out. Tobacco crumbs spilled. The sound of Donatti's fist was very loud in the closed room. The smile remained on his face in spite of the force of the blows, and Morrison was chilled by it. Probably just the effect they want to inspire, he thought.

At last Donatti ceased pounding. He picked up the pack, a twisted and battered ruin. "You wouldn't believe the pleasure that gives me," he said, and dropped the pack into the wastebasket. "Even after three years in the business, it still pleases me."

"As a treatment, it leaves something to be desired," Morrison said mildly. "There's a newsstand in the lobby of this very building. And they sell all brands."

"As you say," Donatti said. He folded his hands. "Your son, Alvin Dawes Morrison, is in the Paterson School for Handicapped Children. Born with cranial brain damage. Tested IQ of 46. Not quite in the educable retarded category. Your wife—"

"How did you find that out?" Morrison barked. He was startled and angry. "You've got no goddamn right to go poking around my—"

"We know a lot about you," Donatti said smoothly. "But, as I said, it will all be held in strictest confidence."

"I'm getting out of here," Morrison said thinly. He stood up.

"Stay a bit longer."

Morrison looked at him closely. Donatti wasn't upset. In fact, he looked a little amused. The face of a man who has seen this reaction scores of times—maybe hundreds.

"All right. But it better be good."

"Oh, it is." Donatti leaned back. "I told you we were pragmatists here. As pragmatists, we have to start by realizing how difficult it is to cure an addiction to tobacco. The relapse rate is almost eighty-five percent. The relapse rate for heroin addicts is lower than that. It is an extraordinary problem. *Extraordinary.*"

Morrison glanced into the wastebasket. One of the cigarettes, although twisted, still looked smokeable. Donatti laughed goodnaturedly, reached into the wastebasket, and broke it between his fingers.

"State legislatures sometimes hear a request that the prison systems do away with the weekly cigarette ration. Such proposals are invariably defeated. In a few cases where they have passed, there have been fierce prison riots. *Riots,* Mr. Morrison. Imagine it."

"I," Morrison said, "am not surprised."

"But consider the implications. When you put a man in prison you take away any normal sex life, you take away his liquor, his politics, his freedom of movement. No riots—or few in comparison to the number of prisons. But when you take away his *cigarettes*—wham! bam!" He slammed his fist on the desk for emphasis.

"During World War I, when no one on the German home front could get cigarettes, the sight of German aristocrats picking butts out of the gutter was a common one. During World War II, many American women turned to pipes when they were unable to obtain cigarettes. A fascinating problem for the true pragmatist, Mr. Morrison."

"Could we get to the treatment?"

"Momentarily. Step over here, please." Donatti had risen and was standing by the green curtains Morrison had noticed yesterday. Donatti drew the curtains, discovering a rectangular window that looked into a bare room. No, not quite bare. There was a rabbit on the floor, eating pellets out of a dish.

"Pretty bunny," Morrison commented.

"Indeed. Watch him." Donatti pressed a button by the windowsill. The rabbit stopped eating and began to hop about crazily. It seemed to leap higher each time its feet struck the floor. Its fur stood out spikily in all directions. Its eyes were wild.

"Stop that! You're electrocuting him!"

Donatti released the button. "Far from it. There's a very low-yield charge in the floor. Watch the rabbit, Mr. Morrison!"

The rabbit was crouched about ten feet away from the dish of pellets. His nose wriggled. All at once he hopped away into a corner.

"If the rabbit gets a jolt often enough while he's eating," Donatti said, "he makes the association very quickly. Eating causes pain. Therefore, he won't eat. A few more shocks, and the rabbit will starve to death in front of his food. It's called aversion training."

Light dawned in Morrison's head.

"No, thanks." He started for the door.

"Wait, please, Mr. Morrison."

Morrison didn't pause. He grasped the doorknob . . . and felt it slip solidly through his hand. "Unlock this."

"Mr. Morrison, if you'll just sit down—"

"Unlock this door or I'll have the cops on you before you can say Marlboro Man."

"Sit down." The voice was cold as shaved ice.

Morrison looked at Donatti. His brown eyes were muddy and frightening. My God, he thought, I'm locked in here with a psycho. He licked his lips. He wanted a cigarette more than he ever had in his life.

"Let me explain the treatment in more detail," Donatti said.

"You don't understand," Morrison said with counterfeit patience. "I don't want the treatment. I've decided against it."

"No, Mr. Morrison. *You're* the one who doesn't understand. You don't have any choice. When I told you the treatment had already begun, I was speaking the literal truth. I would have thought you'd tipped to that by now."

"You're crazy," Morrison said wonderingly.

"No. Only a pragmatist. Let me tell you all about the treatment."

"Sure," Morrison said. "As long as you understand that as soon as I get out of here I'm going to buy five packs of cigarettes and smoke them all on the way to the police station." He suddenly realized he was biting his thumbnail, sucking on it, and made himself stop.

"As you wish. But I think you'll change your mind when you see the whole picture."

Morrison said nothing. He sat down again and folded his hands.

"For the first month of the treatment, our operatives will have you under constant supervision," Donatti said. "You'll be able to spot some of them. Not all. But they'll always be with you. *Always.* If they see you smoke a cigarette, I get a call."

"And I suppose you bring me here and do the old rabbit trick," Morrison said. He tried to sound cold and sarcastic, but he suddenly felt horribly frightened. This was a nightmare.

"Oh, no," Donatti said. "Your wife gets the rabbit trick, not you."

Morrison looked at him dumbly.

Donatti smiled. "You," he said, "get to watch."

After Donatti let him out, Morrison walked for over two hours in a complete daze. It was another fine day, but he didn't notice. The monstrousness of Donatti's smiling face blotted out all else.

"You see," he had said, "a pragmatic problem demands pragmatic solutions. You must realize we have your best interests at heart."

Quitters, Inc., according to Donatti, was a sort of foundation—a nonprofit organization begun by the man in the wall portrait. The gentleman had been extremely successful in several family businesses —including slot machines, massage parlors, numbers, and a brisk (although clandestine) trade between New York and Turkey. Mort "Three-Fingers" Minelli had been a heavy smoker—up in the three-pack-a-day range. The paper he was holding in the picture was a doctor's diagnosis: lung cancer. Mort had died in 1970, after endowing Quitters, Inc., with family funds.

"We try to keep as close to breaking even as possible," Donatti had said. "But we're more interested in helping our fellow man. And of course, it's a great tax angle."

The treatment was chillingly simple. A first offense and Cindy would be brought to what Donatti called "the rabbit room." A second offense, and Morrison would get the dose. On a third offense, both of them would be brought in together. A fourth offense would show grave cooperation problems and would require sterner measures. An operative would be sent to Alvin's school to work the boy over.

"Imagine," Donatti said, smiling, "how horrible it will be for the boy. He wouldn't understand it even if someone explained. He'll only know someone is hurting him because Daddy was bad. He'll be very frightened."

"You bastard," Morrison said helplessly. He felt close to tears. "You dirty, filthy bastard."

"Don't misunderstand," Donatti said. He was smiling sympathetically. "I'm sure it won't happen. Forty percent of our clients never have to be disciplined at all—and only ten percent have more than three falls from grace. Those are reasuring figures, aren't they?"

Morrison didn't find them reassuring. He found them terrifying.

"Of course, if you transgress a *fifth* time—"

"What do you mean?"

Donatti beamed. "The room for you and your wife, a second beating for your son, and a beating for your wife."

Morrison, driven beyond the point of rational consideration, lunged over the desk at Donatti. Donatti moved with amazing speed for a man who had apparently been completely relaxcd. He shoved the chair backward and drove both of his feet over the desk and into Morrison's belly. Gagging and coughing, Morrison staggered backward.

"Sit down, Mr. Morrison," Donatti said benignly. "Let's talk this over like rational men."

When he could get his breath, Morrison did as he was told. Nightmares had to end sometime, didn't they?

Quitters, Inc., Donatti had explained further, operated on a ten-step punishment scale. Steps six, seven, and eight consisted of further trips to the rabbit room (and increased voltage) and more serious beatings. The ninth step would be the breaking of his son's arms.

"And the tenth?" Morrison asked, his mouth dry.

Donatti shook his head sadly. "Then we give up, Mr. Morrison. You become part of the unregenerate two percent."

"You really give up?"

"In a manner of speaking." He opened one of the desk drawers and laid a silenced .45 on the desk. He smiled into Morrison's eyes. "But even the unregenerate two percent never smoke again. We guarantee it."

The Friday Night Movie was *Bullitt,* one of Cindy's favorites, but after an hour of Morrison's mutterings and fidgetings, her concentration was broken.

"What's the matter with you?" she asked during station identification.

"Nothing . . . everything," he growled. "I'm giving up smoking."

She laughed. "Since when? Five minutes ago?"

"Since three o'clock this afternoon."

"You really haven't had a cigarette since then?"

"No," he said, and began to gnaw his thumbnail. It was ragged, down to the quick.

"That's wonderful! What ever made you decide to quit?"

"You," he said. "And . . . and Alvin."

Her eyes widened, and when the movie came back on, she didn't notice. Dick rarely mentioned their retarded son. She came over, looked at the empty ashtray by his right hand, and then into his eyes. "Are you really trying to quit, Dick?"

"Really." And if I go to the cops, he added mentally, the local goon squad will be around to rearrange your face, Cindy.

"I'm glad. Even if you don't make it, we both thank you for the thought, Dick."

"Oh, I think I'll make it," he said, thinking of the muddy, homicidal look that had come into Donatti's eyes when he kicked him in the stomach.

He slept badly that night, dozing in and out of sleep. Around three o'clock he woke up completely. His craving for a cigarette was like a low-grade fever. He went downstairs and to his study. The room was in the middle of the house. No windows. He slid open the top drawer of his desk and looked in, fascinated by the cigarette box. He looked around and licked his lips.

Constant supervision during the first month, Donatti had said. Eighteen hours a day during the next two—but he would never know *which* eighteen. During the fourth month, the month when most clients backslid, the "service" would return to twenty-four hours a day. Then twelve hours of broken surveillance each day for the rest of the year. After that? Random surveillance for the rest of the client's life.

For the rest of his life.

"We may audit you every other month," Donatti said. "Or every other day. Or constantly for one week two years from now. The point is, *you won't know.* If you smoke, you'll be gambling with loaded dice. Are they watching? Are they picking up my wife or sending a man after my son right now? Beautiful, isn't it? And if you do sneak a smoke, it'll taste awful. It will taste like your son's blood."

But they couldn't be watching now, in the dead of night, in his own study. The house was grave-quiet.

He looked at the cigarettes in the box for almost two minutes, unable to tear his gaze away. Then he went to the study door, peered out into the empty hall, and went back to look at the cigarettes some more. A horrible picture came: his life stretching before him and not a cigarette to be found. How in the name of God was he ever going to be able to make another tough presentation to a wary client, without that cigarette burning nonchalantly between his fingers as he approached the charts and layouts? How would he be able to endure Cindy's endless garden shows without a cigarette? How could he even get up in the morning and face the day without a cigarette to smoke as he drank his coffee and read the paper?

He cursed himself for getting into this. He cursed Donatti. And most of all, he cursed Jimmy McCann. How could he have done it? The son of a bitch had *known.* His hands trembled in their desire to get hold of Jimmy Judas McCann.

Stealthily, he glanced around the study again. He reached into the drawer and brought out a cigarette. He caressed it, fondled it. What was that old slogan? *So round, so firm, so fully packed.* Truer words had never been spoken. He put the cigarette in his mouth and then paused, cocking his head.

Had there been the slightest noise from the closet? A faint shifting? Surely not. But—

Another mental image—that rabbit hopping crazily in the grip of electricity. The thought of Cindy in that room—

He listened desperately and heard nothing. He told himself that all he had to do was to go to the closet door and yank it open. But he was too afraid of what he might find. He went back to bed but didn't sleep for a long time.

In spite of how lousy he felt in the morning, breakfast tasted good. After a moment's hesitation, he followed his customary bowl of corn-flakes with scrambled eggs. He was grumpily washing out the pan when Cindy came downstairs in her robe.

"Richard Morrison! You haven't eaten an egg for breakfast since Hector was a pup."

Morrison grunted. he considered *since Hector was a pup* to be one of Cindy's stupider sayings, on a par with *I should smile and kiss a pig.*

"Have you smoked yet?" she asked, pouring orange juice.

"No."

"You'll be back on them by noon," she proclaimed airily.

"Lot of goddamn help you are!" he rasped, rounding on her. "You and anyone else who doesn't smoke, you all think . . . ah, never mind."

He expected her to be angry, but she was looking at him with something like wonder. "You're really serious," she said. "You really are."

"You bet I am." *You'll never know how serious. I hope.*

"Poor baby," she said, going to him. "You look like death warmed over. But I'm very proud."

Morrison held her tightly.

Scenes from the life of Richard Morrison, October-November:

Morrison and a crony from Larkin Studios at Jack Dempsey's bar. Crony offers a cigarette. Morrison grips his glass a little more tightly and says: *I'm quitting.* Crony laughs and says: *I give you a week.*

Morrison waiting for the morning train, looking over the top of the *Times* at a young man in a blue suit. He sees the young man almost every morning now, and sometimes at other places. At Onde's, where he is meeting a client. Looking at 45s in Sam Goody's, where Morrison is looking for a Sam Cooke album. Once in a foursome behind Morrison's group at the local golf course.

Morrison getting drunk at a party, wanting a cigarette—but not quite drunk enough to take one.

Morrison visiting his son, bringing him a large ball that squeaked when you squeezed it. His son's slobbering, delighted kiss. Somehow not as repulsive as before. Hugging his son tightly, realizing what Donatti and his colleagues had so cynically realized before him: love is the most pernicious drug of all. Let the romantics debate its existence. Pragmatists accept it and use it.

Morrison losing the physical compulsion to smoke little by little, but never quite losing the psychological craving, or the need to have something in his mouth—cough drops, Life Savers, a toothpick. Poor substitutes, all of them.

And finally, Morrison hung up in a colossal traffic jam in the Midtown Tunnel. Darkness. Horns blaring. Air stinking. Traffic hopelessly snarled. And suddenly, thumbing open the glove compartment and seeing the half-open pack of cigarettes in there. He looked at them for a moment, then snatched one and lit it with the dashboard lighter. If anything happens, it's Cindy's fault, he told himself defiantly. I told her to get rid of all the damn cigarettes.

The first drag made him cough smoke out furiously. The second made his eyes water. The third made him feel light-headed and swoony. It tastes awful, he thought.

And on the heels of that: My God, what am I doing?

Horns blatted impatiently behind him. Ahead, the traffic had begun to move again. He stubbed the cigarette out in the ashtray, opened both front windows, opened the vents, and then fanned the air helplessly like a kid who has just flushed his first butt down the john.

He joined the traffic flow jerkily and drove home.

"Cindy?" he called. "I'm home."

No answer.

"Cindy? Where are you, hon?"

The phone rang, and he pounced on it. "Hello? Cindy?"

"Hello, Mr. Morrison," Donatti said. He sounded pleasantly brisk and businesslike. "It seems we have a small business matter to attend to. Would five o'clock be convenient?"

"Have you got my wife?"

"Yes, indeed," Donatti chuckled indulgently.

"Look, let her go," Morrison babbled. "It won't happen again. It was a slip, just a slip, that's all. I only had three drags and for God's sake *it didn't even taste good!*"

"That's a shame. I'll count on you for five then, shall I?"

"Please," Morrison said, close to tears. "Please—"

He was speaking to a dead line.

At 5 P.M. the reception room was empty except for the secretary, who gave him a twinkly smile that ignored Morrison's pallor and disheveled appearance. "Mr. Donatti?" she said into the intercom. "Mr. Morrison to see you." She nodded to Morrison. "Go right in."

Donatti was waiting outside the unmarked room with a man who was wearing a SMILE sweatshirt and carrying a .38. He was built like an ape.

"Listen," Morrison said to Donatti. "We can work something out, can't we? I'll pay you. I'll—"

"Shaddap," the man in the SMILE sweatshirt said.

"It's good to see you," Donatti said. "Sorry it has to be under such adverse circumstances. Will you come with me? We'll make this as brief as possible. I can assure you your wife won't be hurt . . . this time."

Morrison tensed himself to leap at Donatti.

"Come, come," Donatti said, looking annoyed. "If you do that, Junk here is going to pistol-whip you and your wife is still going to get it. Now where's the percentage in that?"

"I hope you rot in hell," he told Donatti.

Donatti sighed. "If I had a nickel for every time someone expressed a similar sentiment, I could retire. Let it be a lesson to you, Mr. Morrison. When a romantic tries to do a good thing and fails, they give him a medal. When a pragmatist succeeds, they wish him in hell. Shall we go?"

Junk motioned with the pistol.

Morrison preceded them into the room. He felt numb. The small green curtain had been pulled. Junk prodded him with the gun. This is what being a witness at the gas chamber must have been like, he thought.

He looked in. Cindy was there, looking around bewilderedly.

"Cindy!" Morrison called miserably. "Cindy, they—"

"She can't hear or see you," Donatti said. "One-way glass. Well, let's get it over with. It really was a very small slip. I believe thirty seconds should be enough. Junk?"

Junk pressed the button with one hand and kept the pistol jammed firmly into Morrison's back with the other.

It was the longest thirty seconds of his life.

When it was over, Donatti put a hand on Morrison's shoulder and said, "Are you going to throw up?"

"No," Morrison said weakly. His forehead was against the glass. His legs were jelly. "I don't think so." He turned around and saw that Junk was gone.

"Come with me," Donatti said.

"Where?" Morrison asked apathetically.

"I think you have a few things to explain, don't you?"

"How can I face her? How can I tell her that I . . . I . . . ."

"I think you're going to be surprised," Donatti said.

The room was empty except for a sofa. Cindy was on it, sobbing helplessly.

"Cindy?" he said gently.

She looked up, her eyes magnified by tears. "Dick?" she whispered. "Dick? Oh . . . Oh God . . ." He held her tightly. "Two men," she said against his chest. "In the house and at first I thought they were burglars and then I thought they were going to rape me and then they took me someplace with a blindfold over my eyes and . . . and . . . oh it was *h-horrible—*"

"Shhh," he said. "Shhh."

"But why?" she asked, looking up at him. "Why would they—"

"Because of me," he said. "I have to tell you a story, Cindy—"

When he had finished he was silent a moment and then said, "I suppose you hate me. I wouldn't blame you."

He was looking at the floor, and she took his face in both hands and turned it to hers. "No," she said. "I don't hate you."

He looked at her in mute surprise.

"It was worth it," she said. "God bless these people. They've let you out of prison."

"Do you mean that?"

"Yes," she said, and kissed him. "Can we go home now? I feel much better. Ever so much."

The phone rang one evening a week later, and when Morrison recognized Donatti's voice, he said, "Your boys have got it wrong. I haven't even been near a cigarette."

"We know that. We have a final matter to talk over. Can you stop by tomorrow afternoon?"

"Is it—"

"No, nothing serious. Bookkeeping really. By the way, congratulations on your promotion."

"How did you know about that?"

"We're keeping tabs," Donatti said noncommittally, and hung up.

When they entered the small room, Donatti said, "Don't look so nervous. No one's going to bite you. Step over here, please."

Morrison saw an ordinary bathroom scale. "Listen, I've gained a little weight, but—"

"Yes, seventy-three percent of our clients do. Step up, please."

Morrison did, and tipped the scales at one-seventy-four.

"Okay, fine. You can step off. How tall are you, Mr. Morrison?"

"Five-eleven."

"Okay, let's see." He pulled a small card laminated in plastic from his breast pocket. "Well, that's not too bad. I'm going to write you a prescrip for some highly illegal diet pills. Use them sparingly and according to directions. And I'm going to set your maximum weight at . . . let's see . . ." He consulted the card again. "One eighty-two, how does that sound? And since this is December first, I'll expect you the first of every month for a weigh-in. No problem if you can't make it, as long as you call in advance."

"And what happens if I go over one-eighty-two?"

Donatti smiled. "We'll send someone out to your house to cut off your wife's little finger," he said. "You can leave through this door, Mr. Morrison. Have a nice day."

Eight months later:

Morrison runs into the crony from the Larkin Studios at Dempsey's bar. Morrison is down to what Cindy proudly calls his fighting weight: one-sixty-seven. He works out three times a week and looks as fit as whipcord. The crony from Larkin, by comparison, looks like something the cat dragged in.

Crony: Lord, how'd you ever stop? I'm locked into this damn habit tighter than Tillie. The crony stubs his cigarette out with real revulsion and drains his scotch.

Morrison looks at him speculatively and then takes a small white business card out of his wallet. He puts it on the bar between them. You know, he says, these guys changed my life.

Twelve months later:
Morrison receives a bill in the mail. The bill says:

QUITTERS, INC.

237 East 46th Street
New York, N.Y. 10017

1 Treatment	$2500.00
Counselor (Victor Donatti)	$2500.00
Electricity	$ .50
TOTAL (Please pay this amount)	$5000.50

Those sons of bitches! he explodes. They charged me for the electricity they used to . . . to . . .

Just pay it, she says, and kisses him.

Twenty months later:
Quite by accident, Morrison and his wife meet the Jimmy McCanns at the Helen Hayes Theatre. Introductions are made all around. Jimmy looks as good, if not better, than he did on that day in the airport terminal so long ago. Morrison has never met his wife. She is pretty in the radiant way plain girls sometimes have when they are very, very happy.

She offers her hand and Morrison shakes it. There is something odd about her grip, and halfway through the second act, he realizes what it was. The little finger on her right hand is missing.

A native New Yorker, STANLEY ELLIN *(1916–1986) published fourteen crime novels during his distinguished writing career, most of them characterized by cool, crisp prose and fine style. However, it is as a master of the short story that he will be remembered, even though he produced only an average of one story per year over a long career. His very first published fiction, the immortal "The Specialty of the House" (1948), is one of the most famous stories in the history of crime fiction. He won three Edgar Awards, two for short stories.*

"The Nine-to-Five Man," a deceptively simple story about a working stiff, is one of his best efforts in the genre which owes him so much.

The Nine-to-Five Man
BY STANLEY ELLIN

The alarm clock sounded, as it did every weekday morning, at exactly 7:20, and without opening his eyes Mr. Keesler reached out a hand and turned it off. His wife was already preparing breakfast—it was her modest boast that she had a built-in alarm to get her up in the morning —and a smell of frying bacon permeated the bedroom. Mr. Keesler savored it for a moment, lying there on his back with his eyes closed, and then wearily sat up and swung his feet out of bed. His eyeglasses were on the night-table next to the alarm clock. He put them on and blinked in the morning light, yawned, scratched his head with plea- sure, and fumbled for his slippers.

The pleasure turned to mild irritation. One slipper was not there. He kneeled down, swept his hand back and forth under the bed, and fi- nally found it. He stood up, puffing a little, and went into the bath- room. After lathering his face he discovered that his razor was dull, and discovered immediately afterward that he had forgotten to buy new blades the day before. By taking a few minutes more than usual he managed to get a presentable, though painful, shave out of the old blade. Then he washed, brushed his teeth carefully, and combed his hair. He liked to say that he was in pretty good shape since he still had teeth and hair enough to need brushing.

In the bedroom again, he heard Mrs. Keesler's voice rising from the foot of the stairway. "Breakfast, dear," she called. "It's on the table now."

It was not really on the table, Mr. Keesler knew; his wife would first be setting the table when he walked into the kitchen. She was like that, always using little tricks to make the house run smoothly. But no matter how you looked at it, she was a sweetheart all right. He nodded soberly at his reflection in the dresser mirror while he knotted his tie. He was a lucky man to have a wife like that. A fine wife, a fine mother —maybe a little bit too much of an easy mark for her relatives—but a real sweetheart.

The small annoyance of the relatives came up at the breakfast table.

"Joe and Betty are expecting us over tonight, dear," said Mrs. Keesler. "Betty called me about it yesterday. Is that all right with you?"

"All right," said Mr. Keesler amiably. He knew there was nothing good on television that evening anyhow.

"Then will you remember to pick up your other suit at the tailor's on the way home?"

"For Betty and Joe?" said Mr. Keesler. "What for? They're only in-laws."

"Still and all, I like you to look nice when you go over there, so please don't forget." Mrs. Keesler hesitated. "Albert's going to be there, too."

"Naturally. He lives there."

"I know, but you hardly ever get a chance to see him, and, after all, he's our nephew. He happens to be a very nice boy."

"All right, he's a very nice boy," said Mr. Keesler. "What does he want from me?"

Mrs. Keesler blushed. "Well, it so happens he's having a very hard time getting a job where—"

"No," said Mr. Keesler. "Absolutely not." He put down his knife and fork and regarded his wife sternly. "You know yourself that there's hardly enough money in the novelties line to make us a living. So for me to take in a lazy—"

"I'm sorry," said Mrs. Keesler. "I didn't mean to get you upset about it." She put a consoling hand on his. "And what kind of thing is that to say, about not making a living? Maybe we don't have as much as some others, but we do all right. A nice house and two fine sons in college—what more could we ask for? So don't talk like that. And go to work, or you'll be late."

Mr. Keesler shook his head. "What a softie," he said. "If you only wouldn't let Betty talk you into these things—"

"Now don't start with that. Just go to work."

She helped him on with his coat in the hallway. "Are you going to take the car today?" she asked.

"No."

"All right, then I can use it for the shopping. But don't forget about the suit. It's the tailor right near the subway station." Mrs. Keesler plucked a piece of lint from his coat collar. "And you make a very nice living, so stop talking like that. We do all right."

Mr. Keesler left the house by the side door. It was an unpretentious frame house in the Flatbush section of Brooklyn, and like most of the others on the block it had a small garage behind it. Mr. Keesler unlocked the door of the garage and stepped inside. The car occupied nearly all the space there, but room had also been found for a clutter of tools, metal cans, paint brushes, and a couple of old kitchen chairs which had been partly painted.

The car itself was a four-year-old Chevrolet, a little the worse for wear, and it took an effort to open the lid of its trunk. Mr. Keesler finally got it open and lifted out his big leather sample case, groaning at its weight. He did not lock the garage door when he left, since he had the only key to it, and he knew Mrs. Keesler wanted to use the car.

It was a two-block walk to the Beverly Road station of the I.R.T. subway. At a newsstand near the station Mr. Keesler bought a *New York Times,* and when the train came in he arranged himself against the door at the end of the car. There was no chance of getting a seat during the rush hour, but from long experience Mr. Keesler knew how to travel with the least inconvenience. By standing with his back braced against the door and his legs astride the sample case he was able to read his newspaper until, by the time the train reached 14th Street, the press of bodies against him made it impossible to turn the pages.

At 42nd Street he managed to push his way out of the car using the sample case as a battering ram. He crossed the platform and took a local two stations farther to Columbus Circle. When he walked up the stairs of the station he saw by his wrist watch that it was exactly five minutes to nine.

Mr. Keesler's office was in the smallest and shabbiest building on Columbus Circle. It was made to look even smaller and shabbier by the new Coliseum which loomed over it on one side and by the apartment hotels which towered over it on the other. It had one creaky elevator to service its occupants, and an old man named Eddie to operate the elevator.

When Mr. Keesler came into the building Eddie had his mail all ready for him. The mail consisted of a large bundle of letters tied with a string, and a half dozen small cardboard boxes. Mr. Keesler managed to get all this under one arm with difficulty, and Eddie said, "Well, that's a nice big load the same as ever. I hope you get some business out of it."

"I hope so," said Mr. Keesler.

Another tenant picked up his mail and stepped into the elevator behind Mr. Keesler. "Well," he said, looking at the load under Mr. Keesler's arm, "it's nice to see that somebody's making money around here."

"Sure," said Mr. Keesler. "They send you the orders all right, but when it comes to paying for them where are they?"

"That's how it goes," said Eddie.

He took the elevator up to the third floor and Mr. Keesler got out there. His office was in Room 301 at the end of the corridor, and on its door were painted the words *KEESLER NOVELTIES*. Underneath in quotation marks was the phrase *"Everything for the trade."*

The office was a room with a window that looked out over Central Park. Against one wall was a battered roll-top desk that Mr. Keesler's father had bought when he himself had started in the novelties business along ago, and before it was a large, comfortable swivel chair with a foam-rubber cushion on its seat. Against the opposite wall was a table, and on it was an old L. C. Smith typewriter, a telephone, some telephone books, and a stack of magazines. There was another stack of magazines on top of a large filing cabinet in a corner of the room. Under the window was a chaise-longue which Mr. Keesler had bought second-hand from Eddie for five dollars, and next to the roll-top desk were a wastepaper basket and a wooden coat-rack that he had bought from Eddie for fifty cents. Tenants who moved from the building sometimes found it cheaper to abandon their shopworn furnishings than to pay cartage for them, and Eddie did a small business in selling these articles for whatever he was offered.

Mr. Keesler closed the office door behind him. He gratefully set the heavy sample case down in a corner, pushed open the desk, and dropped his mail and the *New York Times* on it. Then he hung his hat and coat on the rack, checking the pockets of the coat to make sure he had forgotten nothing in them.

He sat down at the desk, opened the string around the mail, and looked at the return address on each letter. Two of the letters were from banks. He unlocked a drawer of the desk, drew out a notebook, and entered the figures into it. Then he tore the receipts into small shreds and dropped them into the wastepaper basket.

The rest of the mail was easily disposed of. Mr. Keesler took each of the smaller envelopes and, without opening it, tore it in half and tossed it into the basket on top of the shredded deposit slips. He then opened the envelopes which were thick and unwieldy, extracted their contents —brochures and catalogues—and placed them on the desk. When he was finished he had a neat pile of catalogues and brochures before him. These he dumped into a drawer of the filing cabinet.

He now turned his attention to the cardboard boxes. He opened them and pulled out various odds and ends—good-luck charms, a souvenir coin, a plastic key-ring, several packets of cancelled foreign stamps, and a small cellophane bag containing one chocolate cracker. Mr. Keesler tossed the empty boxes into the wastepaper basket, ate the cracker, and pushed the rest of the stuff to the back of the desk. The cracker was a little bit too sweet for his taste, but not bad.

In the top drawer of the desk were a pair of scissors, a box of stationery, and a box of stamps. Mr. Keesler removed these to the table and placed them next to the typewriter. He wheeled the swivel chair to the table, sat down, and opened the classified telephone directory to its listing of dentists. He ran his finger down a column of names. Then he picked up the phone and dialed a number.

"Dr. Glover's office," said a woman's voice.

"Look," said Mr. Keesler, "this is an emergency. I'm in the neighborhood here, so can I come in during the afternoon? It hurts pretty bad."

"Are you a regular patient of Dr. Glover's?"

"No, but I thought—"

"I'm sorry, but the doctor's schedule is full. If you want to call again tomorrow—"

"No, never mind," said Mr. Keesler. "I'll try someone else."

He ran his finger down the column in the directory and dialed again.

"This is Dr. Gordon's office," said a woman's voice, but much more youthful and pleasant than the one Mr. Keesler had just encountered. "Who is it, please?"

"Look," said Mr. Keesler, "I'm suffering a lot of pain, and I was wondering if the doctor couldn't give me a couple of minutes this afternoon. I'm right in the neighborhood here. I can be there any time that's convenient. Say around two o'clock?"

"Well, two o'clock is already filled, but I have a cancellation here for three. Would that be all right?"

"That would be fine. And the name is Keesler." Mr. Keesler spelled it out carefully. "Thanks a lot, miss, and I'll be there right on the dot."

He pressed the bar of the phone down, released it, and dialed again. "Is Mr. Hummel there?" he said. "Good. Tell him it's about the big delivery he was expecting this afternoon."

In a moment he heard Mr. Hummel's voice. "Yeah?"

"You know who this is?" asked Mr. Keesler.

"Sure I know who it is."

"All right," said Mr. Keesler, "then meet me at four o'clock instead of three. You understand?"

"I get it," said Mr. Hummel.

Mr. Keesler did not continue the conversation. He put down the phone, pushed aside the directory, and took a magazine from the pile on the table. The back pages of the magazine were full of advertisements for free gifts, free samples, and free catalogues. *Mail us this coupon,* most of them said, *and we will send you absolutely free—*

Mr. Keesler studied these offers, finally selected ten of them, cut out the coupons with his scissors, and addressed them on the typewriter. He typed slowly but accurately, using only two fingers. Then he addressed ten envelopes, sealed the coupons into them, and stamped them. He snapped a rubber band around the envelopes for easier mailing and put everything else in the office back into its proper place. It was now 10:25, and the only thing left to attend to was the *New York Times.*

By twelve o'clock, Mr. Keesler, stretched comfortably out on the chaise-longue, had finished reading the *Times.* He had, however, bypassed the stock market quotations as was his custom. In 1929 his father's entire capital had been wiped out overnight in the market crash, and since that day Mr. Keesler had a cold and cynical antipathy to stocks and bonds and anything connected with them. When talking to people about it he would make it a little joke. "I like to know that my money is all tied up in cash," he would say. But inwardly he had been deeply scarred by what his father had gone through after the debacle. He had been very fond of his father, a gentle and hard-working man, well-liked by all who knew him, and had never forgiven the stock market for what it had done to him.

Twelve o'clock was lunchtime for Mr. Keesler, as it was for almost everyone else in the building. Carrying his mail he walked downstairs along with many others who knew that it would take Eddie quite a while to pick them up in his overworked elevator at this hour. He dropped the letters into a mailbox on the corner, and banged the lid of the mailbox a couple of times for safety's sake.

Near 58th Street on Eight Avenue was a cafeteria which served good food at reasonable prices, and Mr. Keesler had a cheese sandwich, baked apple, and coffee there. Before he left he had a counterman wrap a cinnamon bun in waxed paper and place it in a brown paper bag for him to take along with him.

Swinging the bag in his hand as he walked, Mr. Keesler went into a drug store a block away and bought a roll of two-inch-wide surgical bandage. On his way out of the store he surreptitiously removed the bandage from its box and wrapper and dropped the box and wrapper into a litter basket on the street. The roll of bandage itself he put into the bag containing the cinnamon bun.

He repeated this process in a drug store on the next block, and then six more times in various stores on his way down Eighth Avenue. Each time he would pay the exact amount in change, drop the box and wrappings into a litter basket, put the roll of bandage into his paper bag. When he had eight rolls of bandage in the bag on top of the cinnamon bun he turned around and walked back to the office building. It was exactly one o'clock when he got there.

Eddie was waiting in the elevator, and when he saw the paper bag he smiled toothlessly and said as he always did, "What is it this time?"

"Cinnamon buns," said Mr. Keesler. "Here, have one." He pulled out the cinnamon bun wrapped in its waxed paper, and Eddie took it.

"Thanks," he said.

"That's all right," said Mr. Keesler. "There's plenty here for both of us. I shouldn't be eating so much of this stuff anyhow."

At the third floor he asked Eddie to hold the elevator, he'd be out in a minute. "I just have to pick up the sample case," he said. "Got to get to work on the customers."

In the office he lifted the sample case to the desk, put the eight rolls of bandage in it, and threw away the now empty paper bag into the wastepaper basket. With the sample case weighing him down he made his way back to the elevator.

"This thing weighs more every time I pick it up," he said to Eddie as the elevator went down, and Eddie said, "Well, that's the way it goes. We're none of us as young as we used to be."

A block away from Columbus Circle, Mr. Keesler took an Independent Line subway train to East Broadway, not far from Manhattan Bridge. He ascended into the light of Straus Square, walked down to Water Street, and turned left there. His destination was near Montgomery Street, but he stopped before he came to it and looked around.

The neighborhood was an area of old warehouses, decaying tenements, and raw, new housing projects. The street Mr. Keesler was interested in, however, contained only warehouses. Blackened with age they stood in a row looking like ancient fortresses. There was a mixed smell of refuse and salt water around them that invited coveys of pigeons and sea gulls to fly overhead.

Mr. Keesler paid no attention to the birds, nor to the few waifs and strays on the street. Hefting his sample case he turned into an alley which led between two warehouses and made his way to the vast and empty lot behind them. He walked along until he came to a metal door in the third warehouse down the row. Using a large, old-fashioned key he opened the door, stepped into the blackness beyond it, and closed it behind him, locking it from the inside and testing it to make sure it was locked.

There was a light switch on the wall near the door. Mr. Keesler put down his sample case and wrapped a handkerchief loosely around his hand. He fumbled along the wall with that hand until he found the switch, and when he pressed it a dim light suffused the building. Since the windows of the building were sealed by metal shutters, the light could not be seen outside. Mr. Keesler then put away the handkerchief and carried the sample case across the vast expanse of the warehouse to the huge door of the delivery-entrance that faced on the street.

Near the door was a long plank table on which was a time-stamper, a few old receipt books, and some pencil stubs. Mr. Keesler put down the sample case, took off his coat, neatly folded it and laid it on the table, and placed his hat on top of it. He bent over the sample case and opened it. From it he took the eight rolls of bandage, a large tube of fixative called Quick-Dry, a four-inch length of plumber's candle, two metal cans each containing two gallons of high octane gasoline, six paper drinking cups, a two-yard length of fishline, a handful of soiled linen rags, and a pair of rubber gloves much spattered with drops of dried paint. All this he arranged on the table.

Now donning the rubber gloves he picked up the length of fishline and made a series of loops in it. He fitted a roll of bandage into each loop and drew the string tight. When he held it up at arm's length it looked like a string of white fishing bobbers.

Each gasoline tin had a small spout and looked as if it were tightly sealed. But the lid of one could be removed entirely and Mr. Keesler pried at it until it came off. He lowered the line of rolled bandages into the can, leaving the end of the string dangling over the edge for ready handling. A few bubbles broke at the surface of the can as the gauze bandages started to soak up gasoline. Mr. Keesler observed this with satisfaction, and then, taking the tube of Quick-Dry with him, he made a thoughtful tour of inspection of the warehouse.

What he saw was a broad and high steel framework running through the center of the building from end to end and supporting a great number of cardboard boxes, wooden cases, and paper-covered rolls of cloth. More boxes and cases were stacked nearly ceiling-high against two walls of the room.

He surveyed everything carefully, wrinkling his nose against the sour odor of mold that rose around him. He tested a few of the cardboard boxes by pulling away loose pieces, and found them all as dry as dust.

Then having studied everything to his satisfaction he kneeled down at a point midway between the steel framework and the angle of the two walls where the cases were stacked highest and squeezed some fixative on the wooden floor. He watched it spread and settle, and then went back to the table.

From the pocket of his jacket he drew out a finely whetted penknife and an octagon-shaped metal pencil which was also marked off as a ruler. He looked at his wrist watch, making some brief calculations, and measured off a length of the plumber's candle with the ruler. With the penknife he then sliced through the candle and trimmed away some wax to give the wick clearance. Before putting the knife back into his pocket he cleaned the blade with one of the pieces of cloth on the table.

When he looked into the can which contained the bandages soaking in gasoline he saw no more bubbles. He picked up the can and carried it to the place on the floor where the fixative was spread. Slowly reeling up the string so that none of the gasoline would spatter him he detached each roll of wet bandage from it. He loosened a few inches of gauze from six of the bandages and pressed the exposed gauze firmly into the fixative which was now gummy.

Unspooling the bandage as he walked he then drew each of the six lengths of gauze in turn to a designated point. Three went among the boxes on the framework and three went into the cases along the walls. They were nicely spaced so that they radiated like the main strands of a spider web to points high among the packed cases. To reach the farthest points in the warehouse Mr. Keesler knotted the extra rolls of bandage to two of those which he had pulled out short of the mark. There was a sharp reek of gasoline in the warehouse now, added to its smell of mold.

Where the ends of the bandages were thrust between the boxes, Mr. Keesler made sure that the upper box was set back a little to provide a narrow platform. He took the paper drinking cups from the table, filled each with gasoline, and set it on top of the end of the bandage, resting on this platform.

The fixative was now put to work again. Mr. Keesler squeezed some of it over the juncture of the six bandages on the floor which were sealed there by the previous application. While it hardened he went to the table, took a handful of rags, and brought them to the open gasoline can. He lowered each rag in turn into the can, squeezed some of the excess gasoline back into the can after he pulled it out, and arranged all the rags around the fixative.

Then he took the stump of plumber's candle which he had prepared and pressed it down into the drying fixative. He tested it to make sure it was tightly set into place, looped the gasoline-saturated fishline around and around its base, and pushed the rags close up against it. He made sure that a proper length of candle was exposed, and then stood up to view his handiwork. Everything, as far as he could see, was in order.

Humming a little tune under his breath, Mr. Keesler took the two cans of gasoline and disposed of their contents among the boxes. He handled the cans expertly, splashing gasoline against the boxes where the bandages were attached, pouring it between the boxes wherever he detected a draft stirring in the dank air around him. When the cans were empty he wiped them thoroughly with a rag he had reserved for the purpose and added the rag to the pile around the candle.

Everything that needed to be done had now been done.

Mr. Keesler went back to the table, tightly sealed the gasoline cans, and placed them in the sample case. He pulled off the rubber gloves and put them and the remnant of plumber's candle into the case, too. Then he locked the case and put on his hat and coat.

He carried the case to a point a few feet away from the candle on the floor, set it down, and took out a book of matches from his pocket. Cupping a hand around the matchbox he lit one, and walking with great care while shielding the flame, he approached the candle, bent over it, and lit it. The flame guttered and then took hold.

Mr. Keesler stood up and put out the match, not by shaking it or blowing at it, but by wetting his thumb and forefinger in his mouth and squeezing out the light between them. He dropped the used match into his pocket, went to the back door, switched off the electric light there with his handkerchiefed hand, and drew open the door a few inches.

After peering outside to make sure no one was observing him, Mr. Keesler stepped through the door, locked it behind him, and departed.

He returned to his office by the same route he had come. In the elevator he said to Eddie, "All of a sudden my tooth is killing me. I guess I'll have to run over to the dentist," and Eddie said, "Your teeth sure give you a lot of trouble, don't they?"

"They sure do," said Mr. Keesler.

He left the sample case in his room, washed his hands and face in the lavatory at the opposite end of the hallway, and took the elevator down. The dentist's office was on 56th Street near Seventh Avenue, a few minutes' walk away, and when Mr. Keesler entered the reception room the clock on the wall there showed him that it was two minutes before three. He was pleased to see that the dentist's receptionist was young and pretty and that she had his name neatly entered in her appointment book.

"You're right on time," she said as she filled out a record card for him. She handed him the card. "Just give this to Dr. Gordon when you go into the office."

In the office Mr. Keesler took off his glasses, put them in his pocket, and sat back in the dentist's chair. His feet hurt, and it felt good to be sitting down.

"Where does it hurt?" said Dr. Gordon, and Mr. Keesler indicated the back of his lower right jaw. "Right there," he said.

He closed his eyes and crossed his hands restfully on his belly while the doctor peered into his open mouth and poked at his teeth with a sharp instrument.

"Nothing wrong on the surface," Dr. Gordon said. "Matter of fact, your teeth seem to be in excellent shape. How old are you?"

"Fifty," said Mr. Keesler with pride. "Fifty-one next week."

"Wish my teeth were as good," said the dentist. "Well, it might possibly be that wisdom tooth under the gum that's giving the trouble. But all I can do now is put something soothing on it and take X-rays. Then we'll know."

"Fine," said Mr. Keesler.

He came out of the office at 3:30 with a sweet, minty taste in his mouth and with his feet well-rested. Walking briskly he headed for the B.M.T. subway station at 57th Street and took a train down to Herald Square. He climbed to the street there and took a position among the crowd moving slowly past the windows of R. H. Macy's Department Store, keeping his eyes fixed on the windows as he moved.

At four o'clock he looked at his watch.

At five minutes after four he looked at it with concern.

Then in the window of the store he saw a car coming up to the curb. He walked across the street and entered it, and the car immediately drew away from the curb and fell in with the rest of the traffic on the street.

"You're late, Hummel," said Mr. Keesler to the driver. "Nothing went wrong, did it?"

"Nothing," said Mr. Hummel tensely. "It must have started just about 3:30. The cops called me ten minutes ago to tell me about it. The whole building's going, they said. They wanted me to rush over right away."

"Well, all right," said Mr. Keesler. "So what are you so upset about? Everything is fine. In no time at all you'll have sixty thousand dollars of insurance money in your pocket, you'll be rid of that whole load of stuff you were stuck with—you ought to be a happy man."

Mr. Hummel awkwardly manipulated the car into a turn that led downtown. "But if they find out," he said. "How can you be so sure they won't? At my age to go to jail—!"

Mr. Keesler had dealt with overwrought clients many times before. "Look, Hummel," he said patiently, "the first job I ever did was thirty years ago for my own father, God rest his soul, when the market cleaned him out. To his dying day he thought it was an accident, he never knew it was me. My wife don't know what I do. Nobody knows. Why? Because I'm an expert. I'm the best in the business. When I do a job I'm covered up every possible way—right down to the least little thing. So quit worrying. Nobody will ever find out."

"But in the daytime," said Mr. Hummel. "With people around. I still say it would have been better at night."

Mr. Keesler shook his head. "If it happened at night, the Fire Marshal and the insurance people would be twice as suspicious. And what do I look like, anyhow, Hummel, some kind of bum who goes sneaking around at night? I'm a nine-to-five man. I go to the office and I come home from the office like anybody else. Believe me, that's the best protection there is."

"It could be," said Mr. Hummel, nodding thoughtfully. "It could be."

A dozen blocks away from the warehouse thick, black smoke could be seen billowing into the air above it. On Water Street, three blocks away, Mr. Keesler put a hand on Mr. Hummel's arm.

"Stop here," he said. "There's always marshals and insurance people around the building looking at people, so this is close enough. You can see all you have to from here."

Mr. Hummel looked at the smoke pouring from the building, at the tongues of flame now and then shooting up from it, at the fire engines and tangles of hose in the street, and at the firemen playing water against the walls of the building. He shook his head in awe. "Look at that," he said, marveling. "Look at that."

"I did," said Mr. Keesler. "So how about the money?"

Mr. Hummel stirred himself from his daze, reached into his trouser pocket, and handed Mr. Keesler a tightly folded roll of bills. "It's all there," he said. "I had it made up the way you said."

There were fourteen hundred-dollar bills and five twenties in the roll. Bending low and keeping the money out of sight Mr. Keesler counted it twice. He had two bank deposit envelopes all filled out and ready in his pocket. Into one which credited the money to the account of *K. E. Esler* he put thirteen of the hundred-dollar bills. Into the other which was made out in the name of *Keesler Novelties* he put a single hundred-dollar bill. The five twenties he slipped into his wallet, and from the wallet took out the key to the warehouse.

"Don't forget this," he said, handing it to Mr. Hummel. "Now I have to run along."

"Wait a second," said Mr. Hummel. "I wanted to ask you about something, and since I don't know where to get in touch with you—"

"Yes?"

"Well, I got a friend who's in a very bad spot. He's stuck with a big inventory of fur pieces that he can't get rid of, and he needs cash bad. Do you understand?"

"Sure," said Mr. Keesler. "Give me his name and phone number, and I'll call him up in a couple of weeks."

"Couldn't you make it any sooner?"

"I'm a busy man," said Mr. Keesler. "I'll call him in two weeks." He took out the book of matches and inside it wrote the name and number Mr. Hummel gave him. He put away the matches and opened the door of the car. "So long, Hummel."

"So long, Esler," said Mr. Hummel.

For the second time that day Mr. Keesler traveled in the subway from East Broadway to Columbus Circle. But instead of going directly to his office this time, he turned down Eighth Avenue and dropped the sealed envelope which contained the $1300 into the night-deposit box of the Merchant's National Bank. Across the street was the Columbus National Bank, and into its night-deposit box he placed the envelope containing the hundred dollars. When he arrived at his office it was ten minutes before five.

Mr. Keesler opened his sample case, threw in the odds and ends that had come in the mail that morning, shut the sample case, and closed the roll-top desk after throwing the *New York Times* into the wastebasket. He took a magazine from the pile on the filing cabinet and sat down in the swivel chair while he looked at it.

At exactly five o'clock he left the office, carrying the sample case.

The elevator was crowded, but Mr. Keesler managed to wedge himself into it. "Well," said Eddie on the way down, "another day, another dollar."

In the subway station Mr. Keesler bought a *World-Telegram,* but was unable to read it in the crowded train. He held it under his arm, standing astride the sample case, half dozing as he stood there. When he got out of the station at Beverly Road he stopped at the stationery store on the corner to buy a package of razor blades. Then he walked home slowly, turned into the driveway, and entered the garage.

Mrs. Keesler always had trouble getting the car into the garage. It stood there now at a slight angle to the wall so that Mr. Keesler had to squeeze past it to get to the back of the garage. He opened the sample case, took out the piece of plumber's candle and the tube of Quick-Dry, and put them into a drawer of the workbench there. The drawer was already full of other bits of hardware and small household supplies.

Then he took the two gasoline cans from the sample case and a piece of rubber tubing from the wall and siphoned gasoline from the tank of the car into the cans until they were full. He put them on the floor among other cans which were full of paint and solvent.

Finally he took out the rubber gloves and tossed them on the floor under one of the partly painted chairs. The spatters of paint on the gloves were the exact color of the paint on the chairs.

Mr. Keesler went into the house by the side door, and Mrs. Keesler, who had been setting the kitchen table, heard him. She came into the living-room and watched as Mr. Keesler turned the sample case upside down over the table. Trinkets rolled all over the table, and Mr. Keesler caught the souvenir charm before it could fall to the floor.

"More junk," she said good-naturedly.

"Same as always," said Mr. Keesler, "just stuff from the office. I'll give them to Sally's kids." His niece Sally had two pretty little daughters of whom he was very fond.

Mrs. Keesler put her hand over her mouth and looked around. "And what about the suit?" she said. "Don't tell me you forgot about the suit at the tailor's!"

Mr. Keesler already had one arm out of his coat. He stood there helplessly.

"Oh, no," he said.

His wife sighed resignedly.

"Oh, yes," she said. "And you'll go right down there now before he closes."

Mr. Keesler thrust an arm out behind him, groping for the sleeve of his coat, and located it with his wife's help. She brushed away a speck on the shoulder of the coat, and then patted her husband's cheek affectionately.

"If you could only learn to be a little methodical, dear," said Mrs. Keesler.

Chicago-born ROBERT BLOCH *(1917–) achieved immortality with the film version of his 1959 novel* Psycho. *No other writer has made staying in a motel or taking a shower such a terrifying experience. However,* Psycho *has tended to overshadow his many other excellent suspense novels, which include* Night-World *(1972),* American Gothic *(1976), and* Night of the Ripper *(1984). Long active in Hollywood, Robert Bloch has written scores of scripts for television shows and theatrical films. A modest man, he once said that he has "the heart of a small boy; I keep it in a jar on my desk."*

"The Man Who Collected Poe" is an unforgettable study of obsession, and there is no one better qualified to write a story that centers on that crazed genius.

The Man Who Collected Poe
BY ROBERT BLOCH

During the whole of a dull, dark, and soundless day in the autumn of the year, when the clouds hung oppressively low in the heavens, I had been passing alone, by automobile, through a singularly dreary tract of country, and at length found myself, as the shades of the evening drew on, within view of my destination.

I looked upon the scene before me—upon the mere house, and the simple landscape features of the domain, upon the bleak walls, upon the vacant eye-like windows, upon a few rank sedges, and upon a few white trunks of decayed trees—with a feeling of utter confusion commingled with dismay. For it seemed to me as though I had visited this scene once before, or read of it, perhaps, in some frequently rescanned tale. And yet assuredly it could not be, for only three days had passed since I had made the acquaintance of Launcelot Canning and received an invitation to visit him at his Maryland residence.

The circumstances under which I met Canning were simple; I happened to attend a bibliophilic meeting in Washington and was introduced to him by a mutual friend. Casual conversation gave place to absorbed and interested discussion when he discovered my preoccupation with works of fantasy. Upon learning that I was traveling upon a vacation with no set itinerary, Canning urged me to become his guest for a day and to examine, at my leisure, his unusual display of memorabilia.

"I feel, from our conversation, that we have much in common," he told me. "For you see, sir, in my love of fantasy I bow to no man. It is a taste I have perhaps inherited from my father and from his father before him, together with their considerable acquisitions in the genre. No doubt you would be gratified with what I am prepared to show you, for in all due modesty, I beg to style myself the world's leading collector of the works of Edgar Allan Poe."

I confess that his invitation as such did not enthrall me, for I hold no brief for the literary hero-worshiper or the scholarly collector as a type. I own to a more than passing interest in the tales of Poe, but my interest does not extend to the point of ferreting out the exact date upon which Mr. Poe first decided to raise a moustache, nor would I be unduly intrigued by the opportunity to examine several hairs preserved from that hirsute appendage.

So it was rather the person and personality of Launcelot Canning himself which caused me to accept his proffered hospitality. For the man who proposed to become my host might have himself stepped from the pages of a Poe tale. His speech, as I have endeavored to indicate, was characterized by a courtly rodomontade so often exemplified in Poe's heroes—and beyond certainty, his appearance bore out the resemblance.

Launcelot Canning had the cadaverousness of complexion, the large, liquid, luminous eye, the thin, curved lips, the delicately modeled nose, finely molded chin, and dark, web-like hair of a typical Poe protagonist.

It was this phenomenon which prompted my acceptance and led me to journey to his Maryland estate, which, as I now perceived, in itself manifested a Poe-etic quality of its own, intrinsic in the images of the gray sedge, the ghastly tree stems, and the vacant and eye-like windows of the mansion of gloom. All that was lacking was a tarn and a moat—and as I prepared to enter the dwelling I half-expected to encounter therein the carved ceilings, the somber tapestries, the ebon floors and the phantasmagoric armorial trophies so vividly described by the author of *Tales of the Grotesque and Arabesque*.

Nor upon entering Launcelot Canning's home was I too greatly disappointed in my expectations. True to both the atmospheric quality of the decrepit mansion and to my own fanciful presentiments, the door was opened in response to my knock by a valet who conducted me, in silence, through dark and intricate passages to the study of his master.

The room in which I found myself was very large and lofty. The windows were long, narrow, and pointed, and at so vast a distance from the black oaken floor as to be altogether inaccessible from within. Feeble gleams of encrimsoned light made their way through the trellised panes, and served to render sufficiently distinct the more prominent objects around; the eye, however, struggled in vain to reach the remoter angles of the chamber or the recesses of the vaulted and fretted ceiling. Dark draperies hung upon the walls. The general furniture was profuse, comfortless, antique, and tattered. Many books and musical instruments lay scattered about, but failed to give any vitality to the scene.

Instead they rendered more distinct that peculiar quality of quasi-recollection; it was as though I found myself once again, after a protracted absence, in a familiar setting. I had read, I had imagined, I had dreamed, or I had actually beheld this setting before.

Upon my entrance, Launcelot Canning arose from a sofa on which he had been lying at full length, and greeted me with a vivacious warmth which had much in it, I at first thought, of an overdone cordiality.

Yet his tone, as he spoke of the object of my visit, of his earnest desire to see me, and of the solace he expected me to afford him in a mutual discussion of our interests, soon alleviated my initial misapprehension.

Launcelot Canning welcomed me with the rapt enthusiasm of the born collector—and I came to realize that he was indeed just that. For the Poe collection he shortly proposed to unveil before me was actually his birthright.

Initially, he disclosed, the nucleus of the present accumulation had begun with his grandfather, Christopher Canning, a respected merchant of Baltimore. Almost eighty years ago he had been one of the leading patrons of the arts in his community and as such was partially instrumental in arranging for the removal of Poe's body to the southeastern corner of the Presbyterian Cemetery at Fayette and Green streets, where a suitable monument might be erected. This event occurred in the year 1875, and it was a few years prior to that time that Canning laid the foundation of the Poe collection.

"Thanks to his zeal," his grandson informed me, "I am today the fortunate possessor of a copy of virtually every existing specimen of Poe's published works. If you will step over here"—and he led me to a remote corner of the vaulted study, past the dark draperies, to a bookshelf which rose remotely to the shadowy ceiling—"I shall be pleased to corroborate that claim. Here is a copy of *Al Aaraaf, Tamerlane and other Poems* in the 1829 edition, and here is the still earlier *Tamerlane and other Poems* of 1827. The Boston edition, which, as you doubtless know, is valued today at fifteen thousand dollars. I can assure you that Grandfather Canning parted with no such sum in order to gain possession of this rarity."

He displayed the volumes with an air of commingled pride and cupidity which is ofttimes characteristic of the collector and is by no means to be confused with either literary snobbery or ordinary greed. Realizing this, I remained patient as he exhibited further treasures— copies of the *Philadelphia Saturday Courier* containing early tales, bound volumes of *The Messenger* during the period of Poe's editorship, *Graham's Magazine,* editions of the *New York Sun* and the *New York Mirror* boasting, respectively, of "The Balloon Hoax" and "The Raven," and files of *The Gentleman's Magazine.* Ascending a short library ladder, he handed down to me the Lea and Blanchard edition of *Tales of the Grotesque and Arabesque,* the *Conchologist's First Book,* the Putnam *Eureka,* and, finally, the little paper booklet, published in 1843 and sold for twelve and a half cents, entitled *The Prose Romances of Edgar A. Poe;* an insignificant trifle containing two tales which is valued by present-day collectors at fifty thousand dollars.

Canning informed me of this last fact, and, indeed, kept up a running commentary upon each item he presented. There was no doubt but that he was a Poe scholar as well as a Poe collector, and his words informed tattered specimens of the *Broadway Journal* and *Godey's Lady's Book* with a singular fascination not necessarily inherent in the flimsy sheets or their contents.

"I owe a great debt to Grandfather Canning's obsession," he observed, descending the ladder and joining me before the bookshelves. "It is not altogether a breach of confidence to admit that his interest in Poe did reach the point of an obsession, and perhaps eventually of an absolute mania. The knowledge, alas, is public property, I fear.

"In the early seventies he built this house, and I am quite sure that you have been observant enough to note that it in itself is almost a replica of a typical Poe-esque mansion. This was his study, and it was here that he was wont to pore over the books, the letters, and the numerous mementos of Poe's life.

"What prompted a retired merchant to devote himself so fanatically to the pursuit of a hobby, I cannot say. Let it suffice that he virtually

withdrew from the world and from all other normal interests. He conducted a voluminous and lengthy correspondence with aging men and
women who had known Poe in their lifetime—made pilgrimages to
Fordham, sent his agents to West Point, to England, and Scotland, to
virtually every locale in which Poe had set foot during his lifetime. He
acquired letters and souvenirs as gifts, he bought them, and—I fear—
stole them, if no other means of acquisition proved feasible."

Launcelot Canning smiled and nodded. "Does all this sound strange
to you? I confess that once I, too, found it almost incredible, a frag-
ment of romance. Now, after years spent here, I have lost my own
objectivity."

"Yes, it is strange," I replied. "But are you quite sure that there was
not some obscure personal reason for your grandfather's interest? Had
he met Poe as a boy, or been closely associated with one of his friends?
Was there, perhaps, a distant, undisclosed relationship?"

At the mention of the last word, Canning started visibly, and a
tremor of agitation overspread his countenance.

"Ah!" he exclaimed. "There you voice my own inmost conviction. A
relationship—assuredly there must have been one—I am morally, in-
stinctively certain that Grandfather Canning felt or knew himself to be
linked to Edgar Poe by ties of blood. Nothing else could account for
his strong initial interest, his continuing defense of Poe in the literary
controversies of the day, and his final melancholy lapse into a world of
delusion and illusion.

"Yet he never voiced a statement or put an allegation upon paper—
and I have searched the collection of letters in vain for the slightest
clue.

"It is curious that you so promptly divine a suspicion held not only
by myself but by my father. He was only a child at the time of my
Grandfather Canning's death, but the attendant circumstances left a
profound impression upon his sensitive nature. Although he was immediately removed from this house to the home of his mother's people
in Baltimore, he lost no time in returning upon assuming his inheritance in early manhood.

"Fortunately being in possession of a considerable income, he was
able to devote his entire lifetime to further research. The name of
Arthur Canning is still well known in the world of literary criticism,
but for some reason he preferred to pursue his scholarly examination
of Poe's career in privacy. I believe this preference was dictated by an
inner sensibility; that he was endeavoring to unearth some information

which would prove his father's, his, and for that matter, my own, kinship to Edgar Poe."

"You say your father was also a collector?" I prompted.

"A statement I am prepared to substantiate," replied my host, as he led me to yet another corner of the shadow-shrouded study. "But first, if you would accept a glass of wine?"

He filled, not glasses, but veritable beakers from a large carafe, and we toasted one another in silent appreciation. It is perhaps unnecessary for me to observe that the wine was a fine old amontillado.

"Now, then," said Launcelot Canning. "My father's special province in Poe research consisted of the accumulation and study of letters."

Opening a series of large trays or drawers beneath the bookshelves, he drew out file after file of glassined folios, and for the space of the next half-hour I examined Edgar Poe's correspondence—letters to Henry Herring, to Dr. Snodgrass, Sarah Shelton, James P. Moss, Elizabeth Poe; missives to Mrs. Rockwood, Helen Whitman, Anne Lynch, John Pendleton Kennedy; notes to Mrs. Richmond, to John Allan, to Annie, to his brother, Henry—a profusion of documents, a veritable epistolary cornucopia.

During the course of my perusal my host took occasion to refill our beakers with wine, and the heady draught began to take effect—for we had not eaten, and I own I gave no thought to food, so absorbed was I in the yellowed pages illumining Poe's past.

Here was wit, erudition, literary criticism; here were the muddled, maudlin outpourings of a mind gone in drink and despair; here was the draft of a projected story, the fragments of a poem; here was a pitiful cry for deliverance and a paean to living beauty; here was a dignified response to a dunning letter and an editorial pronunciamento to an admirer; here was love, hate, pride, anger, celestial serenity, abject penitence, authority, wonder, resolution, indecision, joy, and soul-sickening melancholia.

Here was the gifted elocutionist, the stammering drunkard, the adoring husband, the frantic lover, the proud editor, the indigent pauper, the grandiose dreamer, the shabby realist, the scientific inquirer, the gullible metaphysician, the dependent stepson, the free and untrammeled spirit, the hack, the poet, the enigma that was Edgar Allan Poe.

Again the beakers were filled and emptied.

I drank deeply with my lips, and with my eyes more deeply still.

For the first time the true enthusiasm of Launcelot Canning was communicated to my own sensibilities—I divined the eternal fascination found in a consideration of Poe the writer and Poe the man; he who wrote Tragedy, lived Tragedy, was Tragedy; he who penned Mystery, lived and died in Mystery, and who today looms on the literary scene as Mystery incarnate.

And Mystery Poe remained, despite Arthur Canning's careful study of the letters. "My father learned nothing," my host confided, "even though he assembled, as you see here, a collection to delight the heart of a Mabbott or a Quinn. So his search ranged further. By this time I was old enough to share both his interest and his inquiries. Come," and he led me to an ornate chest which rested beneath the windows against the west wall of the study.

Kneeling, he unlocked the repository, and then drew forth, in rapid and marvelous succession, a series of objects each of which boasted of intimate connection with Poe's life.

There were souvenirs of his youth and his schooling abroad—a book he had used during his sojourn at West Point, mementos of his days as a theatrical critic in the form of playbills, a pen used during his editorial period, a fan once owned by his girl-wife, Virginia, a brooch of Mrs. Clemm's; a profusion of objects including such diverse articles as a cravat-stock and, curiously enough, Poe's battered and tarnished flute.

Again we drank, and I own the wine was potent. Canning's countenance remained cadaverously wan, but, moreover, there was a species of mad hilarity in his eye—an evident restrained hysteria in his whole demeanor. At length, from the scattered heap of curiosa, I happened to draw forth and examine a little box of no remarkable character, whereupon I was constrained to inquire its history and what part it had played in the life of Poe.

"In the *life* of Poe?" A visible tremor convulsed the features of my host, then rapidly passed in transformation to a grimace, a rictus of amusement. "This little box—and you will note how, by some fateful design or contrived coincidence it bears a resemblance to the box he himself conceived of and described in his tale 'Berenice'—this little box is concerned with his death, rather than his life. It is, in fact, the selfsame box my grandfather Christopher Canning clutched to his bosom when they found him down there."

Again the tremor, again the grimace. "But stay, I have not yet told you of the details. Perhaps you would be interested in seeing the spot where Christopher Canning was stricken. I have already told you of his madness, but I did no more than hint at the character of his delusions. You have been patient with me, and more than patient. Your understanding shall be rewarded, for I perceive you can be fully entrusted with the facts."

What further revelations Canning was prepared to make I could not say, but his manner was such as to inspire a vague disquiet and trepidation in my breast.

Upon perceiving my unease he laughed shortly and laid a hand upon my shoulder. "Come, this should interest you as an *aficionado* of fantasy," he said. "But first, another drink to speed our journey."

He poured, we drank, and then he led the way from that vaulted chamber, down the silent halls, down the staircase, and into the lowest recesses of the building until we reached what resembled a donjon-keep, its floor and the interior of a long archway carefully sheathed in copper. We paused before a door of massive iron. Again I felt in the aspect of this scene an element evocative of recognition or recollection.

Canning's intoxication was such that he misinterpreted, or chose to misinterpret, my reaction.

"You need not be afraid," he assured me. "Nothing has happened down here since that day, almost seventy years ago, when his servants discovered him stretched out before this door, the little box clutched to his bosom; collapsed, and in a state of delirium from which he never emerged. For six months he lingered, a hopeless maniac—raving as wildly from the very moment of his discovery as at the moment he died, babbling his visions of the giant horse, the fissured house collapsing into the tarn, the black cat, the pit, the pendulum, the raven on the pallid bust, the beating heart, the pearly teeth, and the nearly liquid mass of loathsome—of detestable putridity from which a voice emanated.

"Nor was that all he babbled," Canning confided, and here his voice sank to a whisper that reverberated through the copper-sheathed hall and against the iron door. "He hinted other things far worse than fantasy; of a ghastly reality surpassing all of the phantasms of Poe.

"For the first time my father and the servants learned the purpose of the room he had built beyond this iron door, and learned too what Christopher Canning had done to establish his title as the world's foremost collector of Poe.

"For he babbled again of Poe's death, thirty years earlier, in 1849—of the burial in the Presbyterian cemetery, and of the removal of the coffin in 1874 to the corner where the monument was raised. As I told you, and as was known then, my grandfather had played a public part in instigating that removal. But now we learned of the private part—learned that there was a monument and a grave, but no coffin in the earth beneath Poe's alleged resting place. The coffin now rested in the secret room at the end of this passage. That is why the room, the house itself, had been built.

"I tell you, he had stolen the body of Edgar Allan Poe—and as he shrieked aloud in his final madness, did not this indeed make him the greatest collector of Poe?

"His ultimate intent was never divined, but my father made one significant discovery—the little box clutched to Christopher Canning's bosom contained a portion of the crumbled bones, the veritable dust that was all that remained of Poe's corpse."

My host shuddered and turned away. He led me back along that hall of horror, up the stairs, into the study. Silently, he filled our beakers and I drank as hastily, as deeply, as desperately as he.

"What could my father do? To own the truth was to create a public scandal. He chose instead to keep silence; to devote his own life to study in retirement.

"Naturally the shock affected him profoundly; to my knowledge he never entered the room beyond the iron door, and, indeed, I did not know of the room or its contents until the hour of his death—and it was not until some years later that I myself found the key among his effects.

"But find the key I did, and the story was immediately and completely corroborated. Today I am the greatest collector of Poe—for he lies in the keep below, my eternal trophy!"

This time I poured the wine. As I did so, I noted for the first time the imminence of a storm; the impetuous fury of its gusts shaking the casements, and the echoes of its thunder rolling and rumbling down the time-corroded corridors of the old house.

The wild, overstrained vivacity with which my host hearkened, or apparently hearkened, to these sounds did nothing to reassure me—for his recent revelation led me to suspect his sanity.

That the body of Edgar Allan Poe had been stolen; that this mansion had been built to house it; that it was indeed enshrined in a crypt below; that grandsire, son, and grandson had dwelt here alone, apart, enslaved to a sepulchral secret was beyond sane belief.

And yet, surrounded now by the night and the storm, in a setting torn from Poe's own frenzied fancies, I could not be sure. Here the past was still alive, the very spirit of Poe's tales breathed forth its corruption upon the scene.

As thunder boomed, Launcelot Canning took up Poe's flute, and, whether in defiance of the storm without or as a mocking accompaniment, he played; blowing upon it with drunken persistence, with eerie atonality, with nerve-shattering shrillness. To the shrieking of that infernal instrument the thunder added a braying counterpoint.

Uneasy, uncertain, and unnerved, I retreated into the shadows of the bookshelves at the farther end of the room, and idly scanned the titles of a row of ancient tomes. Here was the *Chiromancy* of Robert Flud, the *Directorium Inquisitorum*, a rare and curious book in quarto Gothic that was the manual of a forgotten church; and betwixt and between the volumes of pseudo-scientific inquiry, theological speculation, and sundry incunabula, I found titles that arrested and appalled me. *De Vermis Mysteriis* and the *Liber Eibon*, treatises on demonology, on witchcraft, on sorcery moldered in crumbling bindings. The books were old, but the books were not dusty. They had been read—

"Read them?" It was as though Canning divined my inmost thoughts. He had put aside his flute and now approached me, tittering as though in continued drunken defiance of the storm. Odd echoes and boomings now sounded through the long halls of the house, and curious grating sounds threatened to drown out his words and his laughter.

"Read them?" said Canning. "I study them. Yes, I have gone beyond grandfather and father, too. It was I who procured the books that held the key, and it was I who found the key. A key more difficult to discover, and more important, than the key to the vaults below. I often wonder if Poe himself had access to these selfsame tomes, knew the selfsame secrets. The secrets of the grave and what lies beyond, and what can be summoned forth if one but holds the key."

He stumbled away and returned with wine. "Drink," he said. "Drink to the night and the storm."

I brushed the proffered glass aside. "Enough," I said. "I must be on my way."

Was it fancy or did I find fear frozen on his features? Canning clutched my arm and cried, "No, stay with me! This is no night on which to be alone; I swear I cannot abide the thought of being alone, I can bear to be alone no more!"

His incoherent babble mingled with the thunder and the echoes; I drew back and confronted him. "Control yourself," I counseled. "Confess that this is a hoax, an elaborate imposture arranged to please your fancy."

"Hoax? Imposture? Stay, and I shall prove to you beyond all doubt" —and so saying, Launcelot Canning stooped and opened a small drawer set in the wall beneath and beside the bookshelves. "This should repay you for your interest in my story, and in Poe," he murmured. "Know that you are the first other person than myself to glimpse these treasures."

He handed me a sheaf of manuscripts on plain white paper; documents written in ink curiously similar to that I had noted while perusing Poe's letters. Pages were clipped together in groups, and for a moment I scanned titles alone.

" 'The Worm of Midnight,' by Edgar Poe," I read, aloud. " 'The Crypt,' " I breathed. And here, " 'The Further Adventures of Arthur Gordon Pym' "—and in my agitation I came close to dropping the precious pages. "Are these what they appear to be—the unpublished tales of Poe?"

My host bowed.

"Unpublished, undiscovered, unknown, save to me—and to you."

"But this cannot be," I protested. "Surely there would have been a mention of them somewhere, in Poe's own letters or those of his contemporaries. There would have been a clue, an indication, somewhere, someplace, somehow."

Thunder mingled with my words, and thunder echoed in Canning's shouted reply.

"You dare to presume an imposture? Then compare!" He stooped again and brought out a glassined folio of letters. "Here—is this not the veritable script of Edgar Poe? Look at the calligraphy of the letter, then at the manuscripts. Can you say they are not penned by the selfsame hand?"

I looked at the handwriting, wondered at the possibilities of a monomaniac's forgery. Could Launcelot Canning, a victim of mental disorder, thus painstakingly simulate Poe's hand?

"Read, then!" Canning screamed through the thunder. "Read, and dare to say that these tales were written by any other than Edgar Poe, whose genius defies the corruption of Time and the Conqueror Worm!"

I read but a line or two, holding the topmost manuscript close to eyes that strained beneath wavering candlelight; but even in the flickering illumination I noted that which told me the only, the incontestable truth. For the paper, the curiously *unyellowed* paper, bore a visible watermark; the name of a firm of well-known modern stationers, and the date—1949.

Putting the sheaf aside, I endeavored to compose myself as I moved away from Launcelot Canning. For now I knew the truth; knew that one hundred years after Poe's death a semblance of his spirit still lived in the distorted and disordered soul of Canning. Incarnation, reincarnation, call it what you will; Canning was, in his own irrational mind, Edgar Allan Poe.

Stifled and dull echoes of thunder from a remote portion of the mansion now commingled with the soundless seething of my own inner turmoil, as I turned and rashly addressed my host.

"Confess!" I cried. "Is it not true that you have written these tales, fancying yourself the embodiment of Poe? Is it not true that you suffer from a singular delusion born of solitude and everlasting brooding upon the past; that you have reached a stage characterized by the conviction that Poe still lives on in your own person?"

A strong shudder came over him and a sickly smile quivered about his lips as he replied. "Fool! I say to you that I have spoken the truth. Can you doubt the evidence of your senses? This house is real, the Poe collection exists, and the stories exist—they exist, I swear, as truly as the body lying in the crypt below!"

I took up the little box from the table and removed the lid. "Not so," I answered. "You said your grandfather was found with this box clutched to his breast, before the door of the vault, and that it contained Poe's dust. Yet you cannot escape the fact that the box is empty." I faced him furiously. "Admit it, the story is a fabrication, a romance. Poe's body does not lie beneath this house, nor are these his unpublished works, written during his lifetime and concealed."

"True enough." Canning's smile was ghastly beyond belief. "The dust is gone because I took it and used it—because in the works of wizardry I found the formulae, the arcana whereby I could raise the flesh, re-create the body from the essential salts of the grave. Poe does not *lie* beneath this house—he *lives!* And the tales are *his posthumous works!*"

Accented by thunder, his words crashed against my consciousness.

"That was the end-all and the be-all of my planning, my studies, of my work, of my life! To raise, by sorcery, the veritable spirit of Edgar Poe from the grave—reclothed and animate in flesh—set him to dwell and dream and do his work again in the private chambers I built in the vaults below—and this I have done! To steal a corpse is but a ghoulish prank; mine is the achievement of true genius!"

The distinct, hollow, metallic, and clangorous yet apparently muffled reverberation accompanying his words caused him to turn in his seat and face the door of the study, so that I could not see the workings of his countenance—nor could he read my own reaction to his ravings.

His words came but faintly to my ears through the thunder that now shook the house in a relentless grip; the wind rattling the casements and flickering the candle flame from the great silver candelabra sent a soaring sighing in an anguished accompaniment to his speech.

"I would show him to you, but I dare not; for he hates me as he hates life. I have locked him in the vault, alone, for the resurrected have no need of food or drink. And he sits there, pen moving over paper, endlessly moving, endlessly pouring out the evil essence of all he guessed and hinted at in life and which he learned in death.

"Do you not see the tragic pity of my plight? I sought to raise his spirit from the dead, to give the world anew of his genius—and yet these tales, these works, are filled and fraught with a terror not to be endured. They cannot be shown to the world, he cannot be shown to the world; in bringing back the dead I have brought back the fruits of death!"

Echoes sounded anew as I moved toward the door—moved, I confess, to flee this accursed house and its accursed owner.

Canning clutched my hand, my arm, my shoulder. "You cannot go!" he shouted above the storm. "I spoke of his escaping, but did you not guess? Did you not hear it through the thunder—the grating of the door?"

I pushed him aside and he blundered backward, upsetting the candelabra, so that flames licked now across the carpeting.

"Wait!" he cried. "Have you not heard his footstep on the stair? *Madman, I tell you that he now stands without the door!*"

A rush of wind, a roar of flame, a shroud of smoke rose all about us. Throwing open the huge, antique panels to which Canning pointed, I staggered into the hall.

I speak of wind, of flame, of smoke—enough to obscure all vision. I speak of Canning's screams, and of thunder loud enough to drown all sound. I speak of terror born of loathing and of desperation enough to shatter all my sanity.

Despite these things, I can never erase from my consciousness that which I beheld as I fled past the doorway and down the hall.

There without the doors there *did* stand a lofty and enshrouded figure; a figure all too familiar, with pallid features, high, domed forehead, moustache set above a mouth. My glimpse lasted but an instant, an instant during which the man—the corpse, the apparition, the hallucination, call it what you will—moved forward into the chamber and clasped Canning to his breast in an unbreakable embrace. Together, the two figures tottered toward the flames, which now rose to blot out vision forevermore.

From that chamber, and from that mansion, I fled aghast. The storm was still abroad in all its wrath, and now fire came to claim the house of Canning for its own.

Suddenly there shot along the path before me a wild light, and I turned to see whence a gleam so unusual could have issued—but it was only the flames, rising in supernatural splendor to consume the mansion, and the secrets, of the man who collected Poe.

MASTERWORKS
OF CRIME
AND DETECTION

Like Dame Ngaio Marsh, SIMON BRETT *(1945–) brings an insider's view of the theater to his crime fiction. His creation, down-on-his-luck actor Charles Paris, is one of the most entertaining detectives to emerge in the mystery fiction of the 1970s. He debuted in* Cast, In Order of Appearance *in 1975 and has since matured (along with his creator) into one of the most popular and original sleuths around. Mr. Brett worked as a radio producer for the BBC in London from 1967 to 1977, when he moved over to London Weekend Television, and his expertise in theatrical productions is one of his great strengths.*

"The Nuggy Bar" is one of those stories that grabs you on the first page and just doesn't let go, and is a superb example of the criminous tale at its best.

The Nuggy Bar
BY SIMON BRETT

Murder, like all great enterprises, repays careful planning; and, if there was one thing on which Hector Griffiths prided himself, it was his planning ability.

It was his planning ability which had raised him through the jungle of the domestic cleaning fluids industry to be Product Manager of the Gliss range of indispensable housewives' aids. His marriage to Melissa Wintle, an attractive and rich widow with a teenage daughter, was also a triumph of planning. Even his wife's unfortunate death two years later, caused by asphyxiation from the fumes of a faulty gas heater while he was abroad on business, could be seen as the product of, if not necessarily planning, then at least serendipity.

But no amount of planning could have foreseen that Melissa's will would have left the bulk of her not inconsiderable wealth to Janet, daughter of her first marriage, rather than to Hector, her second husband.

So when, at the age of fifty-two, Hector Griffiths found himself reduced to his Gliss salary (generous, but by no means sufficient to maintain those little extras—the flat in Sloane Street, the cottage in Cornwall, the Mercedes, the motor-boat—which had become habitual while his wife was alive) and saddled with the responsibility of an unforthcoming, but definitely rich, step-daughter, he decided it was time to start planning again.

Hector Griffiths shared with Moses, Matthew, Mark, Luke, John and other lesser prophets and evangelists the advantage of having written his own Bible. It was a series of notes which he had assembled during the planning build-up to the launch of New Green Gliss—With Ammonia, and he was not alone in appreciating its worth. No less a person than the company's European Marketing Director (Cleaning Fluids) had congratulated him on the notes' cogency and good sense after hearing Hector use them as the basis of a Staff Training Course lecture.

Hector kept the notes, which he had had neatly typed up by his secretary, in a blue plastic display folder, of which favoured Management Trainees were occasionally vouchsafed a glimpse. On its title page were two precepts, two precepts which provided a dramatic opening to Hector's lectures and which, he had to admit, were rather well put.

A. *Even at the cost of delaying the launch of your product, always allow sufficient time for planning. Impatience breeds error, and error is expensive.*

B. *Once you have made your major decisions about the product and the timing of its launch, do not indulge second thoughts. A delayed schedule is also expensive.*

A third precept, equally important but unwritten, dictated that, before any action was taken on a new product, there should be a period of Desk Work, of sitting and thinking, looking at the project from every angle, checking as many details as could be checked, generally familiarizing oneself with every aspect of the job in hand. Thinking at this earlier, relaxed stage made it easier to deal with problems that arose later, when time for thought was a luxury and one had to act on impulse.

It was nearly three months after Melissa's death before Hector had time to settle down to the Desk Work for his new project. He had been busy with the European launch of Gliss Scouring Pads and had also found that clearing a deceased's belongings and sorting out a will, even such a simple and unsatisfactory one as Melissa's, took a surprising amount of time. Janet had also needed attention. Her mother's death had taken place at Easter, which meant that the girl had been home from her Yorkshire boarding school. Janet, now a withdrawn fifteen-year-old, had unfortunately been asleep at the time of Melissa's accident, had heard nothing and so been unable to save her. Equally unfortunately, from her step-father's point of view, she had not been in the bathroom with her mother when the gas fumes started to escape, which would have solved his current difficulties before they arose.

But, as Hector always told the eager young men in beige suits and patterned ties on the Staff Training Courses, success rarely comes easily, and the wise manager will distrust the solution that arrives too readily.

No, Janet was still with him, and he did not regret the time he had devoted to her. His plans for her future had not yet crystallized, but, whatever it was to be, prudence dictated that he should take on the role of the solicitous step-father. Now she was such a wealthy young woman, it made sense that he should earn at least her goodwill.

He smiled wryly at the thought. Something told him he would require more of her than goodwill for the occasional handout. The flat in London, the cottage in Cornwall, the motor-boat and the Mercedes demanded a less erratic income. He needed permanent control of Janet's money.

But he was jumping to conclusions. He always warned Management Trainees against prejudging issues before they had done their Desk Work.

Hector Griffiths opened the blue folder on his desk. He turned over the page of precepts and looked at the next section.

1. Need For Product (Filling market void, increasing brand share)
It took no elaborate research to tell him that the product was needed. Now Melissa was dead, there was a market void, and the product required to fill it was money.

Unwilling to reject too soon any possibility, he gave thought to various methods of money-making. His prospects at Gliss were healthy, but not healthy enough. Even if, when the Marketing Director (U.K.) retired and was replaced by the European Marketing Director (Cleaning Fluids), Hector got the latter's job (which was thought likely), his salary would only rise by some twenty-five per cent, far off parity with the wealth he had commanded as Melissa's husband. Even a massive coincidence of coronaries amongst the senior management of Gliss which catapulted Hector to the Managing Director's office would still leave him worse off.

Career prospects outside Gliss, for a man of fifty-two, however good a planner, offered even less. Anyway, Hector didn't want to struggle and graft. What he had had in mind had been a few more years of patronizing his underlings in his present job and then an early, dignified and leisured retirement, surrounded by all the comforts of Melissa (except for Melissa herself).

So how else did people get money? There was crime, of course—theft, embezzlement and so on—but Hector thought such practices undignified, risky and positively immoral.

No, it was obvious that the money to ease his burdens should be Melissa's. Already he felt it was his by right.

But Janet had it.

On the other hand, if Janet died, the trust that administered the money for her would have to be broken, inevitably to the benefit of her only surviving relation, her poor step-father, desolated by yet another bereavement.

The real product for which there was a market void, and which would undeniably increase Hector Griffiths' brand share, was Janet's death.

2. Specific description of product

Fifteen-year-old girls rarely die spontaneously, however convenient and public-spirited such an action might be, so it was inevitable that Janet would have to be helped on her way.

It didn't take a lot of Desk Work to reach the conclusion that she would have to be murdered. And, following unhappy experiences with the delegation of responsibility over the European launch of Green Gliss Scouring Pads, Hector realized he would have to do the job himself.

3. Timing of Launch

This was the crucial factor. How many products, Hector would rhetorically demand of the ardent young men who dreamt of company Cortinas and patio doors, how many products have been condemned to obscurity by too hasty a schedule? Before deciding on the date of your launch, assess the following three points:

A. *How soon can the production, publicity and sales departments make the product a viable commercial proposition?*

B. *How long will it be before the market forces which revealed a need for the product alter? (N.B. Or before a rival concern also notes the need and supplies it with their own product?)*

 C. *What special factors does your product have which create special needs in timing? (E.g. You do not launch a tennis shoe cleaner in the winter.)*

Hector gave quite a lot of Desk Work to this section. The first question he could not answer until he had done some serious Research and Development into a murder method. That might take time.

But, even if the perfect solution came within days, there were many arguments for delaying the launch. The most potent was Melissa's recent death. Though at no point during the police investigations or inquest had the slightest suspicion attached to him, the coincidence of two accidents too close together might prompt unnecessarily scrupulous inquiry. It also made sense that Hector should continue to foster his image of solicitude for his step-daughter, thus killing the seeds of any subsequent suspicion.

The answer to Question A, therefore, was that a launch should be delayed as long as possible.

But the length of this delay was limited by the answer to Question B. Though with a sedately private matter like the murder of Janet, Hector did not fear, as he would have done in the cut-throat world of cleaning fluids, a rival getting in before him, there was still the strong pressure of market forces. The pittance Melissa had accorded him in her will would maintain his current lifestyle (with a conservative allowance for inflation) for about eighteen months. That set the furthest limit on the launch (though prudence suggested it would look less suspicious if he didn't run right up against bankruptcy).

In answer to Question C (what he humorously referred to, to his Management Trainees, as the "tennis shoe question"), there was a significant special factor. Since Janet was at boarding school in Yorkshire, where his presence would be bound to cause comment, the launch had to be during the school holidays.

Detailed consideration of these and other factors led him to a date of launch during the summer of the following year, some fifteen months away. It seemed a long time to wait, but, as Hector knew, *Impatience Breeds Error.*

4. Research and Development of Product (A. Theoretical)
He was able, at his desk, to eliminate a number of possible murder

methods. Most of them were disqualified because they failed to meet one important specification: that he should not be implicated in any way.

Simplified, this meant either a) that Janet's death should look like an accident, b) that her step-father should have a cast-iron alibi for the time of her death, or, preferably, c) both.

He liked the idea of an accident. Even though he would arrange things so that he had nothing to fear from a murder inquiry, it was better to avoid the whole process. Ideally, he needed an accident which occurred while he was out of the country.

A wry instinct dissuaded him from any plan involving faulty gas heaters. A new product should always be genuinely original.

Hector went through a variety of remotely-controlled accidents that could happen to teenage girls, but all seemed to involve faulty machinery and invited uncomfortably close comparisons with gas heaters. He decided he might have to take a more personal role in the project.

But if he had to be there, he was at an immediate disadvantage. Anyone present at a suspicious death becomes a suspicious person. What he needed was to be both present and absent at the same time.

But that was impossible. Either he was there or he wasn't. His own physical presence was immovable. The time of the murder was immovable. And the two had to coincide.

Or did they?

It was at this moment that Hector Griffiths had a brainwave. They did sometimes come to him, with varying force, but this one was huge, bigger even, he believed, that his idea for the green tear-off tag on the Gliss Table-Top Cleaner sachets.

He would murder Janet and then change the time of her murder.

It would need a lot of research, a lot of reading of books of forensic medicine, but, just as Hector had known with the green tag, he knew again that he had the right solution.

4. Research and Development of Product (B. Practical)
One of Hector's favourite sentences from his Staff Training lecture was: "The true Genesis of a product is forged by the R and D boys in the white heat of the laboratory." Previously, he had always spoken it with a degree of wistfulness, aware of the planner's distance from true creativity, but with his new product he experienced the thrill of being the real creator.

He gave himself a month, the month that remained before Janet would return for her summer holidays, and at the end of that time he wanted to know his murder method. There would be time for refinement of details, but it was important to get the main outline firm.

He made many experiments which gave him the pleasure of research, but not the satisfaction of a solution, before he found the right method.

He found it in Cornwall. Janet had agreed to continue her normal summer practice of spending the month of August at the cottage, and early in July Hector went down for a weekend to see that the place was habitable and to take the motor-boat for its first outing of the season. While Melissa had been alive, the cottage had been used most weekends from Easter onwards and, as he cast off his boat from the mooring in front of his cottage and breathed the tangy air, Hector decided to continue the regular visits.

He liked it down there. He liked having the boat to play with, he liked the respect that ownership of the cottage brought him. Commander Donleavy, with whom he drank in the Yacht Club, would often look out across the bay to where it perched, a rectangle of white on the cliff, secluded but cunningly modernised, and say, "Damned fine property, that."

The boat was a damned fine property, too, and Hector wasn't going to relinquish either of them. Inevitably, as he powered through the waves, he thought of Melissa. But without emotion, almost without emotion now. Typical of her to make a mistake over the will.

She came to his mind more forcibly as he passed a place where they had made love. During the days of their courtship, when he had realised that her whimsical nature would require a few romantic gestures before she consented to marry him, he had started taking her to unlikely settings for love-making.

The one the boat now chugged past was the unlikeliest of all. It was a hidden cave, only accessible at very low tide. He had found it by accident the first time he had gone out with Melissa in the boat. His inexperience of navigation had brought their vessel dangerously close to some rocks and, as he leant out to fend off, he had fallen into the sea. To his surprise, he had found sand beneath his feet and caught a glimpse of a dark space under an arch of rock.

Melissa had taken over the wheel and he had scrambled back on board, aware that the romantic lover image he had been fostering was now seriously dented by his incompetence. But the cave he had seen offered a chance for him to redeem himself.

Brusquely ordering Melissa to anchor the boat, he had stripped off and jumped back into the icy water. (It was May.) He then swam to the opening he had seen and disappeared under the low arch. He soon found himself on a sandy beach in a small cave, eerily lit by reflections of the sun on the water outside.

He had reappeared in the daylight and summoned Melissa imperiously to join him. Enjoying taking orders, she had stripped off and swum to the haven, where, on the sand, he had taken her with apparent, but feigned, brutality. When doing the Desk Work on his project for getting married to Melissa, he had analysed in her taste for Gothic romances an ideal of a dominant, savage lover, and built up the Heathcliff in himself accordingly.

It had worked, too. It was in the cave that she had agreed to marry him. Once the ceremony was achieved, he was able to put aside his Gothic image with relief. Apart from anything else, gestures like the cave episode were very cold.

When, by then safely married, they next went past the cave opening, Melissa had looked at him wistfully, but Hector had pretended not to see. Anyway, there had been no sign of the opening; it was only revealed at the lowest spring tide. Also by then it was high summer and the place stank. The council spoke stoutly of rotting seaweed, while local opinion muttered darkly about a sewage outlet, but, whatever the cause, a pervasively offensive stench earned the place the nickname of "Stinky Cove" and kept trippers away when the weather got hot.

As he steered his boat past the hidden opening and wrinkled his nose involuntarily, all the elements combined in Hector's head, and his murder plan began to form.

4. Research and Development of Product (C. Experimental)
Commander Donleavy was an inexhaustible source of information about things nautical, and he loved being asked, particularly by someone as ignorantly appreciative as Hector Griffiths. He had no problem explaining to the greenhorn all about the twenty-eight-day cycle of the tides, and referring him to the tide tables, and telling him that yes, of course it would be possible to predict the date of a spring tide a year in advance. Not for the first time he marvelled that the government didn't insist on two years in the regular Navy as the minimum qualification for anyone wishing to own a boat.

Still, Griffiths wasn't a bad sort. Generous with the pink gins, anyway. And got that nice cottage over the bay. "Damned fine property, that," said Commander Donleavy, as he was handed another double.

The cycle of the tides did not allow Hector Griffiths to become an "R and D boy" and get back into "the white heat of the laboratory" again until his step-daughter was established in the cottage for her summer holiday. Janet was, he thought, quieter than ever; she seemed to take her mother's death hard. Though not fractious or uncooperative, she seemed listless. Except for a little sketching, she appeared to have no interests, and showed no desire to go anywhere. Better still, she did not seem to have any friends. She wrote duty postcards to two elderly aunts of Melissa in Stockport, but received no mail and made no attempt to make new contacts. All of which was highly satisfactory.

So, on the day of the spring tide, she made no comment on her step-father's decision to take the boat out, and Hector felt confident that, when he returned, he would still find her stretched lethargically in her mother's armchair.

He anchored the motor-boat in shallow water outside the cave entrance, took off his trousers (beneath which he wore swimming trunks), put on rubber shoes, and slipped over the side. The water came just above his knee, and more of the entrance arch was revealed. On his previous visit the tide could not have been at its very lowest. But the entrance remained well hidden; no one who didn't know exactly where it was would be likely to find it by chance.

He had a flashlight with him, but switched it off once he was inside the cave. The shifting ripples of reflection gave enough light.

It was better than he remembered. The cave was about the size, and somehow had the atmosphere, of a small church. There was a high pile of fallen rock and stones up the altar end, which, together with the stained glass window feel of the filtered light, reinforced the image.

But it was an empty church. There was no detritus of beer-cans, biscuit packets or condoms to suggest that anyone else shared Hector's discovery.

Down the middle of the cave a seeping stream of water traversed the sand. Hector trod up this with heavy footsteps, and watched with pleasure as the marks filled in and became invisible.

The pile of rubble was higher than it had at first appeared. Climbing it was hard, as large stones rocked and smaller ones scuttered out under the weight of his feet. When he stood precariously on the top and looked down fifteen feet to the unmarked sand below, he experienced the sort of triumph that the "R and D boys" must have felt when they arrived at the formula for the original Gliss Cleaning Fluid.

In his pocket he found a paper bag and blew it up. Inflated, it was about the size of a human head. He let it bounce gently down to the foot of the rubble pile, and picked up a large stone.

It took three throws before he got his range, but the third stone hit the paper bag right in the middle. The target exploded with a moist thud. Shreds of it lay plastered flat against the damp sand.

Hector Griffiths left the cave and went back to get his step-daughter's lunch.

5. Packaging (What Do You Want the Product to Look Like? What Does the Public Want the Product to Look Like?)
"The appearance of your product is everything," the diligent young men who worried about their first mortgages and second babies would hear. "Packaging can kill a good product and sell a bad one. It can make an original product look dated, and an old one look brand new."

It could also, Hector Griffiths believed, make the police believe a murder to be an accident and an old corpse to be a slightly newer one.

As with everything, he planned well ahead. The first component in his murder machine was generously donated by its proposed victim. Listless and unwilling to go out, Janet asked if he would mind posting her cards to Melissa's aunts in Stockport. She didn't really know why she was writing to them, she added mournfully; they were unlikely ever to meet again now Mummy was dead.

Hector took the cards, but didn't post them. He did not even put stamps on them. You never knew how much postal rates might go up in a year. He put them away in a blue folder.

There wasn't a lot more that could be done at that stage, so he spent the rest of his time in Cornwall being nice to Janet and drinking with Commander Donleavy at the Yacht Club.

He listened to a lot of naval reminiscences and sympathised with the pervading gloom about the way the world was going. He talked about the younger generation. He said he had nothing to complain of with his step-daughter, except that she was so quiet. He said how he tried to jolly her along, but all she seemed to want to do was mope around the cottage or go off on long walks on her own. Oh yes, she did sketch a bit. Wasn't that her in a blue smock out by the back door of the cottage? Commander Donleavy looked through his binoculars and said he reckoned it must be—too far to see her clearly, though.

If he was in the Yacht Club in the evening, Hector might draw the Commander's attention to the cottage lights going off as Janet went to bed. Always turned in by ten-thirty—at least he couldn't complain about late hours. She was a strange child.

Commander Donleavy laughed and said there was no accounting for the ways of women. Good Lord, within a year that little mouse could have turned into a regular flapper, with boyfriends arriving every hour of the day and night.

Hector said he hoped not (without as much vigour as he felt) and laughed (without as much humour as he manifested). So the holidays passed.

When he got back behind his desk at Gliss, he found a letter telling him that an international domestic cleaning exhibition, Intersan, would be held in Hamburg from the 9th to the 17th September the following year.

This was better than he had dared hope. He called in his assistant, a former Management Trainee, who was in charge of undemanding and unexciting Gliss Spot-Remover range and who constantly complained about his lack of responsibility, and asked him to represent the company at the exhibition. Hector knew it was a long way off, but he thought it would give the young man something to look forward to. He was beginning to feel his age, he added tantalizingly, and thought there might be other responsibilities he would soon wish to delegate.

On the 14th September, Hector Griffiths set aside that day's copy of the *'Daily Telegraph.'* He put it with the postcards in the blue folder.

There was little more he could do for the time being, except to go over his planning in detail and check for flaws. He found none, but he still thought there was something missing. He needed one more element, one clinching piece of evidence. Still, no need to panic; it'd come. Just a matter of patient Desk Work. So, while he devoted most of his energies to the forthcoming launch of Gliss Handy Moppits (Ideal for the Kitchen, Nursery or Handbag), he kept a compartment of his mind open to receive another inspiration.

So the months passed. He and Janet spent Christmas quietly in London. To his relief, she did not appear to be fulfilling Commander Donleavy's prognostications; if anything, she was quieter still. The only change was that she said she hated school, was getting nowhere there, and wanted to leave. Her indulgent step-father suppressed his glee, thought about the matter seriously, and finally agreed that she should leave at the end of the summer term, then join him for August at the cottage, so that they could decide on her future.

6. Publicity (Make Sure Everyone Knows About Your Product Exactly When You Want Them To.)
This was the only one of Hector Griffiths' headings which might, while vital for any Gliss product, seem to be less applicable in the case of a murder.

But publicity is not only making things public; it is also keeping things secret until the time is right, and Hector's experience at Gliss had taught him a great deal about this art. Though lacking the glamour of military secrets, cleaning fluid secrets were still valuable and had been the subjects of espionage. So Hector was trained to keep his plans to himself.

And, anyway, there was going to come a time when publicity of the conventional sort was necessary, indeed essential. If the police never found Janet's body, then the plan was incomplete. Not only might there be difficulties in releasing her money to her step-father, he might also have to suffer the stigma of suspicion. As with the launch of a product, what was important was the moment of public revelation. And the timing of that, with this product as with any other, Hector would dictate personally.

It was, incidentally, while he was thinking of publicity that he came upon the missing element in his campaign. Some months before the launch of Gliss Handy Moppits (Ideal for the Kitchen, Nursery or Handbag) Hector had to go to his advertising agency to agree the publicity campaign for the new product. He enjoyed these occasions, because he knew that he, as Product Manager, was completely in command, and loved to see his account executive fawn while he deliberated.

One particular ploy, which gave him a great deal of satisfaction, was simply delaying his verdict. He would look at the artwork, view the television commercial or listen to the campaign outline, then, after remaining silent for a few minutes, start talking about something completely different. The executive presenting to him, fearful above all else of losing the very lucrative Gliss account, would sweat his way up any conversational alley the Product Manager wished to lead him, until finally Hector relented and said what he thought.

After seeing the television commercial for Gliss Handy Moppits

(Ideal for the Kitchen, Nursery or Handbag), Hector started playing his game and asked what else the executive was working on.

The young man, a fine sweat lending his brow a satisfying sheen, answered sycophantically. His next big job was for one of the country's biggest confectionery firms, the launch of a brand new nut and nougat sweet—the Nuggy Bar. It was going to be a huge nationwide campaign, newspapers, cinema, television, radio, the lot. The product was already being tested in the Tyne-Tees area. Look, would Mr Griffiths like to try one? Nice blue and gold wrapper, wasn't it? Yes, go on, try —we've got plenty—the office is full of them.

Well, what did Mr Griffiths think of it? Pretty revolting? Hmm. Well, never mind. Yes, take one by all means. Well, anyway, whatever Mr Griffiths thought of them, he was going to be hard put to avoid them. After the launch on 10th September, he would see them in every shop in the country.

Hector Griffiths glowed inwardly. Yes, of course there was skill and there was planning, but there was also luck. Luck, like the fact that the old Gliss Floor Polish tin had adapted so easily to metric standards. Luck, like suddenly coming across the Nuggy Bar. It was a magnetism for luck that distinguished a great Product Manager from a good Product Manager.

The Nuggy Bar was secure in his pocket. His mind raced on, as he calmly told the account executive that he found the Gliss Handy Moppits (Ideal for the Kitchen, Nursery or Handbag) commercial too flippant, and that it would have to be remade, showing more respect for the product.

7. Run-Up to Launch (Attend to Details. Check, Check and Recheck.)
Hector Griffiths checked, checked and rechecked.

In June he went to an unfamiliar boat dealer in North London and bought, for cash, an inflatable dinghy and outboard motor.

The next weekend he went down to Cornwall and, after much consultation with Commander Donleavy, bought an identical dinghy and outboard from the boatyard that serviced his motor-boat.

Three days later he bought some electrical time-switches in an anonymous Woolworths.

Then, furtively, in a Soho sex shop, he bought an inflatable woman.

In another anonymous Woolworths, he bought a pair of rubber gloves.

At work, the Gliss Handy Moppits (Ideal for the Kitchen, Nursery

or Handbag) were successfully launched. Hector's assistant, in antici-
pation of his exciting trip to Hamburg for Intersan, took his holiday in
July. One of his last actions before going away was to prepare the
authorization for the continued production of Gliss Spot-Remover.
This was the formal notice to the production department which would
ensure sufficient supplies of the product for November orders. It was
one of those boring bits of paperwork that had to be prepared by the
individual Product Manager and sent to the overall Gliss Product
Manager for signature.

Hector's assistant did it last thing on the day he left, deposited it in
his out-tray, and set off for two weeks in Hunstanton, cheered by the
fact that Griffiths had said he was going to take a longer holiday that
summer, all of August plus two weeks of September. Another indication, like Intersan, that the old man was going to sit back a bit and give
others a chance.

So Hector's assistant didn't see the old man in question remove the
Gliss Spot-Remover authorization from his out-tray. Nor did he see it
burnt to nothing in an ash-tray in the Sloane Street flat.

Janet left her Yorkshire boarding school as quietly as she had done
everything else in her life, and joined her step-father in London. At the
beginning of August they went down to Cornwall.

She remained as withdrawn as ever. Her step-father encouraged her
to keep up her sketching, and to join him in occasional trips in the
motor-boat or his new rubber dinghy. He spoke with some concern to
Commander Donleavy in the Yacht Club about her listlessness. He
pointed her out sketching outside the cottage, and the Commander
almost saw her figure through his binoculars. Once or twice in the
evening, Hector commented to the Commander about the early hour
at which she switched the lights out.

On the 16th August, Hector Griffiths went out fishing on his own
and unfortunately cut both his hands when a nylon line he was reeling
in pulled taut.

That evening he tried to talk to his step-daughter about a career, but
found it hard going. Hadn't she discussed it with friends? With teachers at the school? Wasn't there someone he could ring and talk to about
it?

After a lot of probing, she did give him the name of her French
mistress, who was the only person she seemed to have been even
slightly close to at the school. Had she got her phone number? asked

Hector. Yes. Would she write it down for him? Here, on this scrap of paper.

Reluctantly she did. She didn't notice that the scrap of paper was a piece torn from a copy of the *Daily Telegraph*. Or that the only printing on it was most of the date—"14th September, 19 . . ."

Her step-father continued his uphill struggle to cheer her up. Look, here was something he'd been given. A new sort of chocolate bar, nut and nougat, called the Nuggy Bar. Not even on the market yet. Go on, try a bit, have a bite. She demurred, but eventually, just to please him, did take a bite.

She thought it was "pretty revolting."

8. *The Launch*

The spring tide was to be at its lowest at 19.41 on 17th August, but Hector Griffiths didn't mention this when he persuaded his step-daughter to come out for a trip in the motor-boat at half past six that evening. Janet wasn't keen, but nor was she obstructive, so soon the boat, with its rubber dinghy towed behind, was chugging along towards "Stinky Cove." Her step-father's hands on the wheel wore rubber gloves, to prevent dirt from getting into the wounds made by his fishing line the previous day.

Janet seemed psychologically incapable of enthusiasm for anything, but Hector got very excited when he thought he saw an opening in the rocks. He steered the boat in close and there, sure enough, was an archway. The stench near the rocks was strong enough to deter any but the most ardent speleologist—in fact, there were no other vessels in sight—but Hector still seemed keen to investigate the opening. He anchored the motor-boat and urged Janet into the dinghy. They cast off and puttered towards the rocks.

Instructing his step-daughter to duck, Hector lined the boat up, cut the motor, and waves washed the dinghy through on to the sand of a hidden cave.

With expressions of wonder, Hector stepped out into a shallow stream, gesturing Janet to follow him. She did so with her usual lethargy. Her step-father pulled the dinghy some way up on to the sand. Crowing with childlike excitement about the discovery they'd made, he suggested exploring. Maybe this little cave led to a bigger one. Wasn't that an opening there at the top of the pile of rubble? He set off towards it. Without interest, but cooperative to the last, Janet followed.

It was on the precarious top of the pile that Hector Griffiths appeared to lose his balance and fall heavily against his step-daughter. She fell sideways down the loose surface to the sand of the cave floor. Fortunately she fell face down, so she didn't see the practised aim of the rock that went flying towards her head.

The damp thud of its impact was very similar to that an earlier missile had made against a paper bag, but louder. The commotion was sufficient to dislodge a shower of small stones from the roof of the cave, which gave very satisfactory credibility to the idea that Janet had been killed by a rockfall.

Hector also found it a source of satisfaction that she had landed away from the stream. When her body was finally discovered, he didn't want her clothes to be soaked through; it must be clear that she had entered the cave in the dinghy, in other words, at the lowest ebb of a spring tide.

Hector stepped carefully down the rubble. Keeping his feet in the stream, he inspected Janet. A little blood and brain from her crushed skull marked the sand. She was undoubtedly dead.

With his gloved hands, he slipped the scrap of *Daily Telegraph* with her French mistress's phone number and the opened Nuggy Bar with its blue and gold wrapper into Janet's pocket.

He then walked down the stream to the opening, already slightly smaller with the rising tide, waded into the sea and swam out to the motor-boat.

On board he removed a tarpaulin from his second rubber dinghy, attached its painter to the back of the larger boat and cast it behind. Then he chugged back to his mooring near the cottage, as the tide continued to rise.

9. The Vital First Month (Your Product Is Your Baby—Nurse It Gently.)

Hector Griffiths still had nearly a month of his six-week holiday in Cornwall to go, and he passed it very quietly and peacefully. Much of the time he was in the Yacht Club drinking with Commander Donleavy.

There he would complain to the Commander, and anyone else who happened to be listening, about his step-daughter's reticence and ask advice on what career he should guide her towards. Now and then at lunch-time he would point out the blue smock-clad figure sitting sketching outside the back door of the cottage. At night he might comment on her early hours as he saw the cottage lights go off.

In the mornings, before he went out, he would check the time-switches and decide whether or not to use the inflatable woman. He didn't want the sketching to become too predictable, so he varied the position of the dummy in its smock and frequently just left it indoors. Once or twice, at dusk, he took it out in the dinghy past the harbour and waved to the fishermen on the quay.

At the end of August he posted Janet's cards to Melissa's aunts in Stockport. Their messages had the timeless banality of all postcard communications.

In the first week of September he continued his nautical rounds and awaited the explosion from Gliss.

Because the cottage wasn't on the telephone, the explosion, when it came, on the 5th September, was in the form of a telegram. (Hector had kept the sketching dummy out of the way for a few days in antici-pation of its arrival.) It was from his assistant, saying a crisis had arisen, could he ring as soon as possible.

He made the call from the Yacht Club. His assistant was defiantly guilty. Something had gone wrong with the production authorization for Gliss Spot-Remover. The factory hadn't received it and now there would be no stock to meet the November orders.

Hector Griffiths swore—a rare occurrence—and gave his assistant a lavish dressing-down. The young man protested he was sure he had done the paperwork, but received an unsympathetic hearing. Good God, couldn't he be trusted with the simplest responsibility? Well, there was nothing else for it, he'd have to go and see all the main buyers and apologise. No, letters wouldn't do, nor would the tele-phone. Gliss's image for efficiency was at stake and the cock-up had to be explained personally.

But, the young man whimpered, what about his forthcoming trip to Intersan in Hamburg?

Oh no! Hector had forgotten all about that. Well, it was out of the question that his assistant should go now, far too much mopping-up to be done. Damn, he'd have to go himself. Gliss must be represented. It was bloody inconvenient, but there it was.

After a few more demoralizing expletives, Hector put the phone down and, fuming, joined Commander Donleavy at the bar. Wasn't it bloody typical? he demanded rhetorically, can't trust anyone these days—now he was going to have to cut his holiday short just because of the incompetence of his bloody assistant. Young people had no sense of responsibility.

Commander Donleavy agreed. They should bring back National Service.

Hector made a few more calls to Gliss management people, saying how he was suddenly going to have to rush off to Hamburg. He sounded aggrieved at the change of plan.

On his last day in Cornwall, the 6th September, he deflated the dinghy and the woman. He went a long way out to sea in the motor-boat, weighted them with the outboard motor and a few stones, and cast them overboard. The electrical time-switches and the rubber gloves followed.

That evening he said goodbye to Commander Donleavy in the Yacht Club. He confessed to being a little worried about Janet. Whereas previously she had just seemed listless, she now seemed deeply depressed. He didn't like to leave her in the cottage alone, though she spoke of going up to London, but he wasn't sure that he'd feel happier with her there. Still, he had to go on this bloody trip and he couldn't get her to make up her mind about anything . . .

Commander Donleavy opined that women were strange fish.

As he drove the Mercedes up to London on the 7th September, Hector Griffiths reviewed the necessary actions on his return from Hamburg. Because of the Gliss Spot-Remover crisis, he could legitimately delay going back to Cornwall for a week or two. And, since the cottage wasn't on the phone and she hadn't contacted him, he'd have to write to Janet. Nice, fatherly, solicitous letters.

Only after he had received no reply to two of these would he start to worry and go down to Cornwall. That would get him past the next low tide when the cave was accessible.

On arriving and finding his letters unopened on the mat he would drive straight back to London, assuming that he must somehow have missed his step-daughter there. He would ring her French mistress and Melissa's aunts in Stockport and only after drawing blanks there would he call the police.

When they talked to him, he'd mention Janet's talk of going up to London. He'd also mention her depressed state. He would delay as long as possible mentioning that his rubber dinghy appeared to be missing.

Then, preferably as much as four months after her murder on August 17th, by which time, his reading of forensic medicine told him, it would be difficult to date the death with more than approximate accuracy, he would remember her once mentioning to him a hidden cave she'd found at low tide round "Stinky Cove."

The body would then be discovered.

Because of the lack of accurate timing from its state of decomposition, the police would have to date her death from other clues. The presence of the dinghy and the dryness of her clothes would indicate that she had entered the cave at a low spring tide, which at once limited the dates.

Local people would have seen the dinghy, if not the girl, around until shortly before Hector's departure on the 7th September. But other clues would be found in the girl's pocket. First, a Nuggy Bar, a new nut and nougat confection which was not available in the shops until the 10th September. And, second, a phone number written on a scrap of newspaper dated 14th September. Since that was the date of a spring tide, the police would have no hesitation in fixing the death of Janet Wintle on the 17th September.

On which date her step-father was unexpectedly, through a combination of circumstances he could not have foreseen, in Hamburg at Intersan, an international domestic cleaning exhibition.

So Hector Griffiths would have to come to terms with a second accidental death in his immediate family within two years.

And the fact that he would inherit his step-daughter's not inconsiderable wealth could only be a small compensation to him in his bereavement.

10. Is Your Product a Success? (Are You Sure There's Nothing You've Forgotten?)
On the day before he left for Hamburg, Hector Griffiths had a sudden panic. Suppose one of Melissa's aunts in Stockport had died? They were both pretty elderly and, if it had happened, it was the sort of thing Janet would have known about. She'd hardly have sent a postcard to someone who was dead.

He checked by ringing the aunts with some specious inquiry about full names for a form he had to fill in. Both were safely alive. And both had been so glad to get Janet's postcards. When they hadn't heard from her the previous year, they were afraid she had forgotten them. So it was lovely to get the two postcards.

Two postcards? What, they'd got two each?

No, no, that would have been odd. One each, two in all.

Hector breathed again. He thought it fairly unlikely, knowing Janet's unwillingness to go out, that she'd sent any other postcards, but it was nice to be sure.

So everything was happily settled. He could go abroad with a clear conscience.

He couldn't resist calling Gliss to put another rocket under his assistant and check if there was anything else urgent before he went away.

There was a message asking him to call the advertising agency about the second wave of television commercials for Gliss Handy Moppits (Ideal for the Kitchen, Nursery or Handbag). He rang through and derived his customary pleasure from patronizing the account executive. Just as he was about to ring off, he asked, "All set for the big launch?"

"Big launch?"

"On the 10th. The Nuggy Bar."

"Oh God. Don't talk to me about Nuggy Bars. I'm up to here with Nuggy Bars. The bloody Product Manager's got cold feet."

"Cold feet?"

"Yes. He's new to the job, worried the product's not going to sell."

"What?"

"They've got the report back from the Tyne-Tees area where they tested it. Apparently 47% of the sample thought it was 'pretty revolting.' "

"So what's going to happen?"

"Bloody Product Manager wants to delay the launch."

"Delay the launch?"

"Yes, delay it or cancel the whole thing. He doesn't know what he wants to do."

"But he can't pull out at this stage. The television time's been contracted and the newspapers and—"

"He can get out of most of it, if he doesn't mind paying off the contracts. He's stuck with the magazine stuff, because they go to press so far ahead, but he can stop the rest of it. And, insofar as he's capable of making a decision, he seems to have decided to stop it. Call came through just before lunch—Hold everything—the Nuggy Bar will not be launched on the 10th September!"

The Mercedes had never gone faster than it did on the road down to Cornwall. In spite of the air-conditioning, its driver was drenched in sweat.

The motor-boat too was urged on at full throttle until it reached

"Stinky Cove." Feverishly Hector Griffiths let out the anchor cable and, stripping off his jacket and shoes, plunged into the sea.

The water was low, but not low enough to reveal the opening. Over a week to go to the spring tide. He had to dive repeatedly to locate the arch, and it was only on the third attempt that he managed to force his way under it. Impelled by the waves, he felt his back scraped raw by the rocks. He scrambled up on to the damp sand.

Inside all seemed dark. He cursed his stupidity in not bringing a flashlight. But, as he lay panting on the sand, he began to distinguish the outlines of the church-like interior. There was just enough glow from the underwater arch to light his mission. Painfully, he picked himself up.

As he did so, he became aware of something else. A new stench challenged the old one that gave the cove its name. Gagging, he moved towards its source.

Not daring to look, he felt around in her clothes. It seemed an age before he found her pocket, but at last he had the Nuggy Bar in his hand.

Relief flooded his body and he tottered with weakness. It'd be all right. Back through the arch, into the boat, back to London, Hamburg tomorrow. Even if he'd been seen by the locals, it wouldn't matter. The scrap of *Daily Telegraph* and the dry state of Janet's clothes would still fix the date of her death a week ahead. It'd all be all right.

He waded back into the cold waves. They were now splashing higher up the sand, the tide was rising. He moved out as far as he could and leant against the rock above the arch. A deep breath, and he plunged down into the water.

First, all he saw was a confusion of spray, then a gleam of diluted daylight ahead, then he felt a searing pain against his back and, as his breath ran out, the glow of daylight dwindled.

The waves had forced him back into the cave.

He tried again and again, but each time was more difficult. Each time the waves were stronger and he was weaker. He wasn't going to make it. He lay exhausted on the sand.

He tried to think dispassionately, to recapture the coolness of his planning mind, to imagine he was sitting down to the Desk Work on a cleaning fluid problem.

But the crash of the waves distracted him. The diminishing light distracted him. And, above all, the vile smell of decomposing flesh distracted him.

He controlled his mind sufficiently to work out when the next low tide would be. His best plan was to conserve his strength till then. If he could get back then, there was still a good chance of making the flight to Hamburg and appearing at Intersan as if nothing had happened.

In fact, that was his only possible course.

Unless . . . He remembered his lie to Janet. Let's climb up the pile of rubble and see if there's an opening at the top. It might lead to another cave. There might be another way out.

It was worth a try.

He put the Nuggy Bar in his trouser pocket and climbed carefully up the loose pile of rocks. There was now very little light. He felt his way.

At the top he experienced a surge of hope. There was not a solid wall of rock ahead, just more loose stones. Perhaps they blocked another entrance . . . A passage? Even an old smugglers' tunnel?

He scrabbled away at the rocks, tearing his hands. The little ones scattered, but the bigger ones were more difficult. He tugged and worried at them.

Suddenly a huge obstruction shifted. Hector jumped back as he heard the ominous roar it started. Stones scurried, pattered and thudded all around him. He scrambled back down the incline.

The rockfall roared on for a long time and he had to back nearer and nearer the sea. But for the darkness he would have seen Janet's body buried under a ton of rubble.

At last there was silence. Gingerly he moved forward.

A single lump of rock was suddenly loosed from above. It landed squarely in the middle of his skull, making a damp thud like an exploded paper bag, but louder.

Hector Griffiths fell down on the sand. He died on the 8th September.

Outside his motor-boat, carelessly moored in his haste, dragged its anchor and started to drift out to sea.

It was four months before the police found Hector Griffiths' body. They were led to it eventually by a reference they found in one of his late wife's diaries, which described a secret cave where they had made love. It was assumed that Griffiths had gone there in his dinghy because of the place's morbidly sentimental associations, been cut off by the rising tide and killed in a rockfall. His clothes were soaked with salt water because he lay so near the high tide mark.

It was difficult to date the death exactly after so long, but a check on the tide tables (in which, according to a Commander Donleavy, Griffiths had shown a great interest) made it seem most likely that he had died on the 14th September. This was confirmed by the presence in his pocket of a Nuggy Bar, a nut and nougat confection which was not available in the shops until 10th September.

Because the Product Manager of Nuggy Bar, after cancelling the product's launch, had suddenly remembered a precept that he'd heard in a lecture when he'd been a Management Trainee at Gliss . . .

Once you have made your major decisions about the product and the timing of its launch, do not indulge second thoughts.

So he'd rescinded his second thoughts and the campaign had gone ahead as planned. (It may be worth recording that the Nuggy Bar was not a success. The majority of the buying public found it "pretty revolting.")

The body of Hector Griffiths' step-daughter, Janet Wintle, was never found. Which was a pity for two old ladies in Stockport who, under the terms of a trust set up in her mother's will, stood to inherit her not inconsiderable wealth.

Although he has published a few novels, it is EDWARD D.
HOCH's *(1930–) unbelievable prolificity as a short story writer
that makes him unique in the mystery field. Mr. Hoch is now
approaching seven hundred published short mystery stories, and
at least one story of his has been in every issue of* Ellery Queen's
Mystery Magazine *for many years. And he is not just prolific—
he is very good: no one has sustained the quality he has in the
short story format over such an enormous output. His more
than twenty series characters, which include the wonderful
Nick Velvet, a thief who steals only things of no value, and
Captain Leopold, a police officer in a nameless Eastern city,
have devoted readers all over the world.*

*"The Theft of the Four of Spades" presents Mr. Velvet with
one of his greatest challenges.*

The Theft of the Four of Spades

BY EDWARD D. HOCH

Nick Velvet rarely ventured into Manhattan except on business, so he
could understand Ron Saturn's surprise at encountering him on West
43rd Street during one of New York's periodic spells of late-summer
mugginess.

"Nick!" the little man greeted him. "Nick Velvet! I haven't seen you
in a couple of years, and I sure didn't expect to see you in town on a
day like this! Isn't this weather terrible?"

"I like to see how you city people live," Nick replied with a smile.
Ron Saturn was an aging chorus boy who'd appeared in a few Broadway musicals. But his small stature had kept him from ever hitting it
really big and in recent years he'd turned his talents to assorted confidence games involving wealthy, lonely women.

"We're not living well these days, Nick," Ron replied glumly. "All
the big money's in Saratoga or the Hamptons this month. And the new
musicals don't start rehearsals till October. But what brings you down
here?"

"Nothing shady, Ron. Just a bit of shopping for Gloria's birthday."

"How is she? I miss seeing the two of you."

"She's fine. I'll tell her I ran into you."

Ron Saturn scratched his ear in a gesture Nick remembered from the past. "You know, running into you just might be the answer to my prayers."

"I didn't know you ever prayed, Ron."

"Just a figure of speech, Nick. But look—would you be free for a job this evening? It's for a friend."

Nick hesitated, glancing at his watch. "I generally need more time for planning. I don't know if it could be done that fast."

"Come talk to my friend anyway—okay?"

"Sure, Ron. Anything for a friend."

Nick had known Ron Saturn for so many years, off and on, that it was hard to remember how the friendship had come about. It dated from the years following Nick's army service, when he and Ron had worked together at a marina in Westchester County. They'd taken different paths to success after that, but each had always known that at times the other operated outside the law.

Since Nick had been headed back to Grand Central for the train home, they stopped in the lobby of the Biltmore Hotel for a drink while Ron phoned his friend. He was on the phone for some time before he returned, smiling. "He's on his way over. Cary is—well, difficult at times, but you'll like him."

"Cary?"

"Cary Temple, the actor."

"Oh!" Cary Temple was a vigorous man in his fifties who'd achieved a certain fame in his younger days playing Shakespeare in Central Park and at Jones Beach. He'd even handled the lead in *My Fair Lady* in one of its road companies. But Nick hadn't heard his name mentioned in years. He had truly fallen on hard times if he'd hooked up with Ron Saturn on a confidence scheme.

They were just starting their second drink when Temple arrived. His face had aged a bit and his fine head of hair was an unnatural shade of brown, but his handshake was vigorous and his eyes had all their old matinee sparkle. "Velvet! Ron has always spoken highly of you! A pleasure to meet you at last!"

"The pleasure is mine," Nick murmured. "I've seen you on stage many times."

"Yes." Cary Temple smiled sadly. "Those were better days, I fear. But Ron tells me you can assist with a little enterprise we have going."

"Possibly. I generally need a little time for preparation. You both know my terms, I'm sure." He paused, making sure there was no one close enough to overhear. Then he asked, "What do you want stolen?"

Cary Temple glanced at Ron and cleared his throat.

"The four of spades from a deck of cards. Possibly from several decks of cards."

"That certainly falls within my province of stealing only valueless objects. Where are these cards located?"

"In the Fifth Avenue apartment of Sarah Wentworth."

Nick thought about that. Sarah Wentworth was a revered widow of the former American ambassador to the United Nations. Long active in social and political circles, she'd become a darling of the media since the death of her husband in a plane crash two years earlier. Columnists constantly linked her with eligible middle-aged men—and some not so eligible. "Her place will be well guarded," he said.

"There's heavy security in the building," Temple agreed, "but I can get you in."

"You mentioned several decks of cards. Are they all in one location?"

The actor hesitated. "No, there's a second location involved. The apartment of one Amanda Jones, on 126th Street."

"Harlem?"

"East Harlem, to be exact. I have the address here. In each case you are to steal the four of spades from all decks of cards you find in the apartments. But take nothing else—only the fours of spades. And leave no signs of a robbery."

"What about new, unopened decks of cards?"

"Those too, if you find any. Can you do it?"

"Not by tonight. It would mean casing two layouts. Give me forty-eight hours."

Temple shook his head. "It has to be tonight."

"Sorry." Nick started to rise from the table and Temple turned on Ron Saturn.

"I thought you told me he could do it!"

"He *can,* Cary! Calm down. If anyone in the world can do it, Nick can. Look, Nick, what's your fee now?"

"Twenty-five."

"It's worth thirty to us if you can do it tonight. Right, Cary?"

"That's correct. Thirty thousand."

He moistened his lips as he said it, perhaps remembering better days when he'd earned that much for a week's work on Broadway.

Nick considered the offer. "How would you get me into Sarah Went-worth's apartment?"

"That's the easy part. She's having a cocktail party this afternoon and you could go with me."

"Wouldn't she think that's odd?"

"Not at all, dear fellow. I often bring Ron or someone else. But finding and stealing the cards will be your responsibility."

"The other one—Amanda Jones—has to be done tonight too?"

"That's correct. Shall we be on our way?"

Against his better judgment Nick said, "All right."

There was only time for a quick phone call to Gloria, explaining that he might have to stay in town overnight. "Are you working?" she asked, and when he replied in the affirmative she didn't question him further. She knew she'd hear all about it later.

Ron Saturn left them at the hotel and Temple glanced at his watch. "Just after five. If we take a taxi we should arrive just in time for cocktails."

The apartment, a luxury co-op overlooking Central Park, was already crowded by the time they arrived. Nick recognized some familiar types—show-business people, publishing figures, and a sprinkling from the United Nations. Some wore street clothes because they'd come right from work. The show people, between engagements or awaiting the evening curtain, dressed more elaborately. But the star of the party was the hostess, and Sarah Wentworth was as strikingly lovely in person as on the front page of the latest supermarket tabloid. Still in her early forties, she exuded the sort of fashionable sexuality one usually found in models and starlets still in their twenties. "Nick Velvet?" she repeated, shaking his hand. "I should know you. Are you in the theater?"

"No," he explained. "Cary and I have a mutual friend."

"He's a dear," she confided, patting Temple's cheek as she spoke. "I hope we'll be doing some business together." Then, "Enjoy yourself, Mr. Velvet. I'm so glad you could come."

She moved off to greet other new arrivals and Nick followed Cary Temple through the crowded room to the far end where two bartenders were serving drinks. "You expect me to do the job in a roomful of people?" Nick asked under his breath.

"I'm sure you'll find a way." The actor smiled and accepted a cocktail from the bartender, then went off to join a circle of familiar faces.

Nick stood in the center of the room wondering what to do next.

After a moment Sarah Wentworth approached him again, apparently noticing his hesitation to mingle with the other guests. "What do you do, Mr. Velvet?"

"Card tricks," he answered without really thinking.

"For a living?"

"No, just as a hobby. If you have a deck of cards I can demonstrate."

She smiled just a bit condescendingly. "Perhaps later."

She moved away and mingled with a couple wearing matching pink jackets. They were definitely show-business types, Nick decided. Studying an abstract painting that took up much of one wall, he found his mind wandering to Ron Saturn and Cary Temple, and the sort of scheme they were working. He remembered a movie once where a character under hypnosis was programmed to respond to a certain playing card. But something like that seemed unlikely with Sarah Wentworth. Besides, how would it connect her to a woman in East Harlem, a world away from this Fifth Avenue apartment? He was still puzzling over it as the crowd began to thin out. Obviously the guests were going off to dinner after their cocktails, and soon only a few stragglers remained. The hostess came up to Nick again and said, quite surprisingly, "I believe we're ready for your card tricks now, Mr. Velvet."

"Fine. I know a wonderful trick that can be done with six decks of cards. Would you have that many?"

"I doubt it, but I'll go look."

Cary Temple strolled over to Nick. "Going to entertain us a little?"

"I hope so."

Sarah Wentworth returned holding a boxed double deck used for Canasta, two bridge decks, and a pinochle deck. "I'm afraid these are all the cards I have."

Nick knew there was no four of spades in a pinochle deck, so he immediately set that one aside. "These four will do nicely, thanks." If she had produced more than the six requested decks, he would have found a reason to use them all. As it was he ran through some simple tricks he'd known since high school. They were good enough to impress Sarah Wentworth and that was all that mattered. By the time he carefully returned the cards to their boxes and departed with Cary Temple, the four of spades from each of the four decks was in his pocket.

"You're good with your fingers," Temple admitted. "I was watching you and I didn't see a thing."

"I must have shuffled each deck fifteen or twenty times. I'd spot the four of spades on the bottom or when I was cutting, and slip it off the deck. A couple I palmed. One dropped into my lap and one went up my sleeve. It was perfectly safe. Even if someone noticed they'd just think it was part of the trick."

"Give me the cards," Temple said.

"I think I should get half of the money now."

"You'll get all the money when you finish up later tonight. Ron is rounding it up now."

Nick handed over the cards reluctantly. "Sooner or later she's going to know they're gone."

"They only need to be gone temporarily. Next time I'm up there I may be able to slip them back into the decks. But that's my problem, not yours."

"Are you taking me up to East Harlem now?"

The actor smiled and shook his head. "Now *that* is your problem, not mine. My face is too valuable to risk being worked over by some young punks after money for their next fix. Here's Amanda Jones's address. Good luck."

"Where'll I find you?"

"Phone me at this number. Ron and I will meet you with the money."

"It has to be tonight?"

"It has to be tonight."

Nick took the subway uptown. When he emerged from underground to find a gang of leather-jacketed teenagers taunting passersby, he was immediately sorry he didn't have a weapon on him. But they let him pass without incident and he walked the short block to the address on 126th Street.

It was a ground-floor apartment with a light in the window, and for a moment Nick thought he was in luck. A small sign in the window read: *Amanda Jones—Reader—Adviser.* He walked into the dim hallway, past a man sleeping on the stoop, and knocked on the door.

"What you want?" a voice asked from behind the door.

"A reading. Is Amanda in?"

The door opened a crack. "I'm Amanda."

"Can I come in?"

A brown eye inspected him, then the door opened a bit wider. "Can't be too careful, 'specially at night. Come on in."

Amanda Jones was a fairly young woman with light brown skin and wide eyes that seemed to see everything. Nick thought she could be quite attractive if she dispensed with some of the costume jewelry around her neck and wrists and improved on a hairstyle that could only be called gypsy-wild in its present state. "You want a reading?" she asked. "Is that what you said?"

"Yes."

"Tarot or regular deck?"

That was when Nick realized his luck had run out. There were decks of cards visible everywhere in the small apartment, and many were 78-card tarot decks. How did one steal the four of spades from a deck in which the suits were called, if memory served him, swords, wands, cups, and coins?

"I'm not sure about tarot cards," he admitted. "Does a larger deck make for a more accurate reading?"

"Certainly. Though some customers prefer a reading with an ordinary deck, so they can get the technique and try it at home with their own cards." She smiled ruefully. "I lose more customers that way!"

"Let's try a straight deck first."

She looked him over and said, "That'll be ten dollars. In advance."

"Isn't that a bit steep?" He'd expected to pay twenty.

"Inflation, you know?"

Amanda Jones accepted his money and motioned toward a round table in the center of the room. She dealt out ten cards and arranged them in a careful pattern. After studying it a moment she announced his fate.

"You have a crisis to overcome but you will be successful. I see a great deal of money coming to you—perhaps from your labors or from an inheritance."

"I see. Could you do a tarot reading for me too?"

"That would be another ten dollars."

He laid the bill on the table between them and she rose to get the cards. "Do you get many customers up here?" he asked.

"Off the street, like you? Not too many. A few neighbor women, that's all. But you must be feelin' brave to come up here after dark."

"A friend recommended you."

"Who's that?"

Nick decided to take a chance. "Sarah Wentworth."

"You know Mrs. Wentworth? She's *some* lady! I'm doing a reading for her tomorrow."

"Don't mention I was here," Nick cautioned. "I'm always kidding her about fortune-telling and I don't want her to know I tried it myself."

"That lady doesn't do a *thing* without a reading from the cards! She used to be my mother's customer and now I've got her."

"Your mother died?"

Amanda Jones shrugged. "She's in jail. It's about the same thing."

As she shuffled the tarot deck Nick asked, "These suits correspond to the regular card suits, don't they?"

"Sure. Cups is hearts, coins is diamonds."

"What about spades?"

"Spades correspond to swords in a tarot deck. Clubs are wands." She began to lay out the cards with their strange, garish illustrations. "I can give you a ten-card spread, a seven-card spread, or a royal spread. Which would you like?"

"Royal, I think."

She removed some cards from the deck, then dealt the remainder after first having him choose a king and four other cards. Her reading this time was longer and more complex, but the conclusion was the same. "See here? The ace of coins means riches and great wealth. It is the same money I saw in the spread from the regular deck."

"I guess I have to believe it, then."

"You'd be wise to." She smiled and scooped up the cards. Then, sensing there might be more money to be made, she added, "For an additional fee I can do you a special spread on your sex life."

"Another time, maybe. You probably want to close up and get home."

"I live right here. You wouldn't catch me out on those streets at night."

Nick had been afraid that was the case. Stealing the four of spades from all those decks without her knowing it would definitely present a problem. He thanked her for the readings and departed, hearing the bolts slam shut on the door behind him. Somehow he had to get her out of that apartment, but he didn't know how.

A gentle rain was falling outside, glistening the pavement and making him sorry he hadn't worn a raincoat. The street was nearly deserted, though he could see activity down on 125th Street. Not surprisingly, the gang of leather-jacketed youths still waited in the subway entrance. There were four of them, and Nick approached them warily. "How'd you like to earn some money?" he asked.

"How, man?" the tallest one asked. "By beatin' on your head?" He smiled and lunged forward as he spoke. Nick side-stepped and sent him spinning against the wall of the subway entrance. Then he grabbed the second one and twisted his arm behind his back.

"Listen, you punks! Do what I say and there's a hundred bucks each in it for you. Otherwise I'll hand out a few broken arms."

It was the sort of talk they understood. Nick took a few bills from his pocket, promising the rest later, and explained what he wanted.

Some twenty minutes later there was a disturbance on the sidewalk outside Amanda Jones's apartment. She came to the window, glanced out, and saw four youths fighting in the rain. She saw the glint of a knife reflecting the glow of street lights, and then one of the youths cried out and slid to the sidewalk. The other three took off running.

The wounded youth gasped and dragged himself up the steps to the door of Amanda's building. He managed to ring her bell before he collapsed again. Amanda had watched it all, and now she unbolted her door and moved cautiously toward the front steps. She opened the street door and knelt beside the bloody youth. "Are you hurt bad?" she asked.

"I—I don't think so."

"I'll call an ambulance."

"No! Just get me a bandage for this cut. I'll be okay."

It was dark on the steps and she had trouble examining the wound. "Can you come inside?"

"No. Bring me something out here."

She hurried to do so, forgetting her old fear of the street at night. She was, after all, only in the doorway of her own apartment house. She came back with a wet cloth and a bandage, washing away the blood as best she could. "It doesn't look too bad. Sure you don't want me to call the police?"

"No, I feel better now. Just let me go."

"I don't know. I'd better report this. Those kids could be waitin' for you again."

"I'll be all right." He got to his feet, a bit shaky and started down the steps.

She watched him for a time but he seemed to be walking all right. In fact, after half a block he broke into a run.

She went back inside and locked the door. She'd only been out of her apartment for seven minutes, but that had been long enough for Nick Velvet.

Nick met the four youths back at the subway entrance and paid them the rest of their money. He gave an extra twenty to the kid who'd played the injured one. "You'd make a great actor," he said. Then he caught the subway back downtown, hoping they'd spend their new riches wisely.

Nick had entered the building on 126th Street by picking the lock on the back door. He had then slipped into Amanda's apartment when she went out to help the apparently wounded youth on the front steps. With the apartment door open, Nick was able to hear their conversation and hide in a closet when she returned for the wet cloth and bandages. Then he'd completed his task, left the apartment, and gone down the hall to the back door, while she treated the boy on the front steps. He'd taken the four of spades from seventeen regular decks, and the four of swords from eight tarot decks.

It was after ten when Nick reached Times Square and telephoned Cary Temple. The actor had been waiting for his call, and they arranged a ten-thirty meeting at an Irish bar on Eighth Avenue. The rain had stopped but the pavement was still wet as Nick crossed the street and entered the place. A few customers stood along the bar watching a Friday-night baseball game, but the tables and booths were empty. Nick chose one off in a corner and sat down to wait. He still hoped he could catch a late train and surprise Gloria.

Just after ten-thirty Ron Saturn came in. He was alone.

"Hi, Nick. How'd it go?"

"Fine. Here are the cards."

"Good lord! All from Amanda Jones's place?"

"That's right. I even threw in some fours of swords from various tarot decks she had."

"That's great, Nick!"

"Tomorrow's the big day, eh?"

"What do you mean, Nick?"

"While I was stealing the cards from her I took a second to glance in a couple of books she had on the meaning of the cards. The meaning seems to vary from list to list, but it's generally about the same. The four of spades, or the four of swords in a tarot deck, means *Solitude, exile, retreat.* One book is specific enough to give the meaning as *Have nothing more to do with a certain person about whom you are doubtful.*"

"Yes," Ron agreed. "That's correct."

"And Amanda Jones has a session with Sarah Wentworth tomorrow. Obviously Mrs. Wentworth wants to see what the cards say about a possible business deal with Cary Temple. He's still a charmer, and I imagine between the two of you a great deal of money has been removed from wealthy New York ladies. With a target as important as Sarah Wentworth, you couldn't chance anything going wrong at the last minute. You especially couldn't chance the four of spades turning up in that fortune-telling session tomorrow. There are other bad cards in the deck too, of course, but from your standpoint the four of spades would be the very worst. If she believed it, she'd call off the deal with Temple at once. You couldn't be sure if Amanda would bring her own deck or use one of Sarah's, so I had to steal the four of spades from both their decks."

"You're smart, Nick. You always were."

"You and Temple figured one missing card would never be noticed from the deck—not tomorrow, at least. And if Amanda discovered it later it wouldn't matter."

"That's about it."

"What's the con? What is it that Sarah Wentworth is supposed to dump her money into?"

Ron Saturn grew a bit nervous at the question. "You don't need to know that, Nick. In fact, the less you know the better. You know how these things are."

"All right," Nick agreed. "You've got the cards. Give me my money and I can still catch the late train home."

Saturn produced a thick envelope from an inside pocket. "It's not quite all there, Nick."

"What do you mean?"

"We can't raise the rest of it till Sarah comes through with the money Cary's expecting."

Nick felt a growing anger. "You know that's not the way I work, Ron. How much is here?"

"Ten thousand in small bills."

"Ten—"

"I know, I know! I told Cary you'd be angry. But play along with us, Nick. We'll have the rest of it tomorrow for sure."

"I'm not your partner in this, Ron. I have to be paid up front."

"I know, I know! I told Cary that. But we just couldn't raise that much money tonight. You'll have the rest before the banks close tomorrow."

"Was Temple afraid to be here when you told me?"

"No, he's busy working out the final details of his proposal."

"Since I seem to have become an unwilling partner, suppose you tell me about it."

"Like I said, Nick, you don't need—"

"I need to know if I have to wait till tomorrow for the rest of my money."

"All right," Saturn agreed. "I can tell you in a general way that it involves a performing arts center to be built in a city not far from New York. It would be to the arts what Meadowlands is to sports, drawing people from the entire metropolitan area. Cary approached her for some of the initial financing—a feasibility study to choose the site and determine the method of financing the construction itself. He hopes she'll give him a quarter of a million dollars for a start, with perhaps more later."

"I see. And the study will show the idea isn't feasible at all."

"Who knows? Maybe she'll get back her money and then some. Your thirty comes out of the two-fifty, and we'll spend twenty thousand more on real consultants to make it look good. Cary and I split the other two hundred thousand. But when she told Cary she had to get a reading first from this Amanda Jones, we knew we couldn't take a chance on it coming out wrong."

"Why didn't you just talk to Amanda and offer her a thousand bucks to give a fake reading?"

"How could we risk approaching her? We didn't even know her. If she went running to Mrs. Wentworth, all Cary's months of preparation would go down the drain."

Nick sighed and ordered another drink. He could see he'd have to spend the night in New York after all. "You'll give us till tomorrow?" Ron asked.

"What choice do I have?"

Nick took a room at the Biltmore overnight. In the morning he phoned Ron Saturn and learned they were awaiting a call from Sarah Wentworth. The reading was to be at eleven, and they hoped to have the money by noon.

Noon passed and nothing happened.

Nick phoned again as he was checking out of his room at one o'clock. This time Cary Temple answered.

"Don't worry, Velvet. It's just a slight delay. Ron and I are going over there in an hour."

"Good. I'll be waiting for you at the park entrance across the street."

"It might be wiser to remain at your hotel."

"I'm checking out," Nick replied. "I'll be waiting across the street." He hung up before Temple could respond.

Nick reached Sarah Wentworth's apartment building in the mid-sixties just before two o'clock, in time to see Saturn and Temple leave a taxi and walk past the doorman. He found a bench just inside the park entrance and settled down to wait. Though the sky was cloudy there'd been no further rain and he could hear young voices from the children's zoo nearby.

He waited for over an hour but the two men did not reappear.

He stood up at last and started across the street. Certainly it didn't take this long to give a final pitch and pick up the check. It was time to investigate the possibility of a rear entrance, and the growing suspicion that his old friend Ron Saturn was pulling a double cross.

He'd crossed the street and was starting to circle the building when he saw them coming out the front door—Saturn and Temple, and two other men. One of the men walked to the curb and signaled a waiting car. Nick kept walking. The men were detectives, and Saturn and Temple were almost certainly under arrest.

He didn't see the other person come out of the apartment building, not until Amanda Jones spoke to him. "Well, don't I know you from somewhere?" she asked with a grin.

"I—"

"Were you waiting for your two friends? They had a previous engagement—with the police."

Nick took a deep breath. "I think I'd better buy you a drink."

They walked south a few blocks to a hotel cocktail lounge and Nick ordered the drinks. "Do you want to tell me what happened back there?"

Amanda Jones smiled again, obviously enjoying herself. "What were you after up at my place last night? You were working with those two, weren't you?"

"I did them a favor, yes."

"That boy who got hurt on my doorstep—it was to get me out of my apartment, wasn't it? Fake blood, wasn't it?"

There was no harm in admitting it. Nick nodded and said, "I took the four of spades from all your decks."

She laughed out loud. "Man, that's the craziest thing I ever did hear!"

"They were afraid if the four turned up in your reading for Mrs. Wentworth it would cool her toward Cary Temple's scheme." He took a drink and lit her cigarette. "Now it's your turn. Tell me what happened up there."

"I did her a ten-card reading with my tarot deck like I always do. I'll admit I didn't notice any missing card. But when I spread the deck, card number two, showing the immediate influence on the questioner, was the moon."

"The moon?"

Amanda Jones nodded. "It's a bad card in the tarot deck, signifying deception, trickery, dishonesty, insincerity, double dealing. Mrs. Wentworth took one look at it and decided to call a friend of hers at police headquarters."

"Are you telling me Temple and Saturn were arrested because of a tarot reading?"

"Not entirely. But the police apparently had two other complaints from wealthy women about Temple collecting money for this arts-center scheme. They sent a couple of detectives up to be present when she gave him the money." She was smiling again. "I guess that's the end of this con game for now."

"I didn't know there'd been others," Nick admitted.

"It was all in the cards. They never fail me. That moon card told it all."

"I'll tell you something—they failed you last night when you did my reading and said I'd receive a great deal of money. Your reading for Mrs. Wentworth *cost* me a great deal of money!"

But Amanda Jones was still basking in her triumph and wasn't about to be shaken. "Your trouble was, you just thought too small," she told him.

"How do you mean?"

"You only stole the four of spades when you should have stolen the moon."

SUE GRAFTON *(1940–) is a second generation mystery writer; her father, C. W. Grafton, was an active mystery novelist in the 1940s and 1950s. Rapidly emerging as one of the foremost crime writers of the 1980s, her first novels,* Keziah Dane *and* The Lolly-Madonna War, *were interesting mainstream efforts, but it was her detective creation Kinsey Millhone that shot her to fame. Kinsey appears in books that feature a letter in each of their titles, beginning with "A" Is for Alibi.* "B" Is for Burglar *won the Shamus Award for Best Private Eye Novel from The Private Eye Writers of America in 1985. The next Millhone case,* "C" Is for Corpse, *won an Anthony (awards given by vote of the membership of the annual Bouchercon mystery convention) for Best Hardcover Mystery of 1987. Ms. Kinsey Millhone works out of "Santa Teresa," a thinly disguised Santa Barbara, California. Her most recent case is* "E" Is for Evidence *(1988).*

"The Parker Shotgun" won Sue Grafton an Anthony for Best Short Story of 1986.

The Parker Shotgun

BY SUE GRAFTON

The Christmas holidays had come and gone and the new year was underway. January, in California, is as good as it gets . . . cool, clear and green, with a sky the color of wisteria and a surf that thunders like a volley of gunfire in a distant field. My name is Kinsey Millhone. I'm a private investigator, licensed, bonded, insured; white, female, age 32, unmarried, and physically fit. That Monday morning, I was sitting in my office with my feet up, wondering what life would bring, when a woman walked in and tossed a photograph on my desk. My introduction to the Parker shotgun began with a graphic view of its apparent effect when fired at a formerly nice-looking man at close range. His face was still largely intact, but he had no use now for a pocket comb. With effort, I kept my expression neutral as I glanced up at her.

"Somebody killed my husband."

"I can see that," I said.

She snatched the picture back and stared at it as though she might have missed some telling detail. Her face suffused with pink and she blinked back tears. "Jesus. Rudd was killed five months ago and the cops have done shit. I'm so sick of getting the runaround I could scream."

She sat down abruptly and pressed a hand to her mouth, trying to compose herself. She was in her late twenties, with a gaudy prettiness. Her hair was an odd shade of brown, like cherry coke, worn shoulder length and straight. Her eyes were large, a lush mink brown, her mouth full. Her complexion was all warm tones, tanned, and clear. She didn't seem to be wearing make-up, but she was still as vivid as a magazine illustration, a good four color run on slick paper. She was seven months pregnant by the look of her; not voluminous yet, but rotund. When she was calmer, she identified herself as Lisa Osterling.

"That's a crime lab photo. How'd you come by it?" I said when the preliminaries were disposed of.

She fumbled in her handbag for a tissue and blew her nose. "I have my little ways," she said, morosely. "Actually I know the photographer and I stole a print. I'm going to have it blown up and hung on the wall just so I won't forget. The police are hoping I'll drop the whole thing, but I got news for *them.*" Her mouth was starting to tremble again and a tear splashed onto her skirt as though my ceiling had a leak.

"What's the story?" I said, "The cops in this town are usually pretty good." I got up and filled a paper cup with water from my Sparklett's dispenser, passing it over to her. She murmured a thank you and drank it down, staring into the bottom of the cup as she spoke. "Rudd was a cocaine dealer until a month or so before he died. They haven't said as much, but I know they've written him off as some kind of small-time punk. What do they care? They'd like to think he was killed in a drug deal . . . a double-cross or something like that. He wasn't though. He'd given it all up because of this."

She glanced down at the swell of her belly. She was wearing a kelly green tee shirt with an arrow down the front. The word "Oops!" was written across her breasts in machine embroidery.

"What's your theory?" I asked. Already, I was leaning toward the official police version of events. Drug dealing isn't synonymous with longevity. There's too much money involved and too many amateurs getting into the act. This was Santa Teresa . . . ninety-five miles north of the big time in L.A., but there are still standards to maintain. A shotgun blast is the underworld equivalent of a bad annual review.

"I don't have a theory. I just don't like theirs. I want you to look into it so I can clear Rudd's name before the baby comes."

I shrugged. "I'll do what I can, but I can't guarantee the results. How are you going to feel if the cops are right?"

She stood up, giving me a flat look. "I don't know why Rudd died, but it had nothing to do with drugs," she said. (Largely true as it turned out . . .) She opened her handbag and extracted a roll of bills the size of a wad of socks. "What do you charge?"

"Thirty bucks an hour plus expenses."

She peeled off several hundred dollar bills and laid them on the desk. I got out a contract.

My second encounter with the Parker shotgun came in the form of a dealer's appraisal slip that I discovered when I was nosing through Rudd Osterling's private possessions an hour later at the house. The address she'd given me was on the Bluffs, a residential area on the west side of town, overlooking the Pacific. It should have been an elegant neighborhood, but the ocean generated too much fog and too much corrosive salt air. The houses were small and had a temporary feel to them, as if the occupants intended to move on when the month was up. No one seemed to get around to painting the trim and the yards looked like they were kept by people who spent all day at the beach. I followed her in my car, reviewing the information she'd given me as I urged my ancient VW up Capilla Hill and took a right on Presipio.

The late Rudd Osterling had been in Santa Teresa since the sixties when he migrated to the west coast in search of sunshine, good surf, good dope, and casual sex. Lisa told me he'd lived in vans and communes, working variously as a roofer, tree trimmer, bean picker, fry cook and fork lift operator . . . never with any noticeable ambition or success. He'd started dealing cocaine two years ago, apparently netting more money than he was accustomed to. Then he met and married Lisa and she'd been determined to see him clean up his act. According to her, he'd retired from the drug trade and was just in the process of setting himself up in a landscape maintenance business when someone blew the top of his head off.

I pulled into the driveway behind her, glancing at the frame and stucco bungalow with its patchy grass and dilapidated fence. It looked like one of those households where there's always something under construction, probably without permits and not up to code. In this case, a foundation had been laid for an addition to the garage, but the weeds were already growing up through cracks in the concrete. A wooden out-building had been dismantled, the old lumber tossed in an unsightly pile. Closer to the house, there were stacks of cheap pecan wood paneling, sun-bleached in places and warped along one edge. It was all hapless and depressing, but she scarcely looked at it.

I followed her into the house.

"We were just getting the house fixed up when he died," she remarked.

"When did you buy the place?" I was manufacturing small talk, trying to cover my distaste at sight of the old linoleum counter where a line of ants stretched from a crust of toast and jelly all the way out the back door.

"We didn't really. This was my mother's. She and my stepdad moved back to the mid-west last year."

"What about Rudd? Did he have any family out here?"

"They're all in Connecticut I think, real la-di-dah. His parents are dead and his sisters wouldn't even come out to the funeral."

"Did he have a lot of friends?"

"All cocaine dealers have friends."

"Enemies?"

"Not that I ever heard about."

"Who was his supplier?"

"I don't know that."

"No disputes? Suits pending? Quarrels with the neighbors? Family arguments about the inheritance?"

She gave me a "no" on all four counts.

I had told her I wanted to go through his personal belongings so she showed me into the tiny back bedroom where he'd set up a card table and some cardboard file boxes. A real entrepreneur. I began to search while she leaned against the door frame, watching.

I said, "Tell me about what was going on the week he died." I was sorting through cancelled checks in a Nike shoe box. Most were written to the neighborhood supermarket, utilities, telephone company.

She moved to the desk chair and sat down. "I can't tell you much because I was at work. I do alterations and repairs at a dry cleaner's up at Presipio Mall. Rudd would stop in now and then when he was out running around. He'd picked up a few jobs already, but he really wasn't doing the gardening full time. He was trying to get all his old business squared away. Some kid owed him money. I remember that."

"He sold cocaine on *credit?*"

She shrugged. "Maybe it was grass or pills. Somehow the kid owed him a bundle. That's all I know."

"I don't suppose he kept any records."

"Nuh-un. It was all in his head. He was too paranoid to put anything down in black and white."

The file boxes were jammed with old letters, tax returns, receipts. It all looked like junk to me.

"What about the day he was killed? Were you at work then?"

She shook her head. "It was a Saturday. I was off work, but I'd gone to the market. I was out maybe an hour and a half and when I got home, police cars were parked in front, and the paramedics were here. Neighbors were standing out on the street." She stopped talking and I was left to imagine the rest.

"Had he been expecting anyone?"

"If he was, he never said anything to me. He was in the garage, doing I don't know what. Chauncy, next door, heard the shotgun go off, but by the time he got here to investigate, whoever did it was gone."

I got up and moved toward the hallway. "Is this the bedroom down here?"

"Right. I haven't gotten rid of his stuff yet. I guess I'll have to eventually. I'm going to use his office for the nursery."

I moved into the master bedroom and went through his hanging clothes. "Did the police find anything?"

"They didn't look. Well, one guy came through and poked around some. About five minutes worth."

I began to check through the drawers she indicated were his. Nothing remarkable came to light. On top of the chest was one of those brass and walnut caddies where Rudd apparently kept his watch, keys, loose change. Almost idly, I picked it up. Under it, there was a folded slip of paper. It was a partially completed appraisal form from a gun shop out in Colgate, a township to the north of us. "What's a Parker?" I said when I'd glanced at it. She peered over at the slip.

"Oh. That's probably the appraisal on the shotgun he got."

"The one he was killed with?"

"Well, I don't know. They never found the weapon, but the homicide detective said they couldn't run it through ballistics anyway . . . or whatever it is they do."

"Why'd he have it appraised in the first place?"

"He was taking it in trade for a big drug debt and he needed to know if it was worth it."

"Was this the kid you mentioned before or someone else?"

"The same one, I think. At first, Rudd intended to turn around and sell the gun, but then he found out it was a collector's item so he decided to keep it. The gun dealer called a couple of times after Rudd died, but it was gone by then."

"And you told the cops all this stuff?"

"Sure. They couldn't have cared less."

I doubted that, but I tucked the slip in my pocket anyway. I'd check it out and then talk to Dolan in homicide.

The gun shop was located on a narrow side street in Colgate just off the main thoroughfare. Colgate looks like it's made up of hardware stores, u-haul rentals and plant nurseries; places that seem to have half their merchandise outside, surrounded by chain link fence. The gun shop had been set up in someone's front parlor in a dinky white frame house. There were some glass counters filled with gun paraphernalia, but no guns in sight.

The man who came out of the back room was in his fifties, with a narrow face and graying hair, gray eyes made luminous by rimless glasses. He wore a dress shirt with the sleeves rolled up and a long gray apron tied around his waist. He had perfect teeth, but when he talked I could see the rim of pink where his upper plate was fit and it spoiled the effect. Still, I had to give him credit for a certain level of good looks, maybe a seven on a scale of ten. Not bad for a man his age. "Yes ma'am," he said. He had a trace of an accent, Virginia, I thought.

"Are you Avery Lamb?"

"That's right. What can I help you with?"

"I'm not sure. I'm wondering what you can tell me about this appraisal you did." I handed him the slip.

He glanced down and then looked up at me. "Where did you get this?"

"Rudd Osterling's widow," I said.

"She told me she didn't have the gun."

"That's right."

His manner was a combination of confusion and wariness. "What's your connection to the matter?"

I took out a business card and gave it to him. "She hired me to look into Rudd's death. I thought the shotgun might be relevant since he was killed with one."

He shook his head. "I don't know what's going on. This is the second time it's disappeared."

"Meaning what?"

"Some woman brought it in to have it appraised back in June. I made an offer on it then, but before we could work out a deal, she claimed the gun was stolen."

"I take it you had some doubts about that."

"Sure, I did. I don't think she ever filed a police report and I suspect she knew damn well who took it, but didn't intend to pursue it. Next thing I knew, this Osterling fellow brought the same gun in. It had a beavertail forend and an English grip. There was no mistaking it."

"Wasn't that a bit of a coincidence? His bringing the gun in to you?"

"Not really. I'm one of the few master gunsmiths in this area. All he had to do was ask around the same way she did."

"Did you tell her the gun had showed up?"

He shrugged with his mouth and a lift of his brows. "Before I could talk to her, he was dead and the Parker was gone again."

I checked the date on the slip. "That was in August?"

"That's right and I haven't seen the gun since."

"Did he tell you how he acquired it?"

"Said he took it in trade. I told him this other woman showed up with it first, but he didn't seem to care about that."

"How much was the Parker worth?"

He hesitated, weighing his words. "I offered him six thousand."

"But what's its value out in the market place?"

"Depends on what people are willing to pay."

I tried to control the little surge of impatience he had sparked. I could tell he'd jumped into his crafty negotiator's mode, unwilling to tip his hand in case the gun showed up and he could nick it off cheap. "Look," I said, "I'm asking you in confidence. This won't go any further unless it becomes a police matter and then neither one of us will have a choice. Right now, the gun's missing anyway so what difference does it make?"

He didn't seem entirely convinced, but he got my point. He cleared his throat with obvious embarrassment. "Ninety-six."

I stared at him. "Thousand dollars?"

He nodded.

"Jesus. That's a lot for a gun, isn't it?"

His voice dropped. "Ms. Millhone, that gun is priceless. It's an A-1 Special 28-gauge with an extra set of barrels. There were only two of them made."

"But why so much?"

"For one thing, the Parker's a beautifully crafted shotgun. there are different grades, of course, but this one was exceptional. Fine wood. Some of the most incredible scrollwork you'll ever see. Parker had an Italian working for him back then who'd spend sometimes 5000 hours on the engraving alone. The company went out of business around 1942 so there aren't any more to be had."

"You said there were two. Where's the other one, or would you know?"

"Only what I've heard. A dealer in Ohio bought the one at auction a couple years back for ninety-six. I understand some fella down in Texas has it now, part of a collection of Parkers. The gun Rudd Osterling brought in has been missing for years. I don't think he knew what he had on his hands."

"And you didn't tell him."

Lamb shifted his gaze. "I told him enough," he said carefully. "I can't help it if the man didn't do his homework."

"How'd you know it was the missing Parker?"

"The serial number matched and so did everything else. It wasn't a fake either. I examined the gun under heavy magnification, checking for fill-in welds and traces of markings that might have been over-stamped. After I checked it out, I showed it to a buddy of mine, a big gun buff, and he recognized it, too."

"Who else knew about it besides you and this friend?"

"Whoever Rudd Osterling got it from, I guess."

"I'll want the woman's name and address if you've still got it. Maybe she knows how the gun fell into Rudd's hands."

Again, he hesitated for a moment and then he shrugged. "I don't see why not." He made a note on a piece of scratch paper and pushed it across the counter to me. "I'd like to know if the gun shows up," he said.

"Sure, as long as Mrs. Osterling doesn't object."

I didn't have any other questions for the moment. I moved toward the door, then glanced back at him. "How could Rudd have sold the gun if it were stolen property? Wouldn't he have needed a bill of sale for it? Some proof of ownership?"

Avery Lamb's face was devoid of expression. "Not necessarily. If an avid collector got hold of that gun, it would sink out of sight and that's the last you'd ever see of it. He'd keep it in his basement and never show it to a soul. It'd be enough if he knew he had it. You don't need a bill of sale for that."

I sat out in my car and made some notes while the information was fresh. Then, I checked the address Lamb had given me and I could feel the adrenaline stir. It was right back in Rudd's neighborhood.

The woman's name was Jackie Barnett. The address was two streets over from the Osterling house and just about parallel; a big corner lot planted with avocado trees and bracketed with palms. The house itself was yellow stucco with flaking brown shutters and a yard that needed mowing. The mailbox read "Squires" but the house number seemed to match. There was a basketball hoop nailed up above the two-car garage and a dismantled motorcycle in the driveway.

I parked my car and got out. As I approached the house, I saw an old man in a wheelchair planted in the side yard like a lawn ornament. He was parchment pale, with baby fine white hair and rheumy eyes. The left half of his face had been disconnected by a stroke and his left arm and hand rested uselessly in his lap. I caught sight of a woman peering through the window, apparently drawn by the sound of my car door slamming shut. I crossed the yard, moving toward the front porch. She opened the door before I had a chance to knock.

"You must be Kinsey Millhone. I just got off the phone with Avery. He said you'd be stopping by."

"That was quick. I didn't realize he'd be calling ahead. Saves me an explanation. I take it you're Jackie Barnett."

"That's right. Come on in if you like. I just have to check on him," she said, indicating the man in the yard.

"Your father?"

She shot me a look. "Husband," she said. I watched her cross the grass toward the old man, grateful for a chance to recover from my gaffe. I could see now that she was older than she'd first appeared. She must have been in her fifties—at that stage where women wear too much make-up and dye their hair too bold a shade of blonde. She was buxom, clearly overweight, but lush. In a seventeenth century painting, she'd have been depicted supine, her plump naked body draped in sheer white. Standing over her, something with a goat's rear end would be poised for assault. Both would look coy but excited at the prospects. The old man was beyond the pleasures of the flesh, yet the sounds he made . . . garbled and indistinguishable because of the stroke . . . had the same intimate quality as someone in the throes of passion, a disquieting effect.

I looked away from him, thinking of Avery Lamb instead. He hadn't actually told me the woman was a stranger to him, but he'd certainly implied as much. I wondered now what their relationship consisted of.

Jackie spoke to the old man briefly, adjusting his lap robe. Then she came back and we went inside.

"Is your name Barnett or Squires?" I asked.

"Technically, it's Squires, but I still use Barnett for the most part," she said. She seemed angry and I thought at first the rage was directed at me. She caught my look. "I'm sorry," she said, "but I've about had it with him. Have you ever dealt with a stroke victim?"

"I understand it's difficult."

"It's impossible! I know I sound hard-hearted, but he was always short tempered and now he's frustrated on top of that. Self-centered, demanding. Nothing suits him. Nothing. I put him out in the yard sometimes just so I won't have to fool with him. Have a seat, hon."

I sat. "How long has he been sick?"

"He had the first stroke in June. He's been in and out of the hospital ever since."

"What's the story on the gun you took out to Avery's shop?"

"Oh, that's right. He said you were looking into some fellow's death. He lived right here on the Bluffs, too, didn't he?"

"Over on Whitmore . . ."

"That was terrible. I read about it in the papers, but I never did hear the end of it. What went on?"

"I wasn't given the details," I said briefly. "Actually, I'm trying to track down a shotgun that belonged to him. Avery Lamb says it was the same gun you brought in."

She had automatically proceeded to get out two cups and saucers so her answer was delayed until she'd poured coffee for us both. She passed a cup over to me and then she sat down, stirring milk into hers. She glanced at me self-consciously. "I just took that gun to spite *him,*" she said with a nod toward the yard. "I've been married to Bill for six years and miserable for every one of them. It was my own damn fault. I'd been divorced for ages and I was doing fine, but somehow when I hit fifty, I got in a panic. Afraid of growing old alone, I guess. I ran into Bill and he looked like a catch. He was retired, but he had loads of money, or so he said. He promised me the moon. Said we'd travel. Said he'd buy me clothes and a car and I don't know what all. Turns out he's a penny-pinching miser with a mean mouth and a quick fist. At least he can't do that any more." She paused to shake her head, staring down at her coffee cup.

"The gun was his?"

"Well, yes it was. He has a collection of shotguns. I swear he took better care of them than he did of me. I just despise guns. I was always after him to get rid of them. Makes me nervous to have them in the house. Anyway, when he got sick, it turned out he had insurance, but it only paid eighty per cent. I was afraid his whole life savings would go up in smoke. I figured he'd go on for years, using up all the money, and then I'd be stuck with his debts when he died. So I just picked up one of the guns and took it out to that gun place to sell. I was going to buy me some clothes."

"What made you change your mind?"

"Well, I didn't think it'd be worth but eight or nine hundred dollars. Then Avery said he'd give me six thousand for it, so I had to guess it was worth at least twice that. I got nervous and thought I better put it back."

"How soon after that did the gun disappear?"

"Oh gee, I don't know. I didn't pay much attention until Bill got out of the hospital the second time. He's the one who noticed it was gone," she said. "Of course, he raised plu-perfect hell. You should have seen him. He had a conniption fit for two days and then he had another stroke and had to be hospitalized all over again. Served him right if you ask me. At least I had Labor Day week-end to myself. I needed it."

"Do you have any idea who might have taken the gun?"

She gave me a long candid look. Her eyes were very blue and couldn't have appeared more guileless. "Not the faintest."

I let her practice her wide-eyed stare for a moment and then I laid out a little bait just to see what she'd do. "God, that's too bad," I said. "I'm assuming you reported it to the police."

I could see her debate briefly before she replied. Yes or no. Check one. "Well, of course," she said.

She was one of those liars who blush from lack of practice.

I kept my tone of voice mild. "What about the insurance? Did you put in a claim?"

She looked at me blankly and I had the feeling I'd taken her by surprise on that one. She said, "You know, it never even occurred to me. But of course he probably would have had it insured, wouldn't he?"

"Sure, if the gun's worth that much. What company is he with?"

"I don't remember off-hand. I'd have to look it up."

"I'd do that if I were you," I said. "You can file a claim and then all you have to do is give the agent the case number."

"Case number?"

"The police will give you that from their report."

She stirred restlessly, glancing at her watch. "Oh lordy, I'm going to have to give him his medicine. Was there anything else you wanted to ask while you were here?" Now that she'd told me a fib or two, she was anxious to get rid of me so she could assess the situation. Avery Lamb had told me she'd never reported it to the cops. I wondered if she'd call him up now to compare notes.

"Could I take a quick look at his collection?" I said, getting up.

"I suppose that'd be all right. It's in here," she said. She moved toward a small paneled den and I followed, stepping around a suitcase near the door.

A rack of six guns was enclosed in a glass-fronted cabinet. All of them were beautifully engraved, with fine wood stocks and I wondered how a priceless Parker could really be distinguished. Both the cabinet and the rack were locked and there were no empty slots. "Did he keep the Parker in here?"

She shook her head. "The Parker had its own case." She hauled out a fine leather trunk case from behind the couch and opened it for me, demonstrating its emptiness as though she might be setting up a magic trick. Actually, there was a set of barrels in the box, but nothing else.

I glanced around. There was a shotgun propped in one corner and I picked it up, checking the manufacturer's imprint on the frame. A. H. Fox. Too bad. For a moment, I'd thought it might be the missing Parker. I'm always hoping for the obvious. I set the Fox back in the corner with regret.

"Well, I guess that'll do," I said. "Thanks for the coffee."

"No trouble. I wish I could be more help." She started easing me toward the door.

I held out my hand. "Nice meeting you," I said, "Thanks again for your time."

She gave my hand a perfunctory shake. "That's all right. Sorry I'm in such a rush, but you know how it is when you have someone sick."

Next thing I knew, the door was closing at my back and I was heading toward my car, wondering what she was up to.

I'd just reached the driveway when a white Corvette came roaring down the street and rumbled into the drive. The kid at the wheel flipped the ignition key and cantilevered himself up onto the seat top. "Hi. You know if my mom's here?"

"Who, Jackie? Sure," I said, taking a flyer. "You must be Doug."

He looked puzzled. "No, Eric. Do I know you?"

I shook my head. "I'm just a friend passing through."

He hopped out of the Corvette. I moved on toward my car, keeping an eye on him as he headed toward the house. He looked about seventeen, blond, blue-eyed, with good cheek bones, a moody sensual mouth, lean surfer's body. I pictured him in a few years, hanging out in resort hotels, picking up women three times his age. He'd do well. So would they.

Jackie had apparently heard him pull in and she came out on the porch, intercepting him with a quick look at me. She put her arm through his and the two moved into the house. I looked over at the old man. He was making noises again, plucking aimlessly at his bad hand with his good one. I felt a mental jolt, like an interior tremor shifting the ground under me. I was beginning to get it.

I drove the two blocks to Lisa Osterling's. She was in the back yard, stretched out on a chaise in a sunsuit that made her belly look like a watermelon in a laundry bag. Her face and arms were rosy and her tanned legs glistened with tanning oil. As I crossed the grass, she raised a hand to her eyes, shading her face from the winter sunlight so she could look at me. "I didn't expect to see you back so soon."

"I have a question," I said, "and then I need to use your phone. Did Rudd know a kid named Eric Barnett?"

"I'm not sure. What's he look like?"

I gave her a quick run-down, including a description of the white Corvette. I could see the recognition in her face as she sat up.

"Oh him. Sure. He was over here two or three times a week. I just never knew his name. Rudd said he lived around here somewhere and stopped by to borrow tools so he could work on his motorcycle. Is he the one who owed Rudd the money?"

"Well, I don't know how we're going to prove it, but I suspect he was."

"You think he killed him?"

"I can't answer that yet, but I'm working on it. Is the phone in here?" I was moving toward the kitchen. She struggled to her feet and followed me into the house. There was a wall phone near the back door. I tucked the receiver against my shoulder, pulling the appraisal slip out of my pocket. I dialed Avery Lamb's gun shop. The phone rang twice.

Somebody picked up on the other end. "Gun shop."

"Mr. Lamb?"

"This is Orville Lamb. Did you want me or my brother Avery?"

"Avery, actually. I have a quick question for him."

"Well, he left a short while ago and I'm not sure when he'll be back. Is it something I can help you with?"

"Maybe so," I said. "If you had a priceless shotgun . . . say, an Ithaca or a Parker, one of the classics . . . would you shoot a gun like that?"

"You could," he said dubiously, "but it wouldn't be a good idea, especially if it was in mint condition to begin with. You wouldn't want to take a chance on lowering the value. Now if it'd been in use previously, I don't guess it would matter much, but still I wouldn't advise it . . . just speaking for myself. Is this a gun of yours?"

But I'd hung up. Lisa was right behind me, her expression anxious. "I've got to go in a minute," I said, "but here's what I think went on. Eric Barnett's stepfather has a collection of fine shotguns, one of which turns out to be very, very valuable. The old man was hospitalized and Eric's mother decided to hock one of the guns in order to do a little something for herself before he'd blown every asset he had on his medical bills. She had no idea the gun she chose was worth so much, but the dealer recognized it as the find of a lifetime. I don't know whether he told her that or not, but when she realized it was worth more than she thought, she lost her nerve and put it back."

"Was that the same gun Rudd took in trade?"

"Exactly. My guess is that she mentioned it to her son who saw a chance to square his drug debt. He offered Rudd the shotgun in trade and Rudd decided he better get the gun appraised, so he took it out to the same place. The gun dealer recognized it when he brought it in."

She stared at me. "Rudd was killed over the gun itself, wasn't he," she said.

"I think so, yes. It might have been an accident. Maybe there was a struggle and the gun went off."

She closed her eyes and nodded. "Okay. Oh, wow. That feels better. I can live with that." Her eyes came open and she smiled painfully. "Now what?"

"I have one more hunch to check out and then I think we'll know what's what."

She reached over and squeezed my arm. "Thanks."

"Yeah, well it's not over yet, but we're getting there."

When I got back to Jackie Barnett's, the white Corvette was still in the driveway, but the old man in the wheelchair had apparently been moved into the house. I knocked and after an interval, Eric opened the door, his expression altering only slightly when he saw me.

I said, "Hello again. Can I talk to your mom?"

"Well, not really. She's gone right now."

"Did she and Avery go off together?"

"Who?"

I smiled briefly. "You can drop the bullshit, Eric. I saw the suitcase in the hall when I was here the first time. Are they gone for good or just for a quick jaunt?"

"They said they'd be back by the end of the week," he mumbled. It was clear he looked a lot slicker than he really was. I almost felt bad that he was so far outclassed.

"Do you mind if I talk to your stepfather?"

He flushed. "She doesn't want him upset."

"I won't upset him."

He shifted uneasily, trying to decide what to do with me.

I thought I'd help him out. "Could I just make a suggestion here? According to the California penal code, grand theft is committed when the real or personal property taken is of a value exceeding two hundred dollars. Now that includes domestic fowls, avocados, olives, citrus, nuts and artichokes. Also shotguns and it's punishable by imprisonment in the county jail or state prison for not more than one year. I don't think you'd care for it."

He stepped away from the door and let me in.

The old man was huddled in his wheelchair in the den. The rheumy eyes came up to meet mine, but there was no recognition in them. Or maybe there was recognition, but no interest. I hunkered beside his wheelchair. "Is your hearing okay?"

He began to pluck aimlessly at his pant leg with his good hand, looking away from me. I've seen dogs with the same expression when they've done pottie on the rug and know you've got a roll of newspaper tucked behind your back.

"Want me to tell you what I think happened?" I didn't really need to wait. He couldn't answer in any mode that I could interpret. "I think when you came home from the hospital the second time and found out the gun was gone, the shit hit the fan. You must have figured out that Eric took it. He'd probably taken other things if he'd been doing cocaine for long. You probably hounded him until you found out what he'd done with it and then you went over to Rudd's to get it. Maybe you took the A. H. Fox with you the first time or maybe you came back for it when he refused to return the Parker. In either case, you blew his head off and then came back across the yards. And then you had another stroke."

I became aware of Eric in the doorway behind me. I glanced back at him. "You want to talk about this stuff?" I asked.

"Did he kill Rudd?"

"I think so," I said. I stared at the old man.

His face had taken on a canny stubbornness and what was I going to do? I'd have to talk to Lieutenant Dolan about the situation, but the cops would probably never find any real proof and even if they did, what could they do to him? He'd be lucky if he lived out the year.

"Rudd was a nice guy," Eric said.

"God, Eric. You *all* must have guessed what happened," I said snappishly.

He had the good grace to color up at that and then he left the room. I stood up. To save myself, I couldn't work up any righteous anger at the pitiful remainder of a human being hunched in front of me. I crossed to the gun cabinet.

The Parker shotgun was in the rack, three slots down, looking like the other classic shotguns in the case. The old man would die and Jackie'd inherit it from his estate. Then she'd marry Avery and they'd all have what they wanted. I stood there for a moment and then I started looking through the desk drawers until I found the keys. I unlocked the cabinet and then unlocked the rack. I substituted the A. H. Fox for the Parker and then locked the whole business up again. The old man was whimpering, but he never looked at me, and Eric was nowhere in sight when I left.

The last I saw of the Parker shotgun, Lisa Osterling was holding it somewhat awkwardly across her bulky midriff. I'd talk to Lieutenant Dolan all right, but I wasn't going to tell him everything. Sometimes justice is served in other ways.

LINDA BARNES *(1949–), a Boston area writer, is one of the best of the excellent group of mystery writers who debuted in the 1980s. She has published three books featuring Michael Sprague, a wealthy actor who doubles as a detective. These books, the most recent of which is* Cities of the Dead *(1986), reflect her own experiences in the theater. "Lucky Penny" marks the debut of a new sleuth, Carlotta Carlyle, a private detective and former Boston police officer, whose experience and six-foot-one-inch frame make her a formidable presence. Carlotta's first novel-length case is documented in* A Trouble of Fools *(1987).*

The award-winning "Lucky Penny" finds Ms. Carlyle driving a cab between cases and really earning her fare.

Lucky Penny
BY LINDA BARNES

Lieutenant Mooney made me dish it all out for the record. He's a good cop, if such an animal exists. We used to work the same shift before I decided—wrongly—that there was room for a lady PI in this town. Who knows? With this case under my belt, maybe business'll take a 180-degree spin, and I can quit driving a hack.

See, I've already written the official report for Mooney and the cops, but the kind of stuff they wanted: date, place, and time, cold as ice and submitted in triplicate, doesn't even start to tell the tale. So I'm doing it over again, my way.

Don't worry, Mooney. I'm not gonna file this one.

The Thayler case was still splattered across the front page of the *Boston Globe.* I'd soaked it up with my midnight coffee and was puzzling it out—my cab on automatic pilot, my mind on crime—when the mad tea party began.

"Take your next right, sister. Then pull over, and douse the lights. Quick!"

I heard the bastard all right, but it must have taken me thirty seconds or so to react. Something hard rapped on the cab's dividing shield. I didn't bother turning around. I hate staring down gun barrels.

I said, "Jimmy Cagney, right? No, your voice is too high. Let me guess, don't tell me—"

"Shut up!"

"Kill the lights, *turn off* the lights, okay. But *douse* the lights? You've been tuning in too many old gangster flicks."

"I hate a mouthy broad," the guy snarled. I kid you not.

"Broad," I said. "Christ! *Broad?* You trying to grow hair on your balls?"

"Look, I mean it, lady!"

"Lady's better. Now you wanna vacate my cab and go rob a phone booth?" My heart was beating like a tin drum, but I didn't let my voice shake, and all the time I was gabbing at him, I kept trying to catch his face in the mirror. He must have been crouching way back on the passenger side. I couldn't see a damn thing.

"I want all your dough," he said.

Who can you trust? This guy was a spiffy dresser: charcoal-gray three-piece suit and rep tie, no less. And picked up in front of the swank Copley Plaza. *I* looked like I needed the bucks more than he did, and I'm no charity case. A woman can make good tips driving a hack in Boston. Oh, she's gotta take precautions, all right. When you can't smell a disaster fare from thirty feet, it's time to quit. I pride myself on my judgment. I'm careful. I always know where the police check-points are, so I can roll my cab past and flash the old lights if a guy starts acting up. This dude fooled me cold.

I was ripped. Not only had I been conned, I had a considerable wad to give away. It was near the end of my shift, and like I said, I do all right. I've got a lot of regulars. Once you see me, you don't forget me —or my cab.

It's gorgeous. Part of my inheritance. A '59 Chevy, shiny as new, kept on blocks in a heated garage by the proverbial dotty old lady. It's the pits of the design world. Glossy blue with those giant chromium fins. Restrained decor: just the phone number and a few gilt curlicues on the door. I was afraid all my old pals at the police department would pull me over for minor traffic violations if I went whole hog and painted "Carlotta's Cab" in ornate script on the hood. Some do it anyway.

So where the hell were all the cops now? Where are they when you need 'em?

He told me to shove the cash through that little hole they leave for the passenger to pass the fare forward. I told him he had it backwards. He didn't laugh. I shoved bills.

"Now the change," the guy said. Can you imagine the nerve?

I must have cast my eyes up to heaven. I do that a lot these days.

"I mean it." He rapped the plastic shield with the shiny barrel of his gun. I checked it out this time. Funny how big a little .22 looks when it's pointed just right.

I fished in my pockets for change, emptied them.

"Is that all?"

"You want the gold cap on my left front molar?" I said.

"Turn around," the guy barked. "Keep both hands on the steering wheel. High."

I heard jingling, then a quick intake of breath.

"Okay," the crook said, sounding happy as a clam, "I'm gonna take my leave—"

"Good. Don't call this cab again."

"Listen!" The gun tapped. "You cool it here for ten minutes. And I mean frozen. Don't twitch. Don't blow your nose. Then take off."

"Gee, thanks."

"Thank *you,*" he said politely. The door slammed.

At times like that, you just feel ridiculous. You *know* the guy isn't going to hang around, waiting to see whether you're big on insubordination. *But,* he might. And who wants to tangle with a .22 slug? I rate pretty high on insubordination. That's why I messed up as a cop. I figured I'd give him two minutes to get lost. Meantime I listened.

Not much traffic goes by those little streets on Beacon Hill at one o'clock on a Wednesday morn. Too residential. So I could hear the guy's footsteps tap along the pavement. About ten steps back, he stopped. Was he the one in a million who'd wait to see if I turned around? I heard a funny kind of whooshing noise. Not loud enough to make me jump, and anything much louder than the ticking of my watch would have put me through the roof. Then the footsteps patted on, straight back and out of hearing.

One minute more. The only saving grace of the situation was the location: District One. That's Mooney's district. Nice guy to talk to.

I took a deep breath, hoping it would have an encore, and pivoted quickly, keeping my head low. Makes you feel stupid when you do that and there's no one around.

I got out and strolled to the corner, stuck my head around a building kind of cautiously. Nothing, of course.

I backtracked. Ten steps, then whoosh. Along the sidewalk stood one of those new "Keep Beacon Hill Beautiful" trash cans, the kind with the swinging lid. I gave it a shove as I passed. I could just as easily have kicked it; I was in that kind of funk.

Whoosh, it said, just as pretty as could be.

Breaking into one of those trash cans is probably tougher than busting into your local bank vault. Since I didn't even have a dime left to fiddle the screws on the lid, I was forced to deface city property. I got the damn thing open and dumped the contents on somebody's front lawn, smack in the middle of a circle of light from one of those snooty Beacon Hill gas street-lamps.

Halfway through the whiskey bottles, wadded napkins, and beer cans, I made my discovery. I was doing a thorough search. If you're going to stink like garbage anyway, why leave anything untouched, right? So I was opening all the brown bags—you know, the good old brown lunch-and-bottle bags—looking for a clue. My most valuable find so far had been the moldy rind of a bologna sandwich. Then I hit it big: one neatly creased bag stuffed full of cash.

To say I was stunned is to entirely underestimate how I felt as I crouched there, knee-deep in garbage, my jaw hanging wide. I don't know what I'd expected to find. Maybe the guy's gloves. Or his hat, if he'd wanted to get rid of it fast in order to melt back into anonymity. I pawed through the rest of the debris. My change was gone.

I was so befuddled I left the trash right on the front lawn. There's probably still a warrant out for my arrest.

District One headquarters is off the beaten path, over on New Sudbury Street. I would have called first, if I'd had a dime.

One of the few things I'd enjoyed about being a cop was gabbing with Mooney. I like driving a cab better, but, face it, most of my fares aren't scintillating conversationalists. The Red Sox and the weather usually covers it. Talking to Mooney was so much fun, I wouldn't even consider dating him. Lots of guys are good at sex, but conversation— now there's an art form.

Mooney, all six-foot-four, 240 linebacker pounds of him, gave me the glad eye when I waltzed in. He hasn't given up trying. Keeps telling me he talks even better in bed.

"Nice hat," was all he said, his big fingers pecking at the typewriter keys.

I took it off and shook out my hair. I wear an old slouch cap when I drive to keep people from saying the inevitable. One jerk even misquoted Yeats at me: "Only God, my dear, could love you for yourself alone and not your long red hair." Since I'm seated when I drive, he missed the chance to ask me how the weather is up here. I'm six-one in my stocking feet and skinny enough to make every inch count twice.

I've got a wide forehead, green eyes, and a pointy chin. If you want to be nice about my nose, you say it's got character.

Thirty's still hovering in my future. It's part of Mooney's past.

I told him I had a robbery to report and his dark eyes steered me to a chair. He leaned back and took a puff of one of his low-tar cigarettes. He can't quite give 'em up, but he feels guilty as hell about 'em.

When I got to the part about the bag in the trash, Mooney lost his sense of humor. He crushed a half-smoked butt in a crowded ashtray.

"Know why you never made it as a cop?" he said.

"Didn't brown-nose enough."

"You got no sense of proportion! Always going after crackpot stuff!"

"Christ, Mooney, aren't you interested? Some guy heists a cab, at gunpoint, then tosses the money. Aren't you the least bit *intrigued?*"

"I'm a cop, Ms. Carlyle. I've got to be more than intrigued. I've got murders, bank robberies, assaults—"

"Well, excuse me. I'm just a poor citizen reporting a crime. Trying to help—"

"Want to help, Carlotta? Go away." He stared at the sheet of paper in the typewriter and lit another cigarette. "Or dig me up something on the Thayler case."

"You working that sucker?"

"Wish to hell I wasn't."

I could see his point. It's tough enough trying to solve any murder, but when your victim is *the* Jennifer (Mrs. Justin) Thayler, wife of the famed Harvard Law prof, and the society reporters are breathing down your neck along with the usual crime-beat scribblers, you got a special kind of problem.

"So who did it?" I asked.

Mooney put his size twelves up on his desk. "Colonel Mustard in the library with the candlestick! How the hell do I know? Some scumbag housebreaker. The lady of the house interrupted his haul. Probably didn't mean to hit her that hard. He must have freaked when he saw all the blood, 'cause he left some of the ritziest stereo equipment this side of heaven, plus enough silverware to blind your average hophead. He snatched most of old man Thayler's goddamn idiot artworks, collections, collectibles—whatever the hell you call 'em—which ought to set him up for the next few hundred years, if he's smart enough to get rid of them."

"Alarm system?"

"Yeah, they had one. Looks like Mrs. Thayler forgot to turn it on.

According to the maid, she had a habit of forgetting just about anything after a martini or three."

"Think the maid's in on it?"

"Christ, Carlotta. There you go again. No witnesses. No fingerprints. Servants asleep. Husband asleep. We've got word out to all the fences here and in New York that we want this guy. The pawnbrokers know the stuff's hot. We're checking out known art thieves and shady museums—"

"Well, don't let me keep you from your serious business," I said, getting up to go. "I'll give you the collar when I find out who robbed my cab."

"Sure," he said. His fingers started playing with the typewriter again.

"Wanna bet on it?" Betting's an old custom with Mooney and me.

"I'm not gonna take the few piddling bucks you earn with that ridiculous car."

"Right you are, boy. I'm gonna take the money the city pays you to be unimaginative! Fifty bucks I nail him within the week."

Mooney hates to be called "boy." He hates to be called "unimaginative." I hate to hear my car called "ridiculous." We shook hands on the deal. Hard.

Chinatown's about the only chunk of Boston that's alive after midnight. I headed over to Yee Hong's for a bowl of wonton soup.

The service was the usual low-key, slow-motion routine. I used a newspaper as a shield; if you're really involved in the *Wall Street Journal,* the casual male may think twice before deciding he's the answer to your prayers. But I didn't read a single stock quote. I tugged at strands of my hair, a bad habit of mine. Why would somebody rob me and then toss the money away?

Solution Number One: He didn't. The trash bin was some mob drop, and the money I'd found in the trash had absolutely nothing to do with the money filched from my cab. Except that it was the same amount— and that was too big a coincidence for me to swallow.

Two: The cash I'd found was counterfeit and this was a clever way of getting it into circulation. Nah. Too baroque entirely. How the hell would the guy know I was the pawing-through-the-trash type?

Three: It was a training session. Some fool had used me to perfect his robbery technique. Couldn't he learn from TV like the rest of the crooks?

Four: It was a frat hazing. Robbing a hack at gunpoint isn't exactly in the same league as swallowing goldfish.

I closed my eyes.

My face came to a fortunate halt about an inch above a bowl of steaming broth. That's when I decided to pack it in and head for home. Wonton soup is lousy for the complexion.

I checked out the log I keep in the Chevy, totaled my fares: $4.82 missing, all in change. A very reasonable robbery.

By the time I got home, the sleepiness had passed. You know how it is: one moment you're yawning, the next your eyes won't close. Usually happens when my head hits the pillow; this time I didn't even make it that far. What woke me up was the idea that my robber hadn't meant to steal a thing. Maybe he'd left me something instead. You know, something hot, cleverly concealed. Something he could pick up in a few weeks, after things cooled off.

I went over that backseat with a vengeance, but I didn't find anything besides old Kleenex and bent paperclips. My brainstorm wasn't too clever after all. I mean, if the guy wanted to use my cab as a hiding place, why advertise by pulling a five-and-dime robbery?

I sat in the driver's seat, tugged my hair, and stewed. What did I have to go on? The memory of a nervous thief who talked like a B movie and stole only change. Maybe a mad toll-booth collector.

I live in a Cambridge dump. In any other city, I couldn't sell the damned thing if I wanted to. Here, I turn real estate agents away daily. The key to my home's value is the fact that I can hoof it to Harvard Square in five minutes. It's a seller's market for tarpaper shacks within walking distance of the Square. Under a hundred thou only if the plumbing's outside.

It took me a while to get in the door. I've got about five locks on it. Neighborhood's popular with thieves as well as gentry. I'm neither. I inherited the house from my weird Aunt Bea, all paid for. I consider the property taxes my rent, and the rent's getting steeper all the time.

I slammed my log down on the dining room table. I've got rooms galore in that old house, rent a couple of them to Harvard students. I've got my own office on the second floor, but I do most of my work at the dining room table. I like the view of the refrigerator.

I started over from square one. I called Gloria. She's the late-night dispatcher for the Independent Taxi Owners Association. I've never seen her, but her voice is as smooth as mink oil and I'll bet we get a lot of calls from guys who just want to hear her say she'll pick 'em up in five minutes.

"Gloria, it's Carlotta."

"Hi, babe. You been pretty popular today."

"Was I popular at one-thirty-five this morning?"

"Huh?"

"I picked up a fare in front of the Copley Plaza at one-thirty-five. Did you hand that one out to all comers or did you give it to me solo?"

"Just a sec." I could hear her charming the pants off some caller in the background. Then she got back to me.

"I just gave him to you, babe. He asked for the lady in the '59 Chevy. Not a lot of those on the road."

"Thanks, Gloria."

"Trouble?" she asked.

"Is mah middle name," I twanged. We both laughed and I hung up before she got a chance to cross-examine me.

So. The robber wanted my cab. I wished I'd concentrated on his face instead of his snazzy clothes. Maybe it was somebody I knew, some jokester in mid-prank. I killed that idea; I don't know anybody who'd pull a stunt like that, at gunpoint and all. I don't want to know anybody like that.

Why rob my cab, then toss the dough?

I pondered sudden religious conversion. Discarded it. Maybe my robber was some perpetual screwup who'd ditched the cash by mistake.

Or . . . Maybe he got exactly what he wanted. Maybe he desperately desired my change.

Why?

Because my change was special, valuable beyond its $4.82 replacement cost.

So how would somebody know my change was valuable?

Because he'd given it to me himself, earlier in the day.

"Not bad," I said out loud. "Not bad." It was the kind of reasoning they'd bounced me off the police force for, what my so-called superiors termed the "fevered product of an overimaginative mind." I leapt at it because it was the only explanation I could think of. I do like life to make some sort of sense.

I pored over my log. I keep pretty good notes: where I pick up a fare, where I drop him, whether he's a hailer or a radio call.

First, I ruled out all the women. That made the task slightly less impossible: sixteen suspects down from thirty-five. Then I yanked my hair and stared at the blank white porcelain of the refrigerator door. Got up and made myself a sandwich: ham, Swiss cheese, salami, lettuce and tomato, on rye. Ate it. Stared at the porcelain some more until the suspects started coming into focus.

Five of the guys were just plain fat and one was decidedly on the hefty side; I'd felt like telling them all to walk. Might do them some good, might bring on a heart attack. I crossed them all out. Making a thin person look plump is hard enough; it's damn near impossible to make a fatty look thin.

Then I considered my regulars: Jonah Ashley, a tiny blond southern gent; muscle-bound "just-call-me-Harold" at Longfellow Place; Dr. Homewood getting his daily ferry from Beth Israel to MGH; Marvin of the gay bars; and Professor Dickerman, Harvard's answer to Berkeley's sixties radicals.

I crossed them all off. I could see Dickerman holding up the First Filthy Capitalist Bank, or disobeying civilly at Seabrook, even blowing up an oil company or two. But my mind boggled at the thought of the great liberal Dickerman robbing some poor cabbie. It would be like Robin Hood joining the sheriff of Nottingham on some particularly rotten peasant swindle. Then they'd both rape Maid Marian and go off pals together.

Dickerman *was* a lousy tipper. That ought to be a crime.

So what did I have? Eleven out of sixteen guys cleared without leaving my chair. Me and Sherlock Holmes, the famous armchair detectives.

I'm stubborn; that was one of my good cop traits. I stared at that log till my eyes bugged out. I remembered two of the five pretty easily; they were handsome and I'm far from blind. The first had one of those elegant bony faces and far-apart eyes. He was taller than my bandit. I'd ceased eyeballing him when I noticed the ring on his left hand; I never fuss with the married kind. The other one was built, a weight lifter. Not an Arnold Schwarzenegger extremist, but built. I think I'd have noticed that bod on my bandit. Like I said, I'm not blind.

That left three.

Okay. I closed my eyes. Who had I picked up at the Hyatt on Memorial Drive? Yeah, that was the salesman guy, the one who looked so uncomfortable that I'd figured he'd been hoping to ask his cabbie for a few pointers concerning the best skirt-chasing areas in our fair city. Too low a voice. Too broad in the beam.

The log said I'd picked up a hailer at Kenmore Square when I'd let out the salesman. Ah, yes, a talker. The weather, mostly. Don't you think it's dangerous for you to be driving a cab? Yeah, I remembered him, all right: a fatherly type, clasping a briefcase, heading to the financial district. Too old.

Down to one. I was exhausted but not the least bit sleepy. All I had to do was remember who I'd picked up on Beacon near Charles. A hailer. Before five o'clock, which was fine by me because I wanted to be long gone before rush hour gridlocked the city. I'd gotten onto Storrow and taken him along the river into Newton Center. Dropped him off at the BayBank Middlesex, right before closing time. It was coming back. Little nervous guy. Pegged him as an accountant when I'd let him out at the bank. Measly, undernourished soul. Skinny as a rail, stooped, with pits left from teenage acne.

Shit. I let my head sink down onto the dining room table when I realized what I'd done. I'd ruled them all out, every one. So much for my brilliant deductive powers.

I retired to my bedroom, disgusted. Not only had I lost $4.82 in assorted alloy metals, I was going to lose fifty dollars to Mooney. I stared at myself in the mirror, but what I was really seeing was the round hole at the end of a .22, held in a neat, gloved hand.

Somehow, the gloves made me feel better. I'd remembered another detail about my piggy-bank robber. I consulted the mirror and kept the recall going. A hat. The guy wore a hat. Not like my cap, but like a hat out of a forties gangster flick. I had one of those: I'm a sucker for hats. I plunked it on my head, jamming my hair up underneath—and I drew in my breath sharply.

A shoulder-padded jacket, a slim build, a low slouched hat. Gloves. Boots with enough heel to click as he walked away. Voice? High. Breathy, almost whispered. Not unpleasant. Accentless. No Boston *r*.

I had a man's jacket and a couple of ties in my closet. Don't ask. They may have dated from as far back as my ex-husband, but not necessarily so. I slipped into the jacket, knotted the tie, tilted the hat down over one eye.

I'd have trouble pulling it off. I'm skinny, but my build is decidedly female. Still, I wondered—enough to traipse back downstairs, pull a chicken leg out of the fridge, go back to the log, and review the feminine possibilities. Good thing I did.

Everything clicked. One lady fit the bill exactly: mannish walk and clothes, tall for a woman. And I was in luck. While I'd picked her up in Harvard Square, I'd dropped her at a real address, a house in Brookline: 782 Mason Terrace, at the top of Corey Hill.

JoJo's garage opens at seven. That gave me a big two hours to sleep.

I took my beloved car in for some repair work it really didn't need yet and sweet-talked JoJo into giving me a loaner. I needed a hack, but not mine. Only trouble with that Chevy is it's too damn conspicuous.

I figured I'd lose way more than fifty bucks staking out Mason Terrace. I also figured it would be worth it to see old Mooney's face.

She was regular as clockwork, a dream to tail. Eight-thirty-seven every morning, she got a ride to the Square with a next-door neighbor. Took a cab home at five-fifteen. A working woman. Well, she couldn't make much of a living from robbing hacks and dumping the loot in the garbage.

I was damn curious by now. I knew as soon as I looked her over that she was the one, but she seemed so blah, so *normal*. She must have been five-seven or -eight, but the way she stooped, she didn't look tall. Her hair was long and brown with a lot of blond in it, the kind of hair that would have been terrific loose and wild, like a horse's mane. She tied it back with a scarf. A brown scarf. She wore suits. Brown suits. She had a tiny nose, brown eyes under pale eyebrows, a sharp chin. I never saw her smile. Maybe what she needed was a shrink, not a session with Mooney. Maybe she'd done it for the excitement. God knows, if I had her routine, her job, I'd probably be dressing up like King Kong and assaulting skyscrapers.

See, I followed her to work. It wasn't even tricky. She trudged the same path, went in the same entrance to Harvard Yard, probably walked the same number of steps every morning. Her name was Marcia Heidegger and she was a secretary in the admissions office of the college of fine arts.

I got friendly with one of her coworkers.

There was this guy typing away like mad at a desk in her office. I could just see him from the side window. He had grad student written all over his face. Longish wispy hair. Gold-rimmed glasses. Serious. Given to deep sighs and bright velour V necks. Probably writing his thesis on "Courtly Love and the Theories of Chrétien de Troyes."

I latched onto him at Bailey's the day after I'd tracked Lady Heidegger to her Harvard lair.

Too bad Roger was so short. Most short guys find it hard to believe that I'm really trying to pick them up. They look for ulterior motives. Not the Napoleon type of short guy; he assumes I've been waiting years for a chance to dance with a guy who doesn't have to bend to stare down my cleavage. But Roger was no Napoleon. So I had to engineer things a little.

I got into line ahead of him and ordered, after long deliberation, a BLT on toast. While the guy made it up and shoved it on a plate with three measly potato chips and a sliver of pickle you could barely see, I searched through my wallet, opened my change purse, counted out silver, got to $1.60 on the last five pennies. The counterman sang out, "That'll be a buck, eight-five." I pawed through my pockets, found a nickel, two pennies. The line was growing restive. I concentrated on looking like a damsel in need of a knight, a tough task for a woman over six feet.

Roger (I didn't know he was Roger then) smiled ruefully and passed over a quarter. I was effusive in my thanks. I sat at a table for two, and when he'd gotten his tray (ham-and-cheese and a strawberry ice cream soda), I motioned him into my extra chair.

He was a sweetie. Sitting down, he forgot the difference in our height, and decided I might be someone he could talk to. I encouraged him. I hung shamelessly on his every word. A Harvard man, imagine that. We got around slowly, ever so slowly, to his work at the admissions office. He wanted to duck it and talk about more important issues, but I persisted. I'd been thinking about getting a job at Harvard, possibly in admissions. What kind of people did he work with? Were they congenial? What was the atmosphere like? Was it a big office? How many people? Men? Women? Any soulmates? Readers? Or just, you know, office people?

According to him, every soul he worked with was brain dead. I interrupted a stream of complaint with "Gee, I know somebody who works for Harvard. I wonder if you know her."

"It's a big place," he said, hoping to avoid the whole endless business.

"I met her at a party. Always meant to look her up." I searched through my bag, found a scrap of paper and pretended to read Marcia Heidegger's name off it.

"Marcia? Geez, I work with Marcia. Same office."

"Do you think she likes her work? I mean I got some strange vibes from her," I said. I actually said "strange vibes" and he didn't laugh his head off. People in the Square say things like that and other people take them seriously.

His face got conspiratorial, of all things, and he leaned closer to me.

"You want it, I bet you could get Marcia's job."

"You mean it?" What a compliment—a place for me among the brain dead.

"She's gonna get fired if she doesn't snap out of it."

"Snap out of what?"

"It was bad enough working with her when she first came over. She's one of those crazy neat people, can't stand to see papers lying on a desktop, you know? She almost threw out the first chapter of my thesis!"

I made a suitably horrified noise and he went on.

"Well, you know, about Marcia, it's kind of tragic. She doesn't talk about it."

But he was dying to.

"Yes?" I said, as if he needed egging on.

He lowered his voice. "She used to work for Justin Thayler over at the law school, that guy in the news, whose wife got killed. You know, her work hasn't been worth shit since it happened. She's always on the phone, talking real soft, hanging up if anybody comes in the room. I mean, you'd think she was in love with the guy or something, the way she . . ."

I don't remember what I said. For all I know, I may have volunteered to type his thesis. But I got rid of him somehow and then I scooted around the corner of Church Street and found a pay phone and dialed Mooney.

"Don't tell me," he said. "Somebody mugged you, but they only took your trading stamps."

"I have just one question for you, Moon."

"I accept. A June wedding, but I'll have to break it to Mother gently."

"Tell me what kind of junk Justin Thayler collected."

I could hear him breathing into the phone.

"Just tell me," I said, "for curiosity's sake."

"You onto something, Carlotta?"

"I'm curious, Mooney. And you're not the only source of information in the world."

"Thayler collected Roman stuff. Antiques. And I mean old. Artifacts, statues—"

"Coins?"

"Whole mess of them."

"Thanks."

"Carlotta—"

I never did find out what he was about to say because I hung up. Rude, I know. But I had things to do. And it was better Mooney shouldn't know what they were, because they came under the heading of illegal activities.

When I knocked at the front door of the Mason Terrace house at 10:00 A.M. the next day, I was dressed in dark slacks, a white blouse, and my old police department hat. I looked very much like the guy who reads your gas meter. I've never heard of anyone being arrested for impersonating the gasman. I've never heard of anyone really giving the gasman a second look. He fades into the background and that's exactly what I wanted to do.

I knew Marcia Heidegger wouldn't be home for hours. Old reliable had left for the Square at her usual time, precise to the minute. But I wasn't 100 percent sure Marcia lived alone. Hence the gasman. I could knock on the door and check it out.

Those Brookline neighborhoods kill me. Act sneaky and the neighbors call the cops in twenty seconds, but walk right up to the front door, knock, talk to yourself while you're sticking a shim in the crack of the door, let yourself in, and nobody does a thing. Boldness is all.

The place wasn't bad. Three rooms, kitchen and bath, light and airy. Marcia was incredibly organized, obsessively neat, which meant I had to keep track of where everything was and put it back just so. There was no clutter in the woman's life. The smell of coffee and toast lingered, but if she'd eaten breakfast, she'd already washed, dried, and put away the dishes. The morning paper had been read and tossed in the trash. The mail was sorted in one of those plastic accordion files. I mean, she folded her underwear like origami.

Now coins are hard to look for. They're small; you can hide 'em anywhere. So this search took me one hell of a long time. Nine out of ten women hide things that are dear to them in the bedroom. They keep their finest jewelry closest to the bed, sometimes in the nightstand, sometimes right under the mattress. That's where I started.

Marcia had a jewelry box on top of her dresser. I felt like hiding it for her. She had some nice stuff and a burglar could have made quite a haul with no effort.

The next favorite place for women to stash valuables is the kitchen. I sifted through her flour. I removed every Kellogg's Rice Krispy from the giant economy-sized box—and returned it. I went through her place like no burglar ever will. When I say thorough, I mean thorough.

I found four odd things. A neatly squared pile of clippings from the *Globe* and the *Herald,* all the articles about the Thayler killing. A manila envelope containing five different safe-deposit-box keys. A Tupperware container full of superstitious junk, good luck charms mostly, the kind of stuff I'd never have associated with a straight-arrow like Marcia: rabbits' feet galore, a little leather bag on a string that looked like some kind of voodoo charm, a pendant in the shape of a cross surmounted by a hook, and, I swear to God, a pack of worn tarot cards. Oh, yes, and a .22 automatic, looking a lot less threatening stuck in an ice cube tray. I took the bullets; the loaded gun threatened a defenseless box of Breyers' mint chocolate-chip ice cream.

I left everything else just the way I'd found it and went home. And tugged my hair. And stewed. And brooded. And ate half the stuff in the refrigerator, I kid you not.

At about one in the morning, it all made blinding, crystal-clear sense.

The next afternoon, at five-fifteen, I made sure I was the cabbie who picked up Marcia Heidegger in Harvard Square. Now cabstands have the most rigid protocol since Queen Victoria; you do not grab a fare out of turn or your fellow cabbies are definitely not amused. There was nothing for it but bribing the ranks. This bet with Mooney was costing me plenty.

I got her. She swung open the door and gave the Mason Terrace number. I grunted, kept my face turned front, and took off.

Some people really watch where you're going in a cab, scared to death you'll take them a block out of their way and squeeze them for an extra nickel. Others just lean back and dream. She was a dreamer, thank God. I was almost at District One headquarters before she woke up.

"Excuse me," she said, polite as ever, "that's Mason Terrace in *Brookline.*"

"Take the next right, pull over, and douse your lights," I said in a low Bogart voice. My imitation was not that good, but it got the point across. Her eyes widened and she made an instinctive grab for the door handle.

"Don't try it, lady," I Bogied on. "You think I'm dumb enough to take you in alone? There's a cop car behind us, just waiting for you to make a move."

Her hand froze. She was a sap for movie dialogue.

"Where's the cop?" was all she said on the way up to Mooney's office.

"What cop?"

"The one following us."

"You have touching faith in our law-enforcement system," I said.

She tried a bolt, I kid you not. I've had experience with runners a lot trickier than Marcia. I grabbed her in approved cop hold number three and marched her into Mooney's office.

He actually stopped typing and raised an eyebrow, an expression of great shock for Mooney.

"Citizen's arrest," I said.

"Charges?"

"Petty theft. Commission of a felony using a firearm." I rattled off a few more charges, using the numbers I remembered from cop school.

"This woman is crazy," Marcia Heidegger said with all the dignity she could muster.

"Search her," I said. "Get a matron in here. I want my four dollars and eighty-two cents back."

Mooney looked like he agreed with Marcia's opinion of my mental state. He said, "Wait up, Carlotta. You'd have to be able to identify that four dollars and eighty-two cents as yours. Can you do that? Quarters are quarters. Dimes are dimes."

"One of the coins she took was quite unusual," I said. "I'm sure I'd be able to identify it."

"Do you have any objection to displaying the change in your purse?" Mooney said to Marcia. He got me mad the way he said it, like he was humoring an idiot.

"Of course not," old Marcia said, cool as a frozen daiquiri.

"That's because she's stashed it somewhere else, Mooney," I said patiently. "She used to keep it in her purse, see. But then she goofed. She handed it over to a cabbie in her change. She should have just let it go, but she panicked because it was worth a pile and she was just baby-sitting it for someone else. So when she got it back, she hid it some-where. Like in her shoe. Didn't you ever carry your lucky penny in your shoe?"

"No," Mooney said. "Now, Miss—"

"Heidegger," I said clearly. "Marcia Heidegger. She used to work at Harvard Law School." I wanted to see if Mooney picked up on it, but he didn't. He went on: "This can be taken care of with a minimum of fuss. If you'll agree to be searched by—"

"I want to see my lawyer," she said.

"For four dollars and eighty-two cents?" he said. "It'll cost you more than that to get your lawyer up here."

"Do I get my phone call or not?"

Mooney shrugged wearily and wrote up the charge sheet. Called a cop to take her to the phone.

He got JoAnn, which was good. Under cover of our old-friend-long-time-no-see greetings, I whispered in her ear.

"You'll find it fifty well spent," I said to Mooney when we were alone.

JoAnn came back, shoving Marcia slightly ahead of her. She plunked her prisoner down in one of Mooney's hard wooden chairs and turned to me, grinning from ear to ear.

"Got it?" I said. "Good for you."

"What's going on?" Mooney said.

"She got real clumsy on the way to the pay phone," JoAnn said. "Practically fell on the floor. Got up with her right hand clenched tight. When we got to the phone, I offered to drop her dime for her. She wanted to do it herself. I insisted and she got clumsy again. Somehow this coin got kicked clear across the floor."

She held it up. The coin could have been a dime, except the color was off: warm, rosy gold instead of dead silver. How I missed it the first time around I'll never know.

"What the hell is that?" Mooney said.

"What kind of coins were in Justin Thayler's collection?" I asked. "Roman?"

Marcia jumped out of the chair, snapped her bag open, and drew out her little .22. I kid you not. She was closest to Mooney and she just stepped up to him and rested it above his left ear. He swallowed, didn't say a word. I never realized how prominent his Adam's apple was. JoAnn froze, hand on her holster.

Good old reliable, methodical Marcia. Why, I said to myself, *why* pick today of all days to trot your gun out of the freezer? Did you read bad luck in your tarot cards? Then I had a truly rotten thought. What if she had two guns? What if the disarmed .22 was still staring down the mint chocolate-chip ice cream?

"Give it back," Marcia said. She held out one hand, made an impatient waving motion.

"Hey, you don't need it, Marcia," I said. "You've got plenty more. In all those safe deposit boxes."

"I'm going to count to five—" she began.

"Were you in on the murder from day one? You know, from the planning stages?" I asked. I kept my voice low, but it echoed off the walls of Mooney's tiny office. The hum of everyday activity kept going in the main room. Nobody noticed the little gun in the well-dressed lady's hand. "Or did you just do your beau a favor and hide the loot after he iced his wife? In order to back up his burglary tale? I mean, if Justin Thayler really wanted to marry you, there is such a thing as divorce. Or was old Jennifer the one with the bucks?"

"I want that coin," she said softly. "Then I want the two of you"— she motioned to JoAnn and me—"to sit down facing that wall. If you yell, or do anything before I'm out of the building, I'll shoot this gentleman. He's coming with me."

"Come on, Marcia," I said, "put it down. I mean, look at you. A week ago you just wanted Thayler's coin back. You didn't want to rob my cab, right? You just didn't know how else to get your good luck charm back with no questions asked. You didn't do it for money, right? You did it for love. You were so straight you threw away the cash. Now here you are with a gun pointed at a cop—"

"Shut up!"

I took a deep breath and said, "You haven't got the style, Marcia. Your gun's not even loaded."

Mooney didn't relax a hair. Sometimes I think the guy hasn't ever believed a word I've said to him. But Marcia got shook. She pulled the barrel away from Mooney's skull and peered at it with a puzzled frown. JoAnn and I both tackled her before she got a chance to pull the trigger. I twisted the gun out of her hand. I was almost afraid to look inside. Mooney stared at me and I felt my mouth go dry and a trickle of sweat worm its way down my back.

I looked.

No bullets. My heart stopped fibrillating, and Mooney actually cracked a smile in my direction.

So that's all. I sure hope Mooney will spread the word around that I helped him nail Thayler. And I think he will; he's a fair kind of guy. Maybe it'll get me a case or two. Driving a cab is hard on the backside, you know?

Greenwich Village-based DONALD E. WESTLAKE *(1933–) is a true master of the modern crime story. Perhaps no other writer has so successfully and skillfully worked in as many different subgenres, and so prolifically. As "Richard Stark," he wrote numerous novels about a serious, talented thief named Parker; as "Tucker Coe," he launched a series about Mitch Tobin, an ex-police officer who works a beat similar to that of Ross Macdonald's Lew Archer; and under his own name, he has produced many novels that are outstanding examples of the mystery writer's craft. In addition, he is the author of several novels about a band of outrageous thieves that are classics of the "comic caper" book.*

Donald Westlake has written a fair number of short crime stories, none better or more clever than "Never Shake a Family Tree."

Never Shake a Family Tree
BY DONALD E. WESTLAKE

Actually, I was never so surprised in my life, and I seventy-three my last birthday and eleven times a grandmother and twice a great-grandmother. But never in my life did I see the like, and that's the truth.

It all began with my interest in genealogy, which I got from Mrs. Ernestine Simpson, a widow I met at Bay Arbor, in Florida, when I went there three summers ago. I certainly didn't like Florida—far too expensive, if you ask me, and far too bright, and with just too many mosquitoes and other insects to be believed—but I wouldn't say the trip was a total loss, since it did interest me in genealogical research, which is certainly a wonderful hobby, as well as being very valuable, what with one thing and another.

Actually, my genealogical researches have been valuable in more ways than one, since they have also been instrumental in my meeting some very pleasant ladies and gentlemen, although some of them only by postal, and of course it was through this hobby that I met Mr. Gerald Fowlkes in the first place.

But I'm getting far ahead of my story, and ought to begin at the beginning, except that I'm blessed if I know where the beginning actually is. In one way of looking at things, the beginning is my introduction to genealogy through Mrs. Ernestine Simpson, who has since passed on, but in another way the beginning is really almost two hundred years ago, and in still another way the story doesn't really begin until the first time I came across the name of Euphemia Barber.

Well. Actually, I suppose, I ought to begin by explaining just what genealogical research is. It is the study of one's family tree. One checks marriage and birth and death records, searches old family Bibles and talks to various members of one's family, and one gradually builds up a family tree, showing who fathered whom and what year, and when so-and-so got married, and when so-and-so died, and so on. It's really fascinating work, and there are any number of amateur genealogical societies throughout the county, and when one has one's family tree built up for as far as one wants—seven generations, or nine generations, or however long one wants—then it is possible to write this all up in a folder and bequeath it to the local library, and then there is a *record* of one's family for all time to come, and I for one think that's important and valuable to have even if my youngest boy, Tom, does laugh at it and say it's just a silly hobby. Well, it *isn't* a silly hobby. After all, I found evidence of murder that way, didn't I?

So, actually, I suppose the whole thing really begins when I first come across the name of Euphemia Barber. Euphemia Barber was John Anderson's second wife. John Anderson was born in Goochland County, Virginia, in 1754. He married Ethel Rita Mary Rayborn in 1777, just around the time of the Revolution, and they had seven children, which wasn't at all strange for that time, though large families have, I notice, gone out of style today, and I for one think it's a shame.

At any rate, it was John and Ethel Anderson's third child, a girl named Prudence, who is in my direct line on my mother's father's side, so of course I had them in my family tree. But then, in going through Appomattox County records—Goochland County being now a part of Appomattox, and no longer a separate county of its own—I came across the name of Euphemia Barber. It seems that Ethel Anderson died in 1793, in giving birth to her eighth child—who also died—and three years later, 1796, John Anderson remarried, this time marrying a widow named Euphemia Barber. At that time he was forty-two years of age, and her age was given as thirty-nine.

Of course, Euphemia Barber was not at all in my direct line, being John Anderson's second wife, but I was interested to some extent in her pedigree as well, wanting to add her parents' names and her place of birth to my family chart, and also because there were some Barbers fairly distantly related on my father's mother's side, and I was wondering if this Euphemia might be kin to them. But the records were very incomplete, and all I could learn was that Euphemia Barber was not a native of Virginia, and had apparently only been in the area for a year or two when she married John Anderson. Shortly after John's death in 1798, two years after their marriage, she sold the Anderson farm, which was apparently a somewhat prosperous location, and moved away again. So that I had neither birth nor death records on her, nor any record of her first husband, whose last name had apparently been Barber, but only the one lone record of her marriage to my great-great-great-great-great-grandfather on my mother's father's side.

Actually, there was no reason for me to pursue the question further, since Euphemia Barber wasn't in my direct line anyway, but I had worked diligently and, I think, well, on my family tree, and had it almost complete back nine generations, and there was really very little left to do with it, so I was glad to do some tracking down.

Which is why I included Euphemia Barber in my next entry in the *Genealogical Exchange*. Now, I suppose I ought to explain what the *Genealogical Exchange* is. There are any number of people throughout the country who are amateur genealogists, concerned primarily with their own family trees, but of course family trees do interlock, and any one of these people is liable to know about just the one record which has been eluding some other searcher for months. And so there are magazines devoted to the exchanging of such information, for nominal fees. In the last few years I had picked up all sorts of valuable leads in this way. And so my entry in the summer issue of the *Genealogical Exchange* read:

BUCKLEY, Mrs. Henrietta Rhodes, 119A Newbury St., Boston, Mass. Xch data on *Rhodes, Anderson, Richards, Pryor, Marshall, Lord.* Want any info Euphemia *Barber,* m. John Anderson, Va. 1796.

Well. The *Genealogical Exchange* had been helpful to me in the past, but I never received anywhere near the response caused by Euphemia Barber. And the first response of all came from Mr. Gerald Fowlkes.

It was a scant two days after I received my own copy of the summer issue of the *Exchange.* I was still poring over it myself, looking for people who might be linked to various branches of my family tree, when the telephone rang. Actually, I suppose I was somewhat irked at being taken from my studies, and perhaps I sounded a bit impatient when I answered the phone.

If so, the gentleman at the other end gave no sign of it. His voice was most pleasant, quite deep and masculine, and he said, "May I speak, please, with Mrs. Henrietta Buckley?"

"This is Mrs. Buckley," I told him.

"Ah," he said. "Forgive my telephoning, please, Mrs. Buckley. We have never met. But I noticed your entry in the current issue of the *Genealogical Exchange—*"

"Oh?" I was immediately excited, all thought of impatience gone. This was surely the fastest reply I'd ever had to date!

"Yes," he said. "I noticed the reference to Euphemia Barber. I do believe that may be the Euphemia Stover who married Jason Barber in Savannah, Georgia, in 1791. Jason Barber is in my direct line, on my mother's side. Jason and Euphemia had only the one child, Abner, and I am descended from him."

"Well," I said. "You certainly do seem to have complete information."

"Oh, yes," he said. "My own family chart is almost complete. For twelve generations, that is. I'm not sure whether I'll try to go back farther than that or not. The English records before 1600 are so incomplete, you know."

"Yes, of course," I said. I was, I admit, taken aback. Twelve generations! Surely that was the most ambitious family tree I had ever heard of, though I had read sometimes of people who had carried particular branches back as many as fifteen generations. But to actually be speaking to a person who had traced his entire family back twelve generations!

"Perhaps," he said, "it would be possible for us to meet, and I could give you the information I have on Euphemia Barber. There are also some Marshalls in one branch of my family; perhaps I can be of help to you there, as well." He laughed, a deep and pleasant sound, which reminded me of my late husband, Edward, when he was most particularly pleased. "And, of course," he said, "there is always the chance that you have some information on the Marshalls which can help me."

"I think that would be very nice," I said, and so I invited him to come to the apartment the very next afternoon.

At one point the next day, perhaps half an hour before Gerald Fowlkes was to arrive, I stopped my fluttering around to take stock of myself and to realize that if ever there were an indication of second childhood taking over, my thoughts and actions preparatory to Mr. Fowlkes' arrival were certainly it. I had been rushing hither and thither, dusting, rearranging, polishing, pausing incessantly to look in the mirror and touch my hair with fluttering fingers, all as though I were a flighty teenager before her very first date. "Henrietta," I told myself sharply, "you are seventy-three years old, and all that nonsense is well behind you now. Eleven times a grandmother, and just look at how you carry on!"

But poor Edward had been dead and gone these past nine years, my brothers and sisters were all in their graves, and as for my children, all but Tom, the youngest, were thousands of miles away, living their own lives—as of course they should—and only occasionally remembering to write a duty letter to Mother. And I am much too aware of the dangers of the clinging mother to force my presence too often upon Tom and his family. So I am very much alone, except of course for my friends in the various church activities and for those I have met, albeit only by postal, through my genealogical research.

So it *was* pleasant to be visited by a charming gentleman caller, and particularly so when that gentleman shared my own particular interests.

And Mr. Gerald Fowlkes, on his arrival, was surely no disappointment. He looked to be no more than fifty-five years of age, though he swore to sixty-two, and had a fine shock of gray hair above a strong and kindly face. He dressed very well, with that combination of expense and breeding so little found these days, when the well-bred seem invariably to be poor and the well-to-do seem invariably to be horribly plebeian. His manner was refined and gentlemanly, what we used to call courtly, and he had some very nice things to say about the appearance of my living room.

Actually, I make no unusual claims as a housekeeper. Living alone, and with quite a comfortable income having been left me by Edward, it is no problem at all to choose tasteful furnishings and keep them neat. (Besides, I had scrubbed the apartment from top to bottom in preparation for Mr. Fowlkes' visit.)

He had brought his pedigree along, and what a really beautiful job he had done. Pedigree charts, photostats of all sorts of records, a running history typed very neatly on bond paper and inserted in a loose-leaf notebook—all in all, the kind of careful, planned, well-thought-out perfection so unsuccessfully striven for by all amateur genealogists.

From Mr. Fowlkes, I got the missing information on Euphemia Barber. She was born in 1765, in Salem, Massachusetts, the fourth child of seven born to John and Alicia Stover. She married Jason Barber in Savannah in 1791. Jason, a well-to-do merchant, passed on in 1794, shortly after the birth of their first child, Abner. Abner was brought up by his paternal grandparents, and Euphemia moved away from Savannah. As I already knew, she had gone to Virginia, where she had married John Anderson. After that, Mr. Fowlkes had no record of her, until her death in Cincinnati, Ohio, in 1852. She was buried as Euphemia Stover Barber, apparently not having used the Anderson name after John Anderson's death.

This done, we went on to compare family histories and discover an Alan Marshall of Liverpool, England, around 1680, common to both trees. I was able to give Mr. Fowlkes Alan Marshall's birth date. And then the specific purpose of our meeting was finished. I offered tea and cakes, it then being four-thirty in the afternoon, and Mr. Fowlkes graciously accepted.

Before leaving, Mr. Fowlkes asked me to accompany him to a concert on Friday evening, and I very readily agreed. And so began the strangest three months of my entire life.

It didn't take me long to realize that I was being courted. Actually, I couldn't believe it at first. After all, at *my* age! But I myself did know some very nice couples who had married late in life—a widow and a widower, both lonely, sharing interests, and deciding to lighten their remaining years together—and looked at in that light it wasn't at all as ridiculous as it might appear at first.

Actually, I had expected my son Tom to laugh at the idea, and to dislike Mr. Fowlkes instantly upon meeting him. I suppose various fictional works that I have read had given me this expectation. So I was most pleasantly surprised when Tom and Mr. Fowlkes got along famously together from their very first meeting, and even more surprised when Tom came to me and told me Mr. Fowlkes had asked him if he would have any objection to his, Mr. Fowlkes', asking for my hand in matrimony. Tom said he had no objection at all, but actually thought it a wonderful idea, for he knew that both Mr. Fowlkes and myself were rather lonely, with nothing but our genealogical hobbies to occupy our minds.

As to Mr. Fowlkes' background, he very early gave me his entire history. He came from a fairly well-to-do family in upstate New York, and was himself now retired from his business, which had been a stock brokerage in Albany. He was a widower these last six years, and his first marriage had not been blessed with any children, so that he was completely alone in the world.

The next three months were certainly active ones. Mr. Fowlkes—Gerald—squired me everywhere, to concerts and to museums and even, after we had come to know one another well enough, to the theater. He was at all times most polite and thoughtful, and there was scarcely a day went by but what we were together.

During this entire time, of course, my own genealogical researches came to an absolute standstill. I was much too busy, and my mind was much too full of Gerald, for me to concern myself with family members who were long since gone to their rewards. Promising leads from the *Genealogical Exchange* were not followed up, for I didn't write a single letter. And though I did receive many in the *Exchange,* they all went unopened into a cubbyhole in my desk. And so the matter stayed, while the courtship progressed.

After three months Gerald at last proposed. "I am not a young man, Henrietta," he said. "Nor a particularly handsome man"—though he most certainly was very handsome, indeed—"nor even a very rich man, although I do have sufficient for my declining years. And I have little to offer you, Henrietta, save my own self, whatever poor companionship I can give you, and the assurance that I will be ever at your side."

What a beautiful proposal! After being nine years a widow, and never expecting even in fanciful daydreams to be once more a wife, what a beautiful proposal and from what a charming gentleman!

I agreed at once, of course, and telephoned Tom, the good news that very minute. Tom and his wife, Estelle, had a dinner party for us, and then we made our plans. We would be married three weeks hence. A short time? Yes, of course, it was, but there was really no reason to wait. And we would honeymoon in Washington, D.C., where my oldest boy, Roger, has quite a responsible position with the State Department. After which, we would return to Boston and take up our residence in a lovely old home on Beacon Hill, which was then for sale and which we would jointly purchase.

Ah, the plans! The preparations! How newly filled were my so recently empty days!

I spent most of the last week closing my apartment on Newbury Street. The furnishings would be moved to our new home by Tom, while Gerald and I were in Washington. But, of course, there was ever so much packing to be done, and I got at it with a will.

And so at last I came to my desk, and my genealogical researches lying as I had left them. I sat down at the desk, somewhat weary, for it was late afternoon and I had been hard at work since sunup, and I decided to spend a short while getting my papers into order before packing them away. And so I opened the mail which had accumulated over the last three months.

There were twenty-three letters. Twelve asked for information on various family names mentioned in my entry in the *Exchange,* five offered to give me information, and six concerned Euphemia Barber. It was, after all, Euphemia Barber who had brought Gerald and me together in the first place, and so I took time out to read these letters.

And so came the shock. I read the six letters, and then I simply sat limp at the desk, staring into space, and watched the monstrous pattern as it grew in my mind. For there was no question of the truth, no question at all.

Consider: Before starting the letters, this is what I knew of Euphemia Barber: She had been born Euphemia Stover in Salem, Massachusetts, in 1765. In 1791 she married Jason Barber, a widower of Savannah, Georgia. Jason died two years later, in 1793, of a stomach upset. Three years later Euphemia appeared in Virginia and married John Anderson, also a widower. John Anderson died two years thereafter, in 1798, of stomach upset. In both cases Euphemia sold her late husband's property and moved on.

And here is what the letters added to that, in chronological order:

From Mrs. Winnie Mae Cuthbert, Dallas, Texas: Euphemia Barber, in 1800, two years after John Anderson's death, appeared in Harrisburg, Pennsylvania, and married one Andrew Cuthbert, a widower and a prosperous feed merchant. Andrew died in 1801, of a stomach upset. The widow sold his store, and moved on.

From Miss Ethel Sutton, Louisville, Kentucky: Euphemia Barber, in 1804 married Samuel Nicholson of Louisville, a widower and a well-to-do tobacco farmer. Samuel Nicholson passed on in 1807, of a stomach upset. The widow sold his farm and moved on.

From Mrs. Isabelle Padgett, Concord, California: In 1808 Euphemia Barber married Thomas Norton, then Mayor of Dover, New Jersey, and a widower. In 1809 Thomas Norton died of a stomach upset.

From Mrs. Luella Miller, Bicknell, Utah: Euphemia Barber married Jonah Miller, a wealthy shipowner of Portsmouth, New Hampshire, a widower, in 1811. The same year Jonas Miller died of a stomach upset. The widow sold his property, and moved on.

From Mrs. Lola Hopkins, Vancouver, Washington: In 1813, in southern Indiana, Euphemia Barber married Edward Hopkins, a widower and a farmer. Edward Hopkins died in 1816 of a stomach upset. The widow sold the farm, and moved on.

From Mr. Roy Cumbie, Kansas City, Missouri: In 1819 Euphemia Barber married Stanley Thatcher of Kansas City, Missouri, a river barge owner and a widower. Stanley Thatcher died, of a stomach upset, in 1821. The widow sold his property, and moved on.

The evidence was clear, and complete. The intervals of time without dates could mean that there had been other widowers who had succumbed to Euphemia Barber's fatal charms, and whose descendants did not number among themselves an amateur genealogist. Who could tell just how many husbands Euphemia had murdered? For murder it quite clearly was, brutal murder, for profit. I had evidence of eight murders, and who knew but what there were eight more, or eighteen more. Who could tell, at this late date, just how many times Euphemia Barber had murdered for profit, and had never been caught?

Such a woman is inconceivable. Her husbands were always widowers, sure to be lonely, sure to be susceptible to a wily woman. She preyed on widowers, and left them all, a widow.

Gerald.

The thought came to me, and I pushed it firmly away. It couldn't possibly be true; it couldn't possibly have a single grain of truth.

But what did I know of Gerald Fowlkes, other than what he had told me? And wasn't I a widow, lonely and susceptible? And wasn't I financially well off?

Like father, like son, they say. Could it be also, like great-great-great-great-great-grandmother, like great-great-great-great-great-grandson?

What a thought! It came to me that there must be any number of widows in the country, like myself, who were interested in tracing their family trees. Women who had a bit of money and leisure, whose children were grown and gone out into the world to live their own lives, and who filled some of the empty hours with the hobby of genealogy. An unscrupulous man, preying on well-to-do widows, could find no better introduction than a common interest in genealogy.

What a terrible thought to have about Gerald! And yet I couldn't push it from my mind, and at last I decided that the only thing I could possibly do was try to substantiate the autobiography he had given me, for if he had told the truth about himself, then he could surely not be a beast of the type I was imagining.

A stockbroker, he had claimed to have been, in Albany, New York. I at once telephoned an old friend of my first husband's, who was himself a Boston stockbroker, and asked him if it would be possible for him to find out if there had been, at any time in the last fifteen or twenty years, an Albany stockbroker named Gerald Fowlkes. He said he could do so with ease, using some sort of directory he had, and would call me back. He did so, with the shattering news that no such individual was listed!

Still I refused to believe. Donning my coat and hat, I left the apartment at once and went directly to the telephone company, where, after an incredible number of white lies concerning genealogical research, I at last persuaded someone to search for an old Albany, New York, telephone book. I knew that the main office of the company kept books for other major cities, as a convenience for the public, but I wasn't sure they would have any from past years. Nor was the clerk I talked to, but at last she did go and search, and came back finally with the 1946 telephone book from Albany, dusty and somewhat ripped, but still intact, with both the normal listings and the yellow pages.

No Gerald Fowlkes was listed in the white pages, or in the yellow pages under Stocks & Bonds.

So. It was true. And I could see exactly what Gerald's method was. Whenever he was ready to find another victim, he searched one or another of the genealogical magazines until he found someone who shared one of his own past relations. He then proceeded to effect a meeting with that person, found out quickly enough whether or not the intended victim was a widow, of the proper age range, and with the properly large bank account, and then the courtship began.

I imagined that this was the first time he had made the mistake of using Euphemia Barber as the go-between. And I doubted that he even realized he was following in Euphemia's footsteps. Certainly, none of the six people who had written to me about Euphemia could possibly guess, knowing only of the one marriage and death, what Euphemia's role in life had actually been.

And what was I to do now? In the taxi, on the way back to my apartment, I sat huddled in a corner, and tried to think.

For this *was* a severe shock, and a terrible disappointment. And how could I face Tom, or my other children, or any of my friends, to whom I had already written the glad news of my impending marriage? And how could I return to the drabness of my days before Gerald had come to bring me gaiety and companionship and courtly grace?

Could I even call the police? I was sufficiently convinced myself, but could I possibly convince anyone else?

All at once, I made my decision. And, having made it, I immediately felt ten years younger, ten pounds lighter, and quite a bit less foolish. For, I might as well admit, in addition to everything else, this had been a terrible blow to my pride.

But the decision was made, and I returned to my apartment cheerful and happy.

And so we were married.

Married? Of course. Why not?

Because he will try to murder me? Well, of course, he *will* try to murder me. As a matter of fact, he has already tried, half a dozen times.

But Gerald is working at a terrible disadvantage. For he cannot murder me in any way that looks like murder. It must appear to be a natural death, or, at the very worst, an accident. Which means that he must be devious, and he must plot and plan, and never come at me openly to do me in.

And there is the source of his disadvantage. For I am forewarned, and forewarned is forearmed.

But what, really, do I have to lose? At seventy-three, how many days on this earth do I have left? And how *rich* life is these days! How rich compared to my life before Gerald came into it! Spiced with the thrill of danger, the excitement of cat and mouse, the intricate moves and countermoves of the most fascinating game of all.

And, of course, a pleasant and charming husband. Gerald *has* to be pleasant and charming. He can never disagree with me, at least not very forcefully, for he can't afford the danger of my leaving him. Nor can he afford to believe that I suspect him. I have never spoken of the matter to him, and so far as he is concerned I know nothing. We go to concerts and museums and the theater together. Gerald is attentive and gentlemanly, quite the best sort of companion at all times.

Of course, I can't allow him to feed me breakfast in bed, as he would so love to do. No, I told him, I was an old-fashioned woman, and believed that cooking was a woman's job, and so I won't let him near the kitchen. Poor Gerald!

And we don't take trips, no matter how much he suggests them.

And we've closed off the second story of our home, since I pointed out that the first floor was certainly spacious enough for just the two of us, and I felt I was getting a little old for climbing stairs. He could do nothing, of course, but agree.

And, in the meantime, I have found another hobby, though of course Gerald knows nothing of it. Through discreet inquiries, and careful perusal of past issues of the various genealogical magazines, and the use of the family names in Gerald's family tree, I am gradually compiling another sort of tree. Not a family tree, no. One might facetiously call it a hanging tree. It is a list of Gerald's wives. It is in with my genealogical files, which I have willed to the Boston library. Should Gerald manage to catch me after all, what a surprise is in store for the librarian who sorts out those files of mine! Not as big a surprise as the one in store for Gerald, of course.

Ah, here comes Gerald now, in the automobile he bought last week. He's going to ask me again to go for a ride with him.

But I shan't go.

URSULA CURTISS *(1923–) comes from a mystery-writing family—her mother, Helen Reilly, and her sister, Mary McMullen, are both notable mystery authors. Ms. Curtiss' speciality is the mystery with a gothic slant, often involving threatened women, vengeance, and surprise endings. Among her best books are* Widow's Web *(1956),* The Wasp *(1963),* In Cold Pursuit *(1977), and the brilliant* Dog in the Manger *(1982).*

"The Marked Man" is a hunted man, and also a very careful one.

The Marked Man
BY URSULA CURTISS

Outside, in the cold rush of the night air, the left side of Walter's face felt iridescent with pain. The just-inflicted scratches seemed to seethe and simmer like neon tubing and at an occasional pair of oncoming headlights, he'd swing his head sharply out of the glare, as if he were summoning a laggardly dog in the shadows. His heart hammered as though he'd been running, which was the one thing he should not do.

The service station where the girl attendant lay unconscious on the floor—the girl who had astonishingly revealed herself as such only when her billed cap flew off with the suddenness of her jump at him—was now six or seven blocks behind him, and there was still no sound of a siren, no racing, revolving ambulance light. But the expectation of them was like an aimed gun, because although Walter had already disposed of the cheap dark mail-order wig, he was literally a marked man. For the first time in his life he needed a safe place to hide for a few days, and to find that he had to locate a telephone booth, and fast.

Gulping for air even at his only brisk walking pace, he arrived at a telephone booth at the entrance to a closed and spectrally lit shopping plaza. He ruffled through the L's in the chained directory, was seized with panic when he appeared not to have a single coin, finally dredged up a quarter, dropped it in, and dialed. A kind of desperate confidence had carried him this far, but the moment of panic had undermined it and let in a thought that he had kept at bay since he'd fled from the service station: *What if Dex was out of town? Or had moved?*

His face flamed while he waited; he hoped viciously that the girl on the concrete floor was dead. Then an elderly female voice quavered a hello into his ear and he asked for Dex.

The voice hesitated. "He's—busy right now. Could I have him call you back—say, tomorrow?"

A party? No, but something was going on—he heard a low mutter of background sounds. "I'm just passing through. Tell him it's Walt," said Walter firmly, and a moment later the familiar voice was saying warily, unwelcomingly, "Hi, Walt."

A measure of Walter's usual cockiness came back, even in the middle of this crisis. Good old Dex, met at the reformatory in the southern part of the state, where Walter had been sent for aggravated assault and Dex for theft during one of his many flights from a broken home. Dex was twenty-four now, the older by a year, but like most essentially gentle people he was vulnerable. He was also married, with a baby, and assistant manager of his father-in-law's small but thriving grocery store. It had been very clear to Walter, who took care to keep in touch with anyone potentially useful, that neither Dex's prim little wife nor his hatchet-faced father-in-law knew of his reformatory past.

Now, tersely and without details, Walter told the other man that he was in a jam and needed a place to stay—garage, woodshed, anywhere —for a couple of days. Dex replied with the caution of someone with a listener beside him that he wished he could put Walter up but the fact was that his wife's mother had passed away the day before and Walter could see that, uh . . .

"Say, that's an idea. Your wife has lived in this town all her life. She'd probably know of some empty house for sale or something, wouldn't she, if you asked her? I mean if you told her it was for an old friend?"

For a dangerous interval of silence Walter was afraid he had gone too far with the implied threat. Then Dex said in a driven voice, "There's one place that might—where are you now?"

While he waited for the car, Walter tidied up the telephone booth, a process he had automatically begun while talking to Dex. Brought up by an elderly aunt as clean and joyless as bleach, further stampeded by the harsh institutional years, he had an active unease—almost a fear— of dirt and disorder. Although he himself was hardly aware of it, public places like washrooms and park benches and telephone booths were always the cleaner for Walter's passing. By the time Dex's car arrived, two cigarette butts, three matches, two gum wrappers, and a paper cup had been amalgamated into a small neat ball and thrown outside into a litter basket.

After a single instantly averted glance at the bloody marks on Walter's face, Dex confined himself to essentials. The house he had in mind would be empty for a week because the owners had gone deer hunting; he knew this because the woman, a Mrs. Patterson, had been in the store yesterday buying supplies and he had heard her talking to the checkout girl. He didn't think there was a dog. He had brought a flashlight. Beyond that, Walter was on his own.

As he finished these stony announcements a siren commenced to shriek miles away to the south, the urgent sound carrying on the cold dry air. Dex kept his eyes unflickeringly on the road ahead, his only and instinctive reaction a sudden pressure on the gas pedal. Rejection came from him almost as visibly as the simmers of heat from above the radiator, but he said nothing until he pulled in without warning under cottonwoods.

"Far as I go," he said then. "Second house on the right. For God's sake watch it."

"Don't worry," Walter told him, confident because of the distance between him and the siren. "You've got nothing to do with this, right? Somebody else overheard the woman and the checkout girl. So long, Dex."

"Goodbye," said Dex tightly, and drove away.

It was a very good house for the purpose, twenty-five yards back from the road with at least that much separation from its neighbors on both sides, and cupped in trees. If the neighbors had dogs they were the sleepy overfed kind: the only sound Walter could hear as he advanced cautiously on the grass was a faint twiggy rustle of wind high above him.

He melted to the rear of the house, his now-adjusted vision able to pick out details other than the black shine of panes. The back door was sturdily resistant; the windows appeared to be the kind that louvered out. Walter traveled along the wall and presently found another door opening on what felt like flagstones. The lock here gave with only a minimum of attention from his knife and he was inside in total darkness and utter silence.

A faint trace of perfume on the air, a fluffiness underfoot: although both were alien to Walter, he knew that this must be a bedroom. After moments of testing with all his senses—not that he believed Dex daring enough for treachery—he aimed the flashlight cautiously between shielding fingers, snapped it instantly off again, stood frozen with the image of the rumpled double bed still seared on his vision. The illusion of a suspicious householder risen to investigate the rooms within was fleetingly so strong that Walter's hand shot behind him for the doorknob.

But nothing happened; the darkness and silence remained tranquil. After a guarded moment he tiptoed through the open doorway that the brief spurt of light had showed him, found himself in a hall, and listened again. Then, because alarm had made his face blaze as though the girl's nails had just bitten into it, he fumbled his way to a bathroom, ran the cold water boldly, and held his dripping palms to it.

He had committed several robberies before this one, and in fact served a short jail term; but until tonight he had never used more than the threat of violence. He had never had to: his victims had the impression—false, as it happened—that he was completely irresponsible, and heedless as to the consequences of his actions.

As a result, he was suddenly so exhausted that he did not even count the bills wadded deep in his jacket pocket under his gloves. He lay down on the unmade bed, faintly shocking to his neat nature even through his fatigue, and was asleep almost at once.

In the morning Walter took an appraising look around the bedroom and discovered that the untidy Pattersons were well off—not that it mattered to him, as his object was to leave this place without a trace as soon as his scratches were healed enough to be disguised with makeup. He also learned that the money the girl had defended so wildly and stupidly amounted to eighty-one dollars.

—The girl who (the bedroom clock-radio informed him through the open doorway while he shaved and washed his damaged cheek with care) is still unconscious and in critical condition in a local hospital. Her head injuries indicate that she was flung with considerable violence against the corner of a metal filing cabinet. The robbery, which occurred at some time between 10:30 and 10:50 P.M. appears thus far to have gone unwitnessed. Police are continuing their inquiries in the area—

Walter turned the radio off. The fact that Dex had undoubtedly been listening to the news did not worry him in the least; if anything, the fact of the girl's condition would make the other man all the more sweatingly anxious that his own part in this never came out.

And when—and if—the girl recovered consciousness she could only describe her assailant as having dark hair and brows. Walter's hair was fair, and without the burnt-match coloring his eyebrows were almost invisible. When the scratches had healed he would be able to saunter down to the bus station, retrieve his shabby suitcase from the locker there, use his already-bought ticket to Denver, and be on his way—free as air. Cheered, Walter set out for the first time to explore his temporary domain.

Three minutes later he almost called Dex at the grocery store; only the realization that it might be dangerous for anyone to find this number busy stopped him. Because something very strange had happened in this house.

If it had been another kind of house, Walter would have said jeeringly to himself that they had had some party the night before. But in that case you would expect to see liquor bottles about—and something told him that people who lived in houses like this did not give parties like that.

There were two bedrooms, apparently occupied by children, besides the one by which he had entered, and another smaller bath; a long deep kitchen, a dining room with three railed steps down into a big living room; and opening off that, a den.

Everywhere there were costly looking mirrors and rugs and pictures —and everywhere, drawers were not quite closed on their brimming contents and cabinets hung slightly open. In one child's room a sharp scuffle had evidently taken place, knocking the sliding closet doors off their runners and dragging the bedclothes half onto the floor.

Stunned, frightened, careful to stay out of range of the windows that faced the road, Walter checked the front-door lock and then the one in the rear. Both were firmly set. Then how—?

An echo of his own soothing words to Dex came back: "Somebody else overheard the woman and the checkout girl." Somebody had, and had got in somehow, and the thing right now was to make sure that they didn't return. His back prickling whenever he had to turn it on an open doorway, Walter explored deeper and found, in a utility room off the kitchen, a wall ladder which led up into a little room apparently used by a child at some time. There was a canvas cot, a vase of long-dead flowers, a faded cloth doll. And a door, now stirring gently in the morning air, that gave on the long flat roof and the accommodating branches of a cottonwood tree.

Kids, thought Walter with a great rush of relief as he fastened the hook-and-eye that secured the door. Seeing the Patterson family depart in a laden car or camper, deciding that the coast was clear for some casual mischief or vandalism: you read about such things in the newspapers almost daily. That explained the strange disorder below, and also the apparent lack of theft—Walter had counted two television sets, at least three radios, and a typewriter in the bedroom.

The active threat that the house had seemed to contain was now gone. Descending to the kitchen, Walter investigated the refrigerator and found the remnants that a woman might decide were too little to take on a camping trip and too much to throw away: half a loaf of bread, a half stick of butter, four eggs, a partly used jar of strawberry jam. No milk. Walter drank his instant coffee black, scrambled two eggs, and put jam on a slice of bread.

He cleaned up carefully after himself, not touching the litter he found on the long cream-colored formica counters; the earlier intruders, possibly known to the Pattersons, might admit to the soup—there was a pot with withering dregs—and the generous strewings of orange peel. Distasteful though it was, Walter had to leave the disorder alone.

And he would certainly not allow his nerves to be ruffled by the untidiness everywhere else.

But it was a long day. The graveled crescent driveway crunched noisily three times—twice with cars turning around, once with a panel truck disgorging a boy who trundled around to the rear of the house with a sack of whatever they put in water-softeners. Walter held himself flinchingly still against a wall, expecting a knock at the back door; but there was a distant thump and bang and the boy returned to the truck and drove away.

According to the three o'clock news the girl in the service station, Emma Bothwell, had not regained consciousness and was in surgery. A hospital spokesman said there was evidence she had marked her assailant.

Angry at that all over again, Walter went and inspected his scratches, three and a trailing fourth. They had dried and darkened a little, which he took to be a healthy sign, and there was no spreading redness. He then roamed the house at a safe distance from the windows, and grimly did not restore to its rack a man's tie flung over one of the sapphire-upholstered dining-room chairs, did not snatch the weird collection of rubber bands out of the silver tray on the table, or brush off what looked like a wanton sprinkle of sugar on the table top.

At a quarter of five, because he would not be able to move about freely after dark, he opened a can of chili and ate it cold. At five o'clock the telephone rang for the first time.

The sound was terrifying in this refuge, carrying as it did a suggestion that someone was testing the emptiness of this house—or that Dex was warning him of imminent capture. But Dex would know that Walter couldn't lift the receiver. Dex would come himself.

If he had time to.

What if the Pattersons had cut their hunting trip short for some reason and had just stopped at Dex's grocery store for things like milk and butter and eggs? What if this were Dex with a helpless message?- - "They're on their way home."

Walter had actually taken a step toward the telephone when it cut itself off in midscream. Some friend of the Pattersons who didn't know they were away, he told himself—telephones must be ringing constantly in empty houses—but he put on his jacket and stood tensely in the now-dark dining room, gazing through the half-drawn curtains at occasional passing headlights.

At the end of a long half hour he considered himself safe from this particular threat, but the deep uneasiness stayed with him and carried over into his sleep.

It was a cold windy night, and the trees around the house creaked with a sound like keys being inserted into locks. The faraway howl of a dog became a woman's advancing voice and brought Walter sitting up with his heart pounding. At some black hour later he came fully awake again with a thought that must have been hovering around the edges of his mind all day.

There was, he was almost sure, something called immunity—some means by which police protected informers. Walter's sole guarantee of Dex's continuing silence was the other man's fear at being an accessory; but mightn't the police shut their eyes to that in return for Walter, in view of all the fuss being kicked up about the girl? Dex wasn't very bright—anyone with brains would have told his wife about the reformatory at the outset, so as to remove that hold; but it might still occur to him that he could lead the police to Walter at almost no risk to himself. He might even emerge looking like a hero, reformatory or not.

By midmorning of his second day in it, Walter had developed a personal hatred for the Patterson house. He had told himself that he would not let the general dishevelment get on his nerves, but in his restless wandering he yanked the door of the child's room shut; that was one place he didn't have to look at. A genuine rage at the marauders rose up in him, accompanied by a woolly feeling that he was missing some very important point.

Twice before noon he was startled by crunching tires in the drive, but although the cars passed close to the front windows they went by at undiminished speed. This seemed to be a natural turning-around spot, and Walter added it to his list of grievances against the house.

After his lunch—at least the pantry was well stocked—he made the ritual inspection of his scratches and experimented with some liquid makeup he found on a bathroom shelf. The scratches stared through, and the trouble was that they did not look like an encounter with a cat or some barbed wire; they looked exactly like what they were. Walter added another layer of makeup and thought that by tomorrow night . . .

The one o'clock news, which he watched on the television set in the curtained bedroom, jarred him to total attention, because the girl in the hospital was holding a news conference. With a thin prominent-jawed face surmounted by bandages, she looked more like a boy than ever. Blurred backs kept getting in the way as she spoke—eerily, for this was the first time Walter had heard her voice.

"I think he was about twenty-one or twenty-two. He had dark hair. He had on a dark jacket—I don't remember what color his pants were. Yes, he was wearing gloves, darkish gloves I think," she said to some off-camera question, "and when he told me to give him the money he took one glove off, I don't know why. I jumped at him, because I knew my uncle kept a gun in the desk—that was behind him—and I thought—"

Walter had stopped listening. He was staring at the television screen in a paralysis of horror. Once again, in a sick dream that sent the blood to his face and made the scratches flame, he felt the tiny menacing prick in the palm of his right glove as he opened the office door—was it a tumbleweed thorn? In the same awful slow motion he watched the girl's submissiveness at the cash register, although he hadn't known she was a girl then, and saw himself remove the glove with its threatening little stab so that he could more securely take the bills she was about to hand him.

But no matter how hard he tried, he did not see himself put on the glove after that lightning attack. Instead, he felt the dry slither of the money he had fumbled out with his bare and shaking hand.

What had he done then? Closed the cash drawer? Touched anything else? Out of that tiny interval of unexpected violence and pain and everything gone wrong, it was impossible for him to remember.

As though he could silence the girl forever, Walter leaped to the television set and snapped it off. His hands had begun to tremble, and he locked them tightly together and walked calmingly up and down. *This* was the blurry issue he hadn't quite grasped earlier, this was what had to be faced. Would the Pattersons, returning to their untidy house, accept it for the mischief it was—or, having picked up a newspaper or listened to a car radio, assume at once that a fugitive had been in hiding there, and send for the police?

Walter's fingerprints were a matter of record, and there was hardly a place in the house where he hadn't left them. The robbery would be secondary to the police by now; they would be haring after him for aggravated assault, at the least.

Wait. All this presumed that the Pattersons found their home in this shocking condition. What if they *didn't* find it in a shocking condition? Walter certainly couldn't leave it exactly as they left it, but first impressions would probably be clouded by the commotion of a return with children. By the time Mrs. Patterson's eye fell on something odd in the arrangement of her ashtrays or frying pans, Walter's fingerprints would have been smeared and overlaid and polished out of existence.

With a vast relief he began to clean up the house.

It was a staggering job, but his spirits began to lift as he got the surface disorder—the staggering tie, a ball of string, the bunched rubber bands, an empty flowerpot—out of the living and dining rooms and into what he hoped were appropriate places. With a little forcing he coaxed drawers and cabinets to close everywhere. When he had swept the floors, the rugs seemed to have a visible overlay of tiny confetti-like debris and he had to get out the vacuum cleaner.

The cleared tops of tables showed strange little sticky places which required sponging, and only the extreme urgency of his situation made Walter tackle the worse of the two children's rooms. His ingrained vision here was of taut tight mitred sheets and blankets, with toys and games, if any, tucked out of sight. It did not include spilled popcorn, an empty Coca-Cola can stuck jauntily in an open bureau drawer, or a yawning closet which looked as though it had been stirred by an eggbeater.

It was almost dark when Walter finished, but the dining-room table gleamed, the living-room couches were unsullied, the floor shone.

The house would certainly not have passed the antiseptic eye of Walter's aunt or the grim glare of the matrons in the reformatory, but nobody entering it would cry out in shock. Exhausted but pleased, his nerves quieted by the new orderliness, Walter consumed a can of the Pattersons' soup and went to bed.

In the morning he heard, but was not alarmed by, one more turning-around car that crunched, paused, and crunched away again . . .

Anne Merrick had swung her little car briskly into her sister's drive-way. The hunting trip, irresistible to the Pattersons, would be followed in less than a week by a visit from the senior Pattersons, a gentle and elderly couple from New Jersey who had never been allowed to see the house in its normal state. There were things to be done before even the stoutest-hearted cleaning woman could be brought in. Anne had vol-unteered.

The Pattersons lived in a manner uniquely their own, only partly explained by the fact that Betsy was a free-lance writer. They had tree surgeons to minister to their trees and sent their Orientals off to be cleaned at the proper intervals; occasionally, after some unheralded visitor had happened in on a scene of chaos, they laid down stern rules for their three young children: no eating in the living room, keep your bedroom tidy, hang up your clothes.

For perhaps forty-eight hours both the children and the parents observed these strictures, and then fell back into their cheerful disor-derly habits. Once every six months, for a week at a time, Betsy Patter-son and a cleaning woman attacked the bulging closets and brimming drawers, and then the tranquil process of deterioration began all over again.

Anne, remembering the condition of the house three mornings ago when she had helped Betsy and Rob and the children get packed and away, thought now that a fast hour ought to do it. She wasn't aiming at actual cleanliness, after all, but only at the impression that rational people lived here. Bare surfaces were marvelously deceptive. If she made a lightning sweep through the living room and the—

—dining room, with the curtains at its low window half drawn to reveal the shining black-walnut table and the immaculate sapphire chairs. Anne's hand stopped sharply before taking out the ignition key.

Three days ago the dining-room table had worn a heavy sprinkle of salt—Adam, the youngest of the children, could never pass a salt-cellar without upending it—but now the table gleamed. So did the silver tray, innocent of the rubber bands dumped into it at the last minute because Betsy had said firmly she would not travel in a vehicle containing children *and* rubber bands. And what had become of Rob's discarded tie, which Anne remembered clearly because the burgundy and gray stripes had looked so decorative against the sapphire chairs?

For a sickening second it was almost as though the Pattersons themselves had been wiped and polished away. Anne's impulse was to race out of the driveway; instead, because it seemed imperative for some reason, she forced herself to leave at the same speed at which she had entered. Two minutes later, at a telephone in the next house, she explained matters to a bewildered voice at the Sheriff's office.

"*Not* ransacked, you say," repeated the deputy uncomprehendingly; without knowing it, he was much in Walter's position. "Then what seems to be the trouble?"

"The trouble is that my sister's house *always* looks ransacked, and now it *doesn't* and there has to be something very wrong," said Anne, unfairly impatient. "There's been someone in there, don't you see? I wish to heaven you'd hurry. They might still be there—"

Walter was feeling almost tranquil as he applied a second coat of liquid makeup to his nearly healed cheek; the order around him, after the antic condition of the house, was like balm. Even when he heard a brisk sound from the region of the front door, a sound of entry, his heart gave a horrible knock but he did not panic.

A friend or relative with a key? The Pattersons themselves, returning earlier than planned? No matter; his foresight and drudgery of the night before had insured against an immediate alarm, and he had a choice of two rear doors.

He used the door in the bedroom, closed it soundlessly behind him, backed over flagstones into the chest of a man as careful and quiet as he. But this one—how could it *be,* after all his labor?—this one had a badge and a hand at his holstered hip.

One of the most enjoyable female sleuths to emerge in the last decade is television reporter Jemima Shore, the creation of LADY ANTONIA FRASER *(1932–) one of the very few titled (before achieving fame as a writer) women to produce mystery fiction. Her writing career debuted in 1977 with* Quiet as a Nun, *and she has since produced some half-dozen additional books, all of which feature the resourceful Ms. Shore. Earlier, Lady Antonia was known for her nonfiction books, including* A History of Toys, *and* King Charles II, *and she remains a noted historian of the British monarchy.*

"Have a Nice Death" is a wonderful puzzle story that has no sleuth, although the reader can have great fun playing the part.

Have a Nice Death
BY ANTONIA FRASER

Everyone was being extraordinarily courteous to Sammy Luke in New York.

Take Sammy's arrival at Kennedy Airport, for example: Sammy had been quite struck by the warmth of the welcome. Sammy thought: how relieved Zara would be! Zara (his wife) was inclined to worry about Sammy—he had to admit, with some cause; in the past, that is. In the past Sammy had been nervous, delicate, highly strung, whatever you liked to call it—Sammy suspected that some of Zara's women friends had a harsher name for it; the fact was that things tended to go wrong where Sammy was concerned, unless Zara was there to iron them out. But that was in England. Sammy was quite sure he was not going to be nervous in America; perhaps, cured by the New World, he would never be nervous again.

Take the immigration officials—hadn't Sammy been warned about them?

"They're nothing but gorillas"—Zara's friend, wealthy Tess, who traveled frequently to the States, had pronounced the word in a dark voice. For an instant Sammy, still in his nervous English state, visualized immigration checkpoints manned by terrorists armed with machine guns. But the official seated in a booth, who summoned Sammy in, was slightly built, perhaps even slighter than Sammy himself, though the protection of the booth made it difficult to tell. And he was smiling as he cried:

"C'mon, c'mon, bring the family!" A notice outside the booth stated that only one person—or one family—was permitted inside at a time. "I'm afraid my wife's not traveling with me," stated Sammy apologetically.

"I sure wish my wife wasn't with me either," answered the official, with ever-increasing bonhomie.

Sammy wondered confusedly—it had been a long flight after all— whether he should explain his own very different feelings about his wife, his passionate regret that Zara had not been able to accompany him. But his new friend was already examining his passport, flipping through a large black directory, talking again:

"A writer . . . Would I know any of your books?"

This was an opportunity for Sammy to explain intelligently the purpose of his visit. Sammy Luke was the author of six novels. Five of them had sold well, if not astoundingly well, in England and not at all in the United States. The sixth, *Women Weeping,* due perhaps to its macabrely fashionable subject matter, had hit some kind of publishing jackpot in both countries. Only a few weeks after publication in the States its sales were phenomenal and rising; an option on the film rights (maybe Jane Fonda and Meryl Streep as the masochists?) had already been bought. As a result of all this, Sammy's new American publishers believed hotly that only one further thing was necessary to ensure the vast, the *total* success of *Women Weeping* in the States, and that was to make of its author a television celebrity. Earnestly defending his own position on the subject of violence and female masochism on a series of television interviews and talk shows, Sammy Luke was expected to shoot *Women Weeping* high, high into the best-seller lists and keep it there. All this was the firm conviction of Sammy's editor at Porlock Publishers, Clodagh Jansen.

"You'll be great on the talk shows, Sammy," Clodagh had cawed down the line from the States. "So little and cute and then—" Clodagh made a loud noise with her lips as if someone was gobbling someone else up. Presumably it was not Sammy who was to be gobbled. Clodagh was a committed feminist, as she had carefully explained to Sammy on her visit to England, when she had bought *Women Weeping,* against much competition, for a huge sum. But she believed in the social role of best-sellers like *Women Weeping* to finance radical feminist works. Sammy had tried to explain that his book was in no way anti-feminist, no way at all, witness the fact that Zara herself, his Egeria, had not complained . . .

"Save it for the talk shows, Sammy," was all that Clodagh had replied.

While Sammy was still wondering how to put all this concisely, but to his best advantage, at Kennedy Airport, the man in the booth asked: "And the purpose of your visit, Mr. Luke?"

Sammy was suddenly aware that he had drunk a great deal on the long flight—courtesy of Porlock's first class ticket—and slept too heavily as well. His head began to sing. But whatever answer he gave, it was apparently satisfactory. The man stamped the white sheet inside his passport and handed it back. Then:

"Enjoy your visit to the United States of America, Mr. Luke. Have a nice day now."

"Oh I will, I know I will," promised Sammy. "It seems a lovely day here already."

Sammy's experiences at the famous Barraclough Hotel (accommodation arranged by Clodagh) were if anything even more heart-warming. Everyone, but everyone at the Barraclough wanted Sammy to enjoy himself during his visit.

"Have a nice day now, Mr. Luke": most conversations ended like that, whether they were with the hotel telephonists, the agreeable men who operated the lifts or the gentlemanly *concierge*. Even the New York taxi drivers, from whose guarded expressions Sammy would not otherwise have suspected such warm hearts, wanted Sammy to have a nice day.

"Oh I will, I will," Sammy began by answering. After a bit he added: "I just adore New York," said with a grin and the very suspicion of an American twang.

"This is the friendliest city in the world," he told Zara down the long-distance telephone, shouting, so that his words were accompanied by little vibratory echoes.

"Tess says they don't really mean it." Zara's voice in contrast was thin, diminished into a tiny wail by the line. "They're not sincere, you know."

"Tess was wrong about the gorillas at Immigration. She could be wrong about that too. Tess doesn't *own* the whole country, you know. She just inherited a small slice of it."

"Darling, you do sound funny," countered Zara; her familiar anxiety on the subject of Sammy made her sound stronger. "Are you all right? I mean, are you all right over there all by yourself—?"

"I'm mainly on television during the day," Sammy cut in with a

laugh. "Alone except for the chat show host and forty million people."
Sammy was deciding whether to add, truthfully, that actually not all
the shows were networked; some of his audiences being as low as a
million, or, say, a million and a half, when he realized that Zara was
saying in a voice of distinct reproach:

"And you haven't asked after Mummy yet." It was the sudden illness of Zara's mother, another person emotionally dependent upon
her, which had prevented Zara's trip to New York with Sammy, at the
last moment.

It was only after Sammy had rung off—having asked tenderly after
Zara's mother and apologized for his crude crack about Tess before
doing so—that he realized Zara was quite right. He *had* sounded
rather funny: even to himself. That is, he would never have dared to
make such a remark about Tess in London. Dared? Sammy pulled
himself up.

To Zara, his strong and lovely Zara, he could of course say anything.
She was his wife. As a couple, they were exceptionally close as all their
circle agreed; being childless (a decision begun through poverty in the
early days and somehow never rescinded) only increased their intimacy. Because their marriage had not been founded on a flash-in-the-
pan sexual attraction but something deeper, more companionate—sex
had never played a great part in it, even at the beginning—the bond
had only grown stronger with the years. Sammy doubted whether
there was a more genuinely united pair in London.

All this was true; and comforting to recollect. It was just that in
recent years Tess had become an omnipresent force in their lives: Tess
on clothes, Tess on interior decoration, especially Tess on curtains, that
was the real pits—a new expression which Sammy had picked up from
Clodagh; and somehow Tess's famous money always seemed to rein-
force her opinions in a way which was rather curious, considering
Zara's own radical contempt for unearned wealth.

"Well, I've got money now. Lots and lots of it. Earned money,"
thought Sammy, squaring his thin shoulders in the new pale blue
jacket which Zara, yes Zara, had made him buy. He looked in one of
the huge gilded mirrors which decorated his suite at the Barraclough,
pushing aside the large floral arrangement, a gift from the hotel manager (or was it Clodagh?) to do so. Sammy Luke, the conqueror of
New York, or at least American television; then he had to laugh at his
own absurdity.

He went on to the little balcony which led off the suite's sitting room and looked down at the ribbon of streets which stretched below; the roofs of lesser buildings; the blur of green where Central Park nestled, at his disposal, in the center of it all. The plain truth was that he was just very, very happy. The reason was not purely the success of his book, nor even his instant highly commercial fame, as predicted by Clodagh, on television, nor yet the attentions of the press, parts of which had after all been quite violently critical of his book, again as predicted by Clodagh. The reason was that Sammy Luke felt loved in New York in a vast, wonderful, impersonal way: Nothing was demanded of him by this love; it was like an electric fire which simulated red-hot coals even when it was switched off. New York glowed but it could not scorch. In his heart Sammy knew that he had never been so happy before.

It was at this point that the telephone rang again. Sammy left the balcony. Sammy was expecting one of three calls. The first, and most likely, was Clodagh's daily checking call: "Hi, Sammy, it's Clodagh Pegoda . . . listen, that show was great, the one they taped. Our publicity girl actually told me it didn't go too well at the time, she was frightened they were mauling you . . . but the way it came out . . . Zouch!" More interesting sounds from Clodagh's mobile and rather sensual lips. "That's my Sam. You really had them licked. I guess the little girl was just protective. Sue-May, was it? Joanie. Yes, Joanie. She's crazy about you. I'll have to talk to her; what's a nice girl like that doing being crazy about a man, and a married man at that. . . ."

Clodagh's physical preference for her own sex was a robust joke between them; it was odd how being in New York made that, too, innocuous. In England Sammy had been secretly rather shocked by the frankness of Clodagh's allusions: more alarmingly she had once goosed him, apparently fooling, but with the accompanying words "You're a bit like a girl yourself, Sammy," which were not totally reassuring. Even that was preferable to the embarrassing occasion when Clodagh had playfully declared a physical attraction to Zara, wondered—outside the money that was now coming in—how Zara put up with Sammy. In New York, however, Sammy entered enthusiastically into the fun.

He was also pleased to hear, however lightly meant, that Joanie, the publicity girl in charge of his day-to-day arrangements, was crazy about him; for Joanie, unlike handsome, piratical, frightening Clodagh, was small and tender.

The second possibility for the call was Joanie herself. In which case she would be down in the lobby of the Barraclough, ready to escort him to an afternoon taping at a television studio across town. Later Joanie would drop Sammy back at the Barraclough, paying carefully and slightly earnestly for the taxi as though Sammy's nerves might be ruffled if the ceremony was not carried out correctly. One of these days, Sammy thought with a smile, he might even ask Joanie up to his suite at the Barraclough . . . after all what were suites for? (Sammy had never had a suite in a hotel before, his English publisher having an old-fashioned taste for providing his authors with plain bedrooms while on promotional tours.)

The third possibility was that Zara was calling him back: their conversations, for all Sammy's apologies, had not really ended on a satisfactory note; alone in London, Zara was doubtless feeling anxious about Sammy as a result. He detected a little complacency in himself about Zara: after all, there was for once nothing for her to feel anxious about (except perhaps Joanie, he added to himself with a smile).

Sammy's complacency was shattered by the voice on the telephone:

"I saw you on television last night," began the voice—female, whispering. "You bastard, Sammy Luke, I'm coming up to your room and I'm going to cut off your little—" A detailed anatomical description followed of what the voice was going to do to Sammy Luke. The low, violent obscenities, so horrible, so surprising, coming out of the innocent white hotel telephone, continued for a while unstopped, assaulting his ears like the rustle of some appalling cowrie shell; until Sammy thought to clutch the instrument to his chest, and thus stifle the voice in the surface of his new blue jacket.

After a moment, thinking he might have put an end to the terrible whispering, Sammy raised the instrument again. He was in time to hear the voice say:

"Have a nice death, Mr. Luke."

Then there was silence.

Sammy felt quite sick. A moment later he was running across the ornate sitting room of the splendid Barraclough suite, retching; the bathroom seemed miles away at the far end of the spacious bedroom; he only just reached it in time.

Sammy was lying, panting, on the nearest twin bed to the door—the one which had been meant for Zara—when the telephone rang again. He picked it up and held it at a distance, then recognized the merry, interested voice of the hotel telephonist.

"Oh, Mr. Luke," she was saying. "While your line was busy just now, Joanie Lazlo called from Porlock Publishers, and she'll call right back. But she says to tell you that the taping for this afternoon has been canceled, Max Syegrand is still tied up on the Coast and can't make it. Too bad about that, Mr. Luke. It's a good show. Anyway, she'll come by this evening with some more books to sign . . . Have a nice day now, Mr. Luke." And the merry telephonist rang off. But this time Sammy shuddered when he heard the familiar cheerful farewell.

It seemed a long time before Joanie rang to say that she was downstairs in the hotel lobby, and should she bring the copies of *Women Weeping* up to the suite? When she arrived at the sitting room door, carrying a Mexican tote bag weighed down by books, Joanie's pretty little pink face was glowing and she gave Sammy her usual softly enthusiastic welcome. All the same Sammy could hardly believe that he had contemplated seducing her—or indeed anyone—in his gilded suite amid the floral arrangements. That all seemed a very long while ago.

For in the hours before Joanie's arrival, Sammy received two more calls. The whispering voice grew bolder still in its descriptions of Sammy's fate; but it did not grow stronger. For some reason, Sammy listened through the first call to the end. At last the phrase came: although he was half expecting it, his heart still thumped when he heard the words:

"Have a nice death now, Mr. Luke."

With the second call, he slammed down the telephone immediately and then called back the operator:

"No more," he said loudly and rather breathlessly. "No more, I don't want any more."

"Pardon me, Mr. Luke?"

"I meant, I don't want any more calls, not like that, not now."

"Alrighty." The operator—it was another voice, not the merry woman who habitually watched television, but just as friendly. "I'll hold your calls for now, Mr. Luke. I'll be happy to do it. Goodbye now. Have a nice evening."

Should Sammy perhaps have questioned this new operator about his recent caller? No doubt she would declare herself happy to discuss the matter. But he dreaded a further cheerful, impersonal New York encounter in his shaken state. Besides, the very first call had been put through by the merry television-watcher. Zara. He needed to talk to Zara. She would know what to do; or rather she would know what *he* should do.

"What's going on?" she exclaimed. "I tried to ring you three times and that bloody woman on the hotel switchboard wouldn't put me through. Are you all right? I rang you back because you sounded so peculiar. Sort of high, you were laughing at things, things which weren't really funny; it's not like you, is it; in New York people are supposed to get this energy, but I never thought . . ."

"I'm not all right, not all right at all," Sammy interrupted her; he was aware of a high, rather tremulous note in his voice. "I was all right then, more than all right, but now I'm not, not at all." Zara couldn't at first grasp what Sammy was telling her, and in the end he had to abandon all explanations of his previous state of exhilaration. For one thing, Zara couldn't seem to grasp what he was saying, and for another Sammy was guiltily aware that absence from Zara's side had played more than a little part in this temporary madness. So Sammy settled for agreeing that he had been acting rather oddly since he had arrived in New York, and then appealed to Zara to advise him how next to proceed.

Once Sammy had made this admission, Zara sounded more like her normal brisk but caring self. She told Sammy to ring up Clodagh at Porlock.

"Frankly, Sammy, I can't think why you didn't ring her straight-away." Zara pointed out that if Sammy could not, Clodagh certainly could and would deal with the hotel switchboard, so that calls were filtered, the lawful distinguished from the unlawful.

"Clodagh might even know the woman," observed Sammy weakly at one point. "She has some very odd friends."

Zara laughed. "Not *that* odd, I hope." Altogether she was in a better temper. Sammy remembered to ask after Zara's mother before he rang off; and on hearing that Tess had flown to America on business, he went so far as to say that he would love to have a drink with her.

When Joanie arrived in the suite, Sammy told her about the threatening calls and was vaguely gratified by her distress.

"I think that's just dreadful, Sammy," she murmured, her light hazel eyes swimming with some tender emotion. "Clodagh's not in the office right now, but let me talk with the hotel manager right away. . . ." Yet it was odd how Joanie no longer seemed in the slightest bit attractive to Sammy. There was even something cloying about her friendliness; perhaps there was a shallowness there, a surface brightness concealing nothing; perhaps Tess was right and New Yorkers were after all insincere. All in all, Sammy was pleased to see Joanie depart with the signed books.

He did not offer her a second drink, although she had brought him an advance copy of the *New York Times* Book Section for Sunday, showing that *Women Weeping* had jumped four places in the best-seller list.

"Have a nice evening, Sammy," said Joanie softly as she closed the door of the suite. "I've left a message with Clodagh's answering service and I'll call you tomorrow."

But Sammy did not have a very nice evening. Foolishly he decided to have dinner in his suite; the reason was that he had some idiotic lurking fear that the woman with the whispering voice would be lying in wait for him outside the Barraclough.

"Have a nice day," said the waiter, automatically, who delivered the meal on a heated trolley covered in a white damask cloth, after Sammy had signed the chit. Sammy hated him.

"The day is over. It is evening." Sammy spoke in a voice which was pointed, almost vicious; he had just deposited a tip on the white chit. By this time the waiter, stowing the dollars rapidly and expertly in his pocket, was already on his way to the door; he turned and flashed a quick smile.

"Yeah. Sure. Thank you, Mr. Luke. Have a nice day." The waiter's hand was on the door handle.

"It is evening here!" exclaimed Sammy. He found he was shaking. "Do you understand? Do you agree that it is *evening?*" The man, mildly startled, but not at all discomposed, said again: "Yeah. Sure. Evening. Goodbye now." And he went.

Sammy poured himself a whiskey from the suite's mini-bar. He no longer felt hungry. The vast white expanse of his dinner trolley depressed him, because it reminded him of his encounter with the waiter; at the same time he lacked the courage to push the trolley boldly out of the suite into the corridor. Having avoided leaving the Barraclough he now found that even more foolishly he did not care to open the door of his own suite.

Clodagh being out of the office, it was doubtless Joanie's fault that the hotel operators still ignored their instructions. Another whispering call was let through, about ten o'clock at night, as Sammy was watching a movie starring the young Elizabeth Taylor, much cut up by commercials, on television. (If he stayed awake till midnight, he could see himself on one of the talk shows he had recorded.) The operator was now supposed to announce the name of each caller, for Sammy's inspection; but this call came straight through.

There was a nasty new urgency in what the voice was promising: "Have a nice death now. I'll be coming by quite soon, Sammy Luke."

In spite of the whiskey—he drained yet another of the tiny bottles—Sammy was still shaking when he called down to the operator and protested: "I'm still getting these calls. You've got to do something. You're supposed to be keeping them away from me."

The operator, not a voice he recognized, sounded rather puzzled, but full of goodwill; spurious goodwill, Sammy now felt. Even if she was sincere, she was certainly stupid. She did not seem to recall having put through anyone to Sammy within the last ten minutes. Sammy did not dare instruct her to hold all calls in case Zara rang up again (or Clodagh, for that matter; where was Clodagh, now that he needed protection from this kind of feminist nut?) He felt too desperate to cut himself off altogether from contact with the outside world. What would Zara advise?

The answer was really quite simple, once it had occurred to him. Sammy rang down to the front desk and complained to the house manager who was on night duty. The house manager, like the operator, was rather puzzled, but extremely polite.

"Threats, Mr. Luke? I assure you you'll be very secure at the Barraclough. We have guards naturally, and we are accustomed . . . but if you'd like me to come up to discuss the matter, why I'd be happy to. . . ."

When the house manager arrived, he was quite charming. He referred not only to Sammy's appearance on television but to his actual book. He told Sammy he'd loved the book; what was more he'd given another copy to his eighty-three-year-old mother (who'd seen Sammy on the *Today* show) and she'd loved it too. Sammy was too weary to wonder more than passingly what an eighty-three-year-old mother would make of *Women Weeping*. He was further depressed by the house manager's elaborate courtesy; it wasn't absolutely clear whether he believed Sammy's story, or merely thought he was suffering from the delightful strain of being a celebrity. Maybe the guests at the Barraclough behaved like that all the time, describing imaginary death threats? That possibility also Sammy was too exhausted to explore.

At midnight he turned the television on again and watched himself, on the chat show in the blue jacket, laughing and wriggling with his own humour, denying for the tenth time that he had any curious sadistic tastes himself, that *Women Weeping* was founded on any incident in his private life.

When the telephone rang sharply into the silence of the suite shortly after the end of the show, Sammy knew that it would be his persecutor; nevertheless the sight of his erstwhile New York self, so debonair, so confident, had given him back some strength. Sammy was no longer shaking as he picked up the receiver.

It was Clodagh on the other end of the line, who had just returned to New York from somewhere out of town and picked up Joanie's message from her answering service. Clodagh listened carefully to what Sammy had to say and answered him with something less than her usual loud-hailing zest.

"I'm not too happy about this one!" she said after what—for Clodagh—was quite a lengthy silence. "Ever since Andy Warhol, we can never be quite sure what these jokers will do. Maybe a press release tomorrow? Sort of protect you with publicity *and* sell a few more copies. Maybe not. I'll think about that one, I'll call Joanie in the morning." To Sammy's relief, Clodagh was in charge.

There was another pause. When Clodagh spoke again, her tone was kindly, almost maternal; she reminded him, surprisingly, of Zara.

"Listen, little Sammy, stay right there and I'll be over. We don't want to lose an author, do we?"

Sammy went on to the little balcony which led off the sitting room and gazed down at the streetlights far far below; he did not gaze too long, partly because Sammy suffered from vertigo (although that had become much better in New York) and partly because he wondered whether an enemy was waiting for him down below. Sammy no longer thought all the lights were twinkling with goodwill. Looking downwards he imagined Clodagh, a strong Zara-substitute, striding towards him, to save him.

When Clodagh did arrive, rather suddenly at the door of the suite— maybe she did not want to alarm him by telephoning up from the lobby of the hotel?—she did look very strong, as well as handsome, in her black designer jeans and black silk shirt; through her shirt he could see the shape of her flat, muscular chest, with the nipples clearly defined, like the chest of a young Greek athlete.

"Little Sammy," said Clodagh quite tenderly. "Who would want to frighten you?"

The balcony windows were still open. Clodagh made Sammy pour himself yet another whiskey and one for her too (there was a trace of the old Clodagh in the acerbity with which she gave these orders). Masterfully she also imposed two mysterious bomb-like pills upon Sammy which she promised, together with the whiskey, would give him sweet dreams "and no nasty calls to frighten you."

Because Clodagh was showing a tendency to stand very close to him, one of her long arms affectionately and irremovably round his shoulders, Sammy was not all that unhappy when Clodagh ordered him to take both their drinks on to the balcony, away from the slightly worrying intimacy of the suite.

Sammy stood at the edge of the parapet, holding both glasses, and looked downwards. He felt better. Some of his previous benevolence towards New York came flooding back as the whiskey and pills began to take effect. Sammy no longer imagined that his enemy was down there in the street outside the Barraclough, waiting for him.

In a way of course, Sammy was quite right. For Sammy's enemy was not down there in the street below, but standing silently right there behind him, on the balcony, black gloves on her big, capable, strong hands where they extended from the cuffs of her chic black silk shirt.

"Have a nice death now, Sammy Luke." Even the familiar phrase hardly had time to strike a chill into his heart as Sammy found himself falling, falling into the deep trough of the New York street twenty-three stories below. The two whiskey glasses flew from his hands and little icy glass fragments scattered far and wide, far far from Sammy's tiny slumped body where it hit the pavement; the whiskey vanished altogether, for no one recorded drops of whiskey falling on their face in Madison Avenue.

Softhearted Joanie cried when the police showed her Sammy's type-written suicide note with that signature so familiar from the signing of the books; the text itself, the last product of the battered, portable typewriter Sammy had brought with him to New York. But Joanie had to confirm Sammy's distressed state at her last visit to the suite; an impression more than confirmed by the amount of whiskey Sammy had consumed before his death—a glass in each hand as he fell, said the police—to say nothing of the pills.

The waiter contributed to the picture too.

"I guess the guy seemed quite upset when I brought him his dinner." He added as an afterthought: "He was pretty lonesome too. Wanted to talk. You know the sort. Tried to stop me going away. Wanted to have a conversation. I shoulda stopped, but I was busy." The waiter was genuinely regretful.

The hotel manager was regretful too, which considering the fact that Sammy's death had been duly reported in the press as occurring from a Barraclough balcony, was decent of him.

One of the operators—Sammy's merry friend—went further and was dreadfully distressed: "Jesus, I don't believe it. For Christ's sake, I just saw him on television!" The other operator made a calmer statement simply saying that Sammy had seemed very indecisive about whether he wished to receive calls or not in the course of the evening.

Zara Luke, in England, told the story of Sammy's last day and his pathetic tales of persecution, not otherwise substantiated. She also revealed—not totally to the surprise of her friends—that Sammy had a secret history of mental breakdowns and was particularly scared of traveling by himself.

"I shall always blame myself for letting him go," ended Zara, brokenly.

Clodagh Jansen of Porlock Publishers made a dignified statement about the tragedy.

It was Clodagh, too, who met the author's widow at the airport when Zara flew out a week later to make all the dreadful arrangements consequent upon poor Sammy's death.

At the airport Clodagh and Zara embraced discreetly, tearfully. It was only in private later at Clodagh's apartment—for Zara to stay at the Barraclough would certainly have been totally inappropriate—that more intimate caresses of a richer quality began. Began, but did not end: neither had any reason to hurry things.

"After all, we've all the time in the world," murmured Sammy's widow to Sammy's publisher.

"And all the money too," Clodagh whispered back; she must remember to tell Zara that *Women Weeping* would reach the Number One spot in the best-seller list on Sunday.

MARK TWAIN *(1835–1910) remains one of the most influential figures in American literature. Since the pursuit of the American Dream was one of the main themes in his work, his fiction often touched upon criminal activity. "The Stolen White Elephant" is a wonderful story that combines stolen goods with broad humor.*

The Stolen White Elephant
BY MARK TWAIN

The following curious history was related to me by a chance railway acquaintance. He was a gentleman more than seventy years of age, and his thoroughly good and gentle face and earnest and sincere manner imprinted the unmistakable stamp of truth upon every statement which fell from his lips. He said:

You know in what reverence the royal white elephant of Siam is held by the people of that country. You know it is sacred to kings, only kings may possess it, and that it is indeed in a measure even superior to kings, since it receives not merely honor but worship. Very well; five years ago, when the troubles concerning the frontier line arose between Great Britain and Siam, it was presently manifest that Siam had been in the wrong. Therefore every reparation was quickly made, and the British representative stated that he was satisfied and the past should be forgotten. This greatly relieved the king of Siam, and partly as a token of gratitude, but partly also, perhaps, to wipe out any little remaining vestige of unpleasantness which England might feel toward him, he wished to send the queen a present—the sole sure way of propitiating an enemy, according to Oriental ideas. This present ought not only to be a royal one, but transcendently royal. Wherefore, what offering could be so meet as that of a white elephant? My position in the Indian civil service was such that I was deemed peculiarly worthy of the honor of conveying the present to her majesty. A ship was fitted out for me and my servants and the officers and attendants of the elephant, and in due time I arrived in New York harbor and placed my royal charge in admirable quarters in Jersey City. It was necessary to remain a while in order to recruit the animal's health before resuming the voyage.

All went well during a fortnight—then my calamities began. The white elephant was stolen! I was called up at dead of night and informed of this fearful misfortune. For some moments I was beside myself with terror and anxiety; I was helpless. Then I grew calmer and collected my faculties. I soon saw my course—for indeed there was but the one course for an intelligent man to pursue. Late as it was, I flew to New York and got a policeman to conduct me to the headquarters of the detective force. Fortunately I arrived in time, though the chief of the force, the celebrated Inspector Blunt, was just on the point of leaving for his home. He was a man of middle size and compact frame, and when he was thinking deeply he had a way of knitting his brows and tapping his forehead reflectively with his finger, which impressed you at once with the conviction that you stood in the presence of a person of no common order. The very sight of him gave me confidence and made me hopeful. I stated my errand. It did not flurry him in the least; it had no more visible effect upon his iron self-possession than if I had told him somebody had stolen my dog. He motioned me to a seat, and said calmly—

"Allow me to think a moment, please."

So saying, he sat down at his office table and leaned his head upon his hand. Several clerks were at work at the other end of the room; the scratching of their pens was all the sound I heard during the next six or seven minutes. Meantime the inspector sat there, buried in thought. Finally he raised his head, and there was that in the firm lines of his face which showed me that his brain had done its work and his plan was made. Said he—and his voice was low and impressive—

"This is no ordinary case. Every step must be warily taken; each step must be made sure before the next is ventured. And secrecy must be observed—secrecy profound and absolute. Speak to no one about the matter, not even the reporters. I will take care of *them;* I will see that they get only what it may suit my ends to let them know." He touched a bell; a youth appeared. "Alaric, tell the reporters to remain for the present." The boy retired. "Now let us proceed to business—and systematically. Nothing can be accomplished in this trade of mine without strict and minute method."

He took a pen and some paper. "Now—name of the elephant?"

"Hassan Ben Ali Ben Selim Abdallah Mohammed Moisé Alhammal Jamsetjejeebhoy Dhuleep Sultan Ebu Bhudpoor."

"Very well. Given name?"

"Jumbo."

"Very well. Place of birth?"

"The capital city of Siam."

"Parents living?"

"No—dead."

"Had they any other issue besides this one?"

"None. He was an only child."

"Very well. These matters are sufficient under that head. Now please describe the elephant, and leave out no particular, however insignificant—that is, insignificant from *your* point of view. To men in my profession there *are* no insignificant particulars; they do not exist."

I described—he wrote. When I was done, he said—

"Now listen. If I have made any mistakes, correct me."

He read as follows:

"Height, nineteen feet; length from apex of forehead to insertion of tail, twenty-six feet; length of trunk, sixteen feet; length of tail, six feet; total length, including trunk and tail, forty-eight feet; length of tusks, nine and a half feet; ears in keeping with these dimensions; footprint resembles the mark left when one upends a barrel in the snow; color of the elephant, a dull white; has a hole the size of a plate in each ear for the insertion of jewelry, and possesses the habit in a remarkable degree of squirting water upon spectators and of maltreating with his trunk not only such persons as he is acquainted with, but even entire strangers; limps slightly with his right hind leg, and has a small scar in his left armpit caused by a former boil; had on, when stolen, a castle containing seats for fifteen persons, and a gold-cloth saddleblanket the size of an ordinary carpet."

There were no mistakes. The inspector touched the bell, handed the description to Alaric, and said—

"Have fifty thousand copies of this printed at once and mailed to every detective office and pawnbroker's shop on the continent." Alaric retired. "There—so far, so good. Next, I must have a photograph of the property."

I gave him one. He examined it critically, and said—

"It must do, since we can do no better; but he has his trunk curled up and tucked into his mouth. That is unfortunate, and is calculated to mislead, for of course he does not usually have it in that position." He touched his bell.

"Alaric, have fifty thousand copies of this photograph made, the first thing in the morning, and mail them with the descriptive circulars."

Alaric retired to execute his orders. The inspector said—

"It will be necessary to offer a reward, of course. Now as to the amount?"

"What sum would you suggest?"

"To *begin* with, I should say—well, twenty-five thousand dollars. It is an intricate and difficult business; there are a thousand avenues of escape and opportunities of concealment. These thieves have friends and pals everywhere—"

"Bless me, do you know who they are?"

The wary face, practiced in concealing the thoughts and feelings within, gave me no token, nor yet the replying words, so quietly uttered:

"Never mind about that. I may, and I may not. We generally gather a pretty shrewd inkling of who our man is by the manner of his work and the size of the game he goes after. We are not dealing with a pickpocket or a hall thief, now, make up your mind to that. This property was not 'lifted' by a novice. But, as I was saying, considering the amount of travel which will have to be done, and the diligence with which the thieves will cover up their traces as they move along, twenty-five thousand may be too small a sum to offer, yet I think it worth while to start with that."

So we determined upon that figure, as a beginning. Then this man, whom nothing escaped which could by any possibility be made to serve as a clue, said:

"There are cases in detective history to show that criminals have been detected through peculiarities in their appetites. Now, what does this elephant eat, and how much?"

"Well, as to *what* he eats, he will eat *anything.* He will eat a man, he will eat a Bible, he will eat anything *between* a man and a Bible."

"Good, very good indeed, but too general. Details are necessary— details are the only valuable things in our trade. Very well—as to men. At one meal—or, if you prefer, during one day—how many men will he eat, if fresh?"

"He would not care whether they were fresh or not; at a single meal he would eat five ordinary men."

"Very good; five men; we will put that down. What nationalities would he prefer?"

"He is indifferent about nationalities. He prefers acquaintances, but is not prejudiced against strangers."

"Very good. Now, as to Bibles. How many Bibles would he eat at a meal?"

"He would eat an entire edition."

"It is hardly succinct enough. Do you mean the ordinary octavo, or the family illustrated?"

"I think he would be indifferent to illustrations; that is, I think he would not value illustrations above simple letter-press."

"No, you do not get my idea. I refer to bulk. The ordinary octavo Bible weighs about two pounds and a half, while the great quarto with the illustrations weighs ten or twelve. How many Doré Bibles would he eat at a meal?"

"If you knew this elephant, you could not ask. He would take what they had."

"Well, put it in dollars and cents, then. We must get at it somehow. The Doré costs a hundred dollars a copy, Russia leather, beveled."

"He would require about fifty thousand dollars' worth—say an edition of five hundred copies."

"Now that is more exact. I will put that down. Very well; he likes men and Bibles; so far, so good. What else will he eat? I want particulars."

"He will leave Bibles to eat bricks, he will leave bricks to eat bottles, he will leave bottles to eat clothing, he will leave clothing to eat cats, he will leave cats to eat oysters, he will leave oysters to eat ham, he will leave ham to eat sugar, he will leave sugar to eat pie, he will leave pie to eat potatoes, he will leave potatoes to eat bran, he will leave bran to eat hay, he will leave hay to eat oats, he will leave oats to eat rice, for he was mainly raised on it. There is nothing whatever that he will not eat but European butter, and he would eat that if he could taste it."

"Very good. General quantity at a meal—say about—"

"Well, anywhere from a quarter to half a ton."

"And he drinks—"

"Everything that is fluid. Milk, water, whiskey, molasses, castor oil, camphene, carbolic acid—it is no use to go into particulars; whatever fluid occurs to you set it down. He will drink anything that is fluid, except European coffee."

"Very good. As to quantity?"

"Put it down five to fifteen barrels—his thirst varies; his other appetites do not."

"These things are unusual. They ought to furnish quite good clues toward tracing him."

He touched the bell.

"Alaric, summon Captain Burns."

Burns appeared. Inspector Blunt unfolded the whole matter to him, detail by detail. Then he said in the clear, decisive tones of a man whose plans are clearly defined in his head, and who is accustomed to command—"Captain Burns, detail Detectives Jones, Davis, Halsey, Bates, and Hackett to shadow the elephant."

"Yes, sir."

"Detail Detective Moses, Dakin, Murphy, Rogers, Tupper, Higgins, and Bartholomew to shadow the thieves."

"Yes, sir."

"Place a strong guard—a guard of thirty picked men, with a relief of thirty—over the place from whence the elephant was stolen, to keep strict watch there night and day, and allow none to approach—except reporters—without written authority from me."

"Yes, sir."

"Place detectives in plainclothes in the railway, steamship, and ferry depots, and upon all roadways leading out of Jersey City, with orders to search all suspicious persons."

"Yes, sir."

"Furnish all these men with photograph and accompanying description of the elephant, and instruct them to search all trains and outgoing ferry boats and other vessels."

"Yes, sir."

"If the elephant should be found, let him be seized, and the information forwarded to me by telegraph."

"Yes, sir."

"Let me be informed at once if any clues should be found—footprints of the animal, or anything of that kind."

"Yes, sir."

"Get an order commanding the harbor police to patrol the frontages vigilantly."

"Yes, sir."

"Dispatch detectives in plainclothes over all the railways, north as far as Canada, west as far as Ohio, south as far as Washington."

"Yes, sir."

"Place experts in all the telegraph offices to listen to all messages; and let them require that all cipher dispatches be interpreted to them."

"Yes, sir."

"Let all these things be done with the utmost secrecy—mind, the most impenetrable secrecy."

"Yes, sir."

"Report to me promptly at the usual hour."

"Yes, sir."

"Go!"

"Yes, sir."

He was gone.

Inspector Blunt was silent and thoughtful a moment, while the fire in his eye cooled down and faded out. Then he turned to me and said in a placid voice—

"I am not given to boasting, it is not my habit; but—we shall find the elephant."

I shook him warmly by the hand and thanked him; and I *felt* my thanks, too. The more I had seen of the man the more I liked him, and the more I admired him and marveled over the mysterious wonders of his profession. Then we parted for the night, and I went home with a far happier heart than I had carried with me to his office.

Next morning it was all in the newspapers, in the minutest detail. It even had additions—consisting of Detective This, Detective That, and Detective The Other's "theory" as to how the robbery was done, who the robbers were, and whither they had flown with their booty. There were eleven of these theories, and they covered all the possibilities; and this single fact shows what independent thinkers detectives are. No two theories were alike, or even much resembled each other, save in one striking particular, and in that one all the eleven theories were absolutely agreed. That was, that although the rear of my building was torn out and the only door remained locked, the elephant had not been removed through the rent, but by some other (undiscovered) outlet. All agreed that the robbers had made that rent only to mislead the detectives. That never would have occurred to me or to any other layman, perhaps, but it had not deceived the detectives for a moment. Thus, what I had supposed was the only thing that had no mystery about it was in fact the very thing I had gone furthest astray in. The eleven theories all named the supposed robbers, but no two named the same robbers; the total number of suspected persons was thirty-seven. The various newspaper accounts all closed with the most important opinion of all—that of Chief Inspector Blunt. A portion of this statement read as follows:

The chief knows who the two principals are, namely, "Brick" Duffy and "Red" McFadden. Ten days before the robbery was achieved he was already aware that it was to be attempted, and had quietly proceeded to shadow these two noted villains; but unfortunately on the night in question their track was lost, and before it could be found again the bird was flown—that is, the elephant.

Duffy and McFadden are the boldest scoundrels in the profession; the chief has reasons for believing that they are the men who stole the stove out of the detective headquarters on a bitter night last winter—in consequence of which the chief and every detective present were in the hands of the physicians before morning, some with frozen feet, others with frozen fingers, ears, and other members.

When I read the first half of that I was more astonished than ever at the wonderful sagacity of this strange man. He not only saw everything in the present with a clear eye, but even the future could not be hidden from him. I was soon at his office, and said I could not help wishing he had had those men arrested, and so prevented the trouble and loss; but his reply was simple and unanswerable:

"It is not our province to prevent crime, but to punish it. We cannot punish it until it is committed."

I remarked that the secrecy with which we had begun had been marred by the newspapers; not only all our facts but all our plans and purposes had been revealed; even all the suspected persons had been named; these would doubtless disguise themselves now, or go into hiding.

"Let them. They will find that when I am ready for them my hand will descend upon them, in their secret places, as unerringly as the hand of fate. As to the newspapers, we *must* keep in with them. Fame, reputation, constant public mention—these are the detective's bread and butter. He must publish his facts, else he will be supposed to have none; he must publish his theory, for nothing is so strange or striking as a detective's theory, or brings him so much wondering respect; we must publish our plans, for these the journals insist upon having, and we could not deny them without offending. We must constantly show the public what we are doing, or they will believe we are doing nothing. It is much pleasanter to have a newspaper say, 'Inspector Blunt's ingenious and extraordinary theory is as follows,' than to have it say some harsh thing, or, worse still, some sarcastic one."

"I see the force of what you say. But I noticed that in one part of your remarks in the papers this morning you refused to reveal your opinion upon a certain minor point."

"Yes, we always do that; it has a good effect. Besides, I had not formed any opinion on that point, anyway."

I deposited a considerable sum of money with the inspector, to meet current expenses, and sat down to wait for news. We were expecting the telegrams to begin to arrive at any moment now. Meantime I reread the newspapers and also our descriptive circular, and observed that our twenty-five-thousand-dollar reward seemed to be offered only to detectives. I said I thought it ought to be offered to anybody who would catch the elephant. The inspector said:

"It is the detectives who will find the elephant, hence the reward will go to the right place. If other people found the animal, it would only be by watching the detectives and taking advantage of clues and indications stolen from them, and that would entitle the detectives to the reward, after all. The proper office of a reward is to stimulate the men who deliver up their time and their trained sagacities to this sort of work, and not to confer benefits upon chance citizens who stumble upon a capture without having earned the benefits by their own merits and labors."

This was reasonable enough, certainly. Now the telegraphic machine in the corner began to click, and the following dispatch was the result.

> Flower Station, N.Y., 7:30 A.M.
> Have got a clue. Found a succession of deep tracks across a farm near here. Followed them two miles east without result; think elephant went west. Shall now shadow him in that direction.
>
> Darley, Detective

"Darley's one of the best men on the force," said the inspector. "We shall hear from him again before long."

Telegram number two came:

> Barker's, N.J., 7:40 A.M.
> Just arrived. Glass factory broken open here during night, and eight hundred bottles taken. Only water in large quantity near here is five miles distant. Shall strike for there. Elephant will be thirsty. Bottles were empty.
>
> Baker, Detective

"That promises well, too," said the inspector. "I told you the creature's appetites would not be bad clues."

Telegram number three:

> Taylorville, L.I., 8:15 A.M.
> A haystack near here disappeared during night. Probably eaten. Have got a clue, and am off.
>
> Hubbard, Detective

"How he does move around!" said the inspector. "I knew we had a difficult job on hand, but we shall catch him yet."

> Flower Station, N.Y., 9 A.M.
> Shadowed the tracks three miles westward. Large, deep, and ragged. Have just met a farmer who says they are not elephant tracks. Says they are holes where he dug up saplings for shade-trees when ground was frozen last winter. Give me orders how to proceed.
>
> Darley, Detective

"Aha! a confederate of the thieves! The thing grows warm," said the inspector.

He dictated the following telegram to Darley:

> Arrest the man and force him to name his pals. Continue to follow the tracks—to the Pacific, if necessary.
>
> Chief Blunt

Next telegram:

> Coney Point, Pa., 8:45 A.M.
> Gas office broken open here during night and three months' unpaid gas bills taken. Have got a clue and am away.
>
> Murphy, Detective

"Heavens!" said the inspector; "would he eat gas bills?"

"Through ignorance, yes; but they cannot support life. At least, unassisted."

Now came this exciting telegram:

Ironville, N.Y., 9:30 A.M.

Just arrived. This village in consternation. Elephant passed through here at five this morning. Some say he went east, some say west, some north, some south—but all say they did not wait to notice particularly. He killed a horse; have secured a piece of it for a clue. Killed it with his trunk; from style of blow, think he struck it left-handed. From position in which horse lies, think elephant traveled northward along line of Berkley railway. Has four and a half hours' start, but I move on his track at once.

Hawes, Detective

I uttered exclamations of joy. The inspector was as self-contained as a graven image. He calmly touched his bell.

"Alaric, send Captain Burns here."

Burns appeared.

"How many men are ready for instant orders?"

"Ninety-six, sir."

"Send them north at once. Let them concentrate along the line of the Berkley road north of Ironville."

"Yes, sir."

"Let them conduct their movements with the utmost secrecy. As fast as others are at liberty, hold them for orders."

"Yes, sir."

"Go!"

"Yes, sir."

Presently came another telegram:

Sage Corners, N.Y., 10:30

Just arrived. Elephant passed through here at 8:15. All escaped from the town but a policeman. Apparently elephant did not strike at policeman, but at the lamp-post. Got both. I have secured a portion of the policeman as clue.

Stumm, Detective

"So the elephant has turned westward," said the inspector. "However, he will not escape, for my men are scattered all over that region."

The next telegram said:

Glover's, 11:15

Just arrived. Village deserted, except sick and aged. Elephant passed through three-quarters of an hour ago. The antitemperance mass meeting was in session; he put his trunk in at a window and washed it out with water from cistern. Some swallowed it—since dead; several drowned. Detective Cross and O'Shaughnessy were passing through town, but going south—so missed elephant. Whole region for many miles around in terror—people flying from their homes. Wherever they turn they meet elephant, and many are killed.

Brant, Detective

I could have shed tears, this havoc so distressed me. But the inspector only said—

"You see—we are closing in on him. He feels our presence; he has turned eastward again."

Yet further troublous news was in store for us. The telegraph brought this:

Hoganport, 12:19

Just arrived. Elephant passed through half an hour ago, creating wildest fright and excitement. Elephant raged around streets; two plumbers going by, killed one—other escaped. Regret general.

O'Flaherty, Detective

"Now he is right in the midst of my men," said the inspector. "Nothing can save him."

A succession of telegrams came from detectives who were scattered through New Jersey and Pennsylvania, and who were following clues consisting of ravaged barns, factories, and Sunday school libraries, with high hopes—hopes amounting to certainties, indeed. The inspector said—"I wish I could communicate with them and order them north, but that is impossible. A detective only visits a telegraph office to send his report; then he is off again, and you don't know where to put your hand on him."

Now came this dispatch:

Bridgeport, Ct., 12:15

Barnum offers rate of $4000 a year for exclusive privilege of using elephant as traveling advertising medium from now till

detectives find him. Wants to paste circus posters on him.
Desires immediate answer.

Boggs, Detective

"That is perfectly absurd!" I exclaimed.

"Of course it is," said the inspector. "Evidently Mr. Barnum, who
thinks he is so sharp, does not know me—but I know him."

Then he dictated this answer to the dispatch:

Mr. Barnum's offer declined. Make it $7,000 or nothing.

Chief Blunt

"There. We shall not have to wait long for an answer. Mr. Barnum is
not at home; he is in the telegraph office—it is his way when he has
business on hand. Inside of three—"

Done—P. T. Barnum

So interrupted the clicking telegraphic instrument. Before I could
make a comment upon this extraordinary episode, the following dispatch carried my thoughts into another and very distressing channel:

Bolivia, N.Y., 12:50

Elephant arrived here from the south and passed through
toward the forest at 11:50, dispersing a funeral on the way,
and diminishing the mourners by two. Citizens fired some
small cannonballs into him, and then fled. Detective Burke
and I arrived ten minutes later, from the north, but mistook
some excavations for footprints, and so lost a good deal of
time; but at last we struck the right trail and followed it to the
woods. We then got down on our hands and knees and continued to keep a sharp eye on the track, and so shadowed it into
the brush. Burke was in advance. Unfortunately the animal
had stopped to rest; therefore, Burke having his head down,
intent upon the track, butted up against the elephant's hind
legs before he was aware of his vicinity. Burke instantly rose
to his feet, seized the tail, and exclaimed joyfully, "I claim the
re——" but got no further, for a single blow of the huge trunk
laid the brave fellow's fragments low in death. I fled rearward,
and the elephant turned and shadowed me to the edge of the

wood, making tremendous speed, and I should inevitably have been lost, but that the remains of the funeral providentially intervened again and diverted his attention. I have just learned that nothing of that funeral is now left; but this is no loss, for there is an abundance of material for another. Meantime, the elephant has disappeared again.

Mulrooney, Detective

We heard no news except from the diligent and confident detectives scattered about New Jersey, Pennsylvania, Delaware, and Virginia—who were all following fresh and encouraging clues—until shortly after 2 P.M., when this telegram came:

Baxter Center, 2:15

Elephant been here, plastered over with circus bills, and broke up a revival, striking down and damaging many who were on the point of entering upon a better life. Citizens penned him up, and established a guard. When Detective Brown and I arrived, some time after, we entered enclosure and proceeded to identify elephant by photograph and description. All marks tallied exactly except one, which we could not see—the boil scar under armpit. To make sure, Brown crept under to look, and was immediately brained—that is, head crushed and destroyed, though nothing issued from debris. All fled; so did elephant, striking right and left with much effect. Has escaped, but left bold blood track from cannon wounds. Rediscovery certain. He broke southward, through a dense forest.

Brent, Detective

That was the last telegram. At nightfall a fog shut down which was so dense that objects but three feet away could not be discerned. This lasted all night. The ferry boats and even the omnibuses had to stop running.

Next morning the papers were as full of detective theories as before; they had all our tragic facts in detail also, and a great many more which they had received from their telegraphic correspondents. Column after column was occupied, a third of its way down, with glaring headlines, which it made my heart sick to read. Their general tone was like this:

THE WHITE ELEPHANT AT LARGE! HE MOVES UPON HIS FATAL MARCH! WHOLE VILLAGES DESERTED BY THEIR FRIGHT-STRICKEN OCCUPANTS! PALE TERROR GOES BEFORE HIM, DEATH AND DEVASTATION FOLLOW AFTER! AFTER THESE, THE DETECTIVES. BARNS DESTROYED, FACTORIES GUTTED, HARVESTS DEVOURED, PUBLIC ASSEMBLAGES DISPERSED, ACCOMPANIED BY SCENES OF CARNAGE IMPOSSIBLE TO DESCRIBE! THEORIES OF THIRTY-FOUR OF THE MOST DISTINGUISHED DETECTIVES ON THE FORCE! THEORY OF CHIEF BLUNT!

"There!" said Inspector Blunt, almost betrayed into excitement, "this is magnificent! This is the greatest windfall that any detective organization ever had. The fame of it will travel to the ends of the earth, and endure to the end of time, and my name with it."

But there was no joy for me. I felt as if I had committed all those red crimes, and that the elephant was only my irresponsible agent. And how the list had grown! In one place he had "interfered with an election and killed five repeaters." He had followed this act with the destruction of two poor fellows, named O'Donohue and McFlannigan, who had "found a refuge in the home of the oppressed of all lands only the day before, and were in the act of exercising for the first time the noble right of American citizens at the polls, when stricken down by the relentless hand of the Scourge of Siam." In another, he had "found a crazy sensation-preacher preparing his next season's heroic attacks on the dance, the theater, and other things which can't strike back, and had stepped on him." And in still another place he had "killed a lightning-rod agent." And so the list went on, growing redder and redder, and more and more heartbreaking. Sixty persons had been killed, and two hundred and forty wounded. All the accounts bore just testimony to the activity and devotion of the detectives, and all closed with the remark that "three hundred thousand citizens and four detectives saw the dread creature, and two of the latter he destroyed."

I dreaded to hear the telegraphic instrument begin to click again. By and by the messages began to pour in, but I was happily disappointed in their nature. It was soon apparent that all trace of the elephant was lost. The fog had enabled him to search out a good hiding place unobserved. Telegrams from the most absurdly distant points reported that a dim vast mass had been glimpsed there through the fog at such and such an hour, and was "undoubtedly the elephant." This dim vast mass had been glimpsed in New Haven, in New Jersey, in Pennsylvania, in interior New York, in Brooklyn, and even in the city of New York itself! But in all cases the dim vast mass had vanished quickly and left no trace. Every detective of the large force scattered over this huge extent of country sent his hourly report, and each and every one of them had a clue, and was shadowing something, and was hot upon the heels of it.

But the day passed without other result.

The next day the same.

The next just the same.

The newspaper reports began to grow monotonous with facts that amounted to nothing, clues which led to nothing, and theories which had nearly exhausted the elements which surprise and delight and dazzle.

By advice of the inspector I doubled the reward.

Four more dull days followed. Then came a bitter blow to the poor, hard-working detectives—the journalists declined to print their theories, and coldly said, "Give us a rest."

Two weeks after the elephant's disappearance I raised the reward to seventy-five thousand dollars by the inspector's advice. It was a great sum, but I felt that I would rather sacrifice my whole private fortune than lose my credit with my government. Now that the detectives were in adversity, the newspapers turned upon them, and began to fling the most stinging sarcasms at them. This gave the minstrels an idea, and they dressed themselves as detectives and hunted the elephant on the stage in the most extravagant way. The caricaturists made pictures of detectives scanning the country with spyglasses, while the elephant, at their back, stole apples out of their pockets. And they made all sorts of ridiculous pictures of the detective badge—you have seen that badge printed in gold on the back of detective novels, no doubt—it is a wide-staring eye, with the legend, WE NEVER SLEEP. When detectives called for a drink, the would-be facetious barkeeper resurrected an obsolete form of expression and said, "Will you have an eye-opener?" All the air was thick with sarcasms.

But there was one man who moved calm, untouched, unaffected, through it all. It was that heart of oak, the chief inspector. His brave eye never drooped, his serene confidence never wavered. He always said—

"Let them rail on; he laughs best who laughs last."

My admiration for the man grew into a species of worship. I was at his side always. His office had become an unpleasant place to me, and now became daily more and more so. Yet if he could endure it I meant to do so also; at least, as long as I could. So I came regularly, and stayed—the only outsider who seemed to be capable of it. Everybody wondered how I could; and often it seemed to me that I must desert, but at such times I looked into that calm and apparently unconscious face, and held my ground.

About three weeks after the elephant's disappearance I was about to say, one morning, that I should *have* to strike my colors and retire, when the great detective arrested the thought by proposing one more superb and masterly move.

This was to compromise with the robbers. The fertility of this man's invention exceeded anything I have ever seen, and I have had a wide intercourse with the world's finest minds. He said he was confident he could compromise for one hundred thousand dollars and recover the elephant. I said I believed I could scrape the amount together, but what would become of the poor detectives who had worked so faithfully? He said—

"In compromises they always get half."

This removed my only objection. So the inspector wrote two notes, in this form:

> Dear Madam,
> Your husband can make a large sum of money (and be entirely protected from the law) by making an immediate appointment with me.
>
> Chief Blunt

He sent one of these by his confidential messenger to the "reputed wife" of Brick Duffy, and the other to the reputed wife of Red McFadden.

Within the hour these offensive answers came:

> Ye owld fool:
> brick McDuffys bin ded 2 yere.
>
> Bridget Mahoney

Chief Bat,
Red McFadden is hung and in heving 18 month. Any Ass but a detective knose that.

Mary O'Hooligan

"I had long suspected these facts," said the inspector; "this testimony proves the unerring accuracy of my instinct."

The moment one resource failed him he was ready with another. He immediately wrote an advertisement for the morning papers, and I kept a copy of it:

A. — xwblv. 242 N. Tjnd—fz328wmlg. Ozpo,—; 2 m! ogw. Mum.

He said that if the thief was alive this would bring him to the usual rendezvous. He further explained that the usual rendezvous was a place where all business affairs between detectives and criminals were conducted. This meeting would take place at twelve the next night.

We could do nothing till then, and I lost no time in getting out of the office, and was grateful indeed for the privilege.

At eleven the next night I brought one hundred thousand dollars in banknotes and put them into the chief's hands, and shortly afterward he took his leave, with the brave old undimmed confidence in his eye. An almost intolerable hour dragged to a close; then I heard his welcome tread, and rose gasping and tottered to meet him. How his fine eyes flamed with triumph! He said—

"We've compromised! The jokers will sing a different tune tomorrow! Follow me!"

He took a lighted candle and strode down into the vast vaulted basement where sixty detectives always slept, and where a score were now playing cards to while the time. I followed close after him. He walked swiftly down to the dim remote end of the place, and just as I succumbed to the pangs of suffocation and was swooning away he stumbled and fell over the outlying members of a mighty object, and I heard him exclaim as he went down—

"Our noble profession is vindicated. Here is your elephant!"

I was carried to the office above and restored with carbolic acid. The whole detective force swarmed in, and such another season of triumphant rejoicing ensued as I had never witnessed before. The reporters were called, baskets of champagne were opened, toasts were drunk, the handshakings and congratulations were continuous and enthusiastic. Naturally the chief was the hero of the hour, and his happiness was so complete and had been so patiently and worthily and bravely won that it made me happy to see it, though I stood there a homeless beggar, my priceless charge dead, and my position in my country's service lost to me through what would always seem my fatally careless execution of a great trust. Many an eloquent eye testified its deep admiration for the chief, and many a detective's voice murmured, "Look at him—just the king of the profession—only give him a clue, it's all he wants, and there ain't anything hid that he can't find." The dividing of the fifty thousand dollars made great pleasure; when it was finished the chief made a little speech while he put his share in his pocket, in which he said, "Enjoy it, boys, for you've earned it; and more than that you've earned for the detective profession undying fame."

A telegram arrived, which read:

> Monroe, Mich., 10 P.M.
> First time I've stuck a telegraph office in over three weeks. Have followed those footprints, horseback, through the woods, a thousand miles to here, and they get stronger and bigger and fresher every day. Don't worry—inside of another week I'll have the elephant. This is dead sure.
> Darley, Detective

The chief ordered three cheers for "Darley, one of the finest minds on the force," and then commanded that he be telegraphed to come home and receive his share of the reward.

So ended that marvelous episode of the stolen elephant. The newspapers were pleasant with praises once more, the next day, with one contemptible exception. This sheet said, "Great is the detective! He may be a little slow in finding a little thing like a mislaid elephant—he may hunt him all day and sleep with his rotting carcass all night for three weeks, but he will find him at last—if he can get the man who mislaid him to show him the place!"

Poor Hassan was lost to me forever. The cannon shots had wounded him fatally, he had crept to that unfriendly place in the fog, and there, surrounded by his enemies and in constant danger of detection, he had wasted away with hunger and suffering till death gave him peace.

The compromise cost me one hundred thousand dollars; my detective expenses were forty-two thousand dollars more; I never applied for a place again under my government; I am a ruined man and a wanderer in the earth—but my admiration for that man, whom I believe to be the greatest detective the world has ever produced, remains undimmed to this day, and will so remain unto the end.

When someone asked ISAAC ASIMOV *(1920–) if he would write better if he wrote more slowly, he replied that that would be like "asking a sprinter if he would run better if he ran more slowly." His books now number over 370, the vast majority of them nonfiction about science. As a writer of fiction, he is best known for science fiction works such as* The Foundation Trilogy *and* I, Robot. *Issac Asimov was among the first writers to combine science fiction with the mystery story, and his novels featuring a human-android detective team,* The Caves of Steel *(1954) and* The Naked Sun *(1957), are considered prototypes of the form.*

His "straight" mysteries—primarily those found in two series, the Black Widowers and the Union Club stories—have a huge following. They are major contributions to the history of the armchair detective story, being fascinating puzzle tales that always play fair with the reader. "The Cross of Lorraine" shows the Widowers (all except the character Henry are based on real people) faced with one of their most difficult and intriguing cases.

The Cross of Lorraine
BY ISAAC ASIMOV

Emmanuel Rubin did not, as a general rule, ever permit a look of relief to cross his face. Had one done so, it would have argued a prior feeling of uncertainty or apprehension, sensations he might feel but would certainly never admit to.

This time, however, the relief was unmistakable. It was monthly banquet time for the Black Widowers. Rubin was the host and it was he who was supplying the guest. And here it was twenty minutes after seven and only now—with but ten minutes left before dinner was to start—only now did his guest arrive.

Rubin bounded toward him, careful, however, not to spill a drop of his second drink.

"Gentlemen," he said, clutching the arm of the newcomer, "my guest, The Amazing Larri—spelled L-A-R-R-I." And in a lowered voice, over the hum of pleased-to-meet-yous, "Where the hell were you?"

Larri muttered, "The subway train stalled." Then he returned smiles and greetings.

"Pardon me," said Henry, the perennial—and nonpareil—waiter at the Black Widower banquets, "but there is not much time for the guest to have his drink before dinner begins. Would you state your preference, sir?"

"A good notion, that," said Larri gratefully. "Thank you, waiter, and let me have a dry martini, but not too darned dry—a little damp, so to speak."

"Certainly, sir," said Henry.

Rubin said, "I've told you, Larri, that we members all have our *ex officio* doctorates, so now let me introduce them in nauseating detail. This tall gentleman with the neat mustache, black eyebrows, and straight back is Dr. Geoffrey Avalon. He's a lawyer and he never smiles. The last time he tried, he was fined for contempt of court."

Avalon smiled as broadly as he could and said, "You undoubtedly know Manny well enough, sir, not to take him seriously."

"Undoubtedly," said Larri. As he and Rubin stood together, they looked remarkably alike. Both were the same height—about five feet five—both had active, inquisitive faces, both had straggly beards, though Larri's was longer and was accompanied by a fringe of hair down both sides of his face as well.

Rubin said, "And here, dressed fit to kill anyone with a *real* taste for clothing, is our artist-expert, Dr. Mario Gonzalo, who will insist on producing a caricature of you in which he will claim to see a resemblance. —Dr. Roger Halsted inflicts pain on junior high-school students under the guise of teaching them what little he knows of mathematics. —Dr. James Drake is a superannuated chemist who once conned someone into granting him a Ph.D. —And finally, Dr. Thomas Trumbull, who works for the government in an unnamed job as a code expert and who spends most of his time hoping Congress doesn't find out."

"Manny," said Trumbull wearily, "if it were possible to cast a retroactive blackball, I think you could count on five."

And Henry said, "Gentlemen, dinner is served."

It was one of those rare Black Widower occasions when lobster was served, rarer now than ever because of the increase in price.

Rubin, who as host bore the cost, shrugged it off. "I made a good paperback sale last month and we can call this a celebration."

"We can celebrate," said Avalon, "but lobster tends to kill conversation. The cracking of claws and shells, the extraction of meat, the dipping in melted butter—all that takes one's full concentration." And he grimaced with the effort he was putting into the compression of a nutcracker.

"In that case," said the Amazing Larri, "I shall have a monopoly of the conversation," and he grinned with satisfaction as a large platter of prime rib-roast was dexterously placed before him by Henry.

"Larri is allergic to seafood," said Rubin.

Conversation was indeed subdued, as Avalon had predicted, until the various lobsters had been clearly worsted in culinary battle, and then, finally, Halsted asked, "What makes you Amazing, Larri?"

"Stage name," said Larri. "I am a prestidigitator, an escapist extraordinary, and the greatest living exposer."

Trumbull, who was sitting to Larri's right, formed ridges on his bronzed forehead. "What the devil do you mean by 'exposer'?"

Rubin beat a tattoo on his water glass at this point and said, "No grilling till we've had our coffee."

"For God's sake," said Trumbull, "I'm just asking for the definition of a word."

"Host's decision is final," said Rubin.

Trumbull scowled in Rubin's direction. "Then I'll *guess* the answer. An exposer is one who exposes fakes—people who, using trickery of one sort or another, pretend to produce effects they attribute to supernatural or paranatural forces."

Larri thrust out his lower lip, raised his eyebrows, and nodded. "Very good for a guess. I couldn't have put it better."

Gonzalo said, "You mean that whatever someone did by what he claimed was real magic, you could do by stage magic?"

"Exactly," said Larri. "For instance, suppose that some mystic claimed he had the capacity to bend spoons by means of unknown forces. I can do the same by using natural force, this way." He lifted his spoon and, holding it by its two ends, he bent it half an inch out of shape.

Trumbull said, "That scarcely counts. Anyone can do it that way."

"Ah," said Larri, "but this spoon you saw me bend is not the amazing effect at all. That spoon you were watching merely served to trap and focus the ethereal rays that did the real work. Those rays acted to bend *your* spoon, Dr. Trumbull."

Trumbull looked down and picked up his spoon, which was bent nearly at right angles. "How did you do this?"

Larri shrugged. "Would you believe ethereal forces?"

Drake laughed, and pushing his dismantled lobster toward the center of the table, lit a cigarette. He said, "Larri did it a few minutes ago, with his hands, when you weren't looking."

Larri seemed unperturbed by exposure. "When Manny banged his glass, Dr. Trumbull, you looked away. I had rather hoped you all would."

Drake said, "I know better than to pay attention to Manny."

"But," said Larri, "if no one had seen me do it, would you have accepted the ethereal forces?"

"Not a chance," said Trumbull.

"Even if there had been no other way in which you could explain the effect? —Here, let me show you something. Suppose you wanted to flip a coin—"

He fell silent for a moment while Henry passed out the strawberry shortcake, pushed his own serving out of the way, and said, "Suppose you wanted to flip a coin without actually lifting it and turning it—this penny, for instance. There are a number of ways it could be done. The simplest would be merely to touch it quickly, because, as you all know, a finger is always slightly sticky, especially at meal time, so that the coin lifts up slightly as the finger is removed and can easily be made to flip over. It is tails now, you see. Touch it again and it is heads."

Gonzalo said, "No prestidigitation there, though. We see it flip."

"Exactly," said Larri, "and that's why I won't do it that way. Let's put something over it so that it can't be touched. Suppose we use a—" He looked around the table for a moment and seized a salt shaker. "Suppose we use this."

He placed the salt shaker over the coin and said, "Now it is showing heads—"

"Hold on," said Gonzalo. "How do we know it's showing heads? It could be tails and then, when you reveal it later, you'll say it flipped, when it was tails all along."

"You're perfectly right," said Larri, "and I'm glad you raised the point. —Dr. Drake, you have eyes that caught me before. Would you check this on behalf of the assembled company? I'll lift the salt shaker and you tell me what the coin shows."

Drake looked and said, "Heads," in his softly hoarse voice.

"You'll all take Dr. Drake's word, I hope, gentlemen? —Please, watch me place the salt shaker back on the coin and make sure it doesn't flip in the process—"

"It didn't," said Drake.

"Now to keep my fingers from slipping while performing this trick, I will put this paper napkin over the salt shaker."

Larri folded the paper napkin neatly and carefully around the salt shaker, then said, "But, in manipulating this napkin, I caused you all to divert your attention from the penny and you may think I have flipped it in the process." He lifted the salt shaker with the napkin around it, and said, "Dr. Drake, will you check the coin again?"

Drake leaned toward it. "Still heads," he said.

Very carefully and gently Larri put back the salt shaker, the paper napkin still folded around it and said, "The coin remained as is?"

"Still heads," said Drake.

"In that case, I now perform the magic." Larri pushed down on the salt shaker and the paper napkin collapsed. There was nothing inside.

There was a moment of shock, and then Gonzalo said, "Where's the salt shaker?"

"In another plane of existence," said Larri airily.

"But you said you were going to flip the coin."

"I lied."

Avalon said, "There's no mystery. He had us all concentrating on the coin as a diversion tactic. When he picked up the salt shaker with the napkin around it to let Jim look at the coin, he just dropped the salt shaker into his hand and placed the empty, folded napkin over the coin."

"Did you see me do that, Dr. Avalon?" asked Larri.

"No. I was looking at the coin too."

"Then you're just guessing," said Larri.

Rubin, who had not participated in the demonstration at all, but who had eaten his strawberry shortcake instead, said, "The tendency is to argue these things out logically and that's impossible. Scientists and other rationalists are used to dealing with the universe, which fights fair. Faced with a mystic who does not, they find themselves maneuvered into believing nonsense and, in the end, making fools of themselves.

"Magicians, on the other hand," Rubin went on, "know what to watch for, are experienced enough not to be misdirected, and are not impressed by the apparently supernatural. That's why mystics generally won't perform if they know magicians are in the audience."

Coffee had been served and was being sipped, and Henry was quietly preparing the brandy, when Rubin sounded the water glass and said, "Gentlemen, it is time for the official grilling, assuming you idiots have left anything to grill. Jeff, will you do the honors tonight?"

Avalon cleared his throat portentously and frowned down on The Amazing Larri from under his dark and luxuriant eyebrows. Using his voice in the deepest of its naturally deep register, he said, "It is customary to ask our guests to justify their existences, but if today's guest exposes phony mystics even occasionally, I, for one, consider his existence justified and will pass on to another question.

"The temptation is to ask you how you performed your little disappearing trick of a few moments ago, but I quite understand that the ethics of your profession preclude your telling us—even though everything said here is considered under the rose, and though nothing has ever leaked, I will refrain from that question.

"Let me instead ask about your failures. —Sir, you describe yourself as an exposer. Have there been any supposedly mystical demonstrations you have not been able to duplicate in prestidigitous manner and have not been able to account for by natural means?"

Larri said, "I have not attempted to explain all the effects I have ever encountered or heard of, but where I have studied an effect and made an attempt to duplicate it, I have succeeded in every case."

"No failures?"

"None."

Avalon considered that, but as he prepared for the next question, Gonzalo broke in. His head was leaning on one palm, but the fingers of that hand were carefully disposed in such a way as not to disarray his hair.

He said, "Now, wait, Larri, would it be right to suggest that you tackled only easy cases? The really puzzling cases you might have made no attempts to explain?"

"You mean," said Larri, "that I shied away from anything that might spoil my perfect record or that might upset my belief in the rational order of the universe? —If so, you're quite wrong, Dr. Gonzalo. Most reports of apparent mystical powers are dull and unimportant, crude and patently false. I ignore those. The cases I do take on are precisely the puzzling ones that have attracted attention because of their unusual nature and their apparent divorce from the rational. So, you see, the ones I take on are precisely those you suspect I avoid."

Gonzalo subsided and Avalon said, "Larri, the mere fact that you can duplicate a trick by prestidigitation doesn't mean that it couldn't also have been performed by a mystic through supernatural means. The fact that human beings can build machines that fly doesn't mean that birds are man-made machines."

"Quite right," said Larri, "but mystics lay their claims to supernatural powers on the notion, either expressed or implicit, that there is no other way of producing the effect. If I show that the same effect *can* be produced by natural means, the burden of proof then shifts to them to show that the effect can be produced after the natural means are made impossible. I don't know of any mystic who has accepted the conditions set by professional magicians to guard against trickery and who then succeeded."

"And nothing has ever baffled you? Not even the tricks other magicians have developed?"

"Oh, yes, there are effects produced by some magicians that baffle me in the sense that I don't know quite how they do it. I might duplicate the effect by perhaps using a different method. In any case, that's not the point. As long as an effect is produced by natural means, it doesn't matter whether I can reproduce it or not. I am not the best magician in the world. I am just a better magician than any mystic is."

Halsted, his high forehead flushed, and stuttering slightly in his eagerness to speak, said, "But then nothing would startle you? No disappearance like the one involving the salt shaker?"

"You mean that one?" asked Larri, pointing. There was a salt shaker in the middle of the table, but no one had seen it placed there.

Halsted, thrown off a moment, recovered and said, "Have you ever been *startled* by any disappearance? I heard once that magicians have made elephants disappear."

"Actually, making an elephant disappear is childishly simple. I assure you there's nothing puzzling about disappearances performed in a magic act." And then a peculiar look crossed Larri's face, a flash of sadness and frustration. "Not in a magic act. Just—"

"Yes?" said Halstead. "Just what?"

"Just in real life," said Larri, smiling and attempting to toss off the remark lightheartedly.

"Just a minute," said Trumbull, "we can't let that pass. If there has been a disappearance in real life you can't explain, we want to hear about it."

Larri shook his head. "No, no, Dr. Trumbull. It is not a mysterious disappearance or an inexplicable one. Nothing like that at all. I just—well, I lost something and can't find it and it—saddens me."

"The details," said Trumbull.

"It wouldn't be worth your attention," said Larri, embarrassed. "It's a—silly story and somewhat—" He fell into silence.

"Damn it," thundered Trumbull, "we all sit here and voluntarily refrain from asking anything that might result in your being tempted to violate your ethics. Would it violate the ethics of the magician's art for you to tell this story?"

"It's not that at all—"

"Well, then, sir, I repeat what Jeff has told you. Everything said here is in absolute confidence, and the agreement surrounding these monthly dinners is that all questions must be answered. —Manny?"

Rubin shrugged. "That's the way it is, Larri. If you don't want to answer the question we'll have to declare the meeting at an end."

Larri sat back in his chair and looked depressed. "I can't very well allow that to happen, considering the fine hospitality I've been shown. I will tell you the story, but you'll find there's not much to it. I met a woman quite accidentally; I lost touch with her; I can't locate her. That's all there is."

"No," said Trumbull, "that's not all there is. Where and how did you meet her? Where and how did you lose touch with her? Why can't you find her again? We want to know the details."

Gonzalo said, "In fact, if you tell us the details, we may be able to help you."

Larri laughed sardonically. "I think not."

"You'd be surprised," said Gonzalo. "In the past—"

Avalon said, "Quiet, Mario. Don't make promises we might not be able to keep. —Would you give us the details, sir? I assure you we'll do our best to help."

Larri smiled wearily. "I appreciate your offer, but you will see that there is nothing you can do merely by sitting here."

He adjusted himself in his seat and said, "I was done with my performance in an upstate town—I'll give you the details when and if you insist, but for the moment they don't matter, except that this happened about a month ago. I had to get to another small town some hundred and fifty miles away for a morning show and that presented a little transportation problem.

"My magic, unfortunately, is not the kind that can transport me a hundred and fifty miles in a twinkling, or even conjure up a pair of seven-league boots. I did not have my car with me—just as well, for I don't like to travel strange roads at night when I am sleepy—and the net result was that I would have to take a bus that would take nearly four hours. I planned to catch some sleep while on wheels and thus make the trip serve a double purpose.

"But when things go wrong, they go wrong in battalions, so you can guess that I missed my bus and that the next one would not come along for two more hours. There was an enclosed station in which I could wait, one that was as dreary as you could imagine—with no reading matter except some fly-blown posters on the wall—no place to buy a paper or a cup of coffee. I thought grimly that it was fortunate it wasn't raining, and settled down to drowse, when my luck changed.

"A woman walked in. I've never been married, gentlemen, and I've never even had what young people today call a 'meaningful relationship.' Some casual attachments, perhaps, but on the whole, though it seems trite to say so, I am married to my art and find it much more satisfying than women, generally.

"I had no reason to think that this woman was an improvement on the generality, but she had a pleasant appearance. She was something over thirty, and was just plump enough to have a warm, comfortable look about her, and she wasn't too tall.

"She looked about and said, smiling, 'Well, I've missed my bus, I see.'

"I smiled with her. I liked the way she said it. She didn't fret or whine or act annoyed at the universe. It was a good-humored statement of fact, and just hearing it cheered me up tremendously because actually I myself was in the mood to fret and whine and act annoyed. Now I could be as good-natured as she and say, 'Two of us, madam, so you don't even have the satisfaction of being unique.'

" 'So much the better,' she said. 'We can talk and pass the time that much faster.'

"I was astonished. She did not treat me as a potential attacker or as a possible thief. God knows I am not handsome or even particularly respectable in appearance, but it was as though she had casually penetrated to my inmost character and found it satisfactory. You have no idea how flattered I was. If I were ten times as sleepy, I would have stayed up to talk to her.

"And we did talk. Inside of fifteen minutes I knew I was having the pleasantest conversation in my life—in a crummy bus station at midnight. I can't tell you all we talked about, but I can tell you what we *didn't* talk about. We didn't talk about magic.

"I can interest anyone by doing tricks, but then it isn't me they're interested in; it's the flying fingers and the patter they like. And while I'm willing to buy attention that way, you don't know how pleasant it is to get the attention without purchasing it. She apparently just liked to listen to me; I know I liked to listen to her.

"Fortunately, my trip was not an all-out effort, so I didn't have my large trunk with the show-business advertising all over it, just two rather large valises. I told her nothing personal about myself, and asked nothing about her. I gathered briefly that she was heading for her brother's place, that it was right on the road, that she would have to wake him up because she had carelessly let herself be late—but she only told me that in order to say that she was glad it had happened. She would buy my company at the price of inconveniencing her brother. I liked that.

"We didn't talk politics or world affairs or religion or the theater. We talked people—all the funny and odd and peculiar things we had observed about people. We laughed for two hours, during which not one other person came to join us. I had never had anything like that happen to me, had never felt so alive and happy, and when the bus finally came at 1:50 A.M., it was amazing how sorry I was. I didn't want the night to end.

"When I got onto the bus, of course, it was no longer quite the same thing, even though we found a double seat we could share. After all, we had been alone in the station and there we could talk loudly and laugh. On the bus people were sleeping.

"Of course it wasn't all bad. It was a nice feeling to have her so close to me. Despite the fact that I'm rather an old horse, I felt like a teenager—enough like a teenager, in fact, to be embarrassed at being watched.

"Immediately across the way was a woman and her young son. He was about eight years old, I should judge, and *he* was awake. He kept watching me with his sharp little eyes. I could see those eyes fixed on us every time a street light shone into the bus and it was very inhibiting. I wished he were asleep but, of course, the excitement of being on a bus, perhaps, was keeping him awake.

"The motion of the bus, the occasional whisper, the feeling of being quite out of reality, the pressure of her body against mine—it was like confusing dream and fact, and the boundary between sleep and wakefulness just vanished. I didn't intend to sleep, and I started awake once or twice, but then finally, when I started awake one more time, it was clear there had been a considerable period of sleep, and the seat next to me was empty."

Halsted said, "I take it she had gotten off."

"I didn't think she had disappeared into thin air," said Larri. "Naturally, I looked about. I couldn't call her name, because I didn't know her name. She wasn't in the rest room, because its door was swinging open.

"The little boy across the aisle spoke in a rapid high treble—in French. I can understand French reasonably well, but I didn't have to make any effort, because his mother was now awakened and she translated. She spoke English quite well.

"She said, 'Pardon me, sir, but is it that you are looking for the woman that was with you?'

" 'Yes,' I said. 'Did you see where she got off?'

" 'Not I, sir. I was sleeping. But my son says that she descended at the place of the Cross of Lorraine.'

" 'At the what?'

"She repeated it, and so did the child, in French.

"She said, 'You must excuse my son, sir. He is a great hero worshipper of President Charles de Gaulle and though he is young he knows that tale of the Free French forces in the war very well. He would not miss a sight like a Cross of Lorraine. If he said he saw it, he did.'

"I thanked them and then went forward to the bus driver and asked him, but at that time of night the bus stops wherever a passenger would like to get off, or get on. He had made numerous stops and let numerous people on and off, and he didn't know for sure where he had stopped and whom he had left off. He was rather churlish, in fact."

Avalon cleared his throat. "He may have thought you were up to no good and was deliberately withholding information to protect the passenger."

"Maybe," said Larri despondently, "but what it amounted to was that I had lost her. When I came back to my seat, I found a little note tucked into the pocket of the jacket I had placed in the rack above. I managed to read it by a streetlight at the next stop, where the French mother and son got off. It said, 'Thank you so much for a delightful time. Gwendolyn.' "

Gonzalo said, "You have her first name anyway."

Larri said, "I would appreciate having had her last name, her address, her telephone number. Having only a first name is useless."

"You know," said Rubin, "she may deliberately have withheld information because she wasn't interested in continuing the acquaintance-ship. A romantic little interlude is one thing; a continuing danger is another. She may be a married woman."

"Have you done anything about trying to find her?" asked Gonzalo.

"Certainly," said Larri sardonically. "If a magician is faced with a disappearing woman he must understand what has happened. I have gone over the bus route twice by car, looking for a Cross of Lorraine. If I had found it, I would have gone in and asked if anyone there knew a woman by the name of Gwendolyn. I'd have described her. I would have gone to the local post office or the local police station."

"But you have not found a Cross of Lorraine, I take it," said Trumbull.

"I have not."

Halsted said, "Mathematically speaking, it's a finite problem. You could try every post office along the whole route."

Larri sighed. "If I get desperate enough, I'll try. But, mathematically speaking, that would be so inelegant. Why can't I find the Cross of Lorraine?"

"The youngster might have made a mistake," said Trumbull.

"Not a chance," said Larri. "An adult, yes, but a child, never. Adults have accumulated enough irrationality to be very unreliable eyewitnesses. A bright eight-year-old is different. Don't try to pull any trick on a bright kid; he'll see through it.

"Just the same," he went on, "nowhere on the route is there a restaurant, a department store, or anything else with the name Cross of Lorraine. I've checked every set of yellow pages along the entire route."

"Now wait a while," said Avalon, "that's wrong. The child wouldn't have seen the words because they would have meant nothing to him. If he spoke and read only French, as I suppose he did, he would know the phrase as 'Croix de Lorraine.' The English would have never caught his eyes. He must have seen the symbol, the cross with the two horizontal bars, like this." He reached out and Henry obligingly handed him a menu.

Avalon turned it over and on the blank back drew the following:

"Actually," he said, "it is more properly called the Patriarchal Cross or the Archiepiscopal Cross since it symbolized the high office of patriarchs and archbishops by doubling the bars. You will not be surprised to hear that the Papal Cross has three bars. The Patriarchal Cross was used as a symbol by Godfrey of Bouillon, who was one of the leaders of the First Crusade, and since he was Duke of Lorraine, it came to be called the Cross of Lorraine. As we all know, it was adopted as the emblem of the Free French during the Hitlerian War."

He coughed slightly and tried to look modest.

Larri said, a little impatiently, "I understand about the symbol, Dr. Avalon, and I didn't expect the youngster to note words. I think you'll agree, though, that any establishment calling itself the Cross of Lorraine would surely display the symbol along with the name. I looked for the name in the yellow pages and for the symbol on the road."

"And you didn't find it?" said Gonzalo.

"As I've already said, I didn't. I was desperate enough to consider things I didn't think the kid could possibly have seen at night. I thought, who knows how sharp young eyes are and how readily they may see something that represents an overriding interest? So I looked at signs in windows, at street signs—even at graffiti."

"If it were a graffito," said Trumbull, "which happens to be the singular form of graffiti, by the way, then, of course, it could have been erased between the time the child saw it and the time you came to look for it."

"I'm not sure of that," said Rubin. "It's my experience that graffiti are never erased. We've got some on the outside of our apartment house—"

"That's New York," said Trumbull. "In smaller towns there's less tolerance for these evidences of anarchy."

"Hold on," said Gonzalo, "what makes you think graffiti are necessarily signs of anarchy? As a matter of fact—"

"Gentlemen! Gentlemen!" And as always, when Avalon's voice was raised to its full baritone, a silence fell. "We are not here to argue the merits and demerits of graffiti. The question is: how can we find this woman who disappeared? Larri has found no restaurant or other establishment with the name of Cross of Lorraine; he has found no evidence of the symbol along the route taken. Can we help him?"

Drake held up his hand and squinted through the curling smoke of his cigarette.

"Hold on, there's no problem. Have you ever seen a Russian Orthodox Church? Do you know what its cross is like?" He made quick marks on the back of the menu and shoved it toward the center of the table. "Here—"

He said, "The kid, being hipped on the Free French, would take a quick look at that and see it as the Cross of Lorraine. So what you have to do, Larri, is look for a Russian Orthodox Church en route. I doubt there would be more than one."

Larri thought about it, but did not seem overjoyed. "The cross with that second bar set at an angle would be on the top of the spire, wouldn't it?"

"I imagine so."

"And it wouldn't be floodlighted, would it? How would the child be able to see it at three or four o'clock in the morning?"

Drake stubbed out his cigarette. "Well, now, churches usually have a bulletin board near the entrance. There could have been a Russian Orthodox cross on the—"

"I would have seen it," said Larri firmly.

"Could it have been a Red Cross?" asked Gonzalo feebly. "You know, there might be a Red Cross headquarters along the route. It's possible."

"The RED Cross," said Rubin, "is a Greek Cross with all four arms equal. I don't see how that could possibly be mistaken for a Cross of Lorraine by a Free French enthusiast. Look at it—"

Halsted said, "The logical thing, I suppose, is that you simply missed it, Larri. If you insist that, as a magician, you're such a trained observer that you *couldn't* have missed it, then maybe it was a symbol on something movable—on a truck in a driveway, for instance—and it moved on after sunrise."

"The boy made it quite clear that it was at the *place* of the Cross of Lorraine," said Larri. "I suppose even an eight-year-old can tell the difference between a place and a movable object."

"He spoke French. Maybe you mistranslated."

"I'm not that bad at the language," said Larri, "and besides, his mother translated and French is her native tongue."

"But English isn't. *She* might have gotten it wrong. The kid might have said something else. He might not even have said the Cross of Lorraine at all."

Avalon raised his hand for silence and said, "One moment, gentlemen. I see Henry, our esteemed waiter, smiling. What is it, Henry?"

Henry, from his place at the sideboard, said, "I'm afraid that I am amused at your doubting the child's evidence. It is quite certain, in my opinion, that he did see the Cross of Lorraine."

There was a moment's silence and Larri said, "How can you tell that, Henry?"

"By not being too subtle, sir."

Avalon's voice boomed out. "I knew it! We're being too complicated. Henry, how is it possible for us to achieve greater simplicity?"

"Why, Mr. Avalon, the incident took place at night. Instead of looking at all signs, all places, all varieties of cross, why not begin by asking ourselves what very few things *can* be easily seen on a highway at night?"

"A Cross of Lorraine?" asked Gonzalo incredulously.

"Certainly," said Henry, "among other things. Especially, if we don't call it a Cross of Lorraine. What the youngster saw as a Cross of Lorraine, out of his special interest, we would see as something else so clearly that its relationship to the Cross of Lorraine would be invisible. What has been happening just now has been precisely what happened earlier with Mr. Larri's trick with the coin and the salt shaker. We concentrated on the coin and didn't watch the salt shaker, and now we concentrate on the Cross of Lorraine and don't look for the alternative."

Trumbull said, "Henry, if you don't stop talking in riddles, you're fired. What the hell is the Cross of Lorraine, if it isn't the Cross of Lorraine?"

Henry said gravely, "What is this?" and carefully he drew on the back of the menu—

Trumbull said, "A Cross of Lorraine—tilted."

"No, sir, you would never have thought so, if we hadn't been talking about the Cross of Lorraine. Those are English letters and a very common symbol on highways if you add something to it—" He wrote quickly and the tilted Cross became:

"The one thing," said Henry, "that is designed to be seen without trouble, day or night, on any highway, is a gas-station sign. The child saw the Cross of Lorraine in this one, but Mr. Larri, retracing the route, sees only a double X, since he reads the entire sign as Exxon. All signs showing this name, whether on the highway, in advertisements, or on credit cards, show the name in this fashion."

Now Larri caught fire. "You mean, Henry, that if I go into the Exxon stations en route and ask for Gwendolyn—"

"The proprietor of one of them is likely to be her brother, and there would not be more than a half dozen or so at most to inquire at."

"Good God, Henry," said Larri, "you're a magician."

"Merely simple-minded," said Henry, "though not, I hope, in the pejorative sense."

Detective teams are fairly common in mystery fiction, although in America the strong tendency is for a single investigator to walk down those dark streets alone, even if the dark street is in a rural village. In England, a pattern for partnerships was established in the 1880s by the immortal team of Holmes and Watson, although Watson didn't contribute much to the act of deduction.

Britain's REGINALD HILL *(1936–) created the team of Detective Supervisor Andrew Dalziel and Detective Inspector Peter Pascoe who constitute one of the very best detective pairs in contemporary crime writing. They are very different physically, emotionally, and intellectually, yet they grow to respect each other as they progress through the books from* A Clubbable Woman *(1970) to* A Pinch of Snuff *(1978). Mr. Hill had also written many other crime novels under his own name and as Patrick Ruell; each book is unique and maintains a high level of excellence.*

"The Worst Crime Known to Man" is an excellent example of the crime story with a sports setting, and quite simply the best crime story about tennis ever written.

The Worst Crime Known to Man
BY REGINALD HILL

"A middle-aged man was removed from the Center Court crowd yesterday for causing a disturbance during a line-call dispute."

On summer evenings when I was young, I used to sit with Mamma on the verandah of our bungalow and watch the flamingoes gliding over the tennis court to roost on the distant lake.

This was my favourite time of day and the verandah was my favourite place. It was simply furnished with a low table, a scatter of cane chairs, and an old English farmhouse rocker with its broad seat moulded and polished by long use.

This was Father's special chair. At the end of the day he would fold his great length into it, lean back with a sigh of contentment, and more often than not say, "This was your grandfather's chair, Colley, did I ever tell you that?"

"Yes, Father."

"Did I? Then probably I told you what it was my father used to tell me while sitting in this chair."

"Life is a game and you play to the rules, and cheating's the worst crime known to man," I would chant.

"Good boy," he would exclaim, laughing and glancing at Mamma, who would smile sweetly, making me smile too. I always smiled when Mamma smiled. She seemed to me then a raving beauty, and she was certainly the most attractive of the only three white women within five hundred square miles. I suppose she seemed so to many others too. "Boff" Gorton, a young District Officer from a better school than Father, used to tell her so after his third gin and tonic, and she would smile and my father would laugh. Boff came round quite a lot, ostensibly to check that all was well (there had already been the first stirrings of the Troubles) and to have a couple of sets on our lush green tennis court. I was too young to wonder how serious Boff's admiration of Mamma really was. During one of his visits, when Father had been held up in the bush, I got up in the night for a drink of water and heard a noise of violent rocking on the verandah. When I went to investigate I discovered Mamma relaxing in the rocking chair and Boff, flushed and rather breathless, sitting on the floor. Curiously, Boff's situation struck me as less remarkable than Mamma's. This was the first time in my life I had ever known her to occupy the rocker.

Father's attitude to Boff was that of an older and rather patronisingly helpful brother. Only on the tennis court did anything like passion show, and that may have been due to natural competitiveness rather than jealousy. At any rate, their games were gargantuan struggles, with Boff's youth and Father's skill in such balance that the outcome was always in doubt.

The court itself was beautiful, a rectangle of English green it had taken ten years to perfect. It was completely enclosed in a cage of wire mesh, erected more to keep wildlife out than balls in. Human entry was effected through a small, tight-fitting gate, shut at night with a heavy chain and large padlock.

Father and Boff played their last match there one spring afternoon that had all the warmth and richness of the best of English summer evenings. Mamma was away superintending the *accouchement* of our nearest female neighbour, who had foolishly delayed her transfer down-country overlong. Curiously, Mamma's absence seemed to stir things up between the two men more than her presence ever did, and Father's invitation to Boff to play tennis came out like a challenge to a duel.

Boff tried to lighten matters by saying to me, "Colley, old chum, why don't you come along and be ball boy?"

"Yes, Colley," said Father. "You come along. You can be umpire too, and see fair play."

"I say," said Boff, flushing. "Do we need an umpire? I mean, neither of us is likely to cheat, are we?"

"Life is a game and you play to the rules and cheating's the worst crime known to man," I piped up.

"How right you are, Colley," said Father, observing Boff grimly. "You umpire!"

There was no more discussion, but even in the pre-match knock-up I recognized a ferocity that both excited and disturbed me. And when the match proper began it was such a hard-fought struggle that for a long time none of us noticed the arrival of the spectators. Usually only the duty houseboy watched from a respectful distance, waiting to be summoned forward with refreshing drinks, though occasionally some nomadic tribesmen would gaze from the fringes of the bush with courteous puzzlement. But this was different. Suddenly I realized that the court was entirely surrounded. There must have been two hundred of them, all standing quietly enough, but all marked with the symbols of their intent and bearing its instruments—machetes and spears.

"Father!" I choked out.

The two men glanced toward me, then saw what I had seen. For a second no one moved; then, with a fearsome roar, the natives rushed forward. Boff hurled himself towards the gate in the fence, and for a moment I thought he was making a suicidal attempt at flight. But District Officers are trained in other schools than that, and the next minute I saw he had seized the retaining chain, pulled it round the gate post and snapped shut the padlock.

The enemy was locked out. At the same time, of course, we were locked in.

If they had been carrying guns, in, out, it would have made no difference. Fortunately they were not, and the mesh was too close for the broad heads of their throwing spears. Even so, they could soon have hacked a way through the wire had not Boff for the second time revealed the quality of his training. Father in his eagerness for the fray had come from the house unarmed, but Boff had brought his revolver, and as soon as a group of our invaders began to hack at the fence he took careful aim and shot the most enthusiastic of them between the eyes.

They fell back in panic, but only for a moment. When they realized that Boff wasn't following up his attack, they returned to the fence, but no one offered to lead another demolition attempt.

"I've got just five bullets left," murmured Boff. "The only thing holding these chaps back is that they know the first to make a move will certainly die. But eventually not even that will matter."

"Why don't we make a dash for the house?" asked Father. "It's only fifty yards. And once we get to the rifles . . ."

"For God's sake!" said Boff. "Don't you understand? Outside this fence we're finished! And please don't talk about rifles. Once one of this lot gets that idea . . ."

Suddenly there came a great cry from the direction of the bungalow and I thought someone *had* got the idea. But a puff of smoke and a sudden tongue of flame revealed the truth, at the same time better and worse. Worse, because my home was going up in flames; better, because this act of arson would destroy their only source of weaponry and might even attract attention to our plight.

Father, perhaps feeling annoyed at the lead Boff had taken in dealing with the situation, suddenly picked up his racket.

"We might as well do something till help comes," he said. "My service, I believe."

It may have started as a gesture, but very rapidly that match developed into the hard, bitter struggle it had promised to be before the attack. I stood at the net holding the revolver, at first keeping an eye on the enemy outside. But soon my judgment of line calls and lets was being required so frequently that I had to give my full attention to the game.

But the most curious thing of all was the reaction of the rebels. At first there'd been some jabbering about ways of winkling us out. Then they fell silent except for one man, some renegade houseboy, I presume, who rather self-importantly began to offer a mixture of explanation of, and commentary on, the game, till his voice too died away; and at four-all in the first set I realized they had become as absorbed in the match as the players themselves. It was quite amazing, like watching a highly sunburned Wimbledon crowd. The heads moved from side to side following the flight of the ball, and at particularly strong or clever shots they beat their spear shafts against the earth and made approving booming noises deep in their throats.

Father took the first set seven-five, and looked as if he might run away with the second. But at one-four Boff's youth began to tell, and suddenly Father was on the defensive. At four-four he seemed to fold up completely, but I guessed that he was merely admitting the inevitable and taking a rest with a view to the climax.

The policy seemed to pay off. Boff won that set six-four, but now he too seemed to have shot his bolt and neither man could gain an ascendancy in the final set. Six-six it went, seven-seven, eight-eight, nine-nine, then into double figures. The light was fading fast.

"Look," said Boff coming up to the net and speaking in a low voice. "Shall we try to keep it going as long as possible? I don't know what these fellows may do when we finish. All right?"

Father didn't answer, but returned to the base line to serve. They came hard and straight, four aces. The crowd boomed. I forgot my official neutrality and joined in the applause. Father stood back to receive service.

I don't know. Perhaps he *was* trying to keep the match going. Perhaps he just intended to give away points by lashing out wildly at Boff's far from puny service. But the result was devastating. Three times in a row the ball streaked from his racket quite unplayably, putting up baseline chalk Love-forty. Three match points. Father settled down, Boff served. Again the flashing return, but this time Boff, driven by resentment or fear, flung himself after it and sent it floating back. Father smashed, Boff retrieved. Father smashed. Boff retrieved again.

"For God's sake!" he pleaded.

Father, at the net, drove the ball deep into the corner and Boff managed to reach this only by flinging himself full length across the grass. But what a shot he produced! A perfect lob, drifting over Father's head and making for the extreme backhand corner.

Father turned with a speed I had not believed him capable of and went in pursuit. There was topspin on the ball. Once it bounced, it would be away beyond mortal reach. The situation looked hopeless.

But Father had no intention of letting it bounce. I drew in my breath as I saw he was going to attempt that most difficult of shots, a reverse backhand volley on the run. I swear the spectating natives drew in their breath too.

Father stretched—but it wasn't enough. He leapt. He connected. It was superb. The ball floated towards Boff, who still lay prostrate on the base line, and bounced gently a couple of feet from his face.

"Out!" he called desperately.

Father's roar of triumph turned to a howl of incredulity.

"Out?" he demanded. *"Out?"*

He turned to me and flung his arms wide in appeal. Boff called to me.

"Please, Colley. It *was* out, wasn't it? It *was!"*

He spoke with all the authority of a District Officer. But I was the umpire and I knew that in this matter my powers exceeded his. I shook my head.

"In!" I called. "Game, set and match to . . ."

With a cry of triumph, Father jumped over the net. And at the same moment a big black fellow with a face painted like a Halloween lantern twisted his spear butt in the chain till it snapped, and the howling mob poured in.

They were only inside the fence for about ten seconds before the first Land Rover full of troops arrived. But in that time they managed to carve the recumbent Boff into several pieces. Father on his feet and wielding his racket like a cavalry sabre managed to get away with a few unpleasant wounds, while I—perhaps because I still held the revolver, though I was too petrified to use it—escaped without threat, let alone violence.

On her return Mamma was naturally upset. I would have thought the survival of her husband and only son would have compensated for the loss of the house, but the more this was urged, the greater waxed her grief. Later, when I told the story of the match, describing with the detail befitting a noble death how Boff had so heroically attempted to keep the final game going, she had a relapse. When she recovered, things changed. I don't think I ever saw her smile again at Father's jokes.

Not that there were many more to smile at. One of Father's wounds turned septic and he had to have his right arm amputated just above the elbow. He tried to learn to play left-handed thereafter, but it never amounted to more than pat ball, and within a twelvemonth only the metal supports rising from the luxuriant undergrowth showed where the tennis court had been.

Soon after that I was sent back to the old country for schooling, and midway through my first term the Head sent for me to tell me there'd been a tragic accident. Father had been cleaning a gun and it had gone off. Or perhaps my mother had been cleaning the gun. Or perhaps, as they both died, they'd both been cleaning guns. I never discovered any details. Out there in the old days they still knew how to draw a decent veil over such things.

I was deeply grieved, of course, but school's a good place for forgetting and I never went back. Sending me to England had been their last known wish for my future. I did not feel able to go against it, not even when I was old enough to have some freedom of choice. And I have been happy enough here with my English job, English marriage, English health. I dig my little patch of garden, read political biographies, play a bit of golf.

But no tennis. I never got interested at school somehow, and I don't suppose I would ever have bothered with tennis again if my managing director hadn't offered me a spare Centre Court ticket. Well, I had to be in town anyway, and it seemed silly to miss the chance of visiting Wimbledon.

I was enjoying it thoroughly too, enjoying the crowd and the place and the game, here, now, with never a thought for the old days, till the Australian played that deep cross-court lob which sent the short-tempered American sprawling.

Then suddenly I saw it all again.

The white ball drifting through the richly scented, darkling air.

The outstretched figure on the baseline.

The pleading, despairing look on Boff's face as he watches the ball bounce out of his reach.

And with it his youth and his hopes and his life.

I saw the same anguish on the American's face today, heard the same accusing disbelief in his voice.

Of course, it wasn't his life and hopes and youth that were at stake. But as Father used to say, life is a game, and you play to the rules, and cheating's the worst crime known to man.

And the American and Boff did have one thing in common.

Both balls were a good six inches out.

PATRICIA MOYES *(1923–), a resident of the British Virgin Islands, has been called the last of the Golden Age writers because her mysteries are in the tradition of Agatha Christie, Dorothy L. Sayers, and the other greats who published between WWI and WWII. She emphasizes well-plotted, clever stories with fully realized characters. All of her more than sixteen novels feature the husband-and-wife team of Henry and Emmy Tibbett; in Moyes' later books, Henry is a Detective Chief Superintendent of Scotland Yard, while Emmy assists him and sometimes leads him through his cases. Among her flawlessly plotted books are* Death on the Agenda *(1962),* Season of Snows and Sins *(1971), and* A Six-Letter Word for Death *(1983).*

Patricia Moyes' short stories are also excellent, and the present selection, which concerns a blackmailer with principles, was one of the best mystery stories published in 1982.

The Honest Blackmailer
BY PATRICIA MOYES

Any young man starting out in life to be a serious blackmailer should realize that he is entering a very delicate and possibly dangerous profession, requiring great judgment, finesse, and knowledge of human nature. Above all, he must learn not to be greedy. If Harry Bessemer had not been greedy, he might still be pursuing his lucrative career in London.

Harry came to his chosen profession in a conventional, almost classic way. His parents were blunt, North country, lower middle-class people, and they were proud, in a way, when Harry—after an adequate but not brilliant school career—informed them that he intended to go to London. Shows the lad has spunk, independence. They were even more pleased when he wrote to tell them that he had been accepted by the Metropolitan Police as a trainee. A right good start for the boy—shows you what he's made of. End up Chief Inspector, I wouldn't wonder.

In fact, Harry did not enjoy his years on the Force—for his taste, the work was too hard, the hours too long and the pay inadequate. However, it provided him with precious experience and training, so that when he resigned from the police he had no difficulty in getting a job as an investigator for a highly reputable firm of private detectives.

At the beginning there was a lot of tedious legwork on divorce cases —British law in those days still demanded the kind of sordid evidence that only a hired detective could produce. However, he worked doggedly and well, and in time was promoted to more sensitive and interesting cases, involving important and wealthy clients who for one reason or another did not care to call in the law. What he discovered on those cases—the vulnerability of human beings, however exalted—finally decided him to become a blackmailer.

It was, of course, vital that he should lay hands on and keep the tangible evidence that he was sent out to locate—letters, photographs, and even tapes, although he never found them very satisfactory. He would report back to his firm that he had had no success in finding the required evidence. The client might go away happily, convinced that the incriminating document no longer existed; on the other hand, the client might decide to call in another firm of private detectives, and it was imperative that they, too, should find nothing.

There remained the question of where to store these valuable documents until he was ready to use them. Harry moved from the small suburban house which he was renting to another, similar one on the other side of London, which he rented under an assumed name. Here, in the cellar, he installed an efficient safe, a photocopier, and basic darkroom equipment for developing and printing photographs. When he had a sizable collection of potentially damaging evidence in his hands, he resigned from his job as investigator and set up privately as a professional blackmailer.

It is a moot point whether a career blackmailer should marry or remain single. A wife may provide a useful cloak of respectability—on the other hand, it admits another person into that very private world. Harry made a nice compromise. With his savings, together with the small legacy left by his parents, he bought a small dry-cleaning establishment in yet another London suburb, which included living accommodations over the shop. He then married a nice, pretty but not very bright girl named Susan. She ran the shop and did a fair amount of perfectly legitimate business.

Susan had no knowledge of the rented house in the distant suburb, and she genuinely believed that Harry's fairly frequent absences from home were connected with some vague real-estate business up North. This, in her simple mind, accounted for the comparative affluence in which she and her husband lived, which could hardly have been produced by the small dry-cleaning establishment.

Harry knew very well that one of the big difficulties a blackmailer has to overcome is the actual transfer of money from the blackmailee, without any obvious contact between himself and his victim, and, of course, without any written or bank records. His terms, which were reasonable, were strictly cash; and for this, the dry-cleaning shop provided an ingenious front. He bought a van with the name—Clean-U-Quik—painted on the side of it. He himself drove the van to make special pickups and deliveries, exclusively to the homes of his various victims.

Posing as a mere driver, in the employment of Clean-U-Quik, he identified himself by a different and assumed name to each of his prospects. The system was simple. He made a weekly or fortnightly call, the victim's clothes were actually cleaned and returned, and there was always an envelope—ostensibly with a check for the cleaning bill—left for Harry to pick up. It contained the required sum in cash. Thus, if his clients were rich enough (and most of them were) to employ a domestic staff, the latter had no suspicion of what was going on. Harry felt justifiably proud of his scheme.

For some years all went well. Then Harry became aware of a growing worry about the permissiveness of modern London society. He soon realized that actors and actresses, rich though they might be, were useless prospects. They would merely laugh in his face, having probably already sold the scandalous story to a newspaper for a large amount of money. Even the aristocracy had become, by Harry's strict standards, notoriously lax, and were only of any practical use if they were closely connected in some way with the royal family. Income-tax dodgers were still a possibility, but unfortunately the Inland Revenue Service was becoming altogether too efficient at catching its own offenders. Homosexuality was no longer a crime, and eminent people were jostling each other to get out of the closet. About the only promising prospects left were politicians and diplomats. What with all this, and inflation too, the life of an honest blackmailer was becoming more difficult by the day.

One of Harry's good, solid clients who never let him down was the Right Honourable Mr.—better call him X. Mr. X was a Member of Parliament, Under-Secretary of State for something or other, eminently respectable, married to a rich and aristocratic wife, and known for his implacable stand against the Provisional I.R.A. in Northern

Ireland. Harry had acquired beautiful evidence—both photographs and letters—to show that Mr. X in fact enjoyed a homosexual relationship with a young Irishman, whom he kept in a discreet apartment on the fringes of Islington, in East London, well away from his stylish West London house in Kensington. What was more, the young Irishman was strongly suspected of having illegal connections with Ulster terrorists. It was, from Harry's point of view, an ideal setup.

What was even more, a sense of confidence—you could almost call it friendship—sprang up between Harry and Mr. X. Harry's fortnightly demand was a perfectly reasonable sum to pay for his discretion, and he did not abuse it. Moreover, he made a special point of seeing that Mr. and Mrs. X's clothes were impeccably cleaned and pressed. The arrangement would have gone along very satisfactorily for a long time if Harry had not become greedy.

The unfortunate fact was that, in a single week, Harry lost two steady clients. One was a bestselling writer of tough, macho novels who suddenly burst into print with details of his love affair with a private in the Royal Marines. This doubled his sales, and rendered Harry's compromising photograph worthless. The other was a Member of Parliament—a tax-evasion case which the authorities had not spotted, but Harry had—who was blown up when he opened one of the letterbombs which Irish terrorists had taken to sending to politicians known to oppose their views.

This double blow to Harry's finances made him take a drastic step. He wrote a letter to the Rt. Hon. Mr. X., addressed to the House of Commons and purporting to come from one of Mr. X's constituents. It requested an urgent interview with the Member concerning rates and taxes in the constituency. Every British voter has the right to speak to his M.P. on such questions, and private rooms in the House are set aside for such meetings. It was in this way that Harry had made his original contact with Mr. X, and of course he signed the letter with the name by which Mr. X knew him. By return of post Harry received a letter from Mr. X's secretary, granting him an interview the following week.

The Right Honourable Mr. X was not a fool. He had a shrewd suspicion of what was coming, and he was right. In the privacy of the interview room Harry told him bluntly that the fortnightly bills for dry-cleaning were to be trebled, starting from the next pickup day, at the end of the week.

Mr. X smiled, as he always did. He agreed with Harry that these were inflationary times, and that an increase was only to be expected. Harry was momentarily taken aback, feeling that he had trodden on a stair which was not there. He had expected at least a show of opposition.

"There's just one snag, though," Mr. X went on. "The banks are closed for today, and I'm off to Belgium for that NATO conference tomorrow morning. Would you take a check?"

"You know my terms," said Harry, smelling a rat. "Cash only."

"Well . . ." Mr. X sighed. "I don't see how it can be done. If you'd wait until next month—"

"I said this week and I mean this week," said Harry, who had financial troubles of his own.

A sudden light broke upon Mr. X. "I know," he said. "There are banks at London Airport which will be open tomorrow before I have to board my plane. I'll draw the money there and send it to you."

"Send it?"

"By post. If you'll just give me your address—"

"Oh, no," said Harry. "I don't want cash like that arriving at the shop."

"Then perhaps you have another address—a private one?"

"You don't catch me like that," said Harry. "I pick the money up at your house—in cash."

"Oh, Harry," said Mr. X, full of regret, "don't you see I'm trying to help you? After all, we trust each other, don't we?"

"Up to a point," said Harry cautiously.

"Ah, well now, how's this for an idea? I'll mail the money from London Airport in an envelope addressed to myself, at my home. I'll have to disguise my handwriting, of course, but that won't be too difficult. I'll mark the envelope Private and Confidential, and I'll underline the word Private three times. That way, you'll be able to recognize it at once."

"How do you mean?"

"Well, while I'm away, my mail will be waiting for me on the marble table in the hall. You know the one. When the butler goes off to collect the clothes for cleaning, you can just pick up the envelope and slip it in your pocket. How's that?"

"Not bad," said Harry, nodding slowly. "Not bad." He smiled. "It's a real pleasure to do business with you, sir. You're a real gentleman."

That evening Mr. X said to his young Irish boy friend, "You know,

Paddy, I think it might not be a bad idea if I got one of those let-terbombs."

"But—"

"Oh, don't worry. I'll be able to identify it, and take it straight to the police. But there are rumors going round that perhaps I'm not so unsympathetic to the provisionals as I appear to be—"

"Okay," said Paddy, who was a practical young man. "What do you want?"

"It must be posted tomorrow morning at London Airport," said Mr. X.

"Hey, that doesn't give me much time—"

"You can arrange it," said Mr. X.

"Well—yes, okay. I suppose I can."

"I'll address the envelope myself. Get me one—not too small."

"Yes, *sir,*" said Paddy, with an impish grin and a mock salute. He brought a large envelope.

Mr. X. began writing, in apparently uneducated capital letters, his own name and address. He added Private and Confidential in the top left-hand corner and underlined the word Private three times. Then he handed the envelope to Paddy. "Make sure the device is well-padded with newspaper or something," he said. "It should look as though the envelope was pretty full. Got it? All clear?"

"Yes, *sir,*" said Paddy again. He took the envelope. "I'll be getting around to the boys to get this done right away."

"You're a good lad," said Mr. X.

Three days later Harry turned up in his dry-cleaning van at the Kensington house, as usual. As usual, the butler asked him to wait in the hall while he went to get the dirty clothes. It was a great trial to the butler, who had been trained in a grand house, that the mews cottage at the back had been sold for an enormous sum, so that tradesmen had to be admitted through the front door.

As soon as the butler had gone, Harry went to the hall table. Sure enough, there was the envelope, well-stuffed, written in a hand which, from long experience, he could recognize was that of the Right Hon-ourable Mr. X., thinly disguised. He picked up the envelope and put it in his pocket, just as the butler returned with his laundry bag.

"I'll have these back by Tuesday," said Harry cheerfully, as he went out the front door. He could hardly have been more wrong. As soon as he got into the van, he could not resist opening the envelope. He, the van, the clothes, and part of Mr. X's front steps were blown to smithereens.

Harry had made another grave error, as great as his sin of greed. He had not bothered to check that there was no conference in Belgium that week. The Right Honourable, who had simply gone to stay for a few days with his sister in the country, came back to London at once when he heard the news, expressing profound shock and surprise.

The police were efficient—they were becoming accustomed to dealing with such incidents. They found a few fragments of the envelope, and the butler affirmed that he had noticed, after the explosion, that an envelope marked Private and Confidential, which had been on the table awaiting Mr. X's return, had disappeared. He could only conclude that the dry-cleaning man had taken it—either to steal it, but more likely in mistake for an exactly similar one which was still there, marked Clean-U-Quik, and containing Mr. X's check for three pounds and thirty pence for cleaning, as per invoice.

Since poor Harry was dead, the police decided to give him the benefit of the doubt, and concluded that it had been an error on his part to take the wrong envelope. They congratulated Mr. X on his fortunate escape.

The terrorists, however, took a different point of view. Paddy stood a lot higher in the organization than Mr. X had ever realized, and he began to be worried. If the rumors that Mr. X was playing a double game were so prevalent that Mr. X had actually suggested an apparent letterbomb attack on himself, then Mr. X ceased to be an asset and became a positive danger. The Right Honourable Mr. X, having disposed of Harry, was in a light-hearted mood—even possibly in a state of grace—when he opened an innocuous-looking letter in his mail at the House of Commons a couple of weeks later, and had his head blown off. So a rough sort of justice may be said to have been done.

BILL PRONZINI *(1943–) a life-long resident of the San Francisco Bay area, is a prolific crime fiction author with some forty
novels and collections and hundreds of short stories to date. He
is equally proficient in the hardboiled, puzzle, and suspense
subgenres, and has now emerged as an important influence in
the field. His most notable series character has no name—at
least no reference is made to a name in the novels and stories
about him—although Mr. Pronzini has made it clear that the
character is modeled in part on himself. Among the best of
Nameless cases are* Blowback *(1977),* Biddlestiff *(1983), and*
Deadfall *(1985). In addition to his mysteries, Mr. Pronzini has
written excellent Western, fantasy, and science fiction stories.*

*"Nameless" remains a most convincing private eye, and no
one has written about locations in and around San Francisco
with better ability than his creator, as the following "Nameless"
adventure attests.*

Cat's-Paw
BY BILL PRONZINI

There are two places that are ordinary enough during the daylight
hours but that become downright eerie after dark, particularly if you
go wandering around in them by yourself. One is a graveyard; the
other is a public zoo. And that goes double for San Francisco's Fleishhacker Zoological Gardens on a blustery winter night when the fog
comes swirling in and makes everything look like capering phantoms
or two-dimensional cutouts.

Fleishhacker Zoo was where I was on this foggy winter night—
alone, for the most part—and I wished I was somewhere else instead.
Anywhere else, as long as it had a heater or a log fire and offered
something hot to drink.

I was on my third tour of the grounds, headed past the sea-lion tank
to make another check of the aviary, when I paused to squint at the
luminous dial of my watch. Eleven forty-five. Less than three hours
down and better than six left to go. I was already half frozen, even
though I was wearing long johns, two sweaters, two pairs of socks,
heavy gloves, a woolen cap, and a long fur-lined overcoat. The ocean
was only a thousand yards away, and the icy wind that blew in off of it
sliced through you to the marrow. If I got through this job without

contracting either frostbite or pneumonia, I would consider myself lucky.

Somewhere in the fog, one of the animals made a sudden roaring noise; I couldn't tell what kind of animal or where the noise came from. The first time that sort of thing had happened, two nights ago, I'd jumped a little. Now I was used to it, or as used to it as I would ever get. How guys like Dettlinger and Hammond could work here night after night, month after month, was beyond my simple comprehension.

I went ahead toward the aviary. The big wind-sculpted cypress trees that grew on my left made looming, swaying shadows, like giant black dancers with rustling headdresses wreathed in mist. Back beyond them, fuzzy yellow blobs of light marked the location of the zoo's cafe. More nightlights burned on the aviary, although the massive fenced-in wing on the near side was dark.

Most of the birds were asleep or nesting or whatever the hell it is birds do at night. But you could hear some of them stirring around, making noise. There were a couple of dozen different varieties in there, including such esoteric types as the crested screamer, the purple gallinule, and the black crake. One esoteric type that used to be in there but wasn't any longer was something called a bunting, a brilliantly colored migratory bird. Three of them had been swiped four days ago, the latest in a rash of thefts the zoological gardens had suffered.

The thief or thieves had also got two South American Harris hawks, a bird of prey similar to a falcon; three crab-eating macaques, whatever they were; and half a dozen rare Chiricahua rattlesnakes known as *Crotalus pricei*. He or they had picked the locks on buildings and cages, and got away clean each time. Sam Dettlinger, one of the two regular watchmen, had spotted somebody running the night the rattlers were stolen, and given chase, but he hadn't got close enough for much of a description, or even to tell for sure if it was a man or a woman.

The police had been notified, of course, but there was not much they could do. There wasn't much the Zoo Commission could do either, beyond beefing up security—and all that had amounted to was adding one extra night watchman, Al Kirby, on a temporary basis; he was all they could afford. The problem was, Fleishhacker Zoo covers some seventy acres. Long sections of its perimeter fencing are secluded; you couldn't stop somebody determined to climb the fence and sneak in at night if you surrounded the place with a hundred men. Nor could you effectively police the grounds with any less than a hundred men; much of those seventy acres is heavily wooded, and there are dozens of grottos, brushy fields and slopes, rush-rimmed ponds, and other areas simulating natural habitats for some of the zoo's 1400 animals and birds. Kids, and an occasional grownup, have gotten lost in there in broad daylight. A thief who knew his way around could hide out on the grounds for weeks without being spotted.

I got involved in the case because I was acquainted with one of the commission members, a guy named Lawrence Factor. He was an attorney, and I had done some investigating for him in the past, and he thought I was the cat's nuts when it came to detective work. So he'd come to see me, not as an official emissary of the commission but on his own; the commission had no money left in its small budget for such as the hiring of a private detective. But Factor had made a million bucks or so in the practice of criminal law, and as a passionate animal lover, he was willing to foot the bill himself. What he wanted me to do was sign on as another night watchman, plus nose around among my contacts to find out if there was any word on the street about the thefts.

It seemed like an odd sort of case, and I told him so. "Why would anybody steal hawks and small animals and rattlesnakes?" I asked. "Doesn't make much sense to me."

"It would if you understood how valuable those creatures are to some people."

"What people?"

"Private collectors, for one," he said. "Unscrupulous individuals who run small independent zoos, for another. They've been known to pay exorbitantly high prices for rare specimens they can't obtain through normal channels—usually because of state or federal laws protecting endangered species."

"You mean there's a thriving black market in animals?"

"You bet there is. Animals, reptiles, birds—you name it. Take the *pricei,* the Southwestern rattler, for instance. Several years ago, the Arizona Game and Fish Department placed it on a special permit list; people who want the snake first have to obtain a permit from the Game and Fish authority before they can go out into the Chiricahua Mountains and hunt one. Legitimate researchers have no trouble getting a permit, but hobbyists and private collectors are turned down. Before the permit list, you could get a *pricei* for twenty-five dollars; now, some snake collectors will pay two hundred and fifty dollars and up for one."

"The same high prices apply on the other stolen specimens?"

"Yes," Factor said. "Much higher, in the case of the Harris hawk, because it is a strongly prohibited species."

"How much higher?"

"From three to five thousand dollars, after it has been trained for falconry."

I let out a soft whistle. "You have any idea who might be pulling the thefts?"

"Not specifically, no. It could be anybody with a working knowledge of zoology and the right—or wrong—contracts for disposal of the specimens."

"Someone connected with Fleishhacker, maybe?"

"That's possible. But I damned well hope not."

"So your best guess is what?"

"A professional at this sort of thing," Factor said. "They don't usually rob large zoos like ours—there's too much risk and too much publicity; mostly they hit small zoos or private collectors, and do some poaching on the side. But it *has* been known to happen when they hook up with buyers who are willing to pay premium prices."

"What makes you think it's a pro in this case? Why not an amateur? Or even kids out on some kind of crazy lark?"

"Well, for one thing, the thief seemed to know exactly what he was after each time. Only expensive and endangered specimens were taken. For another thing, the locks on the building and cage doors were picked by an expert—and that's not my theory, it's the police's."

"You figure he'll try it again?"

"Well, he's four-for-four so far, with no hassle except for the minor scare Sam Dettlinger gave him; that has to make him feel pretty secure. And there are dozens more valuable, prohibited specimens in the gardens. I like the odds that he'll push his luck and go for five straight."

But so far the thief hadn't pushed his luck. This was the third night I'd been on the job and nothing had happened. Nothing had happened during my daylight investigation either; I had put out feelers all over the city, but nobody admitted to knowing anything about the zoo thefts. Nor had I been able to find out anything from any of the Fleishhacker employees I'd talked to. All the information I had on the case, in fact, had been furnished by Lawrence Factor in my office three days ago.

If the thief was going to make another hit, I wished he would do it pretty soon and get it over with. Prowling around here in the dark and the fog and that damned icy wind, waiting for something to happen, was starting to get on my nerves. Even if I was being well paid, there were better ways to spend long, cold winter nights. Like curled up in bed with a copy of *Black Mask* or *Detective Tales* or one of the other pulps in my collection. Like curled up in bed with my lady love, Kerry Wade . . .

I moved ahead to the near doors of the aviary and tried them to make sure they were still locked. They were. But I shone my flash on them anyway, just to be certain that they hadn't been tampered with since the last time one of us had been by. No problem there, either.

There were four of us on the grounds—Dettlinger, Hammond, Kirby, and me—and the way we'd been working it was to spread out to four corners and then start moving counterclockwise in a set but irregular pattern; that way, we could cover the grounds thoroughly without all of us congregating in one area, and without more than fifteen minutes or so going by from one building check to another. We each had a walkie-talkie clipped to our belts so one could summon the others if anything went down. We also used the things to radio our positions periodically, so we'd be sure to stay spread out from each other.

I went around on the other side of the aviary, to the entrance that faced the long, shallow pond where the bigger tropical birds had their sanctuary. The doors were also secure. The wind gusted in over the pond as I was checking the doors, like a williwaw off the frozen Arctic tundra; it made the cypress trees genuflect, shredded the fog for an instant so that I could see all the way across to the construction site of the new Primate Discovery Center, and clacked my teeth together with a sound like rattling bones. I flexed the cramped fingers of my left hand, the one that had suffered some nerve damage in a shooting scrape a few months back; extreme cold aggravated the chronic stiffness. I thought longingly of the hot coffee in my thermos. But the thermos was over at the zoo office behind the carousel, along with my brown-bag supper, and I was not due for a break until one o'clock.

The path that led to Monkey Island was on my left; I took it, hunching forward against the wind. Ahead, I could make out the high dark mass of man-made rocks that comprised the island home of sixty or seventy spider monkeys. But the mist was closing in again, like wind-driven skeins of shiny gray cloth being woven together magically; the building that housed the elephants and pachyderms, only a short distance away, was invisible.

One of the male peacocks that roam the grounds let loose with its weird cry somewhere behind me. The damned things were always doing that, showing off even in the middle of the night. I had never cared for peacocks much, and I liked them even less now. I wondered how one of them would taste roasted with garlic and anchovies. The thought warmed me a little as I moved along the path between the hippo pen and the brown-bear grottos, turned onto the wide concourse that led past the front of the Lion House.

In the middle of the concourse was an extended oblong pond, with a little center island overgrown with yucca trees and pampas grass. The vegetation had an eerie look in the fog, like fantastic creatures waving their appendages in a low-budget science fiction film. I veered away from them, over toward the glass-and-wire cages that had been built onto the Lion House's stucco facade. The cages were for show: inside was the Zoological Society's current pride and joy, a year-old white tiger named Prince Charles, one of only fifty known white tigers in the world. Young Charley was the zoo's rarest and most valuable possession, but the thief hadn't attempted to steal *him*. Nobody in his right mind would try to make off with a frisky, 500-pound tiger in the middle of the night.

Charley was asleep; so was his sister, a normally marked Bengal tiger named Whiskers. I looked at them for a few seconds, decided I wouldn't like to have to pay their food bill, and started to turn away.

Somebody was hurrying toward me, from over where the otter pool was located.

I could barely see him in the mist; he was just a moving black shape. I tensed a little, taking the flashlight out of my pocket, putting my cramped left hand on the walkie-talkie so I could use the thing if it looked like trouble. But it wasn't trouble. The figure called my name in a familiar voice, and when I put my flash on for a couple of seconds I saw that it was Sam Dettlinger.

"What's up?" I said when he got to me. "You're supposed to be over by the gorillas about now."

"Yeah," he said, "but I thought I saw something about fifteen minutes ago, out back by the cat grottos."

"Saw what?"

"Somebody moving around in the bushes," he said. He tipped back his uniform cap, ran a gloved hand over his face to wipe away the thin film of moisture the fog had put there. He was in his forties, heavyset, owl-eyed, with carrot-colored hair and a mustache that looked like a dead caterpillar draped across his upper lip.

"Why didn't you put out a call?"

"I couldn't be sure I actually saw somebody and I didn't want to sound a false alarm; this damn fog distorts everything, makes you see things that aren't there. Wasn't anybody in the bushes when I went to check. It might have been a squirrel or something. Or just the fog. But I figured I'd better search the area to make sure."

"Anything?"

"No. Zip."

"Well, I'll make another check just in case."

"You want me to come with you?"

"No need. It's about time for your break, isn't it?"

He shot the sleeve of his coat and peered at his watch. "You're right, it's almost midnight—"

And something exploded inside the Lion House—a flat, cracking noise that sounded like a gunshot.

Both Dettlinger and I jumped. He said, "What the hell was that?"

"I don't know. Come on!"

We ran the twenty yards or so to the front entrance. The noise had awakened Prince Charles and his sister; they were up and starting to prowl their cage as we rushed past. I caught hold of the door handle and tugged on it, but the lock was secure.

I snapped at Dettlinger, "Have you got a key?"

"Yeah, to all the buildings . . ."

He fumbled his key ring out, and I switched on my flash to help him find the right key. From inside, there was cold dead silence; I couldn't hear anything anywhere else in the vicinity either, except for faint animal sounds lost in the mist. Dettlinger got the door unlocked, dragged it open. I crowded in ahead of him, across a short foyer and through another door that wasn't locked, into the building's cavernous main room.

A couple of the ceiling lights were on; we hadn't been able to tell from outside because the Lion House had no windows. The interior was a long rectangle with a terra cotta tile floor, now-empty feeding cages along the entire facing wall and the near side wall, another set of entrance doors in the far side wall, a kind of indoor garden full of tropical plants flanking the main entrance to the left. You could see all of the enclosure from two steps inside, and there wasn't anybody in it. Except—"

"Jesus!" Dettlinger said. "Look!"

I was looking, all right. And having trouble accepting what I saw. A man was lying sprawled on his back inside one of the cages diagonally to our right; there was a small glistening stain of blood on the front of his heavy coat and a revolver of some kind in one of his outflung hands. The small access door at the front of the cage was shut, and so was the sliding panel at the rear that let the big cats in and out at feeding time. In the pale light, I could see the man's face clearly: his teeth were bared in the rictus of death.

"It's Kirby," Dettlinger said in a hushed voice. "Sweet Christ, what—?"

I brushed past him and ran over and climbed the brass railing that fronted all the cages. The access door, a four-by-two-foot barred inset, was locked tight. I poked my nose between two of the bars, peering in at the dead man. Kirby, Al Kirby. The temporary night watchman the Zoo Commission had hired a couple of weeks ago. It looked as though he had been shot in the chest at close range; I could see where the upper middle of his coat had been scorched by the powder discharge.

My stomach jumped a little, the way it always does when I come face to face with violent death. The faint, gamy, big-cat smell that hung in the air didn't help it any. I turned toward Dettlinger, who had come up beside me.

"You have a key to this access door?" I asked him.

"No. There's never been a reason to carry one. Only the cat handlers have them." He shook his head in an awed way. "How'd Kirby get in there? What *happened?*"

"I wish I knew. Stay put for a minute."

I left him and ran down to the doors in the far side wall. They were locked. Could somebody have had time to shoot Kirby, get out through these doors, then relock them before Dettlinger and I busted in? It didn't seem likely. We'd been inside less than thirty seconds after we'd heard the shot.

I hustled back to the cage where Kirby's body lay. Dettlinger had backed away from it, around in front of the side-wall cages; he looked a little queasy now himself, as if the implications of violent death had finally registered on him. He had a pack of cigarettes in one hand, getting ready to soothe his nerves with some nicotine. But this wasn't the time or the place for a smoke; I yelled at him to put the things away, and he complied.

When I reached him I said, "What's behind these cages? Some sort of rooms back there, aren't there?"

"Yeah. Where the handlers store equipment and meat for the cats. Chutes, too, that lead out to the grottos."

"How do you get to them?"

He pointed over at the rear side wall. "That door next to the last cage."

"Any other way in or out of those rooms?"

"No. Except through the grottos, but the cats are out there."

I went around to the interior door he'd indicated. Like all the others, it was locked. I said to Dettlinger, "You do have a key to this door?"

He nodded, got it out, and unlocked the door. I told him to keep watch out here, switched on my flashlight, and went on through. The flash beam showed me where the light switches were; I flicked them on and began a quick, cautious search. The door to one of the meat lockers was open, but nobody was hiding inside. Or anywhere else back there.

When I came out I shook my head in answer to Dettlinger's silent question. Then I asked him, "Where's the nearest phone?"

"Out past the grottos, by the popcorn stand."

"Hustle out there and call the police. And while you're at it, radio Hammond to get over here on the double—"

"No need for that," a new voice said from the main entrance. "I'm already here."

I glanced in that direction and saw Gene Hammond, the other regular night watchman. You couldn't miss him; he was six-five, weighed in at a good two-fifty, and had a face like the back end of a bus. Disbelief was written on it now as he stared across at Kirby's body.

"Go," I told Dettlinger. "I'll watch things here."

"Right."

He hurried out past Hammond, who was on his way toward where I stood in front of the cage. Hammond said as he came up, "God—what happened?"

"We don't know yet."

"How'd Kirby get in there?"

"We don't know that either." I told him what we did know, which was not much. "When did you last see Kirby?"

"Not since the shift started at nine."

"Any idea why he'd have come in here?"

"No. Unless he heard something and came in to investigate. But he shouldn't have been in this area, should he?"

"Not for another half-hour, no."

"Christ, you don't think that he—"

"What?"

"Killed himself," Hammond said.

"It's possible. Was he despondent for any reason?"

"Not that I know about. But it sure looks like suicide. I mean, he's got that gun in his hand, he's all alone in the building, all the doors were locked. What else could it be?"

"Murder," I said.

"How? Where's the person who killed him, then?"

"Got out through one of the grottos, maybe."

"No way," Hammond said. "Those cats would maul anybody who went out among 'em—and I mean anybody; not even any of the handlers would try a stunt like that. Besides, even if somebody made it down into the moat, how would he scale that twenty-foot back wall to get out of it?"

I didn't say anything.

Hammond said, "And another thing: why would Kirby be locked in this cage if it was murder?"

"Why would he lock himself in to commit suicide?"

He made a bewildered gesture with one of his big hands. "Crazy," he said. "The whole thing's crazy."

He was right. None of it seemed to make any sense at all.

I knew one of the homicide inspectors who responded to Dettlinger's call. His name was Branislaus and he was a pretty decent guy, so the preliminary questions-and-answers went fast and hassle-free. After which he packed Dettlinger and Hammond and me off to the zoo office while he and the lab crew went to work inside the Lion House.

I poured some hot coffee from my thermos, to help me thaw out a little, and then used one of the phones to get Lawrence Factor out of bed. He was paying my fee and I figured he had a right to know what had happened as soon as possible. He made shocked noises when I told him, asked a couple of pertinent questions, said he'd get out to Fleishhacker right away, and rang off.

An hour crept away. Dettlinger sat at one of the desks with a pad of paper and a pencil and challenged himself in a string of tic-tac-toe games. Hammond chain-smoked cigarettes until the air in there was blue with smoke. I paced around for the most part, now and then stepping out into the chill night to get some fresh air: all that cigarette smoke was playing merry hell with my lungs. None of us had much to say. We were all waiting to see what Branislaus and the rest of the cops turned up.

Factor arrived at one-thirty, looking harried and upset. It was the first time I had ever seen him without a tie and with his usually immaculate Robert Redford hairdo in some disarray. A patrolman accompanied him into the office, and judging from the way Factor glared at him, he had had some difficulty getting past the front gate. When the patrolman left I gave Factor a detailed account of what had taken place as far as I knew it, with embellishments from Dettlinger. I was just finishing when Branislaus came in.

Branny spent a couple of minutes discussing matters with Factor. Then he said he wanted to talk to the rest of us one at a time, picked me to go first, and herded me into another room.

The first thing he said was, "This is the screwiest shooting case I've come up against in twenty years on the force. What in bloody hell is going on here?"

"I was hoping maybe you could tell me."

"Well, I can't—yet. So far it looks like a suicide, but if that's it, it's a candidate for Ripley. Whoever heard of anybody blowing himself away in a lion cage at the zoo?"

"Any indication he locked himself in there?"

"We found a key next to his body that fits the little access door in front."

"Just one loose key?"

"That's right."

"So it could have been dropped in there by somebody else after Kirby was dead and after the door was locked. Or thrown in through the bars from outside."

"Granted."

"And suicides don't usually shoot themselves in the chest," I said.

"Also granted, although it's been known to happen."

"What kind of weapon was he shot with? I couldn't see it too well from outside the cage, the way he was lying."

"Thirty-two Iver Johnson."

"Too soon to tell yet if it was his, I guess."

"Uh-huh. Did he come on the job armed?"

"Not that I know about. The rest of us weren't, or weren't supposed to be."

"Well, we'll know more when R and I finishes running a check on the serial number," Branislaus said. "It was intact, so the thirty-two doesn't figure to be a Saturday Night Special."

"Was there anything in Kirby's pockets?"

"The usual stuff. And no sign of a suicide note. But you don't think it was suicide anyway, right?"

"No, I don't."

"Why not?"

"No specific reason. It's just that a suicide under those circumstances rings false. And so does a suicide on the heels of the thefts the zoo's been having lately."

"So you figure there's a connection between Kirby's death and the thefts?"

"Don't you?"

"The thought crossed my mind," Branislaus said dryly. "Could be the thief slipped back onto the grounds tonight, something happened before he had a chance to steal something, and he did for Kirby—I'll admit the possibility. But what were the two of them doing in the Lion House? Doesn't add up that Kirby caught the guy in there. Why would the thief enter it in the first place? Not because he was trying to steal a lion or a tiger, that's for sure."

"Maybe Kirby stumbled on him somewhere else, somewhere nearby. Maybe there was a struggle; the thief got the drop on Kirby, then forced him to let both of them into the Lion House with his key."

"Why?"

"To get rid of him where it was private."

"I don't buy it," Branny said. "Why wouldn't he just knock Kirby over the head and run for it?"

"Well, it could be he's somebody Kirby knew."

"Okay. But the Lion House angle is still too much trouble for him to go through. It would've been much easier to shove the gun into Kirby's belly and shoot him on the spot. Kirby's clothing would have muffled the sound of the shot; it wouldn't have been audible more than fifty feet away."

"I guess you're right," I said.

"But even supposing it happened the way you suggest, it *still* doesn't add up. You and Dettlinger were inside the Lion House thirty seconds after the shot, by your own testimony. You checked the side entrance doors almost immediately and they were locked; you looked around behind the cages and nobody was there. So how did the alleged killer get out of the building?"

"The only way he could have got out was through one of the grottos in back."

"Only he *couldn't* have, according to what both Dettlinger and Hammond say."

I paced over to one of the windows—nervous energy—and looked out at the fog-wrapped construction site for the new monkey exhibit. Then I turned and said, "I don't suppose your men found anything in the way of evidence inside the Lion House?"

"Not so you could tell it with the naked eye."

"Or anywhere else in the vicinity?"

"No."

"Any sign of tampering on any of the doors?"

"None. Kirby used his key to get in, evidently."

I came back to where Branislaus was leaning hipshot against somebody's desk. "Listen, Branny," I said, "this whole thing is *too* screwball. You know that as well as I do. Somebody's playing games here, trying to muddle our thinking—and that means murder."

"Maybe," he said. "Hell, probably. But how was it done? I can't come up with an answer, not even one that's believably farfetched. Can you?"

"Not yet."

"Does that mean you've got an idea?"

"Not an idea; just a bunch of little pieces looking for a pattern."

He sighed. "Well, if they find it, let me know."

"They'll find it sooner or later. I seem to have that sort of devious mind."

"You and Sam Spade," he said.

When I went back into the other room I told Dettlinger that he was next on the grill. Factor wanted to talk some more, but I put him off. Hammond was still polluting the air with his damned cigarettes, and I needed another shot of fresh air; I also needed to be alone for a while, so I could cudgel that devious mind of mine. I could almost feel those little random fragments bobbing around in there like flotsam on a heavy sea.

I put my overcoat on and went out and wandered past the cages where the smaller cats were kept, past the big open fields that the giraffes and rhinos called home. The wind was stronger and colder than it had been earlier; heavy gusts swept dust and twigs along the ground, broke the fog up into scudding wisps. I pulled my cap down over my ears to keep them from numbing.

The path led along to the concourse at the rear of the Lion House, where the open cat-grottos were. Big, portable electric lights had been set up there and around to the front so the police could search the area. A couple of patrolmen glanced at me as I approached, but they must have recognized me because neither of them came over to ask what I was doing there.

I went to the low, shrubberied wall that edged the middle cat-grotto. Whatever was in there, lions or tigers, had no doubt been aroused by all the activity; but they were hidden inside the dens at the rear. These grottos had been newly renovated—lawns, jungly vegetation, small trees, everything to give the cats the illusion of their native habitat. The side walls separating this grotto from the other two were man-made rocks, high and unscalable. The moat below was fifty feet wide, too far for either a big cat or a man to jump; and the near moat wall was sheer and also unscalable from below, just as Hammond and Dettlinger had said.

No way anybody could have got out of the Lion House through the grottos, I thought. Just no way.

No way it could have been murder then. Unless—

I stood there for a couple of minutes, with my mind beginning, finally, to open up. Then I hurried around to the front of the Lion House and looked at the main entrance for a time, remembering things.

And then I knew.

Branislaus was in the zoo office, saying something to Factor, when I came back inside. He glanced over at me as I shut the door.

"Branny," I said, "those little pieces I told you about a while ago finally found their pattern."

He straightened. "Oh? Some of it or all of it?"

"All of it, I think."

Factor said, "What's this about?"

"I figured out what happened at the Lion House tonight," I said. "Al Kirby didn't commit suicide; he was murdered. And I can name the man who killed him."

I expected a reaction, but I didn't get one beyond some widened eyes and opened mouths. Nobody said anything and nobody moved much.

But you could feel the sudden tension in the room, as thick in its own intangible way as the layers of smoke from Hammond's cigarettes.

"Name him," Branislaus said.

But I didn't, not just yet. A good portion of what I was going to say was guesswork—built on deduction and logic, but still guesswork—and I wanted to choose my words carefully. I took off my cap, unbuttoned my coat, and moved away from the door, over near where Branny was standing.

He said, "Well? Who do you say killed Kirby?"

"The same person who stole the birds and other specimens. And I don't mean a professional animal thief, as Mr. Factor suggested when he hired me. He isn't an outsider at all; and he didn't climb the fence to get onto the grounds."

"No?"

"No. He was *already* in here on those nights and on this one, because he works here as a night watchman. The man I'm talking about is Sam Dettlinger."

That got some reaction. Hammond said, "I don't believe it," and Factor said, "My God!" Branislaus looked at me, looked at Dettlinger, looked at me again—moving his head like a spectator at a tennis match.

The only one who didn't move was Dettlinger. He sat still at one of the desks, his hands resting easily on its blotter; his face betrayed nothing.

He said, "You're a liar," in a thin, hard voice.

"Am I? You've been working here for some time; you know the animals and which ones are both endangered and valuable. It was easy for you to get into the buildings during your rounds: just use your key and walk right in. When you had the specimens you took them to some prearranged spot along the outside fence and passed them over to an accomplice."

"What accomplice?" Branislaus asked.

"I don't know. You'll get it out of him, Branny; or you'll find out some other way. But that's how he had to have worked it."

"What about the scratches on the locks?" Hammond asked. "The police told us the locks were picked . . ."

"Red herring," I said. "Just like Dettlinger's claim that he chased a stranger on the grounds the night the rattlers were stolen. Designed to cover up the fact that it was an inside job." I looked back at Branislaus. "Five'll get you ten Dettlinger's had some sort of locksmithing experience. It shouldn't take much digging to find out."

Dettlinger started to get out of his chair, thought better of it, and sat down again. We were all staring at him, but it did not seem to bother him much; his owl eyes were on my neck, and if they'd been hands I would have been dead of strangulation.

Without shifting his gaze, he said to Factor, "I'm going to sue this son of a bitch for slander. I can do that, can't I, Mr. Factor?"

"If what he says isn't true, you can," Factor said.

"Well, it isn't true. It's all a bunch of lies. I never stole anything. And I sure never killed Al Kirby. How the hell could I? I was with this guy, *outside* the Lion House, when Al died inside."

"No you weren't," I said.

"What kind of crap is that? I was standing right next to you, we both heard the shot—"

"That's right, we both heard the shot. And that's the first thing that put me onto you, Sam. Because we damned well *shouldn't* have heard it."

"No? Why not?"

"Kirby was shot with a thirty-two caliber revolver. A thirty-two is a small gun; it doesn't make much of a bang. Branny, you remember saying to me a little while ago that if somebody had shoved that thirty-two into Kirby's middle, you wouldn't have been able to hear the pop more than fifty feet away? Well, that's right. But Dettlinger and I were a lot more than fifty feet from the cage where we found Kirby—twenty yards from the front entrance, thick stucco walls, a ten-foot foyer, and another forty feet or so of floor space to the cage. Yet we not only heard a shot, we heard it loud and clear."

Branislaus said, "So how is that possible?"

I didn't answer him. Instead I looked at Dettlinger and I said, "Do you smoke?"

That got a reaction out of him. The one I wanted: confusion. "What?"

"Do you smoke?"

"What kind of question is that?"

"Gene must have smoked half a pack since we've been in here, but I haven't seen you light up once. In fact, I haven't seen you light up the whole time I've been working here. So answer me, Sam—do you smoke or not?"

"No, I don't smoke. You satisfied?"

"I'm satisfied," I said. "Now suppose you tell me what it was you had in your hand in the Lion House, when I came back from checking the side doors?"

He got it, then—the way I'd trapped him. But he clamped his lips together and sat still.

"What are you getting at?" Branislaus asked me. "What *did* he have in his hand?"

"At the time I thought it was a pack of cigarettes; that's what it looked like from a distance. I took him to be a little queasy, a delayed reaction to finding the body, and I figured he wanted some nicotine to calm his nerves. But that wasn't it at all; he wasn't queasy, he was scared—because I'd seen what he had in his hand before he could hide it in his pocket."

"So what was it?"

"A tape recorder," I said. "One of those small battery-operated jobs they make nowadays, a white one that fits in the palm of the hand. He'd just picked it up from wherever he'd stashed it earlier—behind the bars in one of the other cages, probably. I didn't notice it there because it was so small and because my attention was all on Kirby's body."

"You're saying the shot you heard was on tape?"

"Yes. My guess is, he recorded it right after he shot Kirby. Fifteen minutes or so earlier."

"Why did he shoot Kirby? And why in the Lion House?"

"Well, he and Kirby could have been in on the thefts together; they could have had some kind of falling out, and Dettlinger decided to get rid of him. But I don't like that much. As a premeditated murder, it's too elaborate. No, I think the recorder was a spur-of-the-moment idea; I doubt if it belonged to Dettlinger, in fact. Ditto the thirty-two. He's clever, but he's not a planner, he's an improviser."

"If the recorder and the gun weren't his, whose were they? Kirby's?"

I nodded. "The way I see it, Kirby found out about Dettlinger pulling the thefts; saw him do the last one, maybe. Instead of reporting it, he did some brooding and then decided tonight to try a little shakedown. But Dettlinger's bigger and tougher than he was, so he brought the thirty-two along for protection. He also brought the recorder, the idea probably being to tape his conversation with Dettlinger, without Dettlinger's knowledge, for further blackmail leverage.

"He buttonholed Dettlinger in the vicinity of the Lion House, and the two of them went inside to talk it over in private. Then something happened. Dettlinger tumbled to the recorder, got rough, Kirby pulled the gun, they struggled for it, Kirby got shot dead—that sort of scenario.

"So then Dettlinger had a corpse on his hands. What was he going to do? He could drag it outside, leave it somewhere, make it look like the mythical fence-climbing thief killed him; but if he did that he'd be running the risk of me or Hammond appearing suddenly and spotting him. Instead he got what he thought was a bright idea: he'd create a big mystery and confuse hell out of everybody, plus give himself a dandy alibi for the apparent time of Kirby's death.

"He took the gun and the recorder to the storage area behind the cages. Erased what was on the tape, used the fast-forward and the timer to run off fifteen minutes of tape, then switched to record and fired a second shot to get the sound of it on tape. I don't know for sure what he fired the bullet into; but I found one of the meat-locker doors open when I searched back there, so maybe he used a slab of meat for a target. And then piled a bunch of other slabs on top to hide it until he could get rid of it later on. The police wouldn't be looking for a second bullet, he thought, so there wasn't any reason for them to rummage around in the meat.

"His next moves were to rewind the tape, go back out front, and stash the recorder—turned on, with the volume all the way up. That gave him fifteen minutes. He picked up Kirby's body . . . most of the blood from the wound had been absorbed by the heavy coat Kirby was wearing, which was why there wasn't any blood on the floor and why Dettlinger didn't get any on him. And why I didn't notice, fifteen minutes later, that it was starting to coagulate. He carried the body to the cage, put it inside with the thirty-two in Kirby's hand, relocked the access door—he told me he didn't have a key, but that was a lie—and then threw the key in with the body. But putting Kirby in the cage was his big mistake. By doing that he made the whole thing too bizarre. If he'd left the body where it was, he'd have had a better chance of getting away with it.

"Anyhow, then he slipped out of the building without being seen and hid over by the otter pool. He knew I was due there at midnight, because of the schedule we'd set up; and he wanted to be with me when that recorded gunshot went off. Make me the cat's-paw, if you don't mind a little grim humor, for what he figured would be his perfect alibi.

"Later on, when I sent him to report Kirby's death, he disposed of the recorder. He couldn't have gone far from the Lion House to get rid of it; he did make the call, and he was back within fifteen minutes. With any luck, his fingerprints will be on the recorder when your men turn it up.

"And if you want any more proof that I'm on the right track, I'll swear in court I didn't smell cordite when we entered the Lion House; all I smelled was the gamy odor of jungle cats. I should have smelled cordite if that thirty-two had just been discharged. But it hadn't, and the cordite smell from the earlier discharges had already faded."

That was a pretty long speech and it left me dry-mouthed. But it had made its impression on the others in the room, Branislaus in particular.

He asked Dettlinger, "Well? You have anything to say for yourself?"

"I never did any of those things he said—none of 'em, you hear?"

"I hear."

"And that's all I'm saying until I see a lawyer."

"You've got one of the best sitting next to you. How about it, Mr. Factor? You want to represent Dettlinger?"

"Pass," Factor said thinly. "This is one case where I'll be glad to plead bias."

Dettlinger was still strangling me with his eyes. I wondered if he would keep on proclaiming his innocence even in the face of much stronger evidence than what I'd just presented. Or if he'd crack under the pressure, as most amateurs do.

I decided he was the kind who'd crack eventually, and I quit looking at him and at the death in his eyes.

"Well, I was wrong about that much," I said to Kerry the following night. We were sitting in front of a log fire in her Diamond Heights apartment, me with a beer and her with a glass of wine, and I had just finished telling her all about it. "Dettlinger hasn't cracked and it doesn't look as if he's going to. The D.A.'ll have to work for his conviction."

"But you *were* right about the rest of it?"

"Pretty much. I probably missed on a few details; with Kirby dead, and unless Dettlinger talks, we may never know some of them for sure. But for the most part I think I got it straight."

"My hero," she said, and gave me an adoring look.

She does that sometimes—puts me on like that. I don't understand women, so I don't know why. But it doesn't matter. She has auburn hair and green eyes and a fine body; she's also smarter than I am—she works as an advertising copywriter—and she's stimulating to be around. I love her to pieces, as the boys in the back room used to say.

"The police found the tape recorder," I said. "Took them until late this morning, because Dettlinger was clever about hiding it. He'd buried it in some rushes inside the hippo pen, probably with the idea of digging it up again later on and getting rid of it permanently. There was one clear print on the fast-forward button—Dettlinger's."

"Did they also find the second bullet he fired?"

"Yep. Where I guessed it was; in one of the slabs of fresh meat in the open storage locker."

"And did Dettlinger have locksmithing experience?"

"Uh-huh. He worked for a locksmith for a year in his mid-twenties. The case against him, even without a confession, is pretty solid."

"What about his accomplice?"

"Branislaus thinks he's got a line on the guy," I said. "From some things he found in Dettlinger's apartment. Man named Gerber—got a record of animal poaching and theft. I talked to Larry Factor this afternoon and he's heard of Gerber. The way he figures it, Dettlinger and Gerber had a deal for the specimens they stole with some collectors in Florida. That seems to be Gerber's usual pattern of operation, anyway."

"I hope they get him, too," Kerry said. "I don't like the idea of stealing birds and animals out of the zoo. It's . . . obscene, somehow."

"So is murder."

We didn't say anything for a time, looking into the fire, working on our drinks.

"You know," I said finally, "I have a lot of sympathy for animals myself. Take gorillas, for instance."

"Why gorillas?"

"Because of their mating habits."

"What *are* their mating habits?"

I had no idea, but I made up something interesting. Then I gave her a practical demonstration.

No gorilla ever had it so good.

Georgia-born and a resident of Virginia, NEDRA TYRE *(1921–)*
brings a strong regional flavor to her mystery and suspense
fiction. Her novels feature gripping suspense, and often endan-
gered children, the elderly, and the disadvantaged. Death of an
Intruder *(1953),* Journey to Nowhere *(1954), and* Everyone
Suspect *(1964) are particularly outstanding, but her real forte*
is the short story, of which unfortunately there has never been a
collection.
"A Nice Place to Stay" is written in the first person, and has
one of the best endings in modern crime fiction.

A Nice Place to Stay
BY NEDRA TYRE

All my life I've wanted a nice place to stay. I don't mean anything
grand, just a small room with the walls freshly painted and a few neat
pieces of furniture and a window to catch the sun so that two or three
pot plants could grow. That's what I've always dreamed of. I didn't
yearn for love or money or nice clothes, though I was a pretty enough
girl and pretty clothes would have made me prettier—not that I mean
to brag.

Things fell on my shoulders when I was fifteen. That was when
Mama took sick, and keeping house and looking after Papa and my
two older brothers—and of course nursing Mama—became my responsibility. Not long after that Papa lost the farm and we moved to
town. I don't like to think of the house we lived in near the C & R
railroad tracks, though I guess we were lucky to have a roof over our
heads—it was the worst days of the Depression and a lot of people
didn't even have a roof, even one that leaked, plink, plonk; in a heavy
rain there weren't enough pots and pans and vegetable bowls to set
around to catch all the water.

Mama was the sick one but it was Papa who died first—living in
town didn't suit him. By then my brothers had married and Mama and
I moved into two back rooms that looked onto an alley and everybody's garbage cans and dump heaps. My brothers pitched in and gave
me enough every month for Mama's and my barest expenses even
though their wives grumbled and complained.

I tried to make Mama comfortable. I catered to her every whim and
fancy. I loved her. All the same, I had another reason to keep her alive

as long as possible. While she breathed I knew I had a place to stay. I was terrified of what would happen to me when Mama died. I had no high-school diploma and no experience at outside work and I knew my sisters-in-law wouldn't take me in or let my brothers support me once Mama was gone.

Then Mama drew her last breath with a smile of thanks on her face for what I had done.

Sure enough, Norine and Thelma, my brothers' wives, put their feet down. I was on my own from then on. So that scared feeling of wondering where I could lay my head took over in my mind and never left me.

I had some respite when Mr. Williams, a widower twenty-four years older than me, asked me to marry him. I took my vows seriously. I meant to cherish him and I did. But that house we lived in. Those walls couldn't have been dirtier if they'd been smeared with soot and the plumbing was stubborn as a mule. My left foot stayed sore from having to kick the pipe underneath the kitchen sink to get the water to run through.

Then Mr. Williams got sick and had to give up his shoe repair shop that he ran all by himself. He had a small savings account and a few of those twenty-five-dollar government bonds and drew some disability insurance until the policy ran out in something like six months.

I did everything I could to make him comfortable and keep him cheerful. Though I did all the laundry I gave him clean sheets and clean pajamas every third day and I think it was by my will power alone that I made a begonia bloom in that dark back room Mr. Williams stayed in. I even pestered his two daughters and told them they ought to send their father some get-well cards and they did once or twice. Every now and then when there were a few pennies extra I'd buy cards and scrawl signatures nobody could have read and mailed them to Mr. Williams to make him think some of his former customers were remembering him and wishing him well.

Of course, when Mr. Williams died his daughters were johnny-on-the-spot to see that they got their share of the little bit that tumbledown house brought. I didn't begrudge them—I'm not one to argue with human nature.

I hate to think about all those hardships I had after Mr. Williams died. The worst of it was finding somewhere to sleep; it all boiled down to having a place to stay. Because somehow you can manage not to starve. There are garbage cans to dip into—you'd be surprised how wasteful some people are and how much good food they throw away. Or if it was right after the garbage trucks had made their collections and the cans were empty I'd go into a supermarket and pick, say, at the cherries pretending I was selecting some to buy. I didn't slip their best ones into my mouth. I'd take either those so ripe that they should have been thrown away or those that weren't ripe enough and shouldn't have been put out for people to buy. I might snitch a withered cabbage leaf or a few pieces of watercress or a few of those small round tomatoes about the size of hickory nuts—I never can remember their right name. I wouldn't make a pig of myself, just eat enough to ease my hunger. So I managed. As I say, you don't have to starve.

The only work I could get hardly ever paid me anything beyond room and board. I wasn't a practical nurse, though I knew how to take care of sick folks, and the people hiring me would say that since I didn't have the training and qualifications I couldn't expect much. All they really wanted was for someone to spend the night with Aunt Myrtle or Cousin Kate or Mama or Daddy; no actual duties were demanded of me, they said, and they really didn't think my help was worth anything except meals and a place to sleep. The arrangements were pretty makeshift. Half the time I wouldn't have a place to keep my things, not that I had any clothes to speak of, and sometimes I'd sleep on a cot in the hall outside the patient's room or on some sort of contrived bed in the patient's room.

I cherished every one of those sick people, just as I had cherished Mama and Mr. Williams. I didn't want them to die. I did everything I knew to let them know I was interested in their welfare—first for their sakes, and then for mine, so I wouldn't have to go out and find another place to stay.

Well, now, I've made out my case for the defense, a term I never thought I'd have to use personally, so now I'll make out the case for the prosecution.

I stole.

I don't like to say it, but I was a thief.

I'm not light-fingered. I didn't want a thing that belonged to anybody else. But there came a time when I felt forced to steal. I had to have some things. My shoes fell apart. I needed some stockings and underclothes. And when I'd ask a son or a daughter or a cousin or a niece for a little money for those necessities they acted as if I was trying to blackmail them. They reminded me that I wasn't qualified as a practical nurse, that I might even get into trouble with the authorities if they found I was palming myself off as a practical nurse—which I wasn't and they knew it. Anyway, they said that their terms were only bed and board.

So I began to take things—small things that had been pushed into the backs of drawers or stored high on shelves in boxes—things that hadn't been used or worn for years and probably would never be used again. I made my biggest haul at Mrs. Bick's, where there was an attic full of trunks stuffed with clothes and doodads from the Twenties all the way back to the Nineties—uniforms, ostrich fans, Spanish shawls, beaded bags. I sneaked out a few of these at a time and every so often sold them to a place called Way Out, Hippie Clothiers.

I tried to work out the exact amount I got for selling something. Not, I know, that you can make up for the theft. But say I got a dollar for a feather boa belonging to Mrs. Bick: well, then I'd come back and work at a job that the cleaning woman kept putting off, like waxing the hall upstairs or polishing the andirons or getting the linen closet in order.

All the same, I *was* stealing—not everywhere I stayed, not even in most places, but when I had to I stole. I admit it.

But I didn't steal that silver box.

I was as innocent as a baby where that box was concerned. So when that policeman came toward me grabbing at the box I stepped aside, and maybe I even gave him the push that sent him to his death. He had no business acting like that when that box was mine, whatever Mrs. Crowe's niece argued.

Fifty thousand nieces couldn't have made it not mine.

Anyway, the policeman was dead and though I hadn't wanted him dead I certainly hadn't wished him well. And then I got to thinking: well, I didn't steal Mrs. Crowe's box but I had stolen other things and it was the mills of God grinding exceeding fine, as I once heard a preacher say, and I was being made to pay for the transgressions that had caught up with me.

Surely I can make a little more sense out of what happened than that, though I never was exactly clear in my own mind about everything that happened.

Mrs. Crowe was the most appreciative person I ever worked for. She was bedridden and could barely move. I don't think the registered nurse on daytime duty considered it part of her job to massage Mrs. Crowe. So at night I would massage her, and that pleased and soothed her. She thanked me for every small thing I did—when I fluffed her pillow, when I'd put a few drops of perfume on her earlobes, when I'd straighten the wrinkled bedcovers.

I had a little joke. I'd pretend I could tell fortunes and I'd take Mrs. Crowe's hand and tell her she was going to have a wonderful day but she must beware of a handsome blond stranger—or some such foolishness that would make her laugh. She didn't sleep well and it seemed to give her pleasure to talk to me most of the night about her childhood or her dead husband.

She kept getting weaker and weaker and two nights before she died she said she wished she could do something for me but that when she became an invalid she had signed over everything to her niece. Anyway, Mrs. Crowe hoped I'd take her silver box. I thanked her. It pleased me that she liked me well enough to give me the box. I didn't have any real use for it. It would have made a nice trinket box, but I didn't have any trinkets. The box seemed to be Mrs. Crowe's fondest possession. She kept it on the table beside her and her eyes lighted up every time she looked at it. She might have been a little girl first seeing a brand-new baby doll early on a Christmas morning.

So when Mrs. Crowe died and the niece on whom I set eyes for the first time dismissed me, I gathered up what little I had and took the box and left. I didn't go to Mrs. Crowe's funeral. The paper said it was private and I wasn't invited. Anyway, I wouldn't have had anything suitable to wear.

I still had a few dollars left over from those things I'd sold to the hippie place called Way Out, so I paid a week's rent for a room that was the worst I'd ever stayed in.

It was freezing cold and no heat came up to the third floor where I was. In that room with falling plaster and buckling floorboards and darting roaches, I sat wearing every stitch I owned, with a sleazy blanket and a faded quilt draped around me waiting for the heat to rise, when in swept Mrs. Crowe's niece in a fur coat and a fur hat and shiny leather boots up to her knees. Her face was beet-red from anger when she started telling me that she had traced me through a private detective and I was to give her back the heirloom I had stolen.

Her statement made me forget the precious little bit I knew of the English language. I couldn't say a word, and she kept on screaming that if I returned the box immediately no criminal charge would be made against me. Then I got back my voice and I said that box was mine and that Mrs. Crowe had wanted me to have it, and she asked if I had any proof or if there were any witnesses to the gift, and I told her that when I was given a present I said thank you, that I didn't ask for proof and witnesses, and that nothing could make me part with Mrs. Crowe's box.

The niece stood there breathing hard, in and out, almost counting her breaths like somebody doing an exercise to get control of herself.

"You'll see," she yelled, and then she left.

The room was colder than ever and my teeth chattered.

Not long afterward I heard heavy steps clumping up the stairway. I realized that the niece had carried out her threat and that the police were after me.

I was panic-stricken. I chased around the room like a rat with a cat after it. Then I thought that if the police searched my room and couldn't find the box it might give me time to decide what to do. I grabbed the box out of the top dresser drawer and scurried down the back hall. I snatched the back door open. I think what I intended to do was run down the back steps and hide the box somewhere, underneath a bush or maybe in a garbage can.

Those back steps were steep and rose almost straight up for three stories and they were flimsy and covered with ice.

I started down. My right foot slipped. The handrail saved me. I clung to it with one hand and to the silver box with the other hand and picked and chose my way across the patches of ice.

When I was midway I heard my name shrieked. I looked around to see a big man leaping down the steps after me. I never saw such anger on a person's face. Then he was directly behind me and reached out to snatch the box.

I swerved to escape his grasp and he cursed me. Maybe I pushed him. I'm not sure—not really.

Anyway, he slipped and fell down and down and down, and then after all that falling he was absolutely still. The bottom step was beneath his head like a pillow and the rest of his body was spread-eagled on the brick walk.

Then almost like a pet that wants to follow its master, the silver box jumped from my hand and bounced down the steps to land beside the man's left ear.

My brain was numb. I felt paralyzed. Then I screamed.

Tenants from that house and the houses next door and across the alley pushed windows open and flung doors open to see what the commotion was about, and then some of them began to run toward the back yard. The policeman who was the dead man's partner—I guess you'd call him that—ordered them to keep away.

After a while more police came and they took the dead man's body and drove me to the station where I was locked up.

From the very beginning, I didn't take to that young lawyer they assigned to me. There wasn't anything exactly that I could put my finger on. I just felt uneasy with him. His last name was Stanton. He had a first name, of course, but he didn't tell me what it was; he said he wanted me to call him Bat like all his friends did.

He was always smiling and reassuring me when there wasn't anything to smile or be reassured about, and he ought to have known it all along instead of filling me with false hope.

All I could think was that I was thankful Mama and Papa and Mr. Williams were dead and that my shame wouldn't bring shame on them.

"It's going to be all right," the lawyer kept saying right up to the end, and then he claimed to be indignant when I was found guilty of resisting arrest and of manslaughter and theft or robbery—there was the biggest hullabaloo as to whether I was guilty of theft or robbery. Not that I was guilty of either, at least in this particular instance, but no one would believe me.

You would have thought it was the lawyer being sentenced instead of me, the way he carried on. He called it a terrible miscarriage of justice and said we might as well be back in the Eighteenth Century when they hanged children.

Well, that was an exaggeration, if ever there was one; nobody was being hung and nobody was a child. That policeman had died and I had had a part in it. Maybe I had pushed him. I couldn't be sure. In my heart I really hadn't meant him any harm. I was just scared. But he was dead all the same. And as far as stealing went, I hadn't stolen the box but I had stolen other things more than once.

And then it happened. It was a miracle. All my life I'd dreamed of a nice room of my own, a comfortable place to stay. And that's exactly what I got.

The room was on the small side, but it had everything I needed in it, even a wash basin with hot and cold running water, and the walls were freshly painted, and they let me choose whether I wanted a wing chair with a chintz slipcover or a modern Danish armchair. I even got to decide what color bedspread I preferred. The window looked out on a beautiful lawn edged with shrubbery, and the matron said I'd be allowed to go to the greenhouse and select some pot plants to keep in my room. The next day I picked out a white gloxinia and some russet chrysanthemums.

I didn't mind the bars at the windows at all. Why, this day and age some of the finest mansions have barred windows to keep burglars out.

The meals—I simply couldn't believe there was such delicious food in the world. The woman who supervised their preparation had embezzled the funds of one of the largest catering companies in the state after working herself up from assistant cook to treasurer.

The other inmates were very friendly and most of them had led the most interesting lives. Some of the ladies occasionally used words that you usually see written only on fences or printed on sidewalks before the cement dries, but when they were scolded they apologized. Every now and then somebody would get angry with someone and there would be a little scratching or hair pulling, but it never got too bad. There was a choir—I can't sing but I love music—and they gave a concert every Tuesday morning at chapel, and Thursday night was movie night. There wasn't any admission charge. All you did was go in and sit down anywhere you pleased.

We all had a special job and I was assigned to the infirmary. The doctor and nurse both complimented me. The doctor said that I should have gone into professional nursing, that I gave confidence to the patients and helped them get well. I don't know about that but I've had years of practice with sick people and I like to help anybody who feels bad.

I was so happy that sometimes I couldn't sleep at night. I'd get up and click on the light and look at the furniture and the walls. It was hard to believe I had such a pleasant place to stay. I'd remember supper that night, how I'd gone back to the steam table for a second helping of asparagus with lemon and herb sauce, and I compared my plenty with those terrible times when I had slunk into supermarkets and nibbled overripe fruit and raw vegetables to ease my hunger.

Then one day here came that lawyer, not even at regular visiting hours, bouncing around congratulating me that my appeal had been upheld, or whatever the term was, and that I was as free as a bird to leave that minute.

He told the matron she could send my belongings later and he dragged me out front where TV cameras and newspaper reporters were waiting.

As soon as the cameras began whirring and the photographers began to aim, the lawyer kissed me on the cheek and pinned a flower on me. He made a speech saying that a terrible miscarriage of justice had been rectified. He had located people who testified that Mrs. Crowe had given me the box—she had told the gardener and the cleaning woman. They hadn't wanted to testify because they didn't want to get mixed up with the police, but the lawyer had persuaded them in the cause of justice and humanity to come forward and make statements.

The lawyer had also looked into the personnel record of the dead policeman and had learned that he had been judged emotionally unfit for his job, and the psychiatrist had warned the Chief of Police that something awful might happen either to the man himself or to a suspect unless he was relieved of his duties.

All the time the lawyer was talking into the microphones he had latched onto me like I was a three-year-old that might run away, and I just stood and stared. Then when he had finished his speech about me the reporters told him that like his grandfather and his uncle he was sure to end up as governor but at a much earlier age.

At that the lawyer gave a big grin in front of the camera and waved goodbye and pushed me into his car.

I was terrified. The nice place I'd found to stay in wasn't mine any longer. My old nightmare was back—wondering how I could manage to eat and how much stealing I'd have to do to live from one day to the next.

The cameras and reporters had followed us.

A photographer asked me to turn down the car window beside me, and I overheard two men way in the back of the crowd talking. My ears are sharp. Papa always said I could hear thunder three states away. Above the congratulations and bubbly talk around me I heard one of those men in back say, "This is a bit too much, don't you think? Our Bat is showing himself the champion of the senior citizen now. He's already copped the teenyboppers and the under thirties using methods that ought to have disbarred him. He should have made the gardener and cleaning woman testify at the beginning, and from the first he should have checked into the policeman's history. There ought never to have been a case at all, much less a conviction. But Bat wouldn't have got any publicity that way. He had to do it in his own devious, spectacular fashion." The other man just kept nodding and saying after every sentence, "You're damned right."

Then we drove off and I didn't dare look behind me because I was so heartbroken over what I was leaving.

The lawyer took me to his office. He said he hoped I wouldn't mind a little excitement for the next few days. He had mapped out some public appearances for me. The next morning I was to be on an early television show. There was nothing to be worried about. He would be right beside me to help me just as he had helped me throughout my trouble. All that I had to say on the TV program was that I owed my freedom to him.

I guess I looked startled or bewildered because he hurried on to say that I hadn't been able to pay him a fee but that now I was able to pay him back—not in money but in letting the public know about how he was the champion of the underdog.

I said I had been told that the court furnished lawyers free of charge to people who couldn't pay, and he said that was right, but his point was that I could repay him now by telling people all that he had done for me. Then he said the main thing was to talk over our next appearance on TV. He wanted to coach me in what I was going to say, but first he would go into his partner's office and tell him to take all the incoming calls and handle the rest of his appointments.

When the door closed after him I thought that he was right. I did owe my freedom to him. He was to blame for it. The smart-alec. The upstart. Who asked him to butt in and snatch me out of my pretty room and the work I loved and all that delicious food?

It was the first time in my life I knew what it meant to despise someone.

I hated him.

Before, when I was convicted of manslaughter, there was a lot of talk about malice aforethought and premeditated crime.

There wouldn't be any argument this time.

I hadn't wanted any harm to come to that policeman. But I did mean harm to come to this lawyer.

I grabbed up a letter opener from his desk and ran my finger along the blade and felt how sharp it was. I waited behind the door and when he walked through I gathered all my strength and stabbed him. Again and again and again.

Now I'm back where I want to be—in a nice place to stay.

*The historical mystery novel is very much in vogue at the pres-
ent time, and the form owes a debt to* LILLIAN DE LA TORRE
*(1902–), whose stories about Dr. Sam: Johnson as told by his
biographer, James Boswell, set the tone for what she aptly
dubbed the work of the "histo-detector." Her three novels,* Elizabeth Is Missing *(1945),* The Heir of Douglas *(1952), and*
The Truth About Belle Gunness *(1955), also involve real historical figures. Ms. de la Torre was an active playwright, and
some of her produced work is based on actual crimes, most
notably* The Coffee Cup *(1955). The adventures of Dr. Sam:
Johnson can be found in four collections, most recently in* The
Exploits of Dr. Sam: Johnson *(1985).*

*Here the good doctor encounters a fascinating but scandal-
ous lady, a character based on the real life Elizabeth
Chudleigh, who* may *have been the Duchess of Kingston or
perhaps the Countess of Bristol.*

Milady Bigamy

(as told by James Boswell, Spring, 1778)

BY LILLIAN DE LA TORRE

"I have often thought," remarked Dr Sam: Johnson, one Spring
morning in the year 1778, "that if I kept a seraglio—"

He had often thought!—Dr. Sam: Johnson, moral philosopher, de-
fender of right and justice, *detector* of crime and chicane, had often
thought of keeping a seraglio! I looked at his square bulk, clad in his
old-fashioned full-skirted coat of plain mulberry broadcloth, his strong
rugged countenance with his little brown scratch-wig clapped on
askew above it, and suppressed a smile.

"I say, sir, if I kept a seraglio, the houris should be clad in cotton
and linen, and not at all in wool and silk, for the animal fibres are
nasty, but the vegetable fibres are cleanly."

"Why sir," I replied seriously, "I too have long meditated on keeping a seraglio, and wondered whether it may not be lawful to a man to
have plurality of wives, say one for comfort and another for shew."

"What, sir, you talk like a heathen Turk!" growled the great Cham,
rounding on me. "If this cozy arrangement be permitted a man, what
is to hinder the ladies from a like indulgence?—one husband, say, for
support, and 'tother for sport? 'Twill be a wise father then that knows

his own heir. You are a lawyer, sir, you know the problems of filiation. Would you multiply them? No, sir: bigamy is a crime, and there's an end on't!"

At this I hastily turned the topick, and of bigamy we spoke no more. Little did we then guess that a question of bigamy was soon to engage my friend's attention, in the affair of the Duchess of Kingsford—if Duchess in truth she was.

I had first beheld this lady some seven years before, when she was Miss Bellona Chamleigh, the notorious Maid of Honour. At Mrs. Cornelys's Venetian ridotto she flashed upon my sight, and took my breath away.

Rumour had not exaggerated her flawless beauty. She had a complection like strawberries and cream, a swelling rosy lip, a nose and firmset chin sculptured in marble. Even the small-pox had spared her, for the one mark it had left her touched the edge of her pouting mouth like a tiny dimple. In stature she was low, a pocket Venus, with a bosom of snow tipped with fire. A single beauty-spot shaped like a new moon adorned her perfect navel—

I go too far. Suffice it to say that for costume she wore a girdle of silken fig-leaves, and personated Eve—Eve after the fall, from the glances she was giving her gallants. One at either rosy elbow, they pressed her close, and she smiled upon them impartially. I recognised them both.

The tall, thin, swarthy, cadaverous apparition in a dark domino was Philip Piercy, Duke of Kingsford, once the handsomest Peer in the Kingdom, but now honed to an edge by a long life of dissipation. If he was no longer the handsomest, he was still the richest. Rumour had it that he was quite far gone in infatuation, and would lay those riches, with his hand and heart, at Miss Bellona's feet.

Would she accept of them? Only one obstacle intervened. That obstacle stood at her other elbow: Captain Aurelius Hart, of H.M.S. *Dangerous,* a third-rate of fifty guns, which now lay fitting at Portsmouth, leaving the gallant Captain free to press his suit.

In person, the Captain was the lady's match, not tall, but broad of shoulder, and justly proportioned in every limb. He had farseeing light blue eyes in a sun-burned face, and his expression was cool, with a look of incipient mirth. The patches of Harlequin set off his muscular masculinity.

With his name too Dame Rumour had been busy. He had won the

lady's heart, it was averred; but he was not likely to win her hand, being an impecunious younger son, tho' of an Earl.

So she passed on in her nakedness, giving no sign of which lover—if either—should possess her.

A black-avised young fellow garbed like the Devil watched them go. He scowled upon them with a look so lowering I looked again, and recognised him for Mr. Eadwin Maynton, Kingsford's nephew, heir-presumptive to his pelf (tho' not his Dukedom), being the son of the Duke's sister. If Bellona married his Uncle, it would cost Mr. Eadwin dear.

The audacity of the Maid of Honour at the masquerade had been too blatant. She was forthwith banished from the Court. Unrepentant, she had rusticated herself. Accompanied only by her confidential woman, one Ann Crannock, she slipped off to her Aunt Hammer's country house at Linton, near Portsmouth.

Near Portsmouth! Where lay the Captain's ship! No more was needed to inflate the tale.

"The Captain calls daily to press his suit."

"The Captain has taken her into keeping."

"There you are out, the Captain has wedded her secretly."

"You are all misled. The *Dangerous* has gone to sea—the Captain has deserted her."

"And serve her right, the hussy!"

The hussy Maid of Honour was not one to be rusticated for long. Soon she was under their noses again, on the arm of the still infatuated Duke of Kingsford. Mr. Eadwin Maynton moved Heaven and earth to forestall a marriage, but only succeeded in mortally offending his wealthy Uncle. Within a year of that scandalous masquerade, Miss Bellona Chamleigh was Duchess of Kingsford.

Appearing at Court on the occasion, she flaunted herself in white sattin encrusted with Brussels point and embroidered with a Duke's ransom in pearls. She would give the world something to talk about!

They talked with a will. They talked of Captain Hart, jilted on the Jamaica station. They talked of Mr. Eadwin Maynton, sulking at home. They were still talking several years later when the old Duke suddenly died—of his Duchess's obstreperous behaviour, said some with a frown, of her amorous charms, said others with a snigger.

It was at this juncture that one morning in the year '78 a crested coach drew rein in Bolt Court and a lady descended. From an upper window I looked down on her modish tall powdered head and her furbelowed polonaise of royal purple brocade.

I turned from the window with a smile. "What, sir, you have an assignation with a fine lady? Am I *de trop?*"

"You are never *de trop,* Bozzy. Pray remain, and let us see what this visitation portends."

The Duchess of Kingsford swept in without ceremony.

"Pray forgive me, Dr. Johnson, my errand is to Mr. Boswell. I was directed hither to find him—I *must* have Mr. Boswell!"

"And you *shall* have Mr. Boswell," I cried warmly, "tho' it were for wager of battle!"

"You have hit it, sir! For my honour, perhaps my life, is at stake! You shall defend me, sir, in my need—and Dr. Johnson," she added with a sudden flashing smile, "shall be our counsellor."

"If I am to counsel you, Madam, you must tell me clearly what is the matter."

"Know then, gentlemen, that in the winter last past, my dear husband the Duke of Kingsford died, and left me inconsolable—inconsolable, yet not bare, for in token of our undying devotion, he left me all that was his. In so doing, he cut off his nephew Eadwin with a few guineas, and therein lies the difficulty. For Mr. Eadwin is no friend to me. He has never spared to vilify me for a scheaming adventuress. And now he has hit upon a plan—he thinks—in one motion to disgrace me and deprive me of my inheritance. He goes about to nullify my marriage to the Duke."

"How can this be done, your Grace?"

"He has resurrected the old gossip about Captain Hart, that we were secretly married at Linton long ago. The whole town buzzes with the tale, and the comedians lampoon me on the stage as Milady Bigamy."

"What the comedians play," observed Dr. Johnson drily, "is not evidence. Gossip cannot harm you, your Grace—unless it is true."

"It is false. There was no such marriage. There might have been, it is true (looking pensive) had he not abandoned me, as Aeneas abandoned Dido, and put to sea in the *Dangerous*—leaving me," she added frankly, "to make a better match."

"Then where is the difficulty?"

"False testimony is the difficulty. Aunt Hammer is dead, and the clergyman is dead. But his widow is alive, and Eadwin has bought her. Worst of all, he has suborned Ann Crannock, my confidential woman that was, and she will swear to the wedding."

"Are there marriage lines?"

"Of course not. No marriage, no marriage lines."

"And the Captain? Where is he?"

"At sea. He now commands a first-rate, the *Challenger,* and wins great fame, and much prize money, against the French. I am well assured I am safe in that quarter."

"Then," said I, "this accusation of bigamy is soon answered. But I am not accustomed to appear at the Old Bailey."

"The Old Bailey!" cried she with scorn. "Who speaks of the Old Bailey? Shall a Duchess be tried like a greasy bawd at the Old Bailey? I am the Duchess of Kingsford! I shall be tried by my Peers!"

"If you are Mrs. Aurelius Hart?"

"I am not Mrs. Aurelius Hart! But if I were—Aurelius's brothers are dead in the American war, his father the Earl is no more, and Aurelius is Earl of Westerfell. As Duchess or as Countess, I shall be tried by my Peers!"

Flushed and with flashing eyes, the ci-devant Maid of Honour looked every inch a Peeress as she uttered these words.

" 'Tis for this I must have Mr. Boswell. From the gallery in the House of Lords I recently heard him plead the cause of the heir of Douglas: in such terms of melting eloquence did he defend the good name of Lady Jane Douglas, I will have no other to defend mine!"

My new role as the Duchess's champion entailed many duties that I had hardly expected. There were of course long consults with herself and her solicitor, a dry, prosy old solicitor named Pettigree. But I had not counted on attending her strolls in the park, or carrying her band-boxes from the milliner's.

"And to-morrow, Mr. Boswell, you shall squire me to the ridotto."

"The masquerade! Your Grace jests!"

"Far from it, sir. Edwin Maynton seeks to drive me under ground, but he shall not succeed. No, sir; my heart is set on it, and to the ridotto I will go!"

To the ridotto we went. The Duchess was regal in a domino of Roman purple over a gown of lavender lutestring, and wore a half-mask with a valance of provocative black lace to the chin. I personated a wizard, with my black gown strewn with cabbalistick symbols, and a conical hat to make me tall.

It was a ridotto *al fresco,* in the groves of Vauxhall. In the soft May evening, we listened to the band of musick in the pavilion; we took a syllabub; we walked in the allées to hear the nightingale sing. It was pleasant strolling beneath the young green of the trees by the light of a thousand lamps, watching the masquers pass: a Boadicea in armour, a Hamlet all in black, an Indian Sultana, a muscular Harlequin with a long-nosed Venetian mask, a cowled monk—

"So, Milady Bigamy!" The voice was loud and harsh. "You hide your face, as is fit; but we know you for what you are!"

Passing masquers paused to listen. Pulling the mask from her face, the Duchess whirled on the speaker. A thin swarthy countenance glowered at her under the monk's cowl.

"Eadwin Maynton!" she said quietly. "Why do you pursue me? How have I harmed you? 'Twas your own folly that alienated your kind Uncle."

" 'Twas your machinations!" He was perhaps inebriated, and intent on making a scene. More listeners arrived to enjoy it.

"I have irrefutable evidences of your double dealing," he bawled, "and when it comes to the proof, I'll unduchess you, Milady Bigamy!"

"This fellow is drunk. Come, Mr. Boswell."

The Duchess turned away contemptuously. Mr. Eadwin seized her arm and swung her back. The next minute he was flat on the ground, and a menacing figure in Harlequin's patches stood over him.

"What is your pleasure, Madam?" asked the Harlequin calmly. "Shall he beg pardon?"

"Let him lie," said the Duchess. "He's a liar, let him lie."

"Then be off!"

Maynton made off, muttering.

"And you, ladies and gentlemen, the comedy is over."

Behind the beak-nosed mask, light eyes of ice-blue raked the gapers, and they began to melt away.

"I thank you, my friend. And now, as you say, the comedy is over," smiled the Duchess.

"There is yet a farce to play," said the Harlequin. *The Fatal Marriage.* He lifted his mask by its snout, and smiled at her. "Who, unless a husband, shall protect his lady wife?"

The Duchess's face stiffened.

"I do not know you."

"What, forgot so soon?" His glance laughed at her. "Such is the fate of the sailor!"

"Do not mock me, Aurelius. You know we are nothing to one another."

"Speak for yourself, Bellona."

"I will speak one word, then: Good-bye."

She reached me her hand, and I led her away. Captain Hart watched us go, his light eyes intent, and a small half-smile upon his lips.

That was the end of Milady Duchess's ridotto. What would come of it?

Nothing good, I feared. My fears were soon doubled. Returning from the river one day in the Duchess's carriage, we found ourselves passing by Mr. Eadwin Maynton's lodging. As we approached, a man issued from the door, an erect figure in nautical blue, whose ruddy countenance wore a satisfied smile. He turned away without a glance in our direction.

"Aurelius calling upon Eadwin!" cried the Duchess, staring after him. "What are they plotting against me?"

To this I had no answer.

Time was running out. The trial was looming close. In Westminster Hall, carpenters were knocking together scaffolding to prepare for the shew. At Kingsford House, Dr. Johnson was quoting Livy, I was polishing my oration, and old Pettigree was digging up learned instances.

"Keep up your heart, your Grace," said the solicitor earnestly in his rusty voice, "for should the worst befall, I have instances to shew that the penalty is no longer death at the stake—"

"At the stake!" gasped the Duchess.

"No, your Grace, certainly not, not death by burning. I shall prove it, but meerly branding on the hand—"

"Branding!" shrieked the Duchess. Her white fingers clutched mine.

"No *alibi,*" fretted old Pettigree, "no testimony from Linton on your behalf, Captain Hart in the adverse camp—no, no, your Grace must put your hope in me!"

At such Job's comfort Dr. Johnson could scarce repress a smile.

"Hope rather," he suggested, "in Mr. Boswell, for if these women lie, it must be made manifest in cross-examination. I shall be on hand to note what they say, as I once noted the Parliamentary debates from the gallery; and it will go hard but we shall catch them out in their lies."

Bellona Chamleigh lifted her head in a characteristick wilful gesture.

"I trust in Mr. Boswell, and I am not afraid."

Rising early on the morning of the fateful day, I donned my voluminous black advocate's gown, and a lawyer's powdered wig that I had rented from Tibbs the perruquier for a guinea. I thought that the latter well set off my dark countenance, with its long nose and attentive look. Thus attired, I posted myself betimes outside Westminster Hall to see the procession pass.

At ten o'clock it began. First came the factotums and the functionaries, the yeoman-usher robed, heralds in tabards, serjeants-at-arms with maces in their hands. Then the Peers paced into view, walking two and two, splendid in their crimson velvet mantles and snowy capes of ermine powdered with black tail-tips. Last came the Lord High Steward, his long crimson train borne up behind him, and so they passed into Westminster Hall.

When I entered at last, in my turn as a lowly lawyer, the sight struck me with something like awe. The noble hall, with its soaring roof, was packed to the vault with persons of quality seated upon tier after tier of scaffolding. Silks rustled, laces fluttered, brocades glowed, high powdered foretops rose over all. Around three sides of the level floor gathered the Peers in their splendid robes.

All stood uncovered as the King's Commission was read aloud and the white staff of office was ceremoniously handed up to the Lord High Steward where he sat under a crimson canopy. With a sibilant rustle, the packed hall sat, and the trial began.

"Oyez, oyez, oyez! Bellona, duchess-dowager of Kingsford, come into court!"

She came in a little procession of her own, her ladies of honour, her chaplain, her physician and her apothecary attending; but every staring eye saw her only. Old Pettigree had argued in vain that deep mourning was the only wear; she would have none of it. She walked in proudly in white sattin embroidered with pearls, that very court-dress she had flaunted as old Kingsford's bride: "In token of my innocence," she told old Pettigree.

With a deep triple reverence she took her place on the elevated platform that served for a dock, and stood with lifted head to listen to the indictment.

"Bellona, duchess-dowager of Kingsford, you stand indicted by the name of Bellona, wife of Aurelius Hart, now Earl of Westerfell, for that you, in the eleventh year of our sovereign lord King George the Third, being then married and the wife of the said Aurelius Hart, did marry and take to husband Philip Piercy, Duke of Kingsford, feloniously and with force and arms—"

Though it was the usual legal verbiage to recite that every felony was committed "with force and arms," the picture conjured up of little Bellona, like a highwayman, clapping a pistol to the old Duke's head and marching him to the altar, was too much for the Lords. Laughter swept the benches, and the lady at the bar frankly joined in.

"How say you? Are you guilty of the felony whereof you stand indicted, or not guilty?"

Silence fell. Bellona sobered, lifted her head, and pronounced in her rich voice: "Not guilty!"

"Culprit, how will you be tried?"

"By God and my Peers."

"Oyez, oyez, oyez! All manner of persons that will give evidence on behalf of our sovereign lord the King, against Bellona, duchess-dowager of Kingsford, let them come forth, and they shall be heard, for now she stands at the bar upon her deliverance."

Thereupon Edward Thurlow, Attorney General, came forth, formidable with his bristling hairy eyebrows and his growling voice like distant thunder.

He began with an eloquent denunciation of the crime of bigamy, its malignant complection, its pernitious example, *et caetera, et caetera.* That duty performed, he drily recited the story of the alleged marriage at Linton as, he said, his witnesses would prove it.

"And now, my Lords, we will proceed to call our witnesses. Call Margery Amys."

Mrs. Amys, the clergyman's widow, was a tall stick of a woman well on in years, wearing rusty bombazine and an old-fashioned lawn cap tied under her nutcracker chin. She put a gnarled hand on the Bible the clerk held out to her.

"Hearken to your oath. The evidence you shall give on behalf of our sovereign lord the King's majesty, against Bellona duchess-dowager of Kingsford, shall be the truth, the whole truth, and nothing but the truth, so help you God."

The old dame mumbled something, and kissed the book. But when the questions began, she spoke up in a rusty screech, and graphically portrayed a clandestine marriage at Linton church in the year '71.

"They came by night, nigh upon midnight, to the church at Linton, and desired of the late Mr. Amys that he should join them two in matrimony."

Q. Which two?

A. Them two, Captain Hart and Miss Bellona Chamleigh.

Q. And did he so unite them?

A. He did so, and I stood by and saw it done.

Q. Who was the bride?

A. Miss Bellona Chamleigh.

Q. Say if you see her now present?

A. (pointing) That's her, her in white.

The Duchess stared her down contemptuously.

As I rose to cross-examine, I sent a glance to the upper tier, where sat Dr. Johnson. He was writing, and frowning as he wrote; but no guidance came my way. Making up with a portentous scowl for what I lacked in matter, I began:

Q. It was dark at midnight?

A. Yes, sir, mirk dark.

Q. Then, Mrs. Amys, how did you see the bride to know her again?

A. Captain Hart lighted a wax taper, and put it in his hat, and by that light they were married, and so I know her again.

Q. (probing) You know a great deal, Madam. What has Mr. Eadwin Maynton given you to appear on his behalf?

A. Nothing, sir.

Q. What has he promised you?

A. Nothing neither.

Q. Then why are you here?

A. (piously) I come for the sake of truth and justice, sir.

And on that sanctimonious note, I had to let her go.

"Call Ann Crannock!"

Ann Crannock approached in a flurry of curtseys, scattering smiles like sweetmeats. The erstwhile confidential woman was a plump, round, rosy little thing, of a certain age, but still pleasing, carefully got up like a stage milkmaid in snowy kerchief and pinner. She mounted the platform with a bounce, and favoured the Attorney General with a beaming smile.

The Duchess hissed something between her teeth. It sounded like "Judas!"

The clerk with his Bible hastily stepped between. Ann Crannock took the oath, smiling broadly, and Thurlow commenced his interrogation:

Q. You were the prisoner's woman?

A. Yes, sir, and I loved her like my own child.

Q. You saw her married to Captain Hart?

A. Yes, sir, the pretty dears, they could not wait for very lovesickness.

Q. That was at Linton in July of the year 1771?

A. Yes, sir, the third of July, for the Captain sailed with the Jamaica squadron on the fourth. Ah, the sweet poppets, they were loath to part!

Q. Who married them?

A. Mr. Amys, sir, the vicar of Linton. We walked to the church together, the lady's Aunt Mrs. Hammer, and I myself, and the sweet lovebirds. The clock was going towards midnight, that the servants might not know.

Q. Why must not the servants know?

A. Sir, nobody was to know, lest the Captain's father the Earl cut him off for marrying a lady without any fortune.

Q. Well, and they were married by Mr. Amys. Did he give a certificate of the marriage?

A. Yes, sir, he did, he wrote it out with his own hand and I signed for a witness. I was happy for my lady from my heart.

Q. You say the vicar gave a certificate. (Thurlow sharply raised his voice as he whipped out a paper.) Is this it?

A. (clasping her hands and beaming with pleasure) O sir, that is it. See, there is my handwriting. Well I mind how the Captain kissed it and put it in his bosom to keep.

"Tis false!"

The Duchess was on her feet in a rage. For a breath she stood so in her white sattin and pearls; then she sank down in a swoon. Her attendants instantly raised her and bore her out among them. I saw the little apothecary hopping like a grasshopper on the fringes, flourishing his hartshorn bottle.

The Peers were glad enough of an excuse for a recess, and so was I. I pushed my way to the lobby in search of Dr. Johnson. I was furious. "The jade has lied to us!" I cried as I beheld him. "I'll throw up my brief!"

"You will do well to do so," murmured the Attorney General at my elbow. He still held the fatal marriage lines.

"Pray, Mr. Thurlow, give me a sight of that paper," requested Dr. Johnson.

"Dr. Johnson's wish is my command," said Thurlow with a bow: he had a particular regard for the burly philosopher.

Dr. Johnson held the paper to the light, peering so close with his near-sighted eyes that his lashes almost brushed the surface.

"Aye, sir, look close," smiled Thurlow. " 'Tis authentick, I assure you. I have particular reason to know."

"Then there's no more to be said."

Thurlow took the paper, bowed, and withdrew.

All along I had been conscious of another legal figure hovering near. Now I looked at him directly. He was hunched into a voluminous advocate's gown, and topped by one of Mr. Tibbs's largest wigs; but there was no missing those ice-blue eyes.

"Captain Hart! You here?"

"I had a mind to see the last of my widow," he said sardonically. "I see she is in good hands."

"But to come here! Will you not be recognised, and detained, and put on the stand?"

"What, Peers detain a Peer? No, sir. While the House sits, I cannot be summoned: and when it rises, all is over. Bellona may be easy; I shan't peach. Adieu."

"Stay, sir—" But he was gone.

After an hour, the Duchess of Kingsford returned to the hall with her head held high, and inquiry resumed. There was not much more harm Mistress Crannock could do. She was led once more to repeat: she saw them wedded, the sweet dears, and she signed the marriage lines, and that was the very paper now in Mr. Thurlow's hand.

"You say this is the paper? That is conclusive, I think. (smiling) You may cross-examine, Mr. Boswell."

Ann Crannock smiled at me, and I smiled back, as I began:

Q. You say, Mistress Crannock, that you witnessed this marriage?

A. Yes, sir.

Q. And then and there you signed the marriage lines?

A. Yes, sir.

Q. On July 3, 1771?

A. Yes, sir.

Q. Think well, did you not set your hand to it at some subsequent date?

A. No, sir.

Q. Perhaps to oblige Mr. Eadwin Maynton?

A. No, sir, certainly not. I saw them wedded, and signed forthwith.

Q. Then I put it to you: *How did you on July 3, 1771, set your hand to a piece of paper that was not made at the manufactory until the year 1774?*

Ann Crannock turned red, then pale, opened her mouth, but no

sound came. "Can you make that good, Mr. Boswell?" demanded
Thurlow.

"Yes, sir if I may call a witness, tho' out of order."

"Aye, call him—let's hear him—" the answer swept the Peers'
benches. Their Lordships cared nothing for order.

"I call Dr. Samuel Johnson."

Dr. Johnson advanced and executed one of his stately obeisances.

"You must know, my Lords and gentlemen," he began, "that I have
dealt with paper for half a century, and I have friends among the
paper-makers. Paper, my Lords, is made by grinding up rag, and wetting it, and laying it to dry upon a grid of wires. Now he who has a
mind to sign his work, twists his mark in wire and lays it in, for every
wire leaves its impression, which is called a watermark. With such a
mark, in the shape of an S, did my friend Sully the paper-maker sign
the papers he made before the year '74.

"But in that year, my Lords, he took his son into partnership, and
from thenceforth marked his paper with a double S. I took occasion
this afternoon to confirm the date, 1774, from his own mouth. Now,
my Lords, if you take this supposed document of 1771 (taking it in
hand) and hold it thus to the light, you may see in it the double S
watermark: which, my Lords, proves this so-called conclusive evidence
to be a forgery, and Ann Crannock a liar!"

The paper passed from hand to hand, and the Lords began to seethe.

"The Question! The Question!" was the cry. The clamour persisted,
and did not cease until perforce the Lord High Steward arose, bared
his head, and put the question:

"Is the prisoner guilty of the felony whereof she stands indicted, or
not guilty?"

In a breathless hush, the first of the barons rose in his ermine. Bellona lifted her chin. The young nobleman put his right hand upon his
heart and pronounced clearly:

"Not guilty, upon my honour!"

So said each and every Peer:

"Not guilty, upon my honour!"

My client was acquitted!

At her Grace's desire, I had provided means whereby, at the trial's
end, come good fortune or ill, the Duchess might escape the press of
the populace. A plain coach waited at a postern door, and thither, her

white sattin and pearls muffled in a capuchin, my friend and I hurried her.

Quickly she mounted the step and slipped inside. Suddenly she screamed. Inside the coach a man awaited us. Captain Aurelius Hart in his blue coat lounged there at his ease.

"Nay, sweet wife, my wife no more," he murmured softly, "do not shun me, for now that you are decreed to be another man's widow, I mean to woo you anew. I have prepared a small victory feast at my lodgings, and I hope your friends will do us the honour of partaking of it with us."

"Victory!" breathed Bellona as the coach moved us off. "How could you be so sure of victory?"

"Because," said Dr. Johnson, "he brought it about. Am I not right, sir?"

"Why, sir, as to that—"

"As to that, sir, there is no need to prevaricate. I learned this afternoon from Sully the paper-maker that a seafaring man resembling Captain Hart had been at him last week to learn about papers, and had carried away a sheet of the double S kind. It is clear that it was you, sir, who foisted upon Eadwin Maynton the forgery that, being exposed, defeated him."

All this while the coach was carrying us onward. In the shadowy interior, Captain Hart frankly grinned.

" 'Twas easy, sir. Mr. Eadwin was eager, and quite without scruple, and why should he doubt a paper that came from the hands of the wronged husband? How could he guess that I had carefully contrived it to ruin his cause?"

"It was a bad cause," said Dr. Johnson, "and he is well paid for his lack of scruple."

"But, Captain Hart," I put in, "how could you be sure that we would detect the forgery and proclaim it?"

"To make sure, I muffled up and ventured into the lobby. I was prepared to slip a billet into Mr. Boswell's pocket; but when I saw Dr. Johnson studying the watermark, I knew that I need not interfere further."

We were at the door. Captain Hart lifted down the lady, and with his arm around her guided her up the stair. She yielded mutely, as in a daze.

In the withdrawing room a pleasing cold regale awaited us, but Dr.

Johnson was in no hurry to go to table. There was still something on his mind.

"Then, sir, before we break bread, satisfy me of one more thing. How came Ann Crannock to say the handwriting was hers?"

"Because, sir," said Captain Hart, with a self-satisfied look, "It was so like her own. I find I have a pretty turn for forgery."

"That I can believe, sir. But where did you find an exemplar to fashion your forgery after?"

"Why, sir, I—" The Captain darted a glance from face to face. "You are keen, sir. There could only be one document to forge after—and here it is (producing a folded paper from his pocket). Behold the true charter of my happiness!"

I regarded it thunderstruck. A little faded as to ink, a little frayed at the edges, there lay before us a marriage certificate in due form, between Miss Bellona Chamleigh, spinster, and Captain Aurelius Hart, bachelor, drawn up in the Reverend Mr. Amys's wavering hand, and attested by Sophie Hammer and Ann Crannock, July 3, 1771!

"So, Madam," growled Dr. Johnson, "you were guilty after all!"

"Oh, no, sir! 'Twas no marriage, for the Captain was recalled to his ship, and sailed for the Jamaica station, without—without—"

"Without making you in deed and in truth my own," smiled Captain Hart.

At this specimen of legal reasoning, Dr. Johnson shook his head in bafflement, the bigamous Duchess looked as innocent as possible, and Captain Hart laughed aloud.

" 'Twas an unfortunate omission," he said, "whence flow all our uneasinesses, and I shall rectify it this night, my Countess consenting. What do you say, my dear?"

For the first time the Duchess looked directly at him. In spite of herself she blushed, and the tiny pox mark beside her lip deepened in a smile.

"Why, Aurelius, since you have saved me from branding or worse, what can I say but yes?"

"Then at last," cried the Captain, embracing her, "you shall be well and truly bedded, and so farewell to the Duchess of Kingsford!"

It seemed the moment to withdraw. As we descended we heard them laughing together.

"Never look so put about, Bozzy," murmured Dr. Johnson on the stair. "You have won your case; justice, tho' irregularly, is done; the malignancy of Eadwin Maynton has been defeated; and as to the two above—they deserve each other."

LAWRENCE BLOCK *(1938–) began his writing career with* Death Pulls a Doubled Cross *in 1961 and labored for some fifteen years under his own name and several pseudonyms in the paperback original market writing crime novels. In the mid-1970s he emerged as a major figure in American crime fiction with two excellent but widely different series—novels featuring Matthew Scudder, an ex–New York City police officer whose problems with alcohol are a central feature of these books, and novels starring Bernie Rhodenbarr, a thief who is forced to solve crimes to clear himself, always in a broadly humorous fashion. One of Mr. Block's recent Matthew Scudder novels,* When the Sacred Gin Mill Closes *(1986), is certainly one of the finest works of crime fiction of the last decade.*

Lawrence Block is also a prolific short story writer, and his collection Sometimes They Bite *(1983) contains some of his finest work, including "One Thousand Dollars a Word," a title with which every professional writer can identify.*

One Thousand Dollars a Word

BY LAWRENCE BLOCK

The editor's name was Warren Jukes. He was a lean sharp-featured man with slender long-fingered hands and a narrow line for a mouth. His black hair was going attractively gray on top and at the temples. As usual, he wore a stylish three-piece suit. As usual, Trevathan felt logy and unkempt in comparison, like a bear having trouble shaking off the torpor of hibernation.

"Sit down, Jim," Jukes said. "Always a pleasure. Don't tell me you're bringing in another manuscript already? It never ceases to amaze me the way you keep grinding them out. Where do you get your ideas, anyway? But I guess you're tired of that question after all these years."

He was indeed, and that was not the only thing of which James Trevathan was heartily tired. But all he said was, "No, Warren. I haven't written another story."

"Oh?"

"I wanted to talk with you about the last one."

"But we talked about it yesterday," Jukes said, puzzled. "Over the telephone. I said it was fine and I was happy to have it for the magazine. What's the title, anyway? It was a play on words, but I can't remember it offhand."

" 'A Stitch in Crime,' " Trevathan said.

"Right, that's it. Good title, good story and all of it wrapped up in your solid professional prose. What's the problem?"

"Money," Trevathan said.

"A severe case of the shorts, huh?" The editor smiled. "Well, I'll be putting a voucher through this afternoon. You'll have the check early next week. I'm afraid that's the best I can do, Jimbo. The corporate machinery can only go so fast."

"It's not the time," Trevathan said. "It's the amount. What are you paying for the story, Warren?"

"Why, the usual. How long was it? Three thousand words, wasn't it?"

"Thirty-five hundred."

"So what does that come to? Thirty-five hundred at a nickel a word is what? One seventy-five, right?"

"That's right, yes."

"So you'll have a check in that amount early next week, as soon as possible, and if you want I'll ring you when I have it in hand and you can come over and pick it up. Save waiting a couple of days for the neither-rain-nor-snow people to get it from my desk to yours."

"It's not enough."

"Beg your pardon?"

"The price," Trevathan said. He was having trouble with this conversation. He'd written a script for it in his mind on the way to Jukes's office, and he'd been infinitely more articulate then than now. "I should get more money," he managed. "A nickel a word is . . . Warren, that's no money at all."

"It's what we pay, Jim. It's what we've always paid."

"Exactly."

"So?"

"Do you know how long I've been writing for you people, Warren?"

"Quite a few years."

"Twenty years, Warren."

"Really?"

"I sold a story called 'Hanging by a Thread' to you twenty years ago last month. It ran twenty-two hundred words and you paid me a hundred and ten bucks for it."

"Well, there you go," Jukes said.

"I've been working twenty years, Warren, and I'm getting the same money now that I got then. Everything's gone up except my income. When I wrote my first story for you I could take one of those nickels that a word of mine brought and buy a candy bar with it. Have you bought a candy bar recently, Warren?"

Jukes touched his belt buckle. "If I went and bought candy bars," he said, "my clothes wouldn't fit me."

"Candy bars are forty cents. Some of them cost thirty-five. And I still get a nickel a word. But let's forget candy bars."

"Fine with me, Jim."

"Let's talk about the magazine. When you bought 'Hanging by a Thread,' what did the magazine sell for on the stands?"

"Thirty-five cents, I guess."

"Wrong. Twenty-five. About six months later you went to thirty-five. Then you went to fifty, and after that sixty and then seventy-five. And what does the magazine sell for now?"

"A dollar a copy."

"And you still pay your authors a nickel a word. That's really wealth beyond the dreams of avarice, isn't it, Warren?"

Jukes sighed heavily, propped his elbows on his desk top, tented his fingertips. "Jim," he said, dropping his voice in pitch, "there are things you're forgetting. The magazine's no more profitable than it was twenty years ago. In fact we're working closer now than we did then. Do you know anything about the price of paper? It makes candy look pretty stable by comparison. I could talk for hours on the subject of the price of paper. Not to mention all the other printing costs, and shipping costs and more other costs than I want to mention or you want to hear about. You look at that buck-a-copy price and you think we're flying high, but it's not like that at all. We were doing better way back then. Every single cost of ours has gone through the roof."

"Except the basic one."

"How's that?"

"The price you pay for material. That's what your readers are buying from you, you know. Stories. Plots and characters. Prose and dialogue. Words. And you pay the same for them as you did twenty years ago. It's the only cost that's stayed the same."

Jukes took a pipe apart and began running a pipe cleaner through the stem. Trevathan started talking about his own costs—his rent, the price of food. When he paused for breath Warren Jukes said, "Supply and demand, Jim."

"What's that?"

"Supply and demand. Do you think it's hard for me to fill the magazine at a nickel a word? See that pile of scripts over there? That's what this morning's mail brought. Nine out of ten of those stories are from new writers who'd write for nothing if it got them into print. The other ten percent is from pros who are damned glad when they see that nickel-a-word check instead of getting their stories mailed back to them. You know, I buy just about everything you write for us, Jim. One reason is I like your work, but that's not the only reason. You've been with us for twenty years and we like to do business with our old friends. But you evidently want me to raise your word rate, and we don't pay more than five cents a word to anybody, because in the first place we haven't got any surplus in the budget and in the second place we damn well don't *have* to pay more than that. So before I raise your rate, old friend, I'll give your stories back to you. Because I don't have any choice."

Trevathan sat and digested this for a few moments. He thought of some things to say but left them unsaid. He might have asked Jukes how the editor's own salary had fluctuated over the years, but what was the point of that? He could write for a nickel a word or he could not write for them at all. That was the final word on the subject.

"Jim? Shall I put through a voucher or do you want 'A Stitch in Crime' back?"

"What would I do with it? No, I'll take the nickel a word, Warren."

"If there was a way I could make it more—"

"I understand."

"You guys should have got yourselves a union years ago. Give you a little collective muscle. Or you could try writing something else. We're in a squeeze, you know, and if we were forced to pay more for material we'd probably have to fold the magazine altogether. But there are other fields where the pay is better."

"I've been doing this for twenty years, Warren. It's all I know. My God, I've got a reputation in the field, I've got an established name—"

"Sure. That's why I'm always happy to have you in the magazine. As long as I do the editing, Jimbo, and as long as you grind out the copy, I'll be glad to buy your yarns."

"At a nickel a word."

"Well—"

"Nothing personal, Warren. I'm just a little bitter. That's all."

"Hey, think nothing of it." Jukes got to his feet, came around from behind his desk. "So you got something off your chest, and we cleared the air a little. Now you know where you stand. Now you can go on home and knock off something sensational and get it to me, and if it's up to your usual professional standard you'll have another check coming your way. That's the way to double the old income, you know. Just double the old production."

"Good idea," Trevathan said.

"Of course it is. And maybe you can try something for another market while you're at it. It's not too late to branch out, Jim. God knows I don't want to lose you, but if you're having trouble getting by on what we can pay you, well—"

"It's a thought," Trevathan said.

Five cents a word.

Trevathan sat at his battered Underwood and stared at a blank sheet of paper. The paper had gone up a dollar a ream in the past year, and he could swear they'd cheapened the quality in the process. Everything cost more, he thought, except his own well-chosen words. They were still trading steadily at a nickel apiece.

Not too late to branch out, Jukes had told him. But that was a sight easier to say than to do. He'd tried writing for other kinds of markets, but detective stories were the only kind he'd ever had any luck with. His mind didn't seem to produce viable fictional ideas in other areas. When he'd tried writing longer works, novels, he'd always gotten hopelessly bogged down. He was a short-story writer, recognized and frequently anthologized, and he was prolific enough to keep himself alive that way, but—

But he was sick of living marginally, sick of grinding out story after story. And heartily sick of going through life on a nickel a word.

What would a decent word rate be?

Well, if they paid him twenty-five cents a word, then he'd at least be keeping pace with the price of a candy bar. Of course after twenty years you wanted to do a little better than stay even. Say they paid him a dollar a word. There were writers who earned that much. Hell, there were writers who earned a good deal more than that, writers whose books wound up on best-seller lists, writers who got six-figure prices for screenplays, writers who wrote themselves rich.

One thousand dollars a word.

The phrase popped into his mind, stunning in its simplicity, and before he was aware of it his fingers had typed the words on the page before him. He sat and looked at it, then worked the carriage return lever and typed the phrase again.

One thousand dollars a word.

He studied what he had typed, his mind racing on ahead, playing with ideas, shaking itself loose from its usual stereotyped thought patterns. Well, why not? Why shouldn't he earn a thousand dollars a word? Why not branch out into a new field?

Why not?

He took the sheet from the typewriter, crumpled it into a ball, pegged it in the general direction of the wastebasket. He rolled a new sheet in its place and sat looking at its blankness, waiting thinking. Finally, word by halting word, he began to type.

Trevathan rarely rewrote his short stories. At a nickel a word he could not afford to. Furthermore, he had acquired a facility over the years which enabled him to turn out acceptable copy in first draft. Now, however, he was trying something altogether new and different, and so he felt the need to take his time getting it precisely right. Time and again he yanked false starts from the typewriter, crumpled them, hurled them at the wastebasket.

Until finally he had something he liked.

He read it through for the fourth or fifth time, then took it from the typewriter and read it again. It did the job, he decided. It was concise and clear and very much to the point.

He reached for the phone. When he'd gotten through to Jukes he said, "Warren? I've decided to take your advice."

"Wrote another story for us? Glad to hear it."

"No," he said, "another piece of advice you gave me. I'm branching out in a new direction."

"Well, I think that's terrific," Jukes said. "I really mean it. Getting to work on something big? A novel?"

"No, a short piece."

"But in a more remunerative area?"

"Definitely. I'm expecting to net a thousand dollars a word for what I'm doing this afternoon."

"A thousand—" Warren Jukes let out a laugh, making a sound similar to the yelp of a startled terrier. "Well, I don't know what you're up to, Jim, but let me wish you the best of luck with it. I'll tell you one thing. I'm damned glad you haven't lost your sense of humor."

Trevathan looked again at what he'd written. *"I've got a gun. Please fill this paper sack with thirty thousand dollars in used tens and twenties and fifties or I'll be forced to blow your stupid head off."*

"Oh, I've still got my sense of humor," he said. "Know what I'm going to do, Warren? I'm going to laugh all the way to the bank."